Metaphorosis

2018

Also from Metaphorosis

Score – an SFF symphony

Reading 5X5: Readers' Edition
Reading 5X5: Writers' Edition

Best Vegan Science Fiction & Fantasy
Best Vegan SFF 2018
Best Vegan SFF 2017
Best Vegan SFF 2016

Metaphorosis Magazine
Metaphorosis: Best of 2018
Metaphorosis: Best of 2017
Metaphorosis: Best of 2016

Metaphorosis 2018: The Complete Stories
Metaphorosis 2017: The Complete Stories
Metaphorosis 2016: Nearly Complete Stories

Monthly issues

by B. Morris Allen
Susurrus
Allenthology: Volume I
Tocsin: and other stories
Start with Stones: collected stories
Metaphorosis: a collection of stories

Metaphorosis

The Complete Stories
2018

edited by
B. Morris Allen

ISSN: 2573-136X (online)
ISBN: 978-1-64076-126-1 (e-book)
ISBN: 978-1-64076-127-8 (paperback)
ISBN: 978-1-64076-128-5 (hardback)

from
Metaphorosis Publishing

Neskowin

Contents

From the Editor

2018 was a mammoth year for Metaphorosis. Whereas in 2016 and 2017 we published about 240,000 words each year, in 2018 we published a whopping 330,000!

The increase took off in January, with Michael Gardner's novelette, "This Side of the Wall", and I consciously extended the notion with February's David and Goliath issue – long stories by various Davids. After that, the thing somehow took on a life of its own, but it wasn't until the end of the year that I realized just how long the stories had become.

The result is that you have in your hands a lot of reading pleasure. The stories range from whimsical contemporary fantasy to heart-wrenching science fiction, and pretty much everything in between.

Last year was also the first that we started issuing monthly print issues. While when I started the magazine, I had no plan for 'issues' at all, I tested out the idea in 2017 and fell in love with the little 4x6 inch paperback format – the perfect size to stick in your pocket and carry around for regular or emergency reading. While I'm a convert to e-books for a number of reasons – convenience, ecology, cost – there's no denying the pleasure of holding a physical book in your hands, and they show off the great art we've had during the year as well. The print books are a little more expensive than I'd like, but the price is as low as we can make it while keeping it stable between issues.

The combination of print issues and longer stories means each monthly book has had a solid 20-40,000 words or so – pretty substantial. Ironically, however, it's cheaper to get individual copies from retailers than it is for us to send them out from us. We also tried an experiment with subscription, but the process was so convoluted – EPUBs converted to PDFs and reconverted to e-book form – and the result so inconsistent, that we gave it up. For now, the best way to subscribe to e-books is through Patreon – patrons get the e-books on the first of the month, automatically. I'll keep working on a solution for print subscriptions.

On the submissions front, things have been remarkably steady. From the very first year, we've received an average of 5 stories per day, now up to 6. I'm happy to say after two years of makeshift, partially-blind reading, we finally moved to a fully blind reading process. Not only is it now a far more convenient process, it's more truly blind – before, I would sometimes inadvertently see an author's name. Now, I can't. I believe in blind reading, and I'm glad to have a process that fully supports it at last.

In early 2018, we published the *Reading 5X5* anthology – a collection of great stories by 25 Metaphorosis authors, in which groups of five each wrote a variant story from the same story seed. It's a great way to examine how different authors approach the same idea. It's also a great tool for aspiring authors – the *Writer's Edition* has the original briefs and notes by each author on their process.

Also in 2018, we started work on *Score – an SFF symphony* – an anthology by about twenty Metaphorosis authors. *Score*'s premise is that the anthology as a whole is based on an emotional score – much like a piece of music, but with major and minor emotional themes and cues instead of audible ones – an emotion of anthology, if you will. *Score* came out in early 2019.

Overall 2019 is shaping up to be just as good a year as 2018. But for the moment, sit back and enjoy a mountain of quality SFF.

Morris Allen
Editor
1 April 2019

January

The Seer at Sunset Hills Shopping Plaza

Katherine Perdue

"A woman's been murdered!"

That was Theodora Yates for you: always jumping to conclusions, bless her heart, and that conclusion most often of all. But there was no talking her out of it once she'd made up her mind, so I said, without bothering to ask any questions, "Then we must go to the Seer at once!"

My granddaughter, Katie, she didn't think much of us going to the Seer. She grew up in this new world: it was no more magical or difficult for her than breathing air. Once, she asked me, "Granny, how much did you just pay that woman for something they'd give you for free at the library? Or you could do it yourself. I'll teach you how to Google if you want." She waved a tiny glowing screen in front of my face.

"You can't Boolean with Google," I said, deeply offended.

"Granny!" She stretched out the word so that I would understand her exasperation. "You don't even know what that means!"

"No, I don't. But it's what the Seer says, and I trust her."

Katie wasn't exactly wrong about the library. Theodora and I used to go round there every time she got it in her head that someone had been murdered, but there were a great many things that the librarians believed were none of our business. And what about the police, you might wonder? Well, they were worse than the librarians. They always just called Katie to come get us and take us home. We never had problems like that with the Seer.

It was a hike to get there. The Seer worked out of a strip mall just off the highway on the edge of town, and I didn't drive anymore because of my cataracts. We looked into getting one of those new-fangled automated cars, but it turned out you still needed a license to operate one of them, though I couldn't guess why. The doctor took my license away years ago. Theodora's doctor told her she shouldn't drive; the exact reason escaped her. She still had her license though. Her doctor was nicer than mine and took pity when she said she needed it for emergencies, since she didn't have any family.

Going to the Seer about a murder never qualified as an emergency, so we took the bus halfway and then we walked, even though there was no sidewalk. A couple of cars honked at us, but I shook my cane at them and they kept on going.

Theodora told me about the murder on the way. It seemed a car had been left parked in her driveway overnight.

"The same one as last week?" I interrupted. Theodora lived near campus. Students were always leaving their cars anywhere they could fit them and you know the sort of hours students keep. About noon or one o'clock, they would stagger back and drive off, unless the car had been towed. You wouldn't believe how persecuted they proclaimed themselves to be if the owner of the driveway had the effrontery to tow their car!

But Theodora never called the tow truck. She always assumed that the owner of the car had been murdered.

"Last week? Was there one last week? No, I don't think it's the same."

"Don't you think it's just another student?"

"No, I do not," said Theodora with a particularly forceful thrust of her cane. I had offended her and she wouldn't say another word to me till we got to the Seer's.

Strip malls are always dreary, but Sunset Hills Shopping Plaza took the cake. The empty husk of a now defunct supermarket dominated the row. "Closed for Renovation," the sign said. I knew that's what it said because I read it back when it was new. All you could tell now is that one of the letters printed on it might have been an 'R'.

Next to it was Video World; vacant, of course. Then a vending machine selling camera film. We'd seen the truck come by to restock it. Sunset Hills was the kind of place that drew lost things like that. Lost people too. There was always a huddle of them in the mornings and the evenings near the old supermarket, waiting eagerly to press around the occasional pickup truck that stopped there to take aboard a lucky few. Migrants, I assumed. People who'd left their homes behind but never quite found one here.

At the end of the row there was a Chinese restaurant that was still in business, although I'd never seen anyone go in it. And across from that was the Seer.

We didn't know her name. She said she didn't tell anybody. Knowing a person's true name gave you power over that person. No one had power over the Seer.

She had a wooden sign that swung back and forth eerily and creaked a bit — when the wind was right. It was purple with a moon and some stars rising above a crystal ball with an open palm beneath it. And, decorated with gold-trimmed purple cloth: a computer monitor. She had all that in neon on her window too, and the words:

Psychic, Palm Reading, Digital Second Sight, Computer Repair. The Seer did a bit of everything.

We went in the plate glass door and through a beaded curtain into a room where the air was thick with incense and the walls were all lined with dark curtains. Mystical symbols were painted on the ceiling and there was a black-light to make them glow. We headed for the back room, which was an ordinary office with a desk and a computer, an antique flat-screen with an ancient keyboard dating back from the time when people thought all computer equipment had to be grey. There was a couch for clients and a straight-backed chair that the Seer put in just for Theodora because she couldn't sit on a couch with her back the way it was. The Seer knew we didn't need any of that nonsense in the front room. When we came, it was for real magic.

She stood up as we came in. "I foresaw your coming and made tea," she said solemnly and went to pour it for us. She had a security camera set up in the parking lot, so she did a lot of very localized foreseeing. I think she knew Theodora and I knew, but we never said anything about it. We didn't want to take away her fun. And we liked having the tea ready. "I take it there has been another murder?"

"Yes," I said. "Terrible affair. Theodora, tell her about it."

"Well," said Theodora, with a bit of a quaver in her voice. "I don't know that there's so much to tell. There was a car left in my driveway last night. It's still there."

"She says it isn't the same one as last week," I added.

Theodora gave me a glare. "Don't be spiteful, Nancy. It's different this time. When I found it, the door was open. And someone had knocked out the window. It's a stolen car, I'm sure of it. And someone just left it in my driveway."

"It just sounds to me like someone broke in while it was in your driveway," I said. "Nothing you've said makes it sound stolen."

Theodora crossed her arms and said nothing, turning a long-suffering gaze in appeal to our host.

The Seer ran a hand over the small crystal ball she kept on her desk. "If someone had broken the window in the driveway, there would have been glass all over the seat. And there was no glass, was there?" Theodora smirked. "Do you have the license plate for me?"

"And the VIN. I know you like to have the true names of things." She passed a slip of paper to the Seer.

"Very good." The Seer laid her hands down reverently upon the keyboard, whereupon it began to glow softly, while at the same time the lights in the room dimmed and just a touch of fog began to drift across the desk.

"Nice," I commented. The Seer just smiled and started typing.

"It *is* a stolen car," she said after a moment. "Belongs to a Mr. James P. Garst. Not from around here. He reported it missing yesterday."

"That doesn't make any sense," Theodora muttered.

The Seer held out her hand and looked at Theodora. Theodora gave her the driver's license she had found on the front seat. "It's what made me think there must be something really wrong. You wouldn't just leave your license like that unless there were something wrong."

"'Hailey Grace Garst,'" the Seer read off the card. "Well, let's see what we can find out about Hailey Grace." Again she stretched out her hands and the keyboard lit. A few keystrokes later, she frowned. "She's been cursed."

"Cursed?" Theodora and I chorused. We'd heard of curses—who hadn't?—but usually they fell upon especially sanctimonious politicians or corporations that had angered the more anarchist factions of the web. This was the first we'd seen one used against an ordinary private citizen.

"Yes," said the Seer, turning the screen so that we could see. "You're looking at the Shallows right now. What anybody would see if they ran a search on Hailey Grace Garst. The first result:" she clicked and we saw it. Medical records. "If this is to be believed, Hailey Grace was committed to Spring Creek Psychiatric Hospital when she was fifteen for severe depression and suicidal ideation." She scrolled. "Released when she was sixteen. The doctors gave her a good report. Prescribed antidepressants. Pronounced her cured."

The Seer hit the back button. "And this is the second result." She clicked.

"Dearie me," said Theodora.

The photographs had been labeled helpfully in big, bold, red print with an arrow and the caption: "NOT HER HUSBAND!!!"

"That could explain the curse," I said.

The Seer clicked back again and showed us the rest of the results. Page after page of forum posts titled things like: "DO NOT HIRE THIS WOMAN!!!" and "DO NOT TRUST MENTAL PATIENT WITH UR KIDS".

"Well, maybe they shouldn't," I said. Theodora gave me a look.

"That is what a reasonable person might conclude if her access were limited to the Shallows," said the Seer. I believe it was meant as a gentle reproof to the both of us, but Theodora puffed up with vindication.

"But we're not confined to the Shallows!" added the Seer with enthusiasm. She waved her hands a bit theatrically and the air seemed almost to shimmer for a moment, as though the universe had just blinked. I'm not sure how she did it. "Behold!"

On the screen in the corner, there was a clock, and as she spoke, it began to tick backwards. "If we had looked yesterday, this is what we would have seen." The page was the same. The clock spun faster. "A week ago. A month ago. Six." And then, in a stage whisper, "Before the curse."

The clock stopped. The Seer clicked. We watched a video of a bride and groom waltzing under a banner that read, "Welcome to the wedding scrapbook of Hailey Grace Lowell Garst and James Prichard Garst. Congratulations Hailey and Jim!" The video was dated five years ago.

"She stole the car from her husband, then?" I asked.

Theodora was shaking her head. "She was carjacked in her husband's car and then murdered!"

The Seer smiled her patient smile and said nothing.

The next result was the divorce case. It had been ugly. But there was no mention of infidelity. The Seer checked the dates on the incriminating photographs. "Taken after the divorce," she said. "The man in the pictures may not have been her husband, but at the time, no man was."

"What about the medical records?" I asked. "Were they real?"

The Seer nodded. She was still looking at the court page. "It seems that after the divorce, Hailey Grace sued James Garst for defamation and for publishing private health records. But they couldn't prove anything because whoever laid the curse did it from a public computer. And it turns out that Spring Creek Psychiatric Hospital accidentally published all of its patients' records online three years ago. They've since apologized and taken them down, but who knows who could have copied them while they were up."

"Did she sue the hospital too?"

"There's a class-action going on. I would guess that in ten years or so she might get ten bucks off that. In the meantime…"

She showed us a page from the Springfield Herald Tribune. The headline read, 'Parents Raise Outcry Over Kindergarten Teacher's Mental Health'.

"She resigned a week later."

"Because of the curse," I said.

"Because of the curse."

"What about the baby?" Theodora asked, out of the blue, like she always did.

The Seer and I demanded together, "What baby?"

Theodora apologetically drew a few photographs out of her purse. Polaroids as usual. She had a huge stockpile of film cartridges in her basement and I suppose if she ever ran out, there was that vending machine. She gave each one a good shake before laying it down on the desk for us to see, though the image was already as clear as it would ever be.

First: the car in the driveway, the rear passenger-side door hanging open and the driver's window empty of glass.

Next: the license lying abandoned on the seat. The keys were still in the ignition.

And last, Theodora held it back a moment and when she finally laid it on the desk, her hand hesitated before pulling back to let us see: a baby seat strapped in the back on the passenger's side, next to the open door.

The Seer and I stared at it a moment and then she turned back to the screen. The keys clattered, the mouse wheel clicked. "She lost custody," the Seer said in a flat voice. "She'd lost her job and was struggling to pay rent on her apartment. Every new job she applied to, they ran a search on her and the curse took them in its thrall. She never even got an interview. And she couldn't move to a cheaper apartment because landlords wouldn't rent to her unless she had a job. She presented all this in court and the judge was sympathetic, but she said it wasn't a healthy environment for a child."

She turned the screen towards us again. On it was a picture of Hailey Grace holding her infant son. She wore a long green dress, cut a bit like a robe. Long dark hair in braids fell down her back. She was gaunt and beautiful in a Pre-Raphaelite way; it made her seem frail. But the way she looked at her son, the joy and the pride, the possessive way she held him, it devoted me to her cause that instant.

"So it was a kidnapping," Theodora said slowly, "not a murder at all. What are we going to do?"

"Notify the police," said the Seer, at exactly the same time that I said, "We can't tell the police." We frowned at each other. Usually if anyone wanted to go to the police, it was me. Usually Theodora's murders turned out to be nothing and no one said anything at all about going to the police.

"What do you think?" I asked Theodora. She'd be on my side, of course. Nobody on earth had a softer heart than Theodora.

But I was wrong. "I suppose it is a crime," she said slowly.

"You would take a child away from his own mother?" I demanded. "I know you never had any children yourself, but I thought you'd at least understand —"

"I understand being alone," she said. And she did. She'd never married. She used to teach English at the university and she'd told me then that she didn't need children; she had students. But students weren't the same. She realized that after she retired. "I don't want to take a child away from his mother. Nor do I want to take him away from his father, his grandparents, his aunts and uncles, his whole life. That's what we're really talking about here, Nancy."

I said nothing. There was nothing to argue with in what she'd said.

"We don't know that James Garst isn't a wonderful father," she continued.

"But he cursed her!" I said.

"We don't know that. If we did — Can you find out?" she asked the Seer. "Was James Garst really the one who laid the curse?"

"Maybe." The Seer pursed her lips and turned back to the computer. There were no special effects this time. She typed and scrolled and glowered at the monitor and typed some more, the rhythm of tapped keys as steady and soothing as rain. Theodora and I waited and sipped our tea. Then she let out a quiet "a-ha."

"It was him," she said. "He signed on to his email while he was doing it. One of the forums he posted on followed his cookie crumbs back to his email and sold the information to advertisers. And to me."

"Then we can't go to the police," said Theodora. "It's black magic, cursing people. James Garst took that woman's whole future from her. He poisoned her very identity. You wouldn't give a child back to someone like that."

"No," said the Seer, "I wouldn't. But I am not a judge and don't want to be one."

"You are though," I said. "There's no middle ground in this. Can't cut the baby in half. Call the police, Hailey Grace goes to jail, and you've chosen the father's side. Don't call, and you've chosen the mother's."

The Seer looked unhappy.

"Lift the curse," said Theodora. "You can, can't you? No, better than that, can you make her invisible? Maybe post an obituary?"

"I'm not sure that's not black magic." The Seer looked again at the screen. It was back to the picture of mother and child. "I could make it as though she never existed. Delete every reference to her everywhere; all the court documents, credit reports, student loans, everything. Every record of that car ever existing too."

"A fresh start," I said.

"No start at all. Maybe when you were both young, it was possible to move to a new place with a new name and reinvent yourself, no documentation required. Not anymore. She couldn't get by just being *no one*. She'd need to find a person like me to make her into *someone*, and people like me charge a lot of money for a thing as precious as a new name and new life to go with it. We don't do it for charity and we don't always have a person's best interest at heart."

"You would do it for charity," I persisted.

The Seer laughed. "I would do it for my usual fee. But the thing is, I can't. Erasing her is powerful magic. Dangerous. Criminal, of course, though that's no concern of mine. Still, it's simple and I could do it in a day. But building her back up is something else: alchemy. It takes time and affinity. I cannot do it from a distance. I cannot do it without her consent and cooperation."

Theodora and I didn't see the problem. "So we find her and bring her to you," I said. "It shouldn't be hard. This isn't a big place and she doesn't have a car. She must be nearby." We dismissed the objection that she could have gotten on a bus. They checked IDs on buses nowadays. The Seer was right. Having no identity was worse than having a cursed one.

She rested her chin upon her fist and sat for a while in thought. "You really think you can find her?"

"Yes," I said, and then, sensing that she was wavering and pressing my advantage, I went too far. "You said it yourself. We pay your fee, and this is what we're asking you to do."

There was a long silence. I held my breath. Finally she said, "The customer is always right, or so I've been told. I'll do it. It'll take me all night. In the meantime, you'd better get rid of that car."

We drove it into the lake. Well, Theodora drove it, since she had her license. I told her that it was silly to care about licenses when you were driving a stolen car into the lake, but she held firm. And the next day we went back to the Seer's and she showed us: Hailey Grace Lowell Garst had been erased. Searching for her in the Shallows brought up nothing at all. The divorce case was gone. When we put in the case number, an entirely different case came up.

"Won't they have backups?" I asked.

"I have my ways of getting to them as well," said the Seer.

"And when James Garst goes to the police station to report his son missing?"

She smiled. "They won't be able to help him. They'll find no record in any database that he ever had a son. When he gives them social security numbers for the boy and Hailey Grace, they'll come up invalid. The only records are on paper, and no one cares about paper anymore. It isn't real if it isn't digital."

All the next week I kept expecting the police to show up on our doorsteps looking for Hailey Grace. Nothing happened. Nor, for all that we turned over every stone and branch, did we find any sign of our missing mother and child. Whenever I thought of them, I worried that we had not done them a kindness in the end.

We didn't go back to the Seer's for some time after that. We were embarrassed that we hadn't lived up to our end of the bargain and for me, it was more than that. I was worried we'd make it to Sunset Hills and find the Seer's shop just as empty as Video World. That was the way of places like hers, appearing suddenly out of nothing and gone again without warning or trace. I'd crossed a line with her by insisting, and I wasn't sure she'd forgive it.

But days went by, then a month, and inevitably Theodora had new mysteries to investigate. I could only put her off for so long. So we made the long trek back to the strip mall and I'd never been so glad in my life to see purple velvet and lit neon.

As we were crossing the parking lot, I saw a waitress taking her break outside the Chinese restaurant. She was thin and had long dark hair. She looked familiar. I only caught a glimpse of her before she went back inside, but the Seer looked awfully jolly about something she'd seen on her security camera when we came in.

"How'd you find her?" I asked, expecting some grand feat of magic, something far beyond my abilities. But the answer was simpler than that.

"I looked out my window," said the Seer, "and there she was, standing in the parking lot with all the others looking for work. I waited till she was one of the only ones left; she doesn't have the right build for hard labor. Then I went out and asked if she'd ever done any waitressing. Xiaomi is a friend of mine and I knew she had an opening."

She hesitated a moment, looking a little unsure of her ground. Up until that point, our relationship had always been strictly business. "Either of you care to get lunch after we're done here? The Chinese place is actually pretty good and I'd like to introduce you to Hailey. It's traditional for fairy godmothers to come in threes."

About the story

The idea for this story came to me while working at the library reference desk. An undergraduate asked me a simple question. I looked up the answer. The student thanked me a thousand times and was in awe as though I'd performed some sophisticated magic. I thought about it for a while and realized, it's not that different from magic. It follows the same rules. If you know the true name of something—the correct subject heading for library materials, a good keyword for a search engine—that's all you need to summon it forth.

I was also doing a lot of programming at the time and there the connection is even clearer. With words alone, with code, you can compose a spell that has some physical effect on the world, whether that's changing the color of pixels on a screen or animating a robot.

We all use this kind of "magic" day in and day out. We don't notice the miracles in front of us. I wanted to tell a story about characters who do notice them and who afford them the same awe as that undergraduate at the reference desk.

A question for the author

Q: Do you use music for inspiration? If so what do you listen to?

A: Yes. Sometimes this is straightforward. If I'm trying to write something sad, I don't choose upbeat music. If it's difficult to write, then I avoid distractingly catchy lyrics. But I also find that if I've written productively while listening to something before, especially if more than once, that piece of music gets imbued with the moment, becomes a kind of talisman.

So that if I want to write that way again, with that kind of focus, I have but to listen to it. As for what kind? You name it: opera, bluegrass, rock, gamelan, all kinds.

About the author

Katherine Perdue lives in Virginia with her two cats and many fish and works as a librarian at a small university. She loves linguistics, live music, and tropical plants.

Jewel/Gem Offering

Emily McIntyre

It is dawn in the half-world of Varuzza, and the sun strikes the woman's face in strips of meat red and blue. Around her still-trim waist she wears a leather belt holstering the latest shiny aggro-tech; old lace kisses pearls around her neck and in her hand is a pot holding the tender sprig of a rose with deep purple thorns and a bud the color of midnight on the old Home World. Two days ago, she left the technological nightmare of Greatcity behind and turned the nose of her hovercraft north, toward a backwater of the universe. The rose fills the cab with a young, piney poison but she no longer notices; until the moment she relinquishes it she is impervious.

Years as a high-paid whore in the faraway Wilder West world taught her to seize her joy where she found it; a lifetime of governmental intrigue confirmed joy is an illusion. Still, she feels a choke of emotion when she sees the curving dome of her daughter's holdfast clinging to blasted earth with the same kind of tenacity with which she herself has clung to vestiges of freedom gathered through the years in dribs and drabs of pilfered data.

Like any stranger, she waits in a generic room after the vac-lock. Remnants of her beauty veil her still, but they are drawn taut, like the pale skin on her cheekbones. Waiting, hardly a breath stirs her. Seven years of searching and a lifetime of regret culminate in this moment, in the hiss of the door as a small woman enters with a line of half-hostile puzzlement creasing between her winglike brows and a dowdy turquoise tunic straining over her belly. The traveler stands and extends the rose sprig; automatically the other woman takes it and the fingers of her right hand close against its stem; the left cup its pot. The single black bud glows against the synthetic fabric covering her breasts. The two women stand like that for long breaths, waiting for a script that does not exist. Finally, the traveler says, "You know who I am." It sounds like a statement, but her voice carries bald hope.

In answer there is only silence. The rose between them is a banner of failure. Infinite potential ignored for too long; the rose-magic heritage that should be passed in whispers and rituals between the generations instead handed over like a reluctant hostage at the end. The daughter looks down at the rose. Her hair is parted in a meandering line and has not been washed recently. The long pause causes the older woman to stir on her feet, to cock her head so that one dangling russet jewel brushes her shoulder.

"I learned you married an itinerant," she says, her prejudice coloring her voice and bringing an angry flush to the other woman's cheek. An itinerant, scum, a meandering prophet with nothing to his name but this desolate holding far away from everything that matters, on the harshest inhabited planet in the multiverse.

The younger woman's eyes narrow along her fine cheekbones— familiar cheekbones. The rose twitches with her tightened grasp, sends eddies of its rich perfume through the room. "Why do you care?" The perfume makes the traveler dizzy, now that she is not the rose's mistress and is susceptible to its power. She struggles to find coherence. Fear chokes her more surely than any over-zealous client ever has.

I care, she thinks to say, because my daughter deserves better. I care, she almost answers, because he will leave you broken and alone and you will regret your life like I regret mine. You can never count on men. But she says only, "Because I cannot help it." She lost the right to care the same day she delivered a mewling girl to the harsh world in a rush of blood and forgetfulness. The day she rose from her bed and disappeared to start her life over on another planet—the day she broke the chain of magic that extended hundreds of years back through the women of her line. She can feel the bitterness twisting her once-famed lips.

At least let her leave well. She steps toward her daughter. "You know what the rose is?" She almost thinks the rose listens, that its poisonous thorns tremble a little at the thought of leaving her. That the Jewel/Gem yearns for its former caretaker; but that is foolish. Magical/chemical or not, a rose is just a plant, not a friend. Not a friend, just a poison so subtle it is imbued with the very desires of its keeper and so old it is undetectable by all modern poison-sniffers.

Her daughter opens her mouth to answer and thinks better of it. She swallows her words, tucks her nail-bitten fingers together around the slick belly of the flower pot. It is clear she knows exactly what she holds; maybe her blood sparks with recognition the way the traveler's did the day her mother died and left her holding the pot. Maybe she has heard the rumors; when you hold the plant the Emperor would trade his planet for, you don't need to say much. When you hold a magic so potent a single drop can change history, you can straighten your back a little. You have, you might think, a way out. A second chance. A fallback.

A child cries, closer now. The younger woman shivers as if waking from a dream, but before she can turn to leave, the traveler reaches out one hand and traces the sweet curve of her daughter's cheek for the second time in her life. The cheek is not so soft as it was in the moment of birth and forgetting, but it is still softer than anything the traveler has felt before. As her hand falls it catches, too familiar, on the spiky edges of Jewel/Gem and she leaves a pendant drop of blood there, cradled against one of the dark thorns which have never pricked her before. Perhaps it was intentional. Once she held her daughter's fate in her hands; now the roles are reversed.

Even after she leaves, she feels the softness lingering on her fingers for hours, like the familiar scent of Jewel/Gem poison now growing and filling her lungs. Her breathing grows thick—the tendons stand out on her long neck with the effort of it. This is, it seems, her daughter's wish; Jewel/Gem is merely an extension of its caretaker's will. She accepts the knowledge and the poison. It is her time.

She is a legend on six planets within her lifetime. All forgotten now; forgotten except the softness of her daughter's cheek on the tips of her fingers. Joy is hard to recognize—she's had so little practice— but perhaps it is joy that fills her when she points her hovercraft into oblivion and lowers the sunshield. Perhaps it is joy she feels in the sacred moment before her skin chars and the pearls melt into her neck. That, or a commonplace kind of redemption.

About the story

Summer in Portland is a riot of roses. Funereal roses, scattering their fragile petals around them like Miss Havisham's train; glowing roses like tiny sun-bits just waiting to be noticed; classic tea roses whispering of the past. I spend a lot of time on my bike in the summer in this city, thinking while I ride, and occasionally I pull over and lose myself in one of the many rose parks in the city. I set my helmet to the side and lie on my back so the sun and filter through the serrated leaves to kiss my cheeks.

Summer 2017 I had about three weeks when everything seemed a rose-scented dream. I remembered the family legend of my great-great-great grandmother's pink rose, which she brought down the Ohio river with her, and which nearly every female family member has grown from a little slip in a Mason jar of water. (I've killed two in my many cross-country moves.) I began to think about the way the things we inherit from our families are rarely the things we want, but sometimes the things we need. I thought about my own writer-mother, and my storytelling daughter. I wondered what would happen if roses were magical, and only women could wield them? And then I thought of the strange way desire and betrayal seem wound into every interaction we have with our parents, our children, and that was the beginning of "Jewel/Gem Offering".

I still envision exploring the concept more thoroughly. A book would be a better idea, but I love flash fiction and all it hides and reveals. This was my first sci-fi story and I had to laugh when I realized it still had magic in it. I guess I'm an inveterate magic-seeker, wherever my imagination takes me.

A question for the author

Q: Why fantasy?

A: Ignoring the fact that Jewel/Gem is a sci-fi story (my first, possibly my last), I choose to write fantasy not just because it's cool—like fezzes are cool—but because life, through the lens of fantasy, is a little richer. Through fantasy I can take a stab at the 'why' behind the 'how', and often neglect the 'how' entirely. In fantasy we can tackle tough topics with just enough distance to stay safe until the fatal moment that truth stabs us in the heart and we find that, like all good literature, this story has changed us somehow. We're bigger. Deeper. Angrier.

Fantasy helps us live.

About the author

A globe-trotting coffee entrepreneur by day and a diehard fantasy writer/reader by night, Emily McIntyre lives in Portland, Oregon.

@mcintyrewrites

This Side of the Wall

Michael Gardner

Today was my day to choose a disease.

"Fennel," Mama called up from the kitchen. "Breakfast's near ready."

"Coming, Mama," I yelled back as I pulled a simple, blue dress over my head. I tied my hair back tight, laced up my shoes and then ran down the stairs to the kitchen.

Mama was heavily pregnant again. She was stirring a large pot that bubbled away on the stove, filling the air with the aroma of milk and oats. Sage, Lentil, and Chilli were crawling around Mama's ankles, squealing. Strawberry, Colander, Rosemary, and Tommy sat at the table, spoons in hands, waiting for their porridge.

Mama had the birthing disease. "When you have the birthing disease," Mama would say, "you don't have time to dilly dally picking out the perfect name for your little uns. I like to look at what's nearby when the baby comes and pick a name that way." Mama had been cooking just before I was born on the kitchen floor. Mama had been cooking before most of our births.

Pa sat at the head of the table, stiff backed. His raw, cracked hands rested in bowls of ice and his stone-grey eyes watched the children. I gave his hard shoulder a squeeze as I walked past him and made my way to the opposite end of the table.

Pa had laid-to-waste disease. He worked in demolition, destroying buildings with his rock-hard hands. When he was young, those hands had been harder than diamonds. But not anymore. As he grew older, it was like the hardness in his hands had begun to leak from where he needed it and, instead, it was spreading slowly but surely up his arms and across his chest and face. The money was too good to stop working, so Pa persisted, despite the toll on his body, despite the stiffness in his joints and the limited movement. I guess it made me sad, though Mama said it shouldn't. We all have to bear our diseases, the good and the bad.

Pa directed his grey gaze at me and cleared his throat. He didn't speak much normally — the hardness in his jaw made talking difficult. But he would speak today, I knew. He would give me the same speech he had given to my older brothers and sisters. The one he reserved for all of our sixteenth name days.

His jaw cracked loudly as he forced his mouth open. His lips were brittle and dry and hard flakes of grey skin fell as he spoke.

"Happy … name day … Fennel," he forced out. "I don't know … how much longer … I can earn … for the family," he rasped. I craned forward to listen. "So now … it's time for you … to give back." A dry red tongue darted out and flicked at his lips, but it barely wet the surface. "Take this money … and invest it … in a disease … that will allow you … to earn for the family." He removed a wet hand from the ice and reached into his pocket. He withdrew five one hundred dollar notes and pushed them roughly towards the middle of the table. "Invest it wisely, Fennel … like your brothers … like your sisters." He dipped his hand back into the ice, grimacing as the cold bit into his wounds.

I reached for the money on the table. More money than I had ever seen. Enough to buy any disease I wanted.

"What are you going to contract, Fennel?" Rosemary asked as she stared at her reflection in her spoon.

"Yeah, Fennel. What are you gonna get?" chimed in Tommy. "A taking disease like Knife?"

My brother Knife was only a year older than me. We'd always been close, even sharing a room up until he'd contracted the taking disease and moved out on his own. Now, people paid him to bear diseases they had contracted that just didn't work out like they thought they should. He'd done well for the family, but I couldn't see him lasting more than another year or two. It was a wealthy, but short life for him. I'd miss him, I knew. I'd miss him most of all.

"I don't know what I'll contract," I said, turning the hundred dollar notes in my hands. "I think I'll take my time, listen to the pitches, decide what's best for me and the family."

Mama removed the pot from the stove and waddled to the table. She began to ladle hot porridge into the bowls, starting with Pa's. "You'll do what's best for the family first, young lady. If it works out for you too, then good, but family first," she said, as she plopped a large portion of porridge in my bowl.

I said nothing. I dipped my spoon into the thick, creamy oats and began to swirl them absently.

"What disease do the people in the Compound have, Mama?" Strawberry asked. "I'd like that disease."

Mama guffawed.

"That ain't no disease. Those people are just born rich and lucky. They live up in their nice houses in Eastern Heights, looking down on us carriers, but they need us. We provide their food, and build their fancy houses and make their fancy clothes."

"I heard some of them used to be like us, but they managed to buy their way into the Compound. Not with money, but with deeds," I said quickly.

Mama ladled porridge into Tommy's bowl and then pointed the ladle at me.

"Where did you hear that rubbish?"

"Jillian told me. She heard that —"

"She heard wrong is what she heard. There's no buying your way into the Compound. That's wishful thinking right there. They have the money, we have the diseases. They get our deeds just fine with coin. So get any wishful thinking of buying your way into the Compound out of that head. You just focus on contracting the right disease for this family, missy."

"Yes, Mama," I replied hastily, lowering my eyes to my food.

I'd been watching the Compound from the outside for years. I knew when the Compound gates would open briefly to accept deliveries. I knew all of the spots around Central where you could peek over the Compound walls. Eastern Heights was beautiful. Neat white homes, green parks and gardens, happy people. If there was a way in, I reckoned I'd have as good a chance as any of finding it. And I wouldn't forget my family. Oh no. I'd look after them, but from inside, not out.

But I knew there was no point telling Mama any of that.

I could have walked directly down Main Street to the Harbourside Disease Markets, but I turned right on Lincoln Street and headed towards the Compound wall. It still took my breath away. It was made of red brick, stood at least a hundred feet tall, and ran as far as you could see — north towards the Harbour and south to the Yarran Ranges. It provided a striking contrast to the mud brick houses of Central.

As I approached the wall, I saw a young man hunched over a pothole, retching up hot tar. It hissed and spat as he coughed the last of it onto the road. Then he picked up his trowel and began to smooth his work.

"Morning," I called out to the retcher as I passed. He wiped some of the tar away from his mouth with the back of his hand and gave me a stained smile.

When I reached the wall, I ran my fingers lightly across the rough bricks, wondering what it would be like to feel the wall from the other side. I smiled, then turned north, keeping to the shadow of the wall.

The morning was quiet. I only passed one person on my way to the quay — a disfigured mutant with tusks, a thick neck and powerful, stumpy legs. It carried bricks in a sling across its hairy back. I gave it a wave and it grunted in return.

I heard the markets before I saw them — a buzz of excited activity. Then the blue expanse of the Harbour opened out before me, seagulls flocking overhead, a couple of small boats bobbing in the water. Running west, along the docks, snaked a multitude of canvas tents and marquees.

I waded into the crowd and it wasn't long before my interest was piqued by the mouth-watering scents of barbecue. I approached the source of the aroma, a marquee manned by five people with the tumours. One of the infected was standing over a BBQ, roasting a large steak cut freshly from a football sized lump on his thigh. God it smelt good, I thought.

"What about you, miss?" a red headed woman with a fist sized tumour growing from the top of her head asked me. "Are you interested in cooking? Grow what you eat, eat what you grow is our motto. We have a franchise opening up in Southwell."

None of my family had ever contracted the tumours. I was curious.

"How much?" I asked, as I looked first at the redhead, then at the meat. I was hoping they'd offer me a free sample.

"Business is booming at the moment, miss. But we could probably do you a deal for four hundred and fifty dollars."

"Hmm, seems a bit steep," I said, as Mama had instructed.

"A high price for a high earner," the redhead replied. "But, tell you what, you have a nice face and I'm in a good mood. So for you, miss, four hundred and twenty five dollars."

Tumour steaks seemed to be more popular than ever. I'd heard orders from the Compound, in particular, had gone crazy, so I believed you could earn plenty. And yet, it was also one of the most physically repugnant diseases. And Jillian had been telling me recently about rumours of kidnappings and a black market trade in organs. Was it worth the risk?

"I'll think on it," I replied, before moving on.

I next passed three people selling the birthing disease from a domed tent. But I wasn't interested in that, thanks. Mama was doing plenty of birthing for the whole family and we needed money now, not more investments.

I passed the laid-to-waste vendor, but that was no good either. Seeing Pa's deterioration up close had helped me make up my mind. No amount of earnings was worth a disease that ruined your latter years like that.

Next to the laid-to-waste stall was a neat tent selling the mutations.

"Hard to say what your specialty will be before the mutation occurs," said a lean man with elongated, muscular legs, "but we guarantee you'll become something of use — all of us mutants do." He pulled out several black and white sketches. "Here we have our farmers," he said, handing me a picture. I took it and looked down at three lovingly rendered mutants. Each had long tusks that they were using to plough the earth. "Labourers," he said, handing me a second picture that showed a powerfully built creature, short and hunched, hauling timber across its shoulders. "And messengers." The next sketch was of a bunch of creatures like the salesman, each with long, muscular legs that looked like they could run all day.

"Do any of these earn well?" I asked.

He cleared his throat.

"Good honest pay, for honest work," he replied smiling. So no, I thought. "But," he continued quickly, "our disease is one of the few that allows a rich, natural lifespan."

Hmm, well I guess that was appealing. But what good was a long lifespan if you were mutated into a dim-witted cretin who carried mud bricks all of your days? So I thanked him, told him I'd consider it, and then moved on.

I walked past stalls selling the taking disease and nymphomaniacism. I listened to retchers, gas breathers, and leather skins, but none of them appealed. And then, sooner than I had expected, I found myself at the end of the markets. Had I missed something? Why didn't any of the diseases stand out for me like they had for my siblings and parents?

Then, as I turned to wander back the way I had come, I spied an old lady sitting on a stool by herself. She didn't have a stall, but next to her was a sign that read: "True sight infection."

Curious, I approached. She appeared normal. No disfiguration, no obvious signs of illness. She was a tiny woman with thin, white hair; the only ailment she appeared to have was old age. But when she looked up at me, I saw her blue eyes were sharp and lively.

"I've never heard of the true sight infection before," I said.

The old lady smiled, papery skin folding around her mouth.

"It's a rare infection."

"And what does it do?"

"It allows you to see into people and know their true self. It lets you see the things that make them who they are — the important memories, the key moments. It lets you see their fears and desires."

"Ok," I said, not fully understanding. "But how do you earn from that?"

The old crone's grin stretched wider. "It's difficult. Not everyone has the ability to use this disease to their advantage. But for the smart ones that do, they can do very well for themselves."

"I'm sorry, but I need to contract something useful for my family. Unless I can be certain of earning from the infection, I'm not interested." I turned to leave.

"It can get you into the Compound," the old lady called after me. I halted mid-stride, and then turned slowly. "That is what you want, isn't it? Your one true desire is to get into the Compound, to become one of the elite, to live as they do in a nice white house with clean children playing in a neat garden."

How did she know that? I thought. But of course I knew. She had said it herself. She could see my desires and fears.

"How would your infection help me do that?" I asked, trying to hold onto my suspicions as Mama had taught me. There had to be a con here somewhere.

"There's only one way to get into the Compound as an outsider and that's to be vouched for by a resident. You find the right resident, you look into their heart, you understand what drives them and what they fear, and you use that knowledge to get your invite. At least that's what I did."

"You've been in the Compound?"

"I lived there for fifteen years, up until my James died. After that, I was forced to leave. But I wouldn't trade those fifteen years for anything."

"But how did you … I mean where … I didn't think the residents ever left Eastern Heights."

"They do, but not often. Enough get the itch to see how we live, just like we get the yearning for their life. Tourists. Some move in plain sight, others disguise themselves. But my infection can help you see them clear as day, whether they are disguised or not," she said, tapping her temple softly.

I stared at the old lady for what seemed like an eternity. And the whole time, her perpetual smile never wavered. She had me and she knew it. I sighed.

"How much?" I asked, feeling nervous and giddy at once.

"For you, three hundred and fifty."

I nodded, knowing Mama was going to be furious. But I reached into my pocket and withdrew my money.

The old lady accepted it with a hand that was missing its pinkie and ring finger. I couldn't help but wonder what had happened, but I wasn't allowed to muse for long. After she deposited my money into a small canvas bag, she took my hand in hers and raised it to her lips. She licked my hand from the wrist to the top of my middle finger, her tongue like sandpaper against my skin. I held still, resisting the urge to recoil. Then, suddenly, she placed her wrinkled lips around the tip of my finger and bit it.

I wrenched my hand back, shocked by the sharp pain. My finger was bleeding and there was a drop of blood on the crone's lips. But then, just as quickly, the pain was gone. Whether it was shock or something else, I didn't know. All I knew was that I saw the old woman differently.

She was a wretched creature. Cold, manipulative, despicable. I saw that she had told the truth about her years in the Compound and that she wanted desperately to return. But she knew she never would, which made her bitter and angry. The smile was for show. There was no mirth behind it, just a well-practiced act. And there was something else about her. Something that had been important once. I'd catch a glimpse of it, but then it would recede from view. It was something precious that she had given up to make her deal to enter the Compound. I almost had it when she spoke.

"You're a beautiful girl, with a beautiful, uncorrupted soul. But all things beautiful grow ugly given enough time."

I choked back my disgust, thanked her like Mama had taught me, and then turned and began walking back through the markets.

They didn't look the same anymore. I was shocked to find so many greedy, ugly, and hateful souls. It was overwhelming. As my pulse pounded in my ears, I dropped my eyes to the ground and rushed as quickly as I could through the throng.

Once home, I was relieved to find that the little uns had nice white souls filled with innocent desires about food, hugs and play. Seeing them calmed me a little which, in hindsight, helped me bear the confrontation to come.

"You contracted what?" roared Mama. Mama's true self was a hideous, writhing beast, filled with greed. My heart raced to look at her.

Mama scooped up Lentil in her arms and put him to her breast. He closed his eyes and began to suck contentedly, his true self glowing with delight. Mama's other breast oozed milk, staining her dress.

"The true sight infection," I repeated.

"I never heard of the true sight infection. How do you earn from that?" she demanded.

I took a deep breath, already knowing Mama wouldn't like what I had to say.

"The old lady said I can use it to find a resident of the Compound and get an invite inside. And once I do, I won't forget you and Pa and the little uns. I'll send money out, I swear."

"Ha," Mama said without mirth. "A resident of the Compound indeed. And here I was thinking you kids might listen to your Mama every once in a while. I told you to put such nonsense out of your head."

"The old lady did it. She lived there for fifteen years. She said she used her true sight infection to —"

But Mama wasn't listening. She cut me off.

"More like the waste of time infection. Your Pa gave you good money to contract a disease that would help you pay your way. And you wasted it on a parlour trick and the promise of a happily ever after. I'm just glad he's at work right now so I don't have to see a good man's heart break. I can't believe I gave birth to such a stupid girl," Mama spat. She pulled Lentil off her breast, turned him around, and then pulled her dress down so he could get at the second.

"You know the rules in this family. You don't earn, you look after yourself," she said sharply, her eyes on the infant in her arms. I tried to swallow but couldn't, my mouth was so dry. I could already see what Mama wanted, she wanted me to leave. She birthed us so we could grow up and then earn for the family. Sentimentality ended there for Mama. I blinked hard to force back my tears as Mama turned her icy gaze upon me.

"I want you gone by tomorrow."

"What about Pa," I said quietly, "what will —"

"Don't you worry about Pa. He and I are one on this. You can stay here tonight, but on the morrow you find a way to look after yourself. We can't afford to keep silly girls who waste our money on a worthless disease."

I didn't know how to say goodbye, and I definitely didn't want to face Mama again, so I left before dawn while everyone was still asleep. I didn't take much with me — the last of my money and a few changes of clothes.

Uncertain what to do next, I wandered, familiarising myself with the effects of my disease. As the sun rose above the horizon, more and more people emerged from their mud brick homes. I was still shocked by the ugly souls I saw, but less so then yesterday. I supposed I was becoming accustomed to the sight. And as I wandered from my house to the Compound wall, to the Harbour and then through Central, I began to see nuances that had not been immediately evident in the aftershock of my contraction.

Not everyone was greedy or angry or hateful. Most people were complex. They displayed a good side and a bad. And the souls themselves differed, I saw. Some were simple, some complex. Some writhed like snakes, some were layered like roses, some were pulsing lights.

I began to realise my sight offered more than just a snapshot of a person. I was soon deciphering the building blocks from which each true self was constructed — the key experiences that made someone who they were. Mistakes, success, love, violence, family, and devastation. I'd catch glimpses of all these things, some clear, others obscured. But each told part of the story of who someone was, and who they were becoming.

Around midday I took my gifts to the Southwell Markets, where the mutant toilers gathered to sell fresh produce and grain along with a few tumour sufferers selling marinated skewers of their flesh. I knew the Compound cart would be loaded in around an hour and I thought that I could talk to the mutant haulers and use my sight to dig out a little information about the residents.

As I strolled through the markets, mutant hawkers hollered in a variety of voices and guttural grunts. Most of the mutants were pleasant to be around. I saw they were generally simpler folk, content with their lives of hard, honest work.

The day was growing hotter, which accentuated the ripe smells of melons, apples, bananas, and pears. Those sweet smells set my empty belly to rumbling. So I bought a shiny red apple from a hunched man with a fulfilled soul and then continued west through the markets.

As I bit into the sweet apple, juice spilling down my chin, I felt like I was almost content in this place. And then, to top it off, I found my resident.

He was sitting on a table wearing a white robe. Behind him stood seven cleans in similar dress. He seemed to have dark hair. I thought he was young. But, to be honest, I found it hard to decipher his physical appearance because I was dazzled by the most beautiful, glowing true self that I had yet seen. It was hard to describe. He was perfect in almost every way. Kind, generous, and loving, with pure motives and matching deeds. And yet I also saw, which confused me greatly, that he was infected. And his key desire was to remain out of the Compound.

My feet took me into the small crowd of diseased that had congregated around the resident. He was speaking to them. To us, I guess.

"A society is not distinct from the people that live in it," he said. "The systems in place, the rules imposed, the sense of community and our place in it are only powerful to the extent that we, the people, accept them.

"Have any of you ever been inside the Compound?" he asked. There were murmurs of no. "And why not?" he continued.

"It's got a big friggin wall for starters," a young, dark haired woman said, drawing laughter from the crowd. The resident smiled.

"But it also has a gate," he said. "Have you ever tried knocking? Or just pushing it open? It's not like it's guarded, is it?"

I saw the woman open her mouth again as if she had thought of something else funny to say, but she stopped, closed it and then shook her head.

"No. You've never tried because you've been brought up with the idea that it is prohibited. But who says? What makes the people out here different to the people in there? Why shouldn't you be allowed to visit the Compound as I am allowed to walk out into Central?"

"What's it like?" I found myself asking.

The young man turned and looked at me, his true self shining brightly, and yet his brow furrowed in concentration and his glowing soul darkened for just a heartbeat. He didn't speak for a time. He just stared, like he knew me. I felt my cheeks redden as he held my gaze. Finally, with an almost imperceptible shake of his head, he spoke again.

"It's very pretty," he answered. "And yet I hate it. Because it's false."

He spoke truly, I saw. He hated the Compound, but why? What did he know that I couldn't see? Every time I'd peeked over the wall it'd looked perfect to me. Heaven next to Central.

The resident turned back to address the wider group.

"Your places as the diseased, mine as the resident, are neither set nor ordained unless we accept them to be so. The system is what we make it. You can survive without earnings. And you can survive without disease. If you wish to try, come with me and I'll show you another way. It's hard work. You'll all labour and you'll all farm and you'll all build and you'll all sew. But you can learn, like I have, and together we can produce enough to subsist happily."

"You said survive without disease," a stunted mutant said.

"Yes. Only one of us needs a disease. I'll take your mutation."

I hadn't expected him to be a taker like Knife. That made even less sense, I thought. But now that he'd said it, I began to notice some of the signs. Elongated eye teeth, black stains around his lips, a bulge on his thigh that might have been a tumour.

"There's always a catch," the mutant said. "How much?"

"I only ask that you give my way a chance. Take the time to learn a skill and then pull your weight in our community. Nothing more."

The crowd erupted into a roar. Some cursed, some laughed, most turned on their heels and wandered back through the markets. But not all of them. Not all of us. I stayed, as did two mutants.

The mutants spoke to the resident first. He talked to them in whispers and soon I saw them nodding. When they were done, two of the nearby cleans led them away from the markets.

Then it was my turn. I didn't know what to say, or what to do, but I stepped closer, drinking in the pureness of his true self. He looked at me again with that uncertain gaze and my stomach fluttered.

"And what disease do you have that you wish me to take?" he asked.

I took a deep breath.

"Actually, I'm happy with my disease."

"Yet curious," the resident said, as he slid from his table onto his feet and took a step towards me, his head tilted slightly to the left. He smelled nice, I thought, like the streets do just after a thunderstorm. Clean and fresh.

"Why would you leave the Compound?" I asked, at which he chuckled. Feeling my cheeks redden, I lowered my gaze.

"No, don't be embarrassed. A pertinent and direct question. I like it. But explaining why is harder than showing. Perhaps you would like to see my community. I think it is far more appealing than the Compound and this city."

I raised my eyes once more and in the dazzling glow of his soul, I saw that he spoke truly. He believed that his community was wonderful. And yet, there was something else. He desperately wanted me to join him there, I saw. But why, I couldn't quite see. I reminded him of someone, or of a particular time in his life, but the experience was from long ago, and was mostly hidden. I couldn't quite untangle it from the rest of him, and that made me more curious if anything.

"No strings attached?" I asked.

"None. A visit only, then you can decide if it is for you or not."

I paused, just like Mama had taught me when negotiating — make them wait. But who was I kidding? I was going to follow this man. Eventually, I bit my lip, nodded. Even if this went nowhere, I rationalized, I could at least use my time to find out a bit more about the Compound from him.

"My name is Lowen," the resident said, holding out a hand to me.

"Fennel," I replied, taking his warm hand in mine.

Lowen lived about an hour's walk from the city — an hour further afield than I'd ever travelled in my life. To be honest, I'd never even contemplated the world existing beyond the city limits. I was surprised by what I found.

It was cooler. Gone was the hot tar, brown buildings and the stink of cohabitation. Instead, I found vast fields of yellowed wheat, rows of green vegetables, and mutants working their land.

It was quiet, and yet I was also assailed by constant noise. I didn't understand how quiet and noise could coexist like that. Long silences were punctuated by insects whirring, birds singing, lizards and field mice scurrying through the plants, and the crunch of gravel under my feet.

After a time, the farms thinned, and then disappeared, replaced with meadows of green grass and yellow flowers, which ran towards the horizon before rising up into undulating hills.

Lowen pointed out his home when we were still a few miles away. It was the only building that marked the landscape for as far as I could see. It was a large, mud brick building, but it was poorly constructed. The western wall was already crumbling in the sun. The roof was thatch, and several spots looked in need of repair. Behind it ran a small creek.

As we turned off the gravel road and onto a dirt path that ran up to the building, I noticed several cleans working in the fields on my left. To my right was a fenced enclosure housing a number of strange, white animals that I had never seen before.

"They're called sheep," Lowen said as we passed them.

"And what do you do with them?" I asked.

"They provide us with wool for our garments, and milk and meat."

"You eat animals," I responded, part horrified, part bemused. The idea had never occurred to me. Lowen laughed.

There were about twenty people working and living in the community. Other than Lowen and the three of us diseased that had followed him home that day, they were all clean.

"This is Robin," Lowen said, introducing me to a girl a few years older than myself. She was short, very slight of build, and she smiled broadly. "Robin joined us a few months ago and she's currently learning how to weave and sew. We make our own clothes and blankets, and trade excess in town for the things we can't yet grow ourselves."

"Nice to meet you," Robin said. Robin's true self showed her as grateful, happy, hopeful, but there were also some scars there, past experiences that had hardened her, and that she was working to forget.

"What if you don't like it?" I blurted out. Lowen chuckled, but urged me to continue. "What if it's too hard, or you miss home or ... I don't know, you just get sick of sewing and want to leave?"

"Then I can go," Robin said, looking to Lowen.

"This isn't a prison, Fennel," he said. "Robin has the same deal as everyone else. I took her disease, and she tries to live clean while she learns the skills needed to survive out here. But no one is keeping her here. Anyone who wants to return to the city, can."

"And has anyone ever left?"

Lowen smiled.

"I'm sure there've been times when people have thought about it. But so far, no one has actually left. They're sticking it out, giving the work a go."

I must have looked doubtful, because Lowen quickly continued.

"It's hard to understand unless you experience it, Fennel," he said. "How about you let Robin show you around tomorrow? She can take you to her classes so you can try things first hand. What do you say?"

I hesitated, looking from Robin, to Lowen, then back again.

"It's not so hard learning to sew," Robin said, smiling. "It just takes a little practice."

I took a breath.

"Ok."

"Great. I'll meet you first thing tomorrow," she said, and soon after she was walking back to the building.

"So, I guess this means you're staying with us," Lowen said.

When I glanced across at him, I saw his heart radiated gold light. At that moment, as a smile danced on his lips and in his eyes, there was nothing more I wanted to do than please him by saying I would stay for good. But that wouldn't be the truth, I knew. I rubbed my fingertips together. They could still feel the rough brick wall of the Compound. I wasn't certain Lowen could or would help me and yet...

"I'll stay for a little while," I said.

The following morning, I sat in the main hall on a mat on the floor, Robin beside me. The trestle tables that were used for meals had been pushed against the walls, the chairs stacked neatly beside them.

Other cleans sat in groups around the hall, like Robin and I. Some sewed, others were peeling vegetables for lunch. Still others were twisting white wool into yarn. Wool that was apparently cut straight from the backs of the sheep out in the paddocks.

Robin was watching intently as I pushed my needle once more through the piece of cloth.

"Good," she said. "Now pull the thread until the stitch is tight."

I did as instructed, the thread making a *whisk* sound. I flipped the material over and looked down at my work. The stitches weren't as neat or as evenly spaced as Robin's, and there was a dot of red in the middle where I'd pricked my finger, but I felt a smile forcing its way to my lips.

"You're a natural, Fennel," Robin said.

When I looked up, I saw her true self filling with pride, in me, her student.

"How did you end up here, Robin?" I asked.

"Same as most people, I guess," she said, turning her attention back to her own sewing. But she wanted to talk, I saw.

"What did you give up?"

"Nymphomaniacism. Before I met Lowen I sold myself in Collins Street."

I looked away from her, embarrassed. I'd never been to the nympho district, but I knew of it. Everybody knew of it. It was good money, it was said.

"I'm sorry."

"No need to be sorry. Lowen saved me," she said. But I was sorry. Because I could see her essence darkening, stained by the memories of despair and dread that she had carried with her in that past life. That she carried still, deep down.

"After my sixteenth name day, I worked the street. It was hard and easy. Hard up here," she said, stopping her work to point to her temple, "because the disease made it easy, made me want to do it, even when I didn't like it, even when I ... even when I began to not like me." She swallowed, eyes down, leaving me to wonder just how bad it had got for her before Lowen came along. I suddenly didn't want to look at her to find out, so I glanced away. She cleared her throat and continued.

"Anyway, I was there around six years before Lowen found me. He told me what he was doing and what he was offering. I didn't think on it for long. I'd been dreaming of an out for a long time, and he brought me a better one than I'd ever contemplated. I came home with him and, well, here I still am."

I looked back at her, her true self lightening as her thoughts turned to Lowen.

"He's quite compelling, isn't he?" I said.

She smiled, bashful, before looking up at me.

"Yes, he is."

Just then, the main doors opened and Lowen entered the hall, all eyes turning towards him. He stood at the edge of the room, searching for a moment until he looked in our direction. Then he was smiling, and approaching quickly.

"We've got a master seamstress in the making here, Lowan," Robin said. I felt my cheeks redden.

"I see," he said, stopping next to us, looking down at my work. "May I?" He held out a hand and I gave him the material. He studied it carefully, as if admiring a work of great art. Then he nodded and handed it back.

"You have a real knack for sewing, Fennel." Then he turned to Robin. "Do you mind if I borrow your student for a while?"

"Not at all," Robin said. "We were due a break."

The sun beat warmly on my back as Lowen led me away from the hall towards fields which emitted a sweet, loamy aroma. The air around me hummed with the drone of bees flying to and fro. A steady clack,

clack, clack rang out from near the road where one of the cleans was using a large mallet to hammer a fence post into the ground.

Lowen stopped just shy of a bed of cabbages. Three cleans were hunched down in various spots, pulling weeds from the rows.

Lowen dropped to his haunches and pulled a weed from between two plants. He tossed it casually aside.

"It looks like hard work," I said, just to fill the silence.

Lowen looked up at me and smiled.

"It is. Very hard. But until you've eaten something you've grown yourself, it's difficult to explain how satisfying hard work can be."

I nodded as if I understood. But I didn't. I got that doing something yourself could give some brief satisfaction, like my sewing, but would that feeling last long enough to warrant giving up all of the conveniences of city life? I wasn't so sure. Standing again, Lowen dusted his hands against each other.

"Tell me about your disease, Fennel," he said.

"I've contracted the true sight infection."

"I don't think I've heard of that before. What are the effects?"

"It allows me to see people truly. Who they are and what they desire."

"Hmm. And what do you see in me?"

I looked at him for a while before answering.

"You're a very, very good man, Lowen," I said.

"Thank you for saying so. What else?"

"I see that you believe in your community, that you consider that this is the true purpose of your life. And ..."

"And what?"

I hesitated, looking again at his hatred of the Compound.

"Why don't you want to return to the Compound?" I asked before I lost the nerve. And as I did, his brow furrowed and, just behind the whiteness of his true self, I saw something darker, something which almost revealed itself, but then slunk away, leaving gold and white.

"You seem to have a fascination with my old home," Lowen said. I didn't deny it. I didn't say anything.

Lowen sighed. "Appearances can be deceiving, Fennel. Particularly when those appearances are manufactured to instil envy and separation.

"What do you know of the origin of diseases?" he asked.

"There's always been disease, hasn't there?"

"Yes and no. Yes, they've always existed. But their willing contraction and exploitation, that's much more recent."

Lowen looked off into the distance, hands twisting within each other as he gathered his thoughts. Finally, he continued.

"Once, those living in Central were not much different to those in Eastern Heights. This was before the wall.

"Eastern Heights always had nicer houses, but anyone could buy one if they had the money. And the way you earned money was to work hard, to be the most skilful builder or artisan or chef. And importantly, back then, anyone could learn those skills.

"After a while though, a group of proud, old families with money — like my own — decided that this 'new money' was not something they wanted to associate with. They didn't like the constant expansion of the elite. And so they came up with an idea. The old families began convincing people in Central that the hardest workers were mutants. That the best clothing wasn't sewn, it was harvested from a leather skin. That the best meat wasn't from sheep, but from tumour sufferers. And as the old families paid for these services, the inhabitants of Central began to contract the diseases sought after by those with the money."

"Only someone who grew up in the Compound, who's never gone without food, would think that was a terrible trade," I blurted out, seeing his true self anger as I spoke the words. I swallowed, watching him wrestle with his beliefs and the realisation that his upbringing might have left him devoid of the life experience of the people he was trying to save. Eventually, the anger dissipated, the white and gold returned. He nodded.

"Ok," he said. "Perhaps I can understand why the poor bought into this system. Perhaps. But the residents could have shared their wealth in other ways. Instead, they created a new class of worker. Workers who would never be like them. Because old money was clean. New money was diseased. And that's why you can only look into the Compound from afar. They created a system that makes you different. The wall just punctuated the declaration."

I looked down at my feet, shuffling in the dirt, watching it form little brown waves that washed over the toes of my shoes.

"But you could change all of that," I said quietly. "You could vouch for me, for all of us, to come back with you."

He stared at me then, emotions chasing themselves across his face — shock, confusion, dismay.

"That wouldn't be change, Fennel."

"So you've never even thought of going home? Don't you still have family there? Friends?"

"No."

I saw he was lying.

"So nothing could make you return?"

He hesitated, looking out over the workers.

"Right now, there's nothing I can envisage that would make me go back. But I'd be naive to say things will never change. Sometimes life steers you towards doing something you don't want to do."

I wasn't certain he was still talking about the future.

"You know, your disease," he said, turning back to me, changing tack. "I don't think you need it."

"Oh really, why's that?" I said, bemused.

"You don't need a disease to see the true self of someone. You just get to know them. At least that's what I do."

The following day, Lowen left for the city with a cohort of cleans, including Robin. He entrusted me to a man called Thomas, the first person who'd agreed to give Lowen his disease.

Thomas' true self was different to Lowen. To Robin as well for that matter. It wasn't imbued with hope, it was just neutral. Neither good, nor bad. Resigned to the fact that this was his life now, and a realisation that this might be as good as it got for him.

We spent the day together weeding vegetable crops. It was monotonous, back breaking work. Down on our knees pulling weeds from rows, being careful not to crush the carrots, cabbages, or whatever other plant we were working between. Within an hour I was sweating, aching and ready to throw it in. But I didn't. I made myself go on. Trying to understand why anyone would do this day in, day out.

"It's better than the pain," Thomas answered when I put the query to him. "Those hawkers in the disease markets never mention it when they're selling the diseases, but most infections bring suffering at one point or another."

"What did you have?"

"The tumours. They were uncomfortable to carry, and they hurt like a bastard when you sliced them. Not as bad as some diseases, but it built up on you. Got so I hated the idea of cooking, of someone approaching my BBQ. But then Lowen did, and he had a different proposal for me."

I shuffled forward, grunting as I shifted position, yanking at another weed and tossing it behind me.

"But let me ask you this. How many hours a day would you have had to cook for to earn enough to survive back in the city? Compared to this, I mean?"

"Oh, I don't know," he said, stopping to wipe his brow and squint up at the cloud mottled sky. "Probably a couple of hours a day and I'd earn enough to eat and pay the rent. Another hour and I could afford a few luxuries."

"And two, three hours of that was worse than ten hours here doing this?"

He looked across at me and just shrugged. But his true self wasn't quite as nonchalant. He'd had similar thoughts, I saw.

Memories of pain faded over time, and he'd sometimes wondered if it had all been as bad as he liked to say.

"I'm not going to lie. I've wanted to go back at times, but I never have."

"Why not?"

"Lowen, mainly. Maybe the pain back there isn't that much worse than the hard life here. Maybe. But I've never known anyone in the city willing to give me as much as Lowen has. And it's not just him taking my disease. It's the time he gives to me, his interest in me as a person. God, sometimes I think he even likes me. No one before Lowen ever made me feel like I might be a better person than I was. Not my Mama, not my ex-wife. No one. I stay for that feeling as much as anything. For a little of Lowen's glow to rub off on me from time to time."

He turned his back on me and hopped over a row of plants, plucking at the ground again.

"Why do you think he did it? Leaving the Compound to begin taking diseases that is?"

For a long time there was silence.

"Don't know," Thomas eventually said without turning back to look at me.

"Aren't you curious?"

"Yep. But Lowen doesn't want to talk about it, so I don't push him. Whatever the reasons, I expect they're personal and none of my damn business."

Which wasn't a good enough answer for me.

"Do you miss it?" I asked Lowen as we walked beside the creek that burbled quietly, whispering to itself.

Friday was a day of rest for the community. I'd been preparing to spend mine in bed, give my aching muscles and raw fingers a chance to recover. But Lowen wouldn't have any of that and so, instead, here I was, forcing movement into my sore body.

"Miss what?" Lowen asked, his true self growing opaque.

The Compound, I wanted to say. *Your neat house, your family.*

"Being clean," I tried instead. I watched him relax again, his essence becoming white, slightly translucent, flowing like the creek.

"Yes, I miss that. Sometimes. But then I remind myself what my disease is achieving."

"Hmm," I said, trying to fight the smirk forming at the corners of my mouth. I didn't succeed, not completely. Lowen saw me smile.

"What?"

"It's just you've been trying to convince me to give up this disease of mine and join the community and, well, here you are spruiking the benefits of your own affliction."

Lowen chuckled, a light throaty guffaw.

"I see. Well, we're all allowed our contradictions, aren't we?"

"I guess," I said, continuing to walk. A breeze erupted from across the stream, poking at the water and blitzing my hair. I brushed my fringe out of my eyes and turned to see Lowen glancing at me, but he turned away quickly as I caught him.

"What about you?" Lowen asked, staring ahead, like he was intentionally avoiding my gaze. "Do you miss being clean?"

I walked for a while, thinking, not exactly sure of my answer until my mouth opened and the words began to spill out.

"Yes and no. Meeting you, meeting Robin, it's nice seeing just how good people can be. On the other hand, it didn't bring me much joy to see how many truly greedy, sad and evil people there were in the city. But if I gave it up, it'd feel like I was just putting my head in the sand and pretending everything was right with the world. I don't know. Part of me wishes I didn't know people could be so bad. Part knows that this disease has opened my eyes to the real world."

"Hmm, the real world," Lowen muttered.

"What?"

"Nothing. It's just the way you talk of the Compound ... You haven't actually seen any residents since contracting your disease, have you?"

"I've seen you."

But I knew that wasn't what he was getting at. I sighed.

"You really believe the residents are despicable, don't you?" I said.

"I know they are. It was better to start again than try and change the lives in there."

"You seem ok," I said, shrugging, smiling.

It was meant to be light hearted but, behind his white soul, I saw a flicker of something black responding to my words. Then Lowen was turning from me and walking ahead, quickly. What had I said? I hurried to catch up with him and then I fell in step alongside. We walked in silence for a while.

"Can I ask you," Lowen said after a time, "how you were intending to survive with your disease? How would you earn?"

From tricking a resident into taking me back, I thought. *Someone like you.*

"I was told if you could discover what someone wants then you could be rewarded for helping them achieve their desire."

Lowen stopped suddenly, his true self lightening again, and then he bent over and splashed some of the creek water into his face. He stood again and turned to look at me.

"What do I want? Right now?" he asked.

I looked at him. I could see his desire to swim, to splash, to cool down in the shallows of the stream.

"You want to bathe."

"And why would I need your gift to help me achieve that?"

I frowned. That wasn't what the old lady meant. Nor was it what I meant.

"I ... I guess ..."

But then he reached down and splashed me with water. And I squealed and frowned and smiled. It felt so cold, and yet good, like I was alive. And soon I was rushing into the stream and kicking water at him. Like a kid. Like we were both kids. Who didn't care what our Mama's would say when we came back cold and wet and dripping.

Walking back to the community, our gowns soaked, smiles still on our faces, I looked at Lowen again and saw his true self buzzing. He was happy. And part of that happiness, I saw, was being with me.

My days continued like that for a while. Sewing garments, pulling weeds, peeling vegetables. My fingers grew calloused, my body began slowly to adjust. I was still bone tired when I'd lay my head down each night, but the aches were less.

Lowen would often seek me out at meal times. And on Fridays we'd go walking for half an hour here, an hour there, whatever he could spare away from his responsibilities.

When I was with him, the community was nice. I could almost forget the drudgery of the work, the repetition, the boredom. I liked our walks. I liked our discussions. Most of all, I enjoyed our arguments about the city and our debates on how life should be lived. What that said about me, I wasn't quite sure.

But then, they'd be over. And I'd go back to sewing, or weeding, or digging. And Lowen would go to town to recruit. Sometimes for a day. Sometimes for a few. And when that happened, my mind would wander. I mean, what else could I do? The work was hardly intellectually stimulating. And by the end of those days I'd have grown tired of it all. I'd despise the place and what I had to do to contribute to the community. And in those moments I'd find myself thinking about my family, and the city, and the wall, and what was waiting for me on the other side of it.

Eventually, I began to realise that nothing had changed inside me, really, despite Lowen's best efforts. I didn't see myself in need of saving like the others did. And I didn't see the same kind of beauty out here that Lowen saw. Or if I did, it was fleeting, and I also saw the hard work as just hard work. And my desire to live more easily back in the city, in the Compound, remained.

I needed to go home, I realised. The surprise in that thought was the sadness that accompanied it.

"What do you want in life, Fennel?" Lowen asked me. I sat across from him at the long table, a bowl of potato soup before me, its earthy scent making my mouth water. I'd miss the food, I knew. It was one thing the community did really well.

I looked up from my bowl and spied something new in his true self. I didn't understand it at first.

"I don't know," I said absently. I dipped my spoon into the soup and then raised it to my mouth. It was warm and creamy with just a hint of smokiness. Delicious.

"You've seen what we can offer here, now. I feel like a choice is nearly upon you. Have you had any thoughts on what you will do? Is this life something you could buy into?"

I looked back at him and, yes, there was something new. Concern? Maybe. Warmness? Yes. And, *oh,* I thought. It was affection. For me. I felt myself blushing and looked away.

"What do you want me to do?" I asked, glancing back at him, my heart racing.

I watched him mull the question over. I watched his affection grow. But there was a nervousness there. This was very important to him, I saw.

"I want you to give me your disease and then stay here with us. With me."

But I didn't want that. What I wanted was for Lowen to take me back home. Back to his real home.

And then I recalled some of his past words. He'd once said that he could never rule out something cropping up in life that would lead him back to the Compound. Could that something be me?

Maybe this was the opportunity the old lady had been talking about. Find a resident, determine his desires and use them. I was Lowen's desire. Rescuing me was something he needed to do. So what if I gave him what he wanted? Gave him my gift to see truly? Wouldn't he then see me like I'd seen him? And once he saw how much I needed the Compound, that it wasn't just fantasies and words, that it was something deeper, in the core of me, well, how could he refuse to take me then if he truly cared?

"Ok," I replied, watching the shock etch his features.

It was gentler than the giving of the true sight.

Lowen led me to the sleeping quarters, which we had to ourselves while the others ate. We sat amongst the bedrolls and faced each other. A crude wall hid us from the common room.

Lowen gave me a gentle kiss and then, with an exchange of breath, I saw him. Not his true self, his physical self. To my shame, my impulse was revulsion.

The golden glow of his beautiful soul no longer obfuscated the tumours that riddled the right side of his face. Nor the black tar that slid unwanted from his mouth. Nor the tusk that poked through his left cheek. Nor the hair on his arms, nor the hunch of his back, nor the rancid smell of his rotting feet. I fought against my urge to retch and forced a smile to my face hoping it didn't look like a grimace. With rheumy eyes, he looked me up and down.

"I see you truly, Fennel," he said.

"And?" I asked.

He hesitated, and then tears budded in his eyes. He cleared his throat, blinking hard.

"There's nothing for you here. Not now, anyway," he croaked, looking away, like he was ashamed of me. Like I'd failed him somehow. Or he'd failed me.

"But, but," I stammered, "but you care for me."

"I do," he said, eyes still averted. A tear rolled down his cheek. "Too much to give you what you want. I can't take you to the Compound."

"But it's your home —"

"This is my home," he cut me off.

I sat there stunned. I wanted to scream. I wanted to demand that he give me what I wanted. But who was I kidding? My plan, if you could even call it that, involved little more than the fancy of a young girl deluding herself that she could be clever. I'd gambled and lost. Lowan would never help me achieve my true desire. And I hated him for that. I hated this place and these crazy people.

Without a word, my rage simmering under a stony exterior, I rose to my feet and left.

It wasn't long before I was back in amongst the heat and noise of the city. It was familiar and yet strange. Like I had immersed myself within a distorted reflection of the place I'd grown up in.

The stench of civilisation assaulted me wherever I went. And people. Everywhere. The sick and diseased jostling, bumping, crowding me. To escape them, at least temporarily, I sought out Western Park. I'd frequented it often when I was younger. It held peace, a little green, and, most importantly, a small hill from which I could just see over a low section of the Compound wall.

I arrived on dusk. It was as I remembered — the copse of elms and oaks, the wide lawns smattered with leaves, a central pond. And dominating the scenery was the red Compound wall. I felt a little gladder to see it. And yet it seemed more distant than ever before now that I'd given up my disease. How had I been so stupid?

I scaled the hill at the far end of the park, reaching the top just as the last of the sun sank below the horizon. I stood, looking over the wall at the tops of the white houses, watching the gas lamps come on like blinking stars as daylight leaked from the world. Finally, when the last of the sunlight was gone and I was left in darkness, when I could see no more of paradise, I sat down on the grass to take stock, removing the last of my money from my pack.

One hundred and forty-nine dollars. I counted it again to be sure. It wasn't enough, I knew. I couldn't start again with that. It wouldn't even be enough to afford the mutations. I sighed, realising I only had one option left. One chance at making something of the mess I'd created for myself.

I stuffed my money back in my pack, and I left the park. I headed south towards the foot of the Yarran ranges, to the edge of Southwell, where the wealthy diseased lived in new homes neatly rendered with dark mud. This was where the takers plied their trade.

I'd only visited once before, but I found the house easily enough. It was at the end of Rosen Street, small for this area, but neat.

I took a deep breath as I approached the front door, and then knocked, suddenly nervous that he wouldn't answer, or that he would and he'd turn me away. I realised I was holding my breath. I exhaled. And then there were the sounds of soft footsteps approaching the door from the inside. And before I could think of what I would say, the door clicked, and was opening. I was met with a look of suspicion, which quickly dissolved into surprise.

"Fennel?" my brother said. I noticed he had a hint of fur poking out from under his collar, and slightly elongated front teeth.

"Hello, Knife."

After I'd told him everything, I waited for Knife to respond. He sat across the wooden table from me, his brow furrowed, his mouth a silent frown.

I took a sip of my tea, grimacing as I realised it had long grown cold. I placed the cup back on the table with a soft clink, and then looked around Knife's kitchen.

The stove was new and clean. It looked like it had rarely been lit. The crockery on the shelves appeared to be for decoration only. I doubt he ate here very often, but I guess he could afford not to. The kitchen opened into a lounge room. A couple of leather couches faced an empty, blackened fireplace.

"So, you want my help, I suppose," Knife said, drawing my attention again.

"No ... I mean, I guess."

He sighed.

"And why should I help you, Fennel? You got yourself into this mess. You picked a disease I've never heard of and then you gave it up. Why? What did Mama teach you?"

I swallowed, trying to force back the lump in my throat.

"I'm sorry, okay? I just ... I just don't know what to do."

He sighed again.

"How much money have you got left?"

"One hundred and forty-nine dollars."

He shook his head.

"I'm such a soft touch," he mumbled to himself, pushing his chair back and rising from the table. I watched him walk into the kitchen and reach under the bench where he withdrew a ceramic jar.

"I'll spot you the cost of a disease," he said, removing the lid from the jar and reaching inside.

"I want to get my true sight infection back. It only cost —"

"A useful disease," he said, cutting me off. "You wasted money once. You aren't wasting mine, okay?"

He stared at me until I looked away. And then I felt my head nodding as I blinked back the tears.

"A friend of mine, Majoris, she trades in leather skins and she's after a new recruit. I'll talk to her tomorrow about a contraction. You can work for her for a while, earn enough to pay me back and then find a place of your own."

I hesitated, swallowing. Of all the diseased, leather skins were the most hideous. More so than mutants, worse than tumour sufferers. I wanted to refuse, I wanted to argue for something better. But I didn't. What choice did I really have? I turned back to Knife and nodded again. He thrust some bills at me, which I accepted, tentatively. I felt the tears then, hot on my cheeks and salty at the corners of my mouth.

Knife's hand was suddenly under my chin, lifting my face to look at him. He wasn't angry anymore, he was just my brother.

"You're really obsessed with this Compound thing, aren't you? Always have been, I guess."

I shrugged. What could I say?

He sighed again.

"Majoris, well, there's something else about her. She sells to the Compound. Her girls get to visit for the harvesting."

A smile must have broken out across my face then, because he smiled too.

"Now don't start getting silly ideas. It isn't what you wanted. You won't get to stay long. But it's the best I can do for you."

When I threw my arms around him and squeezed he stiffened at first, but then he relaxed and returned my embrace. After a while, he pulled back from me, holding me gently at arm's length.

"You can stay here till you find your feet. But it's time to grow up now, Fennel. Time to be responsible. Time to make your own way in the world like the rest of us."

Majoris was a woman in her fifties with brown hair, flecked with grey. Her neck and arms were covered in scars. I presumed they continued under her black tunic, across her chest and back.

She'd been a leather skin most of her life, she told me, but she was clean now. One of my brother's clients. Contracts with the Compound can change a fortune like that. She'd done her time, sold her skin and now, well, others worked for her.

She gave me a good deal, at least that's what Knife said. It was four hundred and fifty dollars for the contraction, and Majoris agreed that any future profits would be split between us sixty, forty — my share being the forty. As I paid the upfront fee, encouraged by Knife, I couldn't help but feel that I was handing over a part of myself to this stranger.

When the transaction was done, Majoris brought one of her girls in from outside. She was short and frumpy, her face tan and rough. Beneath her tunic were misshapen bulges where the excess skin was forming. I tried not to see me in that girl. I tried not to shudder as she pricked my finger and mixed her blood with mine.

"Four weeks," Majoris said, when the girl was done. "I'll be back then to inspect the harvest." She tossed me a small jar containing a pearl coloured, translucent gel. "Rub that into your back, belly and legs when the disease takes hold. It'll keep your skin soft."

I nodded, but couldn't find any words.

"Thank you, Majoris," Knife said on my behalf. "I'll make sure she's ready when you return."

The skin on my belly began to change first. It darkened in colour, and hardened until it didn't feel like me, until it was puckered, and foreign. I applied the gel Majoris had given me to keep the skin supple.

My back followed next. And then my arms, legs, my neck and face. And once the constitution of my epidermis had altered, it began growing.

I watched in horrid fascination as the skin of my belly loosened, bunched, then sagged. It was separating from the fat and muscles beneath, becoming a flesh blanket that folded back on itself. And still it grew bigger, longer, until the skin hung to my waist, then my thighs, my knees. My back followed trend, loosening, expanding, sagging.

I continued to apply the gel, but it became more difficult and time consuming as I had to work my way between folds of the hardened skin.

It was still me under it all, I told myself. But I didn't feel the same. I stopped going outside because, when I did, all I got was stares from passers-by. But even staying locked up in Knife's house didn't protect me from the realisation of what I'd become. Knife tried hard, but he couldn't completely hide the flickers of disgust that flashed across his face when he saw me.

So I kept to myself, I grew, I applied my cream. And as my skin expanded, so did an emptiness inside of me. Would I adjust eventually? I wondered. Would I learn to cope with my new life, my new self? I expected I had too. Everyone else did. And the Compound. I was going to get inside the Compound. It was that thought that kept me going.

Finally, my body having changed, my skin ready, I stood with Majoris outside the Compound gates waiting to be admitted. My stomach roiled and twisted, excited to go inside, nervous about what was to come.

It was just on dusk, but I was still hot under the girdle Majoris had given me to wear beneath my tunic. It allowed me to walk without tripping, as she said it would.

The gates clicked, and then swung inward. My heart accelerated, the sound of it loud in my ears as I took in what I'd longed to see.

The Compound was stunning. The tarred roads of Central ended at the wall, fading into wide, cobbled streets. There were footpaths, and gas lamps creating small pools of illumination. There was grass, and gardens — red and white roses contrasting with dark green foliage. And of course the houses — immaculate, white buildings that lined the streets.

I tried to consume every detail so I could return here in my mind, over and over, after my visit was done. But Majoris didn't allow me to dwell on the scenery for long.

"This is Miss Constrine, my most important client," she said, guiding me inside the gate.

Miss Constrine was tall, with pale skin and a sharp, angular face. Her dark hair was pulled back so tight it looked painful. She wore black leather, I saw.

"Pleased to meet you, ma'am," I said, remembering the manners Mama had taught me.

"Hmm," Miss Constrine said, as if I hadn't spoken. She began to circle me slowly. "Yes, it will do, I think. Very nice. The light colouring, good skin." I stood still as she walked around me. She completed her loop and then stopped, staring at me as if appraising chattels. I suddenly felt self-conscious, unsure of how to hold myself. I felt inferior in this woman's eyes and, unbidden, I recalled how Lowen had always looked at me and realised this resident was nothing like him.

"Come," she demanded. She turned and walked up the cobbled street. Majoris took my arm in hand and led me after her. I wasn't sure I would have voluntarily followed without Majoris' cajoling.

Miss Constrine led us into the yard of a nearby house decorated with elaborate columns. Large, dark windows looked down on me, like the black eyes of some monster. I wondered why there were no lights burning, but I soon realised we weren't heading inside.

I followed Miss Constrine around the back of the home, where there was a second building. It was rendered white like the main house, but the building was small and flat. Barely a room, really. It had no windows, which I thought odd, but a large door was wide open, warm light spilling out.

As I walked inside, my heart beat harder, and I began to feel nauseous. The floor was cement, sloping to a long grate at the back of the room. In the middle stood a large metal table with four cuffs for hands and legs. A smaller metal table, covered in implements, was close by. The room had the faint scent of ammonia.

"This way," Majoris urged, guiding me to the table. My legs were stiff. They felt foreign as I moved. *I'm in the Compound,* I reminded myself. But it no longer seemed important.

Majoris helped me undress as Miss Constrine began inspecting the scalpels, scrapers, and other metal instruments. Eventually, she turned to survey me.

Her gaze across my naked flesh was piercing, appraising. I wondered what I would have seen of her if I still had my true sight. Not the beauty of the Compound gardens, I thought. Not the whiteness of the houses.

"It's ok," Majoris whispered to me. In her eyes I saw understanding. It'd been her on this table years before. "Miss Constrine is a professional. This will be done very quickly. Now, please, lay down on the table."

I looked at it. It was immense. And reflected in its sterile surface was a distorted reflection of my face, frowning, eyes darting to and fro looking for someone to save me. But no one did.

I climbed onto the cold table and lay face down, trembling. Majoris clipped my wrists and ankles into the cuffs. I closed my eyes, willing this to be over as soon as possible.

Miss Constrine was near now, leaning over me. I felt her gaze boring into the back of my head, and then her cold touch in the folds of the skin of my back.

My breathing grew harsh. I could feel it bouncing back from the surface of the table, warm against my cheeks. My body was tense. I knew what was coming, and yet, I knew I didn't really know.

And then it began.

There was an electric pinch high up towards my right shoulder blade, and then it was moving quickly to my left, followed by what felt like a burning hot coal being dragged across my back. I screamed. I couldn't help it.

The skin on my back was wrenched, and I heard tearing, felt the warm blood rolling over my sides, and I screamed again as my back caught alight, fire flickering over the top half. The electric pinch of the scalpel was back, just above my buttocks. I bucked hard, but the restraints held me in place.

There was a clatter as the scalpel was dropped into a tray. I could hear Miss Constrine grabbing another instrument.

Something stabbed my right side then, like a punch in the ribs. I groaned, tears streaming down my face, pooling on the table in front of me.

And then something metal, foreign, was forced into me, under the skin, and worked back and forth, slicing at my nerve endings like someone prodding a rotten tooth. I bucked again, hard, trying to escape the pain. I was on fire, and I could taste copper in my mouth where I'd bitten my tongue. My own screams reverberated around the room.

I couldn't stand this anymore. I wanted the agony to end, God I wanted it to stop. My flesh burned as I felt it all coming loose, being cut and pulled from me as I wailed and wailed and then, thankfully, the world faded, replaced with blackness.

I awoke back in my bed in Knife's house, lying on my side. My body hummed with pain, throbbing. I tried to move, but my back and stomach screamed in protest and I inhaled sharply, my vision jolting as I settled back into the uncomfortable position I'd been left in. I swallowed, took a deep breath, cold sweat beading on my forehead. My throat was parched.

"Knife," I croaked. "Knife."

At first I wondered if he was even at home, the house being so quiet. But then he was standing in the doorway, a glass of water in his hands.

"Hey," he said. He approached, dropped to his knees, and then he awkwardly held the glass to my lips so that I could sip a little coolness into my mouth.

"How did I get here?" I asked when I was done.

"A couple of residents helped Majoris get you back. She applied a poultice to your wounds. You're to leave it on for the next couple of weeks."

I adjusted my head to look at my belly and could see the padding under my tunic. It felt moist. A coolness dousing just the tip of the steady throb of pain that encased me.

"Okay."

"She left your money here. A pretty good haul, three hundred and fifty."

I winced. "Take it. And take the other hundred I owe you from my pack."

He looked at me for a while, then nodded.

"You did good, you know? And it'll get easier. The diseases always do. I took a while to adjust to mine as well. But I learned, as you will. We all have to bear our diseases, the good and the bad," Knife said, repeating Mama's words.

"Do we?" I asked before thinking.

Knife inhaled. I thought he was going to say something reassuring. Something to make me appreciate my new life more. Something that would inspire me.

"Eight weeks, Majoris said. You'll be healed and ready for another harvest then."

My eyes felt hot, and I blinked hard, but a tear escaped anyway and began to roll down my cheek.

"Don't worry, you can stay here till then. After that, you can look for your own place, hey?"

He rose back to his feet and went to the door.

"Why do we have to suffer to earn?" I asked, stopping him halfway out of the room. He turned slowly, looking over at me.

"It is what it is, Fennel. As it always has been. And always will be."

But I wasn't so sure anymore.

It was a week before I got out of bed, two before I could move freely around the house. The pain receded slowly, as Knife said it would. And as my wounds healed, I began to feel more like my old self. Because my skin wasn't growing yet, and I was almost pain free.

If I was to operate on eight week cycles, this was the sweet spot, I realised. This was my window to be me.

The day I left the house, I headed first to the Compound wall, running my fingers lightly against its rough, red surface. I saw the white houses, in my mind, the cobble stoned streets, the gas lamps and gardens. And then I saw the table, Miss Constrine's glare, my terrified reflection clouding with hot breath. I pulled my hand back sharply, shaking my head.

I wandered Central, re-familiarising myself with the town. I had lunch at the harbour, watching birds glide out over the sea.

At two o'clock, I staked out the Compound gates. I saw two mutants admitted to deliver a cart of grain. And as one wandered away from the cart, just slightly, he was quickly surrounded by three large residents, imposing themselves, pointing, cursing, herding the mutant back towards his cart and out the gate. And I felt strange watching the display, the ugly bravado. What did they think he was going to do? Suddenly disappear into the Compound never to be found again?

Afterwards, I found myself back at the entrance to the Southwell Markets. There was a risk of finding Lowen here, I knew. I didn't know how I would feel about that, or what I would say. And yet a small part of me hoped I'd see him again. So I immersed myself in the crowd, inhaling the scents of fresh fruit, losing myself amongst the cries and pitches of the mutant hawkers. It was nice being back.

I made my way to the end of the markets, needing to see if the community were preaching today. And they were.

Robin, who I'd last seen holding needle and thread, sat on a table, some familiar people in white robes standing behind her. She was offering to take diseases from those that had gathered around her.

Where was Lowen, though? I didn't understand what had happened.

I joined the crowd and listened to Robin's spiel. She spoke kindly, she spoke well, but she was no Lowen.

After everyone had finished laughing and cursing and had wandered off, I approached her cautiously, nervously. The disease had darkened my skin, hardened my cheeks, but she recognised me and met me with a smile and a hug. I winced as she squeezed, my body still tender.

"Fennel, it's so amazing to see you. How are you?"

"Good, I'm good," I lied, pulling back from her. "So you take diseases now too?"

Her face grew grave.

"Yes. I have to. Lowen's no longer well enough to recruit, I'm afraid. He doesn't have much time left. But we're making sure his good work will continue."

"Oh," was all I could manage to say. I felt like someone had torn open my intestines and stirred. I hadn't even thought of him dying. I could feel tears stinging the back of my eyes.

"Would you like to see him?" Robin asked. "You could come back with us, just for the night if you like?"

I desperately wanted to go with her and yet I shook my head fiercely.

"No. I can't. I've ..." but I couldn't say anything further. Robin placed a hand on my shoulder, but I shrugged it away and then I turned and moved. She called after me, but I couldn't respond.

I found myself running through the markets, chased by the startled and angry yells of a mutant whose apple cart I'd knocked over as I escaped.

I didn't go out again after that. I locked myself in Knife's house and grew. I applied my cream, and I thought on everything that had happened to me, and I wondered about Lowen and how he was faring. I wondered whether I should go back. I wondered why I couldn't. But mostly, I waited. And waited. Until, eventually, the time for my second harvest was upon me.

Majoris walked quickly, but I forced my weak legs to keep up. It was the middle of the day and it was hot under the bulky girdle that squeezed my folded skin against my body. But that wasn't going to slow me. I marched behind Majoris, determined. *This is the only way,* I repeated Knife's words to myself. The only way. And I almost believed it until the Compound gates came into view.

The feeling of dread that had been building in the pit of my stomach over the last weeks consumed me then, and without consciously willing anything to change, I found myself at a halt, standing in the middle of the road.

Majoris continued to stride ahead for a few paces before she sensed I was no longer following. She pulled up, and then turned to look at me, her expression confused and slightly annoyed.

"We're going to be late, Fennel," she said.

I swallowed, thinking back to my last visit to the Compound. Thinking to the work I'd done in the community. Thinking of Lowen.

"If there'd been another way for you, a way to survive that didn't hurt, that ... that didn't steal so much from you, would you have taken it?"

Majoris stared at me, into me, like she was trying to determine my state of mind.

"This isn't really the time, Fennel. We need to get going."

"Please," I said.

She held my gaze a little longer, but then she glanced away and sighed.

"I had options, other diseases. But they all have costs. And rewards. I sold my skin, but now I'm clean. The same could happen for you if you do your time."

I swallowed again. I didn't believe her, not really.

"What if you could have lived clean from the beginning?"

A laugh escaped her, like something unpleasant she was spitting out.

"Like the residents, you mean? That's not for me."

"Because they wouldn't accept you?" I replied.

She snorted.

"Because even if they did, that's no way to live. They've locked themselves in a prison to keep away from people that they've imagined are beneath them. But we're all the same, really. I prefer to live my life freely, amongst real people."

"But how were you living freely when you sold your skin to them?"

"I'm free now. I'm clean."

"And what about me?" I whispered.

Majoris shrugged.

"You do the best with what you've got."

What did I have, I wondered? Leathered skin for selling, a brain for scheming, hands for sewing, legs to pull a plough. I shook my head.

"Come, we're late."

"No," I stated, and as I did, relief washed over me. "I can't. I'm done."

"Fennel, please. They're ready for us."

"No," I said again, more firmly. Majoris' eyes narrowed in response, and her lips formed a thin, angry line.

"You do this, my door is shut to you. There's no returning if you spurn me now."

"I know."

I stood at the foot of the dirt path looking up towards the ramshackle, mud brick building just shy of the creek. A few workers in white garments stopped to look at me, but they soon returned to their work as I began the trek up the hill.

Knife had tried to talk me out of my decision, but he hadn't succeeded. I knew he'd never understand, but I left him details of where I was going anyway, just in case.

Word of my arrival must have spread for, by the time I reached the top of the path, Robin was waiting for me.

I stopped before her, aware of my rough skin, the mounds of flesh held in place by my girdle. After our last meeting in Southwell, I didn't know what to say. Thankfully, she spoke first.

"I'm glad you came back, Fennel. And so is Lowen. He'd like to see you now if you'd like to see him?"

I nodded, grateful she'd made things easy for me.

I followed Robin into the hall and then through to the sleeping quarters. It was as I remembered, except one corner had been partitioned off with blankets hung from crude beams. It was to that corner that Robin guided me.

She gave me a gentle pat on the shoulder and then pulled the blankets aside.

The scent of rot hit me first and I stalled on the edge of the crude room. A tiny figure was huddled under a white blanket in the far corner, a wooden pail to the right, a jug of water on the left.

"Fennel, is that you?" Lowen croaked, and suddenly the figure moved, rolling onto his back. I took a couple of shallow breaths, then stepped inside and knelt down next to Lowen. Robin allowed the blanket to fall back into place, leaving the two of us alone.

He looked hideous. The top of the blanket was stained black from the tar leaking unbidden from his mouth and nose. His face was a mass of tumours. If he could still see through his yellow, weeping eyes, it couldn't be much. His tusk had grown larger and hair was spreading down his neck. God only knew what his limbs looked like underneath the blankets.

"It's me," I said. "And I'm so sorry. I should have come to see you earlier."

He shook his head.

"You have nothing to apologise for."

"I do. I've been so naive. I thought there was an easier way. But nothing's easy. Nothing."

"No. It's not. But some things are worth working for. A community. A home. Are you coming home now, Fennel?"

I cleared my throat.

"You'd have me back?"

"Of course," he whispered.

I didn't know why, but I burst into tears.

"How can you be so kind?" I blubbered. "How can you still want to help me after what I did, after what you saw of my true self?"

He just smiled again.

"We all make mistakes, Fennel."

"You don't. You were right," I said. "I met another resident. She was nothing like you. Cold, aloof. She looked at me like ... like I was nothing. Like I didn't matter. Like I was just something to use and buy and sell."

"Fennel, she was more like me than you know. At least, the boy I once was."

I sniffed loudly and looked at him, confused. But he didn't hold my gaze. Instead, he closed his eyes tight. I saw a tear escape and roll towards his nose.

"When we first met, you asked me why I left the Compound," Lowen said, his eyes still firmly shut. "I left my home and contracted this disease for penance, Fennel. It was what I had to do to make amends."

He took a deep breath, opened his eyes and looked at me. I could see his pain. His shame. His self-hate.

"When I was young," he began, "I used to tour Central with my friends. It's what the residents did. We would egg each other on, take advantage, lord it over the diseased. But that's no excuse for what we did. What I did." He took a deep breath. "She was about your age, Fennel. And we lied to her. And then we hurt her. We hurt her so badly and —"

I leaned forward and put my finger to his hot, black lips, quietening him.

"I don't need to know," I whispered. "Whatever it was, however horrible, you've changed. You've paid your dues."

More tears surfaced in his eyes and then ran down his cheeks.

"Nothing I have done can ever undo what I did. But I can keep trying. Will you let me keep trying, Fennel? Will you let me take your disease?"

He couldn't forgive himself, I saw. Either that or he wouldn't. But letting him take one last time, well that was something I could do. Something that I wanted to do, for him and me.

"Yes."

Lowen died three days later. The whole community was there to bury him.

Soon after, and I couldn't tell you why, Robin asked me to accompany her into town to help her recruit. Maybe she had good instincts, because it turned out I had a knack for it. While Robin had a kind heart, her spruiking was never as compelling or as passionate as Lowen's. Whereas I had something different to offer. I had the authenticity of an unbeliever. I was the first person ever to experience the community and then leave. And people wanted to know why I returned.

Sure, I still got the laughter and jeers, but a lot of people also listened to what I had to say — about my love of the Compound, my plan to get inside, my diseases, how I had tried the community, left, and then returned when I realised the true cost of participating in the society imposed upon us by the residents.

And each time I spoke, people came back with us.

Lowen started something decent out here. A new way for people to live as people. It's hard work. Really hard. And it's definitely not perfect. But nothing is, I realise now.

Great sacrifice is required, not least from Robin and the other takers who will eventually give up their lives so that we can live ours. But we have no shortage of new recruits. And the bigger we get, the stronger the community grows.

There are going to be struggles to come. The city has begun to take note of us. Just the other day, three cleans were beaten by an angry mob that accused them of taking their children and workers.

But I see that we need to press on. The community was possible because of Lowen's dream and his sacrifice. But it will only live if we live it, and grow if we grow it, by bringing it to those people who don't know this life is an option yet — people like I used to be.

About the story

I read an amazing short story called 'The Wombly' by K. L. Morris (*Shimmer Magazine*, Issue 32). Womblys are strange things that attach themselves to people, turning those people into soap, or metal, or glass, depending on the type of Wombly. A Wombly can be passed to someone else to bear and, once they are, they can't be passed back. The story dealt with a family sharing the burden of a soap Wombly, where a young girl was asked to ultimately bear the affliction for her family.

I thought the concept in 'The Wombly' was fascinating. It led me to imagining some of my own terrible diseases. The first disease I explored was the laid-to-waste disease. I began to pull together a story about a character with this disease – I even wrote a few introductory scenes – but, I ended up putting that story aside as it was becoming a bit too depressing and predictable. Which is when I began to wonder if bearing a disease was all bad. Maybe, diseases could have some useful side effects – useful enough to make money from at least.

So, 'This Side of the Wall' really began with that concept. I thought up a bunch of diseases that were both debilitating and useful, and I created a city around them. I already had a character with the laid-to-waste disease, so I threw him into the story, along with a few others to see how they'd react. And what I discovered was that some of these people were happy to accept a life of disease, while some aspired for more – to join the residents in the Compound, for example – and still others wanted to create a new and better world for themselves.

A question for the author

Q: Do you write things other than speculative fiction?

A: No, not really. Whenever I start developing a story thinking it might not be speculative, at some point my imagination runs away with me and the finished product ends up including something supernatural, or strange, or weird.

It's what I enjoy reading, and it's what I enjoy writing. I love great characters, and reading about interesting people. But I think characters react in even more fascinating ways when you throw them into a speculative world, or you have them face some fantastic or horrifying scenario.

About the author

Michael Gardner is a public servant and economist living in Canberra, Australia with his wife and two kids. He loves contemporary fantasy and horror – really anything strange or weird. And he has a very patient wife who puts up with his taste in TV shows and movies, and lets him spend more time writing then he probably should.

Memory is a Rumor

Yaroslav Barsukov

In the heat, even paper seemed to sweat. Dr. Startsev's fingers left wet stains on the pages of the open notebook, on a number: thirty. Thirty minutes to try and deter the people about to enter his office from doing the irreversible.

He always hoped for thirty; but when the front door in the lobby opened and steps drummed on the laminated floorboards, a resolute ostinato, he corrected himself: at most, twenty.

Then a male voice rang, the barking 'a's and the rolling 'r's, and Startsev was down to fifteen.

Through the blooming headache, he imagined Mr. Turkin answering the receptionist: "I'm here to replace my son."

Something rolled and rumbled in the street, and the noise made Startsev realize that his hand on the table had convulsed into a fist. *What the hell is wrong with you, old boy, calm down, calm down, they aren't even in the room yet.*

Nerves would only hurt the kid's chances.

Mr. Turkin wouldn't say 'replace', of course—people like him never shared Startsev's views on character grafting, people driving imported Bentleys, people sipping Bacardi in sunlit lounges at midday, life's marketers and lenders. The man's knowledge of the procedure likely stemmed from the ads in glossy magazines; Mr. Turkin would say 'enhance.'

The door into the office, opening, threw a shadow over the glass cases on the shelf: butterflies, brush strokes of wings melting in the summer heat. Startsev had started the collection in the third grade; he no longer knew why, but now, as the pieces of the July sun slipped back into the picture-like frames, something stirred in him, and a silly thought occurred: maybe, if he saved the boy, he could remember.

"Good morning, Doctor."

"Good morning, Mr. Turkin, Mrs. Turkin. Kolya. Please, come in, take a sit."

They moved, figures assuming their places on a ghostly chessboard: the father, looking more like a hipster than an oligarch in his slim trousers, designer shorts, and sneakers, put on as though by accident; the mother, in a black-and-white polka-dot dress; and the son, a shorter figure trudging between them, clutching a mechanical dinosaur in his hands.

The boy. Kolya. Startsev's fingers spasmed again, and he forced himself to concentrate, try to piece together the parents' decision process: 'A bit too plump, a bit too passive for his age, stares at his toes all the time.' Over the phone, Mr. Turkin had summed his son up in one word: 'Slow.'

"I wonder if I've seen you before, Doctor." Mrs. Turkin lowered herself into a chair. "On TV, maybe?"

An acute feeling pricked Startsev, of being out of fashion, like an obsolete cell phone.

"Darling, please."

Mr. Turkin remained standing—and so did Kolya, after stealing a glance at his father.

"I'll repeat my question from yesterday: I'd like to know why we've been called here, after all the tests. My son has been through psychological and physical evaluations."

"It's not about tests," Startsev said and cringed inside at his own words. "This is an assessment of you as a family."

"Which our psychologist has already carried out," Mr. Turkin said. "How else could we've gotten a referral to this clinic?"

"We perform random checks to ensure the quality of practicing psychologists' work."

"So we've drawn the wrong ticket." Mr. Turkin nudged Kolya towards a chair and took the place next to him.

Startsev made an effort to smile. "I would look at this rather as an opportunity to get to know each other."

Mrs. Turkin stretched her hand behind Kolya's back to touch her husband's shoulder. She said, "It's fine, Doctor, we'll of course cooperate. And by the way, I'm sure now I've seen you on TV."

Mr. Turkin said, "On *Malakhov's Show,* probably. They like doctors. I take it then you'll be doing the operation?"

"No, I don't operate on patients anymore."

"Then? ..." A hand gesture, as though inviting Startsev to speak.

Then what the hell are you good for? Why are you intruding on my time?

Startsev said, "We're getting ahead of ourselves."

Kolya turned and looked back at the door; perhaps, on an unconscious level, searching for an escape.

A black leather document folder, snapping open. Startsev couldn't beg—a doctor begging just scared people; he had to follow the established dynamic, slide along the accepted routes, play the game. "This photograph. Could you tell me about the man, the donor? I may have seen the face somewhere, but I can't quite place him. Why have you chosen him for the character graft?"

The guy on the picture had a jaw which seemed wider than the rest of his head, a stretched smile turning his eyes into a pair of slits.

"Andrey Arshavin," Mr. Turkin said. "Midfielder in *Zenit*, the best footballer in the game right now."

"Does that mean you're interested in soccer, Kolya?"

The boy pressed the dinosaur against his chest. "Doctor, I—"

"He isn't," Mr. Turkin said.

"Then why this Arshavin fellow?"

Mrs. Turkin produced a neat little smile. "Our psychologist recommended him, and we both like the way Andrey plays."

"Dr. Petrov did a comprehensive analysis," her husband said. "Full mapping of Kolya's brain, plus nine or ten surveys. I mean, put together, how long have you spent in his office, Tatyana?—yeah, at least a day. He said Andrey Arshavin is the perfect donor for the character traits Kolya needs."

The yellow card in the document folder said, 'Resilience, competitiveness, will for success.' A fly, half-comatose from the heat, crawled onto Startsev's hand and stopped between the two bulges of veins. Sweat, palpable against the onset of a headache, burned a line on the back of his neck.

Concentrate, Startsev thought.

He said, "Kolya's eight years old."

The boy drew in a breath. "Eight and a half."

"Please do not interrupt the doctor," Mr. Turkin said.

"He didn't interrupt me at all—and thank you for correcting me, Kolya. At this age, how do you know he's not resilient enough?"

"He's afraid of math tests."

"I probably was too when I was eight."

Mr. Turkin leaned forward. "He's slow, he's not measuring up to his classmates. He has a 'Satisfactory' in math. A 'Satisfactory.'"

Startsev slapped his palm on the desk; he did it to shake off the fly, but the crack of flesh against wood broke some dam inside him. "Then maybe Kolya's the next Mendeleev. Mendeleev had mediocre marks at school. You yourself, Mr. Turkin, did you ever get anything above 'Satisfactory' in math?"

The man leaned forward in his chair. "Doctor, are you *absolutely* sure your guidelines include insulting your customers?"

Back off, rethink. No lashing out, not with these people, old boy. "Please forget what I've said." Startsev fanned his fingers and patted the table. "Must be the heat. The air conditioner's been dead for days."

"To answer your question, Doctor, we *are* certain he's lagging behind," Mr. Turkin said, "because our psychologist has told us that if we don't act now, Kolya would never reach his full potential."

"The potential—I'm sorry, Mr. Turkin, his potential, by definition, is right here in front of you."

Husband and wife stared at him. Kolya turned to look at the door again; no, not the door, Startsev realized: the boy studied the shelf, aquamarine wings in glass cases.

"Do you like my butterflies?"

Kolya jerked his head back around and straightened. He didn't appear frightened, only a little anxious: he must've sensed the tension in the room, but eight years was too gentle an age to comprehend the full gravity of the conversation. His fingers let go of the dinosaur and reached for his mother's hand.

"Go on, answer the question," Mr. Turkin said.

"I love bugs, Doctor. Insects, I mean. They're so different from us, like aliens..."

Something squeezed inside Startsev. *All the little worlds, we step on. That's what we're good at, stepping on precious little worlds, trampling them underfoot.*

You cannot, you cannot beg for him.

Mr. Turkin shrugged. "Spends weekends in the garden—"

Mrs. Turkin said, "We have a big garden."

"—taking pictures of beetles and such, can you imagine that? He takes photos and then, for a whole hour, arranges them on his table."

Without thinking, Startsev said, "I rearrange my butterflies too, every morning."

He immediately regretted the words, a part of himself he hadn't meant to share.

"Why do you rearrange them, Doctor?" the boy said.

"I... Doesn't matter." As though in a dream, Startsev glanced at the butterflies, wishing he could see them through the boy's eyes. Then he caught himself and forced his thoughts onto the more practical rails. "Mr. Turkin, Kolya may become an entomologist or a botanist. You should be proud; most kids of his age have no hobby at all."

The boy batted his eyelashes, and Startsev thought, *They don't praise him even a bit.*

Mr. Turkin sniffed. "Not much of a hobby. I'm not raising him to end up a loser. Ever heard of a millionaire botanist, Doctor? Money and success are in the financial sector."

Mrs. Turkin said in an apologizing tone, "We want him to be a winner."

Startsev rested his head on his fingers—*think, think*—trying to come up with next move the way a chess player would. He wished for the sun to stop, he wished it were evening already. Watercolor wings now seemed like eyes, gazing at him accusingly from the shelf.

"The operation, Kolya," he said, "do you have any idea what it entails?"

The boy hesitated and glanced at his father. "I want to become tough."

Startsev turned to Mr. Turkin. "Could we have a word alone?"

"If we must. Son, sit outside."

Behind the glass panel by the door, Kolya's silhouette slouched into a chair in the lobby. Dangling legs, just long enough for the toes to touch the floor. Hands, fumbling with the leg of the mechanical dinosaur.

Mr. Turkin said, "What kind of family assessment is this? I don't understand what you're trying to achieve, Doctor, but I'm this close to leaving—and then I'm going to have a talk with whoever runs this establishment."

"I'd like to describe the procedure to you," Startsev said. "Because some think we do it with magnets and lasers. What really happens is, we sedate the patient, and then we peel away the skin." He made a gesture as though taking off a hat. "Saw through the bone. Then the surgeon takes the scalpel and makes an incision, cuts into the lump of meat. At this point, the brain is just meat, and you need to cut it for the machines to go in and reshape the neural pathways. The doctor who operates the machines flashes a light into the opening every now and again to make sure nothing got jammed, and if you peek in at that instant, you see metal working inside the brain. Inside the *person*. And in my experience, the *person* who leaves the operation room is never the same one that has entered it. Whatever you may think, it's not an enhancement."

They waited.

"Do you realize how the grafting of character traits came to be?" Startsev said. "It branched off from a different procedure; 'personality transplant' as we called it."

Still, they waited.

"It was conceived as a remedy for schizophrenia."

"I know," said the father. "We researched online before coming here. Character grafts are trivial in comparison. Like, you've rules for it, the graft must not constitute more than ten percent..." He waved his hand.

"Mr. Turkin, as somebody once told me, there's no scientific definition of an individual. No definition of you or me. How much can you replace before the old 'you' ceases to exist? Twenty percent? Forty? Forty-five? If you take your son on a fishing trip, it's the most amazing thing in the world to him, and then a year later he can't even remember the occasion—is he still the same person?"

"We don't do fishing trips," Mr. Turkin said. "Fishing trips are a waste of time."

"Mrs. Turkin," Startsev said, "his dinosaur—the toy—things he loves right now, he may not love them afterwards."

He glimpsed a flash of fear in her eyes, and panic pricked him. How much time did he have left? He'd been wrong, he'd been wrong since the first moment, he should've concentrated on the mother, the mother was the key. Perhaps...

She said, "But he will still love *me?*"

Startsev opened and closed his mouth. Then he dropped his gaze to the documents as though he hoped to find there a cue which would allow him to say 'no.' "Love for one's mother is a deep-going instinct," he said quietly. "Kolya will keep loving you, yes. And yet I'd like you to consider carefully what you're doing. Please. Your son, the one that just exited the room, will die."

She rose her hand to her lips in a quick gesture, then said, "But I thought the mortality rates were zero."

Startsev studied Mr. and Mrs. Turkin: two human beings separated from him by an invisible, impenetrable wall. A decade ago, when that moment had come during his first prep talk, a part of him, inside, screamed, and scratched, and fumed, and fought for the control of the motor neurons—but years dull one's edge. Repetition upon repetition, they wash away everything but the underlying fatigue. He wished it were evening and he could curl in the corner of his office and cease listening, seeing, thinking.

He leaned back in his chair and took out a pen.

That's it, old boy. Let it go.

"This week is booked. I can put you down for next Tuesday."

They signed the papers.

At the door, Mr. Turkin paused, holding his hand on the knob. "This was no family assessment, was it, Doctor?"

"Goodbye, Mr. Turkin."

"I know where Tatyana saw you. I recognize you now. You're one of the graft's fathers. One of the original team? What are you trying to do, sabotage your own work?"

"Goodbye to both of you."

After the door slammed shut, Startsev leaned back in his chair and pressed his fingers against his forehead. *You're right, Mr. Turkin.* Sabotage was a strong word, though; his old colleagues had all but tied his hands—and they would've gladly removed him, too, hadn't he held a significant share of the stock.

What remained were these prep conversations: hardly sabotage, only a tiny chance of dissuading people from making the biggest mistake of their lives.

A handful of successes over a decade of failures—but still, he kept trying: his own private little war against human nature.

Through the glass, he saw the parents talking to Kolya; following an impulse, Startsev stood, picked up a butterfly from the shelf, and went into the lobby.

Behind the window, the far end of the street squirmed in the heat haze. Startsev watched the family exit the hospital; Kolya trudged between his parents, glass case under his arm. He took his mother's hand.

Startsev turned and regarded the insects on the shelf. One was missing now, but he surmised, with weariness, that it would return to its place on Tuesday.

Once, the butterflies had been important to him, but he no longer knew why, and no rearrangement of cases would help that. He didn't remember his own operation; he recalled the rationale—he was a remnant of an age when scientists believed the first test subjects should be themselves—but not the feeling. What had *that man* felt, lying down on the operating table and breathing in the first curls of anesthetic gas?

Memory is an internal rumor, he thought. Perhaps the old Startsev had never existed; perhaps it had always been him, in the white lab coat, in this office, staring at a collection of butterflies that belonged to somebody else.

A question for the author

Q: Have you ever wondered whether ideas are thought waves directed at you by an AI supercomputer located in the distant future?

A: I have, actually. I don't know where ideas come from or why it's sometimes so easy to forget them; it's as though someone would hand you a Post-it note and, in case you don't display an immediate interest, pass it on.

Why does the supercomputer have to reside in the future though? I'm a big proponent of digital physics, Universe as an output of a computer program and all, and I strongly suspect that we and everything around us is a simulation. As soon as I say it, people immediately think *Matrix*; but what if there's nothing else *but* the simulation? What if there's no real us, or beings like us, outside the program's boundaries?

The thought, to me, is too sad not to be true.

About the author

Yaroslav Barsukov is a software engineer from Moscow, currently living in Vienna, Austria. After leaving his ball and chain at the workplace, he goes on to write stories that deal with things he himself, thankfully, doesn't have to deal with.

www.facebook.com/tem.sweenoff, @YBarsukov

February

Love in Its Heart

David Z. Morris

It was the third one. The third ever, all in the same week. On the pipes, grainy handset video showed hulking masses, ungainly, asymmetrical, wobbling out of the sky. Tearing through level after level of the sprawling, towering city, girders screaming through showers of sparks. The first one on a Tuesday, a dozen commerce units over. Then another Friday, a little closer. And then on Saturday, just as the lights came on. Bang. Our zone.

It was still miles from my apartment, and I can't say I felt much fear. In a city of two billion, even the parting of twenty thousand souls seems insignificant. Abstract. I got to the dispatch center by nine. It was in the east 370-by-fifties, perched in the fourth ring of a seven-ring office park, lit by a fairly convincing sun and circling a bedraggled courtyard garden. Better than my place, anyway.

So we all went, called out of our hovels, some still rubbing sleep out of our eyes as we loaded cleanup gear into the eight grey, sharp-angled trucks. Hoses and bins and sacks of absorbent crystals, and newly-scrubbed hazmat suits under the hard benches in the back. We were silent, not grim but indifferent, some managing troubled naps as our convoy navigated the arcing labyrinth of roads toward the crash site.

We unloaded in front of a shattered, three-story hulk. The ship had none of the sheen and polish that the movies would have you expect. It was ugly, had been ugly even before plowing through the anarchic layer-cake of a thousand thousand homes. The giant fragments left, like the cracked shell of a spent egg, were covered in wires and poles and tubes, embedded in mounds of rubble and fresh human corpses, buried and wedged and threaded and impaled. Not built for atmosphere, I could see that much — but I left the question dangling. I wasn't paid to think, so I didn't bother.

What I did notice was the sun — the real, actual sun — emerging from a ragged tunnel torn through forty, maybe fifty stories of solid nested humanity. It seemed to dance over the corpses, giving them in death what they might have gone years without in life. It glinted from the armor of the ranks of Seattle police, and from the nearly-identical gear of the upstanding men of the U.S. Army.

The Tuesday ship had taken out plenty of ups, middles, and masses. But by Saturday the heights were empty — even my two-bit bosses were calling the shots from private bunkers at some unknown depth and distance. The corpses were people like me — too poor to hide or flee, or to have ever travelled to any edge of the city.

Still, just people — what got me was the dogs. Most were close to the surface of the pile, among the twisted remains of the higher levels. Tongues rolling out of crushed and severed heads, eyes still waiting for unworthy masters. To be rich enough to own a dog, and just leave it behind — the thought confused and saddened me.

I fought off feeling, as I fought off theories about all of this. I just bent over, picked up a metal shard and put it in one vacuum chute, or some wet, biotic chunk, and put it in the other one. Three years at Extreme Recoveries, and it almost felt like what I was made for.

Three years of sifting other people's shit and excrescence. Three years of their failed projects, lost hopes, by-products, accidents, leftovers. Like I belonged in the suit, with its empty yellow plastic slickness, a thing that never came to fit. Slogging through cisterns leaking unknown chemicals, pressure-washing breached biological facilities with hydrochloric acid, "remediating" leftover surface-to-space weapon installations.

It wasn't the life I'd hoped for, of course. Who would? I went to school for bioengineering. Life as it existed, and as it could be remade. They had been powerful, those dreams, those ambitions. But they remained vague, and quiet, and unfulfilled.

My parents were of the generation who bought into the myth of equality — born under black presidents, working under black CEOs, a brief dream in a time of plenty. They had begun to forget, begun to think that maybe we didn't have to work twice as hard. Maybe they passed that delusional ease down to me — or maybe I had just let them down. As the world became lean and hungry again, I learned how wrong they were. But not fast enough.

And with a only bachelor's degree in bioengineering, you got to clean up other people's failures.

I'm writing this now, after all that has happened, as the first and last serious product of my bioengineering research "career." It will have no audience, and little scientific value. But it soothes my soul in a time of need.

It was on that day, the third year rounding into the fourth, in the depths of my uncaring, that I reached down and saw something … different. A smooth, chrome egg, no bigger than the palm of a hand, almost blinding in that new sun. Some sort of bomb? An alien grenade? But the army had already swept the place.

Just moments after I picked it up, the egg's gleaming surface opened with a sharp crack. Startled, I looked around, but no one was close enough to hear. It truly was an egg, with a thin shell and inside — something.

A patch of black fur, neutral and mute — but with the aura of life. I picked up the tiny chrome fragment that had fallen away. It seemed machined, unremarkable. Unthinking, I let it drop into the metal chute, which snagged it with a breathy inhalation.

I opened up my suit and my coveralls, just at the neck. I slipped the cracked egg in against my skin, felt its warmth.

In the next second, with the feeling of returning from a dream, I cursed my stupidity. Some robot going through the waste might spot that shell fragment, trace it back to me.

I kept working, picking up stray bits of cabling, the slashed veins of the data pipes. I hadn't had data in my apartment for years.

The chrome egg was still there when I walked off the site, aching, filthy despite the suit layers, back into the truck. Again, we were all silent, exhausted.

"Make a good haul today, ya black bastard?"

Except, of course, for Rollins, who had plenty of energy left to talk. I just barely lifted my gaze to meet that drawn and hungry smile, those hollowed eyes, the spiked ruff of blonde hair.

If you'd asked him, he'd tell you he was just joking, being friendly. When I'd first gotten to Extreme Recoveries, I thought I'd be gone in a few months. So I never bothered educating the man. And now I was just too tired.

"Hey Nixon, c'mon, what's up?" He kicked my boot with his — friendly.

I didn't say anything. Maybe that made me the asshole. I felt a tiny movement against my chest.

"Aw, c'mon man, don't be like that. I'm just fucking around." Even after all these years, he was still confused, maybe even really hurt, when I didn't return his ribbing with a smile. But I didn't need it. Didn't need friends at all, even if someone worthwhile had come along. As much as anything else, I was embarrassed to watch him try, in his painful, perverse way, to win me over.

I turned to catch the last disappearing wisp of natural sun. We rode on in glassy silence.

Back at base, I went into the white-plastic shower room, where I had my one moment of privacy during a ten-hour shift. I opened my shirt and reached in, and found that the shell of the egg had fallen away. I felt bits of it working deeper into the suit, sharp but pliable against my skin.

What lay revealed was black fur, a tiny nose, eyes shut tight to the world. I gently lay the tiny form, still tightly curled, on the shower's cheap plastic bench. Then, perhaps responding to my touch, four paws unfurled from the darkness, huge and searching as black yawns. I watched rapt, while carefully fishing gentle metal shards out of my suit's waistband.

Two pointed ears topped its small, sleek head. A tail twitched out, as long again as the tiny body. Like a kitten — but not quite. Too-long legs, lips that curved the wrong way around, strange, tufted antennae on the ears. I felt no threat.

I scrubbed myself without taking my eyes off of it. Its eyes stayed shut, but its thimble-sized chest rose and fell. Then I turned the water to a warm trickle, thought about it for just a moment, and lifted my charge into the flow. The creature went immediately tense in my hands, and I pulled it out the next instant. Still without opening its eyes, it flicked its head, just so, sending water droplets flying.

However persistent my scientific delusions, I can't help but include the unscientific detail of that head-flick, that single gesture.

Because that was the exact moment it was all over.

I took her home, through the maze of shuttle pods and stairwells and catwalks that bound the city's workers to the lower levels. Red light lit my steps down corridors of cold steel. Clanging boots on the walkways, the rattle of rails, delivery runners, beeping lifters, mumbled talk — the last bits of work mingling with the first bits of trouble.

We were close to the shadowed hellscape of the surface, and we all felt it. Some just schlubs like me. But plenty of predators, who saw the undercity as their safehouse, their escape route. Every time I made it into my single room without having to posture or threaten someone, I was grateful — but this time especially.

Once we were safe, I set her down. She mewled and stumbled around, her eyes still shut tight. I examined her, gently. I immediately sensed her gender, and never doubted my intuition — but there was no evidence to either support or falsify it. When I pressed the pad of one of her paws, a bristle of claws in ranked orders quilled out. I counted carefully — six toes, and hidden in each toe, twenty-eight claws, tiny and delicate. Her teeth, likewise, came in a dozen even ranks, receding back into the depths of her miniscule mouth.

I decided to name her Adesina, a name from far back in my family line. The name given to the first of my family born in America, a message to the rose-tinted future.

I didn't have much to feed her. That first night, I mixed some water and nutrient powder, offered it in a spoon, and she blindly licked at it.

As I fed her, the free pipe news chattered out of its bulletproof screen, a constant educator bolted firmly to the wall. They were talking about the descents, and you could tell that even the government talking heads were scared. Sweat snuck down the anchors' foreheads as they introduced wild speculation from suited experts. It was not just our city — these dead hulks, these uncontrollable wrecks, were hitting Jakarta, Delhi, Osaka, Minsk, Buenos Aires. All of them unoccupied, seemingly inert. They were of no known make or model, no obvious origins. One of the experts insisted it was a Russian ploy, cooked up on Io. Another suggested Chinese. Still a third shouted wildly that they did not come from any Earth culture. Theories sparked and sputtered.

My mind drifted from the debate, and I felt no fear. I caught myself laughing mildly as I watched Adesina soak her muzzle in grainy white liquid. All any of it meant for me was warmth and fur, tentative motions, awkward steps, strange sounds from a secret mouth. Another being. A new life.

The next day, I came directly home and fed her. She blindly pawed her way around my lap. On Tuesday, my day off, I trekked to the desultory, rattling library and read a decades-old book about keeping pets. It said small mammals could drink cow's milk — a tiny cup would cost a week's check. I also used part of my data allotment to browse newer books, but they were clearly for people other than me — a single book on cat care cost more than my entire yearly salary. It wasn't until after I left that I realized I should have pulled up something on xenobiology.

On Wednesday, her eyes opened. They were large, yellow, with square pupils. Almost as soon as they opened, those eyes didn't just observe, but sought. Asked questions. Understood. She would look directly at my face, serious, serene. Her square pupils slid shut like airlock doors at each hint of brightness, so I dimmed the lights.

I thought of my own parents. They were offworld, now — able to give themselves that, at least, thank god. But no work there for me. So we talked at most once a month. They paid for the calls.

She was walking within a week — walking and more. She stalked the place, measuring and testing, pushing behind every piece of furniture. Sometimes she'd go into a tiny frenzy, ricocheting off the walls, clawing at anything soft or dangling. Twice in the first month, I came home from work, exhausted as always, to find the place a wreck, the kitchenette dismembered. Once even the fridge was open and ravaged, plastic wrap shredded, jars shattered on the floor.

Each night when I came in, I'd kneel down and scratch her between the eyes, a gesture I suppose I picked up from old movies. She would speak calmly in a strange, faerie voice. She'd rub her neck against my hand, and arch her back, and twitch her tail.

Then I made the mistake of trying to flip her over on her back and rub her belly. She exploded with rage, her ears furled and her eyes wide as her jaws gaped and her claws fanned out and down into my skin. It pricked and stung and bled, but after a brief retreat she subsided and licked my hand almost clean.

It felt familiar, earthly — but I was careful after that. I watched her with a biologist's eye, feeling old, dry knowledge unfurl within me. She grew too fast, and saw too much. Her waste came in neat, dry pellets — once a week, tiny and uniform and odorless. Within a month, she was as long as my forearm.

She resembled a creature from Earth, but was something else.

I know now how insane this sounds, how selfish and stupid. I sheltered an alien, as my world was under attack by mysterious forces. I said nothing, drew no connections, fed the alien, protected it. My curiosity had curdled years before. And what had this world ever done for me, to expect my loyalty?

I started sitting with her on the landing, in the very early hours, when we could go unnoticed. Then one day she dashed away from me. I searched for her, my gut in a knot — and a few hours later, she showed back up at the door, with a rat as big as herself in her mouth. So I started letting her in and out, at obscure hours we wordlessly agreed upon and kept to like clockwork.

She kept growing, and the ships kept falling — though less frequently. Twice, three times a month, spread out over enough of the planet that any one place began to feel almost safe again. Sometimes they even fell outside the cities, and the free pipes showed panoramas of those awful expanses — lifeless wastelands, glass deserts, glowing with industrial despoliation, crawling with diseased terrors. The greater horror our steel confinement was saving us from.

One afternoon I stood at a hamburger stall, and on a screen above the grill I saw the President. "Our naval laser cannons and detection matrix are now eliminating these threats *before* they enter the American atmosphere. We are keeping America safe for Americans."

But I knew different. I started spending more time at the trash bars — ugly places where trashmen like me were welcome. I'd known about them for years, but never bothered. Too good for them, I'd maybe thought. But now they were invaluable. I acted like other people, sipped beers, played pool, and heard rumors. Cities were still getting hit in America. One or two a month, no matter what the free pipes and the President said. Somehow the ships were dodging the lasers, or evading detection. Or maybe the lasers didn't even exist.

I would come back from my little fact-finding expeditions, sometimes with a warm buzz, a thing I'd not allowed myself for years. And I'd lie down in my narrow, wall-mounted cot, and as I started drifting off, Adesina would pounce on my chest, with a little huffy squeak. She'd settle in, kneading those paws and their pincushion claws gently into my chest, pushing her head up against the bottom of my chin, making a slow, steady noise like the rattling of dry leaves.

Whatever she was, she loved me.

The months stretched into years. A small industry of crashologists sprang up, and Extreme Recoveries was acquired by a descent-consulting conglomerate. The dispatch center was moved into the bottom of a big, shining corporate campus, further up the sprawl. It was a hell of a commute, a daily pilgrimage to a more beautiful world.

There were little descent conferences there — big names on posters, all titles and prefixes. When I saw the posters, I noticed something in my chest — a hollowness, a pull. I thought, maybe in there, they're explaining all of this. And I realized that knowing mattered to me, as it hadn't in some time. Drinking coffee and listening to panel discussions didn't fit into my schedule — but the emptiness remained.

Then, two years after the first descent, with Adesina now as long as my arm, there was a chance. There was a required training on disposal unit protocol, but I knew it like the back of my hand already. And there it was, another poster — "Game Theory and the Descents." A stylized illustration of one of the falling ships. Right in the middle of the training.

So I just left Extreme Recoveries after reporting for the morning, and walked through scrubbed-clean elevated tunnels, glancing out over glowing gardens that hid the slums below. The radiating, white-lit auditorium was at the opposite edge of the campus. I sat in the back, trying not to be seen, hoping my swiveling chair wouldn't squeak.

I was the only person in coveralls. There were others in suits, and a few of that particular breed of indulged slob — the rumpled academic scientists, in wrinkled shorts and flapping buttondowns and beards. I tried to make sense of the swirls of opaquely-worded speculation.

"This is psychological," said one of the suited and slick types. "Some kind of ploy. If they actually wanted to destroy us, there would have been bombs in the ships. Fusion isn't *hard*."

"That's not an answer!" shouted back another man on the dais. "We must assume that this is all *strategic*. I propose this thesis — there is something about the ships we have *missed*. Perhaps a virus. A slow poison. They are a preparation. A vanguard."

I thought then of Adesina. I had considered, of course, telling someone about her. She was information they could use, these big men, trying to crack the case. But I knew they would take her away from me. So I said nothing, to anyone. I began to wonder, very occasionally, if something was wrong with my mind.

But, I thought then, she didn't fit into their war-game scenarios. She wasn't a disease vector. She would never harm anyone. I'd lived in close quarters with her for two years, and I wasn't just healthy, but — I suddenly realized — happy. I would have my curiosity, but the suits and thinkers could go to hell.

Midway through the third or fourth panel, I left. I was halfway back to Extreme Recoveries when a voice rang out behind me.

"Yo, Nixon!" It was Rollins. Jesus.

He peeled towards me from a group of cleaners on their way out of the complex. They must have finished the training early. Rollins smiled broadly, his eyes bright slits over a coathanger smile. "Hey man! You over at that conference?"

I looked him flatly in the eye. Awfully lucky guess. "Yeah. I'm already certified on the new protocol, so Jorgenson said I should go to that thing instead."

"Huh," replied Rollins, rubbing the back of his head, bouncing on the balls of his feet. "Anything interesting?"

"Just a bunch of eggheads," I replied. "They don't know shit."

"The bosses, they gonna make you a scientist or something?" There it was — the aggression masking weakness. I thought of the water-lizard, a lost species which had used a delicate, expansive neck ruff to hide its tiny body.

"I don't have time to let you fuck with me, Rollins." His face collapsed in confusion as I turned to head home.

And of course, that was the day they first followed me. I noticed two men, out of the corner of my eye, like motes or shadows. You get good at that — at first I thought they were muggers. I put my hand in my pocket, making as if I were hefting something there. But they kept their distance, and I lost them.

Adesina pranced to greet me. I made my hands into playful claws and ruffled her head, then turned to the pipe. A descent in China, one outside Lagos (that happened sometimes — a near-miss). None in the U.S. of A, of course. No sir.

It wasn't until the next Sunday that they knocked on my door. I looked out of my peephole and saw them there, in dark blue jumpsuits. No insignia. More than a guy in a suit and tie, or even in body armor, you worried about those blue jumpsuits. Someone must have reported me, but no one knew.

I opened the door just a crack.

They told me my name. They said nothing about the conference, or the training I'd missed. They told me where I'd been and what I'd been doing two years before — cleaning up Descent Number Three.

Then they stopped telling, and started asking. I told them yes, I'd been on that site, but no, I didn't remember tagging or chuting anything unusual, no. They asked if they could come in, and I told them, no, I'm really sorry, but I've got a guest in here, and I made with some eye-bugging and an uncomfortable laugh and a sleepy lascivious grin. It would have made my grandfather roll over in his grave twice — he was the Attorney General of Nevada.

They looked at each other, and I saw them thinking just what I wanted them to — these lower-level boys, they got nothing on their minds but pussy. One of them shrugged and tapped something on his wrist, and they left. Of course, the truth was I hadn't had a girl around in years, but getting those jumpsuits off my doorstep felt better than any lay I could remember.

When I closed the crack of the door and turned around, though, Adesina had her back up against the far wall, her entire body arched and tense, her claws out in their terrifying ranks, her eyes glowing gold so bright it was almost blinding. Just as I shut the door to the outside world, her mouth opened and I saw her hundreds of razor-shard teeth, and a sound came out like the shattering of a tiny planet. It pushed me back against the door, knocked cans from a shelf.

Something changed after that. Snoop-theories started flowing through the trash bars — the jumpsuits were asking everybody questions, all the crews, and they all had their own ideas about why. For me it was a relief — they weren't targeting me. They didn't know about my Adesina.

But she started growing again. She'd still lie on my chest, her eyes closed as I stroked her. But within weeks of that unwelcome visit, her head tucked right under my chin and she stretched all the way down over my hips. By then she weighed nearly forty pounds. I got short of breath with her on top of me, and so I started pushing her off, leaving her to squeeze narrowly onto one side of the cot. She got used to it, I guess.

Things were even trickier when we played. One day I ruffled her ears, and she swatted at me, and I swatted back, and in the next second I noticed that the flesh between my thumb and forefinger was open like a wet mouth, a steady trickle of blood dropping to the floor. She hadn't even tried to hurt me.

I was used to no one giving a damn about me, so I didn't think twice about showing up to work with a bandaged hand. But Rollins noticed. I saw him stare at it — but he didn't say anything. He had gotten quieter, and I started seeing something in his eyes beyond half-friendly stupidity. Something inquiring.

Men started following me home more regularly. I stopped letting Adesina out. She turned moody, would spend hours curled up in a corner, alone, uninterested in me, one sleeping eye open. But she kept growing, and started eating so much I had to feed her cheap cultured food — the sort of flavorless pseudo-protein paste the Light Church fed to indigents. She didn't seem to care. Just kept staring at the door.

Then one night, she leapt up to join me on the cot — and the wall creaked. She halfheartedly tried to find a place to lay, but there was nowhere for her. I looked at her standing above me, searching, confused, and saw her as if I'd never seen her before.

The tiny thing I'd pulled out of a metal egg was now a hundred or a hundred and twenty pounds. Five feet long from nose to tail. And beneath that black coat I still thought of as warm and comforting — muscle, as hard as my own. Without leaving the room, without good food, she had grown into a creature of the jungle. Of another world's jungle.

That night, she slept on the floor. I made a nest for her out of blankets. But we couldn't stay. The net was closing.

I thought about it for days, on my way to and from Extreme Recoveries, watching over my shoulder, in and out of the dark hole I called home. The free pipes regularly streamed their panoramas of the desolate and unlivable land beyond the city. But there were different stories in the streets, in the trash bars. I'd heard them from my family, too, as a kid — tales of places beyond the city, where people could go. Some said they even knew people who had gone — people who were never heard from again. Nothing more than vague whispers passed among the cities' dreaming miscreants. A talisman of hope, like an unscratched lottery ticket.

It wasn't a good option.

I packed up a few things, put on a long coat. We left in the latest part of night, climbed down stairways that became more and more rickety, jumped across jagged walkway gaps, until I was finally climbing hand over hand down masses of rebar, tangled through skeletal steel frames that cut and ripped and shuddered with my weight.

I worried at first what Adesina would make of this place, how she would behave, whether she would even stay with me — but she followed without hesitation or confusion. Where I panted and teetered and hurled my body like a wobbling football, she gracefully arced through the darkness, flowed with light feet down impossible rails, dropped with cold certainty into one black pit after another, and waited for me, unscathed, at the bottom.

We were alone for a time, but as we went deeper, we began to see others. These were the scarred and twisted denizens of the lowest places, unwanted by anyone or anyplace else, even in the vastness of the city. There were lean-tos of blue tarpaulin, wrapped tight into hovels and wedged against pilings. Under them sat men with no noses, no eyes, no hands. We saw huddled clutches of children, naked and squalling like puppies at their dying mothers' dry teats.

And of course, there were the other kinds of outcasts — the toughs who banded together here, out of sight of the authorities. We glimpsed neon now and again, heard voices raised in brittle revelry. The welcome warning of danger.

But we couldn't avoid all trouble. From above, I'd spotted a rope bridge, a delicate pathway over a seemingly bottomless chasm — and at its head, a massive, hooded figure, holding a spiked iron club in one meaty, deformed hand. I scouted for ways around, but there was no other path.

So I approached him, and was relieved when Adesina seemed to disappear. I held myself straight, my arms at my side, unsure even of how to look menacing.

"There's a toll here," said the hulking man, a not-quite-human voice emerging from the darkness of the hood. But before I could reply, Adesina emerged beside me, her shoulder now as high as my elbow.

The tollman regarded her coolly for a moment, in shock or indifference. Then she stepped forward mildly, dropping her head as her jaw unfurled, and loosed that planet-splitting hurricane of a roar.

The brutish tollman tumbled back, his club ricocheting into the chasm as he scrambled to keep his balance. Then he turned and fled across the bridge, into the shadows. We didn't see him again.

And then finally, finally we reached it — the muck on which the city floated, the end of our descent. The light here was red and thin, like sickly blood. There was dirt — not the groomed dirt of an elevated garden, with its fluffy clumps that rolled out of your hand. This was dead earth, sticky, frozen in glutinous waves, full of bits of garbage fallen from higher levels; iron bars and rusted car parts and split batteries spilling acid; glowing slicks of strange lace over every diseased surface.

Great lichen grew on the carcasses of ancient traincars. Tremendous, pale-eyed rodents gnawed at tangles of rust — and fled at Adesina's scent. Every twenty yards stood the mass girders, so often hidden on the higher levels. Like steel tree trunks, forty feet around, spattered with filth and hard-earned graffiti — the foundations of the world.

This, certainly, looked like the outside world shown on the free pipes — nothing but mud and the skeletons of a dead past. Still, we were lucky. It was January, cool and dry. Three months later, the place became a floodcatch for the summer.

Adesina moved through it all with such smooth and untroubled confidence that I couldn't shake the suspicion that she had been there before, somehow — that she had gone far beyond the boundaries of the neighborhood on those early morning wanderings, that she had dreamed her way here as she lay entombed in my bedsit.

But still, she was alert, orbiting me like a nervous moon, flitting from one shadow to the next, disappearing and reappearing as I moved in the vague direction of a half-heard memory.

Any threats were gone before I knew. More than once, I felt the air go tense, heard an abbreviated grunt or hiss, and waited as she slunk back to my side, breathing heavily, her jaws dripping.

We moved for days, barely stopping to rest. There was no change in the light — not even the half-imagined traces of sun I treasured at high noon on a low city Saturday. I had only ever moved through the city on lifts and trams and winding walkways, and had no sense of when we might reach its edge. After ten days, I was out of food. After two weeks, when she brought me the corpses of sick and diseased and horrible creatures, I shared them with her, gratefully.

On the fifteenth day, or the twentieth, we rounded a corner — I in front, and Adesina roaming loosely at my heels — and there was a huge black shape there, and something flashed white in it, and I felt a violent blast to my chest. There were sharp pinpricks as I fell back, then rending pain — and then came another blunt impact, lifting the weight from me.

I scrambled to my knees, and saw Adesina grappling, hissing, clawing with a ferocity I'd never dreamed of — tangled with another creature that looked exactly like her.

In the next second, another figure emerged, running — a woman with red hair, matted and tangled, her round, defeated face contorted in panic and sadness as she ran towards the enraged pair of beasts.

"Stop, stop!" she cried, and she threw herself into the fray, and somehow she wrapped one of them in a bear hug (I could not tell them apart) and separated them bodily, even as claws and spittle flew around her.

She lay there, panting, not half as big as the creature she gripped. It roared and twisted and flailed, but the woman did not let go, though a flap of her face lay open like a curtain, streaming blood.

I stood, stunned, my mind reeling. The other creature backed nervously towards me, away from the entwined pair, and I thought it must be Adesina. I put my hand on her head, gently, and she calmed. I saw she was missing tufts of hair.

Then the other two slowed, untangled, and turned to face us. We all panted.

I looked at Adesina, and at the other creature. This was not how animals worked. Not how life worked. Variation was the heart of any natural species — different tones, eyes, shapes, angles. But these two were not simply of the same kind — they were truly identical. The same size, precisely. Their ears tufted in the same strange way, twitching with the same tension. Their eyes were the same shape and size. They were indistinguishable — except that Adesina now hugged close to my side.

"What ... what is this?" It was all I could manage.

The woman ignored her mauled face, staring numbly at the ground, not meeting my confused eyes. Her clothes were ragged and torn, and stained with blood all over. I thought of my hand, still carrying its accidental scar.

"You haven't seen others, then," she said, not a question, but an inflection of disconnected madness echoing sorrow into the space between us. "They are Drexal," she continued. "They are heralds. Bait. Traps."

Her hand rested on the other creature's head, and absently scratched between its eyes. It stared at Adesina, and Adesina stared back.

"Did you find an egg?" I dared to ask.

"It found me," she said, her lips moist and loose. "They found us." Then I saw the tag on her wrist — a medical designation of some sort, condemning its wearer to one of the towers for the sick or disturbed. The woman was on the verge of tears. "She made me happy, damn her."

And with that, she backed away, eyes darting. The great beast backed after her, its head low and haunches tense, its eyes not leaving us until it had disappeared into the bloody shadows.

We travelled for many more days after that. I became wasted and sick with bad food and poisonous water. But finally, a thing began to happen that I could hardly fathom — the city began to fade above us. When I looked up, I could distinguish the shadow of one looming tower from the next. During the day, true light began to reach us, first in a putrid yellow wash — and then, one day, there was a dusty, golden sunbeam, and I stood and let it warm my face for three hours.

There were scraps of grass, then plants, and then, as if in a dream, we were *outside.* And it was nothing like the pipes showed. It was like a platform garden that went on and on. The wind was an animal, playing against my face. In the distance, during the daytime, I saw the earth rising to meet the sky, covered in more green than I had ever seen, but also brown, and far away, farther away than my eyes had ever reached before, beautiful rising angles of grey and blue and white.

Adesina was unnerved. She twitched at every waving blade of grass, ripped bushes from their roots when they brushed her flanks, pawed at pools of water and hissed at her own image. But before long, she once again wandered far afield, and hunted, and brought me a new kind of prey — rabbits and birds, things out of books, more and better food than I had ever known. I knew that we were supposed to cook them, but I had no clue how — and they were still delicious.

I regained my strength, and then some. With Adesina curled beside me, I slept in beds of grass, and dreamed shapeless, vertiginous dreams. The world inside my head expanded to fill the world outside.

Then I thought of something, and for the first time looked back at the city. It was a massive aberration, smoking, flashing. It revolted me — but day by day it shrank behind us, until it was no bigger than the distant mountains.

I thought about the woman, and what she'd said. Adesina, and the other one like her — the woman had called them Drexal. They had found us. She'd been a madwoman. Yet she had pushed me closer to a certain dark knowledge. But now more than ever, I needed my strange companion, and I evaded that knowledge fiercely — just as I now saw, for the first time in the flesh, rabbits and grouse frantically evading eagles.

After leaving the shadow of the city, Adesina had grown again, now to six or seven feet long. We moved easily over the rolling, open land, unconcerned for many days about anything but the ground beneath our feet, and where the whispered promised land might show itself. But then, one morning, there was a low whirring in the air — a mechanical sound that drew me jarringly back to the city. I hissed at Adesina, who disappeared, and hid myself behind a rocky outcropping.

It was a large delivery drone, hefting a man-sized crate beneath its rotors. I watched its path, and when it was gone, we moved cautiously to follow it, keeping a lower profile. We spotted two more craft in the next few days, one some kind of menacing scanner luckily spotted from afar — but one a passenger vehicle, a large clear bubble showing the profile of dozens of people. It was hard to be sure, but I caught an impression of leisure from within that bubble.

It was not long before we came upon its destination. In a valley, a wandering row of boxes spread along a river and up an embankment — buildings, the kind that were common before the cities rose. From a faraway perch, I saw opulent silver statues and expansive gardens, carefully sculpted paths, playing fields and geometric pools of water. More drones came and went, in many directions, as tiny human shapes moved among it all. And, intermittently, a menacing laser would scan the surroundings, or a martial robot fly or roll into sight. We retreated before we could be spotted, taking a wide circle around the place.

This, I realized, was what the ups were hiding, why the free pipes insisted that the world outside the city was poison. I imagined dozens of opulent settlements like this, escapes from the city and its rabble. We kept the engines pumping for them, ran the hydroponic farms and the toothbrush factories, programmed the drones and crafted vapid distractions for the premium pipes. We stayed out of the way, confining our trouble to the lower levels of pocket worlds, while they wandered the unspoiled earth. I hoped that these were not the Edens that had been whispered of, for my soul knew they would execute me on sight.

So we moved on and on, and my clothes had nearly fallen away by the time we saw the first people. They appeared far in the distance, on a green expanse, and I felt Adesina hide herself. Over the next day, I spotted them again and again, moving closer, and I walked towards them, Adesina trailing invisibly behind. Finally, we met, and they approached me openly, easily and calmly — a group of four men. They carried long spears, and the tallest among them held a primitive gun. Their hair was matted and wild, their skin darkened by the sun, and they wore beards — all now true of me, as well.

When they were thirty feet away, they stopped, and then I stopped. There was something joyous about their manner, nothing of threat or anxiety.

"Hello," the tallest one said. "Do you mean us harm?"

"None," I replied. And I held out my naked palms.

"Then welcome."

The village was crude, but beautiful — buildings of wood and stone, touching the earth, full of children. It was surrounded by lush farmland, and I adapted quickly to tending the plants, mending tools, digging trenches to carry water from streams and wells into the rows. Some of the people had childhood memories of the city, but most had been born in this place. They listened to my descriptions of life in that tangle of metal and electricity with rapt horror.

Adesina disappeared after I went with the men — but I knew she hadn't gone far. A week after I arrived, as I tentatively explored the forest near the village, she quietly emerged from the shadow of a massive tree to meet me. She was larger still, now — her shoulders as high as mine, her body ten feet long, her ear-tufts brushing the lower branches. But she lowered her head, and I rubbed between her eyes, and she butted me in the chest playfully. Then she sat, looking down on me, her eyes more gentle and sad than I had ever seen.

We continued to meet there, in the woods, but she never showed herself to the villagers, and I never spoke of her. So we lived separately for those months, and I imagined her joyful life in the wild as I reveled in the warmth of the village. Extreme Recoveries, the falling ships, Rollins and all he stood for, seemed like distant things. Nothing but stories. I spent my nights welcomed in the modest huts of my new family, nestling into my new life.

I had been the first arrival from the city in half a generation — but suddenly, more began to come. First two, then five, then ten. The village took them in as they had me, and like me, they rejoiced in the place, and there was no strife.

But these new arrivals also shared stories explaining their exodus, huddled around fires like the primitives of the deep past.

"All the same. No motive, no suspect, just piles of gore, heads severed. High up or low down, doesn't matter a bit," said an old woman, a miracle she'd made it out.

"They found my son, in the play yard, he was ..." The young mother couldn't finish.

"I walked into the garden, he had just been out to tend the tomatoes. He loved a fresh tomato." I loathed the widowed heiress, even as I pitied her.

Blood dried into ribbons across the streets, unnumbered thousands cut down.

"Even on the elite pipes, we pay good money for information, and they gave us nothing — NOTHING." The businessman, in the soiled remnants of the suit he had worn in his rush to flee, was indignant and terrified. "Dark shapes, they say. Huge but unseen. The ramblings of a bunch of lower-level drunks," he huffed. Then, remembering himself, he apologized with his wounded eyes.

I wondered if his world was more shattered than mine.

"It isn't the murders," said a preternaturally calm young man, the fire glinting against his cracked spectacles. "A thousand deaths, ten thousand — who would notice? The problem is the unknown. The paranoia. Panic is starting to set in. Streetcorner doomsayers. New cults, dark prophecies. Hate groups, blaming the gays, blaming the blacks ..." And he trailed off, looking at me, as if this would surprise me in the least.

Again my mind dredged up the sick woman, with her madness and her medical tag, and Adesina's furious twin. Yet I refused to understand. I see that now, and I blame myself — but what could I have done?

So I continued to farm, began to think of the rest of my life out there in beauty, let the city and its problems devolve to someone else. I built a hut of my own, a crude thing of mud and thatch, at the edge of the woods.

Still Adesina came to me when I went into the trees, and lowered her head, and sometimes we even wrestled, and she was gentle and joyful. She seemed to sense when I was alone in my hut, and some nights she wriggled through the door, and lay next to me as we once had — but now she cradled me on her rising and falling chest. I had never slept so well.

Then the final new arrival came. He stumbled across the grasslands, just as all the others had — and I carried a spear as we went to meet him. He looked at me, and looked at the others with me, and I saw in his wide eyes wonder, fear, disbelief, suspicion, hope. It was Rollins, the edges of his face softer, the angle of his body opened. I felt a tiny curl of the past rise in my chest, but said nothing as we took him back. All that was over now.

He also said nothing, did not nod or wink or smile. He only spoke of the city, lost, toppled, burning. It was not the descents, no — the cults had risen, fear had taken hold, chaos reigned. Refugees had fled in every direction, he said, more bloodshed as the remnants of the police and army tried to stop them, penning them in the cities 'for their own protection.' When we retired that night, I was worried no more or less than the rest of the villagers.

The next morning, he was at the door of my hut, polite and still. I didn't let him in, because Adesina was inside, breathing deeply, curled against the length of two walls. But we sat in the grass, and he asked me about my life here. I told him I was happier than I had ever been, and the sadness that washed over him, the sudden tenderness of him, surprised me.

But suddenly the past came back to me, in the form of paranoia. "How ... how did you come *here*? Of all the directions to flee, how did you choose this one?"

"Oh, you know," he said, "Just street rumors." He gave a forced laugh, and something flared red within me.

"I have to ask you something, too." He plucked at the grass with a wonder only barely overshadowed by some other darkness.

"Go ahead," I replied, old caution suddenly remembered.

"You found one, didn't you? One of the eggs."

He watched my face. After years of control, of yes sirs, of the mask — in that moment, when I needed it most, my face betrayed me.

He looked back down. "I'm sorry we couldn't be friends, Nixon. I tried. But I tried wrong, I know that now." He paused for another moment, looking up at the clear morning sun.

"I really hoped we could be friends. But they didn't give me any choice."

And then I saw them — a dozen men in blue jumpsuits, carrying heavy packs, hefting black guns, flanked by robots crawling on six legs. They appeared over a gentle rise, as if from nowhere.

Rollins stood. From somewhere, he pulled a pistol and trained it on me. His hand shook.

"They told me you have one of the ... the creatures that's doing this," said Rollins, his eyes weirdly distant, his voice taut and fearful. "They have to be stopped. You left before they made their move — you're a sharp one, I always knew that."

Two soldiers seized me from behind, and two others advanced on my hut, hunched as turtles, large guns held before them like holy relics.

My knees were weak. "Rollins ... Rollins, what have you done?" Of course, I knew the answer. But I had nothing else to say.

Adesina rocketed from the door of the hut, and there was only one tiny, pitiful pop before the advancing men lay dead, obscenely mauled. The soldiers holding me dropped my arms and scrambled for weapons.

She moved like water, like smoke. She crushed one of their heads in her jaws, the metal of his helmet plinking with a hundred diamond punctures. I heard a horrendous sound, like a wet mattress tearing, and felt a spray. I looked, and saw Rollins holding his spewing guts as if cradling a baby. Adesina flowed sinuously towards the woods.

As Rollins lay down to bleed to death, I saw more shapes moving in the woods — and in the village. The soldiers raised their guns, trained them on my daughter, my love — and the villagers rushed the soldiers. In moments, dozens lay dead or dying. But I saw Adesina's shadow move smoothly into the trees.

Rollins was whispering something through bubbling blood. "There are hundreds of them ... thousands." He coughed and shuddered. "Help. Find them. Save us." And then he died.

Then came the firestorm. Over the next few days I saw more and more of Adesina's kin, if that was the right word. Black monsters, roaming freely now — all of them identically long and clawed and tufted. Impossibly identical. Such uniformity could not even be engineered, by any means I'd ever heard of. The environment had too much impact on a growing creature; even clones wound up slightly different.

But not these. Identical in form, and in function. Fighting the soldiers, fighting the villagers — though fighting wasn't the right word. Killing everything. The robots, the armor, the machine guns were useless.

Then came thundering choppers, hovering as they spewed lasers at the Drexal — but again and again, I saw the great beasts unleash their unnatural roars into the sky, saw the craft judder and slide to the ground.

Then came the jets and bombers, and when each missile or explosive whistled its descent, their targets fled into the trees faster than the wind, leaving the bombs to destroy only the land, to kill more and more of the survivors.

In all of this, some of the creatures were harmed — but not many.

I watched as the battle decimated the village, and watched the flashes of other battles, across the plains, on the flanks of the distant mountains. I knew I could do nothing to save my new family. Even the ups, in their mountainside playgrounds, would barely outlast the cities. But Adesina endured, appearing, covered in gore and radiating violence, to stop every threat that neared my hut.

Her protectiveness remained — but her affection was gone. And that is the truth of the Drexal. They found us in our deepest need — a need that was everywhere. They found homes, they found love — real love, I still choose to believe. The Drexal (I will never know where the name came from, whether the ramblings of a madwoman, or some secret singular connection to its source) did not know what plan they were a part of. Their lives, for them, were not stratagems or affectations — they loved, and were loved, in the way they had been made. This, I still choose to believe.

But the Drexal's love was destined to take on the enraged and defensive character of our own selfish regard. To feed terror with passion. When the time came, they showed their love in the way our world had taught them. They settled scores. They cleared ledgers. They protected — with a determination that was final.

This was how they were made. And how we made them.

So I sit to write this, as death mounts ever higher. I sit, and I wait, in this village, desolated like villages and hovels and secret resorts and burning cities across a world bigger and more beautiful than I had ever imagined.

I am alone now, save for Adesina. All I see of the final few beloved are the Drexal that roam on their behalf. They rage against each other, too — though always to a stalemate. Adesina comes back to me wounded, slinking, and with the last of each day's strength she fetches some new corpse — beasts, men, women, children. Unloved. I cannot scold her, I cannot stop her — she is fifteen feet long, and must weigh nearly five thousand pounds.

And I am hungry beyond reason, so with a heart full of horror, I eat what she brings me, and nestle in her blood-drenched fur.

I wait eagerly for those who gave us these gifts. Not because I long for an end — but because I long to know the shape of what we've invited.

What will the ships be like? The real ships — not the shattered eggs that ferried the hidden Drexal to the surface, but the chariots of their masters? Will they glitter fearsomely, as they descend onto this forsaken planet? Will they be black and unreflecting? Will they open to reveal something with limbs, and heads, and eyes? Or will there be something more terrible, something shapeless, or spaceless — something unlovable, twisting out of lost dimensions to take its prize?

Will we even know them when they come? Perhaps they are already here. Perhaps they are nothing but the return of this darkness to my heart.

Adesina, my dearest, our love has burned a path.

Let the bastards have what's left.

About the story

This story was inspired directly by a real cat named Nebula. My wife badly wanted a cat, but this one was practically demonic- the incidents of accidental mutilation in the story, but also the sense of deep attachment to something dangerous- came from Nebula. She disappeared when we briefly left a window open on a hot Tampa night.

The story's themes of race, exploitation, and alienation are lifelong concerns of mine. I grew up partly in Japan in the early '90s, where being a white person made me stand out dramatically. That's a very different matter than being black in the United States, since it comes with at least as much privilege as alienation. But I was followed suspiciously around toy stores as a child, and strangers often wanted to touch my and my brothers' hair. It wasn't oppression, but it was deeply and permanently unnerving.

I've since devoted most of my life to understanding how people treat those they see as different. This story was first drafted in 2014, but even then I was skeptical of the idea that America was moving past its founding racial crimes. I'm saddened, but not surprised, that the cycle of history has made this story more obviously relevant now than it was when I started working on it.

The writing of the story was one of those moments you treasure- it all essentially came out at once, even at a time when I was under a huge amount of stress. I'd just left my career as an academic researcher to write full-time, and was patching together a living with freelance gigs and commercial copywriting. I've come a long way since then, but I think the story reflects the real economic anxiety I was feeling at the time, and which, frankly, most people in the U.S. and around the world now live with permanently.

So obviously, it's a dark story, with some dark predictions- but I want to be clear that I'm not an advocate of nihilism in any form. Despite our many anxieties, we still live in the most prosperous time in human history, and in many ways the most just. We can't give in to bitterness over the ways our world still isn't perfect, or abandon hope when we see what look like impossible problems. We will absolutely assure our destruction if we refuse to see it coming- but acknowledging our failures is not the same as accepting them as inevitable.

A question for the author

Q: If you could have a meal with a character from any classic novel, whom would you choose?

A: It would be Samuel Beckett's Watt. We would share a single bean, thinly sliced.

About the author

David Z. Morris is a fiction writer, journalist, and social scientist. He lived in Fort Worth, Nagoya, Austin, Tokyo, and Tampa before making it to New York City. He is married to the painter Georgia Hourdas and holds a PhD from the University of Iowa.

www.davidzmorris.com, @davidzmorris

Cheminagium

David Gallay

Pain, true pain, lives outside of time. It arrives in a shear of liminal precognition, the thudding sky before the storm. We formulate routes of escape, believing that the visitor darkening our door could be turned away with the right words. It doesn't matter what we do, what we say, whether the heart is flooded by prayers or screams.

Pain is patient.

The door always opens.

Col is only an arm's length away, huddled in his bed, a naked foot dangling over an empty boot, but I can't hear him. The ringing migraine swallows every word he says.

I press my thumbs to my ears and shake my head until my jaw clicks.

" … worse today?"

"I'm fine."

I make my way over to the window and rest my forehead on the cold glass. Outside, the first wisps of snow kick through the leaves. My eyes drift up from a patch of wildflowers sheltering in the lee of the woodpile, over the dawn-gilt crowns of linden, towards the towering heart of Spire Iberos. I squint into the glazed eyes of the keep. Usually they are dead as a fish, but this morning, there is movement. A candle floats from room to room like a stray thought.

"Our guest appears to have settled in," Col says. "He stopped by last night, while you were out. Nothing like the shaggy weed I remember. Barely recognized him. Twice, I mistook him for Mislav and had to bite my tongue. Remember that one, our bald cousin?"

Of course, I do. Mislav was once a frequent visitor to Iberos, related to us by some stray weave of marriage. His head gleamed like sea-glass. We used to wonder if he shaved it every morning or if that was simply his skull, painted and polished. He vanished out on the Ore-Fist curs a long time back.

In the keep, the candle flickers out.

"If you're looking for an excuse," Col says, "the mules he rode in on have been rooting up and down the hill, careless for next season's crop. Remind him where the stables are, make sure the bolts aren't rusted."

"Eir or Adal can take care of it."

A flash of annoyance crosses his face. He's always been ambivalent to our huldufólk, giving their ancient, withered bodies no more thought than one would a chair or broom.

"They have their own responsibilities," he sighs. "And you need a breath of light. Go see him."

There's nothing more he'd like than to shove me out the door, into the snow. But he can barely stand. Although we are brothers in decrepitude, his ruin exceeds my own. Instead, he rolls back to his patchwork map of Casses, our domain, our country, an island beset on all compass points by unpassable seas. The map is scored with pale chalk lines, one for each mystic curs seared into the landscape. These invisible rivers of velti old-magic radiate from the wellsprings of the Blessed: Spire Centonica at the tip of the southern archipelago, Spire Palus deep in the wild cliffs, and our home, Spire Iberos, an old iron nail struck into the toes of the northern mountains. Practiced travelers like Col can ride the curses from coast to coast without missing a meal. Used to be he'd be gone for weeks cataloguing those liminal pathways. Wearing his chalks down to the nub. Whenever I assumed the worst, that he'd finally lost himself to the blur of obsession, I'd inevitably find him curled up in bed, snoring that same musical wheeze from the days we shared a twin's crib, when his lungs were clean and his linens free of red.

The swallowing chain. A fish you cannot see. Yearning for the unlit taper. To crawl beneath your own spine. A long visit from a bad friend. Sleeping in the nailed bed. An argument with birth. The Blessed have a thousand words to describe suffering and just as many reasons given for it to exist. Pain is the cost of vigilance, for we Blessed stand watch on the bridge between Casses and darker countries beyond the sea, under the hills. Others believe that pain is a burden, a punishment, passed down from mark to mark, throat to throat. A reminder that the velti was never meant for us.

I learned most of this from my mother. As she tapped drops of poppy milk onto her lips, I asked how it was possible her Blessing brought her so much misery. After all, she could swim through the air as easily as an otter through the water. How could that be anything but joyful?

She gazed out the window. Her jaw already trembled from the bone-fever.

I yearn to touch the sun, she said. *I would give up everything. The desire consumes every spare thought. I dream of plunging my head into its fire, letting it consume me. I've flown so high that I could see over the mountains, to the sea. I would have gone further if my body let me, if my waking mind didn't froth into oblivion. Judoc, my darling, I would stab you in the heart right now if it offered even the slightest chance.*

Col was right about the mules. One has already breached the neighboring meadow, its flanks thick with burrs, while the other nearly snapped a leg by lodging its hoof down a rabbit burrow. With a calm but firm hand, I prod them uphill to the stalls. While drawing up a bucket from a well rimed with ice, I become aware of a figure crouched on the hill. He has a feral aspect, like a crow eying the seed in your palm.

"I had forgotten all about the mules," he says. "Seems I'm a bit fog-brained today."

"No worries. The curses can suck the wind from you."

Stig stands and approaches. He seems taller than I remember, or perhaps just thinner, stretched out. A worn cloak drapes off his lanky shoulders like moss from an alder. At the last moment he remembers to raise his chin up for a formal greeting. The mark on his throat is a scorch in the sand, mirrored glyphs of fortune. I desperately want to touch it. Instead, I mirror his posture so that he can acknowledge my own mark.

"My dearest, my Judoc. What brings that look of disbelief? Is it this?" he asks, rubbing his scalp. "Or this?" He taps his mark.

"That you're here at all."

"When I heard about Col –"

"Is that the nature of your Blessing? To hear the death clarion from the far side of Casses? Or perhaps you came to spark the kindling on his funeral pyre?"

The stinging words fly faster than I can swallow them back down. Stig accepts each blow.

"That would be something, wouldn't it? No, my gift deals with the flow of reason. Watch …"

He bends down and plucks a dead leaf off the ground. He makes a fist and crushes it inside, close to my face so that I can hear the dry crackling of its destruction. A pattern of greenish burn scars scores his knuckles and wrists, in some places carved down to the bone.

When he opens his hand, there are only flakes of copper.

"What do you see?" he asks.

"Nothing," I say, cautiously. "Dust."

"Then we agree, it was once one thing and now is another. What compelled that transformation?"

"You did. With your hands."

I sense a child's trick, such as when Col juggles acorns and they vanish in midair, only to reappear days later in my boots. Velti magic runs through the veins of the Blessed like a translucent thread. Col's acorns, the suck of breath when my mother's feet lifted from the ground, every curs weaving its way across the earth, the hum of rooted bones and witch-ravens weeping in the cliffs. I have my own meager gifts, and it appears Stig has found his as well, although I'm at a loss how. The mark is a birthright of the Blessed. It can neither be earned nor forged.

"Before the movement, before the thought, there was the intention. An intention birthed by your presence."

The migraine, absent until now, begins to make itself known again.

"You're saying I crushed the leaf."

"That's one way of putting it. I could also blame the mules, at which point I would have to blame myself, and then so on, and so forth. We can follow the water upstream and never reach the source."

"Then what does it matter?"

"Let's say I returned home a season ago?" He takes my hand, sweeps the remains of the leaf into my palm.

Before I can answer, he covers my hands with his own.

He closes his eyes. Fog drifts from his lips.

When it is over, I am holding neither dust nor the dead leaf reconstituted.

It is a honeybee, shivering in the wind. I protectively cup my fingers around it.

"The sun is peaking," he says and there's that half-smile I remember, those exquisite angles hiding under the softness of age. "Best get on with the day. I do promise to keep more watchful eye on the mules."

"Right. There's should be some chestnuts in the storehouse that haven't moldered yet. Keep them away from the western slope, there's a line of belladonna that'll turn them into frothing bags. If you want, I can send up a hulda to help. You remember Adal, don't you? He still has a touch with animals."

"No. Your huldufólk won't be necessary."

As I make my way down the hill, he calls after me.

"I searched for you last night, up in the keep, but the other chambers were all bolted or destitute. If my arrival has brought you any discomfort – "

A tingling pain flares in the crease of my palm. Stinger torn away, the bee curls up and dies. I scuff a hole in the dirt with my heel and gently place it inside.

"I forgot, you weren't here," I answer without turning around. "The bone fever consumed our parents, one after the other. That was a long time ago. Me and Col ... we sleep in the common halls now. The keep belongs to the spiders."

The last time Stig and I spoke, adolescence still dripped from our noses. We were deep in the trenches of another Iberos winter. Despite the freezing bite of the clearing sky, the walls of the kitchens were already sweating. Stig stood at the cutting board, thin as a reed, hunched over a platter of smoked eel. Focused on the sweep of the butcher's blade, he noted my approach with a sarcastic bob of deference.

I didn't expect to see you, divine one, he said between decapitations. *Rumor was you'd taken to your blankets again.*

Most unmarked wouldn't dare speak to a Blessed with such brazenness; it was only our friendship that granted him protection. As my own parents were often preoccupied and Col had grown bored with entertaining his smaller brother, most of my childhood lingered with Stig and his clan. His uncle especially treated us both like sons. We sat at his feet as he worked the potter's wheel and regaled us with stories of his people, gods and queens, pirates and demons. Me and Col spent a hundred afternoons staring at the treasures paraded across the shelves of his uncle's shop, ancient relics to be revered but never touched. Whenever our friendship bore injuries over the jagged shoals of boyhood, his uncle reminded us that good men are strengthened by their scars.

Col must have already been through here, I said. *No doubt spreading rumors of my condition while picking bones from his own teeth.*

Not my place to say, Stig laughed. *Fact is you look rotted. Let's take care of that.*

With three knocks on the wall, Maeija appeared out of the gloom. Like most huldufólk, she was a shrunken, pitiful creature, swathed in linens that barely disguised her oaken complexion and the weeping wounds of blue gaslight. While Spire Iberos may have had many tenants over its life, lore had Maeija a constant fixture, serving drinks and scrubbing floors back to the primordial mud. I would not be surprised if she was there to greet the first Blessed when they descended onto Casses in a storm of falling stars.

Of course, Maeija never bowed to me. A hulda has no need to acknowledge its rung on the ladder. With the buzz of cicadas under her breath, she addressed me in their strange backwards language, where tomorrow has already happened and yesterday is yet to come.

My Blessed, I recalled this threshing in your skull. If I served you better, would the pain have fled more swiftly?

Without another word, she slipped away and returned with an ivory cup. Her tea smelled foul, with bits of unidentifiable gray matter settling to the bottom, and drinking it felt like wires drawn across the tongue.

From one blink to the next, the ringing quieted. Maeija inspected my face. I often wonder what she saw there.

Better, mayfly?

Before I could answer, Stig nudged a bowl of eel bones towards her newly emptied hands.

Well, what are you waiting for, beastie? Ah, never mind, I'll do it myself.

Stig beckoned me to escort him outside. We walked against the wind, our fists clenched against the warmth of our stomachs. In the shelter of a shivering linden, Stig tossed the bones in the snow and withdrew a clay pipe. I once owned its twin, both sculpted by Stig's uncle. It's long gone now. We stood apart from each other, teeth chattering.

Sure you can't wiggle up a spark of velti fire? He nudged me on the shoulder. I flinched. *The tea usually lasts longer, yeah? Or perhaps it's your brother's wanderings biting at your ankles? Don't waste a worry. Col could walk with Death under the hills and find his way back blindfolded.*

That's not an exaggeration. I still remember the first time Col invited me along to walk the curses with him. He made it seem so easy, striding into the unknown, feet barely touching the ground. I only made it a few miles before keeling over to empty the contents of my stomach. He hooted, not out of cruelty but for the simple joy of having me along. I didn't see it that way. After that, I avoided the curses, which meant avoiding Col. We became strangers to each other.

Which is to say, lingering outside the kitchens on that frozen morning, I wasn't thinking of my brother at all.

Despite all the tearstained promises made in the summer dark, the inequities between me and Stig had become unavoidable. Our boyish defiance snapped too easily under the heel of that imbalance. Although I reassured him it would be many, many years before I would receive my Blessing – ah, it hurts now to think how wrong I was! – he pled with me to refuse it.

I explained the Blessing was not simply a tradition, that without the mark to give release to the magic burning in my veins, it would eventually curdle both body and soul. Anyone who ignores the velti surrenders to the red hands of disease or despair.

And still, hearing all this, he continued to accuse me of selfish deformity!

We spoke in circles, grinding our arguments down to insults, to venom, to daggers. Did I suggest he should leave the Spire for various hells? And if I did, was it to hurt or liberate? I truly don't know. The forests of the past are unforgiving.

Well, plenty more fish to gut, Stig mumbled, the unlit pipe bobbing between his teeth. Then he clasped my hand and offered a startlingly genuine bow. The drumbeat of the velti pounded against my ribs. My last memory of him before he left Spire Iberos without word or warning was his gangly body slipping into the labyrinth of massive ovens with the ease of a fawn into the woods.

"I found it! Come on, stop dreaming. Wake up!"

Col stands over me, grinning madly, shards of pinking twilight caught in his hair. Before I can resist, he has me on my feet, a ratty cloak tossed over my shoulders. Insults curdle on my tongue before I remember his condition. Damn it. How is he standing? Where is he going? I push into my boots and chase him outside, past the fences and into the crackling frost. The trees thin out, their branches heavy with black leaves bowing inwards as we pass into the ephemeral corridor of the Grave-Green, one of the oldest curses.

Wheezing, he crouches in the snow. From above, I see lesions snaking down his neck, remnants of the latest huldufólk remedies.

"Let's go back," I say. "You can tell me about what you found, and I swear we can come back … later in the season … on a better day …"

Col pulls himself back up. His eyes reflect the blood-dark spectrum of the sky.

He offers me his hand.

How can I refuse?

As we walk into the curs, the ground seems to speed from beneath us, as if every step doubles its distance. The trees whistle a strange tune. *Remember to breathe.* From Grave-Green, we pivot into other overlapping pathways – Serpents-Feast, Gallow-Seed, Ore-Fist, Tooth-Hook. The world fogs around us as we flicker, ghostlike, through wood and meadow, our feet barely touching the cobbled streets of distant Spires, our eyes blinking from flashing of rivers, lakes, sheets of ice crawling down the mountain. Occasionally, other travelers flit by us, women and men, Blessed and unmarked. I can still smell their skin long after their shades have passed. Perfume. Sweat. Wine. Disease. All of Casses flows through my lungs. *Remember to breathe.* At Col's insistence, we move faster and faster, until nothing remains other than buzzing smears of color. I cover my face with my hands, preferring the darkness.

"That wasn't so bad," Col says. He coughs into his hand and discretely wipes it under his arms.

The sun, returned a full hands-width up from the horizon, shines from a different direction. Instead of ice, the canopy drips with wet rubies of late autumn. It's difficult to determine exactly where we have alit; somewhere close to the southern rim I imagine. I begin to unpeel my cloak from the spreading tack of sweat, but Col stops me.

"Quiet. Listen."

The birds. Their song has changed from melody to keen. And there's this smell. Burning wood. The trees fall away as we step out onto a wide, rocky beach. The ocean surf inhales and exhales, pulling with it the smoke of a small campfire built at the edge of the tideline. Two figures kneel before the flames, warming themselves. Col strides towards them, palms facing out in in friendly surrender, those damn manic teeth wide and bright.

"You wouldn't mind if my brother and I join you?"

I shuffle in behind him, an afterthought. As we near the fire, my eyes pull apart more details about the strangers; their odd, hunchbacked posture and stunted proportions.

A moment of panic seizes my chest.

Wild huldufólk. Not the servile creatures of the Spire. No, these hulda are proudly undomesticated — no rags conceal their wizened bodies, no attempt to meet the delicate standards of human agreeability. It is a stark reminder that these are the aboriginal inhabitants of this place, long before the Blessed and the shipwrecked. Their kind were here when Casses was a nameless rock and likely will be when it is again.

The larger hulda, a female, lopes over to Col. She draws a claw across his chest and sniffs it. For his part, he doesn't flinch.

"My friends, last we met you claimed knowledge of a hidden road," he says. "A way across the waters?"

Before they can answer, I pull Col aside.

"You've been here before? When?"

"I go where the velti leads me, little brother." He punctuates the last two words with an acidity that leaves me mute. He spins back to the hulda patiently waiting out our human melodrama. "Well? The curs?"

"Whale-Breath," nods the smaller creature. I notice that the tone and texture of his skin has changed to match the rocks beneath us. "I recall you paid the cheminage this time."

I watch with increasing trepidation as Col makes a show of wagging his fingers, clucking his tongue. The velti charges with an odor of overripe fruit. The hulda seems not to notice. With a snap, two silver coins appear in the air, already spinning in the light. Col rolls the coins up and down his knuckles like a street performer.

"A trick my mother taught me. Here's your toll."

The hulda pass the coins between themselves. Appeased, they snuff the fire and lead further along the coast, into the marshlands. It occurs to me that the landscape's contours are not entirely natural. What initially appears to be a mound of earth transforms into the underbelly of an overturned ship. The further inland we push, the more displaced vessels we pass, like abandoned toys in a dredged pond. I can trace the outline of their unusual prows beneath the vines, intricate sculptures of wood and iron — the fangs of serpents, the talons of eagles, a wyrm caught in metamorphosis. We hike around the broken face of an angel, slugs and beetles cozying between her stoic lips.

The migraine returns, pressing the thumbs of my eyes into my brain. I grab a branch from the ground and nervously roll it between my thumb and forefinger. My Blessing, brought to boiling by the velti fires in my skull, whittles away the wood like an axe, sharpening it to a knitting needle, a porcupine quill, a surgeon's pin. I hone it down to nothing, and the ache whittles away with it.

We arrive at a pair of obsidian sarsens rising out of the earth like the fingers of a buried god. Weathered runes swirl across them, a language I don't recognize. The hulda fall to their knobby knees and offer petitions to the massive stones. The sun is now just an amber shard snagged on dimming felt.

"Now what?" Col asks.

"You stepped between them."

Grinning madly, his molars grinding, Col walks forward between the sarsens. I wait for the bitter tang of the curs to sweep him away.

Nothing happens.

Col looks around, confused.

Then the hulda do something I've never seen before. They laugh.

It's horrifying.

Infuriated, Col tears the scarf away to reveal his mark. "I demand you reveal the curs to me. We are the Blessed. The open wounds of heaven!"

This only makes them cackle harder. They remind me of imps scribbled in the margins of a holy text.

"What do you want?" Col snarls. "What is it? More silver?"

His hands clench tight, gripping the velti so hard I feel it shift in my marrow. A coin falls from the sky and hits the sand with soft thud. Then another. And another. A clamor of raining metal fills the air as Col's deluge crashes around us, bouncing off the sarsens, breaking through the trees, pelting the shoulders and backs of the hulda. Their merriment pitches into hysterics as the rain becomes a gale, then a hurricane of silver.

I should try to pull Col away. I should beg him to stop.

With a word, I could end this.

Wait. Listen to the velti delighting in the music of its own song.

How could I ever deny him this moment of rapture?

Instead, I find a half-buried wreck and cower in its berth. I close my eyes and pretend the drum of coins against the wooden beams is the thunder of a summer squall.

The heavy rain slows, stops. A lone crow coughs into the widening silence.

"Judoc," Col says after some interminable time.

As we make our way back to the homeward curs, I hazard a quick glance back. The sarsens stand against the night like silent judges, passively watching over the unmoving shapes of the hulda. Then I turn my gaze back to Col, carefully reading the tremors rippling outward from the marrow of his shoulders, the rasping of his chest, the blood freckling across his chin. Ironic that for a miraculous moment, my own head is clean from pain. I can see every leaf turning white in the moonlight. I hear the pads of our feet, the movement of tiny insects, the fading breath of the endless, unrelenting sea.

While my mother accepted the pains, named them like pets, my father refused to acknowledge them.

His mark granted the gift of prosperity. Anything he touched thrived. Fruit trees. Wheat. Horses. Exotic orchids that had no right surviving through the Casses winters. His own children, born dark-haired and opal-eyed. He inherited a crumbling outpost and nurtured it into a beacon of opulence. Both Blessed and unmarked came to tend their gardens within our walls.

How quickly fecundity can turn cancerous.

Within a few years, thorny vines strangled the orchards. Gluttonous rats ate through our granary. The horses tore their ropes and disappeared into the woods. The orchids, so frail and delicate, gave birth to evil smelling tumors.

We had to burn it all.

Stig watches with curiosity as I light the candles, set out the linens and washing basins, wave away the cobwebs. Eir scuttles in with a decanter of wine, pungent with acorns and cloves.

Eir fills my glass, but ignores the other.

I raise my hand to the reprimand the hulda, but Stig gently restrains me.

"Come now, poor Adal is nearly blind with age."

"That's Eir."

"Oh, well, I could never tell them apart." He toasts me with his empty glass. "Now, I thought you didn't come up into the keep anymore. Just me and the spiders?"

A second pouring loosens my voice enough to tell Stig everything; the cackling hulda, the forest of shipwrecks, the storm of coins. He listens carefully until it's all spilled.

"You see ... Col's gift is to surface the lost and forgotten ... could be anything ... but he always comes back to the curses."

"Yeah, even as a wild-runt, I remember him being waist-deep in those weird roads. Can only imagine how it was after a Blessing like that. Did he find what he was looking for?"

"Yes," I say. "All of them. A completed map of Casses sits in his brain like a pulsing rot. So ... I suggested that perhaps there were some secret curs leading ... elsewhere. The gamble worked ... for a while ... but ... my efforts may have only thickened the poison ..."

"Easy, easy. You stutter as if you plucked the strings of his fate."

He means it as an absolution but it only pricks my temper.

As if cued, Eir returns with a pewter serving dishes balanced on root-gnarled elbows. The hulda spoons out fragrant servings of cooked fruit, again only for me, before scuttling back downstairs. I slide my plate over to Stig.

He smiles, teeth jeweled by candlelight. "I have something to show you."

He pulls a figurine from his pocket, a primitive bird-like totem, its silver feathers smoothed away by the centuries. His uncle claimed it was an ancestral heirloom, passed down from the survivors of the apocryphal landfall that introduced their bloodline to Casses. When no one was looking, Stig would steal it from its high shelf for our garden games.

"I took it before I left," Stig says. "Do you recall the hours we spent play acting with clay dolls from uncle's scraps? I would pluck a cob-spider to play the álfar, wicked prince of the small folk, and this was its witch-raven. And you would be the great and powerful sorcerer from the wild cliffs ... what was his name?"

"Lord Ormstunga."

"Yes! Serpent-Tongue! And you hunted down the álfar, threw it in uncles' kiln. We watched it burn until we couldn't take the heat. Remember? So, tell me, what is your Blessing, divine one? Can you drag down the stars? Can you reduce men to their bloody bones?"

I explain my gift to sharpen a thing to its finest edge. Metal, yes, glass, wood, a knife, a sword, a needle. Also, sight, a dream, a song. Joy. Grief.

"Ah, what a waste!" he exclaims. "So many dull knives could have used your attention back when I worked the kitchens. I snuck down there today, you know. Thought I'd pinch a flask of gray tea for you. What a sight. Ovens dead, pantries furred with dust."

His mention of Maeija's tea rattles craving's cage. I ease the conversation back to the missing years.

"I meant to prove my own way in the world," he says, biting into a steaming pear. "I was an idiot. Barely a month on the road and I blistered through two pairs of boots and nearly starved. It was a miracle that your cousin stumbled over me."

Bells ring deep in my ears, metal on bone.

"Mislav found you?"

He laughs. "Even before taking pity on my empty stomach, the old man shaved my head to clean out the ticks. When he realized I wouldn't be whimpering back home, he let me wander the wilderness with him. In return I shouldered his library and offered up my meager culinary skills. But, Judoc, let's not be coy. You don't really care about all that. You want to know about my mark. Been staring at it all night."

No reason to deny it. "Yes."

"I don't know if you recall the huldufólk Mislav traveled with. Vile, scheming little beasts. No doubt relatives of your tricksters in the woods. One night, I caught them sitting on his chest, suckling the velti from his mark as he slept. I had just been working a rabbit, still carrying the butcher knife. And. Well." He glances down at his scarred hands. The smile remains, but his words struggle like a moth in the rain. "You've not felt pain until you've been kissed by that blue fire they bleed."

Stig refuses to divulge any details, other than that when it was all over, the impossible had happened; his throat burned with the mark. Since then he's been traveling between the Spires, unlocking the secrets of this strange and inexplicable Blessing.

I ask him if the Blessing hurts. How he deals with the pain.

He acts as if he can't hear me. A sour draft whistles through cracks in the wall.

"Look. Here I am, to rescue you from this dour pile of rocks. Don't you see? We're the same now, nothing left to stop — oy! Be careful! Your hand!"

"What?"

Did I spill the wine? Bright drops of red roll off my fingers. No, not wine. There's a flap of skin hanging off my thumb, sliced neatly by the lip of the glass, whose edge I've idly sharpened to a near invisibility. Strange, how it doesn't hurt. The cut is too clean. Stig leaps from his chair and quickly wraps the wound with linen. Roses soak through.

"Here, let me help," he says, grabbing my hand. He concentrates on the injury. The velti gathers around him, not naturally like iron to the lodestone, but with great resistance. I can taste its resentment. Its loathing.

Finally, Stig gives up and runs downstairs, calling my brother's name. I try to follow him, but somehow end up going the wrong way, stumbling down the steps leading out into the courtyard. The frigid night jabs through the bloodied linen. I thrust my hand into the frost to numb the wound. Framed in the windows of the keep, the hulda glare down at me. From here, their faces are unreadable, statues in the moonlight.

When the paradise of Iberos began to rot, my family followed close behind.

Our father withdrew into himself, hoping that his inattention might restore nature's balance. But even abstinence tills our flesh into fertile soil for all manner of affliction. As with my mother, bone-fever took root in his velti's abscesses. As winter crept in, they became haunts of themselves, Lord and Lady of a fallen Spire.

Col spent more and more time away from home, walking the curses.

Stig and I remained inseparable, even as our quarrels grew teeth. Weeks went by without me speaking a single word to my parents.

When our cousin Mislav offered to relieve us of a few hulda, the decision was easy. At a whim, my mother gave him Vigdis, a spry imp from the gardens, and Maeija. From what I heard, they did not complain as he led them into the woods.

I was not there, of course.

It was the evening of Stig's disappearance.

I had retreated to the darkness of the keep, heartache and hatred crashing through me like lightning and thunder.

With the caress of morning's cold incandescence, Spire Iberos shudders into snappish wakefulness like a dog yet to slip into its housebroken mask. The few remaining inhabitants amble outside, women and men, half-dressed, snorting clouds of vapor, to dump the contents of their night buckets into the weeds or knock the icicles from their roofs. Some face down the rising sun with clenched lips. With neither Blessed nor hulda in sight, the unmarked bask in a world where merely human is enough.

Stig joins me at the window. He follows the activity below us with the genial indifference you might have for an ant crawling across your arm.

"Col is waiting for us in the next chamber."

"Then you've seen him in the daylight. The shaking, the bruises? It's just how my mother was, at the end."

"And when he's gone, what will you do?"

A roar kindles in my head, bells within bells. I grab Stig by the shoulders and shove him towards the exit. It's shocking to feel the warmth of his skin through his shirt.

"You haven't asked about your uncle."

"No."

"Ulcer-blossoms of the stomach," I sneer, tongue sharpened for cruelty. "Died sobbing and alone."

He flinches but doesn't budge. "Join us at the hearth. Bring your blankets. Col could use some more."

When our mother died, my father stood with us at the edge of the cremation pit. As both flesh and disease burned away, he refused to watch as Col breathed in the smoke, sucking it deep into his lungs, blacking his teeth to ashen gravestones. His eyes were showing their whites when the smoldering mark finally appeared on his throat. First, the stave for hunter, overlapped by the sign of the underground. Finder of the hidden and lost. His Blessing.

My father whispered something into the ear of his eldest son. Then he walked down into the fire. He didn't scream and he didn't look back.

Col rested his hands on my shoulders.

It was my turn.

I wasn't ready. I tried to run away, to do what Stig had begged of me so many times, to forgo family, destiny, to remain a child.

Col braced me and held my head into the grim cloud that my father was becoming.

Breathe, he commanded.

I struggled to twist out of his grip.

No!

He jammed his fingers into my mouth, gagging me. In that moment, with ashes crusting in my nose, I hated Col, a hate that still scratches at the back of my throat.

Breathe.

I had no choice but to relent to the fire and the cinders and the heat of velti released with my father's final heartbeats. His ashes filled me, Blessed me, marked me, and when I was sure I couldn't take any more was when my brother urged me to breathe deeper.

"And here comes our little Lord Serpent-Tongue," Col says.

Stig offers me a half-empty bottle of wine like the taper of a supplicant. When I don't move to take it, Col smirks and draws the blankets tighter around him. A bruise spreads across his face, dark as ink in the dim firelight. Several more of his teeth have fallen out.

Spots of dread whirl at the edge of my vision. How long have they been conspiring? A tight knot cannot be unraveled in the dark, but if enough hands tug the strings it may be undone by accident.

"Brother, let me help you back downstairs —"

Col glares at me. "No. You need to listen."

"To him?" I try to hide the urgency in my voice, even as the edges brighten, the pressure builds. "He's a kitchen boy who stumbled his way into his mark."

Stig runs a scarred finger around the bottles lip, making it sing. The spots pulse faster, dark feathers against my temple. "Transiency is the natural state of all things," he says. "Even the hardest, oldest stone is remade by a single drop of rain. It's a difficult lesson to learn." He passes his hand over the bottle, and the velti reduces it to a pile of quartz-glinted sand. "Or that might all be poetic nonsense. What do I know? Maybe you're right and all I'm good at is scaling a fish before it stops gulping for air."

Despair slips into the room like a ghost. It stares into the fire. Finally. I've been waiting for you. I don't care if the velti starves for attention, if it eternally pries its fingernails into the seams of my skull.

Nothing would make me happier.

Then another coughing fit rakes out from Col's lungs. Before his voice falls apart, he manages a hoarse whisper into my ear. "Don't you dare give up on me. Not yet."

After finally convincing Col to return to his bed, I peel back the wrappings around my thumb. The cut shines in its rawness. Some scabbing at the edges, the rest gapes like a drowning fish. Without asking, Stig inspects the wound for any slickness of infection. Why does such a simple act nearly bring me to tears?

I take my hand back and ask Stig why he believes he can save Col rather than be the final tap of false hope that nudges him over the edge.

As an answer, he produces a slight book, clasped in bronze, bound in pebble-gray reptilian leather. If my face betrays any reaction, he doesn't notice.

"It's an ancient war-tongue," he explains, tracing its spidery script. "Mislav claimed no knowledge of this book, that he had never set eyes on it before. Must have been a lie. Right? Yes. That's how I knew it was important."

"And he taught you how to read it?"

"No, he never had the chance. I taught myself – or, rather, I used my Blessing to transform into someone who always could read it. A small adjustment, really."

A small adjustment. That's how it always starts. Maybe just a taste, enough to prove it to yourself. A taste leads to a morsel to a meal to a bottomless feast, eat, eat or ache, eat or wither, until you realize, too late, that perhaps it's *you* that the velti has been devouring all along.

"There's a ritual described inside," Stig continues. "To carve out a new curs. It requires certain forms of velti, which we have between the three of us. And I know the perfect place to try it." He picked at the scars on his hands. "I'm sorry, should have told you right away. Not sure why I didn't."

"It's fine."

"Judoc, don't you think, now that we are both Blessed, there shouldn't be any more secrets between us? There doesn't need to be. Right? There's something I should tell you, about your cousin. Mislav, he didn't find me. I was waiting for him. I swear, I only wanted his guidance –"

Before he can speak another word, I take his damaged hands in mine. "It's fine."

With enough practice, any lie can be sharpened into the truth.

In all those years, away, did I think of you?

Stig, why don't you ask?

Then I could tell you.

Yes. Constantly.

I obsessed over you the way Col does his maps.

What you might look like, what you might be doing, where you might be. I saw you sleeping in a night-blue forest of pines. I heard you walking the marble streets of Spire Palus. I tasted the salt of the western sea on your teeth.

Visions of you sparked against a constantly spinning whetstone of resentment. I would wake up in the middle of the night, velti currents knotted in my hands.

I would tell you how strange it was, as Iberos collapsed, as my parents burned and my brother sank into desolation, that I remained healthy, even as I rarely exercised my Blessing.

How, in all that time, I never felt a drop of pain.

Not until the day you returned.

The tall grass snaps underfoot as we march through the fields. Our boots glitter with ice. We suck cold air through our teeth, where it warms along the roof of our mouths before rolling down into our lungs. Stig pauses occasionally to tug his cap back over his reddening scalp.

"Almost there," he says, multiple times, first as a joke, then more serious as familiar woodlands thin out to a horizon of cobalt stone. There is nothing alive out here, not a single sparrow, hare or beetle.

Col seems oblivious to the cold. Hope rouges his cheeks. I bet he's already imagining names for this new curs.

Approaching the mountains, the trail shakes off its snowpack to reveal crests of shale, uneven steps as likely to cast an unlucky traveler off as carry them forward. Up here, the hissing wind becomes more insistent. It seeks out any patch of exposed skin, groping at us, promising cool, dry kisses, if we only take off our cloaks, our scarves, our boots.

Stig pauses to gauge the way ahead.

"See those twin ridges of rock jutting out? My uncle called them the Sleeping Dogs. First time he brought me out here, I was certain that wolves or mud-snakes would devour us in the night. Nothing happened though. I suppose even devils find it too cold up here to bother."

Evening drops quickly. Other than a hazel shaft of sunlight pricking over the mountains, nightfall drains the world of color.

A coin flashes in Col's palm, then disappears again.

We reach a flattened palm of untouched snow sheltered between a copse of ice-heavy alder on one side and the elbow of a Sleeping Dog on the other. There's a stillness here, the quietude of an ancient chapel, present and sacred, nature holding its breath.

We are exactly where we need to be.

"We best start," Stig says. "Before we lose the light entirely."

Col tastes the air. Nods. The lines of his body grow rigid, even the creases on his face, his grimace sharp as a scythe.

Stig sidles up to me and pulls my face close to his.

"Are you ready, divine one?"

He's giving me one more chance. To stop everything, to turn around and trudge back down the mountain and let events unfold as they should, a story already written where the Blessed of Spire Iberos fade away, our inheritance reclaimed by the ivy, the moss, the worms, our lineage forgotten to everyone except the huldufólk who had yet to meet us. Before our extinction, there might even be a time of warmth, rising from the decay in a rush of wine and tea, blood to blood, the sighs of aging friends.

And if I can see that possibility, so can Stig.

Above us, dark clouds churn through each other, trapped between the dusk and the mountains. As if driven by instinct, we concentrate our Blessings. The velti responds. Even as the pain flickers away, I start to say something, I can't even tell what, a dozen shapeless words rising from my ribs, when the sun goes rust and velti wildfire leaps from Col's throat, to Stig's, to mine. Magic pops and spurts between us, burning away our emotions, its alchemy shifting the elements to air, to water, to glass.

I was a babe when Maeija came to me.

She looked then exactly as she does now, as she probably did when the earth itself slipped the fiery cowl of its birth. She crept into my chambers in the middle of a moonless night with what would be the first of many cups of gray tea. As my headache dulled, she climbed up onto my bed. I will never forget the jab of her knees through the blankets. The smell of her breath, like the heavy air from a cavern deep underground. The rough brush of her bark-scaled lips against my ear.

There, as I laid in the darkness, paralyzed by terror, she related the entirety of my life, backwards.

You rose from a broken corpse, she said, *up, up, into the keep, through that very window on the other side of this room. The sickness shook you like a doll, softer and softer, through a winter and a summer. Then you barely felt the fever at all, other than a twinge in your jaw. Yes, just like you see in your mother's jaw now. Then, your brother walked out of the ocean, relief turned to anger, to despondency. He can barely remember being dead, all those guts eaten by crabs. He rejoined you here in the Spire for many years, some happy, others less so. The bone-fever burned brightly in him, before fading, before your mother and father pulled themselves out of the ashes ...*

Please, enough, I wept. *I don't want to know this.*

Don't be frightened, mayfly. It is a story already told, a stone resting at the bottom of the sea.

It's horrible.

She drew her claws through my hair, gentle as a kitten.

Perhaps, together, we tipped the stone as it settled? Speak truthfully. What else could you have done for your own blood? Was it all worth it to take away their pain?

All I had was family. They were my whole world. Even Stig, despite all his charms, could never grasp the beautiful and terrible magic that stitched the Blessed together in threads of white and black.

Anything, I said. *I would do anything to save them.*

In that way, we were the same. She pressed a thin book into my hands. It felt oddly alive. I swear there was a fading pulse under its skin. *This came back to me in the cage of a corpse. It wrote itself. You slipped it in with others of its kind. You chose a darling of unlike blood carry it. You kept it hidden for a hundred turns of the moon.*

As she climbed off my bed, I asked her how this could possibly save my family.

Left alone, a quiet love retained its simple form. Hit with an axe, it shattered to dust. But, carefully fletched, whittled over time, you turned a green sapling to a needle, its life sharpened to pierce the world's skin.

Me? I will cure them? That is to be my Blessing?

It was too dark to see, yet I knew she was grinning.

Mayfly, that was my weapon.

Stig screams into the unnatural gale swirling around us.

"Col, now!"

My brother, weak, skeletal, raises his hands into the velti. It appears first as a smudge, then a shadow, then a shape. Massive. Dark. It crashes to the ground and I recognize it as one of the obsidian sarsens from the forest of shipwrecks. It totters precipitously over us like a finger about to crush a beetle, before settling into the snow. The second sarsen arrives with a thunderclap, taking its place by its twin.

Col collapses in exhaustion, tongue lolling.

I look over to Stig. He's concentrating on the empty space between the sarsens. Under his guidance, the air dulls like a cataract, softening the sharp angles of the mountains beyond. With a final grunt of effort, he becomes midwife to a shivering curs that limps and lurches out from the gap.

The velti seethes around us. Col grimaces, lips wet with bile.

"Behold," he cries triumphantly, "I name thee the Broken-World curs."

It is not complete. To enter now would be like walking into oblivion.

A tempting thought.

According to the book, three Blessings are required to create a new curs. Col's gift of finding brought the sarsens to this location. Stig changed history, making it as if this end of the curs were always tethered to the stones.

As for reaching the other side ...

Stig hands me the bird-like totem, our witch-raven, the relic of a distant continent. Sparks roll down its silver wings.

I take the totem and roll it between my velti-slicked palms until it softens like wax, keep spinning until it forms a rod, then a spear. With shaking hands, I aim the tip towards the curs. The velti wind draws it forward as if pulled by a string.

The curs ripples at the impact. But it does not open.

I knew it wouldn't.

"Oh," Stig says.

"Your uncle probably thought it was real."

Col has curled up in a soft pile of snow rusted with vomit. He's barely breathing.

"It's over," I say. "Help me carry him home. Better to die in his own bed than out here."

Stig looks to Col, then to me.

Many strains of acquaintance may sprout in the thin soil of our footsteps; comradery, love, lust. Friendships blossom like wildflowers. However, a perfect bond, a heart that returns to your side through seasons of pain and selfishness? One that, when presented with the opportunity, would choose to sacrifice itself for your own happiness? Infinitesimally rare. Like my father's impossible gardens, it must be meticulously cultivated. Take a scythe to the weeds, to the stragglers, to the less desirable offshoots. Creation is an act of cutting away all other possibilities.

"Something else we can try ..."

There's a thousand things I should say now. I have been practicing them all my life.

Stig, perhaps, once, you truly were a friend to a monk who found you in the woods. Perhaps, once, he died peacefully in his sleep, and you stood too close to his funeral pyre. A smudge of the velti singed your throat. Enough to taste. To want more. To abandon what you were and eventually, through slaughter and desperation, to dream yourself to my equal.

Stig, you always were my equal.

Stig, don't make me choose.

Stig, the truth is, I chose this a long time ago.

My lips refuse to speak, even as Stig embraces me and his mouth covers mine, as his breath fills my lungs, as he draws the velti from me, Ormstunga, Serpent-Tongue. He already understands. Perhaps he knew from the moment I agreed to come to this barren place. What portion of our lives is constructed from such feints to ignorance, burying our wet natures to play the roles required? We tell ourselves we can step off the stage at any time. But controlling our story takes an act of creative violence, one whose expanding design refuses easy perception, even as it alters everything it touches.

While it's undeniable that all humans are alien to Casses, via some unnatural symbiosis the Blessed anchored themselves to this rock. Stig's people never had that chance. We bound their identity to exclusion. Their blood. Shipwrecked. Unmarked.

He is the shape hidden in the wood.

I am the blade with which to carve it out.

"Wait," is all I manage to say before the velti reads our intent and explodes with a prehistoric wail, rooting out from the marks in our throats, encircling us, forcing us closer, pressing my hands to his chest, then sinking into his chest, one knuckle, two. He buckles as his knees fuse together. His ribs explode outward, the bones jutting from the skin in a spray of red. A sheen of moss crawls upwards from where his feet used to be, bursting from the muscles beneath. That's when he finally screams.

Ever since Maeija's prophecy, I have only prayed for one thing; that this moment would be painless.

I should have known better.

Stig, my darling. This is our Blessing.

His face is last to transform. His eye sockets pinch shut. Teeth crack. Muscles harden. He has become a milestone of bone and flesh. As the velti lifts him up and carries him into the white maw of the curs, I can still see a hint of his smile in the scratching runes.

The Broken-World curs erupts into brilliance. A corridor of light pours out like a crimson thread from the needles eye. It effortlessly flows across the rough, between the ears of the Sleeping Dogs, presumably crossing the mountains and the ice freckled waters beyond.

Through the warped glass of the curs, plagues of flies rumble over a wasteland of sand and vermillion scrub. No, not flies, distant warships, floating in the air. Entire armadas of those carved totems skate across the surface of a burning horizon, just as my mother did, that effortless glide. Will they become the wrecks in the marshlands? Am I seeing the past or the future?

It doesn't matter.

Pain exists outside of time.

The curs warbles. Something emerges from the other side. It is difficult to look at. My eyes slide off its shifting collection of limbs, arms and legs, intertwined with serpentine roots of gaslight. It takes no heed of me or Col as it picks through the snow, constantly changing shape, shrinking, hardening, a liquid mandala becoming stone.

I know what this is.

Prince of the small folk. Mythic creature of pure velti.

Álfar.

It pauses at the bloody pile of rags that were Stig's clothes. A sinuous claw plucks the leather book out from the carnage and gently attaches it to a weeping sore of matching shape on its flank.

Then it sees me.

Orbs of blue flame flicker in its sockets.

"Judoc of Iberos. Your life made a nice splash dropping into the pond of time, mayfly."

My mouth goes numb with the taste of gray tea.

"Maeija?"

"A good name. Perhaps I will take it one day."

A thousand questions sting my tongue to silence. All I can manage is stutter.

The álfar whispers into my ear.

"The knife in its velvet sheath needed not know why it was made, or in whose forge it was birthed. It only needed to know how to cut."

A second phantom steps through the curs, then a dozen more, a hundred, an upended waterfall of thrashing shadows pouring from the curs and spilling across the mountains. Horror clamps my ribs. Is this an invasion? A plague?

A reclamation?

An invisible wind takes them up, light as spiderlings, and carries them into the night. As fast as they arrived, they are gone. Gone into our dead past, their future.

Stars prick through the thin clouds.

I crawl over to Col and press my ear to his chest. Still breathing. I leverage him over my shoulder and make my way towards the curs. My arms brush against the milestone. It is warm, slightly yielding. It reminds me of when Stig and I sat on our hands and watched his uncle work the sculptor's wheel. It always fascinated me to see a simple lump of clay transformed by nothing other than his naked hands. He didn't need the velti to infuse the inanimate with grace and beauty. Once, he sculpted us miniature replicas of ourselves, perfectly detailed down to the fingernails. I remember Stig cradling his brittle boy in his hands. I remember crushing mine under my heel, not for the sin of accepting gifts from the unmarked, but for the unfairness of it being unfeeling clay all the way through.

I drag my brother's limp body past the milestones, into the curs, toward the ragged dawn of a distant shore.

About the story

This story began with the image of a two men standing before a gate in the mountains. At their feet was a body, crumpled in the snow. I knew the two men were brothers. The body remained a mystery until I heard someone define "cheminage" on the radio, as an old word for a toll to pass through the forest. That's exactly what the body was. Everything else flowed from the tension of that triangle and the strange red sky on the other side of that gate.

A question for the author

Q: What kind of pieces are the most fun to write (action, lyrical, etc.)?

A: The human mind has an underrated capacity for acceptance. The pieces I find the most fun to write are those that arise from characters placed in unexpected, uncomfortable or even horrific situations and then watching them navigate their way through it. No matter how dark or bizarre the circumstances, the act of living always finds its own lyric beauty.

About the author

David Gallay is a writer of speculative fiction and horror. After receiving a B.A in Creative Writing from Binghamton University, and currently resides in Wisconsin where he leads a double life as an IT SysAdmin.

@svengali

Hold This Star For Me

Mark David Adam

When David got to work that morning, he discovered a large shell on his desk holding down errant pieces of paper. He smiled. His coworkers were always razzing him about how messy his desk was and now, it seemed, someone had taken it upon themselves to assist him.

He picked up the seashell; it was as big as his fist. It didn't have pointy bits like a conch but was smooth, almost like a marshmallow that had been melted and stirred then set again.

He lifted the shell to his ear, something he had not done since he was a boy. He half expected the old notion that you could hear the ocean in an empty shell to have gone the same way as the Easter bunny and other childhood things, but he did hear waves, like the whispering of a giant.

He closed his eyes and found himself thinking of a beach side motel he and his mother had stayed at when he was around six. He hadn't thought of that time in years but now an unusually vivid memory rose in him. It was of standing on the beach, listening to the crash of waves, while sand blew against his legs. The sand had felt like the pricks of insect bites and as a child he had been confused by this. He had seen bugs, ugly bugs, hopping out of a washed up tangle of kelp he'd poked with a stick. He hadn't seen the bugs clearly, been too repulsed to get too close, but he had dimly seen, or perhaps imagined, that they had tusks of all things, and in his mind that meant they should be much larger than him not jumping about at his feet. When he felt the pricks of the sand he had thought they were the same bugs, now even smaller.

He opened his eyes and laughed, recalling how he had screamed and cried, telling his mother giant shrunken bugs were eating him.

That night, laying in bed, reflecting on how different his thinking and perception had been as a child, he had the growing feeling there was another memory in him wanting to surface. As sleepless hours went by, he became more and more convinced that something else had happened at the motel, something that — unlike the crawling insects and blown sand which he could reconfigure with an adults understanding — would be more strange if remembered now, not less. A child's whole world is largely of unknowns. He could, he was sure, have witnessed something and not seen it for what it was, a truly unusual event.

When dawn arrived before sleep he got up, sent a message to work saying he wouldn't be in, then drove to his mother's, arriving in time for lunch.

"I can't recall," his mother said, taking the kettle off the stove.

"I think I was six," he said. "So I guess it was before we moved here." He thought about how the wind had been cold; had it been early spring or fall?

His mother set a tea pot on the table.

"A motel?" she asked, turning back to the cupboard and taking out a package of Peek Frean cookies. She shook the package before opening the top and looking inside.

"It was on the ocean," he said. He had a clear image in his mind. "There were sliding glass doors and just a bit past the back deck you could walk to the beach."

"Oh, you must mean Taylor Bay," she said, opening the trash can and throwing the empty package out.

"No," he replied.

"You used to love going to Taylor Bay," she said, opening another cupboard.

"It wasn't Taylor Bay."

"You sure David? You were quite young, weren't you?"

He knew it wasn't, and if his mother thought about it at all, she would know that not only had they never stayed at Taylor Bay, there were no motels there.

He didn't think too much of this discrepancy in recall with his mother. She had never been one for details or direction. Even now, after having lived in the same house for twenty years, she could get disoriented and find herself driving out of town instead of to her local shopping centre. And she still told her friends that he'd studied anthropology at university, her memory sealed by his description of an early course he had taken.

David took a sip of tea and wondered if his mother's poor recall had inspired him to look more closely at his own memories. He didn't think so; it didn't explain the pull he felt.

The next morning, while waiting to pay for fuel at a gas station, he pulled a road map off a rack and examined it, but the lines of highways and names of towns did not evoke anything. Back in his car he found himself driving towards the coast. He didn't think it likely that the motel, which he remembered as being old back then, would still be there. Still, he always had liked road trips and the possibility of finding the same beach excited him.

And then, after a morning of driving through forests and farmlands, it happened.

He rounded a corner and the highway broke through to an open view of the sea from atop a high cliff. As he began his descent to the coast, he recognized the bay below him, remembered seeing it for the first time as a young boy. He felt this so strongly it was as if his younger self was riding in the car beside him.

He remembered rolling down his window (his mother had complained about her hair getting in her eyes) and sticking his head out, imagining he was flying over the ground like superman.

He smiled, opened his window, extended his hand, and moved it like a rolling wave against the rushing air.

After many switch backs, the road levelled out and he drove past houses, cabins, craft stores, a gas station, and motels. And yes, after he had driven the whole length of the bay, he found *the* motel.

The sign, which he had had absolutely no memory of a moment before, he immediately recognized. He remembered looking at it while waiting in the car as his mother went inside. It was of a large seahorse, painted gold and green: the Seahorse Motel.

He pulled in and peered at the buildings in front of him. He could see now that he had not remembered it right. He had thought it had been like most motels, one long building with adjoining rooms, but it wasn't. There were three small cottages that he could see, possibly more behind.

The place was not well kept. The paint on the cottages was sun bleached and flaking. Some of the pale roof tiles on the cottage in front of him had come loose, revealing their original colour beneath to have been a dark green. And there were dandelions everywhere. They rimmed the foundations of the cottages and flowed out over the gravel parking lot as if they were running from under the buildings, attempting to flee.

He looked past the cottages; unable to see the ocean he opened his door and got out.

Wind, not strong but full and steady, blew off the ocean, cool like it had been in his memory. His sense of smell had never been strong, but he had no problem perceiving the scent of the sea. And he heard it, the low thrush of waves falling on sand.

He walked to the end of the parking lot, stepped onto an old log, and looked at the horizon. The sun was low, hidden in clouds far out from land. The sea was not blue, but reflected the clouds above; it was the colour of concrete and appeared tired. Everything was so muted he felt like an actor in a black and white film.

He heard a screen door bang shut behind him. Turning he saw a man walking towards him.

When the man was about ten feet away he stopped. He gazed above David's head as if examining something. David turned, wondering if perhaps a bird had caught the man's interest, but somehow he didn't think so, and looking he saw nothing in the sky. When he turned back, the man came closer.

"Hello," the man said, his eyes the blue the sky and water should be.

"Hello," David replied.

"You looking to stay?"

He had not had time to think of that.

"You have a cottage available?"

The man waved his hand.

"Take your pick," he said. "The newer motels drop their rates at this time of year and the few people who come through at this time stay elsewhere. I can let you stay for half our usual."

David made a show of looking around, but he already knew he would.

David slid back the glass door and let the wind and the sound of the sea enter the cottage. The deck before him looked small, but he was certain this was the same cottage he had stayed in as a boy. Before him, dandelions seemed to be in conflict with another plant. A single golden flower grew up through a tangle of wild succulents, while other dandelions watched from around the edge of the cottage. Were the dandelions advancing? he wondered. Or was this other foliage? Was the lone dandelion making headway into indigenous terrain, or was it the first to be attacked by invaders from the shore?

It didn't appear, as he drove looking for a place to eat, that there was any real town. There was no shopping centre, no grocery or drug store. The gas station where he stopped to refuel had a few shelves on which, besides the usual chips and chocolate bars, sat two lonely loaves of white bread and various summer-time condiments. The fridge held ice and pop, a single carton of eggs, and empty racks where a twisted sign indicated wieners had been displayed and probably would be again when summer returned. He was told by the teenager behind the counter that he would have to drive half an hour south to buy more substantial fare. Similarly, the first restaurant he came across was closed, and the second. He drove the whole length of the bay until at the end he found one that was open.

It did not look promising.

Walking up to the front doors David saw only one other parked car, and the motel the restaurant was attached to showed no signs of activity. He was not greeted by people or sounds when he entered. He walked past an unmanned reception desk and down a narrow unlit hallway till he emerged into a surprisingly bright and pleasant room. The front wall was not straight but curved like the prow of a ship, with full windows facing towards the ocean. Outside, the horizon glowed softly. It was not a vivid and spectacular sunset. No rays pierced the clouds, which held only the slightest tinge of orange, but it was beautiful in a calm, assured way.

A man sat at a table facing the view, a glass of beer in his hand. His light hair looked like a crashing wave caught in a photo; it rolled up off his forehead, gaining height as it drifted towards the back of his head. David heard a cup connect with plate and turned to his left. Another man, fingers pinched delicately through the small handle of a coffee cup, was staring at him, as was the man who sat across from him. They both had on dark suits, not expensive, nor had they recently seen the inside of a dry cleaner. The men did not nod a greeting, nor go back to their half eaten pies, but stared at him unblinking. David imagined that if he had a better sense of smell, he would be able to detect a lingering touch of embalming fluid emanating from them.

He moved towards a table on the other side of the room, but as he passed the man with wavy hair, he saw that the table next to him also had a better view of the setting sun.

As David sat down, the man turned and looked at him lazily, or perhaps drunkenly, his smile friendly enough, and a sharp contrast to the two men at the table behind, who had swivelled their heads and were still watching him intently, unconcerned or unconscious of being rude.

"Hello," David said to the man with wavy hair as he sat down.

"Hello," the man said, pointing his beer towards him before lifting it to his mouth. The man looked at David while he drank, keeping his eyes on him until his beer, which had been half full, was all gone. When the man had finished drinking, he put his glass down, smiled as if at some private reminiscence, then startled David by bellowing out, "Sarah."

This produced no immediate results, but after several long moments, moments in which the man continued to hold his gaze, David heard footsteps in the hall.

Over the man's shoulder, he saw a woman around his own age enter the room, her dark hair close on either side of her face, like stage curtains closing. She wore a simple, light blue dress and had a beer in one hand, evidently familiar with the wants of the man who had yelled.

The woman stopped when she saw David, stopped like a bird hitting glass. The men in suits swivelled their heads between her startled stance and David.

It was for only a moment that the woman stood still and their eyes connected, but that moment seemed larger and fuller than the time accorded it. If he were to learn it had lasted centuries unchanging, waiting for the machinery of time to begin to roll again, he would not have been surprised.

The woman walked past the men at the table and it seemed to David that he saw a flicker of fear in her eyes and that her shoulders were taut in the anticipation of trouble.

She placed the beer in front of the man beside David, picked up his empty glass and held it lightly, as if weighing its potential as a weapon.

"Perhaps this man would like a menu," the man said reaching for his beer, "or a drink."

"Kitchen's closed," she said.

The man turned to her. "Surely a sandwich is in the realm of possibility. He appears to have travelled far."

Sarah looked down. The room, as when he had first entered, as when she had first entered, was thickly silent. Words, footsteps, were the anomalies, allowed, but visitors with few rights.

Sarah lifted her gaze back to David. This time, instead of fear, her eyes narrowed and her mouth tightened with what he thought was a trace of anger.

"I don't want to be a bother," he said quietly.

Their eyes locked.

In David's mind there appeared a scene of being at the beach, of patting a small, blue, upside down pail with his hands and then lifting it gingerly to reveal a compressed tower of sand. A hand, not his, came into view and placed a shell on top.

"I can make a sandwich," she said.

"That would be nice."

"Roast beef?"

He nodded.

"Anything to drink?"

"Could I have some tea?"

"Regular?"

He nodded again. In his mind he saw a hand holding thin seaweed, the kind of sea weed that you can almost see through when you hold it up to the sun. The hand placed the sea weed around the base of the small sand tower.

She turned away; her thin dress billowing slightly as she did so. She walked past the men at the table, who had not stopped staring. One was slowly lifting a sliver of pie towards his mouth. His eyes on the woman, his aim was low; the fork hit his lip as she walked past. The man pushed the piece of pie into his mouth, then turned to David with blue smeared lips.

David adjusted his chair so that it pointed away from the men at the table and out at the view. As he sat waiting for his sandwich, he was unsure if the silence was more uncomfortable than it would be to have a conversation with the man beside him considering the audience they had. When the man did not speak, but stared as raptly at the ocean as he had before, David followed his example.

When Sarah returned with his sandwich and tea, she placed them on the table without speaking. She also brought another beer for the man, at which he smiled and drained the one in his hand. When David had finished half his sandwich, he heard the rub of chairs on the floor behind him. He did not turn and look. He was certain the men in suits were standing, staring at him. He took two bites of his sandwich before he heard footsteps walking away and then he did turn, making sure that the men in crumpled suits were truly gone. He wanted to comment to his neighbour on the men's strange manner, but the words did not come to him. He looked towards the man beside him who, continuing to stare out the window at the sea and sky, much darker than they had been, said, "Maybe tomorrow night?"

Before David could answer, or even begin to speculate on what this meant, the man stood, held his beer up to the departed sun, drank the last of it, then turned and walked out.

The woman, Sarah, did not return.

When David had eaten his sandwich and drank his tea, he got up and called tentatively into the hall. There was no response. He sat back down, tested the small stainless teapot she had brought to see if there was anything left and, discovering it empty, got back up.

"Hello," he called again into the hall.

He walked to the reception desk.

"Hello," he tried again.

When no one answered, and he heard no sound of movement, he returned to the dining room, took out a ten dollar bill — it was either that or a twenty and he did not feel the dry sandwich and tea deserved it — and placed it under a knife beside his plate and left.

At his car, he turned and looked back. He wasn't sure, but the curtains of an upstairs window moved as if a hand had been holding them to the side and had just let go.

Sleep did not come easily. The bed was harder than he liked, and cold; it took a long time for his body to warm the sheets. He did like the sound of the ocean though, and the absence of the city noises he usually heard in his apartment.

When he woke, he lay in bed trying to remember his dreams. He felt they had been important. There was something about a door but, in the way of dreams, the door, while being a door, had been something other too, like a cat or a tree.

It was a sunny day. Once he got up, he sat on the cottage's back step, rolled up his pant legs, then walked onto the beach barefoot. As bright as it was, he discovered that it was still quite cool and walking barefoot was not as enjoyable as he had hoped it would be. He did venture into the water though, remembering as a child laughing at the feel of outgoing waves eroding the sand beneath his feet. The tide was advancing, though, not retreating, and the sand beneath him stayed firm, while the icy water felt as if it were cutting his skin.

He walked back to the cottage dejected, but not inconsolably so. He decided go into town, have breakfast, come back and explore again properly attired.

As he made his way up from the beach past a ribbon of driftwood to where clumps of succulents appeared like small islands in the sand, a voice called out to him. He hadn't expected to be addressed and at first thought the wind was sending him sounds meant for someone else. Looking up, he saw the man who had rented him the cottage gesturing to him, his movements overly dramatic, as if the two of them were in the midst of gale force winds and he was offering sanctuary.

"Hello," the man said when David had walked up sufficiently close to hear. "Would you like some coffee?"

He did want some coffee, though he stood for a moment without speaking. Here, away from the water, the sand was drier. It blew against his legs and he felt tiny pricks along the back of his calves.

He smiled.

The man smiled back. He had a softness to his face and David sensed a loneliness in him, a long, well-established loneliness.

"Coffee would be great," David said. "I haven't had a chance to get any groceries."

"Come in, come in," the man gestured, again too largely, his arms moving as if they were pulling in a net.

David followed the man stepping up through the sliding door at the back of his cottage.

"Here," the man said, extending a towel towards him with which to wipe his feet. "How do you like your coffee? Cream? Sugar?"

"Black would be fine."

When he was done wiping the sand and moisture from his feet, David looked around the room. Shelves extended from floor to ceiling along one whole wall, filled with all manner of things. David found himself squatting down. On a low shelf, sticking out from behind a piece of driftwood, was a thin gold rod the length of his hand and just slightly wider in diameter than an ink tube from inside a pen.

He picked the rod up. It was light, but he sensed that it would not bend to any pressure his hands could give.

"Here you..."

David looked up. The man, holding a cup of coffee in each hand, was staring at the rod in David's fingers, his mouth open in mid-sentence. David felt that by holding the object he had invaded the man's privacy, had broken ancient rules of guests and hosts.

He did not replace the small rod on the shelf, however. He stood up holding it. The man backed up a few steps, his mouth still hanging open.

Feeling uncomfortable, David turned from the man and looked at the shelves.

Why had he been drawn to this one object out of all that were there before him? At eye level was a beautiful purple spiral of a worn shell, beside it a full wing of a dark feathered bird. Why, and how, had he seen the object that was in his hand? Certainly his eyes should have gravitated towards these other more noticeable and attractive objects first. And now that he looked at the items on the shelves more closely, he saw that what at first he had assumed to be simply interesting pieces of driftwood, were in fact subtly carved. The knots and grains of weather moulded wood had been delicately emphasized, causing faces and animals and birds to appear like shy hallucinations. He knew the man had carved them; they echoed the loneliness David sensed in him. He wished now that he had noticed these figures first and commented on the skill they evinced, but he hadn't, and looking back at the man, he saw it was too late now. There were tears in the man's eyes and — David was not entirely sure if he was imagining it or not — the thin rod in his hand was vibrating with a soft current.

The man composed himself and stepped forward, holding out a cup of coffee.

David took it.

The man kept his hand extended. David looked down at the rod in his hand, then reluctantly gave it to him.

The man slid his hand inside his jacket, depositing the rod into a pocket, then patted his chest over top of where it was.

"She gave it to me and told me to look after it," he said as if this explained everything.

They went outside, sat on low beach chairs, and drank their coffee watching crows along the tide line scratch the sand with their claws and peck at it with their beaks, feeding on creatures buried beneath.

"I had forgotten," the man said after a time. "Well, not forgotten, just stopped thinking about it."

He looked out towards the horizon.

"It's been so long," the man said quietly.

Sitting beside this man, David felt as if he were at the bedside of a loved one in a hospital. He didn't know what to say, but felt it was important he was there.

After David had drunk his coffee, and the cup was becoming cold in his hand, the man spoke again.

"I don't think they remember either," he said sadly. "Things..." his hand fluttered as if picked up by the breeze, "things distract and over time bury the past."

The man looked at David, seeming to need some response. Not knowing what to say, David nodded.

"But you," the man said smiling. "You're here."

David smiled back.

After another long period of silence, David got up.

"Thank you for the coffee," he said.

He stood in front of the man and held out his hand. Like the man's earlier emphatic gestures, the man shook his hand in overly large up and down strokes before stopping and squeezing David's hand firmly.

"Don't let him fool you," the man said looking him in the eye. "He's as dangerous as he ever was."

He went to fetch his mother. He had been exploring the beach and at first that had been preferable to waiting in the cottage for his mother to shower and drink her coffee, but after awhile he felt too alone. It was not enough to chase gulls and cause them to fly; he needed to be seen doing so. It was not enough to be the only one to look at the things he found. He needed his mother to also hold the tiny spirals of broken shells and wonder with him. It was uncomfortable to see something beautiful or interesting on his own; he didn't know how to contain it. So he walked back to the cottage holding some of his best finds: a dried out baby crab fully intact, a piece of rounded green glass, and an oyster shell with sea weed attached to it, looking like a withered hand.

When he was close to the cottage he saw his mother sitting outside, not on a chair, but on the ground, leaning against the sliding glass door, her knees drawn up and her arms resting on them. He called out to her as he approached, excited to show her what he had in his hands. Her head turned so slowly towards him that he in turn slowed his pace and then, when he was still twenty feet or so away, he stopped entirely.

He had never seen his mother, or any adult, cry before. He had not known it was something they did. He did not know how to respond. His mother did not say anything, did not rise to greet him. She looked at him for a moment then leaned her head against the glass behind her and closed her eyes.

It frightened him.

He stood there lost, not able to go to her and not able to leave.

He felt a tug on his shirt.

A girl, a few years older than him, motioned with her hand and, not knowing what else to do, he followed her back to the beach.

They walked until they came to a log, its trunk buried in the sand as if it had been thrown there by some giant. The roots stuck out above the ground and someone had placed a stone in the centre of them, making an eye, turning the sun bleached log into a dragon, its roots now whiskers and teeth, horns and scales.

"Here," the girl said, holding out a plastic blue pail. "Go get some wet sand."

David carefully put down the things he was carrying and did as he was asked.

Later, after he had made a ring of towers and she had decorated them with sea weed and shells and feathers and he had not thought of his mother for quite some time, the girl surprised him by saying, "She wasn't crying because of you."

That thought had never occurred to him.

"She was crying because of your father."

"My father?"

"He's a bad man."

"He is not," David said, feeling attacked.

The girl did not reply, and after a moment David looked up from his moat digging to find her staring at him.

"My father's a bad man too," she said.

David did not know if his father was a bad man, did not think so, but the way she looked at him, he wanted his father to be. He wanted to share this grown-up like seriousness with her.

"My father's a very bad man," the girl said, placing a feather on the castle wall, "and like your mother, I have to do something about it."

He did not go into town for groceries like he'd planned. The thought of leaving the bay and entering the outside world not only did not appeal to him, he felt it might endanger his quest. The past, like a hungry feral cat, was showing itself, but that it would continue to do so was not certain.

He spent the day alternating between strolls. First to the point south of the motel and then, after stopping back at the cottage, where he made himself some tea he found in the cupboard, he walked north towards the end of the bay, but not all the way. He did not want to go as far as the restaurant. Not yet.

After his second, longer walk, he lay on the bed in his cottage and it was then he had remembered meeting the girl and building the sand castle.

And then, standing at the sink, filling a glass with water, looking out at the ocean, an image had surfaced in his mind of her dark hair blown back in the wind as he ran to keep up with her longer legs.

"My father says it's time for us to leave."

"No," he said, grabbing her arm and making her stop.

She looked at him.

"You're right," she said. "We mustn't let him leave. Will you help me?"

He nodded.

"It's....dangerous," she said.

"That's OK," he replied.

She took his hand in hers and squeezed it.

He took a deep breath and felt himself grow larger inside.

When David drove to the restaurant, the same lone car was in the parking lot that had been there the day before and the reception desk was still as lifeless as a museum exhibit.

"Do you like fish? Halibut to be exact?" the man with the wavy hair said the moment David stepped into the dining room.

"Uh...Yes," David answered.

"Good, good," the man nodded. "Caught today by our skilled and dedicated neighbour. Rice? A white marinade sauce?"

"Uh.."

"No. You're right," the man said, jabbing the air with his finger. "Why cover up the natural flavor? Grilled, that's it. With potatoes. Yes, and some pickled cabbage on the side for contrast and digestion." He rubbed his hand in circles across his stomach at the last word.

"Sit."

The man pointed to the table David had eaten at the night before, then disappeared down the hall, singing as he moved away.

The man's voice trailed off, then became loud again as he returned with a beer and a glass and put them on the table.

David looked at them.

"On the house," the man said, patting David's shoulder. Singing again, he turned and left.

When there was only an inch of beer left in his glass, and the sun was a similar visual distance above the horizon, David heard footsteps behind him. He turned, hoping it would be Sarah, but it was the men in suits. They looked at him like he was a strange animal, or perhaps like they were strange animals. They made their way to the same table they had been at the night before. They continued to stare at him as they sat down. The one who had smeared pie on his lips the day before collided with the side of the table. He did not stop looking at David as he slid his hip along the table's edge and lowered himself into a chair.

David found that he was not as disturbed by the men as he had been the night before. He felt no ill intentions towards him from them.

Moments after their arrival, the man returned, expertly carrying five steaming plates, two plates in each hand and one balanced on the crook of his arm. He stopped at the table with the men in suits, who each took a plate, and then came over to David and placed the rest.

"Sarah!" he yelled as he had the night before. The man looked and saw David's nearly empty beer. "Ah yes," he said, and walked away, calling out "Sarah" again when he was in the hallway.

The man returned with a beer in each hand and sat down.

"Bon appetit," he said, toasting David.

David had never thought it before, but he wondered now if his poor sense of smell meant he also had a diminished sense of taste. He had never been one to fuss much over food. He ate what he considered to be a healthy diet but, unlike his friends, he did not become enamoured of certain restaurants or insist on particular coffees or wines. Tonight, however, he was enjoying eating far more than usual. He could taste the freshness of the halibut and felt that with every bite he was taking in some of the strength and mystery of the sea.

They ate without talking; the man emitting slight noises of pleasure as he chewed. Halfway through their meal, Sarah arrived. She sat on the other side of the man with wavy hair, all three of them facing the window. David could not see her without leaning forward and turning his head. He tried to think of things with which to start a conversation and give him a reason to look at her, but he could think of nothing better than "it's a beautiful view," which he finally did say.

"Wait for it," the man responded. "I think we are in luck tonight."

Unlike the night before, it was a clear, cloudless evening. A golden path sparkled along the surface of the sea from the shore beneath them to where the sun touched the horizon. As they watched, the sun moved below the water, but the man beside him did not stop looking, and, when David leaned forward to pick up his glass of beer and use the opportunity to look sideways at Sarah, he saw that she was gazing as intently as the man was. Neither of them was looking at where the sun had been. Instead they were concentrating on a band of green sky between the darker blue of the beginning night and the lighter blue lingering on the horizon.

"There," the man said reverently.

David heard footsteps. The men in suits came and stood by their table, staring as well at the changing colour of the sky.

"There," the man quietly said again. "The colour of home."

Putting his glass back on the table, David stole another sideways glance. The four of them were so still, so absorbed. He felt as he had as a child when adults had been attentive to things he had not understood.

And then that short period of shifting light was over, and Sarah was standing, collecting plates, and the men in suits turned away, not back to their table, but out and down the hall.

Sarah did not return and the man beside him, who had been jovial and friendly earlier, now seemed as welcoming as a sleeping python.

After it was clear that Sarah would not return, and the man beside him was not going to break the silence, David stood, took his wallet out, and put a twenty dollar bill on the table.

This time, when he looked back before entering his car, he did not see the curtain of an upstairs window fall back into place as if someone had been watching him. The curtain was held to the side and she was standing there staring.

"What is that?" he asked, watching her roll the thin, gold coloured rod between her thumb and small fingers, her eyes closed, concentrating.

"An Ancil," she replied.

"What's it for?" he asked.

She didn't answer him, but continued to run it back and forth.

David did not know how long the storm had been going on. He woke to rain battering the sliding door, wind whistling around the corners of the cottage, and waves sounding too close and too large. As he lay there listening, he thought he heard another sound, a voice, coming closer, angry, possibly drunk. The wind and waves were so loud he was not sure if there was a voice, but then the glass door shattered as something heavy crashed on the floor and rolled across the room.

"I know you have it," the man yelled. "Who do you think I am? Did you think I would not know? Come out!"

David scrambled in the dark for his pants and shoes, not that he planned to go outside, but he did not want to meet this threat in his underwear, and he did not want to cut his feet on the shards of glass scattered on the floor.

He managed to slip on pants, but not find his shoes, before the man was there at the mouth of the broken door. David stayed still for a moment, crouched low, hoping to be hidden by shadow. A hand grabbed the back of his t-shirt and pulled him off balance. He fell and felt a sickening jab in his right knee; pain like he had never felt before tore up the inside of his thigh. The man yanked him through the door and dragged him towards the roaring sea. David twisted, trying to grip the ground with his feet. The man pulled him across a log and David fell over the side. His head snapped back, striking the ground, and then he was no longer aware of the rain, the wind, the man, or the glass embedded in his knee.

She came by their cottage just as they were finishing eating a dinner of sandwiches and potato chips. She knocked at the glass door, and his mother rose before he was able to, and invited her in. She saw the half-packed suitcases on the couch.

"You're leaving?" she asked.

"Yes," his mother answered.

"Tomorrow?"

"I'm afraid so."

She looked at David and he felt so guilty — even though there was nothing he could do — that it took all his resolve not to cry and not to turn away.

He put his plate in the sink and went with her outside.

"I'm sorry," he blurted out when they were away from the cottage.

He hadn't known how she had planned to make her own father stay, and his crying and shouting earlier had not had any impact on his mother's decision.

She did not address his apology but instead said, "I'll come tonight; listen for me." She made an O with her mouth and called out like an owl. "When you hear that, come outside. I'll be waiting."

He nodded, though he was not sure how easy that would be. Seeming to sense this, she knelt on the sand and pulled him down to face her.

"Please," she said, and for once she did not seem as strong and sure as she always had. "Will you?" She squeezed his hand. "I need your help."

He nodded. "If my mom wakes up, I'll run and meet you at the castle."

She laughed at this. Not making fun of him, he felt, but because he had surprised and impressed her. She hugged him then, and though he was too young and too small to fall in love, he did. And though he would not think of her when he was older and in the arms of other women, he would always compare those later embraces to this one and be unsatisfied.

That night he tried not to fall asleep. He lay on the couch, staring out the window, until he heard his mother's breathing deepen and small sighs come from where she lay on the bed around the corner of the open room. He woke to a hand shaking his shoulder and his friend standing over him; the finger at her lips barely visible in the dark. He followed her outside, slipping on the shoes he had left there, while she quietly slid the door shut behind them.

"I'm sorry I fell asleep," he whispered. "I'm sorry I didn't hear you call."

She smiled. "It's OK. It took longer than I thought it would."

He looked around and saw that the skyline was starting to glow with a new day.

She took his hand and they walked to the dragon log by which they had built their castle.

She sat down and patted the ground for him to join her.

"I need you to take something with you and hide it for me," she said.

"Will this help keep your father here?"

"He. We. Will be trapped here."

"Trapped?"

"Will you do it?"she asked.

"Yes."

"Lie down," she said.

When he had lain on his back she straddled his chest.

"Keep your eye open," she said.

She held the Ancil just above his left eye. She rolled her finger against her thumb, spinning the small gold rod. From its tip fell a single point of light.

At first all he felt was a slight irritation. He tried to blink, but the fingers of her other hand held his eyelids open.

His eye watered until he could no longer see her face and still his eye watered until it seemed like he was at the bottom of a pool. And there, on top of the pool, a star floated. As he watched, it sank down through the water of his eye, gracefully, slowly, determinedly.

It fell deeper than his vision could follow and he felt it inside, like the touch of the most beautiful note ever played. It moved into him and hid itself in a coral corner of his mind.

He lifted his head and heard his own voice moaning. Sarah was kneeling in front of him, a piece of blood covered glass in one hand, her other hand holding a towel to his knee which throbbed explosively. Behind her David saw the man who had fed him fish, who had dragged him from his cottage. The man was sitting on a chair, his nose bleeding. At his sides, holding an arm each, were the silent staring men in suits. Behind them David saw the shelves he had seen that morning, lined with carvings and gifts of the sea.

"How dare you?" the wavy haired man shouted, struggling. He was larger and stronger looking than the men holding him, but their hands pinioned his arms like vises and his efforts moved them not at all.

"And you," he said, turning to the man whose cottage this was, who held a shovel in his hand, looking quite prepared to use it, had probably used it already, judging by the wavy haired man's broken and bleeding nose. "You're part of this? I will rend you and your ripples. I will tear your threads out of existence. Your kin will never formulate again."

The man, who had looked so tender that morning, was calm and solid in the face of these threats.

"I aligned my threads with yours because you were of the best of us," he said. "But I will stay thick and large till my time is done before I ever let you return and impinge upon the others."

The man strained against his captors, yelling in frustration.

"Release me at once," he said to the men in suits, "and I will only reshape you."

But they did not.

The man noticed David was conscious and glared at him. David felt a small furtive movement somewhere behind his eyes.

"Father," Sarah said. "You can never return."

At this, the man's proud head fell to his chest and he wept loudly, louder than David had ever heard anyone cry. The room filled with his torment. David's skin could not keep it out. It was becoming his own and it was not something he was strong enough to bear.

"Please," the man said, looking at David. "If not me, let her go. It is not right that she no longer moves along the lines. That her grace does not enrich the others."

David found himself agreeing to this plea, but the carver was firm. "You know that can't be," he said.

David, who knew nothing of anything he had heard and only felt the anguish that penetrated him, called out "Why? Why can't it be?"

He looked at the woman who had been his friend when he was a boy and he, like then, was willing to do anything for her, even if it meant his life.

"My father and I are linked," she told him. "With me there, he could always find his way on our shared threads."

There was a flash of green light and before David was knocked backward by the man's body striking him, the room, and everything in it, the walls, the furniture and even those standing, seemed to him, just for a moment, to be like he had been told they were in science class at school, composed primarily of empty space. For just a moment, he could see through everything, as if nothing was in fact there and he was alone, adrift in the void between stars.

Then he was on the ground, the man behind him holding his neck in the crease of his elbow.

Sarah turned and calmly, as if the man's actions were of absolutely no concern, said simply "No."

And the man surprisingly released his grip.

David moved quickly away, turned back and saw the man nod at his daughter.

"I..." the man paused, taking a deep, long breath, "...will let you go."

The man reached out and squeezed his daughter's hand. "You must go. You must be part of home again." He softened his grip. "I'm sorry."

The sky showed the beginning traces of dawn, like it had that morning years before when she had given him the key — that was a grain of sand and also a star — to hold and hide, and take with him.

Gulls circled above as the grey sea crashed against the shore.

David's bare feet were cold; he leaned against the shovel in his hand, taking weight off his wounded knee. The others stood before him in shallow water, Sarah facing her father, her hands in his, he flanked by the silent men.

The man released his daughter's hands, looked at David, gave the slightest of nods to the carver of found wood, then turned, and with one hand in each of the suited men's, the three of them walked into the sea.

"Do you still have the Ancil?" she asked, after they had stared at the sea for a long time

"Of course," the carver said.

He reached into his pocket, pulled out the small golden rod and handed it to her.

She turned to David, took his hand, and led him up the beach.

He had not noticed, and had not thought to look for it, believing that it would have been long gone, but she led him to the log that had once had a head of a dragon. It was buried deeper, and the roots that had been teeth and horns were worn away.

There, behind the log, she sat atop him and held the rod's tip just above his open eye.

"Look," she said. "Look into the Ancil."

And, as when he was a child, she held the lids of his eye open until it watered freely. And moving up from its resting place in the folds of his mind, leaving a wake of childhood memories, a point of light pierced the bottom of his eye, rose up through his vision, floated for a moment on the surface of his world, then disappeared above his tears.

He held himself from asking if she must leave so soon. He knew that for her it was not soon at all and, as much as he wanted to, he would not ask her to linger. He did ask her one question. He was not sure she would be able to answer, but he knew if he didn't ask he would regret it for the rest of his life.

"Where are you from?"

She smiled.

"It's not really a where. Watch," she said.

She took a step back, then another and another, putting one foot behind her at a time. With each step she did not get any further away, but somehow, with each step, she became smaller and smaller, as if he were looking the wrong way through a telescope.

And then she was gone.

About the story

"Hold This Star For Me" started as an exploration of the idea of lost memory. My first draft began with a page and a half of the main character obsessed with the idea of repressed memory, feeling he'd had experiences in childhood he couldn't recall. After the story was finished, I realized this musing about the possibility of repressed memory had been my way into the story but the reader just needed the story, so I cut it all out.

I believe Stephen King in "On Writing" (though I've been scanning his book all morning and haven't found it) relates how Raymond Carver once knew he had a story though he only had the first sentence, something banal like: "She went to the closet and got out the vacuum cleaner." Carver didn't know what the story was about, only that it was there, and that following that first line would lead him to it.

"Hold This Star" was very much like this. I knew the protagonist was on a quest to uncover childhood memories but I had no idea what he was going to find. This makes "Hold This Star For Me" one of my personal favorites. Writing it was an act of discovery, and I was especially excited by how David uncovers two important strands of memories: contact with aliens and the very real human memories of his mother.

A question for the author

Q: When do you decide a story is finished?

A: I often don't know where a story is going, or how it will wrap up, until I get there. I believe that good stories are discoveries, or at least have an unpredictable organic quality, where the characters and events start to chart their own course. While some stories are thought out before I begin writing — or the end is known and it is the journey that needs to be discovered — I am often surprised by the ending and say to myself, "So that's what happens."

In terms of when I consider a story finished, as in, I've worked on it enough, not until it gets published. Almost every time I reread a story, I find something I hadn't noticed before or that I could do better. Each time a story is rejected, I work on it before sending it out again. It is only that final stamp of approval that ends the process.

About the author

Mark David Adam lives on an island off the coast of British Columbia. When he is not foraging for edible and medicinal wild plants, playing funk guitar, or working at his day jobs, he writes short stories.

Hishi

David A. Gray

Hishi's claws ticked on the polished floor as she ran. The sound was barely audible, yet the teeming corridors emptied ahead of her. News had spread through the great city, out and down from the bloody throne room, that a new blend – an Excisor – had been dispatched to seek vengeance. Ten million people wondered who this Excisor was going to kill today. A very few knew, and prepared as best they could.

"Sure as The Scour hunts us all," the old ones whispered as she passed, pointing superstitiously up through the ceiling towards the roiling leaden cloud that blanketed the world. "The bonehawks will feast today."

The bonehawks feasted *every* day, Hishi's glanded memory stacks told her: Portmanteau's dead were rendered to remove every priceless, treacherous trace of metal, and the remains dropped through one of the mile-long vents in the bottom of the track as the gargantuan city rolled along its ancient course. Vast flocks of the vicious four-winged scavengers roosted on Portmanteau's underbelly, swooping down on Funereal days to try and catch the cascade of meat before it reached the steppe far below, there to be fought over by far more deadly competitors.

Hishi cut off the information flood with a thought. She had an Instruction from the Eternal him/herself, and would carry it out in perfectly and literally, as demanded. For the briefest of moments, the little Excisor wondered how things might be were she *not* to do so, and felt the gland at the top of her neck pulse. The surge of shame and contrition was so great that her step faltered and she came to a halt in an arching bloodwood cathedral, saw a flutter of red robes as a group of Spirituals scuttled to get out of her sight-line, never pausing in their endless repetition of the Histories.

"Deadliness and obedience," the Artificer who'd created Hishi had said paternally, not long after decanting. "You are my triumph. I took the best of the Assassin blend, added scar-cat senses and instincts, mixed in some peak-scaler, a touch of Human thinking, some Corrader-root contrariness, and a hundred other secret things. You are the epitome of single-minded loyalty. And," the leathery Agnost-root blender had muttered to himself, heedless of Hishi's keen hearing, "a thing of unsurpassed beauty and potential."

"Show us how lethal you are, how loyal," the masked, slumped figure on the throne had gasped, as Healing blend attendants had stanched the blood seeping through the priceless and ancient metal-ornamented robes. A wounded Courtier had handed The Eternal a long, thin bone pen, and a tiny scrap of parchment on a little tray made from priceless Original plastic. The nib had scratched steadily, ornately, and the Courtier had passed Hishi the completed Instruction. She had unfolded it, read it, carefully refolded the paper and placed it in a little pouch on her hip belt.

Hishi had bowed, turned and loped out of the blood-slicked throne room, as the healthy and walking wounded hurriedly cleared a path for her. She had glanced up once, through the grown crystal dome, past the mist-wreathed spires of this highest part of the city, at the Scour, where it roiled and seethed from horizon to horizon. Olders believed the turbulence moved with you as you walked, Hishi remembered. They believed it watched, and hungered. Hishi saw no such thing, but something deep in her gene memories made her relax a little more when she passed into the roofed corridors again.

Come to a halt in the vaulted church, Hishi replayed events so far, looking for unnoticed details that would aid her. "The past becomes the future," a bone-blade instructor had told her one day, as they'd sat nursing wounds. When Hishi had glared at him, he'd sighed and added: "A small omission one moment is your death the next."

She had not expected to be given an Instruction this day. She was barely out of the tank three months, summoned to an audience in the topmost levels of the city so the unquestioned ruler could give the seal of approval to his/her newest toy in front of fawning courtiers and cowed rivals. The new Artificer, whose blends were causing so much of a stir, had fussed round Hishi beforehand, measuring, assessing, murmuring: "You need to look your best, show them all!"

She had indeed shown them all her best: and her best was killing. No, *excising*. The difference was everything. Those who came before Hishi could *kill*. None could excise. She had showed them the difference.

"Assassins!" a towering gold-crested Courtier blend had shrieked as the group of hooded Maintainers had turned from their supposed duty repairing the floor of the coral floor, to pull stubby, fibrous, electromuscle thorn-throwers from their overalls. Thousands of tiny darts had sprayed the crystal-roofed room, cutting down Warriors alongside Clerks and Courtiers and a dozen more blends. They had killed. And the clumsy big Human-root Bodyguard blends had also killed, had swung bone swords with glacial speed, fired bulky living wood carbines, killed a hand of the attackers even as they were killed. They, and scores of glittering Courtiers, aloof foreign Ambassadors and liveried Servitors. But Hishi had *excised*.

The doomed Courtier had barely uttered the first syllable of its warning when Hishi's world had slowed. People became vectors and possibilities, estimates and presumptions. Thousands of glittering arcs marked the paths of the toxin-laden thorns in the air. Speedy attackers moved as through amber sap, hardened Soldiers lumbered, 1,000-generation-bred Bodyguards fought with steady predictable tedium.

Not Hishi. She'd moved through the slow-moving tableau, dodging deadly thorns, kicked out sideways at an attacker as she ran, seen a bouquet of rusty blood bloom from its neck, raised a long muscled tight-furred arm and sent a score of splinters of bone from her forearm, tiny vanes guiding them to throats, eyes, weak spots, delivering poisons brewed in her glands. A giant Bodyguard had screamed slowly as an assassin's stubby bone blade sliced through a gap in her overlapping chitin scale armor, had clubbed the smaller attacker down even as she fell.

Hishi saw everything, using eyes, ears, scent, bioelectric fields, vibration. She saw the dying attacker's finger squeeze the triggering bud on the pistol, heard 24 tiny darts as they sped out, calculated that five would pose a threat to The Eternal – who had moved not one hair's breadth since the warning scream – and had somersaulted over the stricken pair, taking a spread of darts to her back and shoulder. Her tightly packed layers of scar-cat fur and microfibers had stiffened and the darts had dug deep enough to hurt but not to deliver the poison on their pulsing tips.

Hishi had plotted a course towards the perfectly motionless figure on the throne. But not directly to it. She had discounted obvious threat and tactical considerations, leaving simple defensive reaction to the slow Guards. Hishi's route across the throne room was designed to take her from one attacker to another, to remove them in the simplest, most economical manner possible, then move on to the next. She'd jumped, sliced through an assassin's hood with a claw, felt warm blood that triggered the tiny poison cells in the needle-like tips to dispense targeted toxins. She'd sidestepped a knotted Reaver commander swinging a long diamond-edged blade like a scythe, trying to hold a clot of attackers back even as tiny darts sprang from his face and arms. A frantic Courtier, loyalty coming to the fore where martial skills were lacking, had grappled with a hooded assassin, taking multiple deep slashes to her arms and face. Hishi could have paused, saved her, but that would have cost her an early interception with another attacker who was more likely to reach The Eternal, so she had left the brave servant to die, then had struck her targeted attacker so hard she'd felt its chest cavity collapse, had ripped her hand on its shattered spinebone.

Another had stabbed at Hishi with a long glass blade. She'd taken the strike along her ribs in order to avoid losing momentum, nipped the off-balance attacker with a poison spur on her heel, spun onward. *This* was excising, she had thought triumphantly, danced on, slashed, leaped, kicked, eviscerated.

Suddenly, disappointingly, it had all been over.

Time had sped up again.

A score of attackers had lain dead, and twice as many court officials and guests. The last assassin, laid open from neck to waist by Hishi's retractable claws, had lain bleeding, inches from the edge of The Eternal's robe.

Hishi had felt her ruler's shrouded eyes on her, smelled an unfamiliar musk under a camouflaging perfume, knew she was being studied by a great many senses. She scented blood, too, saw a thin bone handle protruding from the Eternal's chest, heard the slow glutinous trickle of fluids onto the old metal-inset fabric. Hishi felt her gland pulse, thought she would die from shame and guilt. She hadn't seen the knife in play, should have seen it, tracked it. She had gasped in near physical pain at her failure.

The mask had nodded infinitesimally, then a bloodied Soldier had wrenched the dying attacker back, exposed the face, and a chorus of hisses had come from those nearest. It was no Assassin blend, but a hard-edged, scale-skinned rangy blend like none Hishi had seen before. An Ambusher, her glands whispered, and Hishi remembered. The Ambusher blend had been a step too far, at least in Portmanteau and its client cities. They had proven useful in the endless skirmishes with the nomads the city encountered on its long loop through the lowland plains, but conventional wisdom had it that they had been given a little too much native DNA and not enough Original, and they were ... unsettling to be around. *Unsettling,* Hishi thought. I know how that feels. Then the notion evaporated.

The Ambushers had all but vanished, employed now only by some of the more traditional sub-clans in Portmanteau.

This one suddenly stiffened and thrashed in a way it shouldn't have from Hishi's precision strike alone, its double-jointed sinewy limbs hitting the smooth floor so hard she heard them fracture. A suicide trigger, then. Much like her own, only hers was keyed to the displeasure of The Eternal. That last seemed unfair, Hishi thought, but the thought was snatched away before she could even consider it.

A spindly Reader was hurried forwards as Guards held the dying Ambusher down. Long fingers clasped the leathery skull. A moment later, the Ambusher lay still, and the Reader knelt and whispered something to The Eternal Courtier, who in turn leaned close to the wounded ruler and spoke. That was when The Eternal had actually spoken directly to Hishi, reproachfully telling her to prove her lethality. And she'd been handed the Instruction.

"The sponsor for this is Matriarch Eventide," the paper had read. "Excise all responsible."

Hishi, in the gloom of the cathedral, spotted an osmosis port set in the dark wooden wall. She was close to the edge of safe palace territory, and so touched her wrist to the little iris. She was recognized, and a moment later, a warm rush of nutrients and chemicals flowed into her veins, and a torrent of information into her glands and head. Some information seemed extraneous, some vital. She saw her route, already selected to take her through the most public of thoroughfares, the grandest of plazas. She frowned for a moment at the showiness and inefficiency of this, then obedience kicked in. All the new information would take a minute to permeate, infuse and be sorted, so she slowed her triple hearts and let her mind wander. She saw her reflection in the lustrous oiled wood, studied it critically. Small, by most standards, maybe half the height of a towering Soldier blend. A touch feline, she knew, if you took the tight-coiled scar-cat as your base assumption of feline appearance. The genes had been incorporated into previous blends, she remembered, but never with much success, as their implacable and frankly cruel instincts were too ingrained. A true memory, then: the Artificer studying Hishi fresh from the tank and muttering to himself. "Of all the creatures they made and left, of all the monsters and sports and tricks, the scar-cat was the most beautiful and least wise," he'd whispered to no-one. "And you, my dear, *you* are the first to do it justice."

Hishi had some of the scar-cat in her impenetrable dun fur, fast-twitch muscles, and ability to track multiple moving objects. And, for a reason that she knew to be vanity on the part of her maker, a fold to her ears that served no purpose save to mark her as a pet, a project. Hishi understood why she was what she was: a perfect instrument, designed for a role. But something about the knowledge that she had been molded for the esthetic pleasures of another, *that* was wrong. She felt a cold fury rise up at that, then other, saner, Original traits kicked in and reined the scar-cat heritage back, choked it. She saw in the dark mirror the first of a new blend, small, taut, gender-less. An angry thought emerged, was muffled as treacherous.

The tiny osmosis port closed, bringing Hishi back to the moment. Now, it was time to excise. She sped out of the cathedral, heard the Spirituals chanting, wondered if she would be included in their spoken histories of the city.

Two tiers below, Hishi passed out of the palace. The change was not noticeable to the casual eye, not even marked officially. But from here, though the orders of The Eternal were still sacrosanct, his/her will still law, she was in the city proper. And from this point on she would be mingling with teeming millions who cared less for their ruler than themselves, or their own clan leaders. She felt danger, opportunity and freedom. Hishi felt alive.

This close to the royal chambers and receptions, the corridors were wide and clean, decorated with rich coral mosaic and fringed with rare plants. House Eternal Courtiers huddled, watched by Guards, but not so closely they couldn't conduct sensitive business with other city functionaries and visiting envoys. Hishi saw it all with her eyes, knew it all from an endless well of stored and inherited memories. She had only to wonder, and she knew. Knew too much, she suspected, blinking it to a halt so she could focus on the real, the present. And in that moment, she cursed internally. Ahead, a fork in the thoroughfare, the corridor to the left was still emptying, while the one to the right was crowded with people looking her way. Her designated route was to the left.

In the rarefied, scandal-filled tiers of the palace, especially following an assassination attempt on The Eternal, that was only to be expected. There were whispers, coded hand signals, pheromones, and a hundred other ways of passing information fast and unnoticed. But here, she should have been free to travel without anyone knowing. To perform her function. Instead, Hishi realized, she was *expected.* And that could only be intentional. A signal, and an entertainment for the colossal city this day. Hishi felt warring priorities: should she take the route given, presumably by the royal court, knowing it would be slower and offer less chance of success? Or should she Excise with the single-minded goal of fulfilling The Eternal's Instruction? Hishi decided instantly: Excision was everything. She concentrated, pulled a complete map of Portmanteau from her glands, knew every inch of the thousands of miles of corridors, halls, shafts, drains, and highways.

Hishi ran the expected way for a short time, savoring the bubble of solitude that surrounded her, planning. At a narrow intersection of three corridors, she took the one that led up, and back into the palace proper, passing a pair of surprised Soldiers at rest, not pausing, but knowing they would raise some kind of alarm at her change of course.

The challenge was to leave the palace not just unseen, but with some clever misdirection. She sprinted through a small park roofed in cellulose, herds of wandering plants tracking her and instinctively moving in tandem, to the irritation of masked Gardener blends who were trying to trim tiny hard iridescent scales from their crowns.

Down, then, and to a slim grown bone arch whose span narrowed to at its arched peak. At this end, a hulking Guard, standing immobile in chitin plated armor, a serrated coral blade longer than Hishi resting point-first on the floor. At the other, the start of a route that pointed straight to the heart of the distant Caltrop tower.

Hishi could have run past, ducked, but she needed to make a statement, and so feigned a dodge and then, as the Guard lunged, she struck down with one claw, slicing between arm plates as the brute extended its reach. A tiny drop of paralyzing agent, hardly noticed, but staggering the Guard enough that Hishi had plenty of time to strike again, delivering another dose to a momentarily exposed neck. Then to the back of one leg. Again, and the Guard slumped, unconscious. But not for long.

Hishi leaped over the prone figure, ran, and halfway across, dropped off the edge of the unrailed arch, falling a tier to a ledge whose filigreed coral window overlooked a wide spiral stair that led down through the bowels of the city. She glimpsed, saw, heard, felt a dozen Secretaries there, conducting business. The ledge was narrow, crumbling, windblown. Hishi waited, unseen, patient.

This high up she had a clear view between two colossal towers, out across rooftops, out to the planet's surface, the near-flat horizon. The memories formed.

Scour. They'd named the planet after the terror that blanketed it, those unwilling Originals. The spoken litanies preserved by the very Spirituals who chanted without pause somewhere behind Hishi said that the ships had crashed here, eaten and dissolved by the living clouds even as they landed. Everything metal, plastic, contrived, from the ships' hulls to the tiny living machines in many of the Originals' bodies, had been consumed, the remains abraded to bone dust by the swirling storm.

The few survivors, from the 20 remembered old species, had fled, shorn of every tool and device they relied on. There, in the vast plains, dodging the Scour storms that stooped from the sky and dug mile-wide scars from horizon to horizon, they met lethally designed flora and fauna. Vast herds of fast-moving plants with toxins in every leaf, ferocious armored herbivores, flitting razor-beaked flying things and tireless predators on, below, and through the churned soil. All of them living around, dodging, following after, and screaming defiance at the storms. All deadly to the naked arrivals.

Hishi saw a Scour storm moving parallel to the giant city, seemingly blind to its existence, digging a ragged deep trench as it spun, moving, the city whispered to her, away. Fifty miles out, a pair of storms danced around each other, all the while moving in loops towards the northern sea. Hishi's eyes zoomed in, enhancing every detail.

A swarm of jagged little threshers let the wind pull them along in the backwash of the storm, where they tore chunks from creatures dazed from its passing. Preying on them, sucking the jagged omnivores up in wide grinding jaws, a group of reinworms. One of the 40-foot serpents was thrashing up a cloud of ichor and grit as a flock of trepaner birds swooped and plunged hollow sucking lances through its bulbous head. On the outskirts, rippers and spined seers, tearing at stragglers and each other, and following them all, a wide carpet of swaying ambulatory plants, elegant and three times as tall as Hishi, with a spread of pink motile light-gathering fronds on top, and a tangle of dragging roots festooned with paralysis-causing barbed hooks.

The deep wound in the ground would soon be smoothed by rain and wind, dappled with ponds, filled with fast-growing moss and opportunistic wind-blown prey and predators alike. All looking for food, and the tiny – and ever decreasing – amounts of metal left in the soil. The Originals, Hishi recalled, had not just relied on metal and artificial materials, they had contained it in abundance flowing through their blood, rich and versatile. The Scour had devoured them, replenished itself.

Hishi wondered about those memories. How could things so flimsy, so ill-suited to live, have survived here? She felt her Human and other Original genes, enjoyed their cunning and reasoning, but doubted the grandiose stories attributed to those beings, doubted even that there *was* anything above the Scour. How could there be?

The Secretaries moved on, a chattering gaggle. Hishi swung through the window, pushing the coral panel ahead, catching it before it fell, turning and placing it back where it had rested. She ran on, down, unrecognized.

While plugged into the osmosis port, she'd tasked her glands with sending new resources to the tiny distilleries in her hands, feet, glands and elbows, and already she felt hundreds of tiny lethal bone spikes sliding into queued muscle-fired channels powered by one-shot electro cells. Her retractable claws had added layers of extra ceramic to their outer edges, and the little toxin-bulbs around their bases were full. Hishi was not by personality or design prone to boasting, but she felt a certain pride in her abilities, and recognized that she was the pinnacle of the 1,000 generations of gene-tweaking that had followed the discovery of the first Cache. Well, she corrected, not the pinnacle: a pinnacle. It was just that some pinnacles were more fit to the task than others. A gland memory quickly interjected the cautionary tale of the recent Revenant blend attempted in House Astrogator's secondary city. All accounts pointed to that reckless House's attempts at a radical mix of Scholar, Hr'esche root, and the murderous Hook birds, plus some of the still-incompletely-understood strands from the Cache. The Astrogator Emperator had announced that a catastrophic failure in one of Dunedin's axles had caused the small city to stall in the path of a Scour, but a handful of survivors plucked from the grit by House Hood Scavengers told a very different story, of sabotage by panicked Scientificers to try and eliminate the uncontrollable blend before it could take flight.

Hishi paused on the stair. No alarms, no footfalls that spoke of anything out of the ordinary, no wafting pheromone orders. She was free to carry out her duty.

Matriarch Eventide, then, of House Caltrop. Memories bloomed, and Hishi ran on. The old Matriarch would not submit to the Instruction, and Caltrop was a formidable clan. An assassination attempt, while not unheard-of in inner and inter-House politics, was significant, more so in that every House, faction, sub-clan and nomad group would be watching closely to see how The Eternal reacted. On Scour, hesitation meant weakness meant death. The Eternal could have sent a small army rampaging through Portmanteau, but that would have shown a lack of confidence, and over-reacting was another perceived sign of weakness. Also, damaging a city's living structure was unacceptable. Hishi liked that her purpose was to make necessary things happen tidily.

She raced through rooms and chambers, across living stone, warm wood, engineered coral and cellulose, never slowing. She ran with no mind to misdirection; she simply took the fastest way down from the high tiers and inwards to the geographical center of the palace city. Word of her route would spread by mouth, bird, and chem-signal through the palace's sap conduits. But the eventual target would be secret until there were no other possible options. And Hishi had a complex series of bluffs, turns, and evasions prepared.

The ornate tiers slowly gave way to more utilitarian corridors whose dead wood and stone walls dated them to before the pre-Cache explosion in organic building artifice. She slipped unnoticed through halls busy with shift change Administers, the multi-strand and root support cadres that kept House Eternal's gargantuan palace city and its 23 subsidiary and client cities running smoothly. Hishi had been tanked with a complete if simplistic knowledge of the great Houses' affairs, and knew that the cities' survival depended upon a vastly complex system of manufacturing, cultivation, gathering and trading with friend and foe alike. At any given time, a capital city like Portmanteau would have scores of thousands of outriders – Herders, Merchants, Reavers, and Sifters and many more specialties – coming and going via hoists, scoops, drags and the giant access decks found on every hundredth core-stone Track tower.

She passed through the throngs like a wraith, stepping between the heartbeats, dancing through fleeting spaces. To Hishi it felt like an easy run through virtually motionless statues. To the bustling crowds of Administers, slow and deliberate of thought and action, it was as if an outside door had been left ajar and a tiny dusty vortex was whirling through their midst, brushing them no harder than a feather.

Some tiers beneath that, she cut through a broad wet chamber full of moonflowers, their waving pale stalks turning to follow the never-seen satellites claimed to be somewhere above The Scour. Cold, muted, blue light came from a million hair-wide pinprick optic veins that twisted and coiled into thick cables and finally emerged on a flat sky-facing terrace somewhere on the city's skin. Hundreds of Botanicals in white woven coveralls bustled around in the soaking soil, tapping minuscule quantities of metal-rich sap from the root bulbs. They paid Hishi no mind as she raced along narrow raised boards crisscrossing the fields: like many specialties, every successive generation was tending towards more focus on their role, and less interest in society as a whole. Hishi had only a brief sliver of actual life experience to fall back on, but her gene memory told her that the tens of thousands of Botanicals had seldom set foot outside the lower mid-cavern levels these past few generations.

Hishi came to a cargo capillary, where stooped, burly simian/Scour-dragon-stock Workers were racking big seed-pod-shaped containers in front of a bio-valve that opened with a wet suck every few beats, then closed, sending the container down to the bowels of the city. She raised a hand, and the senior Worker dutifully trotted over, his eyes darting up and down Hishi, agitated, unsure but respectful. *Good,* Hishi thought. *I'm faster than word of my description.*

"Duty of The Eternal," she said simply, and the sinewy Worker picked the most reasonable course of action.

"We are honored," he said. "If you can delay by only enough heartbeats to allow this current load to descend, I can clear a pod for you. These are only for kindling seeds, and are volatile from seepage…"

Hishi sniffed, detected a faint, acrid scent, that triggered a new memory. Kindling seeds were collected by nomads and those cities whose tracks arched above the ember forest belt, or passed close by. The flammable, sticky liquid inside the seeds was a volatile and valuable trade commodity, especially when the great cities were in conjunction, and war loomed. And, Hishi knew, Portmanteau was about to converge with House Recurve. Recurve was arguably as powerful as House Eternal, and the last time their vast capital cities had passed at a distance of 40 miles, 100 years ago, casualties on both sides had been high. Very high. Rumor had it that that some facing towers had yet to regrow their full height, but Hishi considered that detail nothing more than an instructional tale for fresh tanklings.

The next convergence of the elevated tracks was this very month. And this time the channels would pass so close that the cities' extremities would be within a hairs-breadth of each other – a ridiculously close 100 paces – for weeks. Yet another puzzle for Historians to study: some Tracks circled the world alone, others intersected and looped close to others, a few even circled on a huge closed perfect circle at one pole. In one place, a Track climbed above another, even, and then there was the Yard, where hundreds of the soaring stone channels met, meshed and joined. The Yard was where the course of a city might change, for the good of the ancient structure, and sometimes the ill of its inhabitants.

Portmanteau's course took it close to other cities quite regularly. Most of those were now clients and satellites. But not Recurve. And few came as close as that behemoth. At such range, a war could reduce them both to three-mile-high ruins, thus the daily exchange of Envoys. But The Eternal was no fool, and House Eternal had not risen to the top of the heap through complacence. As diplomats rode out, so vast trade caravans kept pace below the city, delivering mountains of wartime supplies. The kindling seeds – alongside other nasty chemicals and surprises – were hoisted up to hidden arbalests and throwers, alongside great wound bows and grappling arms. Thousands of Warriors would wait, too, by drawbridges and hoists. The thought thrilled Hishi, and repelled her.

She snapped back to focus, cursing the unasked-for memories for distracting her, when an Assassin might have come on her unprepared. No, never unprepared. But marginally less prepared. And Hishi needed to succeed. The Worker was gesturing to an empty pod, and Hishi got in with a nod. He looked relieved that she was going.

The organic shell sealed with a snick, and a few moments later the translucent casing was dropped into the rhythmically contracting tube. Down, ever down.

Threshold was not for the claustrophobic. Here, the ancient, indestructible core-rock base of the city melded with the less enduring materials added over the eons. The Originals, wandering their murderous new world, had found some of the slow-moving structures to be no more than colossal platforms on slow-turning wheels. Others were motionless, stripped by The Scour after some accident or decision had caused them to stall. Still more had been on the move in various stages of completion.

In Portmanteau's rare case, the city was apparently abandoned near-finished and intact, with living ironwood binding precision-cut stone blocks to form a mile-high fortress, complete with pinprick lights, power, irrigation systems, and still-living protein vats. More vitally, as with all the still-moving cities, enough of the billions of nutrient-fed bio-muscle pistons were functional enough to move turn the core-rock gears and drive shafts that kept the colossus moving.

The survivors, those few who the litanies said lived through the Wandering Time, had scaled a Track tower and moved in. Wary, depleted and grateful, they had vowed never to abandon their new haven.

The structure was now almost four times the initial height and double the width, a dazzling layered puzzle of wood, stone, bone, cell-glass, and coral, and a hundred combinations thereof. Hishi felt pride in the Original City, as such a trait, along with a tightly-linked loyalty to The Eternal, had been deemed useful.

And so as she brushed the last pod fibers from her fur and strode away from the sliced-open container on its landing pad, she was suitably impressed by the mile-wide chamber whose roof arched many hundreds of paces above gigantic stone and wood supporting pillars. Threshold was where the city met, people said. Incoming cargo and trade/war goods and parties were lifted in through massive portals, vast mountains of food and consumables came up and down for packing and distribution, and giant grown parts for the wheels and axles were hauled to access pits in the stone floor. Add to that innumerable shops, stalls, dens, pleasurariums and bio-pits, and teeming crowds, and you had Threshold in all its exciting, seedy, dangerous, opportunistic glory.

Hishi immediately liked it, in the way her scar-cat DNA liked the promise of a dusk hunt. She set off at an easy lope, aware that eyes might already be on her. Hishi took in a thousand scents, hundreds of distinct blends of what were once just those 20 Original races. Giant muscled Porters hauled bales of harvested pelt as big as Dust-Ox, tiny darting Messengers dashed past with secrets, Reavers strutted in long-legged packs, Artificers stood lost in calculation, Ambassadors moved arrogantly like plains-galleons, and visitors gawped at it all. Woven through this tapestry, assassins stalked, spies peered, plotters schemed, and poisoners waited.

Now, Hishi needed to be creative and fast. She knew Caltrop would be waiting: even if they were not aware of the discovery of their guilt, Mistress Eventide would have her people prepared. But if they even relaxed a little, that tipped the odds a fraction. Her presence here in Threshold was no secret, but her destination would still be a matter of debate.

The first attack came in open view of thousands of eager witnesses. A trio of dusty Nomads carrying heavy saddlebags were passing close by Hishi in the throng, when, as one, they shrugged off the bulging leather sacks and lunged at her, short glass blades in each hand. Hishi had no warning, but plenty of time to study her limited options. Nomads were a catch-all name for a whole subset of blends. All of which were designed for harsh conditions outside the cities. These were typical of the type: lean, fast and, Hishi realized as a dodged blade abruptly reversed course and slashed a shallow score across her ribs, double jointed. And, another surprise, possessed of accelerated reactions. That last, as a slash that should have raked out the close-set eyes of the lead attacker, only nicked the wide snout. Hishi had been taken by surprise, and felt humiliation and rage rise up. Her blood roared, glands surged and reduced the world slowed to a crawl, flooded her body with her own, vastly superior accelerants, and Hishi waited, motionless. The Nomads hesitated at that, exchanged the briefest, most fatal of puzzled glances, that allowed Hishi a space between heartbeats. She kicked out, felt tough exoskeleton snap under her heel, fired a brace of targeted darts from her backward-flung balancing arm. Nomads' genes were hardwired to fear toxins, Hishi knew, through hundreds of generations of encounters with the worst that the planet could devise. So even though their rough hides and inbuilt immunity should have had them ignore the darts, they flinched back, attack arcs forgotten. And died gurgling as Hishi turned and leaped, claws bare.

The gathering crowd, well aware of who Hishi was by now, stamped in a thunderous approval. Not necessarily for The Eternal, she understood, but for the raw display. Something in Hishi responded, and an impulse rose, was followed. She bent to slash the nearest satchel, spilling out hundreds of glass beads, the heart of every one holding a tiny grain of reddish metal. Taking a double handful, Hishi threw them in the air, a glittering fountain. The scene turned into a mad scramble, and Hishi ran, unseen for the most part.

Hishi gazed at the three prone guards. Regrettable and messy, as they would be missed, and that would eliminate the element of surprise. But they'd blundered onto the scene when they were meant to be elsewhere. That was troubling. As was her very use of poison so early in her mission: Guards were a hard blend to render unconscious, and she'd been rushed into using a powerful and lethal toxin. They'd dropped the moment she'd raked all three across their vulnerable eye-slits on one motion.

Hishi had been careful, passing under Caltrop's massive turret and heading for the fringes of sub-clan Flint territory. Even when she'd backtracked up the outside of a wind-scarred stone escarpment, she'd angled as if to sneak into the Stirrup embassy, only swinging across a half-mile-deep chasm at the last moment to steal through a narrow window into her real target. She was sure she'd not been tracked. And yet ... she had been met at every step, fought, forced to Excise. No matter. She raced on, up a wide spiral staircase with indentations worn into the stone treads. Ahead, heavy footfalls coming down, a trace of musky sweat containing glanded accelerators: vulpine-blended Caltrop Warriors. Hishi flooded her body with the boosters she would need, snicked long curved claws from their sheaths and squeezed a range of toxins along tiny veins. She flicked a long arm and a hundred tiny guided seed slivers flew out, the native hunting plant-gene twist giving them a heat-seeking hunger. Time slowed, Hishi sped up.

Hishi looked down, a clear mile drop to the Track. She'd never been outside on the facing edge of the city before, never seen the Track through her own eyes, to form real memories. She had to wait out here for long enough that the Caltrop retainers would take the planted clues and assume she'd retreated after the barrack-room battle, to lick her wounds, and would set off in presumed pursuit to finish her. Hishi did need a moment, she admitted, for rents to knit, toxins to flush. She had excised 267 living things thus far, and it was becoming messy, brutal, not beautiful. She'd climbed out of a window, edged up the slick living rock wall and on to a tiny ledge, where she now clung, unseen, battered by the cold wind. Vertigo was not an issue, or fear: Hishi's poise here no different than had she required to walk in a straight line through a genteel garden level. Only the outcome should she make a mistake would differ.

She looked down, ahead. Restorers were visible on the Track, making sure even tiny scrapes and gouges in the mile-wide core-stone channel were smoothed over, clearing any worrisome debris thrown onto the U-shaped canyon. Down in the raw deep wound off to the side were crews of Sifters, alert for any particles of metal not consumed by The Scour, but mostly seeking another Cache. There had only been two such stores found, Hishi knew, in many thousands of years; fragments of whatever civilization had created the great moving cities, then vanished. Each Cache had contained enough specialized knowledge to give the unwilling colonists previously unimaginable advances in genetics and bio technology.

Much further off, Hishi's predator-spliced eyes could see a Scour moving slowly anti-spinward: churning up the Bone Wastes again.

Somewhere in that vast dead expanse sat the shell of the great city the stunned first arrivals had named Necropolis. Hishi had tasted memories of recent travelers who'd seen the colossus, tilted and ruined at the shattered end of a Track, smoothed a little more by every passing Scour it could no longer outrun. Perhaps I can see that for myself some day, she thought, then unwillingly discarded the idea as counterproductive.

When finally she calculated it was safe to drop down and in again, Hishi was stiff with the cold, but alert, and driven by the need to move, to obey the Instruction. The wrecked room had been cleared of the bodies, but not the slick of blood, or the smell. She padded along the edge, and took a small door that led to an unassuming staircase.

Hishi's focus was all on fighting, moving up. Her movements were more spare, to conserve energy and to allow a dozen gashes to heal. Her working memory contracted to snippets. Dropping from a vaulted ceiling onto the helmets of five surprised warriors, claws flashing. Slicing through a toughened cell-glass wall with de-bonding enzymes, through a tanking ward, cutting down a clan Warrior as she raised a razor-edged ceramic blade. A leap across a chasm, claws scrabbling for purchase, a swing into a waste shaft a spliced second before a Guard looked down. A tumbling, chaotic battle with a kilted, gnarled Forager, retired to court duty but still fast as a grit snake and too thick skinned for toxins, requiring a choke hold to make him gasp for air and allow a single drop of deadly oil to be forced in his mouth.

A cold pond room with a dozen lithe junior nobles of Aristocratic blend, a flurry of billowing scarp-scorpion silk robes and thrown crown thorns, falling like leaves in the Scour to Hishi's leaping slashes and strikes. A long bloody score along her back, fast clotted and knitted. 502 excised. Killed, something in her head whispered, and was muffled.

No more stairs. This was the top of Caltrop territory. Hishi stepped over the body of a proud Bodyguard blend, almost sorry to have spattered that fine feathered crest with blood. At the same time, scornful that effort had been wasted on decoration, rather than efficiency. She strode through an old-fashioned grand observatory, the centerpiece of which was a dented, priceless alloy head-sized encased in amber, dead, useless. An Artificed Intelligence, she recalled, supposedly brought by the Originals, wrenched from one of the dissolving starships, the Caltrop, after it smashed on the great plain. Inside the sphere were useless fragments of carbon-cell brain. In as much as Hishi had any interest in ancient history, she wondered at the hopeless naivety of the stranded survivors, to preserve that, when they had had exactly no chance of ever leaving this world.

A rush of near-silent feet, the silken rustle of an Assassin's strangling ropes and thin coated blades. Hishi ached, slowed time, and let the scar-cat loose.

"You are the new Excisor blend, I assume?"

Hishi nodded.

The old Human-root woman pursed pale lips, looked Hishi up and down. "Too much," she said disapprovingly. "Before you do what you must, let us talk?"

Hishi felt no need to talk, but a small, subversive part of her wanted to listen. Eventide was old, near ancient, in fact, as close to an Original as had existed since the Caches were discovered. She had seen many generations come and go, must have traversed this world a hundred times over. Hishi sought completion, but also a *reason*, so she could best understand why she was here, dappled in the blood of hundreds of citizens. Her warring instincts found a truce in common sense: she would use the brief pause to flush some toxins from her blood, saturate her lungs with more air, isolate and eject a hundred slivers and ceramic fragments that had penetrated her body. Her toxin buds were dry, her thorn chambers empty, three claws snapped off, and she ached all over. An ear was ragged, too, which oddly irked Hishi more than the more serious injuries.

She heard a slow regular drip, noticed her own blood falling slowly to the bespattered coral floor. Five Ambushers lay dead around the old wooden chair, alongside a half dozen retainers who'd tried to impede her; a towering Human-elve Counsellor lay bubbling in her own blood. A dozen others poised to make a desperate rush. A fruitless rush. Maybe. She sensed every inch of the modest circular turret room, heard treads thundering up the single staircase, saw the locked hatch to the roof, felt a tiny movement of air through minuscule gaps in the big round window that overlooked the rooftops.

Hishi nodded, noting the beads of sweat on the withered clan ruler's wrinkled face. Eventide was easily over 1,000 years old, one of the early beneficiaries of Cache-given advances that had slowed aging in those few ruling-class specialties deemed fit for the laborious and painful process of re-gening an adult. She was as pure a strain as Hishi had heard of, one of the relative ancients who'd come from basic alterations to make the feeble colonists tough enough to survive. Human look and build, aquatic scales for durability, largish cranium for intelligence, a scattering of strands from winged omnivores for speed and focus, Hishi thought. Definitely live birthed, too.

"Who are you?"

"I am an Excisor," Hishi said, puzzled.

The ancient one scowled impatiently. "No, who are you? I hear you have a name."

"Hishi," she said simply.

"And you chose this name? Or was it that twisted Artificer who made you?"

"I chose."

"Yet you have no siblings, no family, you are also, unless my senses fail me, obedience-bound and genderless. Why do you need a name?"

Hishi felt that sting, though she did not know why. "I will not always be genderless; only for the duration of my service," she said, parroting the words the Artificer had use to her, no, *about* her, to Courtiers and Scientificers. "For clarity of focus and purpose, no distractions. When my service is done, I will choose to be 'she'."

A look of pity crossed Eventide's face. "We've come to this," she said softly. "Sending our children to kill for us. So," Eventide said more gruffly, "that fool of a boy on the throne sent you to try and dispose of me. I knew he would, eventually. The weak ones always do. Did he say why?"

The Eternal was male? And young? Neither had even occurred to Hishi before. Which struck her as odd, also. Curiosity, she had, but not a full range of it. That bothered her, and then it didn't. She almost killed the old woman there and then, loyalty and outrage lifting a hand to strike. But she held back, waiting for an admission of guilt that would end her task cleanly. Also, she was curious.

"Because you tried to kill hi…. The Eternal," Hishi said. "I was Instructed to Excise all responsible."

"Before you do your horrid duty, let me show you something," the old matriarch said in a dry whisper. Hishi paused, clawed hand raised, time crippled to a crawl. Another drip of her own blood slowed in its passage to the bespattered coral floor.

The old lady fished carefully about her plain tunic, keeping lightly scaled hands where Hishi could see them, Hishi noted approvingly. Then Eventide held out a folded scrap of parchment. Hishi didn't take her eyes off the woman, but took the paper between two claws and flicked it open. She glanced at it, fast. The familiar script read: "Assassinate person of Eternal. 7/10 Turn, this day."

Hishi was confused, and in the dissected second her attention was elsewhere, the Matriarch lashed out with surprising speed, a hardened hand striking Hishi in the throat. The blow would have crushed her windpipe had the Excisor not thrown herself backwards as it landed, skidding across the blood-soaked coral-glass floor, gasping for air. The Matriarch's Guards leaped forward to complete the kill, but Hishi used the slick floor's lack of traction and slithered a body-length clear, vaulting to her feet to slash down on a mailed fist where the hand armor and forearm plates met, near-severing the appendage. A thrown bone blade penetrated Hishi's tough layered fur at the shoulder, the point protruding out the back. Her glands shunted the pain away, closed off redundant arteries and in a smooth motion, Hishi gripped the blade in a hand and wrenched it out, continuing the sweep to send it through the eye-slit of the second Guard. She jumped backwards, a flip, landing in front of the defiant Matriarch, and lifted her good hand to strike.

The old woman's face showed no fear. "The Instruction was real, lass. Do with that knowledge what you will."

Hishi struck, tearing the woman's throat open, using the last drops of every toxin she had to ensure no revival was possible. She turned, letting the light old body fall, and saw a wave of furious retainers and Gaurds rushing toward her. Without a thought, Hishi jumped back and through stained-amber window behind the Matriarch's chair. A spray of darts and projectiles caught her as she tumbled, one ripping into the back of her head.

Hishi saw a bottomless chasm, and tried to right herself for a controlled fall. She struck a stone parapet, felt something break, then knew nothing more.

Fascinating, Hishi thought through a haze of pain so great that it almost was surreal enough to be able to pretend it was happening to someone else. Even while unconscious I tracked my own position. I did not know I could do that. She was lying on her back, so could see a tracery of glowing lines stretching up though blackness, like the webs rot-spiders drifted on ahead of a Scour storm. She tried to examine the data and immediately passed out. When she came to again, she was thinking a little more logically and directed her glands to numb the pain and give her stimulants. This was, to Hishi's surprise, only partly effective. Tasks that would have taken a thought, were now beyond her.

She listened, unable to see a thing. Other senses, then. A low hum and constant slight vibration. A very slight breeze on the side of her face. She tried to move, couldn't, and a rare panic took hold. Am I paralyzed? She howled, then, and felt the fur on her back tear out in clumps as she came free of the ground with a sticky ripping sound.

When Hishi came to again, still in pitch black, she moved carefully, found she had some control over limited gland function, and boosted her senses to ultra violet and thermal spectrums, with an active ping added. So, she was lying on core-stone, a curving platform fully 50 paces long that sloped down to left and right. Only a thick accumulation of sticky oil-saturated grit had prevented her from sliding off. Behind Hishi the core-stone wall was moving, smoothly and ceaselessly. Not just moving. Rotating. Hishi could sense heat from a small gap around the semicircular ledge she sat on. Not semicircular, she reasoned. Circular. And huge.

A distant part of her mind finally made sense of the data from her fall, matching course with maps. She'd descended a full, incredible, two miles and some. That she had survived at all was down to the ancient design of Caltrop's fortress: the outer walls were grown and built to be too smooth for interlopers – internal or some of the more enterprising external predators – and like Portmanteau itself, widened as they descended. A full third of Hishi's drop had been down a sloped section of city wall, then the architectural tricks to funnel wind and rain had played in her favor, treating the tiny, broken Excisor like a piece of storm-blown trash, funneling her down and away efficiently.

Hish had bounced from outcrops, slid down a vast fungus-choked air shaft, tumbled across a slope of Dayshade vines, ripped through a wide bio pipe and sluiced down an overflow drain on the resultant nutrient torrent. Ever downward, light and limp, bouncing. And breaking, healing, breaking again, partially healing again as she fell.

And now, Hishi realized with a shock, she was on one of the giant wheel hubs down in Axle. The undercity, off-limits to civilized people. The moving wall was a wheel, stretching up and away, and down to the Track. A few paces to either side and ... Hishi shuddered. Wait: fear? Shock? These emotions should not have been available to an Excisor. She remembered a blow to the back of her head, ceramic slivers from Guards' weapons slicing into her, and reached up with shaky hands. Instead of tight muscle and fur, a jagged sticky mess. She had some glanded abilities, still, but clearly there was serious damage. Also, surprisingly, clear thinking, no, not clear, just not limited. Hishi experimented, imagined The Eternal dying, felt a rush of agony so great she knew she would die too, were it true. So, the suicide gland was still there. But she knew, now, that her crushing loyalty was artificial, glanded, enforced, as was the idiotic idea of her life ending just because The Eternal's did. The fool boy's, she corrected, remembering Eventide's words. Hishi healed fast, knew for sure that she would have a very brief time in which to act to keep her new-found clear-headedness. If she wanted to. Dared to.

Hishi decided, called up the stored plans of her own body and then, looked deep into the schematics for the complex and remarkable gland cluster. Dozens, scores of tiny individual glands and manufactories, all working together. But some wrecked now, and some a hindrance. Hishi took a deep ragged breath, not allowing her conscious mind to catch up, snicked out an undamaged razor-sharp claw and struck deep at the base of her skull. She screamed, then, and dug with brutal precision until the pain stole away her consciousness once more.

Hishi dragged herself up another rung. 3,086. She'd told herself she could climb no more of the narrow stone notches on the dangling stalactite ladder, at 2,000. And at 3,000 had thought she might throw herself backwards, off, down to the wheel again, this time to bounce and die. But she had an Instruction to finish. And the clarity to know how.

3,203: no more rungs. A lichen-covered corridor of wet core-stone, shuffling Axle inhabitants from no specialties Hishi recognized, and some her glanded memories had told her were long-since eradicated. Hands helping her, too weak to fight back, a nutrient tap, a cup. Blackness again.

Hishi came to slowly, tried to spring to her feet, managed only to roll over and vomit on herself in the dark. Her night vision flared too bright, showing a rough-hewn chamber with indistinct figures around her. Then it snapped off and the blackness was total, only to be replaced by an overlap of thermal map and motion vectors from the slow draught of warm stale air. She tried to shake her head, screamed in agony.

Strong hands gripped her head and a cup was held to her bruised lips.

"Don't fight, lass," a grating, slow voice urged. "Someone made a proper mess of the back of your head, near tore that abomination of a manufactory cluster out your head."

"Me," Hishi tried to say, "suicide gland. Take it out." It came out as a whisper but whoever was holding the cup, seemed to understand.

"Thought as much. Well, we don't have The Eternal's Medicants here, lass, but we've some experience in removing the worst of the new tortures. Drink: this will hurt less if you do."

Hishi didn't drink, and as more hands held her, the pain in her head multiplied a thousand-fold. She thrashed and howled but forbade her thorns to fire or her claws to extrude. And in time she passed out.

"How long can they survive?" Hishi and the stooped old Healer called Chirur sat on the edge of Portmanteau's blunt frontal slab, directly above the leading edge of one of the mountainous wheels. Its fellows stretched to both sides, across the width of the stone canyon of the Track. The noise – millions of tons of stone rolling over stone – was less brutal than Hishi had expected, due, Chirur had told her, to the incredible smoothness of the wheels and Track, even after these uncounted centuries. It vibrated every part of you, Hishi thought, reducing you to nothing. A stiff but pleasant wind blew in their faces, dispelling, for a moment, the ever-present Axle levels smell of grease and waste.

She didn't have access to her gland memories any more: that pulsing black organ had been buried in an organic settling bed, Chirur said, to have it do some good at last.

"Why not just kill them?" she asked, as a group of figures far below and a little ahead were prodded off a wooden hoist onto the smooth stone track bottom.

"Where would be the lesson in that?" Chirur replied. "This way, anyone who cares to see The Eternal's mercy for his opponents need only look down."

Most of the 20 or so people were trotting away from the trundling mass of the city, slowly increasing the gap between themselves and the grinding wheels. A few were running towards the distant edges, and the cliffs rising there on both sides. A few simply sat down in the path of the relentless wheels.

"Can they escape?"

"The only escape is under the wheels, or if they're still alive when we go over a vent and they fancy a drop all the way down to the monsters that shadow Portmanteau looking for scraps. And once in a while a hookbill will take one to lay its eggs in."

Hishi shuddered. "How long?"

"How long can they walk without stopping? There are tales of victims – the fleeter, hardier blends – lasting five-days, 100-days, even more."

Hishi perked up. The old exiled healer was fond of telling stories, and in the ten day since Hishi had arrived near death in Axle, he had proven a kind companion. And a vital one in the dark, unmapped, dangerous base levels of the city. Here, Hishi had learned, the detritus, the unwanted, the unsuitable, ended up. Both inorganic and organic. Discontinued blends, fugitives from Eternal justice, illegal immigrants to the city, and more. And, raining down on them, the byproducts of the capital city. Axle was where waste was processed, the endless gears and muscle engines located, the proceeds of illicit deals hidden, swapped, traded, along with lives.

"More?" she prodded gently.

"There are tales of lights, campfires glimpsed way ahead on the long straight sections of the Track, the flames carefully shielded from those gazing down from above, but sometimes visible from way down at our level. People say there are entire tribes living on the Track, who've perfected scavenging from the things that blow, fall, and are trapped in the Track."

"Do you believe those tales?"

The old man smiled: "I believe a lot of things that are not true."

Hishi leaned forward to see one of the people below as the vast turn of the wheel lost them to sight. She'd been shy of going too close to the mountainous stone rollers at first, haunted by a fragmented memory of waking, broken, on the curving axle. Now, she was confident, happy to hang over the drop by a hand to satisfy her curiosity.

Portmanteau trundled ceaselessly on dozens of rows of the polished stone cylinders, each row made up of 20 wide smooth solid wheels, separated from their fellows by a hand's breadth.

Chirur hissed in concern and she smiled inwardly. Once the gland was removed and a ready supply of clean, if illicit nutrients had come her way, Hishi had healed fast. But not totally. She'd lost the tip of an ear, which now delighted her for the anguish it would have caused the Artificer, and had pale scars all over her body. She was close to her old speed and balance, though lacking some of the powerful aids the gland had given her. But though she was free of the compulsion to please, to die for, The Eternal, Hishi was still driven by duty.

"I need to go back," she said bluntly.

Chirur was silent, and instead of answering, nodded out to the right into the foothills. "Recurve coming," he said conversationally, as if discussing the weather. "Convergence in a three-day. Be busy upstairs, with all those Strategists and Soldiers and Diplomats running around."

Hishi nodded. She zoomed in on the distant curve of another elevated Track as it looped round through the plain to run parallel to Portmanteau's course, traced way back to a distant smudge on the horizon.

Chirur continued: "Not so many people know, the traffic that goes back and forth down these levels come a convergence. From the high and mighty doing secret deals, to people looking to start a new life..."

Hishi felt something new, something not hostile. The thought wasn't banished, but neither did she know what to do with it. She touched the old healer softly on the shoulder with a furred hand, and padded away.

The stir was audible when Hishi limped in through the giant double doors of the High Reception. The room was truly grand, a billion shards of Scour-glass covering every span of wall, floor, and vaulted ceiling. Behind the high throne, a stained-crystal coral fan, colored and dyed to show a scene from the story of the Landing, Originals stumbling from a ruined warship even as The Scour's tiny living machines ate it.

The Eternal was surrounded at a respectful distance by whip-smart Strategist blends, and a score of military specialties. At the back, the stooped Artificer who'd made her, and whose name she realized she had never heard. Watching her, expressionless.

The atmosphere was tense but not panicked. And Hishi knew from her lope up through the city that war was, thus far, at arm's length.

The Eternal's Secretary let the babble of voices rise, then snapped a long tendril and there was silence. Hishi knew her appearance broke a score of Court protocols. Bruised and scarred. More deeply than they knew.

She padded forwards, stopping three paces from the throne, noting the Guards, three from before, one new.

The Eternal's ornate mask was fixed on her. The Secretary coughed, and spoke: "The Eternal wishes it to be known that we are pleased to see our loyal instrument returned alive …"

"They knew I was coming. It was a test," Hishi said simply. She stared at the mask. There was an outraged pause, then the Secretary started to puff up to deliver a rebuke. A gloved hand was raised, silencing the courtier. It leaned close to The Eternal, and something passed between them. The courtier straightened and spoke: "Why do you say that?"

Hishi took a breath: this close, The Eternal's presence was almost overpowering. Her conclusions came in a rush: "Because The Eternal didn't move. Not a twitch. Not even to avoid harm. And because I would have seen the blade. And the blood, it smelled … wrong. Old. Not real."

Everything stilled, quieted. Hishi could sense Bodyguards tense, Diplomats watch with feverish interest. She hadn't mentioned Eventide's note, sensed that The Eternal was waiting to find out if she knew. Hishi said nothing and there was a barely perceptible feeling of tension ebbing. The Eternal nodded to the Secretary, and something was whispered.

The Secretary stood tall, spoke loud and clear to the whole room: "A test of loyalty of a new blend, yes, and a lesson at the same time. Matriarch Eventide had questioned our rule, sowed dissent. An example had to be made, that just one loyal servant could excise even the most powerful sub-clan. The completion of the Instruction means…"

"Not completion," Hishi said quietly, and there was a scandalized hush. She sensed a Guard move, a Human-root female.

"'All responsible' not Excised," Hishi said. "Instruction wording very specific."

She sensed The Eternal stir, felt the tissue around the empty suicide gland bud twitch, a knot of scar tissue in her head acknowledge the repeated signal, but no more happened. The Guard hesitated. The Eternal's mask trembled. Time slowed down.

About the story

"Hishi" came from a bunch of directions at once. I was worrying about my daughter and the world I'm raising her in, where rich old white men seem intent on burning it all down and ensuring she has no rights. And where we as a species seem to be sending our kids to war, or to bomb and kill. So I had in mind a character who had all her life ahead, all her potential, but was choked by the actions of these old men. But who would triumph, in the end. Kind of. The world – Scour – was inspired a little by those old stories where we know society is the ruins of an older civilization, a tiny bit by railway tracks (a minor obsession), and a lot by a wish to take an extreme situation and imagine how we'd be after 10,000 years of forced evolution. The things we would do if we had to, then because we could. Also, I'm an avid student of Ottoman history, and of the Crusades, and Europe's Hundred Years War. Imagine, for a moment Constantinople on wheels.

"Hishi" was – and is – a standalone story, but in the process of editing, I realized this is her first chapter as a person in a strange world. I know where she goes next, even if I don't ever write it.

A question for the author

Q: From where you do you draw inspiration for your characters?"

A: I take something from myself at a young age. when I used to stagger home from the library with armfuls of peculiar/comforting-smelling classic sci-fi, full of anticipation and alert for the local crazed bullies. But it's from my kids that I take most, now: that heady mix of potential, hope, happiness and occasional heartbreak. If any of my characters convey even a little of that sense of opportunity amidst the darkness, then I'm flattered and happy.

About the author

Gray is an exiled Scots creative director and journalist living in NYC. He works for a range of print and digital magazines and brands, and every night he climbs to the roof of his Brooklyn apartment building and squints at the Manhattan skyline, wondering how it might look in a century or few. Sometimes he thinks it will be a glittering gem, other times, a flooded ruin. Or maybe a bit of both.

March

Always Dawn to Forever Night

Luke Elliott

Pwela woke to a chill unknown in the Forest of Always Dawn. Tar and peat filled the air, undercutting the perpetual crispness. She shot to her bare feet.

While she slept, the Rot Thing had stolen her warmstone.

Her warmstone sustained her, let her live in the everglow of the forest. Her palms went slick and her breath came short and shallow. She should flee. Run as far and fast as skylight arcing over a cloud. She should, but she would not. She hated the Rot Thing. It had brought unwelcome change to the Continuance.

She could not allow it. She would reclaim her warmstone.

Pwela found Loper resting in a glade of white heather and woke him with a whistle.

"What is it?" he said, jaws cracking with his yawn. The bogcat stretched his long black body, first his back legs, then his front. Extended claws raked the heather, upturning black loam, and a long tail swished high in the air.

"The Rot Thing stole my warmstone."

Loper hissed.

"You smell it, too. Tar and peat." She scratched behind one of his long, feathered ears in the way he liked. She laid her head against his neck, his ghost-striped fur smooth against her bare scalp. "Will you take me after it?"

"Only since it's you asking," he said.

Such a softie. She climbed onto his back, settling between bony spines.

Loper carried her through the Forest of Always Dawn. The orange of the low-roosting sun lit the leaves in its unending glow, dappling the forest floor. Loper darted into the underbrush, then leapt out onto a fir. Long claws sank into its mossy trunk as he bounded off, clearing a sinkhole full of vine snarls. Pwela held fast to the mane of black hair around his neck, her skin blending against his fur. The harmony of their colors was music.

She laughed as they soared, eyes leaking.

Another leap took them into the heart of a familiar glen. But where baby's breath once flourished white and pink, stains now colored flowers with yellow and brown. Wilting from the Rot Thing's passing.

"What is it?" she asked. But she knew.

Loper bent to chew the grass, then spat with a hacking cough. He growled, a rumbly sound from deep within his chest. "Wrongness stains our forest, Pwela."

She sat tall on Loper's back. "The Rot Thing carries stain and wilt and canker. We must drive it out."

"Do you know the Rot Thing?" her friend asked, voice a near-whisper.

She had never met it, but found she did know. "I have long dreamt of it." A shiver shook her small frame.

"As have I," Loper said.

Together, they followed a trail of wrongness in pursuit of the Rot Thing. The thick underbrush and wide trees of the Forest of Always Dawn thinned and lapsed away. Lessening was the way of borders, but swathes of ugly wrongness marred the gentle margins. It hurt her chest to see beauty so wronged.

And so they crossed into the Desert of Only Day. The sun shone savage above, its radiance afire atop the sands.

"The Rot Thing walks the desert," said Loper. "I smell its wrongness, tar and peat." He climbed a dune slowly, paws sinking.

"Shall I walk?"

"The sand is fire, Pwela. Your softness would not long last it." The heat already lashed against her scalp. Oddly, though, a chill remained in her belly.

"You are kind to worry." She let one hand free of his mane to scratch at a long, feathered ear. "But if you tire, my softness will manage." Bogcats were not of the desert. They came from the deep Moor of Forever Night, where they hunted through chill and gloom. Loper had only come to live in the Forest of Always Dawn to be with her, though he grew to love it.

Loper plodded on, persisting against his disharmony with the desert. If he could endure such extremes, she too could reach the gateway, where surely the Rot Thing headed. Its path was no mystery to her, she realized, and that unsettled her stomach. Perhaps she would even discover what lay beyond the gate. Thoughts of what lay beyond filled her with anxiety, a shrill thing. It made her all out of tune.

An immense dune rose above the rolling sands, so tall it brushed the sun. Its sands quivered and roiled.

"What is it?" she said, gasping.

Loper paused. His back hair bristled against her skin. "Come out," he yelled. The bogcat stepped closer to the dune, growling. His ropy muscles coiled beneath her thighs. "You who lurk beneath the sands, come topside."

The dune rippled, and two long eyestalks burst skyward. Each eyestalk reached higher than Pwela would if she stood on Loper's back. Black orbs swelled at their ends.

A voice like an avalanche shook beneath them. "How dare you tread upon our sands, bogcat? And with that wretched manthing clinging to your fur?"

"I tread where I wish, prawn," said proud Loper.

The eyestalks rose higher and an immense horned shell clove the sands. Chitinous legs tipped with forked pincers lifted a carapace half out. Thick antennae whipped the sands, sending Loper back on his haunches. Fetid winds eddied around the creature.

Pwela stifled a gasp.

"We are not prawn." The voice fell over them.

The dune devil was the largest she'd ever seen, perhaps the largest in all the Continuance.

"I am this bogcat's friend, Old One," Pwela said. "Forgive him, please. He can be thorny for a feline."

"Why does the manthing make words at us?"

Loper growled, prowling the sands.

"I am Pwela. I would be your friend as well."

The dune devil's antennae ceased their lashing.

Pwela unslung herself from Loper's back. Her breath hissed at the burning of the desert. The softness of her feet indeed hated the fiery sand. She trudged toward the dune devil, palms raised. "We only seek to cross your dunes and enter the meadow. We chase the Rot Thing."

"Rot Thing?" the old devil demanded. "You are with the Rot Thing?" An enormous claw rose from the sands around Pwela and clamped over her chest. The dune devil drove out her wind. She gasped, fighting for air.

Loper snarled. "Release her, you crusty shrimp."

The dune devil lifted her toward its maw. Hot, dry breath reeking of spoiled fish blasted her from the furnace of the devil's gullet. Arm-like mandibles grasped for her.

"We are not with the Rot Thing," she screamed. "Enemies, enemies!"

The dune devil stopped just shy of biting into her. "We hate the Rot Thing," it said, voice all clacks and clicking. "Look what it did to us." The dune devil rolled onto one side and moved her toward its underbelly. Black stains of ichor marred its orange carapace. The pools spread inky tendrils, even as she watched.

"It's horrible," she said, eyes welling. Dull ache filled her own belly, chilled from within.

The dune devil released her. Before the sands burned her softness, Loper was at her side, head dipped so she could clamber on to his back.

"How do we beat the Rot Thing, old one?" she asked. "How can I save you from its wrongness and destroy it?"

"You cannot," said the dune devil. It quivered, slowly descending back into the sands. "The Rot Thing has always been, though it shifts form."

"I must try," she said, lip thrust out. "I will reclaim my warmstone and not allow wrongness to desolate my Continuance."

"The Continuance is not yours, manthing," said the dune devil. Soon, only its eyestalks remained above the sands. "It is not for belonging. Shared by all and none."

"Once I cast out the Rot Thing, will you heal?" she asked.

"Look to yourself," the dune devil said. Its eyestalks dipped beneath the sands, which stilled as if nothing had ever lurked beneath its shifting layers.

"We must go, Pwela," said Loper. "Even I cannot long withstand the fire." And go they did, across the Desert of Only Day's long reaches, until tufts of sawgrass dotted sand that lapsed into soil. The sun dipped in the crossing, turned purple.

They entered the gentle meadow of the Everdusk.

Though Pwela was most comfortable in the Forest of Always Dawn, she adored the Everdusk. She and Loper had come once before, played on beds of lilac, rolled together beneath the tranquil light. The autumn wind blew songs of sleepiness and slow. The meadow was a place for resting.

But wrongness had come to the Everdusk, too. The lilac sea had wilted, petal clusters browned and decayed. A sign of the Rot Thing's passing.

The path wound down into the moor and out of sight. Her feet tried to follow, but she forced them to halt. She felt the end in her belly, and rested her palm over the chill. The path led, eventually, to the gate.

"What ails you?" Loper asked.

"A chill," Pwela said, peering at her stomach. She gasped. Wrongness marred her as well, spread from her belly in tendrils of sick.

Loper could not see her belly, since she still rode astride his back. "What is it?" he asked.

"I need my warmstone," she said. "The chill runs deep now, and I cannot shake it." She would spare him the truth.

"We should turn back," said Loper. His black paws sank into the wilted sea. "Please, Pwela. No joy or beauty lies ahead."

"I must face it," she whispered. "It has my warmstone, and without it I cannot stay here. You can go back. Return to the Forest of Always Dawn and run among the elm and fir."

"No." Loper flattened his long ears. "I shall carry you all the way."

She scratched those ears while they walked the lilac sea, which shimmered with light and wind, but soon, far too soon, the meadow, too, began to lapse. The purple glow darkened, deepened, until only black remained. A crescent moon hung alone in the sky at the edge of the Moor of Forever Night, shining pale like milk, white like bone. The dying lilacs turned to weeds and snarls and damp.

She had never been so far.

The blackness of Forever Night had haunted her dreams as long as she could remember, beckoning her. It had been the Rot Thing all along, she realized, summoning her to the gate.

Loper sloshed through puddles as dark as his fur, between the shadows of cypress trees like grasping ghouls. The moor was his home, she reminded herself. Bogcats lived in harmony with the darkness at the heart of the Continuance, prowled the paths surrounding the gateway. Loper would protect her.

The swamp stank of tar and peat. Loper raised his head to sniff the air, then bounded forward through the gloom. Eyes glinted back through shadow, reflecting moonlight. Loper did not slow, for his eyes glinted too, and the unseen things did not assail them.

They emerged, at last, onto the bank of a still lake lit only by the crescent moon which dipped low over the water, as if reaching for its own reflection. At the middle of the lake rose an island of pale sand. At its center lay the freestanding gateway, plain and brown, locked and bolted.

As it should be.

But beside it stood a figure dark beyond mere black. It stung her eyes like an inverse sun. The Rot Thing. On the island, the Rot Thing extended white hands holding a shape red and luminous, light stark against its depth of black.

Her warmstone.

The Rot Thing lifted the red rock high and brought it down upon the gateway with a crack that thundered over the still lake, raising low ripples. The gate shook and shuddered.

Loper whimpered. "Turn back, Pwela. I cannot swim."

She climbed off his back. "I know. But you have carried me far. And I *can* swim. Stay here, my friend. I will face it alone. Someone must." Her heart told her so. "Let it be me."

"I... understand." Loper said, dipping his wide head. "Our moments in the forest live eternal, though we've passed them by. I am with you, whether you sense me or not. And if you return, I will find you again on the shore."

Pwela hugged his neck, eyes leaking, then dove into the still waters, breaking them, casting waves across the lake. Cold beyond ice bit her everywhere, though not as cold as the wrongness in her belly, but soon the pain of the chill lapsed too. She swam, arm over arm, legs pumping. She laughed as she sped toward the island, laughed despite it all. The song of the water played in her heart, filling her. When she reached the island, she climbed out, cold and dripping, but full of harmony.

"Let the gateway be," she commanded. "It must remain shut."

The Rot Thing stood with its back to her, hood drawn, looming over the gateway, its huge umbral mass shifting and fluid. It smashed the warmstone against the gateway again with a thunder that forced Pwela to cover her ears. Her red rock broke. The gateway's frame cracked, and the Rot Thing turned, then dropped the shining shards of her warmstone to the pale sand. It returned its long hands to its sides.

"No!" she cried. She dropped to her knees and cupped the fragments. Their light faded and was gone.

She dropped the broken bits and glared at the Rot Thing. Her eyes stung from gazing upon shadow so deep, but they soon adjusted too, even to blinding oblivion. She did not look away.

"You do not belong," she said. "Leave this place and never return."

"None belong. All belong," it said, throwing back its hood. "Look within and know you brought me here." The Rot Thing's voice came as a hollow echo of her own, rebounding from an endless cavern. The head of the Rot Thing was her own bald head, but distorted and immense. Chill radiated from it, sapping her strength. She wanted to scream, to run as far and fast as skylight. She should flee, but she did not.

"You cannot trick me, bastard," she said, rising from the sand. "I did not bring you. You are *not* welcome here. Leave this place!" She set her feet wide and lifted her fists.

"There is only one way." It laid a thin hand against the gateway. "Join me." The Rot Thing's immense face was like her own, but wrongness filled empty eyes above lips blue and frigid.

The gateway opened, and nothing lay beyond. An abyss with no color at all.

She should have never come. The Forest of Always Dawn waited still. Stained though it was, at least it held warmth and sun.

A place for beginnings, not ends.

But no, the wrongness had spread through the heather, through the fir and lilac. To herself.

The Rot Thing held out its hand to her, fingers like white worms.

She searched the far bank for Loper, but the bogcat had gone. It did not anger her. Such things were not easy to witness.

The Rot Thing waited, hand extended.

"I will not go with you," she said, but did not shrink away from the awful hand.

"You will," it said, voice still a hollow echo of her own. "I will not tell you to be unafraid. I will not barter or beg. But you will come."

She stared at the nothing beyond the gate. "What is it? Is there something farther in I cannot see?"

The Rot Thing stood silent, spindle fingers swaying before her. The only way to know was to step through.

She thought of the wilted heather, the browning lilac, the wheezing old dune devil. Loper, so worried for her softness, who had carried her over fire.

"Will you leave the Continuance if I go with you?" she said.

It paused, silent for a time before responding. "I came for you."

Then it was right. "I'm sorry, Loper," she whispered.

She took its hand. Her tiny fingers stuck to the Rot Thing's pallid skin as if it were tar. Near translucent skin. She gasped as black eels wriggled beneath the thin membrane of its being. They coiled beneath her hand, drawn to her warmth.

The crescent moon rent and tumbled from the black. The still lake spilled skyward, rising in a geyser around her.

With one long hand, the Rot Thing pushed through the absence of the gateway and pulled her through with the other, away from the Continuance. She could not stay, only go. And go, she did. Through and beyond into nowhere.

About the story

To tell the story behind "Always Dawn to Forever Night," I need to first share some tragic personal history. My mother died from stage IV brain cancer in 2012 after battling the disease for years exceeding her prognosis. Her passing left me numb as conflicting emotions fought each other once her ordeal was over. I never really dealt with the pain and injustice. I just tried the best I could to carry on.

Then, in 2015, my German-shepherd mix died unexpectedly while in the care of a vet for a minor issue. She was 3 years old. I'd adopted the dog before my mother's death and she had helped me cope when it happened, with her unconditional love. I blamed myself for her death (though I'd done nothing wrong). All the unresolved pain rushed back, combining with the guilt to overwhelm me, and sent me into a depression lasting months.

One night during that depression I dreamt about a young girl who lived on a world where the time of day was linked to geographical location. Only through travel could she witness the passage of time. Her journey began in a warm forest of perpetual dawn and ended in a land of night filled with foreboding. As she drew closer to the end, she became frightened, but continued. The dream ended abruptly without a satisfying conclusion when I woke. The concept of her world stayed with me even as details of the dream faded, so I typed a note in my phone about the potential story idea.

My waking mind connected the dream to the journey of our lives. How we begin young and worry-free and travel toward our twilight years with growing anxiety about what lies beyond. I realized what I'd dreamt was my subconscious trying to grapple with mortality. I didn't know who the girl was, but I sensed that even though she was afraid, she was brave, and willing to face whatever waited for her. The characters of Loper and the Rot Thing took shape as I crafted a story out of the building blocks my subconscious provided.

I wrote the first draft in one sitting and by the end felt euphoric and proud. Still, I'm savvy enough to know that just because you're drunk on a draft doesn't mean the story is good, so I let it sit. My suspicions were right. It needed a lot of work, but its heart was compelling. I rewrote it several times before showing it to my wife, who cried when she read it. Next, I sent it to critique partners, who helped shape it, before the final product was ready to query.

"Always Dawn to Forever Night" represents much I can't put into words about death and my admiration for people brave enough to face it with dignity. Several readers have asked what happens next and I always smile, because the answer haunts me as well.

A question for the author

Q: What do you think is the single most important quality for a good writer to possess?

A: Persistence. There will be days you want to quit. There will be months where you feel like all you are doing is banging your head against the keyboard and producing nothing remotely readable. You will get rejections. Oh, so many rejections. Saying "persistence" might be trite, but as long as you continue to learn and grow, it's the path to success.

About the author

Luke Elliott was born and raised in the suburbs of central Florida. In his late twenties, he travelled across the country with his wife and two dogs to live in Portland, Oregon, where he fell in love with the city and a region with natural beauty as magical as any fantasy world. He has a B.A. in Creative Writing from the University of Florida where he studied and wrote both literature and poetry, and earned a MFA in Writing Popular Fiction from Seton Hill University. Now he writes mostly science fiction, fantasy, and horror, but will go wherever inspiration leads. In August of 2017, he launched the *Ink to Film* podcast with a filmmaker co-host, where he discusses books and their film adaptations from a writer's point of view. In between writing and podcasting, he collects quality single malts and is always happy to pour a dram for company.

www.lukeelliottauthor.com, @luminousluke

Any Old Disease

Dimitra Nikolaidou

"What is *wrong* with him?"

Ada had heard that tone before, the horror of a newly assigned doctor witnessing the Leak for the first time. She waited for the novice's breath to settle.

"He is withering," she said, her gaze fixed upon the man slowly expiring in front of them, his eyes already blinded, his skin paper-thin and stained. "For years on end, he is going to waste away; his remaining senses will dull, his organs will fail and in the end, he will die. This is what doctors here refer to as the Leak. As for what exactly is wrong with him, what the causes are and how it can be stopped — well, this is exactly what we are trying to figure out here, in this Institute. This is why we need you." She let that sink in. This was the make-or-break moment, when someone decided whether they had the stomach to stay and deal with the horror on a daily basis, or walked away and drank themselves to oblivion.

The younger woman crossed her arms in front of her, eyes still fixed on the man beyond the glass. So far, she seemed to take it in better than Ada herself had, so many years ago.

"I will do everything I can to find a cure for this disease," the woman said in the end, and Ada let go of a breath she had not realized she was holding. She had liked this one from the start; it would have been a pity to see her go the way of so many others.

The novice's name was Cybele and now that she had made up her mind to stay, Ada could finally allow herself to get to know her. The two of them rode the glass elevator that went all the way up to the Institute's terrace in silence, emerging as the sun's last rays bled over the snow-covered mountains.

The view was sublime as always, yet it failed to draw a reaction out of the Cybele; she kept staring at her drink instead.

"It gets better," Ada said, after a few moments of silence.

Cybele glanced at her, lips parted, and then turned back to her cup. The signs
of shock were still etched on her face; the sun-tanned skin was now cast in grey, and her green eyes, so bright and curious this morning, had retreated into their sockets.

Ada said no more, let the woman compose her thoughts in peace. To see patients dying of the Leak took the wind out of your lungs; it was not so much the physical decay, the so very slowly crumbling skin, the hair turning to ash. No disease was a pleasant sight, after all. No, there was something else about the Leak, something visceral, whispering threats under your skin, pulling you when common sense told you to run. But then again, common sense was not the strong suit of anyone working at the Institute.

"I apologize." Cybele said eventually. "I thought I was prepared."

"This isn't any old disease. It has that effect on everyone who encounters it. Take your time."

Cybele nodded. Her eyes seemed to take in the landscape around them before settling back on Ada.

"Do they understand what's happening to them?"

"They understand everything at first. Yet by the end, even the mind is gone." Some considered this a blessing. Ada did not.

"Why is this disease so little known outside the Institute?" Cybele asked. "I tried to read up on it before coming up here but there's very little out there. Just a few vague footnotes, and an ancient, inconclusive case study."

Ada shrugged. "Well, this is the rarest of diseases. No known cause, no cure. Every single case is brought to us, and since we still do not know how it spreads, we have chosen to remain as isolated as we can. Plus, for now, we do not want to publish our findings."

"Why not?"

"Institute's policy. As obscure as a black cat's soul."

For the first time after witnessing the Leak, Cybele's eyes came back to focus. "But then, where do the Institute's funds come from? This facility looks anything but cheap."

Ada lifted the cup to her lips. "The Director scored us a government contract, untold eons ago. It means we're under the Health Ministry's thumb, but it's a relief to actually work instead of hunting down funds every second semester."

Cybele did not speak for a moment, then mimicked Ada's shrug. She settled on her chair a little better. "And this?" she asked, looking at Ada's glossy chrome and matte carbon-fiber left hand. "Did you get it working here?"

"This? No... no." Ada clenched the metal fingers, then left them immobile again. "It was a landmine in New Paris." She held the hand up and the fingers caught the last flashes of the setting sun, silver painted molten red. "I can't be a surgeon anymore of course, but it beats a pirate's hook."

Cybele laughed, and Ada smiled back. The memory always summoned pinpricks of fire on her skin, but she sensed the unspoken questions in the air and pressed on.

"We were a bunch of volunteers from the medical faculty, searching for survivors in the ruins. We had gone as far as the Louvre crater, and were looking for a way to pass through when our guide slipped and landed face down on the wrong side of a minefield."

This was as much as she could say for now — perhaps in a few hundred years she would be able to talk about the rest, about flying deafened through the debris and the flame, about landing on her best friend's body, about Milo and Anwuli pulling her away seconds before the collapse, or about or any of the things that came after. For the time being, she just took another gulp.

"Prosthetics are the reason I decided to go into medicine," Cybele said, shifting the subject. Empathy; a useful trait in a doctor. "Everyone else thought I was destined to be a historian, or a journalist. Something with digging up the past, anyway. The world had 10 billion people before the Great Floods, and all their stories are now lost; someone has to find them, and I wanted it to be me. However, in the end I found myself so touched by the engineering feats of prosthetists, that I knew I had to be a part of it."

"Prosthetics don't do anything for them, you know," Ada said, nodding towards the underground labs where the Leak drained their patients away. "Nothing does."

"And they just wither away like that? Till they are gone?"

Ada nodded. "You will get attached to your first. I won't say don't do it; we all did."

Cybele didn't answer. She took another sip, lips tight, fingers tense. She seemed secretive, but it mattered little. Isolated as they were up in the mountain, miles away from any village, everyone opened up eventually, and let go.

After all, they had all the time in the world.

The Institute was a pile of glass boxes, panels, and domes, designed to let as much light as possible slip in through the day. The Leaks, however, were secured underground; they were too fragile, and always cold. As a result, Ada had to spend half her day below the frozen earth with them and at the end of her every shift, no matter how sharp the alpine cold was, she always needed to go outside the crystal walls even for a minute, in order to start breathing again.

"How is the novice doing?"

Milo asked the question as soon as the elevator started moving towards the terrace. In the six months that had passed since she and Cybele had shared their first coffee up there, the days had become much shorter. The sun had already set when they stepped out, but the view remained magnificent; starlight reflected on sculpted snow.

"Better than most," Ada said. The elevator doors closed behind them without a sound and they both let a few moments pass, bathing in the night. So far up the mountains there was almost no wildlife to break the silence —just their own long exhalations, carrying away the day. "She caught up fast, doesn't flinch near the Leaks, even asked a couple of questions that got me thinking."

Milo let a half-laugh out. "Doesn't flinch? Are you sure she's human?"

"Shut up." She just looked at the snow for a moment, half a word riding on each breath but none getting out of her lips. "I wish I knew how she does it. It is getting in the way of our research, the way the disease freaks out the rest of us."

"I know. I know." Levity had been chased away from his tone now. "Hey, if she can do what we can't, we are lucky to have her here. Just... don't blame yourself for not being her."

Her anger evaporated and she sighed. "I know. She just reminded me why I signed up for this in the first place. She cares for them the way I used to care when I first came here – nowadays, I feel I'm just continuing the work out of stubbornness."

"It takes all kinds. The compassionate, the stubborn, the morbidly fascinated and even those of us trapped up here by our bloody contract." He closed his eyes and stretched, head to toe. "Not that I do not share your frustration. Sometimes, for all our hard work, I swear we are just going in circles."

"True." They weren't supposed to talk about work after their shift had ended; eight hours with the Leaks were draining enough. Some days, though, were more intense than others and today, their oldest patient had refused to continue treatment. It would be a matter of days before her clouded eyes closed out the world for good –her life seeping towards the darkness in the center of the earth.

The words snuck out of Ada's mouth. "What if... what if we aren't meant to find the truth?"

"What?"

"Come on. We've circled the issue before, let us say it out loud. There are files missing from the Institute's research. You can tell by the serial numbers. Most of it is older work, but still. Why lock away anything at all, if we 're so desperate for answers?"

Milo looked at her. For a moment, the stars did not blink.

"Are you the one who put Cybele up to it, then?" he asked.

"Up to what?"

"Snooping. Asking to cross-reference old research. Was it you?"

"What? Of course not. When did that happen? And why would I set a newcomer to do my snooping for me? I've been here for ever."

"I'm sorry." He ran his hand through his hair. "You've wondered aloud about the missing files so many times in the past, and the Director never reacts well to the implication, so..."

She waited, but Milo had stopped talking. "So you thought I conned the rookie into asking on my behalf," she said, arms crossed.

"Hey, I would've done it if I were you. Anything to avoid his stare. Noticed how he started locking his office door a month ago? How he revoked half our access codes for no reason? I think he hired extra guards a week ago; some of the faces outside the fence are new. He's getting more paranoid by the day."

Ada had noticed, but she was still pissed at Milo, and chose to leave all his words unanswered.

Three months after that spat, spring rode over the mountain top. Now the third floor cafeteria was always full early in the mornings; nobody wanted to lose a moment of sunlight before heading underground to work. She braced herself for the cheerfulness, but the minute she walked in, everyone stopped talking for the briefest of moments, and then resumed chattering with half an eye turned towards her.

Milo was the only one to keep his eyes on her; she moved towards his table, but then he nodded imperceptibly towards the windows. With one last glance at him, she walked up to the glass, and looked outside.

The sun was melting the scarce snow they had gotten last night, and Cybele was out there, holding the last flakes in her hands. Showing them to a Leak.

Ada sighed on the inside. The new ones always got attached, and then did something stupid about it. The Leaks — *the patients* — were exactly as fragile as they looked. Taking them out of the underground bunker was not doing them any favors. This one seemed so far down the road, that even talking in the chilly air burdened his lungs. On the other hand, they all had done something like that when they were as fresh as Cybele was. Ada would have a talk with her later on.

Ada turned away, only to find herself almost stepping on the Director's toes.

It took her a few more seconds to realize that the cafeteria had fallen silent, everyone staring in their cups, ears cocked to her side.

"Look at her," the Director said, through a mirthless smile. He was a head taller than her, and made of slippery ice. "Brave, isn't she?"

Ada did not answer. Cybele looked up. The Director did not acknowledge her; he brought his cup to his lips but did not drink.

Cybele turned to her patient again, as if he were the only person in the world.

Around them, snow began falling again.

"How do you do this?"

"Do what?" Cybele was several steps ahead as they climbed down the snow-dusted slope, but she stopped and turned.

"Be so comfortable around them." Cybele remained silent, and eventually Ada caught up to her. They stared at the distance for a while. Below them, whiffs of clouds concealed the valley at the feet of the mountains. The pyramidal tip of an old church steeple, probably buried under the ground three thousand years ago, when the Great Floods had covered the old world in water, was the only landmark as far as their eyes could see.

"I don't know," Cybele said at the end. "Why not? In the end, it is just another disease. You get used to the symptoms and proceed to the treatment."

"I know. But for most of us, it took much, much longer."

"So everyone keeps telling me. Sometimes, I think I freak you out as much as the patients do."

"True," Ada said. Cybele looked up at her in surprise; the older woman simply shrugged. It took a few more seconds before they both burst out laughing. "You do score points for constantly aggravating the Director, however."

"Not my intention," said Cybele, and her tone made Ada hold her next words back. Just mentioning the man's name seemed to cast a shadow these days, and the mountain light was receding too fast for comfort anyway.

"So where are you from? I never asked" she said instead, kicking a stone down the slope. It did not even echo as it rolled.

"Northern Greece. The great wind farms. Ever been there?"

"No. Not yet. Perhaps when I am done with the Institute."

"You have a bucket list for afterwards?"

"Not really. Who knows what I will want to do when I'm finished here. Probably just fish in the sun for the next thirty years. Not that my contract expires any time soon."

"Has anyone ever left?"

Ada hesitated. It sounded too sinister to say it out loud that no, nobody ever had. There was work to be done, still, and after so long, the outside seemed distant and noisy. Cybele stared at her a few seconds more, and then turned back to look at the setting sun being impaled on the solitary church steeple.

"Come on, let's walk a bit more" she said. "We don't have much time left."

Shots woke Ada up in the night.

Her eyes opened. She should be startled, should maybe even panic as the dry sounds tore the air. As she reached for the light, though, she realized she had been half-waiting for something big to happen, ever since Cybele had taken the patient out in the snow half a year ago. When you live so long in a place, you can read the change in the air.

There was no alarm going off, no red lights blinking. If she hadn't heard shots before, she might even write the sound off as a distant avalanche and go back to sleep. However, this was not a choice now. She got up, found her morning clothes and slipped her white coat over them— the most useless armor ever.

She cracked her door open and looked across the corridor, at Cybele's room.

The door was half open, and no-one was inside. No laptop on the desk either.

She was preparing to go over when an armed man in black uniform turned the corner. Her heart clenched; the Institute guards did not carry weapons and they had never stepped inside the main building, for as long as she had worked there. This man was military; an outsider.

"Are you all right, Doctor?" he asked, cold in his tracks.

"What is going on?"

"You are not to worry. Please return to your room."

"I need to check on my patients." Cybele was closer to them than to her colleagues; perhaps Ada would find some kind of answer in their quarters. The man was not actively stopping her, but there is a thing about guns, they talk in a way mouths can't. "Getting them upset is not good, for any one."

Yes, he had his guns — but she could always rely on the terrifying aura of the Leak.

It worked. "All right, Doctor. You can go down, but I will need to escort you."

She nodded and walked to the underground entrance, the guard one step behind her, his boots leaving muddied prints on the pristine floor. She had hoped to get rid of him once they reached the basement but of course, no such luck. The accordion doors parted for them, and they entered the underground.

He gasped at the sight of the Leaks behind the glass walls; his sudden shock would be her only chance. She ducked into one of the glass rooms fast, and closed the door before he could gather up the courage to follow. It locked behind her, and she hoped the man would not know how much she was going against the rules by doing this.

She knelt by the bed, and whispered to the patient under the covers. "I'm Cybele's friend. I need to help her. Please, if you do know, tell me what's going on. Is she safe?"

The man was one of their oldest patients; his hair had fallen off long ago and his skin was stained, crumpled paper. He wasn't sleeping; the Leak took their sleep away after a while. Twisted fingers held the covers close to the chest. They were always cold after this stage, no matter the temperature.

She caught herself bending forward, trying to inhale the crumpled skin. The disease beckoned as it always did, and it took all her experience and training to resist. Her fingers touched the covers, twitched as she tried not to touch the patient himself.

"Did she make it out?" the man asked. Their voice was the worst, the disharmony in it. It echoed out of a grave and forced you to come closer, to listen.

"Cybele?" she whispered. The man looked at her. "I'm not sure. I'm her friend, though. Do you know where she is?"

"I know you. I saw you watching us over the deck so many months ago, when she showed me the snowflakes."

She did not answer. His labored breath ticked the seconds off.

"She liked to visit the black church," he said. "She liked to watch the sun rise from there."

Ada waited some more, but the man only exhaled. It wore them out, talking, much as they craved it. And much as she craved an answer, the pull was becoming too much. She stood up and walked out, smoothing her jacket all the way down.

Outside, the soldier was holding on to his gun. He was fighting hard not to vomit, but for the first time in her life, Ada could not conjure any sympathy at all.

"Is he... is he...?"

"Going to be all right? What do you think?" she answered, walking past him and reaching for the stairs.

"And he was born like that?"

It caught up with her, then, compassion. She slowed down, took a breath. "It's a very rare disease, sir. You shouldn't worry— it affects less than one person in ten million. I suggest visiting Dr. Kira here, first thing in the morning. Talk about it. She will help you get it out of your mind."

Her concern shamed him back into stony silence, and they walked out.

Next morning at breakfast, the usual cliques had merged into one big, animated hydra. Ada was expecting them to be awkward with her as

she walked in, cup in hand, but they had all been together for too long; after a second, they circled her, eyes gleaming.

"Have you heard?"

"I only heard the gunshots." They did not believe her; they waited for more. "All right. Anyone care to shock me with the terrible news?"

Milo stepped forward, steaming cup in hand. "Cybele is nowhere to be found. Haven't the guards come to question you yet?"

Question her — odd choice of words.

"Cybele ran off?" She could feel her heart skipping beats, but would not give them the satisfaction. "And why the fuss? She wouldn't be the first to break down in here."

"She did not break down. Or run off. She broke into the Director's office. Using very precise, very professional methods."

She looked at them startled, and they looked back, waiting.

"Did she take anything?"

"He won't tell of course," said Milo. "But she must have. They caught her down the slope, halfway to the river. I heard there was a boat waiting for her there but whoever drove it escaped when the guards grabbed her."

"Where is she now?"

"A government helicopter came for her at sunrise."

"You said government?"

The crack in her voice shut them up. Leaving her cup on the table, she walked outside and, thank their oaths, her colleagues found it in themselves to respect that and leave her alone, till the soldiers came in her room to ask her their empty questions.

"Still thinking about her?"

"You can tell?"

Six months had passed since Cybele was taken away, but Milo knew Ada well enough.

"At least the Director isn't looking at you funny anymore."

"Why would he? He's the one who hired her. And it was his decision to appoint Cybele to me in the first place. It's not like I had anything to do with her schemes."

Milo nodded and laid back. The time had not come yet for a frank discussion, and they both knew it.

Ada got up. "Going for a walk," she said. "Last days of summer."

He raised his cup, and she smiled, buttoned up her coat and walked out of the glass doors. She had been taking walks every day for the past five months, till the guards had eventually stopped tailing her and everyone had started taking her new habit for granted. Only today, instead of going towards the summit, she turned around, and went the way she had been long avoiding, the path down the slope.

The path towards the 'black church'.

It wasn't a church anymore, of course. Ages ago, it might have been the roof of one, probably considered ancient even before the Great Floods swept the old world away. The rest of the building had been submerged in mud but the top, built to withstand hail and stone, had remained, jutting out of the earth, catching the light on its dark tiles.

It took some searching but finally she noticed it, the place where the moss had been disturbed. She knelt and slid her artificial hand over it. The whole tile dislodged and a dew-covered tin caught the sunrays. There was a box there — Cybele's lunch box.

It opened easily under the pressure of her metal fingers, and Ada saw two things inside; a musty book that looked as old as the sunken church itself, and a digital data stick. She picked the tome first and slid her fingers in the old pages, trying not to inhale their rotten scent. The handwriting was hard to read, but she could tell it was some kind of ledger, a list of births and deaths in the small village that used to lie half a mile below, long before the Floods had taken it with them three millennia ago.

Only there was something wrong with the events recorded inside. First of all, it seemed that everyone who had ever been born in that village, had eventually died. Not only that, they had also died very young: at seventy, at eighty, some of them even at sixty. The most peculiar thing, though, was that the archivist had labeled all those premature deaths as 'natural causes.'

It made no sense.

"I am impressed."

The Director's voice, just a few steps behind.

A split second; her sole chance. She dropped the box and as she scrambled to pick it up, she stepped on the data stick and pushed it into the mud.

She turned around and there he was, looking at her, hands behind his back. No armed guards, she noticed. She exhaled, and looked at him; he extended his hand and she handed the book over without shutting it, trying to get a last glimpse at the handwritten litany of death.

For a moment they stood in silence, he reading, and she pushing the stick further into the ground.

"I am sorry for your friend" he said eventually, startling her. His own eyes had not widened as he looked over the ledger. "Had she told you of this?"

"No. I figured it out a few days ago," she half-lied. "Pieced some of the things she had implied together. I wanted to see if I was right."

She could see he did not believe her, and she decided to go all in.

"What does it mean, though?" she asked. "What killed this people? Why natural causes? What happened in this mountain?"

"No idea, Doctor," he smiled through his teeth. "I will study this and let you know when I understand myself."

He turned his back and left, and Ada wanted to knock him over for a moment but then she noticed his shoulders hunching and his steps growing heavy as he walked away. Kneeling to clean her boots, she picked the data stick up.

Security had tightened since Cybele's stunt, but the guard in the gate was used to Ada's artificial hand setting off the alarm; they did not notice the stick tucked inside the glove, chrome on chrome. Back to her room, she sealed the windows, took her tablet to the bathroom, sat on the edge of the bathtub and slid the stick in.

Only one folder inside, untitled. No notes, no documents, only photos: underwater graveyards, larger than anything she had ever seen, and extremely short lifespans carved on each one. Seventy years. Sixty. Forty. Some of them had pictures enshrined in them, and she could see that most of the deceased had fallen victims to the Leak before their deaths: the lined faces, the cloudy eyes, the false teeth.

This made no sense. She was no historian, and even if she were, there was precious little left from the world before the floods. However, even though the waters and the wars that followed had obliterated written records, just as they had swept away everything else, some stories had been recorded a few decades after the disaster, once the few survivors stopped fighting and scraping for food, settled down and started to rebuild over the ruins. They spoke of famine, and salted earth and the fires that broke out in the abandoned cities, consuming what was left. They spoke of the Himalayan ice melting, flooding the world a second time, prolonging their struggle. They spoke of the diseases they had to combat without access to hospitals or medicine, the wounds that took decades to heal, their cancers that had to wait a hundred years for previously known cures to be re-invented. Yet there was no mention of a Leaking epidemic in their scarce tellings, no word of people simply wasting away with time till they were dead.

A knock on her room's door. Oh well. It had taken him long enough.

She got up, opened the bathroom door, crossed the sitting room. The Director was on the outside. Again, no armed guards with him. He inclined his head, and she stepped back to let him in. The door closed behind him.

"So, you really did not know," he pointed out. "I apologize for the bluff. I had to make sure you were not allied with them."

"Them?"

"The Pures. Cybele's little terrorist group." She kept staring at him, and he sighed. "Can I have the data stick, or whatever it was? You would not have given me the book so easily, if you weren't holding on to something else."

"Of course. Can I have an explanation in return? I've been working on the Leak for the last two hundred and seventy-five years. Milo was here a century before me. This," she pointed at the tablet, still sitting on the bathroom sink, "looks like something we should've known."

"I know. I apologize, Doctor; I did not enjoy keeping secrets myself, but the position of the Director came with caveats."

"Yet you let me find it. You could've stopped me before I reached the church."

"Again, I do not enjoy keeping secrets, even as I understand the need for them. They are the death of science. "He leaned on her wall, arms crossed. "Speaking of secrets, by now you might have realized how your protégé had us all fooled. I invited her over after encountering her impressive research on prosthetics and regenerative techniques. And at first, she seemed the most dedicated of all of us. Yet it seems, she never meant to heal the Leak."

"Oh? Then what was she doing up here? The view isn't that magnificent."

He did not crack a smile. "I believe she meant to sneak one of the patients out, or at least secure samples and photos, and spread them into the general population." He paused for a moment, glancing at her, then went on. "You see, the Pures believe the disease and its conclusion, death, to be our natural state — something to strive for, instead of a horrible illness. Which is why Cybele wormed her way up here, so she could find a way to spread the word and, maybe, the disease itself." He scrutinized her face for a moment. "This is the first you are hearing of that."

"It is." Cybele as she knew her was shredded; she would pick the pieces later, rebuild a new Cybele. Out of the maelstrom though, one thing remained. "She did make you wonder, didn't she? You did ponder, could she possibly be right?"

He smiled a tight smile. "Perhaps? Doesn't the sight of the Leak strike a chord a bit too deep for comfort? What other disease does that to us, after so long?" He stopped leaning on the wall, and took a step towards her, hands in his pockets. "Most governments try to keep it under wraps, but the archaeologists do find unsettling bits from time to time, things like the ledger and the graveyards. There are old texts, stories that would only make sense if we were mortal once."

"You mean, if we all eventually contracted the Leak and simply died?"

"Exactly. With our antediluvian history lost, anyone can theorize, can't they? And this is why you and I are paid to stay holed up here: someone always digs something up and starts wondering — and eventually, they become enthralled with this idea of death as the true natural order. Some of them even find our little Institute and crawl to us, like Cybele did. For these people, the Leak is the ultimate confirmation of their theories." He paused for the briefest second. "I admire their perseverance, yet in the end I am a healer, just like you are. No matter what I think of their theories, I do not have the patience to entertain their madness."

"What if they're right? What if this is the way we are meant to end? What if we were short-lived, once, so very long before the Floods that we had lost even the memory of it when the waters came?"

"Care to tell that to the people withering in the basement? That it is all right to suffer as they do, that they are doing their ancestors proud?"

No. The answer came unbidden and she silenced it, but it hung between them for a whole ripe moment before dissipating.

She held back for a second, then another. Finally, she sighed.

"What will happen to her?"

"It is never my decision. All I could do was tell the agents who came to question me that the Leak drives some of us mad and they should take pity on her, see her as another casualty of this disease. I doubt I made any difference, though. The last thing the government wants is more cultists."

"Why hide this truth from us researchers, though? Why not tell us, a few decades in?" And then, "Why not tell everyone in the world about this mortality theory? We are still a democracy, are we not?"

He was silent for a few seconds, and something of this silence crept into her bones.

"Because once the idea gets into someone's head that the Leak is the way things should be, Doctor, ugly things start to happen to the believers. The pull becomes stronger. More visceral. It tugs at people at a whole other level. And for those of us who have looked at a patient's eyes, the sensation becomes irresistible. Do you understand what I am saying?"

She could read between the lines well enough. "We get sick too."

He gave no reply, yet she found the answer in his eyes, and it chilled her.

She did not want the Leak. She did not want to get sick and then waste away. How could she? How could anyone? How could anyone believe, that this horror was the natural order of things? Cybele had been mad to think so. This was a disease, and like every disease it had to have a cure.

"What should I do?"

"Work." His smile startled her. It was not a pretty sight, like light coming down on old ruins. "Work harder than before, to find the cure and prove your friend and the Pures, or any other cultist, wrong. Because if we don't find a cure, Doctor, if there isn't one, then they might be right and the moment you believe that will be a painful one."

No, this could not happen. She had things to do, they all had. A bucket list. Fishing. She looked at him and then nodded, chrome fingers limp at her side.

"Good night, Doctor. I trust you will keep this entirely to yourself. Better not to place any more people in danger, don't you think so?"

"Of course."

She escorted him out, and closed the door.

She would not tell, he was right about that. No reason to drag Milo and the rest into that. No reason to put them in such danger. She would sleep on it, then wake up and start working, really working. Now that she knew, she would request permission again to dig among the Institute's roots. This time, he would not have reason to deny her. She would find out why the Leak called to all of them, the real reason, not Cybele's delusions. After all, what else was left to do?

A chord a bit too deep, the Director had said. She went to pick the tablet, stare at the graves again, but stopped in her tracks.

Tomorrow would come and with it, questions. But tonight, the sky was clear and the Institute was silent. The world's buried truths could wait for one last, peaceful night.

About the story

For a story that deals with death, hope and our human lust for achieving ever more, "Any Old Disease" has decidedly pulp origins. I have never seen 2012, the disaster movie directed by Roland Emmerich, but one image in the trailer stuck to mind: a Tibetan monk, looking up to see a tidal wave dwarfing the Himalaya. A few years later we began playing Ivory Towers, a role-playing game where after a flood, the world has been beautifully rebuilt — by corporations. I played as a soldier who becomes increasingly curious about the lost world that came before him, the world he thinks he knew about.

Thinking of the past as a well-documented time with just a few mysteries sprinkled in-between to keep things spicy, is a common mistake. David Macaulay's *Motel of the Mysteries* illustrates that best: in 4022 a motel is excavated and future archaeologists are excited, interpreting every single thing they find, from a toothbrush to a bathplug, as an important artifact. The picture of the lead archaeologist with a toilet seat on his head, purposely resembling Sophia Schliemann bedecked in Troy's gold, is meant to be humorous but to me, it was a revelation: we can never know what came before and everything we think we know, is covered in our own assumptions. My love of history had suddenly turned from a diligent pursuit of knowledge to a romantic quest.

Not that that I consider this a bad thing.

With these ideas in mind, I began to write a horror story about a mysterious disease, a sinister Director and the stalwart doctor who sets out to discover the truth. Soon though, it mutated into something else.

It might have been the face of my Godfather, a surgeon who has not rested a day since he began work and won't rest as long as someone needs him. Maybe it was the article I wrote on the pursuit of immortality from China's courts to the USSR and up to the transhumanist movement. Or my growing fear of an environmental catastrophe, sweeping us away.

It might also have been that, amidst a deluge of bad news from all over the world, humans keeps insisting on a better future – no matter how badly we mess up our eternal pursuit. After all, I was taught at school that our Greek word for human –anthropos– literally means *looking upwards*.

Of course, as I was writing, none of this entered my mind. I was just following Dr Ada as she unraveled the secrets of her Institute one by one, as familiar faces changed into something unknown and signs of wrongness kept unsettling her, nudging her to find the truth. In a way, it is a gothic tale, a heroine trapped in a mountaintop estate racing to discover its long buried secret before they drive her to an awful fate. While my plot pays homage to its pulp roots, other elements had crept in and made the story mine – as is always the case when you write. And every time someone asks a question about the worldbuilding or the characters, I uncover a new inspiration which I had not even considered in the course of writing.

I can only be grateful so many others have liked it in the meantime.

A question for the author

Q: Are you a Luddite? Or do you have the latest and greatest technology?

A: Not a Luddite at all; I love technology, and recognize it as a major factor in many positive social changes I am now benefiting from. Having said that, I need to step away from my screens more often, before I fuse with them.

About the author

Dimitra Nikolaidou is a PhD candidate, researching role-playing games and speculative fiction at the Aristotle University of Thessaloniki in Thessaloniki, Greece. She is the chief editor and in-house writer for Archetypo Publications. Finally, she teaches creative writing focused on speculative fiction at *Tales of the Wyrd*. She is always planning trips in Europe and excursions in the woods, and sometimes even manages to take them.

@D_Nikolaidou

Velaya, the Dreaming City

Six parts after Dunsany

Beston Barnett

Part 1

I set out for Velaya as a young man, having only just pledged to wed. I was to marry Belqis, flower of our village and light of my eyes, in whose father's orchards I had played since my childhood. Our marriage should have been enough for a lifetime of happiness. But I believed then—as so many young fools do—that dreams were the currency of happiness, and I carried with me dreams as yet unredeemed. And though I tried to conceal it, Belqis, my betrothed, sensed my dissatisfaction and, knowing its source, spoke to me, saying:

"Always you have shared with me your dreams of Velaya. You have whispered to me of silver domes and white carved stone, of miraculous waters which run in aqueducts through strolling parks, of red and gold kites which fly from the cliffs and gild the sky, and of so many other wonders that for me the Dreaming City lives in the sound of your voice. Always it has been your dream to visit far-off Velaya and know its mysteries.

"And yet, once we are married, it is possible that duties to our fields and orchards and to family and to our as yet unborn children— think of our beautiful children, my love!—may keep you from ever travelling to such dreamed-of distant lands. I am selfish and do not wish to bear that disappointment. Therefore, though each day apart will be a trial, I say: go now to Velaya and return to me with eyes brim full of silver and green and red and gold, eyes that have beheld the Dreaming City. For though I love you now and with all I know of my heart, it may be that I will love the man who returns to me from Velaya even more."

Thus—as ever—did Belqis amaze me with her generosity.

Of course, I protested.

I said, "The duties you speak of are to me nothing but joys."

And also, "Our full and happy lives could admit of no regrets."

And also, "My dreams of Velaya are a child's dreams, but my dreams of the coming together of our lives are the dreams of the man I wish to become."

But Belqis knew my heart, and she overcame my protestations. And truthfully—young and foolish though I was—I knew myself blessed even then to be understood so well and trusted so completely.

And so Velaya rose up triumphant in my mind's eye.

I set out by cart and was soon come to lands beyond any I had known. I traveled by overgrown tracks through fields cultivated with grain and by wide highways that the legionnaires had of old hewn through the impassable forests between cities. Coming over rocky wastes and through orchards of olives, I had my first sight of the sea and felt myself remade in its grandeur and its sadness.

And though I was clumsy with the language of the dock-hands in that first port, I was able by signs and nodding to book passage over the sea and to come finally to the yellow shores of that great desert land of which Velaya is the very jewel and heart and center. From there, caravans of camels in long trains came and went daily. Here were found traders, journeymen, diplomats, shepherds, but also pilgrims, and these were my true kin—the pilgrims—those that had been granted visions of Velaya in dreams.

When I had replenished my stores and purchased a blanket and hired a camel-puller, I too joined a caravan and left at dawn for the last four days of my pilgrimage.

That first night in the desert was cold; a cold of open spaces like none I had known. As the drivers settled their camels into corrals, I huddled with three pilgrims around the remnants of our cooking fire, and we drank the clear local liquor called *raktash* and each of us was fired by the *raktash* with bright longing for Velaya.

And out of this bright longing, the woman who had traveled from distant lands far to the West spoke, saying:

Part 2

"It is said of the gods of Velaya that they are fierce but also generous, that their dreams dwell often along the white and shining cliffs, and that in their dreams, miracles are worked. For it is within the power of their miraculous dreams to grant the gift of *flight*.

"Aspirants travel great distances to petition this gift of the gods. Settling in the squatter's quarter known as the Aerie, aspirants build themselves the nests of sticks and mud which will be their homes for at least the next season and often much longer. During the days they lie in their uncovered nests, absorbing the rays of the sun, taking the lightness of the sun into them, willing themselves to lighten. Then in the cool spring evenings, they descend in their white robes to the taverns and meeting places of the city, and there recite the light-filled 'cloud poems' for which Velaya is justly renowned.

"As the sun fills their bodies with lightness, so aspirants fill with a floating feeling, and in the summer they are often seen wearing lead weights around arms and ankles as ballast. Much of their poetry in this season eulogizes the peculiar sensation of untying the weights from their limbs in the evening, of experiencing that weightlessness which presages the hoped-for gift. In this season too they begin work on the red and gold paper constructions which they will fly from the lower cliffs with such drama during the kite festival.

"It is in the autumn that aspirants often decide to petition the gods. It is not a decision shared or discussed, but must be reached alone, known by the lightness in the heart, by the tense spreading of invisible wings. Many, through doubt or humility, never decide. But on a clear morning in the first cool days after summer, a small white-robed figure may be seen climbing alone the Dawn Stair and mounting to the heights of Veliara, tallest of the white cliffs, though it does not face Velaya as the others do, but is hidden and turned away behind a great knee of limestone rubble.

"And what happens then numbers among the great mysteries of Velaya. For it is not known if there is some right phrasing or secret password or if perhaps the heart of the aspirant is weighed against that of a feather or if it is purity or yearning or some inborn talent or simply the dream of gods whose dreams must of necessity be ineffable. The aspirant makes his petition and steps from the cliff. The gods dream and judge. And some aspirants—most, it is said—end there at the base of Veliara, and their bleached bones remain uncounted, for the base of the cliff of Veliara is sacred ground and to visit there is forbidden.

"But there are some—a few? one a year? a decade? a generation? —who are caught in the cupped hands of the gods' dreaming and who fly."

The woman from the distant West paused then and drank. We all drank, each in turn—the *raktash* like hot sand that singes the throat and afterwards consoles it—before she continued.

"And there are those who say that long since passed are the days in which the gods of Velaya heard petitions. The city fills with white-robed aspirants, yet fewer and fewer climb the Dawn Stair each year. *Where are these chosen flyers,* they say, *aloft on god-dreams?* And in the dark corners of taverns there are others who whisper that the gods' interest is only with the pile of aspirant bones at the base of Veliara and not with those that would fly above it.

"But as for me, I am unwavering. From my youngest days have I dreamed of flying and known those dreams to be the best part of myself and true.

"And one day I will take my place among the flyers above Velaya."

We stared into what embers of the fire remained then, each of us inhabiting the image of the city that our minds conjured glowing there in the coals, and I sensed the others drift one by one into sleep.

But I lay awake, I know not how long after, with my mind in the jaws of frightful premonitions. A veil seemed pulled aside, and all was revealed and inverted and churning. *The city is a trap,* I thought, and my thoughts were like jaws that closed and closed again. I saw a procession of young men and women with broken wings, sun-blind, their limbs contorted. *The city is a trap. It calls to the gullible, to the pilgrims, to the dreamers like myself, and it eats their dreams.*

I saw the pile of bones at the base of Veliara, felt myself pressed beneath them.

I slept.

In the morning was a great hubbub of packers and camel-pullers and coffee wallahs calling across the expanse of cold, spent fires. I stood, wrapped in my blanket. In the noise and the smell of the coffee and the gray light of the new day, my last night's imaginings paled. I thought of Velaya and Belqis, the dreamed-of city and my beautiful wife. Both awaited me, and by this I knew myself a pilgrim twice blessed, who followed two stars. Gathering my few belongings, I thought, *And what if the allure of Velaya eclipses that of Belqis? What if its red and gold kites, its white walls, its taverns full of poetry, what if these seduce me and make me forget my heart?* Yet—after one month, after two—I would return to my Belqis and tell her what I had felt and seen, for the tale of such beauty must have an audience, and always Belqis had been that audience for me. I believed that I knew myself; that I would return to her. For though Velaya filled my mind with imagined colors, Belqis still filled my heart.

Velaya might be a trap for some, but not for me.

All that sweltering day I sat and swayed on the princely hump of my camel as the great caravan spread out around me and advanced. And at end of day, we came again to a camp in the desert where the day's caravan heading northward from Velaya met our southward-heading caravan, and again there was the chaos of stocks and tents and animals and cooking fires scattered like a wide mirror of the stars which are themselves scattered in a band across the night sky. And again that evening my three companions and I reclined together around our small fire and ate and passed the local liquor *raktash* that so opens the hearts of travellers, one to another.

Then into that tranquility that descends upon the desert at day's end, the young man from the distant North spoke, saying:

Part 3

"I have heard it said of the gods of Velaya that they are loving but shy. That they love their people is certain, evidenced by the many miracles they have wrought in their city, chiefest among these the Miracle of the Waters, which rise up in the desert city in green pools and playful fountains to delight and succor its people. Yet the gods of Velaya are also shy, timid of applicants, unwilling to reveal themselves except to the most pure and the most devout. But in their love, they have left stones hidden in and below the city which the pure and devout may find and with which they may commune with the gods. For it is thus that the gods find the miracles they bestow upon Velaya: by mining in the hearts of men.

"There was a man stranded at the base of a cliff deep in the desert, lost, dying of thirst; this was the first applicant. How he came to be there, how he came by such purity of heart and devotion of spirit, these things are not known. But there in his distress he found a stone, and this was the first of the Dreaming Stones. It was a sand-smoothed oblong of jade, and through it, clasping it to him, the man communed with a god; this was the first of the gods of Velaya, who is called simply Vel, and who mined in the heart of the man through the Dreaming Stone and found there Velaya's first miracle: the Miracle of the Waters.

"He was the first applicant; since then, there have been many. Successive generations of applicants have come and striven and searched and some—the pure, the devout—have found the stone they sought, and the miracles they carried in their hearts have transformed Velaya into the jewel of the desert. The massive statues of the First Dreamers, the tiered Night Gardens, the filigreed temple of Vel-Abir— all these were miracles wrought by stone-finders of old. The Dawn Stair itself was among the earliest miracles: the heart-wish of a father whose daughter loved above all else the flying of kites; his plain river stone appeared to him one evening at the bottom of a humble pot of soup.

"Many applicants are miners or prospectors or vendors in the gemstone markets for which Velaya is renowned, where they daily handle seraphinite, jade, epidote, chrysoprase, beryl. Others work in infrastructure, shoring up stone work, re-routing water systems, sculpting architectural ornament, or simply cleaning the floors of palaces and homes. Always and at every hour, applicants search for their Dreaming Stone, listening for its distinct call, opening their hearts in purity and devotion. An applicant serves the city and his dearest wish is to have the next great miracle—the cliff statues, the gardens, the stairs—called forth from his heart through the stone of his dreams, and thus to live on forever as a part of the city itself.

"And, yes, there are those who say that many years have come and gone since Velaya was re-fashioned by miracle-stones. They say that the city is too big now, too impure with commerce, or that the last Dreaming Stone has long since been found. Or in darker moods, some mutter that perhaps the gods find their nourishment no longer with the pure and their stones, but with the suffering of the applicant who goes blind cutting gemstones or who is crushed in the mines beneath the city or who is worked to death cleaning, every day, year upon year, the palaces, the walls, the sewers."

The young man paused, and drank as if to rid his mouth of a disagreeable taste.

"But as for me, I am undeterred. Since earliest memory have I dreamed of holding a green stone to my breast, holding it and calling forth wonders. And I believe that one day, when I have hallowed the city in my eye and in my heart—with purity, with devotion, with humility—then shall I find my place among the miracle-workers of Velaya.

"For this was I made."

We lay then silent around the dying fire, each of us awed and entranced by the Northern man's story. The Dreaming City shone before my mind's eye—as I knew it must before the others'—wonderful, exotic, like a child's glass marble given by a parent returning from long travels, alight with possibility.

And yet, as the others drifted into sleep, the image of the city tilted in my mind. I saw it as from below, up from the blackness of the mines that coil through its foundations, and there I saw old men and women, frail and blind, who struggled through those tunnels ceaselessly and in vain. And I saw that those tunnels were the entrails of the city, its very intestines, and all those zealous seekers no more than digesting meat trapped in a horrible peristalsis. *The city is a trap,* I repeated to myself.

The words echoed, the coils tightened. *The city is a trap.*

Somehow I slept.

The next morning broke with the same confusion of activity as before, and yet I felt it overlain with a new sense of urgency and reverence. The Dreaming City waited only two days ride to the South. We pilgrims rode lost in thought as brides to a distant wedding who in their thoughts take leave of their former lives and prepare as best they can to be transformed. And all that sun-bleached day I meditated on what it might mean to be disappointed by Velaya. What if I found its streets dirty, its vistas uninspiring, its palaces gaudy, its gardens wasted, its denizens petty, its meeting places unwelcoming, its waters untended and unclean, and all my many dreams, mirages? What if I found more truth in the eyes of its beggars, than in the hauteur of its gods? These thoughts were terrible. I would be broken. And would I then return to Belqis and ask her to fulfil her vows to a broken man?

And thinking thus I remembered Belqis, my other pilgrim's star. I remembered her not as simply an audience or a symbol of home, but as she truly was—generous and understanding and kind. I knew that she would accept and remake me, that I might be dispirited for a time but that I would be remade in our lives together and in the lives of our children, and that one day we might all smile together at the dreams of my earnest youth. A weight lifted from me, like a fever breaking. I believed I knew myself. I believed I knew Belqis. And as we arrived at the final camp and the porters flew about their accustomed tasks, I thought, *I shall see what there is to be seen of Velaya, whatever that may be, and I shall return to my beloved and tell of it.*

The city might be a trap for some, but not for the man for whom Belqis waits.

And as the preparations for the night's camp began, there were pilgrims who said they could see already the white cliffs of Velaya off to the South, but I could make out only what seemed a sand storm, a shimmering white smudge on the horizon.

Just as in earlier nights, my companions and I built a small fire, spread blankets, and shared out dried apricots and patties of lentils. We passed the local liquor *raktash* in a small gourd between us, hand-to-hand and solemnly: a libation. It would be our last night as a company, and our hearts were so full with the awesome nearness of the Dreaming City that I expected no one to break the thoughtful trance which had come upon us with the cold and the dark. Thus were we all surprised when the silent woman—a woman from far to the East by her clothes, whom I, for one, had assumed spoke none of our common tongues—began to tell of her dreams in a clear and quiet voice, saying:

Part 4

"Among my people we have an idiom: *wary as the gods of Velaya.* We say this of the baker who will not share his recipe with his apprentice, or of the midwife who will teach no one the secrets of her trade. That the gods of Velaya keep secrets is known. Of the secrets of flight and of communion we have had eulogies already; but they keep also secrets for changing lead to gold, and making broken things whole, and living eternally young. And why are these secrets kept so dear? Are the gods given to spite or jealousy? Or might they perhaps be wise to allow only the few and the dedicated to learn the working of such miracles as might undo less worthy supplicants?

"The madrasas of the Dreaming City are built on this simple faith: that both wary *and* wise are the gods of Velaya.

"Students flock to the madrasas from all the lands that we know, and from the moment they step through the East Gate, their lives are bounded by ceremony and study. During their first years, most complement their research by taking apprenticeship with the glassblowers or the metalsmiths or in the guild of the nurses. After graduation, many may take up the mantle of professorship or medical practice, but the final stage in the lives of the scholars of Velaya is always solitary and secret study, for it is in mimicking the gods themselves—*wary and wise*—that they hope to discern that which their dreams have intimated: the recipes, formulas, incantations, codes, and mechanisms of the miraculous.

"Of the great madrasas, two dominate: the alchemists' university and the hospital. At the lower levels, these institutions operate as schools, as wards, as laboratories and libraries; they buzz with students, patients, and journeymen, all moving about their labors. But as scholars attain the higher levels, treading spiral stairs into the towers that sprout from these centers of learning like shoots in spring seeking upward for a purer air, so their silence deepens. In the highest rooms—within the very domes which so distinguish the city—the most learnéd study in deep solitude where the only sound is the turning of pages and the scritching of pen against parchment. And even above that, it is said, there are floating rooms hidden by art of magic in the upper air where adepts neither read, nor write, nor discourse at all, but simply stare into the secret mysteries of the universe.

"Of course, such institutions must have their detractors: students embittered by failed examinations or families dissatisfied with the care given a loved one. The scholars of Velaya, they say, neglect the world around them for the sky above and lose their way in mazes of their own making. In seeking the miraculous, the scholars wish to be gods themselves and so must fail.

"And perhaps, whisper the spiteful to one another, the whole towering hierarchy of study and sacrifice is as a honeypot laid by the gods—oh so wise and wary, the gods—who would lay a honeypot to feed off the best and brightest, their would-be usurpers.

"But as for me, I am undaunted."

Here, the Eastern woman paused and raised the gourd of *raktash* to each of us in turn, looking steadily into each pair of eyes from beneath the folds of her hood before continuing.

"In my dreams, I stand below the silver domes with a balm in my hand, a miraculous balm to heal the sick and make whole the maimed. And in that dream, the sick and the maimed come to me, and I heal them and, by my hand, I make them whole.

"Be it prophecy or be it illusion, I shall follow whither such a dream leads, because it is a good dream, and because it is mine."

Silence settled on us then, and we lay staring into the last lit embers of our fire. The Eastern woman's tale had been so eloquent, her dream so noble, we each of us felt that a grace had been laid upon our little camp and a blessing upon our dreams. I felt certain that the premonitions which had haunted me on previous nights would not recur.

But as the others closed their eyes and the dim fire gave way entirely to the dimmer light of cold desert stars, I began to think of Velaya in the abstract. Of what does it dream?—Velaya—for it is called the Dreaming City, and not the City of Dreams. Are the dreams of the city and of its gods one? And what if the city's dreams are of men that never leave, but circle endlessly its siren streets, seeking but never finding dreams of their own?

Then, of a sudden, the image of Velaya—that image which had been in my mind since my earliest memories and which had grown in these final days of my pilgrimage to fill every corner of my inner sky— that image tilted again. Now I saw it not from belowground, where its mines twisted and turned, but from above, where countless layered labyrinths made of naught but wind and vapor ornamented the air between the domes and radiated outward and upward in towers and coronae. And through these labyrinths, hidden in the air, crawled old men and women, scholars, always alone, always seeking but never finding, their robes too threadbare to keep out the cold. And I saw that if the mines were the digestive tracts of Velaya, then these insubstantial mazes above the city were its brain matter, and the scholars lost there were as its very neurons. And I saw that this beast of a city nourished itself on a steady stream of pilgrims but shat out only bones. And I saw that the great breathing of this parasitic beast, squatting there one day's ride through the desert, was the nightly going out and gathering in of its dreams, dreams like lures, like siren song, like golden netting, and these dream-lures were made in the crucible of its inhabitants' desperation and longing, made under great pressure and flung out in invisible waves from its trembling need.

The city is a trap, I thought, *but not for me. I am neither flyer nor miner nor scholar, and I have Belqis.* I would pass through unharmed, like a white egret that flies over the swamp and returns, unsullied.

My mind calmed. I shifted beneath my blanket and turned on my side and thought that now I would finally rest. A pleasant silence of sleepers and cold stars spread out around me. Tomorrow, all the colors of Velaya awaited.

And with that I came fully awake. Another scenario visited me— a possibility I had not before considered—and it set me shivering, for it had the halo of truth about it. What if Velaya seemed at first a disappointment and, after a week of seeing its uninspired sights, I was ready to depart and prepare what disappointing words I would say to Belqis, but then I spied there something colorful and vibrant, something truly *of* the city of my many dreams? Of course, I would have to stay and explore it—a café where poets gathered or a crumbling temple in the gardens, a place where something unfolded which was worthy of being described to my Belqis. And after I had learned enough of the vain poets or the maudlin temple and was preparing to leave once again, what if I should stumble across some other image or experience which seemed to speak more to the heart of the mystery of the Velaya for which I had first set out? A little girl building a kite with her grandfather perhaps, or a green-robed monk planting a yellow flower, or the great cliffs glowing from a certain perspective in a certain light. Would I not then stay and explore a while longer, if only so that my tales for Belqis would be that much more captivating?

And with each new delay, my absence from Belqis would grow. The longer I was away, the more amazing my stories would have to be on my return. Otherwise, how could I explain to her why I had stayed away so long? I imagined myself desperate—after six months, after a year, after five years—struggling to find something, always just around the corner in Velaya, worthy of telling my Belqis. Something amazing enough to heal the wound of our long separation. After five years, what could possibly be amazing enough? A miraculous balm? A god-stone? A pair of god-gifted wings?

Now was I frozen in fear, feverish, trapped in the coils of my own premonitions. I saw the pile of bones, the mines like intestines, the mazes pulsing in the air, and I saw myself following a trail of glittering clues through the streets, pacing out mandalas, the true Velaya always just ahead, and I, desperate and in despair. And what then would become of my Belqis?

No. Sometime well before dawn, I made a decision. I would not say goodbye. I would not face the disbelief and disappointment of my companions.

I arose and padded through the camp and found my indignant camel-puller and informed him of my change of plans.

I would not venture on to Velaya.

Part 5

And that is the story of my life. The central story, the story on which the rest teeters. A coward's less-than-heroic story about a long journey and an abandoned dream. That is how I viewed it for many years: an abandoned dream.

I returned to my village and married Belqis. At first I lied to everyone: I told fanciful but brief tales of the wonders I had seen. To those who asked why I hadn't stayed longer, I said that the time away from my beloved had been too painful, that I had been eager to start our lives together. This was half true, and Belqis, caught up in the excitement of the wedding, allowed me these half-truths for a time.

But my wife is an observant woman. After we had been living together for some months, she began very delicately to probe my stories, and I broke down almost at once. In real torment of soul, I told how three nights of terrible premonitions in the desert had defeated a lifetime of dreams. I recall how we sat at our little table long after the village slept, drinking the tart early cider our orchards produce in that season and speaking in low tones by the light of a single candle. And how she did not reproach me but looked at me all through our conversation with tender compassion. Yet still I felt myself a failure.

"I failed the first and simplest test of Velaya, a test of the resilience of my dreams. I am revealed a coward."

"My beloved, you were made to choose between the city and me. It is not cowardly to choose love. I honor you."

"And I honor you and love you ... yet I cannot help but feel unworthy now of that love."

And Belqis held my hand and, from that night, she seemed to love me as much as ever she had or even more.

And in the years that followed, our fields were fruitful and our flock thrived and our village prospered. We were blessed with three children, two girls and a boy, all beautiful and full of life. In motherhood, Belqis grew in beauty and wisdom. We were blessed. And yet at times—in truth, *often*—I seemed to see our blessings as through a veil, a veil that separated me from my feelings and from other people. A veil that filtered color from the world. At these times, I felt myself a hollow husband, a hollow father.

Rarely in those years did we mention my journey, and never once did Belqis reproach me for my failures. Never, at least, until the naming of our tavern.

For some time, she had talked of opening a tavern such as our village lacked, a proper place for travelers to eat and pass the evening, and for village meetings and dances in the colder months. I supported her, and when the structure was complete and the first fire was lit in the barroom hearth, Belqis showed me the signboard that would hang above the front door. The board was carved and colored wood, white cliffs against a blue sky, with the words, *The Dreaming City,* engraved across them in painted silver.

It had been so long since those once magical words had passed my lips; I felt stung, mocked. I hesitated, then spoke carefully.

"I did not know you had decided on a name."

Belqis did not look at me, but smiled at the floor. "It is a beautiful name for a tavern," she said. "Travelers will recognize it, and the village will find it exotic and exciting... Do you like it?"

I sensed that she was tense, that maybe the whole project for this tavern had been leading to this moment, to this sign and this name—that now was the time to show my gratitude for her years of forbearance—but I didn't trust myself to speak. Coward that I am, I made an ambivalent "mmm" sound and nodded.

The tavern was a success. Belqis took some pride in preparing the days' meals and the nights' rooms, in welcoming travelers and introducing them to our local cider. She seemed in her element there, a fish in good water. I spent more time in the fields or teaching the children to tend the flock and the garden and the orchards. Of course, I visited the barroom some nights, though I was uncomfortable with the travelers and their talk.

But one cool autumn evening with the fire's warm glow burnishing the few faces in the room, a young man traveling alone began to talk of Velaya, and it was as if his voice spoke to me across space and time, from another fire in the desert far away and years ago, but immediate, present. He said he loved birds and had dreamed as a child that he could speak to them. Later, he had heard that the secret to the language of birds could be found in a distant city far to the South. Many had scoffed, insisting that the birds had no language or that the stories of men who spoke with birds were only legends, but he remained true to his dreams.

I was transfixed.

When he had finished, Belqis looked at me and away—subtly and quick—and then she offered a glass of cider to the young man who loved birds.

To the room, she said, "A glass of cider and a bowl of stew on the house for any traveler who tells a story of the Dreaming City!"

There were no more storytellers that night, but word spread, and eventually our tavern became known throughout the countryside and beyond as a trading post for the lore of Velaya. Pilgrims would travel many miles off their routes to spend an evening or two at *The Dreaming City* and to share a story. We heard from warriors who dreamed of invincible swords, and lovers who dreamed of fairy brides, and would-be wizards who dreamed of taming fiery dragons. And sometimes—as the months became years—if the night was slow or the weather was bad, I might volunteer a story of my own journey. Never of the city itself, but of the dock-hands I had encountered and the sailing ship, or of the sounds and smells of the great caravans.

And am I now content? Am I healed? I am still ashamed of my brush with the city. And yet also I am haunted by a kind of wary nostalgia for the road and its mysteries. I am not entirely content, but neither am I the hollow man I was for a time. There is color again.

And tonight after a late evening of stories in the tavern, as I helped Belqis into bed and lay down beside her—wise Belqis, clever Belqis, flower of our village and light of my eyes—she turned to me and spoke to me softly.

She said, "Our flocks and our orchards do well. The tavern prospers."

"Yes, my love," I said and touched her gray hair.

She said, "Our children are grown and married and have children of their own. You have taught them to tend the farm and I have taught them to tend the tavern, and our children and our grandchildren do these things well and with love."

"Yes, my love," I said and touched her shoulder.

She said, "All these things we have done with love and now we have time."

"Yes, my love," I said and took her hand, though I did not yet know what she meant.

And she said, "We can go to Velaya together."

Part 6

I am Belqis and the dream of Belqis and I am old.

I was old already when we set out. Old and dying, if truth be known, though it had been my constant concern in those last few months to hide my growing infirmity from my husband and my children.

They were not so very difficult to deceive. My children worried about their own children, not about me, and this relieved and comforted me, for it is as things should be between the generations. As for my husband, I believe he saw me still as a young maid—the dream of Belqis he had returned to all those years ago—and I loved him for this harmless delusion and indulged him.

But I could not deceive myself. What had at first seemed the common ache and stiffness of age revealed itself over the course of some months to be a creeping paralysis. I could no longer turn my hips or unbend my back to reach the shelves in the pantry, my ankles would not flex, and my right hand was perfectly wooden, like the false claw of an amputee, so that I poured cider now only with my left. I was become an old fire-ravaged tree. I succumbed branch by branch, the sap hardened, the xylem and cambium no longer coursed with living water: I knew that soon I would be only pith, only dead wood.

And so I determined that we should travel as aged pilgrims to Velaya, to the Dreaming City, where my husband could at last complete the great interrupted arc of his life, and I, like a canny cat that when its time has come slinks away from family and friends, I could go there to die.

We left with fanfare and the blessings of the whole village, and I, swaddled in quilts, waved from our hired carriage and smiled and wept and knew that I was dying and never to see my children again. And that was hard—very hard—but I have always endeavored to live gracefully, and I chose to die gracefully as well.

After only two days, we had traveled farther than I had ever traveled before. After two weeks, nothing at all was recognizable to me: not the language men spoke, not the trees, not the very color of the earth. In the mornings, birds I did not know sang songs I had never before heard. My body continued to stiffen, but through the apertures of my ears and eyes, a new lightness entered me, made of awe and surprise and a comforting sense of our smallness when considered against the expanse of the wide world.

And still I did not speak to my husband of dying. Not until at last I beheld the sea—the true, storied sea, wide, steel gray, implacable, against which all human conceit is but loose sand—only then did my unwillingness to speak of dying fall away from me at last. We booked passage, and there on deck, amid the strange back-and-forth calls of the sailors as they clambered through the rigging and the sharp smell of sea wrack, I pressed my husband's hand.

"Now that we have left the road for the sea and can no more turn back, we must speak of difficult things."

"My love?"

"You know that my body is failing, that I walk only with great difficulty, that my hands have stiffened to such a degree that I can no longer feed myself. You take my arm and you guide me, you put the spoon in my mouth, and you do these things lovingly. I am made to feel young and loved and I am grateful. But we must speak the truth of these things." I held his eyes. "My husband, I am dying."

"Of course you are not... Or we are dying together, yes, and will do so for many happy years. My love, let us not talk of such things, but enjoy the sea breeze and the sun. Here, I will adjust your chair to better catch the light."

I said, "I have a disease. A paralysis is moving through my body, slowly, stilling my hands, my legs, my back. It will reach my lungs or my heart soon. Sooner than you have imagined... I am sorry."

He looked at me, amazed, but I would not look away, though tears started from my eyes. "Then we will turn back," he said. "If it is as you say, I will speak to the captain immediately and we will turn back. I must bear the blame for encouraging this pilgrimage. We will go home where you can rest and you can mend."

And my husband made as if to stand and go, but I spoke softly, so that he bent to hear me.

"I will not mend and there is not time. I am sorry. It has been a good life with you and our families and our children and the orchards and the tavern—a life full of love—but it is ending. And now I wish to see Velaya."

Then he sank before me and held my knees and wept.

We said much more to one another, that day and in the days that followed, but we did not turn around, and gradually my husband came to support my resolve. And though my condition worsened, so that I was more like a bent plank of wood than a woman when finally we made port, he bathed me and cared for me and passed the evenings of our sea voyage with descriptions of the great caravans he had known of old.

But the port town, when we alighted, seemed diminished from the bustling center he had described, and the wide caravanserai with its many stables and markets was pitifully empty. I saw disappointment on my husband's face and also confusion, and I, in my debility, could do little to help. Eventually we found someone in the dusty market who would take us the four days to Velaya on camelback, though our guide's fare was exorbitant and his camel seemed skinny and old, even to one who had never seen a camel before.

We set out the next day, and the going was hard for me. We rode together on the one camel, my husband and I, because I was so light and because I was too stiff to sit without falling, so that my husband had to tie me to him atop that strange fleshy hump. The heat of the day was punishing and the cold of night, bitter. I spoke almost not at all, for my breathing had become shallow and short. I feared that the paralysis had come to my lungs at last, that I might not make it to the city.

On the third morning, we woke alone in the desert with no water —camel and guide gone—and all but one coin stolen from us.

I could not walk. I could barely breathe. But far on the horizon, my husband said he could see white cliffs, and so he hoisted me into the air, as a bridegroom crossing the threshold with his bride, and began to walk. All that day he walked through the broken desert carrying his wife before him like a cord of wood and the sun beating down. And all that night with the cold stars staring. And more than once he stumbled, but never did he let me fall, and I could do nothing to help but to coax my laboring lungs on, and each breath a trial.

At dawn we came to Velaya.

And having never seen the Dreaming City myself, I could not know with certainty that it had fallen, that it was a husk of its former glory. I had heard only stories of Velaya, and who can say what is fantasy and what is real in a story, no matter how earnest the teller.

But the city was certainly a husk. The Northern Gate was pockmarked; its arches had fallen where their keystones no longer held. The domes of the madrasas which had not collapsed had been stripped of their silver. The streets were dusty and steep and uneven and empty of inhabitants except for a few market-folk in colorless rags selling trinkets and dried nuts from the shadow of low doors.

But my husband entered with his head held high in the dawn light and his eyes stern and his dying bride in his arms.

"We are come to Velaya, my love," he whispered.

And on the blanket of a sun-wizened old rag-picker, from among dirty sandstone idols and chipped crockery, my husband chose a small earthenware jar the size of a hen's egg and traded for it our last coin. And squatting there in the street with myself in his lap—never putting me down—he opened the jar, and with his two fingers scooped from it a gray ointment, and opening my thin black robes, he rubbed the ointment onto my chest.

"A balm of Velaya, my love," he whispered.

And at first I felt only a tingle, but then air rushed into my lungs and I breathed as deeply as a child breathes who wakes from a long and untroubled sleep.

And I would have lain there in his lap breathing and praying and giving thanks—for I had surely been touched by a miracle—but my husband stood with me in his arms, and continued walking up the broken street and in his eyes was a burning intensity. The rag-picker called after us, and some children, ragged also and all skinny, came from the doorways out of curiosity or wonder and followed us on up the street, and more joined, until we were leading some dozens of street urchins in a motley parade. And we wound through the abandoned city until we came, all of us, to a wide plaza with a shallow pool at its center, the pool dry and half-filled with wind-blown sand and its tiles all cracked. Then my husband reached down and grasped a pebble that two of the boys had been kicking and raised it to the light for me to see—a piece of broken cobble with green flecks in its clay—and then he held it to my chest and held me close to *his* chest.

"A stone of Velaya, my love," he whispered.

And as he held me to him, water burst forth in a great arcing spray from the center of the pool and the children all screamed and the mist from the spray of water soaked into our robes and into the rags of the children as they ran and jumped and splashed into the pool. But my husband held me and rubbed more of the ointment into my hands, and as he rubbed the sore useless tendons and the stiff little bones, my fingers returned to life and ached and flexed and clutched his fingers in desperate gratitude. We drank from the pool together, cupping our hands, the clear cold water running down our chins and necks, and rainbows danced in the arcing mist.

There were more shouts as the city-folk came running into the plaza, clapping and ululating and wading in. But my husband lifted me again in his arms, though he did not need to do so for the miracle of the ointment was spreading through my body and I felt my knees tingle and my shoulders and my neck, and a great relaxation came over me, like a fist that has been too long clenched finally unclenching. He walked with me up into the city, through abandoned alleys, past temples, past the eroded faces of old stone gods and the disjoint columns of palaces, and as we walked higher and higher, the wind blew across our wet clothes and the sun warmed us and our skins felt magical. And we climbed up into the cliffs above the city by a long white stair cut from the living rock.

"The Dawn Stair of Veliara, my love," he whispered.

Far below us, from the shoulders of the great cliff, we could see the water from the pool as it shimmered in the sun, and the water overflowed into ancient canals and along aqueducts that had run of old throughout the maze-like city, and the spreading of the new water through the city was as the veins of a leaf held to the sky, except that the veins of Velaya were silver and shining. Then my husband set me carefully down, and though my feet had not felt the ground for some days, I was suffused with a curious lightness, as if I floated like a cork on water. We continued on up the stair, hand-in-hand, always higher, and we were not tired, and we climbed until at last we came to the very summit of Veliara and stood at the cliff-edge looking down into the shining maze of the Dreaming City.

And there was no terror and there was no trial. My husband bent and placed upon that high ground the stone and the small jar of balm and then he took up my hand again. We were not judged. We felt no fear and no uncertainty. We felt no need to leap into the unknown, for we rose from that place on wings we had always known we had.

About the story

"Velaya" was very much inspired by Lord Dunsany, who was a writer of quirky little fantasies in the pre-Tolkien era. I had been fooling around with different voices and styles in my writing, and thought Dunsany's high, Biblical language would be interesting to mimic. Of course, what you set out to do is never quite what you do do, which is true for the protagonist of my story as well.

A question for the author

Q: Are titles easy or hard for you? Do you start with the title or the story?

A: Titles are the best! Really, coming up with titles is like coming up with band names: it's pure id. I usually do it after the fact, with an eye to seeing the title in a list of other titles. Something to stand out, but without, I hope, being too obnoxious.

Chapter titles are even better. When I was revising my (unpublished) novel, *A Catalog of Devils,* I suddenly realized that I could give the 40 or so chapters titles. I went through each chapter, looking for my favorite phrase or word and used that. It was like bringing all the best, trickiest bits of my writing to the forefront. It sounds absurd, but out of the year and a half I spent on the novel, that two hours of titling chapters was the emotional highpoint.

About the author

During the day, Beston Barnett designs and builds furniture in San Diego. At night, he plays Romani jazz. The rest of the time he is reading a book, or eating with chopsticks, or—in the best of all possible worlds—doing both at once.

Switch

Lisa Clark

Claudia Campbell shifted in her seat, clutching her oversized pocketbook closer to her chest. She released an audible huff. With all the automation these days, why couldn't they move things along faster?

She dragged a digital magazine off a nearby table, catching the gaze of another woman. She was probably a decade younger than Claudia's ninety-two, though it was increasingly difficult to tell how old people were these days.

For Claudia, age-retarding pharmaceuticals, surgery, and gene therapy had come too late. She was stuck being old.

She swiped on *Full Life: The Digital Magazine for Seniors* and began flicking through pages filled with ads for precision medications, comfort living, designer foods, cyber companions, etc., etc., etc. *Nothing new here,* she told herself. *Move on.*

Nearby, a man sniffed loudly. With sagging skin, pores the size of pennies, and hound dog jowls, he looked at least a hundred. When he coughed, Claudia could envision micro-flecks of sputum hurtling toward her. She tutted quietly.

Waiting for a doctor today was no more desirable than it had been during the last century. True, the natural light and greenery were pleasant, even if they came courtesy of VR. And the cool aqua-toned seating was attractive and comfortable, with sizes and configurations to fit any patient.

But waiting was still waiting.

She returned to the magazine. On the eighth page, an unbelievably handsome holographic figure popped up. Okay. Claudia would stop to savor a piece of eye candy.

"Ever wonder how it would feel to be someone else?" the man asked in a drawn out, sexy tone. Claudia unconsciously leaned in. "Would it change the way you experience the world or relate to others? Would it make you a better person? At Switch, our VR will take you places beyond your dreams." The hologram looked directly at Claudia. "Come. Try Switch. The world will never look the same."

"Claudia Campbell? Is Claudia Campbell here?" a robotic receptionist called out. Its voice was neither high nor low. Its androgynous body was dressed in blue hospital scrubs. Claudia's lips pursed at its flawless skin.

She pushed herself up. "Yes. I'm here. I've been here for almost an hour."

"Excuse us for the wait," the robot replied, "Physio Caretaker  4 will see you now."

"Hey, Grams," Claudia's grandson called out from the other side of the short wall that separated the living room from the front door. A second later, she heard the *thump* of his satchel as he shoved it onto the seat of the antique hall tree.

Next came a *whump* as Jerrod pushed the door shut against its weatherproofed seal. That sound was Claudia's daily reminder of how much the ranch house had changed since she and Dan bought it back in 1965 as newlyweds. When Jerrod moved in five years ago following the death of his parents, he'd insisted on modernizing.

Claudia strained to greet Jerrod pleasantly. A twenty-eight-year-old had better things to do than spend his life watching over his grandmother, waiting for her to die. The least she could do was welcome him home with a smile.

She was thankful Jerrod didn't treat her like the RoboDoc had earlier. Afterwards, she'd felt like a waste of time, space, and resources. Like the planet would be better off without her.

She'd broken down in the exam room. "My back, my neck, and my joints ache so. It's relentless. Can't you do something? Please! You're supposed to be the best Physio Caretaker in the city."

"Now, Claudia," RoboDoc said.

S/he or it (Claudia never knew how to refer to the unisex care provider) always did that. Called her by her given name.

"First, I'm not the best. Every Physio Caretaker is the same. New models are coming, but we'll all be updated." It tilted its head to the side in a gesture of concern. Claudia wanted to whack the thing over the head with her purse.

"Second, I told you the last three times you were in that your chronic pain is a malfunction in perception. It began with one complaint and, because you didn't deal with that properly, it has continued, spread, and escalated. Your brain is now addicted to the pain. If—"

"Addicted to the pain!" she yelped. "Who programmed you, anyway? People are addicted to things they *enjoy,* at least at the beginning. I have never enjoyed being in pain."

"I'm sorry, but you're mistaken," he answered. Impassively. RoboDocs were infuriatingly emotionless. "As I was about to say, if you continue to feed that addiction, it will continue to grow. My advice? Calm down. Think of something else; occupy your brain with other thoughts and the pain will release its hold on you."

"You know," Claudia stood as indignantly as she could with the nagging cramp in her foot, "back in the days when we had *real* doctors —human ones—they were compassionate. They would have found *some* way to help."

"Back in the days when you had human doctors," RoboDoc answered, "you probably would have been taking fifteen different medicines, none of which would have done a thing besides bankrupt you and interact dangerously with each other." He opened the door. "Don't come to see me again about this issue."

As she rode home in the driverless cab, Claudia brooded. She hated robodocs. Human doctors and nurses could commiserate and touch you with warm skin, assuring you that someone cared.

She had resisted going to the Physio Caretaker because of the cost. Politicians still hadn't figured out how to make medical care affordable and Claudia didn't want to weigh Jerrod down with bills. But he had seen her pain and insisted she go. What a waste.

At home, swirling, grimy, depressing thoughts twined around her. Her hope of relief had shattered. What was left? Maybe it wouldn't be such a bad idea if she scheduled a medical suicide. Plenty of other elderly people did it.

But she was too pathetic, too scared, to take that route.

"Hey, Grams," Jerrod repeated as he rounded the corner into the living room.

Claudia could barely find the strength to meet his gaze.

Seconds later, Jerrod was at her side. "Hey, what's wrong?" His voice was gentle as he knelt by the recliner, her daytime perch for a dozen years. He laid his hand on her shoulder. "What happened? Bad news from the doctor?" His face was still boyish, round, with hair that fell across his forehead and sometimes into his eyes. Their deep blue was so like his grandfather Dan's seventy years ago. She wished Jerrod would wrap her in his arms and draw her close. She ached to inhale his hope.

She shook her head. "No. Not really. Just no help."

His hand slipped onto her wrist. Jerrod was kind. She only wished that, occasionally, he would caress her cheek and hold her hand. But then, her dry, prune-skin face and knobby hands didn't exactly welcome touch.

She shrugged resignation to her fate.

"You know what?" His grin was Dan's. How could she choose medical suicide with this memory of her late husband around? "I have a surprise for you!"

She forced a tiny smile.

"Oh, this will make you a lot happier than that!"

He raced to his room at the end of the hallway, returning less than a minute later.

"Happy birthday!" He bowed smartly at the waist and extended his hand like a butler.

Claudia laughed aloud. "It's not my birthday."

"It will be. In a week. But you need this now."

She eyed the reusable envelope, "guaranteed not to crease, stain, or tear." Claudia was sick of high-tech.

"Open it, Grams. You're gonna love it!" He slid back onto the couch.

She drew out a picture of the unnaturally handsome man she'd seen in hologram form earlier. His words were printed this time. "You are the lucky recipient of a Switch session. Book a time today. After Switch, the world will never look the same."

Claudia didn't look up. She didn't want to see the disappointment in Jerrod's eyes when she refused the gift. She thought he knew her better.

"Great, isn't it?"

"I... Jerrod, I can't do Switch. It's for young people."

"No, no," he protested, slipping onto the couch next to her. "This is for anyone. Everyone. Switch has a great track record, Grams. People up to one-hundred fifteen have entered Switch. Wait a second; I'll call up their testimonials." He slipped on a pair of MR glasses and began manipulating a virtual screen with his fingers.

Claudia pulled his hand down. "Don't bother. I'm not interested. I dislike video games."

"This isn't a game. I've done research on it. I've even talked with Switch clients. No one regrets it."

Claudia grew rigid and clenched her jaw. "Even if you spoke to a hundred people, it means nothing. I'm sure there are just as many with the opposite view. Besides, I've heard about Switch, too. They knock you out with drugs. I don't use drugs. At least, not non-medicinal ones."

"It's not like that. It's more like what they do when you have an operation."

"I don't care to be knocked out!"

"Consider it a nap, then!" He sounded annoyed. "You're always complaining about how you can't sleep."

"It's not the same!" She was yelling now. Her voice sounded like one of those old biddies she used to mock years ago. When had she turned into one of them?

"Listen, Grams." Jerrod stood and loomed over her. "I forked over half a week's salary for this. All I ever hear from you is, 'I can't do this. I can't do that.'" His tone was merciless. "I'm sick of your complaining. All I'm asking is that you give this a try. It's not like you have anything better to do. Can't you think of anyone else for a change?"

Then he marched off to the kitchen.

As Jerrod clanged and clattered dishes and silverware, Claudia doused herself with self-pity, brushing away tears. How could he be so cruel? His grandfather had never acted that way.

No. Not true. Dan regularly had bossed and bullied her around, especially when she resisted him. In the end, she always complied.

She just didn't expect such treatment from Jerrod.

"Dinner's ready." Was that disgust in his voice?

Please, she inwardly begged, *don't be angry with me.* She bit back the urge to cry.

"Coming." Her voice was shaky.

She'd do as he said.

Claudia lay on a gurney in a clean room, her breasts and lower body the only parts covered. Two twenty-something techno-medics worked over her, one a woman with a nametag that read *Tania,* the other a man named *Gopal.* Probably Switch thought they were doing clients a favor by providing human techs. For this, Claudia would have preferred a robot.

She clamped her eyes tight while they glued adhesive sensors to her arms, on skin shriveled like a dried streambed, then to lumpy flesh that sagged into rolls on her stomach. To think, Jerrod had *paid* for this humiliation. Tania and Gopal would probably go home and laugh their heads off at her age-spotted skin.

"So," Tania said, her eyes on the alcohol pad she was swiping Claudia's arm with. "I saw that you chose to enter Switch as a six-year-old girl. At a birthday party in 1946, right? How fun!"

Claudia didn't want to hear friendly banter. With stinging eyes, she turned from the girl.

"Okay, Mrs. Campbell," Gopal said after the IV was in place. "You're all set. You're in for a fantastic experience."

He settled a mask on her face. "Easy breaths. Now count to ten for me."

Before she reached two, Claudia was out.

"Smile, Louise!" a woman urged.

Claudia-turned-Louise blinked, confused. Where was she? Who was she? Who were these people?

"Smile for the camera, honey!" the woman said.

To Louise, the woman looked like a stranger. Except for her cotton button-up dress with tiny ruffles down the front. And her hair, parted to the side and bobby-pinned away from her face. Around her ears, frizzy curls blossomed. Oh! It was mommy.

A man holding a black metallic cube to his face peeked at her around the box. "Show me a big six-year-old smile!" His own smile, wide in a thin face, revealed a missing top molar on the left side and another on the bottom right. His white button-up shirt hung large and his belt cinched tightly, creating an elastic-looking waistline. Louise's daddy.

She giggled at her silly confusion and he snapped her. A small *pop* of the flash created a snowy glare in her vision.

Everything was as it should be: a crisp white tablecloth set with good china and silverware. Her baby brother bouncing and slapping his dimpled hands against a highchair tray smeared with smashed peas. Her older brother, wearing a smart plaid suit, honking a noisemaker. Balloons on the table, ruffled sheers on the window, and —Louise reached to make sure—a cardboard crown for her, the birthday girl.

The kitchen door swung open with her grandma singing and carrying a carrot cake decorated with piped rosettes along the top edge and chopped walnuts on the side.

"Blow out the candles and make a wish!" Mommy encouraged.

"Yeah. Hurry up so we can eat cake!" That was her brother.

"I wish I never had to grow up," Louise said.

"Hah! She wants to be Peter Pan!" her brother mocked. "Only now she can't, 'cause she said it out loud."

That bothered Louise as she ate her cake. And again, when she opened her gifts: a pretty dolly whose eyes opened and closed, soft knit slippers, and a red sweater Grandma had knitted with pearly Scottie dogs as buttons.

"Did you have a good birthday, sweetheart?" Mommy asked at bedtime.

"Yes," Louise said. "Except for..."

"Except for what?" Mommy pulled the satiny bedspread up to Louise's chin.

"I don't want to grow up. Now I have to because I said it."

"Not grow up? I thought you wanted to be a mommy."

Louise's brow wrinkled in plump ridges. "I do want to be a mommy."

She woke the next morning with her new doll, a dove cooing outside her window, and a call from downstairs.

"Breakfast!"

The first thing Louise-turned-Claudia noticed as she groggily woke was the odor. A familiar, greasy, old cut-grass scent she couldn't identify.

"Hey, Mrs. Campbell," said an unfamiliar voice. "Welcome back."

Two questions collided in her brain. Why was this stranger urging her from sleep? And where was that disgusting stench coming from?

The woman nudged Claudia's shoulder. "It's time to wake up."

Claudia's eyes fluttered.

"That's it. Welcome back to the world."

Claudia opened her eyes partway. The lights were blinding. And the woman was dressed in white. Had her mother changed her clothes?

Claudia lifted her hand to cover her eyes. They bolted open at the hand coming toward her, shriveled and covered with spots, protruding veins, and swollen knuckles. She lurched upward, only to fall back immediately.

She groaned. Why did her neck feel as though she'd wrenched it?

"No, no." The woman in white—most definitely not Louise's mother—held her down. "Rest a bit. Give yourself time to transition back."

"What? What are you talking about?"

Ten full minutes passed before Claudia's mental fog cleared. Then it all came back, crashing over her like a tsunami.

She was back in the real world.

And that smell? It was her.

"I'll admit I was skeptical about it," Claudia told Jerrod as the taxi whisked them home. The physical contact she'd had inside the program made her crave it again. Why did Jerrod have to sit so far away?

"But you're not now?"

She turned her stiff neck toward him. "It was wonderful to be young again. You have no idea."

He smiled and set his hand on her shoulder. "I'm glad you liked it, Grams."

Her awakening in the clean room after her Switch session didn't return to her fully until the next morning. "Don't worry," the attendant named Destiny had said as she handed Claudia her glasses. "A little confusion is normal, especially after your first session. I'm just glad you're not waking up like the guy last week. Said his whole life had flashed before him." Destiny shook her head. "His Switch session was as a racecar driver. Our medical techs pulled him out of the simulation just before his car crashed. They're very careful to bring people back at any sign of distress. We promise our clients safety, after all." She lifted Claudia's wrist to feel her pulse and nodded a few seconds later. "The only exception was with the guy who signed a waver that said he didn't want to be pulled out early no matter what happened." She leaned forward and said in a hushed voice, "He'd chosen a scenario where he disarmed landmines in a combat zone. He was clearly looking for death by Switch. You know, like people do with police?" Destiny straightened. "The bosses don't allow those types of scenarios anymore."

Claudia often replayed her day in Switch (though, by some computer magic, she knew it had only been an hour in real time). The warmth of her family there. Their closeness. Why had such feelings vaporized in today's world? What was wrong with people these days?

Sometimes, to relive the feel of the red sweater her Switch grandmother had knitted, Claudia closed her eyes and rubbed with withered fingers the afghan draped over her chair arm. But it wasn't the same.

For her birthday, she insisted Jerrod buy her a carrot cake decorated with walnuts.

"*Carrot* cake?" he answered, like she was requesting bugs. "The only kind of cake you'll even touch is dark chocolate."

"I ate it in Switch and have decided that variety is the spice of life."

"All righty, then," he said, holding his hands up in surrender.

She wished she could return to the program to recapture the sensations. To inhale the complex scent of her mother's perfume. Well, Louise's mother.

One day, while Jerrod was at work, Claudia ordered sample vials of fifty vintage perfumes in search of the scent with floral and woody undertones but also powdery and musky. She found it: Lanvin My Sin. One whiff transported her back to the mother that wasn't hers and yet, oddly, had become hers.

"Grams! It smells like an airport duty free shop in here," Jerrod said when he returned home that evening.

She felt like he'd doused her with ditch water.

His brow furrowed. "What?"

She waved him off. How could she explain?

She recalled Louise's downy, unblemished skin and perfect child's body, unmarred by life. Limbs that didn't ache. Eyes that saw without the need of magnification.

As the days passed, Claudia squelched those musings. What a waste of Jerrod's hard-earned money! It was make-believe. If Claudia wanted to pretend, she could read a book or watch TV. That world, that life, that girl—Louise—was merely a construct of computer programmers. How many other people had lived through that exact memory?

Then she remembered. Each Switch scenario was unique; computers designed them based on pre-set parameters, but the program responded to clients' reactions. "When a client acts or speaks, the program goes off in a new direction," the hostess at Switch had explained. "It's never the same, no matter how many people use it."

Which meant the memory of that day and life was Claudia's alone.

Claudia spent most of Thanksgiving Day mourning the family that had been hers for but an hour in the real world.

"What's wrong, Grams?" Jerrod asked.

The lump in her throat made it too difficult to croak out an answer.

She rubbed her throat.

He fetched her lozenges.

The most frightening days—there had only been three—were those when Claudia couldn't stop thinking about reentering Switch. The desire possessed her. Switch could restore to her joy, youth, and connection to people she inexplicably but genuinely loved. She wanted those things so badly she thought her brain might explode if she couldn't have them.

"What's the matter with you, Grams?" Jerrod asked once "You're so irritable."

I'm wishing I could have a life again, she thought. *I'm tired of my body and feeling helpless and useless.*

"Just these old bones getting me down," she said. Her attempted chuckle sounded more like a choke.

"I'm sorry," he said. As though the fault were his. "Work's been crazy. The boss says it should slow down after the holidays. Then I'll be around more."

"I'd like that."

Christmas was near, and Jerrod was feeling guilty about being gone so much. Claudia knew exactly what he could do to assuage his guilt.

"Aren't you going to ask me what I want for Christmas this year?" She pushed aside the lemon cream salmon cannelloni prepared by L'Ultima Chef, Jerrod's favorite kitchen bot. The dish sounded good, but was nothing compared to the home-cooked fare in Switch.

"Ya gotta eat more, Grams," Jerrod grumbled as he scooped up her plate then scraped it into their home composter. When he clicked the button, the machine commenced humming loudly as it began grinding the materials before mixing them into the compost-in-progress. He checked out the temperature inside the device: a bacteria-loving sixty-five degrees Celsius.

Returning to the table, he plunked down. His usually bright eyes were ringed heavily and his face looked drawn. "So, what's this about Christmas? You never have ideas." He ran his fingers through his hair so that it stood straight up for several moments before settling into a style Claudia thought oddly reminiscent of the beehive look of the 1960s. "I haven't had time to think about tomorrow, say nothing of what's coming in two weeks. I'm sorry Grams."

"Don't worry. I've reconciled myself to long periods of isolation." She heaved her shoulders.

Jerrod's face flushed. "Hey, you're not being fair, Grams. This isn't my fault." The deep vertical line between his eyes deepened. It had begun as a shallow depression but had grown more pronounced over the past six months. "How about I check into having a Home Assistant come to spend part of the day with you?" He shook his head miserably. "They're expensive, though."

"I'm not interested in a babysitter!" Claudia snapped.

"How about a senior day care center then?"

"Jerrod Cameron Campbell. *Listen* to me. I'm bringing up Christmas because I have a suggestion for you." Claudia slid her hand across the tabletop. "I wouldn't mind another session at Switch." She made her voice light and nonchalant. "Maybe three hours this time."

Jerrod's jaw dropped.

"You don't have to look so surprised. It's not as though I'm asking you to do something *illegal*."

"No. I mean, of course not."

"I enjoyed it the first time, that's all." She added softly, "It's hard being old and alone."

"Aw, Grams. I understand." He scraped his fingers through his hair again. "Three hours? Whew. That'll cost a lot." He stared silently at the table for several moments. "Are you sure that's what you want?"

She thrust her chin up. "You're always asking for ideas. Now I'm giving you one."

Jerrod shook his head. "Let me think about it." He pushed himself up from the chair. "I gotta get to bed. I need to be at work early again tomorrow."

Two days after Christmas, at the first opening available, Claudia once again lay nearly naked on a gurney in a clean room while two techno-medics attached electrodes to her skin. She squelched her discomfort. She had forgotten what it felt like to have young eyes look at a body she could barely stand the sight of.

Stop it! a voice inside scolded. *So what if they see you? In a few minutes, you'll be in Switch.*

Claudia couldn't wait to be young again. Not a child, though. This time, she would be living inside the body and mind of a newlywed woman. The time frame she'd chosen was different, too. More suited to an adult. What would it be like, she'd wondered, to assume the life of a new wife after the dawning of the sexual revolution? After men understood they could no longer expect their wives to bow to their every demand? After they saw them as equals?

She had considered the 1960s. Then the 70s. In the end, she'd settled on 1975. There, Claudia could enjoy decent music. She'd grown to dislike almost anything new. Disco had been bad enough, but then came heavy metal. And rap? It was the genre she used to measure all others in terms of horridness. Then came electronic, skewed, and now atomic. Dreadful. All of it.

Uncharacteristically, she'd acted spontaneously and ticked "mystery" on the list of elements she wanted in the program.

Claudia ignored the girl technician's friendly banter, choosing instead to daydream about the scenario she would soon enter.

At first, she'd wanted a groom who would resemble her actual husband, Dan. Then she decided she'd like someone different. Someone like Mel Gibson's character in *Forever Young.*

Switch promised authenticity, not enjoyment. What if she ended up with a chauvinistic bigot like Archie Bunker from that old show, *All in the Family*? She eventually decided that even he must have had some endearing qualities in the beginning.

Besides, anyone Switch matched her to would be exciting; she'd be a newlywed, not someone who'd been married fifty years.

For the dozenth time, Claudia clenched long unused muscles in anticipation.

"Okay, Mrs. Campbell," the male tech said after the IV was in place. "You're ready to enjoy three days of adventure!" His eyes were reassuring. Did Switch only choose employees with pleasant personalities? "When I place the mask on your face, I want you to count to ten. Real easy now."

After "one," she was out.

"I want you to see what I see, Peggy," the man hummed into her ear.

Claudia-turned-Peggy opened her eyes to the reflection of a couple in a full-length mirror. His hair of rich caramel was slicked back. Fawn-colored eyes beneath heavy, straight brows bespoke openness; honesty. Though his face was angular, almost sharp, his lips were full. Exquisite, and somehow more so because they surrounded slightly crooked teeth. His white shirt, opened at the collar, set off tawny skin. In front of him and reaching only to his chin, a somewhat younger woman lifted her gaze. Shy eyes, blue-violet and a trifle too deep-set, contrasted with generous curves beneath a two-piece periwinkle dress, closely fitted. An intricate auburn chignon bared her neck. The cast-iron mirror frame, painted cream and embellished with delicate scallops and intricate vines and leaves, captured the pair like an image in a gallery.

Claudia-turned-Peggy squinted for the briefest moment, trying to place the couple before bursting into a full smile, shaking off the feeling of waking from a dream. This was her, Peggy, with Jack Michaels, the man who had, a few hours ago, promised to be hers and hers alone for as long as they lived.

"Just look at you." Jack stood behind her, wrapping her in his arms. One hand caressed her breast while the other gently pressed and spread over her pubic bone. "You're mine now, Peggy. All and only mine."

She glanced at her own hand, at the finger which held proof that what they were doing was all right. *No. Right.* And *good.* For the first time, she could do what she'd been waiting, wanting to do with this man every day for the past six months. She closed her eyes and leaned back into her husband.

As a railroad shipping clerk and his secretary, Jack and Peggy had meager resources for a fancy honeymoon. "We'll go to San Francisco. Stay in a pretty inn. Eat out a few times. Take in a show, maybe," he'd promised her before their wedding. Which was fine with her. All Peggy wanted was to be with this man.

Soon the mirror, bay window, fireplace, and four-poster bed faded away and there was only Jack and how he was touching her, as though his hands, fingers, and mouth were made for her and nobody else.

Later, barefoot and wrapped in a bedspread that draped behind her like a heavy train, Peggy scampered across the chilly floorboards. Light from a full moon slanted through the tilted blinds, casting the room in stripes of blue-gray. Peggy clicked on a lamp, showering the floor with a wide yellow arc. "We should have started a fire."

For the first time, she noticed a small fruit basket on the table by the window.

"I'll warm you up. Come back to bed." Jack propped himself up on an elbow.

"Jack! I'm hungry."

"I am, too." He twitched his brows Groucho Marx-style.

Peggy bit into a green apple. "This is so nice. Do they leave fruit for everyone, or just for newlyweds? Oh, wait. Here's a card."

With apple still in hand, she broke the envelope's seal. A moment later, the apple rolled down the bedspread and *thunk*ed onto the bare floor. The covering slid to her waist and her face twisted in confusion.

"What?" Jack threw back the blanket and padded toward her.

Peggy barely noticed that he was naked. That the skin along one of his sides was peppered with dozens of maroon scars. That he was ready for her again.

"What's wrong?" He wrapped one arm around her and grabbed the card with the other.

Johnny, it said, *Your new wife very pretty, but she know about Linh and Johnny Jr.?*

Jack froze.

"Jack?"

"This is a mistake." He released her to rip the card and toss it into the fireplace. "It has to be. Who's Johnny? And who's Lin? Or however you say that name. Get back in bed, Peggy, and I'll build a fire."

"But—"

"It's mis*take,* honey. Trust me." The way he kissed her, carried her to the bed, and made love to her again made Peggy almost forget the note.

Later, when they left for dinner, Jack slid the fruit basket onto the reception desk. "There's been an error," he said. "This is someone else's."

"But, sir," the manager protested, "someone left it specifically for you,".

"It's not ours."

*

The next morning, Peggy spotted a bakery and Jack a fruit cart at the same time. "Let's surprise each other," she suggested. "You buy fruit. I'll buy pastries."

"Perfect," he agreed. "We can eat in the park."

The selection of freshly made breads and doughnuts kept Peggy in the shop longer than she'd planned.

Finally, balancing a rough cardboard holder for their coffee cups in one hand and a box with enough treats for three days in the other, she swiveled to exit.

Through the window, she spotted Jack with a strange woman.

The small bell above the door tinkled as she pushed it with her shoulder. Jack, several feet away, shot her a glance then hissed something to the woman.

The stranger—some sort of Oriental, Peggy thought—peeked around Jack and sneered at her with such venom that Peggy gasped. The coffee holder wobbled precariously in her hand.

"... sister know... you... must care..." The woman's voice was harsh but indistinct.

As Peggy warily approached, the stranger bustled away, weaving through pedestrians, hustling to their daily grinds.

"Who was that?"

Jack shook his head. "Just a beggar. There are lots of them here."

"But what did she say? Why were you talking to her?"

Jack goggled at Peggy as though she'd accused him of a crime.

"I-I mean," she stuttered, "I was just wondering."

He smiled, but not warmly, then pressed on the small of her back a touch too firmly. "Let's go and eat."

*

Jack was wonderful, mostly, for the rest of the day, and possessive and intense that night. "I love you so much, Peggy. You. Only you," he told her two, three, four times.

Her timid, "I love you, too, Jack," after the last time brought him to tears, though he tried to hide it.

"You're mine and I'm yours. No one else's," were his last words that night.

*

The sights as they hopped off the trolley the next day—signs featuring "imperial," "Chinese," and hanzi characters alongside tall buildings topped with pagodalike roofs—made Peggy glad her aunt had suggested Chinatown. Here they'd find coconut buns, egg yolk almond balls, mooncakes, and who knew what else.

The air vibrated differently here. The fragrance of unfamiliar spices wafted from shops and mixed with crisp, precise music with odd rhythms.

Tomorrow they would drive home. The next day, it was back to work.

Peggy didn't want to miss a thing.

Outside the Far East Café, she decided to use the restroom. "Find a shop we can visit," she said. "I'll be quick."

When she reemerged, Jack wasn't waiting by the door. She scanned the sidewalk to her right, then to her left. No sign of him. Her stomach clenched. What if she couldn't find him?

But that was silly. Jack would never leave her.

She gazed across the street, in the direction of Fisherman's Wharf, already bustling. After a jangling trolley passed, she spotted Jack. Again, with another woman. Was it the one from yesterday? He extracted the wallet from his pocket, glanced nervously around, then handed the woman money.

What was he *doing*? Why was he with her? And why was he giving her money?

Peggy stepped off the curb onto the street, furious, aware of nothing but Jack.

A horn blared at her.

Peggy screamed.

A car screeched, then plowed into her, throwing her to the ground.

The driver jumped out and cursed her. People stopped to watch.

The next moment, Jack was there.

And then he wasn't. Peggy-Claudia was out of Switch.

"Hey, good morning, Grams!" Jerrod clicked off the burner and pivoted from the stovetop, where he was whipping up his favorite weekend concoction: scrambled eggs with garlic, scallions, and jalapenos.

He flicked off the virtual comp display on the table, opened to the news.

"How did your Switch session go?" he asked as she settled into her chair. "I peeked in on you last night when I got home, around nine, but you were already asleep."

"It was good."

"Good. That's great. Would you like some eggs?" He scooped his breakfast onto his plate.

"With hot peppers? No thank you."

"I can make the kind you like."

"No, no, sit." She tapped the table with her fingers, noticing how gnarled they were. So different from yesterday, inside Switch.

Why did she have to return? To wake every day in a ninety-two-year-old body? To constant swollen ankles. To teary eyes. To hauling one leg over the other with both hands, as though performing a herculean chore. To shriveling skin and the inability to stand erect.

Her shuffle down the hallway seemed a trifle longer every day.

What did life offer her besides more pain, more loneliness, and more hopelessness?

Switch delivered her from all that. Her brain stored Switch experiences just like real ones. In fact, memories from Switch were fresher and clearer. That didn't mean she forgot actual people and events from her past. But her Switch family as a child... Her marriage to Jack... How he reinvigorated sensations in this old body of hers... It was squirmingly delightful.

The truth? Claudia had been awake last night when Jerrod came to her door. She'd been reliving Jack's breath on her cheek and neck. His fingers on her skin. The way he possessed her.

Dan had never made her feel like that.

Jerrod handed her a mug of coffee with a splash of coconut milk. "So, tell me about your adventure."

"It was... lovely." She almost cringed. She sounded like such an old lady.

He chuckled and slapped his palm onto the table playfully. "Come *on*, Grams. Details, please."

Claudia felt her face redden and lifted the mug to her mouth. She couldn't remember the last time she'd blushed and that thought almost made her blush again. She sucked in a breath. "Okaaaay. This time I visited San Francisco in 1975."

Jerrod nearly choked on a mouthful of juice. "Are you kidding? I'd love to see Frisco before the earthquake and wildfires destroyed so much of it."

"So, take some time off work."

"Grams," he groaned.

She waved a hand at him that resembled a bundle of twigs.

"What did you do there?"

Hmm. What was she supposed to say? That she had enjoyed the thrill of first-time sex for the second time in her life? About being smitten with Jack? No. Definitely not. She'd improvise.

"I met a young man. And his wife. Newlyweds." She leaned into the table edge, flattening her saggy breasts. "They were lodging in the same guesthouse, and—"

"Oh. What was the guesthouse like?"

"Lovely, dear, but that wasn't the interesting part."

Jerrod rose to clear his plate. "More coffee?"

"Not yet."

He refilled his mug and resettled onto his chair. "You were saying?"

"Well, this husband—we'll call him Jack. And his wife, Peggy."

"What was your name?"

What? Claudia fumbled for a second. "Jill. I was Jill."

"Ha! You shoulda been married to the guy. Jack and Jill. Funny."

Claudia's face warmed again. "Are you going to talk or listen?"

"Geez, Grams. Go on."

Claudia told about the fruit basket, Jack's reaction to it, the whispering woman, and finally the money exchange.

"What were you, a spy? How did you find out about all that?"

"I, um, Jill, I mean Peggy, was my sister. She told me."

"You didn't say you were sisters."

Claudia huffed. "It's a *story,* Jerrod. That's all. I'm just trying to figure out why Jack was hiding information about the woman from his new wife."

Jerrod's eyes narrowed. "I have a feeling you're not telling me everything."

Claudia threw her napkin at him.

"Okay, okay. Maybe he was a Vietnam War vet. The time was right. Maybe the strange woman was Vietnamese, not Chinese. The sister of a woman Jack had met in Vietnam. Maybe they married and had a son. 'Johnny' could be a nickname for 'Jack.' That would fit. When the war ended, Jack had to leave the country, his wife, and his child."

Claudia stared at him. "That must be it." Her brow furrowed. "Jack had another wife."

Jerrod shrugged. "Don't be too hard on the guy. Soldiers get lonely during wartime."

Claudia sighed. "That's true." She pushed herself up from the chair.

"Wait, Grams. Aren't you going to eat?"

She swung her hand behind her. "I'm fine."

But she wasn't fine. Imagining Jack with another woman shook Claudia. Why hadn't he said anything? She would have understood.

She thought she would, anyway.

Halfway to her room, she froze. Jack was not her husband. Not really. He had been a character in a computer simulation. That's all.

Claudia slumped against the wall. *But it's not all. Jack was my husband. Those things happened. They were real.*

By the end of the day, one thought pummeled her: she had to return to Switch, to Jack. She couldn't bear never seeing him again.

"I'm sorry, Ms. Campbell," the woman said. On the virtual screen, she looked pleasant enough, but she was inflexible as a broomstick. "What you're asking for is impossible."

These people had promised a customized experience. Why were they now unwilling to keep that promise?

"Our programs are not reproducible," the woman went on. "I'm sure someone told you that. To work within program parameters, our technology cannot recreate the kind of details you want."

Claudia's shoulders drooped. She did remember that. "You mean," she asked in a tiny voice, "I'll never be able to go back to my husband?"

"Your husband?"

"I mean, my Switch husband."

"Oh. No. I'm sorry." Later, this woman would probably laugh at Claudia for believing in the world and life Switch had created for her. Right now, she sounded compassionate. "Please allow me to make up for the confusion. I can offer you a special deal: one week inside of Switch for the price of four days. You can choose a program similar to the last, if you like. How does that sound?"

It would have to do. "Okay. Mark me down for a week from today."

As she disconnected, the awful truth washed over Claudia. She'd never see Jack again. Never inhale his Old Spice. Or lie by his side.

She'd never find out his secret—or tell him she forgave him for keeping it from her. And her lips would never feel his again.

She touched her lips with her fingers, closed her eyes, and saw Jack's kind face. He seemed to be speaking to her. Telling her to move on.

Could she? If she married again, it wouldn't be as though she'd *lose* Jack. He was in there to stay.

Over the next hours, Claudia's mind created a new wish list for her next Switch session. This time, she'd visit a later timeframe: the 2010s. She wouldn't tick off "mystery" in the story elements. She hated not knowing—never knowing—the truth about the Asian woman. Jerrod might have been right in his conjecture, but he might also have been wrong.

This time... This time... Ohhhhh. Yes! This time, she'd spend her honeymoon in Paris. And *this* time, she would opt for a man with an "intriguing" side to his character. She clenched the muscles she would use to satisfy her new husband and laughed out loud.

Instantly, she slapped her hand over her mouth, forgetting for a moment that Jerrod was at work. Then she laughed again. She could fantasize as much as she liked.

By the end of the day, she had only one problem: where would the money come from? The session would cost a full month of Jerrod's pay and he'd never agree to taking out a loan. She'd figure something out.

"Grams, you're awfully chipper tonight," Jerrod said at least four times that evening. The last time, he followed the comment with, "So, are you going to let me in on your secret?"

No. Absolutely not. The poor boy would probably die of shock. "I'm just happy, that's all."

The next evening, the door clicked open. Jerrod stepped in. "Hey G—" Silence reigned for two seconds. "What?" Five seconds more, and he was around the corner, staring at her.

Claudia glanced up from the electronic book she'd been reading. A trashy romance—the kind she used to consider obscene. Now, it fueled her imagination.

The line between his eyes deepened as Jerrod fisted the hair at the top of his head. "What happened to the hall tree?"

Claudia had expected this. "Well, hello to you, too, dear."

He slipped out of his sleek winter jacket and held it in one hand, letting it drape to the floor as his gaze fixed on her.

They make everything so lightweight these days, Claudia thought, blinking. When she was a child, she remembered piling on so many layers she'd end up clomping around like Frankenstein.

She swiped her book close.

"Where is it, Grams?"

Her shoulders lifted slightly then dropped as she sighed. "I sold it."

"What?" The jacket slipped from Jerrod's fingers.

"I sold it. It was a monstrosity. Besides, it didn't fit in with the rest of our furnishings. You know that. It was old."

Jerrod collapsed onto an easy chair. "I can't believe you did that. *Why?* What were you *thinking*?"

Claudia shrugged and turned instead toward the front window. It was dirty, streaked and splotchy from bugs and rain. She'd noticed that earlier, as the sun set. When had it last been cleaned? Years ago. She never would have let that happen in her younger years.

"Grams!"

The sharpness of his tone made her jerk. She twined her fingers together like grapevines coiled into a wreath.

"That was mine! You know that. Just because it didn't come from your side of the family doesn't mean it wasn't valuable to me. It was the only thing I had of Dad's grandparents."

She shrugged again. "It was ugly, Jerrod. The mirror was blackened in the corners. And those claws meant to hang coats on? There were ridiculous."

"It was an antique! If the piece were restored, it could have sold for more than this house is worth."

"Maybe. But it wasn't restored," she snapped. "I was sick of looking at it."

"So what? I put up with this dust-infused living room set of yours. You don't even sit on it! You perch yourself in that La-Z-Boy like it's some kind of throne."

Claudia supposed he didn't mean to sound so nasty. Still, his words hurt.

After a long pause, she mumbled, "Buy something modern instead. Something you'll enjoy."

"I en*joyed* that. It gave me a connection to the past. Now, tell me what you did with it so I can get it back."

Claudia barked out a laugh. "I have no idea who the buyer was. He didn't leave his name or contact information. I'm sorry."

Jerrod pounded the arm of the chair, sending up a thin mist of dust. "You're not sorry at all!" He bolted out of the chair, swiped his jacket off the floor, glanced around as though trying to find something, then threw it back down. With his back toward her, he said, "You still haven't told me why."

Claudia fiddled with the edge of the arm cover on her chair. It was old, like her, and frayed. Not good for much. "I needed the money," she said, her voice only barely above a whisper.

"What?" He turned slowly.

His tone flipped something inside of Claudia.

"I said I needed the money." Now her voice was defiant.

"For *what?*"

"For returning to Switch, if you must know."

He gaped at her. "You just *had* a session at Switch."

"Well I need to go again. The woman offered me a great deal: a week for the price of four days. I couldn't pass it up. I've already booked a session for next Monday."

Jerrod's head flinched back. "You're going for a *week?* How long is that in Switch time?"

"Roughly six months."

"*Six months?* Are you crazy? Why?"

She swung her head to the side. "You wouldn't understand."

Jerrod said nothing for a long time, but she could feel him gaping. As though she'd just grown horns. Then, shaking his head slowly, he said, "Okay. I won't stop you. Just don't sell any more of my stuff."

That evening, Jerrod ate in his bedroom, Claudia in her La-Z-Boy.

I'll make it up to him, Claudia vowed to herself before drifting off that night.

When Claudia emerged from her week-long Switch session, her eyes sprang open and she surveyed the wake-up room. Within a half a minute, she understood who she was, what the thirty-something male watching over her was doing, and that she was out of the program. Safe.

"Whoa there, Mrs. Campbell," the man said as she jostled to raise herself up on her elbows.

Cursed old age. It was a bother more than anything. There were more important things to do in life than sit around, watching other people live. That's what Damian, her Switch husband for the last six months, used to say. For several moments, the room and attendant vanished as Damian's image filled her inner vision: movie star handsome, dressed in edgy haute couture, holding a champagne glass. And there she was—as Rosa—by his side. Also beautiful. Also dressed in the latest fashion and firmly ensconced in the high life. Wearing a three-carat blue diamond ring, studded with twists of black and white diamonds.

The attendant gentled Claudia onto her back. "Give yourself a little time to readjust. No one's chasing you, you know."

But they were!

Or, they had been. Since Rosa and Damian's honeymoon in Paris, life had become a game of cat and mouse with INTERPOL.

On their wedding night, Rosa had learned that Damian was a fraud artiste (he loved calling himself that; "con man" was too plebeian) and lived luxuriously by scamming people. He mixed both targets and methods frequently to avoid capture. Damian concealed his occupation from friends by claiming to be the obscenely rich heir of a powerful Bulgarian family.

At first, Rosa was horrified. After seeing Damian in action, though, she slowly warmed to his tricks. Soon, she joined him.

The law, never far behind, provided an unending source of adventure.

Their lives together vaporized when she reemerged from Switch.

How could she bear to return to her mundane reality, sitting around, waiting to die?

"Well, your vitals look remarkably good for someone who's been in an induced coma for a week. How do you feel?"

Miserable, she thought. "As well as a ninety-two-year-old can expect, I suppose."

"Excellent!"

"Grams, what's the matter?" Jerrod helped her sit up against the headboard and set a decades-old breakfast-in-bed tray in front of her.

Her lip curled at the black metal surface, decorated with a painted floral design, long-ago faded. Years of dust, miniscule crumbs, and spilled liquids, never thoroughly cleaned from its crevices, made it slightly tacky and thoroughly gross. They should have thrown it out long ago. How could she ever have thought such a cheap, unsophisticated item was charming?

For that matter, how had she lived so long in such an unattractive home, surrounded by things Damian and Rosa would have scorned? The high life was the only life for the person Claudia had become.

She stared at the Saturday morning meal her grandson had prepared for her: a poached egg, fruit bowl, fresh croissant, and steaming mug of coffee. "It looks wonderful, dear." Her voice sounded as bereft of enthusiasm as she felt.

Jerrod scooted the table over a bit and sat on the edge of her bed. She hadn't laundered the sheets, hadn't even changed out of her nightgown for a week. Since her return from Switch.

She must reek. But what difference did it make?

Nothing appealed to her anymore. She dreaded the thought of beginning each day in her drab bedroom, on this old-fashioned bed. Dreaded opening her eyes to another chapter of boredom and pain.

Switch was all she wanted, all she craved. The only thing that could satisfy her.

Jerrod cocked his head to the side and lifted her shriveled hand. *No, that thing isn't a hand; it's a jumble of bones,* she thought. She wiped the corners of her eyes, pretending to be doing what she needed to do dozens of times daily because of her annoying runny eyes.

She was so sick of life.

"I blame myself for your... What is it, Grams? Depression? You haven't been the same since you returned from Switch. You're wasting away. Sometimes I think a stranger has taken over my grandmother's body. What did they do to you?" He was growing agitated. Angry. "Or was the program they plugged you into upsetting? Please! You haven't told me anything."

She smiled at him. Sadly. How could she tell her grandson that she'd embraced a life of crime with a handsome man who was more exciting, more alive than anyone she'd known in real life? That all she wanted was to return to him, knowing she never could?

Jerrod would never agree to fund another Switch session for her. In a way, he *was* responsible for her current state. It was no use telling him that, though. He wouldn't understand.

Claudia's mind flung back to the scene on Rosa and Damian's wedding night as they strolled along a tiny Paris street, alive with bistros and brasseries, toward one of the city's most elegant restaurants.

"Wait here," Damian had told Rosa, who was too surprised to object.

He trotted a half block ahead of her, looking like a model in his well-fitted suit. After crossing the street, he wove around passersby until he reached the sidewalk seating area of a bistro. At the first table, he smiled and, in perfect French, asked if the couple was enjoying their meal. "Oui, oui monsieur," they answered. He bowed his head and moved on to two other tables.

At the third, the dining couple had yet to pay the bill, left in a guest check book on their table. "I hope madam and monsieur were satisfied with their meal and service." "Oui, oui." "Excellent. I'll take this for you." Within three minutes, Damian was at her side again with the man's credit card in his pocket, several hundred meters beyond the restaurant.

Rosa had been mortified.

Damian slowly wore down her objections. "I never hurt anyone," he assured her. To prove it, after paying for their dinner with the stolen card, Damian melted it.

The second scam didn't seem quite as bad to her.

Soon, Rosa was helping Damian conjure up ways to defraud people. Neither of them wanted to destroy people's lives. Their goal was to pilfer only the money people would have wasted anyway.

"I... I'm sorry to worry you, dear," Claudia told Jerrod now. "I'll be okay. Just give me a little time."

Claudia had considered several ways to take money from Jerrod. Scruples weren't the problem; she mainly feared being caught. Plus, well, he *was* her grandson.

It wasn't until that evening, exactly seven days after her return, that Claudia figured out how to reenter Switch. This time, she'd order the longest session available. And she wasn't going to waste it on a quotidian scenario. This time, she'd *really* live.

Again she lay on a gurney in a clean room while two techs bustled around, attaching sensors to her nearly naked form.

She focused on the program ahead. She'd opted for the year 2030, when regular people began skydiving from the edge of space. She'd chosen the program because of its risks, but thinking about them now scared her. She squeezed her eyes tightly.

"Everything all right, Mrs. Campbell?" the young woman asked.

She was *going* to do this. "Yes, I'm okay."

"Almost there," the young man said. Months ago, Claudia would have considered him a boy. That was before she married Jack and Damian.

She shifted her gaze to the wall and again her thoughts raced. Did she really want this? She could be facing a puncture in her jump suit that would create gas bubbles in her bodily fluids. Her blood would literally boil. Or she could end up in a flat spin that would whip her around up to 250 rotations a minute, stealing her breath away or even bursting her eyeballs. A collision or blackout could also take her life.

Actually, a blackout didn't seem so bad. That would be okay.

She hated leaving Jerrod with no explanation. At least she'd met him in the hallway that morning, rising to wish him a good day—a good life, really, though she couldn't say that without alerting him to her plan. She'd set her left hand on his arm. "Don't worry about me, Jerrod. I'll be fine." Thankfully, he didn't register the absence of her wedding ring. Before she sold it, she hadn't taken it off since her wedding day. With the money, she bought a two-week session, which meant a year inside Switch.

"Okay, then," the young woman said. "You're all set."

Claudia inhaled deeply.

"Hope this is your best experience yet." The woman settled the mask on Claudia's face. "Please count to ten for me."

Claudia-turned-Rochelle's eyes opened slowly, as though awakening after a long sleep. After half a second, they popped wide, like a goby fish. Her lips parted to scream, but something was clamped over her mouth, her nose, her chin. Even pulling her head back was impossible.

"Hey, Rochelle. Everything okay?"

Who was Rochelle? And why was a man's voice inside her head? Her focus turned from the visor in front of her face to the view outside. Her heart stopped, or skipped a few beats, or did something else abnormal, because the voice was back.

"Rochelle! Speak to me."

She shut her eyes to block the panorama beyond her face mask: the curvature of Earth; its azure painted with cloudy swirls.

Then her mind cleared. "Um, yeah Phil. I'm fine. I was disoriented for a second. I'm all right now."

Phil was twenty-two-year-old Rochelle Moreau's jump team leader on this, her first dive from near space. This suit, the helmet, visor, gloves, and special boots were her protection from one of the planet's most dangerous climates.

"You're falling at four hundred miles per hour already."

"Cool."

Phil's staccato *ha-ha-ha*s made her smile.

Despite her speed, Rochell's jump—which she remembered now had begun at 135,000 feet above the Earth—felt calm.

"You're up to 600 mph now," Phil said a short time later.

Now Rochelle laughed. This was amazing. She shifted her orientation with a slight movement. During freefalls at lower altitudes, this was easy. Out here, so far from the Earth's surface, it felt different. Her throat constricted at the passing thought of being stranded in space. That was impossible; she wasn't out nearly far enough.

As she plummeted, Rochelle could make out mountains and large bodies of water.

She jostled to the right to try to identify a shape, then something went wrong. An invisible force shoved her. The next moment, she was spinning. No, no, *no*. This was bad. Very bad. If she didn't get herself under control, she'd soon be nothing but sausage in a fancy coat, splatting onto the frying pan of the New Mexican desert floor.

Fear enveloped her. How many rotations a minute was she up to?

"Push against the spin, Rochelle!"

I can't, she thought. *I'm gonna die up here.*

"Spread your arms and legs into a layout position," Phil barked. "Do it now!"

Rochelle obeyed. Almost instantly, her spinning slowed. Soon, the ground was in focus again.

Good thing Phil was such a hard-ass.

She heard him exhale.

"How fast am I going?" Her record before was 500 mph.

"You've reached 800 mph."

She wanted to laugh. Spread-eagle, she spotted fields and rivers below. Then buildings and roads came into focus.

"You're at four minutes, Rochelle. Ten thousand feet. Time to open the chute."

The sudden yank, which always felt gentle at lower altitudes, felt like a punch after freefalling for so long.

Soon, the toe of Rochelle's right boot touched down. She loped clumsily for ten gigantic steps, then threw her arms into the air before falling onto her knees, crying.

She had to do this again.

At the completion of twenty-five successful jumps, Rochelle became a record-holder in the world of space-chuting. By then, she felt invincible.

On her twenty-sixth jump, 363 days after her first, Rochelle Moreau slammed into a flock of migrating Greater Sandhill Cranes at 6,000 feet.

She did not survive.

About the story

"Switch" came to me as a sort of spin-off of the YA SF novel I'm working on called Skin Changers. In that book, teens are the ones to the immersive VR program. Its purpose is to help them grow in empathy.

But what if old people - people like Claudia in "Switch," who grew up before the age of computers - could enter that type of program? What scenarios would they choose? How would it change them? Would reentering "life" again as young people become addictive? So many questions could be explored. Some, in pain and without hope of for a better personal future like Claudia, might use the program as a final solution to their desperation.

A question for the author

Q: What five words describe you?

A: creative, organized, quiet, purposeful, and thoughtful

About the author

If Lisa Clark could enter a program like Switch, she'd go 1) back to Israel 1,999 years ago (but her avatar would have to know the local languages) 2) a thousand years back to sit on Mauna Kea Hawaii to stargaze 3) back to see herself as a teenager (though she's not sure they'd allow that). While waiting for that tech to be developed, she'll try to make the best of the world we've got.

lisakclark.com

The Three Sisters

Keith Azariah-Kribbs

Once upon a time there were three brothers who lived with their parents in the midst of a vast forest. If there were any other people in the forest, they knew nothing of them, for they found no trails other than those they themselves had blazed, and they found no pits for iron in the bogs other than those they themselves had dug, and they discovered no hewn trees other than those they themselves had hewn.

The three young men grew well in the midst of this forest until they had mastered their trades and wanted for nothing. For none could track or hunt or cure hides and weave cloth so well as Wulfstan, and none could forge iron or steel or fire molded clay into vessels so well as Odduin, and none could better coax the barley or the flax from the fields or encourage the ash trees to produce fairer and straighter limbs than Baldry. In their skills they were masters, and their home was filled with carved wood and stone and with jewels and wrought gold and silver the envy of any prince. Other skills they had and shared, but in these, they each were alone the master. But they knew nothing of that, for they supposed themselves alone in the world.

As their lives could not have been bettered with company, it never occurred to the three brothers to wonder why there were no other people in the world. It was just so.

Yet the world could become lonelier still, and the day dawned when the father and mother of Wulfstan, Odduin, and Baldry died. The three brothers found them thus in their bed after the long cool of the night of the autumnal equinox, and straightway prepared for them a suitable burial. Baldry carved a coffin out of a single great branch of a favorite oak, Odduin forged golden hasps, hinges, and handles for the coffin, and Wulfstan fashioned a princely cloak of silver ferrel fur underlain by fine linen and with a clasp of gold adorned with emeralds for their coverlet. And then they placed the coffin to float on the river, and they stood by the bank and watched at twilight until the current carried the coffin so far to the south that the corpse candles over the coffin could no longer be seen in the gathering gloom.

With that, the brothers felt a strange chill fall on their broad shoulders as the dusk descended, and each turned silently to his workshop, but they could not busy themselves with their craft, and instead they sat and wondered at how dark and empty the world suddenly seemed.

For a time and half a time, the three brothers mourned as is fitting, but eventually they decided that the time for mourning was past. And as the strange gloom that had fallen on them had not eased, they took council among themselves.

Odduin, who was regarded as the wisest of the three, gathered his brothers beside the glowing fire of his forge and the warmth of his kiln, and he spoke. "Brothers, we are alone now in the world, and the warmth we had of our family has gone. I can find no joy in my work, for now there is none to take delight in it, no mother to make her presents of golden combs or father to make him gifts of iron tools."

Baldry nodded in agreement. "So it is, brother. What shall I do now with the carved seat I intended for our mother for Yule, or the barley ale I brewed for our father's table?"

"I could make use of that barley ale, if you're truly stuck with it," Wulfstan whispered. "But you're right, brothers. My fine shawls and gowns for our mother—I'm afraid we are going to look very foolish wearing them."

Odduin frowned at his brother, and Baldry laughed, but silently.

"And that is why men marry," Wulfstan declared. "So that they will have someone to please with presents of gold and silks and gems. We must marry."

"But we no longer have mother and father to find us suitable wives," Baldry said.

"And so we must look to this task ourselves," Odduin declared.

"How can we, brother?" Wulfstan replied, "Seeing there are no others in all this great forest wherein we alone wander?"

"We must go beyond the forest, Wulfstan, and seek wives in the wider world. For our father found a wife in this world, unless we are to believe he fashioned her himself out of the clay of the bank or the iron of the bog or the wood of the forest. I will seek to the north, toward the mountains of ice under the pole star. Wulfstan, you shall seek to the west, toward the plains under the setting sun. And you, Baldry, shall seek to the east, toward the hills under the rising sun. We need not search to the south, for we know well that the great forest there is the haunt of demons and dragons and trolls, and we will find no women there."

"Unless there be one there who could daunt demons and dragons and trolls, and she would make a fine, blushing bride, I'd wager," said Wulfstan.

Odduin stood. "For two moons of Islith shall we walk, and then we will return here and we shall know where we are to find our wives."

And so it came to pass. In the morning, Odduin banked the great fire in his forge and closed the flue on his great kiln, Wulfstan set the last of his hides to dry on the racks and doused the fires in his smokehouse and rolled up his great bolts of fine linen, and Baldry harvested the last of the year's grain into his barn and placed a bung in his beer barrel, and then each brother bade the others farewell and they set out.

The moons of Islith passed quickly enough, and at twilight of the last day of the fourth moon, the three brothers stepped from the forest into the clearing alone, and each nodded to the others in mute acknowledgment of the failure of the quest.

Odduin kindled the fires in his forge and his kiln, but he simply sat beside the fire and gazed into its ruddy glow. Wulfstan took up his bow and stepped into the forest to hunt, but he simply sat on a fallen log in the glade until the night's dew covered his shoulders. And Baldry opened his barn, inspected the harvest for mice, and noted that his beer had fermented properly during his absence, though he did not bother to fetch down a mug for himself or his brothers.

The next morning, the three brothers met at the long table and took council.

"Brothers," Odduin said, "In all my wandering I found no women in all the world. I see it is the same with you, Wulfstan, and also with you, Baldry."

"Yet our father had a wife," Baldry observed.

"Even so. It may be that in some way he fashioned her himself. Therefore I propose, brothers, that we do this thing out of our craft. For my part, I am a master of iron and clay. I will set to this task tomorrow morning. I advise you to do likewise. See here. I have returned with the sacred waters taken from the well of Uldar at the foot of the mountains of ice, guarded by the nymphs. It may be that this water will bring life to iron and clay and wood and stone and hide, if we but fashion a suitable vessel to contain it. But be warned, for the nymphs, grudging my taking of their water, warned me that although this water brings life, so also does it assure strife and pain."

"Strife and pain come to all that live, brother," Baldry said. "Except to the nymphs of the well of Uldar. We shall attempt this task."

And so the next morning Odduin set the clay to fire in the kiln and the iron to heat in the forge. Wulfstan took his finest furs and his softest cloth and began to stitch them together, and Baldry began to carve the finest wood, after settling on rowan for his beloved. Into the working of their materials, the brothers mingled the waters stolen from the well of Uldar. And after laboring until dusk on this work, each brother left to take his rest. And so they continued for many days.

Now, it was unfortunate, if understandable, that the brothers had avoided searching the demon and dragon and troll haunted forest to the south, for had they done so, they might have discovered the mighty city of Ib that lay below the great forest. In this evil city there are many women, though few of them honest enough to wed, and many men as well, though few of them suited for much other than craft and intrigue.

The citizens of this city were likewise afraid of the great forest to the north, knowing it to be the haunt of terrible fiends that delighted to rend the flesh of city people particularly. Yet they coveted the lumber of this forest, which they dared not cut. Instead, they gleaned whatever logs floated down the river from time to time, regarding them as gifts from the gods, and the gods were especially generous after the great storms descended from the ice mountains in the far north. And the people of Ib coveted the gold and gems that they found in the gravels and sands along the banks of the river, washed down from hidden veins of untold riches somewhere in that forest.

Thus the people of Ib spent many hours in the reaches of the river just above the city, collecting goods with which to barter or to fashion their cruel idols and elegant seats of power. And so it came to pass that Freydor, the fisher, who cast his nets into the waters of the river just above the city and had occasionally fished as much as a furlong upstream into the forest, though remaining watchful for demons and dragons and trolls along the banks, found the drifting casket containing the remains of the three brothers' parents.

Freydor was astonished at the quality of the casket, the elegantly carved and polished oak wood, each end of the casket decorated with the likeness of a dragon's head, the sides of the vessel adorned with beautiful nymph's faces and terrible wolves, alternating down the sides of the casket. He marveled at the quality of the gold hinges and hasps, each in the shape of a great lion's paw, and he thrilled at the sight of the coverlet, the ferrel furs finer than those worn by the corrupt Prince Ladlow, the linen suitable for Princess Asriel's shift, and the golden clasp, wrought in the likeness of an angel with inlaid silver and crusted with emeralds, more magnificent than the crown that sat atop the dissipated brow of King Durac himself.

Freydor was a craftsman of some repute, but he acknowledged that the men who fashioned this vessel were his masters. And he divined that three separate hands had been at work here, one on the wood, another on the gold, and yet a third on the furs and fabrics.

Now, three was a number of some interest to Freydor, for he had three daughters of surpassing loveliness, and he was loath to see them wed to mere tradesmen of the city of Ib. For the men of Ib were grasping, thoughtless, frivolous creatures, and they required of their women both stature and wealth or they would not take them to wife. Yet Freydor fancied his daughters as far above the noble women of Ib as the soaring hawk is above the humble, if practical, kingfisher. Moreover, Freydor knew his daughters for honest women, and he would not see them bound to the worshippers of the lying god Yerolka, who was currently fashionable in Ib and who gave men mastery over their wives in measure beyond their desert, and who encouraged women to cultivate deceit as their revenge for this abuse.

Thus Freydor pondered this matter deeply for some hours. Then, just as the sun touched the western horizon, he devised his plan to send his daughters to wed these unknown craftsmen. Such men were obviously unwed, for no wife of Ib would approve such an extravagance as this coffin, and they must surely match his daughters well, and in addition, such a match would establish his claim to a share of their wealth. After all, Freydor too was a man of Ib.

So Freydor took the bodies from the casket and brought them to the bank of the river and buried the two passengers with all due rites under a ledge of red sandstone, said to be particularly favored by the dead on account of the fossils of ancient sea creatures it bore. The corpse lights continued to burn over the newly dug grave, so he knew that the rites he performed were acceptable to the dead, who would now rest quietly. Then he concealed the casket under a low hanging bush at the river's edge, and he returned home and called his three daughters to his side.

The first, Mathilda, was tall and pale and had hair the color of flax and cold, blue eyes under a noble, lofty brow. He held out to her a magnificent necklace of silver and diamonds. "Mathilda, this is your dowry. Remember that you are stately, you rise above your peers as an elm tree, yet you are graceful like the willow. Put on your blue gown, adorn yourself with this necklace, and prepare to meet your husband."

To the second, Nerita, voluptuous, green eyed, hair the color of burnished copper, he held out a torque of red gold threads, crusted with rubies and woven around a core of dark utta wood. "Nerita, this is your dowry. Know that you are lithe and supple like the river otter, and as cunning as the mink. Put on your green gown, adorn yourself with this torque, and prepare to meet your husband."

And to the third, Lirila, dark of skin, black eyed, and raven haired, he gave a necklace of onyx set in ebony and iron and hematite. "Lirila, this is your dowry. You are quiet and mindful, yet of the three you are the strongest for those very reasons. Put on your white gown and this necklace of nighted onyx and prepare to meet your husband."

Each of his daughters did as she was commanded, and then they stood before him, each of them more lovely than any other in Hyperborea. "Now, my daughters," Freydor said. "Come with me to the river. I will set you in a vessel and you will sail up the river that enters the great forbidden forest. See that you do not approach the bank, lest you be taken by a demon or a dragon or a troll, but sail straightway until you come to the settlement of your husbands, the men who crafted this vessel, and there will you live. You will know these men by the quality of their houses, the wood, and the iron, and the gold, and the great riches of their home."

And Freydor set a sail on the coffin and a rudder, and then he set his daughters within, and with the first light of the morning and a fair southern wind, they set sail against the current, and Freydor stood on the banks and watched as they disappeared out of his sight, and still he remained on the bank for a long while after. At last, Freydor felt a strange chill fall on his narrow shoulders, and he went silently to his workshop and busied himself with mending his nets. After all, Freydor was a man of Ib.

Mathilda, Nerita, and Lirila found a fair wind behind them, and so after three days they came at last to where the settlement of the three brothers lay, which they knew by virtue of the rich cloth of gold banners fluttering beside the landing and by the pylons topped with great wooden heads of dragons carved in the same fashion as those on either end of the coffin. And it was darkest night, so the sisters ran their boat against the bank and concealed it under a bush, and then they stole silently into the settlement and wondered at the great riches in the carven wood, the stone, and the banners that fluttered below golden lamps affixed to masts of iron.

The three sisters came at last to Baldry's workshop. Within, they found magnificent carvings of wood, figures of beasts and nymphs, angels and demons. Many of the figures were adorned with gilt, or with jewels of rare fire and color that lighted the workshop even in the darkness.

And in the center of the room, they found the figure of a woman carved of rowan wood, seated in an ivory chair, adorned with fine woven linen and crowned with a wreath of willow leaves fashioned from emerald and silver.

"Perhaps it is an image of the maker's goddess," Lirila said.

"Perhaps it is," Mathilda replied. "But this is a rare chance, and I will not let it pass. Would men of such great substance as these take a fisherman's daughter to wife?" And she took the crown from the statue and set it on her own brow. "Here I shall sit until the morning," she announced.

"This is not wise," Lirila warned her sister. "Soon enough the maker will learn the truth of it."

"The craftsman creates the image because he longs for the true. Let him make of it what he will," Mathilda replied.

So her sisters removed the statue to the forest and concealed it beside the boat.

Next they came upon Wulfstan's workshop, and they marveled at the fine furs and the heads of mighty beasts mounted upon the walls. The weapons of the hunt lay upon a table, a long bow and a heavy spear and a great sword. Nerita took up a fur of the lithe cemerr and stroked it against her cheek as they explored. And in the center of the workshop, they found the figure of a women, cleverly stitched together from silken soft hides and fabrics twisted so finely that the threads could not be seen, and this figure was crowned with the hair of the copper colored tira wolf, rarest of all predators. On her brow, she bore a circlet of rude, red hammered gold, set with uncut emeralds. Nerita nodded approval, took the circlet, and set it on her brow. "So it is here just as it was in the other room. Sisters, here I shall sit until the morning." And her sisters removed the figure of furs and hides and silks and concealed it beside the boat.

Lastly they came to Odduin's forge and kiln, the room smoky and dark, a ruddy warm glow filling the air. The walls were lined with weapons of black iron, and the tables laden with gold and silver, wrought in fine wires and in massive plates, and they found jewels, raw and cut, heaped into coffers.

And in the center of the room, they found a statue of a woman, cast of black iron, adorned with dark jewels, onyx and jet and ebony wood. On her dark brow, she wore a circlet of polished black dragonclaw, bearing a single large gem seemingly black, but bearing a red fire that flashed forth at certain angles. Lirila could not resist a smile as she took the circlet and set it on her own brow, where it fit comfortably, but then, ashamed of her boldness, she set the crown aside on a workbench.

"Here you shall sit, Lirila, until the morning," her sisters announced. And her sisters removed the iron figure and concealed it beside the boat.

Then they each returned to the seat each had claimed and remained there until the morning. But Lirila did not place the dragonclaw crown upon her brow.

The pleasures and horrors of Hyperborea may be more clearly illuminated than in other realms, the pain and the ecstasies may be more keenly felt than in more mundane districts, but this they have in common with those of the rest of the world—neither of them lasts forever.

Each of the brothers was astonished at the success he had had in conjuring his wife. Each of these women was more fair than he could have hoped for, and their transformation into beautiful, loving, devoted brides was more complete than any of them had dreamt possible. Even more felicitous, the three wives seemed much at ease with one another, and at this the brothers were most astonished, for had the nymphs of the well of Uldar not warned the brothers that the waters of the well, though they could bring life to mere clay, would also breed enmity and strife?

And so for a time and half a time, the brothers and their wives lived together in complete harmony and bliss. Yet as is the case with such matters, difficulties were bound to arise, and so they did, to the misfortune of all.

And it came about in this way.

Wulfstan it was who first saw the change. For copper-haired Nerita had decided to cut her hair, a custom of her and of her sisters from of old, for their hair grew exceedingly fast and thick, and in the warm months they would often trim their locks to a cooler length. This Nerita did, and upon walking into Wulfstan's workshop, the great hunter, stitching together a fine gown of cemerr trimmed silk, the which her husband intended to present her as a gift, she so surprised him that he drove his needle quite through his thumb.

Bellowing in surprise, his thumb in his mouth, Wulfstan gaped at his wife. "How has your hair come away, my love?" he asked her.

"My hair, my husband?"

"No pelt treated by my hand ever loses its fur, wife. I have seen the beast shed its fur in the warmth of the year, Nerita, but I made you with nothing but winter fur in its richest and fullest state. And see here! Your beautiful hair!"

Instantly Nerita saw that he did not approve, but she was as sinuous as the river otter, both in her limbs and with her tongue. She did not care much for the close examination Wulfstan seemed intent upon making of her, so before he could rise from his work table and approach her, she slipped from his grasp and raised her chin in delicate hurt and turned for the door, stopping only briefly to cast an offended look back at her husband, the first such look of its kind. "If you do not approve of me, you have only yourself to blame, for you yourself fashioned me."

"So I did," Wulfstan said doubtfully, rooted to the floor as she disappeared through the door.

At once, Nerita repented her words, but she did not reply.

Baldry set aside the sapphire adorned silver ring he was polishing, the which he intended to present his wife the next evening, and he examined her curiously as she stood in the doorway to his workshop, the bright sunlight framing her from behind and highlighting her flaxen hair, scintillating with the diamonds he had strung for her willow-green ribbons. At least, he admired what of her hair was left on her head, for, as had her sister, Mathilda had cut her hair short.

"I have seen the willow cast its leaves in the fall, but never in the summer, my love…"

Mathilda raised a golden eyebrow at her husband as a charming blush stole across her pale cheek. "What does my husband mean with this riddle?" she asked.

Baldry stood and crossed the floor to her, and took a shortened lock in his hand, twining it between his fingers lovingly, yet the look on his face was appraising, craftsmanlike. Unwilling to explain herself, she simply turned from Baldry and started for the house, casting but a single glance back at her husband as she said, "If you do not approve of me, you have only yourself to blame, for you yourself fashioned me."

"So I did," Baldry replied slowly.

And Mathilda repented her words, but she did not reply.

Lirila sat before her glass, considering the long black tresses that fell in waves about her shoulders and spilled wantonly down her dark throat and across her breast. When her husband Odduin had first found her in his workshop so many months ago, sitting in the very seat where he had left the iron likeness of a maiden, he believed that his project had succeeded beyond his hopes. Then he looked first into her eyes.

"Your glance is black as pitch, maiden," he had said, knowing well that now she heard his words with living ears. "And yet I do see the fire of the forge in them, burning even now. Will it ever be cooled?"

"It will not, my husband, so long as we love."

"How could I have hoped to have succeeded so wonderfully? Yet, there is more here than iron and clay, I think. I cannot forge a soul in that furnace," Odduin said. His face grew dark and grim. "And it is plain that you are a living soul. There is more here than my craft or the waters of the spring of Uldor."

She wondered if the ruse was a failure. She wanted to reveal the truth to him, willing to take the risk herself, yet she feared for her sisters, and as she was not quite sure what he did suppose her to be, she was afraid to ask.

Odduin drew near and reached out to touch her, his hand drawing near hesitantly, as if he still feared that the fires of her forging might burn within. Yet he found her dark smooth throat warm, her long black hair silken and soft.

Then he fell to his knees and plighted his troth to her that instant. When she received his pledge, he rose and placed the dragonclaw crown upon her head, bearing a single large black gem in the center that cast back no light except, at certain angles, a single flash of deepest garnet red. In placing that crown on her head, she felt a sudden horror, and she would have set the thing aside at once and told him all, but she did not. And she had carried this heavy secret in her heart, for in truth, she loved him well.

And so Lirila now sat before her mirror of polished crystal framed in gold, her silver shears in her hand, and she hesitated.

Her reverie was disturbed by the sound of agitated weeping outside her window, and she crossed the room to look out upon her sisters, wringing their hands upon the paving stones. Fetching them to a quiet grove, she heard their stories.

That night as she slept, Lirila was awakened by the sound of her husband's voice, conferring with his brothers. She recognized Wulfstan's strong grumbling words: "'If you do not approve of me, you have only yourself to blame, for you yourself fashioned me.' That is what she said to me! This woman, divine in form and perfection—she blamed—me!"

"And so it was with Mathilda, just so!" Baldry said, his voice a sinister murmur. "And since then, she has not spoken to me. But Lirila, brother. What of her? Has she too shown any signs of corruption or defect?"

"She has not, nor would I believe that she could, for—for whatever she is, fairy or spirit, there is surely more in her than I could forge with my craft."

"Nonsense. They have said it themselves! She is your work, brother. As is mine and as is Baldry's. We fashioned them to perfection, and so they were perfect. Or, almost perfect. And this must be mended," Wulfstan said.

"And so it must," Baldry agreed. "For mine, a bonfire I think. And from the ashes of her burning I shall create again. I still have some drops of the waters of the spring of Uldor, and my first essay in this craft was so near to perfection…"

"Then it is settled. Our craft is not perfected yet, not worthy of the great task we undertook. We shall begin again, and then we shall have all as it should be."

Lirila was not certain which brother spoke those last words, but she did not wait to inquire further.

She flew to her sisters' sides and drew them down to the riverside wherein they had concealed the effigies so many months ago. There they still lay, hidden in the tangled jasmine alongside the coffin.

"Now, sisters, all is lost. We must fly!"

"Have our husbands discovered our secret?" Mathilda asked, her cheek pale and wan.

Lirila laughed bitterly. "Would they had thought us goddesses, or fishermen's daughters! Our husbands have decided that they must repair their work, and they mean to begin by destroying us that they might create again. Let us replace these images in their workshops and get us gone before they destroy us in their desire to perfect us."

And so they did, but not a moment before time, for just as the first light appeared in the eastern sky, they heard a cry from Baldry's workshop, and then another from Wulfstan's, and at last, a cry from Odduin's forge, and they knew that the images had been discovered.

Lirila wondered at that cry, and she hesitated at the water's edge, but her sisters drew her toward the boat.

And with that, they betook them to the coffin, pushed it out into the current, and began the long journey south toward the evil city of Ib.

The three sisters tarried in Ib for a time and half a time, until even after they had brought forth the children of Odduin, Wulfstan, and Baldry.

Lirila made it her custom to walk along the bank of the great river with her child in the twilight. She was careful to stay clear of the forest, for she would not have her treasure stolen by demon or dragon or troll. She would admire his hair, dark and smooth and fine as if it were onyx spun on a loom of the gods, and his smooth cheek, polished like rosewood from the jungle forest of Umber, and his eyes, burning with the light of Odduin's forge. She wondered if that light would ever be cooled. But she knew it would not, not in this child. For she knew the forge wherein that light had been kindled, and it would never cool.

Yet still the three sisters delayed to return to their husbands, for they fretted about what defect their husbands might still find in their wives.

And the three brothers never repeated their experiment, and they crafted no other images, but rather they adorned the mute things that they had made with their own hands, and remained ever hopeful that one day, they might wake to life again.

But they did not wake to life again, and after a time, it became difficult to imagine that the three women they had fashioned had ever been otherwise.

At last there came a twilight when Lirila espied a craft sailing down the river, and she ran to the bank to see what it might be. She saw that the craft bore the hallmark of the three brothers in the magnificent carven dragon heads at the bow and stern and in the wonderful golden hasps and hinges and in the marvelous silken coverlet that lay over the three figures concealed there. Three corpse lights burned over the princely vessel, and she was filled with horror at the thought of what might lie within. But before she could arrive at the vessel's side, the priests of the lying god Yerolka, at their ritual ablutions in the river, took the vessel and made it fast to the shore and drew back the coverlet to reveal the three effigies the brothers had fashioned.

The priests at once proclaimed this a miracle, for had not the gods sent them their very own images to worship and adore, instead of the vain things before which they had until now prostrated themselves? So they took the images to the temple, cast down the image of Yerolka, and all Ib worshipped the three goddesses in the darkened temple, lit only by the corpse lights that refused to dim.

Lirila brought this news to her sisters at once.

"But what do the burning lights over the figures mean?" Mathilda asked. "That these figures truly lived, after all?"

"Yes, sister," Lirila said. "And ask yourself—what was it that brought life to the effigies?"

And the three sisters, knowing what this must mean, betook themselves to the boat and set sail with their children up the river.

But whether they arrived at last, and what they may have found there, or whether they were taken by a fiend as they sailed through the great forest, none could say. For none in Ib ever ventured into the great forest, knowing it to be the haunt of demons, dragons, and trolls.

About the story

With some stories, I can remember where I was standing when I got the idea. "The Three Sisters" didn't come to me quite so immediately, but seemed to slowly crystallize out of what I have learned from life with my wife and daughters, and about how difficult you can make things for yourself when you worry that you aren't seeing things the way they are. Still, that could be the origin of a lot of stories. The central image of the three women replacing the three brothers' icons with themselves seemed to spring full formed and armored into my head.

A question for the author

Q: What book or books inspired you as a child?

A: There are images in my mind, vague recollections of scenes and settings and disjointed plot fragments really, that I have carried along for as far as my memory goes back. I'm sure that most of them come from traditional fairy stories, Grimm's brothers, Hans Christian Anderson, Appalachian folk tales, and who knows what else. These images seem to be the foundation that underlies everything I write, and I can't even dredge up a recollection of where I got them. I wish I could, for I would love to go back and read them again, but I suspect that what they were wouldn't bear much resemblance to what they have become.

About the author

K.D. Azariah-Kribbs grew up in the hills of east Tennessee, a place where twilight starts early and lasts long. He studied geology in school, but when that didn't answer the big questions he went back for medieval English literature. That didn't quite do it, either. He traveled widely as a prospector, decided southern India has the best climate anywhere, and now writes speculative fiction in Maryland, where it's easy to speculate about how things might have been otherwise.

azariahkribbs.com

April

Bye Bye Skinny Cow

Hamilton Perez

"Excuse me," Cash tried again, "you're not a doctor, are you?" Another bemused look and shake of the head. "Oh, okay, thanks anyway," he said to their backs. The warm bundle in his arms groaned uncomfortably. It was the first Cash had heard from him all day. He took it as a good sign—beggars not choosers and all.

One after the other, people came and went from the office, filtering in and out fluidly by some alien osmosis that always kept Cash at bay. Sure, he could enter. But if he entered uninvited, he might be asked to leave, and then there would be no hope for him.

Cash watched them lead their sick or injured, augmented or gene-spliced companions beside them: furry lizards in need of hormones, bipedal hamsters overdue for flu shots, half-cat half-dog—*cags*—to be spayed or neutered. Unnatural creatures born from science and an excess of money. They all looked at Cash and his raw need with perplexed annoyance.

Are you a doctor? Excuse me, are you a doctor? You're not a doctor, are you? Hey, I'm not asking for money or anything, but are you a doctor?

"I don't carry cash," someone said in passing.

It felt prophetic.

"Young man…" a voice called, "I don't know if you should be out here doing that." An old woman stood behind him, round as Granny Smith apples and just as sour. She was leaving the office with a disgruntled Pekingese in matching attire, and gave Cash a dubious look in passing. "You know there's a shelter just down the street," she said like an accusation.

"Thank you," was all Cash could manage. He didn't want any trouble. He just wanted her to go. Instead she stood there, and Cash felt the weight of her eyes scrub him down from his mop of blond hair to dark-stained pants that quit before his ankles. She sneered at the knobby head of the guitar peeking over his shoulder, and when her eyes fell on the black and white Jack Russell cradled in his arms, she scrunched her face in disapproval. *"Thank you,"* Cash said again to appease her.

Ultimately, the woman merely shook her head and slumped into her car before heading home disgruntled, though Cash felt the itch of her eyes linger on his skin for some time after.

The sun was beginning to set. Business hours were almost up. This was the third office he'd been to today. The others had told him they couldn't help without an appointment. The technician at the last office offered dog treats as a consolation. "He's not eatin…" Cash said on his way out the door.

Now the sky above him reddened and bruised, begged for the cold relief of night. An imminent despair tapped at his back, though still he shook it off. *No… Not yet*, he told it, and occasionally wondered if he'd spoken aloud.

It was almost an hour before a determined looking man in a white button-down and blue tie stepped from the office. His clothes were crisp and perfectly pressed, his shirt tucked flat into his pants. Cash couldn't find so much as a stray dog hair or misplaced button. He was neatness, itself. And that terrified Cash, reminded him of men he'd known growing up: men immaculate on the outside and rotting within.

The man stood before the door, hands on his hips, scanning the strip mall parking lot with furious purpose. When he spotted the trouble, half-hidden behind a stucco pillar, it sent a wave of panic clawing up Cash's spine. Was he about to be berated? Attacked? Asked to leave? *Hey kid, fuck off already*, or *Do you want me to call the police?* A call for help was always a threat. Cash took a deep breath and pulled the Jack Russell in his arms tight against his chest.

"Hi, sir," said Blue-tie, approaching without hesitation. "Can I help you?" The man was on the verge of middle-aged, with crow's feet flanking his eyes and silver creeping through his hair. Still, he called Cash *sir*. Cash didn't know what to make of that—feigned respect or condescension.

"Are you a doctor?" Cash had to force the words from his mouth. He now waited for the inevitable *I'm sorry, you can't be here*, knowing it would break him.

"I am. Who's your friend?"

Cash winced, the response too unexpected. "This is Jack. He's sick." Cash freed one hand to wipe his cheek before it darted back.

The doctor reached out gently and rubbed Jack's head. "Hey, Jack! I'm Doctor Burke." Jack eyed him curiously but otherwise didn't move. He grumbled when the doctor withdrew his hand.

"He says nice to meet you…" Cash muttered.

"What's been wrong with him?"

"He's not eatin…" said Cash. "Then this mornin I couldn't get him to follow me, so I picked him up, but he just fell over. He can't move at all, and I don't have any money or nothin', but I can work. I can brush animals or clean up after em—whatever it takes, I'll do it, you just tell me and I'll do it!"

The doctor raised his hand. "It's okay. Just *breathe...*" Cash didn't argue; he took a breath, and it rattled like loose change all the way down. "Let's not worry about that right now, okay? Let's just take care of Jack. What did you say your name was?"

"Cash," he admitted begrudgingly. The doctor made a face like he misheard him. This was not uncommon. People thought it was a joke. An irony concocted while high. "Like, *Johnny* Cash," he explained.

It was Cash's mother that had named him; she'd always loved the artist more than the arts. When asked why she didn't just name him Johnny, she told him, "Everyone's named Johnny. Nothing special in Johnny. It was always either *Cash* or *Sue*, and your father wasn't about to raise no queer." Cash had long wished they'd gone with Johnny. *Nothing special.*

"Oh, cool!" said the doctor, smiling with straight white teeth. "Well, Cash, why don't you bring Jack inside? I'll take a better look at him there."

The doctor turned back inside, and Cash just stood there paralyzed. Good things were rare enough, and life experience had taught him not to trust them. *There's no cleansing grace but rain*, his father used to say. *And even that can kill you.* Cash felt the fear tugging his arm to go. The soles of his feet itched to leave. But then a wet tongue licked his hand; a soft head nestled in the crook of his arm.

A blonde woman in green scrubs locked the door behind them. She avoided eye contact as they walked past, even when Cash startled at the sharp clack of the bolt. The woman smiled, though not at him.

"Do you want me to wait?" she asked.

"Oh, this shouldn't take long..." said the doctor.

"Thank you! Thank you so much..." said Cash, knowing words were not enough and yet he had nothing else. *Or do I...* he wondered. *Nothing good comes free.* How many times had his father tried to beat that into him? Cash only ever learned the hard way.

The doctor led him down a long hallway, past a never-ending series of closed doors, each one concealing a perfectly useable room, or so Cash figured. They passed an open area where anxious dogs barked from cages and technicians prepped syringes.

An old chocolate lab rose slowly in its cage, opened its mouth to bark, but the sound that escaped was only, "*I love you!*" in a tinny, electric voice. Cash startled at that, and stopped.

"Voice box implantation," said the doctor casually, as though that explained all. He gestured Cash onward.

"*I love you! I love you! I love you!*" said the labrador as they walked away, but the hair raised on its back said otherwise.

At the very end of the hall, a door hung partway open. No light came from within. "In here," said the doctor. Cash wondered if it was an order. He stepped inside anyway, waiting for the light, or else the curtain to draw. For it all to be a joke. A trap. For the rug to be pulled out from under him and take the whole world with it. *Wouldn't be the first time...*

The doctor stepped in behind him.

Click!

And then there was light. Sterile, florescent light. The room was barren, save for a hand-washing sink and stainless steel table. Utilitarian in the extreme with one exception. On one of the vast beige walls hung a small painting: yellow dogs running through green fields, circling a red barn under a blue sky. Everything was in primary colors —simple, unjaded things. It was all very bright and happy.

It was also a lie, thought Cash.

Any moment now, the walls would come alive and swallow him. Undercover cops would appear and arrest him for loitering, for drugs, for disappointing his parents. Men in hazmat suits would charge in, restrain him, and drag him away to be experimented upon. No one wonders about the missing homeless.

The doctor shut the door. Was that a lock he heard?

"Why don't you set him there?" The doctor pointed at the table.

Despite his nerves, Cash didn't argue. He laid Jack gently across the table and stepped back, standing rigid as a scar while awaiting the next command or question. The doctor snapped into his blue latex gloves. *Primary colors*, thought Cash. *Lies...*

The doctor probed Jack's ears, listened to the whisper of his heart, molested him with rubber fingers. Cash watched the doctor closely for sign of trouble or recognition, for some perverse grin or an *Ah-ha!* But the doctor's eyes were too far away to read, as if they were looking at the space between Jack's molecules—analyzing, scrutinizing, dissecting.

"Are you a musician?"

It took Cash a moment to realize the doctor was speaking to him, not Jack. "I'm sorry?" he said, wondering how he had known and whether the doctor had just revealed his hand.

"The guitar..."

Cash had nearly forgotten about the battered acoustic slung across his back. "Oh," he said, feeling so foolish he nearly smiled before catching himself. "Yes."

The doctor grinned and continued the exam, occasionally muttering soft assurances to Jack, who panted and licked his lips. "What sort of music do you play?" said the doctor.

"Uh… Folk songs. Classic rock. I guess." Keep it short, non-committal, thought Cash. People do all kinds of things with personal information, and music was both his income and his passion, the addiction that fed his addiction. The thing that lifted and crushed him. Like teeth, he supposed.

"That's great!" The doctor smiled at him, warm and kind. "Like Bob Dylan, the Stones?"

At their mention, Cash was triggered. So few wanted to talk music with him anymore—about the messy purity of Richards and Jagger, or how Bob Dylan was a prophet straight from Heaven. Cash's walls tumbled down without him even realizing the earth was rumbling.

"Yeah yeah! Stones, CCR, The Doors. Me and my friend Donald play on street corners, and we try to put our own twist on em, you know, cuz you can't just play it straight without a full band. You gotta get creative to make the sound big and full, but when you think of those really great artists, it's usually just one or two people that made it great, you know, so like, why not simplify their—"

"Would you mind playing something?" asked the doctor, staring deep into Jack's eyes.

"What?" Cash was suddenly aware of how much he'd given away. He felt the heat of every bulb boiling microbes on his skin.

"A song. If you don't mind."

"Is that, uh… allowed?"

"Sure! Why not? Jack seems tense. Might calm him down."

Cash sensed a trap in this, but with Jack helpless and immobile in the doctor's hands there was no point in questioning. He swung the guitar around his shoulder. "Any, uh, requests?"

"What does Jack like?"

Cash smiled without realizing it. He gripped the guitar's neck, strummed the opening riff to "Have You Seen the Rain," and soon his voice cut through the chords with that classic Fogerty twang.

With Cash distracted and relaxed, the doctor continued his exam. He snapped his fingers in front of Jack's eyes, measuring their reactions. Jack blinked belatedly and jerked his head. "Has Jack had any recent head trauma?" asked the doctor.

Cash stopped just before the final chorus and stuttered, the guitar hanging in his arms like a dead thing. He didn't want to tell him about the fight he got into with another homeless person. Jack had jumped into the fray, tearing clothes and flesh and catching a wild punch for his trouble.

"He got in a tussle, yeah. With a dog, yeah."

"He may have brain swelling," said the doctor. "That would explain the gradual paralysis."

"Oh." Cash didn't know what to make of *brain swelling*. Was that a cancer-thing? He imagined Jack's brain blowing up like a balloon, pushing against his skull until it popped.

"That seems the likeliest possibility, though there are other, *rarer* maladies as well." Cash stood frozen, listening helplessly. "Fungal infections, slipped disks, brain tumors—Hell, it could be depression?"

"Depression?"

"Yes. It's not just for people."

"So what do I do?"

The doctor stepped back, hands on his hips, considering. "Well, normally I would suggest an MRI to give us a better sense of what's causing this sort of debilitation. Unfortunately, we don't have an MRI scanner. We're still fairly small and scanners are—as you might imagine—quite expensive."

"I understand." Cash didn't understand. Here they treated animals with cybernetic limbs and pets that were made of other pets. How was this so different?

"The good news is it doesn't change our first course of action. I'm going to give you some anti-inflammatories. If it is brain swelling, this should help Jack recover. If not, it won't hurt him, and we can go from there."

Cash was speechless. Indeed, he could barely breathe. This was more than he'd dared hope. His face felt like a black hole, everything collapsing towards the center in sudden relief. Unbidden tears streamed down his face, forming brown specks on the floor. He dug desperately through his pockets for a napkin or handkerchief.

"It's okay," said the doctor, walking over and placing both hands on Cash's shoulders. "I'm glad to help. But I want to make one thing clear: I wouldn't normally release a dog in this state. He should really be at an intensive care facility. Now, my hope is that this will make him feel better and he'll gradually start to recover... But you should consider how you want to move forward if he doesn't improve."

"Oh."

"Listen, I don't want you to worry any more than you're doing. But if it comes to the point that Jack isn't getting better and he still won't eat, just know that you can bring him here and we'll help him pass on peacefully. Okay?"

Okay? That's how the exam went. At once an affirmation and a question, an ellipsis. Some crisis resolved, some threat left hanging.

Okay... Cash felt anything but. *Come back and we'll kill your dog*, they said. *Okay?*

Home was a small park tucked within the curve of the Watt Bridge onramp. Their sleeping bag was laid along the cement wall so that no passing cars or dog-walkers could see or harass them. No one could tell them to leave or go home. That made this home, Cash figured.

Not so very long before, Cash had migrated nightly from couch to couch. At the very least he'd have a pillow and blanket on somebody's floor. But it was hard doing that with a dog, and harder still since he split with the friends he got high with. It was just the two of them now. He looked out for Jack and Jack looked out for him. Better to be clean in the gutter than dirty in the house, though even that sometimes proved too much.

Cash laid against the bushes that blocked out the wind, with Jack curled up beside him. They'd given the first pill back at the office, but Cash worried it had been too late. A hundred questions crept like cockroaches from the shadows of his mind. What if Jack died in his sleep? What would he do with the body? What would he do with himself? And the worst of them wasn't a question at all, but a hard certainty: he would get high.

It was a comfort cold as anything, but at least it numbed him, removed him from the terror of all this. Cash could go back to being a junkie. He had little enough, but he had that—a backdoor escape that was always near to hand no matter how far he ran. It was either that or face the grief that gnawed his heart like a worm through an apple.

Cash stroked Jack's black and white fur, whispering to him words of love and warmth until his speech slurred and his eyelids grew heavy. *"It's okay, skinny cow... You're okay..."*

Several times he startled at some screech of tires, worried Jack had yelped in pain as his heart gave out. Cash only got back to sleep once reassured by the gentle rise and fall, rise and fall of Jack's breathing.

All through the night, Cash shook from the cold and the fear. His dreams were fierce but vague, shadows dancing and blending together. They kept him panicked, kept him trembling and confused. One moment, he floundered and drowned in a cold, roaring current; the next he was carried by an angry mob, their raised torches singeing his flesh. Here he was lost; there he was ferried helplessly away, as impotent in his dreams as in the waking world.

But in the morning, Cash awoke to a wet nose sniffing his face, and it almost made him cry. His companion stood on all fours, as stable now as he'd ever been.

"Jack!" Cash rolled him to his side and kissed his head, while Jack's tail *smack, smack, smacked* the soft earth beneath them. Cash repeated his name again and again, and each time Jack's head swiveled toward him, panting, smiling. A blessed light had shown, and all the fearful questions now scurried back into their shadows, invisible in the black of his mind, to watch and lurk and wait.

"So dey juss gayoo sum druds, uh?" said Donald, another homeless musician plucking his way from meal to meal. He grinned at Cash, who felt uncomfortable despite trying not to. "Spose ah shuh git a dog too." When Donald spoke, all the gravel and dirt of the streets came up through his voice.

"Not those kinda drugs." said Cash, distracting himself by rubbing Jack behind the ears.

The afternoon sun had baked cement and asphalt into a steamy haze, but they'd found some respite in the shade of an empty alleyway.

"Lemme seeyum," said Donald, hand outstretched. Long dark hair hung in inky clumps over Donald's weather-beaten face, melting into a wild thicket of facial hair flecked with debris. But all of this could not hide the grin, nor the mischief fire in his eyes.

Cash tensed. "They're for Jack," he said, hoping it sounded firm. "They're makin him better."

"Ah juss wanna see," Donald insisted, unblinking. He set his guitar in the felt-lined case beside him, his glare striking bone-deep. Who could guess what those eyes unearthed when they squared on you? What weakness, what fear? Cash handed over the small blue bottle. Donald didn't bother reading the label. He popped the tab and fingered through. "Aw hell..." he said. "Ah cun tay dese."

"Don't," said Cash, clutching the worn neck of his guitar.

"Yoo don ian wanna try? Look a' Jack, man! If dese cun mae im bettuh, juss tink wha dey can do fah us! Open new wirls, new chore progressuns, rhyddms, melodees!"

"Doesn' matter..." said Cash. "Those pills are for Jack."

Donald appraised him through the dark strands of hair that glued to his face and, once satisfied, offered a mere chuckle. It was all just a joke. Just play after all. "Ey, man. Ya don' wanem, ya don' wanem." He handed back the pills.

Cash stuffed the bottle back into his pocket, grateful to have avoided conflict. But when he glanced up, he caught Jack watching him with sharp, unblinking eyes that sent a tide of shame rolling over him.

Somehow, Jack understood what was happening whenever he and Donald got high. He'd whine pitifully, passing worried glances between them. Sometimes this was enough to fortify Cash's resolve. To tell Donald no and mean it. But other times, Cash would look away, and for a few hours find a more complete relief than any other. It was a hard thing to refuse when the world was at turns too hot or too cold, and always stingy with its blessings. But when Cash came out of the fog, he always found Jack lying head down, eyes glazed and unwilling to meet him.

The look Jack gave him now was different. It was as if he were studying Cash, absorbing him in some vague but obvious way.

Donald plucked the open strings of his guitar from e to E. "Leds stot," he said, ever the one to lead. Donald strummed a percussive, palm-muted rhythm that invoked the intro to "Sympathy for the Devil." Cash quickly followed, finger-picking both the piano and bass lines in one unified melody.

Though Donald's speech was nigh unintelligible, when he sang his voice reached beyond language, tapping into some incommunicable ache that throbbed at the core of all living things. Cash, himself, was not without his talents: at turns making a guitar drip with heartache and longing, or charging the air with rowdy, joyous chords. He was digging into the lead when Donald called a stop.

"Wassee doin?"

Cash glanced up and found Jack thumping his paws fitfully against the ground. Terrified, Cash stopped playing. Was this a seizure? A stroke? He jumped to his feet, and Jack followed.

"Jack! You okay, skinny cow?!" Cash feared this odd behavior was a symptom of something new bubbling to the surface, but Jack just smiled back at him, panting happily. "Why'd he do that, you think?"

"Ah dunno, man. Look lite he drummin. Ya say dere wuh awl dat shit iniss brain—"

"Swellin..." said Cash distantly.

"Yah, wull mayee now dat dass gone heez learnin frum you. He wanna play, man, leh im play." Donald dug through his mismatched belongings and withdrew a beat-up pair of bongos. "Ere, man. Lettum play withis." Donald set the bongos in front of Jack who sniffed at them, then looked up to Cash. "Play, man! Play!" Donald encouraged. "Giffussum tunes!"

Cash knew better than to trust Donald's ramblings, but right now he needed the odd distraction. Some simple answer to the questions that hounded him. He strummed the chorus of "Wayfaring Stranger" and Jack thumped his paws discordantly against the bongos, just as Donald suggested.

"Eez geddin ih, man! Eez geddin ih!"

Cash watched, amazed. Jack's timing was off, but he was close, which is nearer than most first-timers, and Jack was also a dog. Cash stopped playing, and Jack sat still.

"I toll you, man. Dem druds opun up the mind! Ere, tae duh bongos. Yoo neum mo den ah do rye now."

At first, nothing happened. Cash had left Donald shortly before dark and spent the early evening "home," trying to teach Jack how to play bongos. Cash played his guitar, something with an easy rhythm, but Jack just stared passively. "Come on, skinny cow..." Cash muttered.

Jack whined back at him.

The night was growing late. Already the city slept and dreamed. A lazy wind yawned through the park. Cash rubbed the weariness from his eyes, but found them no less heavy, and his fingers were growing sore.

Cash lifted Jack's paws and physically pressed them against the skins. Jack whined and sat back down. This was ridiculous, Cash thought. He picked his guitar from the ground beside him and began plucking another melody from its strings.

The song was new to him, something sweet and light. But it kept urging him quicker, calling for the panicked clamor of chords between the finger-picking. His easy glide across the guitar's neck became frantic, his hands clawing, clutching, running across the neck.

Up and down and to the sides, the song pulled him—quicker, quicker—as if it were trying to get somewhere. His hand was a raft drifting helpless down the neck, singing its narrow path around discord and calamity.

Cash was so focused on navigating the song he didn't catch when the bongos came in. They popped, cracked, and snapped with life. They gave a perilous timing, like the river of song was urging him towards a fall. The finger-picking turned to hard, crunching chords. But soon even they were blending—sliding and hammering and crashing together.

Together, he and Jack twisted through the melody, pulling something somber and forlorn from its sweet beginnings. They played until Cash grew tired, when the chill of pre-dawn numbed his fingers and only the tears warmed his face. The song ended on a precipice, its fall unwritten—or else, just a bit further downstream.

Cash sighed, wiped his eyes and looked to Jack who watched him curiously, then ran one paw over his own face.

The next day Cash showed Donald all that Jack had learned, and Donald sat back with a smile and said, "Wuh godda drummuh." They practiced all afternoon, tucked away in a dank but undisturbed alley, running through their most popular songs until Jack developed a beat for each one.

Cash showed Jack a few tricks and soon his rhythms became more intricate, his paws crossing over and under each other. He watched the humans carefully as they strummed and plucked their strings. And they watched him also.

Donald laughed between verses, delighted by their new gimmick. Occasionally, he'd change the words and sing his joyful thoughts to Cash. He'd sing of Jack's focus and how you could almost see the wheels turning behind his eyes.

Cash smiled and nodded while he played, but he didn't see any of that. He saw eyes that never blinked or looked away. Eyes that gave nothing—only took.

Around five o'clock, the traffic outside the alley started to pick up, and Donald announced they were ready. "C'mon," he said, grinning. "Almose appy our."

They found a street corner along a popular bar block and claimed it. Occasionally they'd see some other hopeful street performer pass by. "*Kee moothin...*" Donald would growl at them, and Cash was simultaneously grateful and shamed to have Donald there, standing on his side.

Before they started, Cash took Jack into a nearby coffee shop to bathe in the bathroom sink. When a nervous barista stepped up to address him, Cash quickly said, "He's a service animal!" Donald had once told him that businesses couldn't refuse you with a service animal. They couldn't ask for proof or documentation either. They just had to take your word for it. Often enough, this worked, though Cash learned not to try the same place twice.

Cash rinsed his face, arms, and hair. He tried to scrub out the stains in his clothes with little to no success. One thing he'd learned over the years: no one wants to look poverty in the face. The less homeless you looked, the more money you made.

He scrutinized himself there before the mirror. Wondered if he looked truly homeless, or just disheveled, if he was "put together" now. Either way, he felt lighter without the weight of the world's refuse on his shoulders.

He gave Jack a once over with warm water, which Jack groaned passively about. Before they left, he held Jack under the hot air dispenser to dry him off.

"Ya luhk good," said Donald once they emerged.

"Thanks," said Cash, smiling like he'd finally washed out a stain that had stuck to him for years.

"Ah's talkin ta Jack!" Donald had a good laugh at that.

Cash set Jack against the wall of a building and placed the bongos in front of him. He and Donald stood on either side of Jack, guitars slung around their necks like some fateful albatross.

The first piece they played was an old Irish folksong. Donald started off slow and melodic with a thick, husky voice that was made for open fields and foggy days. Then Cash joined in, strumming hard and heavy, and with him was Jack, sitting upright and thumping his skins, as wild and crackly as fire.

People were drawn almost immediately. They stopped from their walks and were late to their dinners and dates. Meanwhile, all three of them dug into the music, grinning like mad ghosts. Jack even bobbed and swayed, just like Cash.

They played old classics and songs they'd written. People sang along to the ones they knew, and a brief community formed there on the streets. Between songs, there was laughter and applause, cheers and flashes of light.

Afterwards, people approached Cash, wanting to know what kind of pet-mod he'd gotten for Jack. *Was it implant or hormone treatment? What did they charge? Who's your doctor?*

Cash just smiled at all their questions and ideas. "Jack's an all-natural skinny cow," he told them proudly. "We don't mess around with those drugs and stuff." Even as he said it, Cash felt the lie of it. But for a moment, he enjoyed the lie—the *What if?*

Several people asked to have their picture taken with Jack. Cash said of course, but Donald cut in: "Pithuhs aw ten dollas." Money poured into the open guitar case, easy as that.

At the end, Donald's case was lined with bills and rattling with change. The two of them felt rich as kings. They ran their hands through it all, not bothering to count their plunder, just taking it in with their fingers and eyes. Jack circled around them, tail wagging. He barked gruffly to be included and threw his own paws in as well.

When they divvied up their spoils for the night, Donald claimed the larger share.

"I don't know if that's right..." Cash tried. "We're partners. And they paid to see Jack play."

"Thass rye," said Donald. "Mah bonjoes."

By the third night, people were waiting on the corner for them to arrive. Cash and Donald didn't know what to make of that, so they smiled uncomfortably, pushed through, and took their places—backs against the wall, as they always were. There was laughter and applause as they set up their instruments, and they didn't know what to make of that either.

Cash didn't like crowds. They made him nervous. In the susurrus of shifting bodies he thought he heard a whisper: *You don't belong.* But when the music started, that sound was stamped out. Jack's drumming popped and cracked and killed the whispers, and Cash dared allow a smile. There were plenty now to go around.

After the show—and the inevitable request for pictures—one man lingered behind. He was dressed in tan slacks, their fold lines raised and prominent, and a pale blue polo buttoned all the way to his neck. Cash recognized him immediately. He was what Donald called an "easy mark."

More than that, Tom Lord was a businessman. He introduced himself and told them he'd recently opened a café downtown. On Tuesday nights, they had live performers but only the bands' friends showed up, and they just took up seats. Tom Lord was in need of something special, something unique, something that would draw people in.

"What do you say, guys? I'd pay you, of course, and you'd get all the coffee you can drink!"

"Sounds great!" said Cash. He couldn't believe how things were turning around for him. At this rate, he could soon afford new clothes, he could get a job, he might finally get him and Jack off the streets. *Clean* was the word, the future he imagined for himself, and it burned at the back of his mind like a stage light.

But Donald shook his head. "Ah dunno ih thass rye fuh us."

Cash looked to him, confused. This offer was only good news for them. Cash wanted to speak up, to take charge, but instead he followed Donald's lead.

Tom Lord looked distressed. "Uh, okay," he said. "How about this! Free meals. Eh? We make a heck of a grilled cheese." He grinned ear to ear, as pleased with himself as his mother surely was.

Things only got better, thought Cash in disbelief. He almost shouted his excitement before Donald spoke again.

"See, da prawlum is, ya don' wan two shlubs lie us comin off da streets ta ya nice estabushmin."

Tom Lord squinted at Donald, as if that would make his words any clearer. "Ah, hmmm, isn't there a shelter you can go to...?"

Cash deflated; Donald would lose this for them. He considered jumping in, accepting Tom Lord's deal in spite of Donald. But if he did that, Donald was like to be spiteful back, to not show up at all, perhaps even demand Cash return the bongos.

"*Shelder?!*" Donald scoffed, waving his hand. "Man, I god shelder. I god shelder wih my oalady! Nehermye. Wuh goud." Donald stomped off, dismissing Tom Lord, and reluctantly Cash followed.

"Wait!" said Tom Lord desperately. "Commit to a few shows and I'll set you up somewhere. You can get clean and have a good night's sleep beforehand."

Donald stopped, so Cash stopped too.

"Eh, ah spoze tha's okay." He looked to Cash thoughtfully and nodded. Cash tried to hide his worry and excitement and nodded. Beside him, Jack nodded as well.

Easy mark or not, Tom Lord was smart enough not to rent an expensive suite on their account. Still, the small two-bed motel room was nicer than any they'd stayed in since making their way to the streets. They were given the room for two nights, one for each show they would perform. Originally, they would only have the first night, but Donald had successfully pushed for a second.

The afternoon before their debut, Tom Lord stopped by with a barber and dog groomer. "All right, boys," he said. "Let's get pretty!"

Donald was first to shower and get trimmed, and disappeared entirely once finished. Meanwhile, the freshly-scrubbed Cash sat with a towel wrapped around his shoulders, waiting patiently for his turn.

"How do you want it?" the barber asked him.

Cash wondered how best to say, *Not homeless.* "Clean?" he shrugged.

The cold steel was sweet on his skin, as were the warm fingers sifting through his hair. Cash couldn't remember the last time anyone touched him like that, or touched him at all, really. He shut his eyes and was so relaxed he near fell asleep. When, at the barber's gentle command, he opened his eyes, Cash didn't recognize the face that met him.

His greasy, twisted hair was cropped short against his scalp, with the top a thick sheen running from front to back. Seeing himself, Cash felt like a new man. Like all the ugly past, the addictions and mistakes now lay behind him. He was *this*—this image of normal. He had a job. He paid his bills. He went home at night. *Surely.*

"I don't have a tip..." he realized, embarrassed.

"That's all been taken care of." The barber gathered his things and left, and Cash felt like he took some part of him too. Some small dignity Cash didn't know he had until it was lost, like a crumpled dollar in a back pocket.

When Jack came trotting out of the bathroom, his white on black coat glistening and smooth, he startled at Cash's new appearance. A low growl built up to a bark.

"Jack! You can't do that here!" Cash walked over and scooped him up, and Jack lay rigid and uncomfortable in his arms. He sniffed Cash but didn't recognize the shampoo smell, and growled again.

Before Cash could scold him, the groomer emerged from the bathroom carrying a used towel and a bag of cleaning products. "Boy, he needed that," she said, wiping her brow with her forearm. "There was fungus growing in his fur!"

"*Homeless,*" Cash shrugged with a grin.

She didn't think it was as funny as he did. Jack still growled, but shrugged as well.

Inside the West Ender Café, a packed house awaited them. Some of the faces Cash recognized—fans and friends that watched them perform on street corners. There was applause as they came in through the side door with Jack trotting behind.

Tom Lord introduced them, giving a name they'd never claimed or asked for: "Give it up for *Skinny Cow and the Street Rights!*" The room erupted with cheers.

Jack started them off with a bongo solo that created an uproar of excitement through the crowd. Donald and Cash came in together on guitar, strumming quick and sweet to Jack's rhythm, while Donald growled the lyrics to "Whiskey in the Jar."

Around them cameras clicked and flashed, people laughed, they clapped, and Cash felt so happy he near collapsed. His face was tingly and warm, his fingers blissful sore. He strummed away, digging into the music and singing along with Donald who glanced back to him, grinning pure and simple. They fed off each other's energy, until even Jack was barking behind them, inspiring gasps and cheers from the crowd.

Afterwards, Tom Lord approached them, giddy as can be. The café was so packed they had to turn people away at the door. He gave them each a hundred dollars in cash, which Donald claimed wasn't enough.

"I believe that's what we agreed upon..." said Tom Lord.

"Fells short ta me. Dey came fuh us," he said, gesturing his hand across the crowded room.

Cash was nervous, feared Donald might lose this for them after all, but he had to trust Donald. Who knows what they might come away with this time.

"Ah tink ih ya wan us ta come back, weh nee a lil more."

Tom Lord looked to Cash who looked to Donald who didn't flinch. A moment later, Tom Lord was counting fifty dollars into Donald's hand.

As they left, Cash applauded Donald's business acumen and asked for his share of the extra money.

"Wha?" Donald looked at him perplexed. "Ah raced the price, I tae duh cut."

They didn't talk all the way back to the motel. Once they got in, Cash couldn't take the quiet and went for another shower—his third that day. He lost all sense of time in there, with the water washing away all his discomfort and ache. The warmth and privacy let him process things without the accompanying stress.

And tonight he was coming to terms with being taken advantage of. It wasn't Donald that troubled him, but Tom Lord. Though they'd never met, he'd recognized the businessman upon sight. In another universe, their lives might have been switched. Either way, they still bowed to anyone that pressed. In Tom Lord, Cash saw all the qualities he disliked most in himself. All the weakness and fear and the pathetic struggle for control.

It had to change, he determined. He would make it change.

When Cash emerged from the bathroom, he found a woman dressed down to her underwear, lying on his bed, petting Jack, who lay beside her.

"Uh, hi," Cash managed to get out.

"Hi." She barely glanced up before turning away, bored.

Cash stood there, confused, not knowing what to say. Donald was missing, but a moment later the door beeped and swung open.

"Finally..." said the girl as Donald entered. "I've been waiting forever." She rolled away from Jack and sat slouched on the edge of the bed.

"W-who's your friend?" asked Cash.

"Aw, sahhy," said Donald, apparently surprised to find Cash standing there. "Dis Cyntia."

"*Cindy*," she said, rolling her eyes.

"*Cinny*." Donald smiled but wouldn't meet Cash's eyes.

"Well, did you get it?" asked Cindy.

"Sha dih, darlin." Donald withdrew a bag from his pocket and sat beside her on the bed.

Cash watched them, speechless and still like a piece of furniture. He looked to Jack, who watched them as well, sniffing the air for hint of what was in the bag.

"Ey, man. C'mon. Wuh godda celebrade. Geh in on dis."

"Uh, I dunno..." He thought a moment. "What is it?"

"Juss coke, man."

Just coke. When Cash was a teenager, he'd gone from coke to crack to heroin, and then back again, thinking if he turned to something less potent it would curb his appetite. No matter how he bounced between them it always ended in him strung out with a tube tied around his arm. Still, he wondered if there weren't some happy middle-ground.

Donald held up the bag to his nose and smelled it. He kissed his finger, dipped it in the bag, and rubbed it across his teeth. Beside him, Cindy or Cynthia leaned close, wrapping her arm around his and staring lustily at the bag, and Cash wondered: *Why shouldn't I take part?*

They were in a safe place, well off the streets. Shouldn't he enjoy himself? Hadn't he earned that by now? It was growing dark in Cash's mind, the cockroaches slipping from their shadows, one by one, to join and mate and spread. Cash stared at the bag in Donald's hands, considering, and just the consideration made him feel weightless and heady, ready to float over, another ghost searching for the light. But a sharp whining pulled him back to his body.

"I think your dog wants some," said the girl, glancing over at Jack who stood at the edge of the bed, whimpering. The girl laughed pathetically. Even her own jokes bored her.

Cash avoided Jack's eyes though. He didn't want to see the desperation, the plea he knew was waiting. Cash had already surrendered to the possibility—the *maybe just tonight*. If he didn't get high now the desire would linger in his skin for days. Jack fidgeted and growled, demanding Cash see him.

But I need it... Cash almost said aloud.

Jack watched him, unblinking, and barked.

"Ee cant do dat ere, man," said Donald, snorting a line from the bedside table.

Suddenly, the seductive hue of getting high turned sour. More dirty than alluring. Like he'd mistaken oil puddles for rainbows. Cash shivered for another shower—where he could be washed clean, or just washed away. Where the desire for drugs would run down the gutters and back down the drain. But there was Jack, caught between him and his addiction.

When Cash picked Jack up from the bed, the girl flinched as if he might come in for a kiss. Donald didn't even look over. Cash almost walked out the door then, returned to the curve of the Watt bridge onramp, leaving the room to Donald and his new friend. But as Cash turned to bow out, he thought once more of Tom Lord—and refused to be him in an instant.

"*YOU* can't do *THAT* in *HERE*," said Cash.

"Do whah?"

"Get high!" Cash hadn't intended to shout, but at least he now had Donald's attention. Jack squirmed uncomfortably under his arm. "You need to send Cindy outta here. And I want my money. We should be 50/50. I want my cut. Now! *Please.*"

Donald chuckled and set another couple of lines.

Cash stepped forward and threw his hand across the table, spraying white granules everywhere. Before Cash knew what was happening, he was knocked onto the other bed while Donald's fists smacked repeatedly against his cheeks. Jack flew over him, yelping as he hit the floor.

Cash didn't know when it stopped. His face throbbed and throbbed like tiny, endless blows. He just became aware he was sprawled across the bed, floating away. When the spinning and throbbing finally stopped, Cash lifted his head as much as he could to look around. Donald and Cindy were gone, with not but a smear of white powder across the nightstand betraying their existence at all. The room was quiet, lonely, and afraid.

"*S'okay, skinny cow.*" Cash slurred before slipping out. "*S'okay.*"

There was no response.

It was early morning when Cash awoke, feeling heavy and sore and hung over. He called for Jack, but Jack didn't come. He called again, feeling something was forgotten or out of place.

Cash rose slowly from the bed, the world spinning and wobbly. He braced himself against the wall until it stabled. "Jack?" he called. But there was nothing. He rubbed his head and called again. A *thump thump thump* came from the other side of the bed. Cash stumbled over quick as he could.

Jack lay on the floor, eyes scanning passively and tail smacking the carpet but otherwise unable to move. All across his body, thin white stalks broke through the fur.

Cash was speechless, the blood and breath fleeing his face to hide in some deep, dark place. He bent over Jack and stroked his fur, moving his lips and trying to find the air for words. "Hey, skinny cow..." His voice was like a whisper on the wind, something carried from very far away. "Donald!" he called. "We gotta get Jack to a vet!" But when he looked to the other bed he remembered that Donald had gone. Remembered the events of the night—why his head ached so sorely and the room felt so cold.

Cash was alone in this.

He scooped Jack in his arms and rushed him from the room. Jack didn't move, but Cash felt thin, spindly stalks slide over his hand, searching the lines and cracks in his skin.

"I need help!" Cash shouted through the lobby, and every suburbanite, technician, purebred, mutt, and mod-pet turned sharply in his direction. People pointed and stared when he walked through the door. They muttered in hushed whispers.

"Excuse me, sir," said a receptionist. He looked ready to lead Cash back out the door when he spotted the white fingers stretching everywhere through Jack's fur. He let out an exasperated breath.

"Okay folks," he said, stealing the room, "I'm sorry but I need everyone to escort their animals out, please. Yes, now. No, I'm sorry, this is not a joke." He directed Cash away from them, kept him sequestered.

Before the lobby had fully emptied, a technician in full hazmat suit appeared from the backroom. The suit was bright yellow. *Everything's okay*, thought Cash forcibly. The hazmat visor was blurry and reflected the fluorescent light, obscuring the face. Cash couldn't see if the technician was man or woman, if they smiled or frowned or had compassion in their eyes. They were just this *suit*.

Jack sat heavy in Cash's arms, and when the technician took him, the sudden relief left Cash feeling hollow, scooped out. The hazmat said something indistinguishable. Probably, *Wait here*. Cash just nodded, ran his hands through his hair, over his face, trying to find some purpose in his body to occupy himself.

Doctor Burke came out, looking concerned as clients rushed their pets out the door. "Cash?" he said, squinting. Cash nodded, figuring the doctor didn't recognize him with a haircut and clean clothes. He hadn't yet realized the right side of his face was swollen like a tumor, as purple as sunset. "*Are you okay?*" the doctor asked with alarm.

"They took Jack... He's got stuff growin..."

Time passed, or didn't. Like the world around him, time was all a blur. Cash wiped his eyes. He sat in one of the comfortable chairs uncomfortably. He hunched forward, then slouched back. He stood up. He paced. He sat back down.

He tried to lose himself in the television where men in suits scoffed at recent politics. He watched the technicians come and go hurriedly, making phone calls and printing charts. Outside the world chugged along, oblivious.

He was alone. Like a castaway on a barren island, contemplating the rough waters and dreaming of some chemical oblivion.

"*Ey Cash, may ah sih wittew?*"

Cash startled and turned. He hadn't noticed Doctor Burke approach. "What?"

"May I sit with you?"

"Okay."

Doctor Burke slowly lowered into the leather chair beside his. "How are you hanging in there?" he asked.

"Okay." It was the only thing Cash could say out without crumbling.

"Before we talk about Jack... Is everything else all right? Are you safe?"

Cash didn't know what to say to that. Right now he felt like the tide was lapping at his feet, calling him in, away from the rough and craggy landscape of survival. "O—" He choked before he finished, tears breaking from his eyes, nose, and mouth. Cash wiped desperately at his face. "Is he dead?" he finally got out.

"That's a difficult one to answer, actually. Cash, do you remember how we thought Jack might just have brain swelling, but I said it could be something else?"

Phycomycosis exemplum was a rare fungal infection that affected cats and dogs. Once rooted in the brain, it bypassed neural pathways, copying the behavior of organisms outside the host to better infiltrate a potential host-group. When fully matured, it spread through the rest of the body until its spores broke through the skin.

"So all that stuff he was doin... playin' bongos was just..."

"*Phycomycosis exemplum,*" said the doctor clinically.

Cash thought to all the ways Jack mimicked him, all the ways his best friend seemed human. Now he was told that wasn't Jack at all but something even further from humanity. Some gross, mindless mockery of it.

"It's impossible to draw a sharp line between what was Jack and what was the infection. But for him to push through in the end would require a tremendous effort of will that we don't often see unless the animal feels threatened."

"What are they doin to him?"

"Right now they're sanitizing Jack, killing the fungus right down to the base."

"So he'll be okay?"

Doctor Burke's face grew long. He looked away. "Perhaps I haven't been clear. The fungus actually *replaces* the brain of its host. It becomes like a copy until it's time to spread. The good news is that, aside from a little confusion, Jack was probably never aware it was happening. But I'm afraid he's been gone for some time..."

Cash felt as though something heavy and important had collapsed inside him. His heart, he thought. But it couldn't be that. That still ached and beat and bled.

He stood up abruptly with nowhere to go, and just as abruptly walked towards where the hazmat had taken Jack. Cash didn't know where he was going or what he was going to do, but he pushed through door after door, past surprised technicians who said he couldn't be there and walls of caged animals who watched him quietly with fear in their eyes.

Doctor Burke ran after him, calling him back and discouraging technicians from getting involved.

Cash came to a dead-end at a large steel door, like a walk-in refrigerator with a big circular window at eye-level. "Cash, don't..." he heard behind him, but he ignored it. Peering inside, Cash saw Jack lying across a stainless steel table. The hazmat circled around him, spraying a white mist from something like a fire extinguisher.

Thin wisps of smoke rose from Jack's fur as the stalks crumpled into dust, leaving red holes freckled over his body. The tail wagged cruelly, thumping once, twice, before the technician sprayed it and it stopped for good.

Cash clutched his scalp, his nails digging into the skin. He needed to get out of there. He thought about finding Donald, losing himself for a while. He'd have to apologize, of course. Make amends. And then he could blast his brain, with all its dolor and woe, so far into oblivion that he wouldn't feel anything but a flicker of nostalgia for better days.

Before Cash turned away, his eyes caught his own reflection, saw the hopelessness and grief and the red welt that bloomed across his face. That's what Donald's friendship had brought him. Suddenly, getting high never felt so low. Going back was just as empty as staying put.

The world lost all sense after that. Time and space fused together or broke entirely apart. He was weeping under florescent lights; he was on the streets alone; he was in the cursed room with Donald and Cindy. People were there beside him one moment, gone the next. Disembodied hands pat his back, led him elsewhere. Stray voices whispered like ghosts.

Every squeak of metal or rubber sole scuffing the floor sounded to him like a yelp, making him turn sharply in search for Jack, only to realize his mistake—the void that now awaited him.

It made that last memory come bubbling up through the grief—Jack standing on the motel bed, begging him not to get high. It was a memory that scared and shamed him. So much hung on the precipice of that moment, and yet all he wanted was to go back to it. If the fungus' goal was to fit in, why hadn't Jack just gotten high with him? Why couldn't they just share that together, him and Jack transcending time and space and all their troubles on a chemical journey?

Doctor Burke's words now came floating back to him: *...to push through in the end would require a tremendous effort of will...*

The realization struck him sudden and unexpected, like garbage thrown from a passing car. The last time Cash saw Jack—the *real* Jack—he was pushing through the fog, doing what he always did for Cash: calling him back from folly. To now go back to Donald, back to the drugs, would be to dishonor this final act. Maybe even his life entire.

"I know this can't be easy for you," said Doctor Burke, appearing beside him. "But with this rare infection in town, there will be others. There will be pets that are scared and families that don't know what to do. We're going to be very busy trying to manage this, and we're going to need help—*lots of help*—taking care of them all. We're going to need someone on staff that understands what's at stake... Someone that cares. Maybe someone looking for a second chance..." He put a warm hand on Cash's back, and for a moment, the world was just a little bit less cold.

In the weeks ahead, sleep was hard to find. Like his prayers to the beyond, it rebuked all his efforts to connect. Though Cash now had a job, a room, a bed, their comfort was too alien to soothe his heartache. At night, he'd toss and turn, shift pillows and blankets about himself, and finally he'd consider sleeping on the streets just to feel a little closer to home.

The cravings kept him anxious, kept him fidgeting and uncomfortable. And the relief was still out there, somewhere, waiting for him. Always ready to take him back, to swallow him and all his grief if he only surrendered. The thought made him ill.

Once sleep finally came, it swept up and dragged Cash away like a current roiling beneath the surface. Cash rarely slept deep enough to dream, and often assured himself he hadn't dreamt at all, only fell into a black stupor. But occasionally he would startle awake, sure he heard Jack whimper, or yawn, or bark, and he'd accept then that he had indeed been dreaming, and dreaming, no less, of Jack.

In that moment, the distance between them didn't feel so far. Cash felt at once comforted and heartbroken then, aching for that connection that seemed so close he swore he heard Jack snuffling before realizing it was just the damp, sweaty sheets sliding over his body. He wept like he only had as a boy—breathy, voiceless, and trembling. Then, freshly exhausted, he curled up with pillows and sheets, shivered once for the warmth they couldn't give, and slept, and dreamed, and recovered.

A question for the author

Q: What's your favorite story?

A: I really love stories about reluctant friendship, where two enemies are forced to work together and over time they begrudgingly start to care. Begrudgement isn't appreciated enough in modern friendships.

About the author

Hamilton Perez is a writer and freelance editor living in Sacramento, California. When not writing, he can be found rolling 20-sided dice or chasing squirrels with the dog. He is also an Associate Editor at *Podcastle*.

hamiltonperez.wordpress.com, @TheWritingHam

Cathedra

M.C. Tuggle

We glided out of the base's garage onto smooth tarmac, but once we hit the icy terrain, things got bumpy. The rover shimmied up a rise pocked with shallow fissures and slowed to a crawl as we neared the crest. I gazed up. Saturn and its massive rings dominated the sky, glowing in the dim bronze light of early morning on Enceladus.

We stopped. Rafferty tapped my shoulder from the rear seat. I was so absorbed in the view she startled me. I turned, and for an awkward moment, we were face to face. Through her crystal-clear helmet, glints of simmering anger flashed in green eyes set off by a mop of red hair. She pointed to a smooth stretch of grey ice in the gorge below and said, "That's it, Kaplan. That's where our friends were working. They never had a chance."

Beside me in the driver's seat, Martinez turned his dark eyes on me, his head tilted back. "Yeah, that's the spot. 'Safe for geothermal drilling,' according to the survey."

Our helmets were equipped with automatic radio comms, as well as audio sensors and external transducers for through-water comms, but I didn't answer. Martinez sat back and kicked the brake. The rover purred down the slope as Martinez jerked the tiller left and right to dodge ice blocks in our way. Even in the tiny moon's low gravity, our loopy course threatened to hurl us out of our seats. My companions seemed to have no difficulty. I tightened my grip on the grab bar.

Martinez shot a look at me. "Better hold on, Kaplan."

The way Martinez was driving, and with no protective sides on the rover, I could've been flung out onto the rock-hard ice. In fact, my two associates might've been hoping to see me take a fall, since everyone on Cassini Base blamed me for the disappearance of two of their coworkers.

Well, that's me. Always the odd man out.

The three of us, me, Martinez, and Rafferty, the electrician's mate, wore white company-issued biosuits, easily the best I'd ever used. They'd been designed to function on surface and underwater, though powerful, shifting currents made it impossible to work in the underground seas. In addition to flex-ballast to simulate 70% g, the suits supplied us with air, and were enviro-adaptable and armored to protect us from Enceladus' hostile environment. So if the journeyman astrogeologist tumbled out of the rover, no one would be reprimanded. In fact, it'd make a great story back at base.

We reached smoother terrain and coasted toward a dozen or more toppled ice columns that looked like a collapsed Stonehenge. Something caught my eye and I twisted around. On the grey horizon, a geyser shot superheated water into space, followed by another. Seconds later, the twin rumbles reached us through the moon's thin atmosphere, registering nearly 50 decibels in my suit's audio sensors. The fountain-like spray rose high, caught the sunlight, and formed a gigantic sparkling cone with Saturn looming in the background like an enormous round agate of gold, blue, and white bands. Most of the propelled water would add to the moon's atmosphere, but some would break free of Enceladus' gravity and become part of Saturn's E ring.

We reached the site where the two men had vanished. Martinez braked the rover, and we clambered out. Rafferty busied herself setting up the 3-D imaging unit we'd brought from the main base, and Martinez followed close behind me.

There was no doubt in my mind that both watched my every move.

The terrain surrounding us was warped and striated with pressure faults, smooth in places, powdery in others. Blunt ice boulders and smaller chunks littered the area. And there it was – in the center of a stretch of ice otherwise smooth as glass, ten feet of a silent drill derrick poking out.

When I turned toward Martinez, he wasn't looking at the accident site. His eyes had narrowed on me.

He nodded toward the drill. "Hasegawa's comm is still active down there." Martinez' tone was icier than the atmosphere. He took a deep breath. "We never heard from Spenser. And that's been almost three months."

"How do you know it's still active?"

Martinez patted the back of his suit. "When you put in a charged lithium pack, your suit is operational about four months, including the radio. The three of us are sending and receiving on frequency Tac 12. But if an activated suit is not in motion more than three minutes, it's assumed you're in trouble, and a dead man circuit kicks in. The helmet comm receives all live transmissions so you can locate help, and broadcasts a directional beacon on the emergency frequency."

Yep. Damn good biosuits. The company takes care of its own.

I recalled this spot from when I conducted my original survey nearly a year ago. We stood at the moon's south pole, one of the most complex and tectonically active regions in the solar system. Enceladus was covered in water ice that hid a liquid sea and hydrothermal flows heated by tidal friction and radioactive decay. The company that had hired me, Xtracta, planned to tap into the moon's vast geothermal reserves and ship charged supercapacitors to power-hungry space outposts. That plan had suffered a major setback when the two crewmembers disappeared. Which was why we were here.

I looked up. The alarm array on a utility pole near a small, nearby mound of dark ice showed no sign of damage. I tapped the touchpad on my wrist and studied the display in my visor. "Strange," I said. "All the sensors and alarms I installed are responding. Everything's working."

Martinez faced me, arms folded across his chest. "Well, Kaplan, then I suppose you're done here. You can go back to the belt and forget about us. Again."

I didn't respond. But something about Martinez' tone got to me. People like Martinez were one of the reasons I preferred working alone as an astrogeologist in the asteroid belt. The asteroid miners kept to themselves and paid well for my surveys. But when Xtracta contacted me about the disappearance of its two crewmembers, I'd felt I had to come back. It had taken nearly three months catching transports, but I was here to do what I could. What I had to do. Anyone who questioned my work was going to hear from me. I'd come back to defend myself.

But now a growing ache in my gut told me I might be responsible for the deaths of two men. An unknown geohazard must've killed them – unknown because I had overlooked it. Nothing else could explain what had happened. The football-sized creatures that raced in the small moon's sub-surface seas were harmless. Cute, even. The miners had dubbed them sea pigs.

My response to Martinez was to march out to the derrick. Martinez dropped his arms to his side and stared at me. Rafferty turned from the equipment she was setting up. Neither wanted to miss the sight of me crashing through the ice.

"It's solid here," I said, stomping my boot. "The alarms would go off if the ice was thinning or under stress." When I touched the drill's control panel, the unit's display lit up, and I squinted at it. The drill had punched through the ice and had penetrated rock, still several meters away from the superheated water that surged below the surface. But the display indicated the wellbore had ruptured. What the hell could've caused that? Squatting, I brushed away blue powder ice from the surface. The solid ice showed signs of stress and rapid re-freezing. "Has anyone tried to retrieve this equipment?"

Martinez remained motionless. "No one's dared. Not after what happened."

"I don't get it," I said. "There's no way hot streams from the interior could breach the surface. Not here. The ice is always at least 30 centimeters. And look at this." I pointed toward the drill's display, but Martinez and Rafferty didn't budge. "The wellbore is still embedded in rock. Don't see how enough hot water could've seeped out to do any damage." After another glance at the drill's display screen, I said, "Rafferty, let's roll out the GPR."

"Hooah." She turned half way, looked back at me, and scurried back to her equipment.

"As soon as the ground penetrating radar maps the interior, I should have a better idea what's down there, maybe even figure out what happened. Then we can power the drill back up and replace the bore."

"What's the map gonna show you?" Martinez folded his arms.

"Hopefully, that it's safe to continue."

Martinez snorted. "You're mighty cautious when it's your butt on the line."

"Yes, I am." I turned away, burning in shame. Why the hell had I said that? I leaned close to the drill's control panel. "There's the main power. If the area's secure, we can continue to drill, finish the job. The one thing we don't want to do is overlook–"

That's when the world I thought I knew disappeared.

A powerful shock wave whipped through my body, and the ice around me pinged and cracked and roared. Something tossed me high over the surface, and I tumbled and dropped among shards of flying ice. The alarm blasted the air, and the crisis alert chime in my suit sounded. I bellyflopped into water, and the instant I hit, something wrapped around me and pulled me down into darkness.

I rocketed through the water at mind-numbing speed. I tried to switch on my suit's light panel, but whatever was pushing me had pinned my arms back. Helpless and terrified, I sped face-first through black water.

Seconds later, as suddenly as it had started, all movement ended. I glanced around, panting. Blood throbbed in my ears. There was no sign of whatever had brought me here, and I drifted in the water. It took a few seconds to control my breathing and orient myself. I was in an underwater cave. My audio sensors picked up the dull thunder of water rushing through a nearby channel, broken every few seconds by the crash of a powerful surge colliding with rock. Several meters away, a dim light flickered through water thick with icy slush. By kicking my legs and pulling myself along the rocks, I glided toward the white glow that gave the chamber its only illumination.

I stopped. A figure in a white biosuit, arms and legs spread-eagled, stared back at me. But when I pulled closer, the suit's sleeves floated free in the current. They were empty. It was just a biosuit and its helmet wedged into the rocks, its fading light panel illuminating the watery chamber. The armor at the chest appeared gouged open. I switched on my own light panel and read the letters "HASEG." A cold shudder shot down my spine.

A voice in my helmet said, "Kaplan, do you copy?"

"Yes, Martinez, I copy."

"I've been trying to reach you. What happened?"

"Something dragged me underwater. What did you see?"

"Water, ice, arms, legs. Where the hell are you? You okay?"

"I'm in a cave, and I'm still in once piece. Martinez – I found Hasegawa's suit and helmet."

"Is he ..."

"There's no sign of his body. And I haven't seen any trace of Spenser." I switched off my suit's light panel. No telling how long I'd be stuck here, so I figured I'd better conserve power.

After a long pause, Martinez said, "What can we do?"

"Say again?"

"Kaplan, I repeat, what can we do?"

"Hold on."

Martinez' voice was echoing in my audio sensor, repeating what I heard over the comm. How was that possible? I turned up the amplitude on my through-water system and heard a team leader bark at workers in the hangar for not moving uncharged supercapacitors into the warehouse. Then I remembered what Martinez had told me about our suits. The dead man circuit in Hasegawa's comm system had triggered, so it repeated all radio conversations in the area.

It was possible a random burst of superheated water had broken the ice I'd been standing on and washed me into this cave. But what had stuffed the helmet and the suit in the rocks? And why?

"Martinez, do you copy?"

"I'm here."

"I'm going to look around, see if there's a way out. Rafferty?"

"Rafferty here."

"Go ahead with the 3D mapping. Look for an opening in the rocks."

"Hooah," she said. "Got it. And good luck, Kaplan."

"Thanks."

This seemed like a good time to check the indicators in my visor display. No telling what might be useful. Trimix replicator: fully functional, so I had plenty of air. Surrounding water: 7 Centigrade, but the suit's enviro regulators checked out. At least I wouldn't be frozen or cooked alive in this crazy stew of freezing and boiling water. Ambient radiation: now that was a problem. The radiation in the cave was high. Deadly high. Nearly 25 Sv. My heart sank as I did the math. I had less than an hour to escape.

Then another problem – the light behind me went out.

I nudged against the rock to turn around, and peered into murky water. Just as I started to power on my own light panel, I realized the light from Hasegawa's suit was still on. Something floated between me and the suit, blocking the light. Something large. And it was only a couple meters away.

This was serious. A breakaway ice column drifting in the powerful currents could crush me. I glanced around the cave searching for an escape route and realized my situation was even worse than I first thought: there were several enormous columns floating in the cave. The moon's wildly elliptical orbit created enormous friction between the ocean and the moon's rocky core, and that friction heated the underground sea. Other streams heated from radioactive decay blended with those currents. If heated waters from another region had shifted, my little underwater cave could suddenly freeze up, and the radioactivity would be the least of my worries.

The column nearest me moved. It didn't lurch in random current, it flexed so that it remained close to me as I drifted. It jerked closer, and when I tried to swim out of its path, it changed course until it was nearly in my face. And it had eyes.

Clicks and deep grumbles sounded through the audio sensors of my through-water comm system, which were answered by eyes opening on the dozens of other large shapes in the cave. The dim glow from the dead man's suit reflected red in the large eyes that surrounded me.

It took me a long moment to comprehend what I faced. These giants weren't friendly little sea pigs.

And here I was trapped in an underwater cave full of them. My heart thumped in my chest, and I took a couple of gulps of air. I had to remain calm. I let myself drift in the water, unsure how any effort to maneuver might be interpreted.

I could tell I was being studied by these aquatic creatures. The one closest to me was at least four meters long, with a thick, streamlined body that glistened like slate in the dim light. It resembled a dolphin with an alligator's thick hide. A row of spikes formed along the spine. Oval, reptilian eyes that blinked from front to back sat high on top of a cone-like head. The blunt jaws, anchored by a massive neck and chest, suggested monstrous power. The creature had two long flippers in front and stubby flukes on its tail. And near the tail, a thick dorsal tentacle swayed menacingly.

Was I in their dining room? Had Hasegawa's suit been mounted in the rocks as a trophy?

Radioactivity was accumulating in my body, so I had to do something. I needed a better idea of my surroundings, and how many mouths were aimed at me. I switched on my light panel at its lowest setting.

Rapid clicks and moans filled the cave. Like a school of fish, the creatures rippled away from the light, but as they retreated, each one formed a fist at the end of its dorsal tentacle. The balled-up tentacle reminded me of the hammer tail of the ankylosaurus, and I had no doubt of the immense power behind each.

The creature next to me nudged forward and faced me. My only weapon was the light panel in my suit. The max setting might blind the creatures. But only some. And then what would I do? I had no idea how to get back to the surface.

The creature opened its mouth, revealing three rows of pointed black teeth. A rapid pulse of clicks sounded from it. Adrenaline fired through me, but I forced myself to remain still and face whatever was about to happen.

Then the creature said, "Have you finished?"

All I could do was stare back. The creature's voice was a bone-rattling bass. I took a deep breath and switched on my external speaker. "Finished what?"

"Mourning your dead self."

I wrestled with a response, but gave up. "Please explain."

"Part of you died. You have seen the shell. The suit." It slowly shut and opened its red, slotted eyes. "Know that the dying was necessary."

So these creatures had killed Spenser and Hasegawa. A knot of fear clenched my stomach.

"How is it you can talk to me?"

It looked at Hasegawa's suit. "We listened."

That was another punch to the gut I wasn't ready for. This creature had learned to speak our language by overhearing the communications on Hasegawa's radio.

"That's – quite an accomplishment."

"We must speak to the beings who feed us, the podfrums, gallytrots, and firedrakes. What you would call our prey."

Predators. They fed on the smaller animals that lived in the underground sea. I had to force myself to breathe deeply. These alien beings possessed an intellect as breathtaking as their physical power. And they were apparently immune to extreme heat, cold, and radioactivity.

Were we considered a new prey species?

Surrounded by intelligent aliens of immense power, and my body absorbing radioactivity at dangerous levels, I had little to lose by interrogating them. More important, the crew at Cassini Base had to know what was down here. My finger tapped the control panel on my arm to transmit our conversation.

"Who are you?"

"We are Of Na. And you are Kaplan."

It had heard my name on Hasegawa's comm when I was talking to Martinez and Rafferty. There was no doubting its intelligence. "You said it was necessary the two men had to die. Did you kill them?"

Of Na blinked its eyes. "That horrid thing they brought to life, your drill, was harming Na, which would deprive Cathedra of her beauty."

"Who are Na and Cathedra?"

"Na is our home, what you call Base. Cathedra is the great One above. You call it Saturn."

"How do you know what's above?"

"We can see through the ice in many places, especially near the geysers. Sometimes pools form near the heated water, letting us look up at Cathedra and its holy circles. And we can open the ice when Na's currents allow us."

So that's what their hammer tails were for. I had to let Martinez and the others know what they were facing.

"Did you break the ice and bring me here?"

"We heard you tell yourself on the comm you were going to bring the horrid drill back to life. The Hasegawa and Spenser parts of you had to be stopped. And you, Kaplan, had to be stopped."

"Why? Why did you have to stop us?"

A long moment passed before Of Na shut its long eyes from front to back. Then it said, "You would have disrupted Na's lifeblood, which we offer to Cathedra. When an offering is accepted, our dead become part of Cathedra's sacred rings."

It shuddered, edged closer, and its broad, powerful mouth hovered inches from my face.

"Your time of mourning is finished."

Before I could answer, the creature's tentacle shot forward and the sledgehammer on the end opened up and engulfed me. Darkness hit me like a falling rock, and we took off. The sudden g-force from shooting through water turned my brain to mush. Seconds later, we stopped. Too lightheaded to react, I drifted in total darkness. The distant roll of surging water rumbled in my through-water comm. I gulped air, found the control for the light panel in my suit, and peered into a pair of long, reptilian eyes. A panicked search of my surroundings revealed we were alone in a water-filled, rocky chamber.

Despite my suit's enviro-regulators, my entire body was slick with sweat.

I started to ask Of Na why it had brought me here, when a rat-like, rust-colored skeleton floated in the light from my suit. Following in its path were dozens of similar remains, some whole, with wide, staring eye sockets, and many others headless. A few meters away, at the fuzzy edge of my beam, a creature like Of Na drifted, its massive jaws gaping as it slowly cartwheeled in an invisible eddy.

"What you call the geyser will soon erupt at this place. We have honored the dead by bringing them here. What is left of their bodies will be sky-scattered."

The small skeletons must've been the sea pigs these creatures hunted. While that thought sank in, my still-addled brain comprehended what Of Na had just said: a geyser was due. In my survey, I'd concluded the geysers erupted irregularly, and other geologists had confirmed that.

"How can you predict a geyser?"

"We listen. We know." Of Na cocked its head and slowly blinked. "The Hasegawa and Spenser parts of you were also sky-scattered, and are now part of Cathedra's rings."

I glared back, so enraged my vision went blurry. "You killed them because they were drilling?"

"You are worse than the podfrums. Even they understand when we explain what has to be done." Of Na shuddered. "We had to stop you from destroying Na's lifeblood, which feeds Cathedra. We did not know you could be killed so easily." It shook itself, edged closer. "But you have said you will drill again, and we have pledged a sacred oath to protect Na. We will surround your mess, your barracks, your rec center, your garage, and your admin building and crush them."

My anger at the planned mass murder crowded out what the creature had claimed about the geyser. The roar and hiss of powerful streams of superheated water crashing against the chamber's walls reminded me, and I checked my visor display. I blinked, and looked at it again. The surrounding water was 98 degrees Celsius, approaching the boiling point.

My heart dropped into my gut when I realized the creature might be right about an imminent geyser. The blast from a geyser eruption would shred and atomize anything in its path. Including me.

Of Na turned around.

"Wait – are you going to leave me here?"

The creature did not face me, but rumbled its reply. "It is our way to give all a proper sky scattering. Whatever good or harm one has done, the story of their life must have a proper end."

My entire body tightened up. I gulped a breath of air. "Of Na."

No response.

"Of Na, you told me you can see Cathedra when the currents allow you to break the ice."

For a long moment, there was no reply. "Yes."

"I – *we* – don't believe you would wrongfully take life. But we don't know how to read the currents. If you told us where it is safe to break the ice and run our generators, there would be no harm to Na. Cathedra would continue to receive your dead."

Of Na turned until we were eye to eye. It gave me a long, slow blink – hopefully a good sign. For the first time since I'd crashed through the ice, the tension that had knotted my stomach relaxed, and I exhaled.

The creature regarded me without moving or speaking.

I said, "We can adapt the comm so you can use it to tell us where it is safe to drill."

Of Na cocked its head. "That would be – impossible, Kaplan."

"Impossible? Why?"

"We have listened to you argue among yourselves. You are too stubborn, too greedy to be trusted. You would not follow our instructions."

"But we would. We will shut down a turbine when you make your offerings. We can switch to different locations so we don't interfere with Na's lifeblood. I promise we will do as you say."

Of Na closed its huge eyes several moments. When its eyes reopened, it stared at me. "What you are saying is pure bullshit."

It had certainly paid attention to the crew's radio chatter. "Of Na, wait – you said you made a sacred oath to protect Na."

"Yes."

"We can make our sacred oath to you."

Of Na studied me without speaking. It opened its mouth and let out a loud stream of clicks. Its eyes opened and closed in a jittery, shaking motion.

Was this its version of laughter?

Not far away, rushing water thundered against rock, and the walls around us groaned. Bubbles fluttered up from the depths. The water was boiling. A glance at my visor display showed the water had reached 102 degrees.

The creature stopped shaking. "Kaplan, I have listened to you many sunrises. You are a contentious, divided people. There is too much mutual distrust for a sacred oath to have any meaning."

"Ah–" I stared back into those probing, alien eyes, my mind racing. There was no way to convince Of Na we could be trusted. And time was up.

Then it hit me.

"Yes, we do." I swam close to the creature's broad face. "We have a sacred oath, and you have heard it. What's more – you have heard us fulfill that oath."

"You really need to cut the crap."

"That oath, which we hold sacred, is –'Hooah.' When we make this oath, it is our duty to do what we say. I'm surprised you haven't recognized that oath for what it is."

The front flippers quivered, and Of Na backed away, its eyes locked on me.

"Of Na, if you destroy the base, more of us will come, and there will only be more damage to Na. Take me to the surface, and I will convince the others what they must do."

Of Na made no reply.

Deep below, something snapped, radiating shock waves through rock, ice, and water. I made the mistake of looking down toward the source. At that instant my head jerked back in my helmet and I plummeted through inky water, the light panel in my suit illuminating knife-like rock shards that flashed bright, then flickered into darkness. I spun at breakneck speed through tight channels of rock and ice, then raced through icy slush.

Suddenly, no more motion. A bone-shaking thump, followed by a metallic crash, and the next thing I knew, I was facing Of Na, who dangled me from its dorsal tentacle. We were nearly eye to eye, and the light from my suit cast deep shadows on Of Na's rock-like, muscular face.

"Kaplan, you will speak to me through the suit we possess before the next sunrise. We will then guide you to a place where you can safely drill."

Reeling and nauseated from hurtling through deadly waters, I held my head as high as I could, took a deep breath, and with my last trace of strength, firmly replied, "Hooah."

Of Na whipped his tentacle and tossed me.

I shot out of the water, slid several meters, and sprawled onto the icy surface. As I staggered to my feet, the flash-frozen water on my suit splintered and cracked in the freezing atmosphere. Lightheaded and stumbling, I searched my surroundings. When I found the place Of Na had hammered through the ice, it had already turned solid. It took a couple of drunken efforts to cut the power to my suit's light panel.

"Martinez? Do you copy?" In all directions, the frozen, twisted terrain stretched toward a black horizon, with no sign of help. "I'm on the surface. Martinez? Rafferty? Cassini Base? Can you hear me?"

A geyser flared and rumbled directly in front of me, shaking the ice under my feet, spewing a giant plume of water, silt, and the remains of dead, alien beings into space. The ice rattled and cracked, but I didn't have the strength to run. I gazed up at the gigantic spray as it caught the sunlight. Saturn, its huge rings nearly a knife edge, loomed overhead, glowing its warm colors.

Never again would I see geysers the way I used to. They were more than interesting displays. The creatures of Enceladus – or should I say Na – were building something – something worth working for. Something worth defending. I understood.

Over the roar of the nearby eruption, Martinez' voice crackled in my helmet. "We've spotted you, Kaplan. We're at bearing 270, and on our way."

I scanned the area. The rover bounced and wobbled toward me at full speed over the rugged surface. Rafferty waved, signaling me to run away from the geyser. I plodded a few steps, slipped, and fell flat on my face. The groaning and trembling in the ice warned of the possibility of fissures opening around me. I pushed myself up on my arms and focused my remaining strength on scrambling to my feet.

Martinez scowled when he stopped the rover. "Damn, Kaplan, get in."

I hobbled forward. Rafferty grabbed my outstretched arm in both hands and hauled me into the back. She scooted into the front seat, and Martinez revved the engine and steered toward base.

The rich hum of the rover's engine turned into a whine as we gained speed. Flat on my back, arms and legs like jelly, I gulped air.

Martinez glanced back at me. "Took you long enough. That was a hell of a geyser blow. We coulda been launched into space."

I didn't say anything. A couple of minutes later, Rafferty turned toward Martinez and must've given him a look, but I couldn't see their faces.

"Thought you'd like to know, I relayed your comms when you were underwater so the whole base knows what happened to you down there." Martinez shifted in his seat, leaned back a bit. "And I just got a priority comm from the commander. After sick bay checks you out, I'm taking you to her office. She wants a full rundown on this deal you want to make with that creature."

I was too beat to answer.

"I wouldn't worry about it," said Martinez. "She's reasonable. And I shouldn't tell you this, but she did tell me we need someone who knows the crazy geology here, someone who can handle our underwater friends."

Rafferty pivoted in the passenger seat, tossing the mane of red curls inside her helmet as she faced me. "Know anyone like that?"

I gave her the strongest grin I could manage. "I'll ask around. But first, I'm taking a long, old-fashioned rest."

Rafferty raised an eyebrow. "I guess you've earned it."

I nodded agreement and shut my eyes and let my bruised body conform to the shape of the back seats. Maybe it was exhaustion, maybe it was the moaning engine harmonizing with the swift beat of the rover gliding over bumpy ice, but I thought I saw the mist from the heart of Na racing through dark space to merge with the rings of Cathedra.

About the story

"Cathedra" is a "hard-science" story, inspired by an article in *Astronomy* magazine on Enceladus, the most promising site for life in our solar system. It's a tale of faith and one's discovery of purpose within society. The title and theme came from this anecdote:

A man came upon a construction site where three people were working. He asked the first, "What are you doing?" and the man replied: "I am laying bricks." He asked the second, "What are you doing?" and the man replied: "I am building a wall." As he approached the third, he heard him humming a tune as he worked, and asked, "What are you doing?" The man stood, looked up at the sky, and smiled, "I am building a cathedral!"

A question for M.C. Tuggle

Q: What kind of non-fiction do you like to read and how does it affect the fiction you write?

A: I enjoy history, especially ancient and American colonial history. Articles on astronomy, evolution, and electronics always grab my attention, and often inspire story ideas.

About M.C. Tuggle

M. C. Tuggle is a writer living and working in Charlotte, North Carolina. In addition to fantasy, science fiction, and crime novels, his reading includes history, especially military history. An avid weightlifter, tennis player, and student of martial arts, he has been married to Julie Tuggle since 1982 and is the proud father of a daughter, Jessica. He blogs at mctuggle.com.

@tuggle_mike

The Cypress and the Rose

Sandi Leibowitz

On her sixteenth birthday, a girl approached her mother, a priestess gifted in prophecy, to learn her name and her fate. The trees of that island country spoke with the people, the priestesses most of all, and taught them things that we, to whom the trees are mostly silent, cannot guess.

"Your true name is Cypress," the mother told her.

"The tree of mourning?"

"The tree of resilience. It is long-lived. And where there is death, the cypress stands vigil, its life in balance with what's been lost. Your destiny, daughter, is to leave our land and find a tower of roses. Then, like a rose, the story of your life will unfold."

"What is a rose?" asked Cypress, for their island, rich in hibiscus, bougainvillea, and a thousand other flowers, had never known roses.

The priestess described them to her daughter, adding, "You must go east, to the crowded realms. That is what the trees tell me."

And so Cypress traveled across the sea, hiking deserts and ice caps, climbing mountains, sailing rivers. It took the better part of a year before she came to the place her mother had foretold: a castle with a garden famed for its rose beds, and more famous still for an ancient tower around which the roses were so thickly planted it was practically smothered in them.

She arrived in autumn, when most flowers were already dead. But the roses of the tower, even at their ebb, still blossomed in a cancerous surfeit of white petals, their perfume sickly sweet like pastries in a house of mourning. Despite those fulsome blossoms, the hedge was more thorn than flower. Cypress could understand the greenspeech of most plants, though trees spoke with the clearest voices and had the most to say, but from the great rose-hedge she heard only an angry humming, as of a hive of bees whose honey has been stolen.

Cypress asked for work and was grudgingly hired as a lowly scullery maid, only because the girl who'd last held that post had run away. The castle folk mistrusted the foreigner for her dark coloring, which they called ugly, though in her own land her cinnamon skin had been praised for its beauty. They thought her oafish and ungainly, for she was tall in the ways of her country-folk, a head or two above the tallest men in the east; the dress they made her wear barely reached her ankles, though it hid the strong legs she'd earned from a lifetime of swimming and running and the full skirts weighed her down, making her slow. The castle folk rarely spoke to her, even Myllem, the cook. Cypress bore all, for this was her fate, and she knew that happiness, or at least some great purpose, awaited her.

Only one other was treated worse. It wasn't Raffin the dim-witted stable boy, for he was Myllem's son, and even his stupidest mistakes were laughed off and forgiven. No, it was Rosabella, the princess.

Her milk-white skin had no bruises, and she was clothed and fed well enough—too well, in fact—but oh, Cypress pitied her. They never let the princess run or ride, or even walk in the sun. The girl had grown plump and soft and so very pale. No one spent time with her except her nurse, a pinched and wizened creature with a voice like a harpy. Cypress only saw the princess at the occasional feast or holy-day, or when visitors came and even the lowest kitchen wenches had to serve in the hall. Rosabella often smiled but never laughed, and her eyes, the scullery maid observed, were always sad. Once, when Cypress had to fetch water from the well, she saw the girl staring out in wonder as snow fell on the ice-silvered rose-canes, their thorns sharp as a wolf's fangs. The gaunt arm of the nurse yanked the princess back inside.

For many years the king and queen had longed for a daughter. They had six fine sons—if by fine one meant richly dressed and sneering. But only the eldest could inherit the tiny kingdom—a ramshackle village and few paltry fields surrounding the castle—and it was costly to find dowries or commissions for the rest. They needed a daughter to sell off in marriage to a wealthy suitor in order to keep the realm solvent. And so Rosabella was swathed in precious silks, bathed in almond milk and crushed flower petals, and stowed away in the rose-choked tower until she could prove her worth.

Cypress worked hard at her lowly chores. In her few spare hours, she wandered in the forest, bringing back to Myllem fresh herbs and hidden gems like chanterelles or wild strawberries. Her gifts added fresh flavors to the meals, so the cook no longer beat her. Cypress brewed tasty tisanes which granted the drinkers restful sleep and sweet dreams. Soon all the servants clamored for them, and even the king and queen called for cups before retiring. The foreigner won new respect, and Myllem no longer thought it beneath her to chat with the girl. Cypress made the kitchen garden flourish, and aided the gardeners with the rose beds and in cutting back the thick canes that threatened to overwhelm Rosabella's tower.

One spring day while Cypress was doing just that, she spoke to the princess. The nurse was away. Now that the princess was almost a grown woman, she often left Rosabella alone for hours at a time, certain she would spend her time suitably; docility had been the primary trait cultivated in her. While Cypress hacked at the canes, her sleeves ripped by the thorns, her arms bleeding, the princess peeked out from the threshold.

Cypress paused in her work. "Wouldn't you like to step outside? It's a fine day."

"I'm not allowed," the princess said meekly.

"Nurse Krimps told me she'd be gone for a few hours."

The girl glanced to her right and left and didn't budge. But she held a hand over her heart and her face was filled with yearning.

"I'll stay by you and protect you," Cypress said, pulling herself up to her full height. She'd grown accustomed to stooping, lest the castle folk feel threatened.

"Would you—could you—take me to the garden?" the princess asked. "I've never seen it."

If Cypress worried about the risk of such an undertaking, the girl's joyful smile made her sorrier she'd never tried before. She held out her arm like a courtier for Rosabella to lean on.

"You go too fast!" the princess complained. "A lady must never take long strides like a man, but show herself to be dainty and fragile." Cypress bit back the desire to argue that the girl was fragile enough. Instead, she shortened her stride and slowed down.

They stepped through the arbor. The garden wasn't much to look at yet; most of the flowers were just green spears poking up from the soil. But the girls bent down to examine each sprout and bud, the patterns of veins on the different leaves, happily comparing all the different varieties of green.

"What do you do all day in that tower?" Cypress asked.

"I learn deportment. How to speak with a soft, silken voice, to say little and listen much. How to smile sweetly but not too broadly. And I embroider. I've embroidered tablecloths and sheets for my trousseau, and thousands of pillow-slips, and ever so many slippers for my ladies in waiting, though I don't have any. Nurse Krimps herself has twenty pairs. My parents send others off to far lands, in the hopes that princes and kings will admire my work and ask for my hand in marriage. I'm rather tired of embroidery, but it does keep me occupied."

"Don't you do anything useful? Sew your own gowns, or card or spin?"

"Princesses aren't supposed to be useful," Rosabella answered, "only beautiful. And of course fetch a good bride price and bear her husband healthy heirs."

"Do you never read? Or sing?"

"Heavens no!" the girl cried. "If I read, my future husband would think me too independent, filled with radical ideas. If he wishes me to know things, he will teach me them himself. As for singing—Nurse Krimps is tone deaf, so she's never taught me any songs. I wish I knew some."

Cypress felt very sorry for the girl indeed, and before she returned her to the tower, vowed that she would visit as often as possible, and help her see a little something of the outside world whenever the nurse was absent.

She was as good as her word. Almost every day, the scullery maid escorted the princess to the garden. Cypress told the Rosabella of her homeland, and taught her many of the island songs. The princess had a lovely voice, faint at first, but gaining in strength over time. Her cheeks no longer resembled the white roses of her tower but the pink ones that now blossomed in the summer garden. She walked briskly, and could even run. She easily learned the names of plants and flowers, and soon her nimble fingers were adept at snapping off dead leaves and spent blooms. She had a quick mind, after all, and had only been trained to be dull. She reminded Cypress of the topiaries that edged the garden walk, twisted out of their true form. But a topiary left unpruned would soon revert to its natural state. Cypress hoped that her friend was now experiencing such a restoration.

One day, when Nurse Krimps was out for most of the day, Cypress brought Rosabella to the woods. She'd told Myllem she would bring back mushrooms and watercress, so she'd been granted three full hours between breakfast and dinner.

"I've never seen so many trees!" the princess exclaimed. "And the light!" She placed her hand in a golden shaft that threaded its way between the trees. Tears starred her cheeks like dewdrops in the morning grass.

That was when Cypress knew she loved her, not merely as a friend, but with a deep, abiding love.

The princess caressed the long needles of a pine. When her fingers came away sticky with sap, she sniffed them. "Will you teach me?" she asked.

"Teach you what?"

"How to hear them. The trees. You said they communicate with you."

"I don't know if they'll speak to your kind," Cypress said. "Besides, it takes years to learn to hear the trees' speech.

"Please, let us try!" the princess begged.

"First you must take off your shoes." Before Rosabella could comply, Cypress bent and removed them herself. The delicate green satin had gotten muddied from their woodland trek, the silk embroidery torn. "Oh, they're ruined! Nurse Krimps will discover our secret and never leave you alone again!"

Rosabella laughed. "I have thousands of slippers. I'll discard these and replace them with another pair; she'll never know. The greenspeech," she insisted.

"Stand with your bare feet on the roots," Cypress instructed. "Wrap your arms around the trunk, your cheek and ear pressed to it. Let it feel and hear your heartbeat, get to know you a little and then listen. Listen hard."

Rosabella did as she was told, her eyes closed, her mouth slightly open. Cypress knew the moment when the princess heard the oak: her eyes flew open and her mouth widened. Her arms tightened around the trunk, her feet pressing deeper against the roots.

When her arms grew slack, Cypress asked, "What did you hear?"

"A song! A song, at first, of sun and the rich taste of soil, and the tickling of ants on bark. And then it spoke to me. It said, *Be brave.* And told me my true, my secret name."

Cypress wondered that the tree would speak so readily to a girl untrained in greenspeech, but then her princess was like none other, and who could hold back their heart from her? "What is it?" she asked, in a hushed voice.

The princess laughed. "Rose. That's hardly a secret name, is it? It's mostly just my real name."

But Cypress knew that trees never err or cheat. The girl was Rose, and though now she most resembled the long-stemmed cultivars of the garden's seemly rows, in her heart of hearts she was like the eglantine that gladdens the forest shadows.

She wished she could tell the princess all that. Instead she asked, "Why are the roses that grow around your tower so strange? I've never seen anything like them."

"They were planted generations ago; the tower was old even then. King Rorum married Queen Merash but he loved another. He waited till she bore him three heirs and then plotted to rid himself of her. He called her mad, shut her in the tower with one of her maids, and wed his paramour. The new queen planted the roses herself, saying they were an offering of love to Merash, white in honor of her purity. But she had knowledge of witchcraft, and the roses grew more quickly than was natural. The thickest hedge was placed before the tower door, the canes climbing and entwining so Merash could never get out."

"So the hedge was built to be her prison," Cypress said.

Rose nodded. "When they put me in the tower, they had to hack away the briers, and remove the bones."

Cypress shuddered. Rose took her hand. "It was long ago. The hedge no longer bars my door."

"You're still a prisoner there."

"I will always be a prisoner." The princess looked up into the boughs of the oak as if she wished she could trade places with it. "When I marry, I'll no longer have this. Or you. Though maybe my husband will be kind to me. Maybe we'll even love each other."

The oak groaned, although there was no wind. *They will choose as her bridegroom old King Mindor, rich and cruel,* it told Cypress. She was glad Rose could no longer hear its voice. *He will not love her. She will exchange one prison for a worse one.*

The castle bustled with activity. The princess would soon reach her majority, and the king and queen were planning a ball — ostensibly to celebrate it, but really to provide her many suitors a last glimpse of her beauty before they offered their bids for her hand. Only Cypress knew the man who'd be accepted. As she scrubbed cauldrons clean, or pruned the tower's rose-canes, she tried to hatch a plan to help Rosabella to escape—if that were what she wished. Surely that was why Cypress' fate had sent her there.

Rose no longer needed to stand on the trees' roots with her bare feet, or even touch them, to hear them. One day when they were in the forest, Rose listened to her oak, the first that had spoken to her. She cried out, tears coursing down her cheeks. And then she laughed loudly, head thrown back.

Cypress wanted to ask what she'd learned but what the trees say to a person is private, only to be shared if the hearer wishes, and Rose didn't offer. *Perhaps,* she thought, *it tells her about my plan to rescue her. Did she weep at the thought of her marriage being prevented? And laugh that my plan would fail?*

"This wedding—it's something you long for?" she asked Rose instead.

"I—no. I have no wish to wed a stranger. If I marry, I would have it be for love and not for gold. I fear finding myself in a worse prison than the one I've lived in all my life. At least here, there is friendship." She smiled at Cypress.

"What if a way could be found to free you—would you take it?"

"And do what? Go where?" The light dimmed from Rose's eyes.

"Wherever you like. I'll take you anywhere you wish to go."

"Like in a tale!" Rose sighed. "It can never be."

"No tale," Cypress said, "though tales will go in the making of my plan. Do you want to hear?"

It took nothing for Cypress to add some extra herbs to her tisanes.

"Nurse Krimps has told me of the princess' curse. How terrible!" she said to Myllem.

"Curse? I never heared o' no curse," the cook replied.

"Why surely you must have been there yourself. Three hedge-witches were invited to her christening but a fourth forgotten. She laid a curse on the infant, saying that she'd prick her finger on a spindle and die on her eighteenth birthday. But one of the other hedge-witches softened the curse, so that instead she'd sleep for a hundred years."

"A hundred years," Myllem went on, as if she'd been the one telling the story in the first place. The tisanes ensured that Cypress' tale was believed and remembered as fact. "I heared the witch meself. That's why they never let the girl spin; embroidery needles is all they let her get at. But prophecies has ways o' makin' themselves happen, mark my word. And woe if the princess' birthday en't soon upon us! A sad thing for Princess Rosabella but worse for the rest of us if the kingdom loses the money her bride price would provide. What's to become of me, I ask you, if the princess sleeps a hundred years, and the castle goes to wrack and ruin?"

"Good thing the spell may break if the right suitor wins his way to the tower," Cypress said.

"Aye, we must pin our hopes on a hero, that's for certain."

"But how will any man get through those hedges?" Cypress continued. "Soon after her sleeping body is discovered, the roses will grow around her, and the thorns turn into spikes."

"Ready to pierce the heroes like pigs on my spit," the cook continued. "I never liked them hedges, but I suppose that's cause I always knew they was cursed. They'll keep out anyone but the right man. And what if he don't come?"

And so the story circulated. All feared for the day when the princess would turn eighteen. While the suitors gathered thick as flies, Cypress and the princess gathered white roses from the tower's hedge. The night before the ball, Cypress stole into the tower. She tiptoed past the room where Nurse Krimps slept to the chamber where the princess waited, candles lit. They strewed the rose petals onto the bed, pouring beeswax from the burning candles onto them. With the wax still hot and pliable, Cypress molded the mixture into the shape of the princess, eyes closed as if in sleep. Soon the effigy no longer looked like a mere doll but so exactly like the princess that Rose glanced at her looking-glass to make certain she still wore her own face. Its waxen skin looked and felt like real flesh, and its breast rose and fell as if it breathed. Cypress placed a spindle by the wax figure's outstretched hand.

They stole from the tower, taking anything useful for a long journey, including several jewels to trade for horses and lodging. As they passed the tower's threshold, the rose-hedge spoke in greenspeech for the first time. *I will give your tale the ring of truth,* it promised, *and grow thorns sharp as swords, hungry to slice into human flesh and drink human blood.*

The next morning, Nurse Krimps discovered the body of the princess, and the vile spindle, and the kingdom mourned—at least for a time. The hedge rose up, true to its vow, stronger than any wall, brandishing foot-long thorns sharper than swords. But although Rosabella could not be married off to King Mindor or any other suitor, the realm flourished, for the king and queen charged a handsome fee to each man who attempted to broach the hedge. Several inns were built at the foot of the tower to house the would-be heroes, which added significant revenues to the local economy. For generations the little kingdom prospered from the heroes' blood—until one day, they say, a man won his way to the tower, kissed the sleeping form, and it crumbled into dust. The hedge receded, the spines retracting, till it looked no more vicious than any ordinary rosebush.

One night, in a forest a day's ride from the coast, Cypress and Rose dismounted. Cypress built a fire and cooked the last of the food she'd stolen from Myllem's kitchen. The next night they would spend in an inn before buying passage on a ship to the former scullery maid's homeland. They ate in silence.

Rose got up to pat the horses, whispering loving words to them, while Cypress warmed her hands at the fire and gathered her courage.

"That first day the oak spoke to you, why did you cry and then laugh? Is it something you can tell me now?"

Rose left the horses and stepped closer, standing behind Cypress. "At first I cried," she said, "because the oak told me your secret. I hadn't known you loved me."

Cypress exhaled slowly, the fog of her cold breath flying up to the stars. Rose kneeled behind her.

"Then it told me that I loved you. And I laughed because I knew that already." She wrapped her arms around Cypress and laid her cheek against her back, as if she were a tree.

About the story

I envisioned this as a feminist re-telling of a certain familiar fairy tale, but I didn't want that to be apparent early on. The hero's name that came to me was Cyprus, who was a boy. Then

I changed it to Cypress, and the tree and plant imagery came to me. That sounded like a girl's name, so I swerved the story into a different direction again--and liked it much better that way.

A question for the author

Q: What's a genre you'd like to write but don't or can't?

A: Interesting question--if I want to do it, I certainly try. I am attempting to write a fantasy novel for children--it's complete, it's even second and third drafted, but it's not ready for prime time yet and I am having to leave it on the back burner for a while till I can grapple with how I do and don't want to change it. I've started a YA novel, about 3/4 through the first draft, and am having trouble with that. And I have many many ideas for other books. So—I am struggling to become a novelist.

About the author

Sandi Leibowitz is a teacher, classical singer, and writer of speculative fiction and poetry. Her works appear in *Mythic Delirium, Liminality,* Ellen Datlow's *Best Horror of the Year 5, Devilfish, Not One of Us,* and elsewhere. She has been nominated for the Rhysling, Pushcart Prize, and Best of the Net awards, and won second- and third-place Dwarf Stars. The author of *The Bone-Joiner,* a collection of poems, she lives in New York.

www.sandileibowitz.com

Koehl's Quality Impressions

Tim McDaniel

Early Wednesday morning, not much past 10:30, I wheezed my way through downtown in my old '31 Ford. Down to White Center, where the city sprawl collided with the suburban rents, resulting in rows of dingy cheap apartment buildings, absentee landlords and the retreats of the old or underemployed. I found the place easily. A building of wooden clapboard, still advertising 'covered parking' even though those parking spaces were filled with rusting Chevys, discarded washing machines, and mildewed mattresses.

I parked along the street and walked up to the front door, then leaned on the button next to the peeling paper with 'Linaman, Manager' penciled on it.

After a long while there was a muffled voice.

"Yeah?"

"Mr. Linaman?"

"Naw, he left months ago."

"You the manager now?"

"Yeah. You a cop or what? No one here been making any calls."

"Nothing like that. I have a small business proposal that you might be interested in."

"A business proposition, huh? So there's money involved?"

"There's money involved." I'd met plenty of guys like him in prison.

"Well come on up, then, I guess. 203."

The door opened, and I climbed the stairs. The thin carpet, perhaps originally a beige sort of color, was held together by stains, and the narrow staircase exuded the tang of cat piss.

Mr. Manager was, as I would have guessed, dressed in an old t-shirt and a pair of sweatpants, and smelled a lot like the staircase. I explained my needs, he articulated his, and we reached an agreement.

I checked out the deceased woman's room next. It was tiny, and the windows didn't open. There were a few sticks of shabby furniture, and one yellowing photograph on a wall, of a young man in a uniform standing in a desert somewhere. The room at least smelled a little better; a lavender-kind of scent lingered there. I closed the door behind me when I left to go back downstairs.

I left the building and took a deep breath. At least the apartment was still vacant. I wouldn't have to make any more deals on behalf of my client. Vampires, we called them, but not the blood-sucking kind. I made a commission on each deal, but they still made me feel like I needed to shower.

"Koehl's Quality Impressions" was stenciled in black gothic letters on the glass of my office door. A little crooked. All it needed was a cheesy little "While U Wait" card taped under it. Well, in this building, this neighborhood, I couldn't expect the clients I used to get at First Impressions; over there, Pichrenn's name still brought in the classy set, even this long after his death.

Was "Quality" accurate? Well, it's not bragging to say that I can raise ghosts with the best of them. I can make latent ghosts visible, clear as day, short-term or long. At least I can when I can afford to lay my hands on quality equipment. The gear I use now is so shoddy I'm lucky if Fred and Mary can even recognize dear jowly Aunt Greta.

So, yeah, clients were not lined up outside my door. I came in every day, though, in at nine or maybe ten or eleven and out at five or maybe four, when I wasn't out on a job. I couldn't afford to miss any walk-ins. I got the occasional referral of a double-booked or cheap client from my old friend Nol at First Imp, and some job orders from a few regulars, vampires, some of whom I knew from my prison days. But walk-ins, impulse buyers, were my main source of income. Sometimes people do act on whims. I stayed in the office daily, watching TV or reading or surfing for obits or drinking until I could justify the return to my apartment.

The glass on the door was at least frosted. A classy touch. Most of my clients didn't particularly want to be seen from the street, no more than I wanted passersby to see my empty reception room.

Empty it was, when I got back from arranging the vampire feeding. I hung my jacket on the rack near the door.

Ah. There was a new message for me on my computer. I went to the desk and jabbed the button.

"Hello, Koehl." I was sitting in the chair, and I didn't remember sitting down. Lindsay. "I have a job I'd like to discuss with you. I can come by tomorrow about eleven, if that's good for you."

I hadn't seen her since... when? Oh, yeah. Not since the trial.

God, how I wanted to see her again. And I also really wished that, tomorrow at eleven or so, I could be somewhere else, far away.

"I need you to come see me." Pichrenn's voice on the phone had been thin and uneven, air forced through rusty valves. I was in the middle of a job, taking the impression of a young couple's son, four years old at the time of death, but this was Pichrenn, so I called Nolan to take over for me.

This kind of thing wasn't unusual. The job I was doing was routine, though never tell a family that, and Pichrenn often called me away from those to attend him on more interesting cases. Or more high-profile. I figured, and hoped, he was grooming me to take over once he passed on.

I apologized to the couple, saying I had a family emergency, and took a cab over to the address Pichrenn had given me. I found him in one of those huge, lavish condos on 12th, squatting in the corner of a bedroom. The equipment was still boxed, lying in its contoured foam.

The room was dominated by an immense bed, brass. A window took up most of one wall, affording an impressive view of the city and the mountain, and ostentatious abstract paintings garnished the other walls.

There was another bit of apparent abstract art on the peach carpet, a dark red Rorshach image, all that physically remained of the room's former occupant: a bloodstain like an obscene starfish that had been crushed into the floor. There were additional random splashes and splatters on the mussed bed, and even on one of the walls.

Well, this family wasn't shy about displaying their money, if they could afford to keep the condo, untenanted (so to speak), for four and a half months after the murder of the husband. No wonder they could afford Pichrenn himself.

He stood up and looked down at the carpet stain, back straight, perfectly still, but his hands, jammed deep into his jacket pockets, were twisting and pinching the material. He did that a lot, as if his hands were the only vents for whatever emotions roiled within.

Lindsay was next to him, sitting on a clean part of the bed, composed and quiet. Her eyes were on Pichnrenn, but she was breathing a little too heavily.

"The Dudanna murder," Pichrenn said. I raised my eyebrows. The story had been a big one.

"The wife was the one who did it," Pichrenn said. "Made it look like a robbery, or tried to."

"Yeah," I said. "I saw it on TV. Hi, Lindsay."

She nodded at me, her eyes flashing secrets over Pichrenn's lowered bald head.

I said, "Our client, then, must be the dear departed's murderer's sister, is that right?"

Pichrenn smiled. "Right. The sister of the killer. That's what makes it interesting, isn't it?"

I squatted on the floor next to him and surveyed the scene. He was waiting, I knew, for me to see it. Our job, if we did it well enough, would be both a reflection on the murder, and a comment on the client. And of course we had to please our client while doing so, which sometimes meant hiding or disguising our own comments. We were portrait artists. Well, that's how we thought of ourselves. We wanted to do more than get a snapshot of a corpse. Our equipment amplified the energies embedded in the walls, the floor, the air, to reveal not a carcass, but the shade of a living man.

"Not a happy family, I take it," I said. "I mean between the sisters."

"I'd guess not."

"The wife got away with a slap on the wrist, as I recall. The best justice money could buy."

Pichrenn said nothing.

"Sis is, of course, married herself. An older gent, if I recall."

"Very happily married. There've been no reports of trouble."

"Right. And so there would be no jealousy of the sister who snagged the young movie-star-handsome millionaire, no sexual tension at family get-togethers, no younger-sister resentments or buried bitternesses."

"These people were the top predators of the social jungle, Scott. We're not talking about trailer trash."

"Course not."

"Would it make a difference if they were trailer trash? People all do the same things to each other, no matter their positions," Lindsay said. "Cheat on each other, sneak around."

I decided to ask Lindsay what she had meant the next time I was alone with her. But I knew I wouldn't. Betrayal was not something I wanted to discuss. And anyway, Lindsay had a way of making me forget scruples, even as they clearly gnawed at her.

But I had to say something. Something safe. "Sure it would," I said. "They couldn't afford us. They'd have to make peace with their dead and move on."

We were all silent for a time, then I stood up and squatted down again next to the box of highlighters. I took the first one out and stood up, looking the room over again. Then I crossed the room to the bedroom door and extended the tripod. After setting it in place, I put another highlighter just behind and to the left of where Pichrenn still stood. He observed my choices.

I pulled a third highlighter out of the box and placed it just in front of the window. I punched in some settings. Then I looked down at Pichrenn. He cocked his head.

"There was a lot of emotion flying around here, before and during," I said. "The whole area is bound to be saturated."

"Then we wouldn't need three highlighters," Pichrenn said. "I can almost see the remnants without the use of even one."

"You're sensitive, so you don't count. I've set up these two —" I pointed at the one near the door and the one near Pichrenn — "with complementary frequencies. They'll nearly cancel each other out, with just enough bleed-through to give us something to work with. As you say, it's so thick in here that even that amount should be plenty."

"Ummm."

"And the third one, near the window, I've set much lower."

"To pick up the background."

"Right," I said. "With only one, and with all the other energies flying around, all it'll probably pick up will be ghostly half-images, like something seen out of the corner of your eye."

"You did that at the Joshi place," Pichrenn said.

"Are you accusing me of repeating myself? But these will probably be a little weaker, more ghostly. I've been thinking about getting the chance to try this since the Caceres job. There, the energies were so weak there that half-images were the best I could get, but I did think the effect was an interesting one."

Pichrenn nodded. "And why here?" he asked. "A neat effect is just so much dazzle without a purpose to it."

"The energies released during the act," I said, "will be powerful, and I'm sure they'll be compelling as all hell. But they're all of violence, and terror, or its aftermath. We're sure to get some striking images. But what interests me just as much is the underlying tension. I doubt the victim was entirely shocked by his wife's deed."

I chanced a glance at Pichrenn, but his gaze remained focused on the floor, his brow creased. I would have given a pinkie to know his thoughts just then, to know why he wanted me there. Just for the job? Or was he sending me another message? "He knew, he must have known," I said, "that she was on the edge. He probably enjoyed baiting her, flirting with the sister, making her feel unwanted, bullying her, whatever. I don't know. But I'm sure there was something there. If we can display some of that, even as — or especially as — ghostly after-images behind the main action, I think it'll be something worth looking at."

"Hmmm," he said. Lindsay was nodding along.

"And I was thinking. They specified suppression of sounds, knocks, smells, temperature variations, I suppose?"

Pichrenn nodded.

"I don't know if it's totally ethical, but if we allowed a little of the subsonics to leak through..."

"Yes," said Lindsay. She looked over at me.

"Unsettling." Pichrenn got up, bones creaking, and shook a leg that had apparently gone numb. "Very interesting, Scott," he said. "You have a good grasp of things. I believe I'll leave this one in your hands."

I kept my face blank. There was no way he could have found out about what Lindsay and I had been up to. He had called to say he'd be late for a meeting up at his cabin, and things had just happened. And then they happened again, in other places at other times.

"The client paid for your personal attention," I said. "She's bound to be upset."

"I'll smooth things over with her," he said. "If she wants to pay for my judgment, she'll have to accept my judgment that you're the best one for this job."

Maybe that was all there was to it — that he thought I was best for the job.

It kind of makes me sorry that I killed the old guy.

Lindsay settled into the chair and leveled her eyes at me. Lindsay Ingham, Charles Pichrenn's former lover, or at least the final one. And mine. She used to breeze through the outer offices on her way to his inner sanctum, slim, elegant, and moneyed, with glossy black hair that bounced off the small of her back.

After Pichrenn's death, she'd pretty much disappeared. At the funeral it seemed to me, at least, that an understanding look had passed between us, an acknowledgement that I was still part of her world. But I had been out on a job when she came by the studio to pick up her mementos. She called me twice. I put off answering. But when she heard that I had taken Pichrenn's impression, she vanished. Felt like I'd betrayed him even unto death. Or maybe it was just guilt that she felt, however unwarranted. Our affair hadn't killed him.

Then the law finally caught up with me, and I saw her in the witness box at the trial, and there was prison. She didn't visit.

And now here she was, in my own little studio, in one of those new skirts that's tight in some places and loose in others, and a black blouse with ruffles around her neck. The air was low in oxygen just then, and my gaze stole back to her face, tracing the line of the chin, her cheeks and eyes and hair, whenever she looked down.

"So. Welcome to Koehl's Quality Impressions," I said. "It's uh, good to see you again, Lindsay."

Lindsay looked around her at the decor — the faded carpet, the Degas print on the wall. "Nice," she said. She didn't say it was nice to see *me* again.

"Yeah," I said. "High class all the way."

"Do you keep your equipment here?" she asked.

"I got a closet. This place came with every convenience. So, what have you been up to?"

"I remember you used to only use the best. You know, Charles really admired your ability to keep all of it in such top shape."

So she didn't want to get personal. No old friends and lovers catching up crap. "That's the trouble with the best stuff," I said. "It's temperamental." Like people. I waited for her to talk.

"Charles used to say you were the best in the studio," she finally said, not looking at me. "No knocks, no temperature swings or stopped clocks when you did a job."

The second mention of Pichrenn. "I miss him too, you know," I said, opening and closing a desk drawer for no reason. "I was there with him from the beginning."

"I know. Until the end. Well, if you miss him so much, stop by his place. You can see him anytime there, right?" Her voice had shifted out of neutral, but not in a direction I liked. "Sorry," she said. "I know you didn't mean... I mean, that you never wanted..."

"Don't worry about it. I'm past that. So what's up, Lindsay?" I leaned back in my chair. It creaked a little. I thought Lindsay had perhaps changed her perfume, but I couldn't be sure.

"I need a job done, Scott."

"And you came here? As far as I know they're still taking commissions at First Impressions. They're the best. And I know you always did like the best." I couldn't look too long into her eyes.

"If you're fishing for a compliment, I've given you too many already. Do you want to take the job?"

"I need to hear a little about it first," I said. A lie, but I didn't want her to know how far I'd sunk and how desperate I'd become. Oh, when I first got out on probation, I was the talk of the town, the indispensable impressionist and party guest. Offers both personal and professional came in the daily email. I had turned them all down; they had all been just a different kind of vampire, getting their jollies with a touch of death. But my fifteen minutes had ended.

Back to business. I clasped my hands on my desk. Clients liked it when you seemed to give them your full attention, and going to an impressionist is a little intimidating to some, like going to confession, or revealing your dirty little secrets to a psychiatrist. People take death seriously, even if it's not their own.

"It's my mother."

"I don't remember you talking much about her."

"No. We didn't have a lot of contact the last few years."

"So you had a fight. Teen angst, I suppose?" She didn't say anything. "But now you decide that you want to raise her. Planning to enact a little posthumous make up session, a sort of after- death mother-daughter heart to heart? You know it doesn't work that way." I don't know why I was being such a bastard.

"Look, I just owe it to her. There's nothing else I can do for her."

"'For her'? How's that? It's just a damn ghost, Lindsay. It's got as much self-awareness as a black and white photograph. Your mom, she's gone."

"Call it a gesture, then. It's too late for anything else." She looked down at the floor, as if the topic were too personal for her to go on. I didn't believe that for a second, but I let it ride. I didn't need to talk myself out of a job.

"OK. You're the customer." I slid a brochure over to her. Nice how desktop printing can make your hole-in-the-wall look like a real-live business. "Here are the rates."

She took it, but she didn't look down at the brochure. At least she didn't crease it; I could use it again next time if she didn't stick it in her purse. "I came to you because you're good. I don't want the effect spoiled by second-rate equipment."

"I don't really have the resources I once did."

"With the advance I'm prepared to pay, you can afford to get some of those resources again." I liked the sound of that; I missed the feel of properly tuned and maintained equipment, its quiet, even hum and ozone smell. The garbage I used now tended to sputter, and the focus kept going out unless you constantly kept on top of it.

Also, an advance that big could pay some of my less important bills, too. Rent and food came to mind.

Lindsay began tapping her code into my paypad.

I forced myself not to look. I pulled up an empty file on the computer, and started filling it out. "I'll need your current address." She took one of her cards out of her purse and passed it to me. I saw that nowadays she was employed at EarthTenders, Inc., a non-profit environmental umbrella. Part-time, no doubt. It was just the kind of feel-good job an over-indulged rich girl would have. It shouldn't have made me so bitter. If she spent her time suckling endangered wildebeest puppies, what was it to me?

"Any other legally interested parties?"

"Mom's latest ex has signed off on it. That satisfies your legal requirements, I believe."

"Sure does." I kept typing. "Visual, audio, olfactory?" Most people want only the visual, even though it's more work to suppress the taps and moans and temperature swings.

"Just the visual."

"Short-term, long-term, or permanent?"

"Short-term."

"OK." I stopped typing and looked at her, but she was doing her stare-at-the-floor act again. I saw a few wrinkles on her face that hadn't been there all those years before.

"I really just have to say goodbye," she said. "I don't need an endlessly repeating exhibition, for people to gawk at." Another little dig at me for raising Pichrenn. So I guess the guilt still gripped her. But I'd show her that nowadays I was immune to that kind of subtle reprimand. I was a businessman now, not some overpaid artiste.

"Short-term it shall be. Cause of death?"

"Her heart."

"OK, good. Place and time of death?"

"June 19th, this year. It was a Saturday. At 9:10 p.m. At 7th and Bell."

I typed. Then, "If the death occurred on the street itself, or in any public area, we'll need all kind of permits."

"That's not a problem. She actually died in a restaurant there, Grasso's. They've already given their permission." She fished some papers out of her purse and passed them across the desk. Standard release forms. The restaurant probably figured a ghost would be good for business, and maybe they were even right, at least for the short term. But I doubted it. "When can you do it?"

I pulled my appointment book out of a desk drawer and made a show of flipping through its blank pages. "How about this Thursday? Say one o'clock."

"That would be fine."

I didn't suppose the restaurant would object to that hour of the day. The raising of a ghost would be good entertainment for their lunch crowd.

After Lindsay left I sat in my chair, blinking. What the hell had I done? She'd reached out – clumsily, indirectly, but she had made contact. And all my defenses had shot up. I'd needed her, on many levels, after Pichrenn died. My friend, my mentor. According to the law, my victim. And I'd had no one to lean on, because she was dealing with her own issues.

I could still smell her. I didn't know if it was a perfume or just her, but now I knew it hadn't changed from back when. The office was suddenly small, dingy, dark and close. I had to get out.

I had to visit Pichrenn again.

The apartment building was now owned by a foundation that had agreed to allow suite 612 to remain vacant. They rented out the other rooms, and probably not one in ten of the current inhabitants knew that the former occupant up there on the sixth floor had not really left.

The doorman knew.

"Mr. Koehl. Good to see you again." Jacob removed his hat and put it under an arm. I noticed that his hair was graying, the tight curls looking like ash.

"Good to see you, Jacob."

Jacob turned to open the door for me. "Time for the renewal, Mr. Koehl?"

"No. Just a visit."

"Ah." Jacob led the way across the plush lobby to the bank of elevators. "Well, that's important. Remembering." He gently pressed the elevator call button, and the doors opened immediately.

"Yeah, I guess so," I said. We entered the elevator. "Many tourists come by lately, Jacob?"

"Not so many. There was an old lady eight, ten days ago, and some art student early this week."

The elevator car stopped. We paced the cream carpet down to 612. Jacob turned the key in the lock, then stepped back. "Have yourself a good visit, now, Mr. Koehl."

He never came in.

"Thank you, Jacob." I opened the door.

Usually he was in the big easy chair, head up, one hand touching his chin. He must have done that a lot, for it to have imprinted so strongly; he couldn't have planned a better portrait.

And, I must admit, I had done well with the material. Nothing flashy here, nothing avant-garde, not for him. A quiet study of a thoughtful, gentle man. I'd let a sound of even breathing come though. The legs were almost invisible, mere suggestions of lines and the drape of his trousers. But his body became more substantial as you moved up, and the chair back was nearly completely obscured by his torso. The head was preternaturally distinct, the dark eyes burning.

God, I missed him.

The foundation kept some equipment in a closet. I set it up the way I always did, going through the motions, and renewed the imprint. It wasn't time yet, I just needed to do something with my hands. Then I sat in a chair for a while. It doesn't do any good to talk to a ghost. I never know what to say, anyway.

I shouldn't have set the appointment for Thursday. It gave me three days to wait. Sure, I had wanted her to think I was busy, but I could've claimed a sudden cancellation. She'd have seen right through me, but then, she almost certainly already had anyway.

There was one thing I could do. I fed her check to my computer. Now I had the money, I could stop using the shoddy broadcasters that spit all over the spectrum, and the tuneless highlighters and the touchy suppressors. Now it would be topline stuff, paid for in full with Lindsay's advance.

At the shop they greeted me like an old friend who'd killed someone — fair enough. But once we got to going over the equipment — oh, the way those new suppressors squelch noise! — all awkwardnesses and discomforts were forgotten, and I walked out of there with the best stuff I'd ever worked with, and slaps on the back.

Then, of course, I had to go to the scene of death, to scout out the territory. I hoped my car still had some juice in the bat.

It was in a good part of town. A very good part, in fact, where I stuck out like a zombie at a wedding. Grasso's was the kind of place a Mafioso would kill to be murdered in — all indirect lighting, widely-spaced tables, dark reflective wood, candles, and hovering waiters. And expensive. Conscious of my old jacket, my shoe with the loose sole, I didn't want to go in.

I knocked on the glass door anyway.

A guy in a billowy white shirt, his tie undone, peered out at me. I flashed him my business card, which should mean nothing, but flash any sort of ID when you aren't being asked to and people just start thinking police or Homeland Security. He opened the door.

"I'm afraid we're closed," he began.

"Yeah, I figured. Lindsay Ingham asked me to stop by."

"One moment, please." He disappeared into the bowels of the restaurant and soon came back with a Mr. Sarkouhi. Apparently there was no Grasso.

"Ms Ingham mentioned you would come to see the site, Mr. Koehl. Thank you for visiting before we open for dinner." Mr. Sarkouhi, comb-over plastered to his wine-colored skull, a thin moustache drooping against jowly cheeks, nodded me inside. "When you have prepared everything, of course, then we will go public, as they say. The table where it occurred is just through here."

Nothing special about the table. It was against one wall, a painting above it. But I saw some interesting possibilities, and the setting was appealing — death and money, death and elegance; these were and remain powerful combinations. They pushed buttons, and I found myself getting excited by the work ahead. Such a change from that which I had been getting lately.

I made some mental notes. Places I could shoot from, surrounding material resonances. I forgot that Mr. Sarkouhi was hovering behind me until he delicately cleared his throat.

"I'm almost finished, Mr. Sarkouhi. Just figuring the angles."

"Of course, Mr. Koehl. The passing of Ms Mehrer in our establishment was, I'm sure you understand, quite a shock."

"I'm sure it was."

"What I mean is, Ms Mehrer was more than a customer here. She was here so often, and she enjoyed a close relationship to those here, the staff and the other diners."

I could see what he was working up to. "Do you suppose they'll enjoy seeing her here again?"

"It might be disquieting to some."

"And yet Lindsay told me you agreed to the raising. She showed me the paperwork."

"Yes, that's true. It's just that, well..."

"I know. I guess you don't say no to Lindsay." I never could, for different reasons. Or maybe they weren't so different. "Mr. Sarkouhi, she's asked for just a temporary raising. I'll make sure it's as tasteful as I can. I don't know what else I can tell you."

"Thank you, Mr. Koehl. And my thanks, again, for coming when we are closed between lunch and dinner. I appreciate that you are trying to minimize the disruption."

"No problem." Actually, I hadn't even thought about the restaurant being open or not.

As Mr. Sarkouhi turned away, a thought struck me. "Mr. Sarkouhi. On the night in question, was Ms Mehrer dining alone?"

Mr. Sarkouhi's face flushed a deeper red. "Ah, no, Mr. Koehl. She was dining with her husband."

Her husband? Lindsay hadn't shown me any paperwork from him. And I would need it. As she well knew.

Back in the office, I called up the news stories about the death of Ms Mehrer on the computer.

Alicia Mehrer had indeed died of a heart attack on June 19th, at 9:10 p.m., at Grasso's. According to witnesses she murmured something, stood up, took a few steps and then collapsed, dying a few moments later.

I wondered at the last name. I looked up Lindsay's bio. Skimpy. She must have paid someone monstrous sums to keep her bio so short. But it did show that her dad, Joseph Ingham, had left the family when she was just seven. The mom remarried two years later. The second husband had died. Cancer. Then mom had married Joseph again, and divorced him again two years after that. Well. Sounded like an interesting family. Money and death, and Lindsay's family had a lot of both. But with a divorce on record, at least I wouldn't have to meet the old man to get a signature.

My computer search turned up plenty of gossip concerning the late Alicia and her ex Joseph. Curiosity got the better of me and I expanded the search a bit and came up with some charming hospital records. All of the sources agreed that Mr. Ingham had been one real bastard. The kind of guy a jury would wink at you for killing.

And yet, even after the abandonment and after the divorce, Alicia had kept coming back for more pain. Again and again.

Sex and death is another powerful combination; the oldest and the strongest of them all.

And why had Lindsay neglected to mention that her dad was with her mom at the time?

Closet skeletons can make a raising a lot more interesting.

Thursday. The restaurant door opened, and Lindsay entered with the grace of a predatory eel, dressed all in satiny black. She stood and watched me work for a while. Of course, a small crowd had already gathered; the equipment summons them as reliably as it summons ghosts. Mr. Sarkouhi stood prominently in the center, his arms folded in pride, surveying the crowd.

Lindsay came closer. "How's it going?" If she was so cool and commanding, why did her fingers clench her bag?

"Just finishing up the underlays now." I tightened a tripod leg, then checked the broadcast shadow.

"I've decided to go long-term, Scott."

I looked up. "What?"

"I said I've decided to go long-term. With an option for permanency."

I looked at Mr. Sarkouhi. "It's all right," Lindsay said. "Mr. Sarkouhi has given us permission."

"I'll need to see that for myself."

"Of course." She opened her purse without looking at it and took some papers out. She held them out to me.

"Why the change in plan?" I left her holding the papers and picked up another broadcaster.

Lindsay was silent for a short time. "Does it matter?" She allowed her hand to drop to her side, the papers slapping against her tailored slacks.

"No, I guess not." I extended the tripod legs on the broadcaster and set it up at a 45-degree angle to the first. I'd put a highlighter just between the two. "You just wanted to say goodbye — wasn't that the purpose of this raising?"

"Maybe I just thought I would need more time with her." I didn't even pretend to look convinced, and she continued, "She *was* my mother, Scott."

I flipped the test switch on the 'caster and checked the levels as it hummed. "Not a very private place for getting in your quality time with mom." I adjusted the levels and checked the output. I looked up at her.

Lindsay looked at me, her eyes just slightly narrowed. I knew why she had chosen me for the job. Not because I was the best, but because she knew that I would do it, that I would gratefully touch things more reputable studios sneered at.

Or there was another reason, but I veered away from that thought.

"Well, if you change your mind, remember I do collapsings, too," I said. "In fact, I lay more ghosts than women." It was a standard joke, and she gave it the response it deserved.

"Are you ready?"

"Another ten, fifteen minutes."

"Fine." Lindsay passed the papers to Mr. Sarkouhi and greeted some oldsters sitting at a nearby table. Mr. Sarkouhi stood there, one hand on his moustache, not looking at anything.

"I guess you'll be getting a permanent tourist attraction, right here at table eight, Mr. Sarkouhi," I said.

"Permanent, maybe." Sarkouhi looked less than thrilled.

"None of my business, but it seems to me that what might attract a crowd for a short while might grate on the nerves of your diners, if it's constantly in view. Of course, you'd be a better judge than me of what might pique a person's appetite."

Sarkouhi narrowed his eyes. "If you talk me into withdrawing my permission, Mr. Koehl, you'll lose the job."

"Last thing on my mind, Mr. Sarkouhi."

"I could revoke permission, though, at a later date. Couldn't I? I read the contract."

"Yeah, maybe. But Lindsay might try to sue if you try it. The lawyers would have to decide what your contract actually says. Better to just curtain off the table."

Sarkouhi met my eyes briefly, then nodded thoughtfully.

Memories intrude like unwanted ghosts.

The day Pichrenn died, I'd gone to see him at home. That memory was a persistent visitor. He'd been sick for some time, and he'd had his bedroom outfitted with all kinds of medical equipment and monitors. The place smelled of disinfectants and futility, and Pichrenn lay in his huge bed, looking over at me with eyes too bright in a head become too large.

His voice was as weak as his body, but he could still speak, was still coherent.

"Art," he told me. "That's been my life, Scott, these last thirty years."

"And you've done well," I said. "You know how impressions were looked at before you got into the field. Dodgy at best. You made a whole new artform. I guess not many can claim that distinction."

Pichrenn smiled sickly, not falling for the flattery, sincere though it was. "And now this." With an arm little more than papery skin stretched over knobby bones, he gestured at the IV feeds, the machine that beeped his heart along. "They tell me I could live ten more years like this."

What could I say to that?

"They're making advances all the time."

"So maybe I'll only lie here for eight years, or six. That's no way to be, Scott. But the law says I can't take the easy way out, with ten 'good' years ahead of me. Damn Republicans."

I looked away.

"Help me, Scott." He whispered it.

And then, "Make me a work of art."

"Huh?" But I knew.

There is no kind of death that can compare with a properly-conducted suicide. Despair, desperation, pain, a reckless courage, and even a strange sort of hope: that someone will stop you, that you'll be delivered into heaven, whatever. It makes for one hell of an impression.

And it's almost as hard to kevork as it is to do it yourself. Sure, lots of laws make it all right to kill someone, if they really want you to, and if the doctors have signed off on the sign-off. But that's not what Pichrenn was asking for, a sterile room and a certifiably painless fade out. My way would be less clinical.

But afterwards, I made the impression, and it's still drawing the occasional connoisseur. Maybe Pichrenn, or part of him, thought he was doing me a favor, giving me so much pain to work with.

Lindsay came over, ushered by a hostess. "Everything's ready?"

"Yep."

"Fine. Let's do this."

Sarkouhi raised his eyebrows at me. I nodded.

"I think your host would like to get everyone here for the unveiling," I said. "That's his payoff, right? That he can show this off to his customers."

"Who knows why anyone does anything. He gave his permission. That's all I needed."

"Still, we can give him a minute to get his people assembled." I made some final, unnecessary adjustments. "I have to say that I don't feel this will be representative of my best work, Lindsay. The image is fairly clear and sharp, but the background hum is, at best, just..."

"I don't need art. I just want to see Mother."

"Well, then everything's fine."

Sarkouhi, all smiles and broad gestures, led a small group of his well-fed and overdressed patrons into a semicircle around the table. I showed them where they could stand for the best view, then stood before them. I waited for their gossiping to slow to a trickle, their eyes to wander to me.

"Before I unveil this, I'd like to clear up a few common misconceptions about my craft, for those who may not be as deeply involved in the netherworld as I am," I said. I saw that Lindsay was annoyed with my delay, but hell, this was too good a chance to pass up. I just might pick up some high-class clients.

"First, what this is not." I started passing out business cards. "Ghosts are not self-aware, they're not beings. They can't see you or hear you. They're simply impressions, imprinted on the local area by the trauma of death. Or by other trauma, or other emotion. That's why you sometimes see ghosts of the living." I'd passed out all my cards. Time to wrap it up.

"The impressions are often of the moment of death, but not always." I went back to my equipment. "Dominant feelings, commitments left unfulfilled, unsaid messages, all these things can and do show up, and it's up to the artist to see that they do. And that's all I have to say. Let's see what we can see."

I checked my viewer. Yeah, I was satisfied with what I had called forth. I flipped the final switch.

At first there was nothing, except for the low hum of the 'caster. The smell of ozone grew in the air. Slowly an image started to form, in mid-air next to the table. It started as a grainy mist, like fine television snow, a vague human shape. It slowly intensified and clarified as the highlighters brought more of the energy out into visible forms, kicking it to the focusers. All this was needed to get the image formed in the first place — although of course natural ghosts do form, usually of an inferior quality, and with odd, annoying, aural and temperature effects — but once it was there, it would stay until properly laid, as long as it got boosted now and then.

The image continued to clear, and soon we were looking at a woman. It was a loop. Not uncommon. She moved, in jerky, uncertain movements, from the table to a spot a few feet away. Then suddenly we would see her lying on the floor, face down. Then she would be up again, moving around, as if confused. Her death had obviously come as a shock to her.

Her body, her clothes, were not too distinct — vague suggestions of a matronly form, decked out in some kind of conservative dark dress. Maybe the neckline was a bit lower, the dress a bit tighter, than society would choose to dictate. Was that a string of pearls around the fleshy neck? It was hard to tell.

But none of that mattered. Because the face — the face was clear, very clear. Real.

It was an aged face, but not heavily lined; Lindsay's mother would have been happy to hear that her face-lifts had survived her death. The forehead, fringed by curled white hair, was nearly smooth, the cheeks still full, the chin small and weak but still single.

You could see all that eventually. But it took time to take in, because what caught the attention were the ghost's eyes. They were startlingly blue in that papery face, and as the woman paced they sought something, something to be wary of. You could almost see a hunched form, a shadow, a dark aura, hovering at her back. And the expression in Mrs. Mehrer's eyes—

They were imploring. That's the word. But why? Was Ms Alicia Mehrer asking for mercy, for freedom? Or for understanding, compassion? There was shame in those eyes, too.

Even in death, she remained in thrall to her husband, bound to him by pain and need.

I couldn't have manufactured such a thing. But an impressionist can choose what to highlight — lives are complicated things — and I'd made sure that sick dependency came through. Call it art, showing a truth in place of the prettified picture that was asked for. Call it a stab at Lindsay. I don't know.

Maybe it was just what Lindsay had wanted to see. I had to look over at her. Her expression was at first smug, then horrified, lips parted and wide-eyed, but soon a mask slid down over her face. Her eyes narrowed and the right edge of her mouth curved up slightly. She coolly surveyed the onlookers; before her eyes met mine, I quickly looked down.

Then I looked at the crowd. I'd seen the same reactions a hundred times before. Some looked on in horror, lips curled, and clutched at the arms of those next to them. Some tried to avert their eyes, as if embarrassed, but their gazes were continually drawn back to the apparition before them. And some few leaned forward, drinking in the death.

Sarkouhi was watching the crowd, too. He seemed less than pleased. He saw me looking at him and walked over to me.

"Is this normal?" he asked in a low voice. "I mean, will it do anything else?"

"Some few do seem to react to things near them. Some look like they are trying to talk to you — the impressions can react to the impressed energies of those still living. Some act out the worries on their minds at the moment of death. Sometimes they even communicate what that was. Or try to. But, to answer your question, no. This is it. It's a fairly short action loop this time. She wasn't here long enough to lay down much more narrative."

Sarkouhi looked back at the impression, his face sour. I began packing up my stuff. Sarkouhi looked back at me.

"You're leaving?"

"Yep. Job's done."

"And this will just go on, repeating here in my place?"

"That's right." I folded a tripod and laid it gently in its foam-lined case. "I've pumped a lot of energy into the floor and walls, enough to keep it going for at least five or six weeks. And after that, I'll come back and pump it up some more. Can I use your phone? I have to call to have this stuff picked up." I couldn't just toss equipment of this caliber into my trunk, but it was humiliating to have to ask.

"Of course." He handed it over and I turned to the wall to give the man a moment, and sure enough, Sarkouhi went to talk to Lindsay.

Their conversation apparently didn't last too long, because when I clicked off and resumed packing, Sarkouhi was over by the other restaurant patrons. I guess he was trying to put a good face on the show, but the diners weren't buying. Several had already left, and a few in the back were realizing that they would have to pass uncomfortably close to the ghost to get to the door.

"Mrs. Sorensen!" Lindsay called, and one of the biddies looked up. A much younger man, his hair still dark, put a protective arm on her shoulder.

Lindsay made no attempt to get closer to her. "Enjoying the show, Mrs. Sorensen?"

"It's, ah..."

"Not sure? Perhaps your latest young man has an opinion — what's this one's name?"

The man scowled, whispered something to Mrs. Sorensen, and they turned away. Then she pulled away from him and looked back.

"I didn't know, Lindsay. I swear, I didn't know what he was doing to her." She turned and walked away.

Lindsay looked after them, her mouth fixed in its smile, her eyes full of hate.

Then she blinked and looked back at her mother for a moment. She strolled over to me. "Good work, as always."

"Thanks. And the rest of the money will be in my account when, exactly?"

"Oh, how you've come down in the world, Scott." She fished around in her purse and then started writing out a check.

"Yep. All the way down to the bottom line." I swiped her check through my reader. "Pleasure doing business. Please remember me whenever a loved one dies on you." I went back to the packing.

"This is my mother, Scott. You make me sound like one of your ghouls."

I folded a tripod and lay it gently in its foam. "The term is 'vampire.' But you're right. I know that you had me do this out of the love and respect you hold for your dear mom."

Lindsay moved in front of me, and spat her words. "You, of all people, have no right to judge me. I paid you for the job, and you did it. You didn't complain."

"I'm no judge, Lindsay." I closed and locked the lid on the case. I stood up. "They are, though." I nodded over to the last of the restaurant patrons. "You've given them a good show." I couldn't resist. "Was it the one you wanted?" I really was curious about that.

"You're done here, I think," she said, and walked out of the restaurant, almost striding through her mother's image.

Lindsay, Lindsay, Lindsay. Our shared betrayal of Pichrenn had eaten away at us both. Maybe my time in prison had given me a chance to let it go just a little more than she had, had convinced me that she was now out of reach, a subject of wistfulness and what-if. And how did she feel, now? No way would she think of me as out of her league; she could scrape me off the sidewalk any time she felt like it. But having me in her life would just remind her of what we had done to Pichrenn, how our relationship had been tainted from the start by that duplicity.

Sarkouhi headed over to me. I was getting downright popular. "This," he said, "is a bad business."

"Disappointed with the show? You're not alone."

"Oh, Mr. Koehl, I'm sure you have done an excellent job. But this is... It's not dignified."

"Death usually isn't."

He looked at me. "This isn't just death. How can I serve food, with this obscene thing here?"

Dear, dead Ms Mehrer continued her routine.

He hadn't thought of that before? Just what kind of idiot was he? Or, more to the point, what had Lindsay done or said to him? "You'd be surprised," I said. "This kind of show does bring a certain subset of the population. Not like your current crowd, though." I waved a hand at the people. "Like I said, you can always withdraw permission, Mr. Sarkouhi. These things are a lot easier to collapse than they are to bring out. And I work for reasonable rates."

"Ah. Mr. Koehl. As you reminded me, Lindsay Ingham has very many friends."

"She can make trouble for you, is that it? Not just legally."

"That is it."

"Looks like she's making trouble for you, anyway, Mr. Sarkouhi."

"That she is, Mr. Koehl."

As I climbed into my car I saw Lindsay watching the ghost through the window of the doorway, smoking an actual cigarette, the smoke making her features a little unclear. You can't do that in a restaurant. It's slow suicide. That wouldn't bother anyone, but even worse, it's public suicide.

The next day I was sitting in my office, staring out the window. I felt like shit. With the money and new stuff, paid bills, I should have felt like a pop star. Instead I kept seeing Ms Mehrer's face, and I felt like a whore.

The phone buzzed. I picked it up, and there was my vampire, Justin Hoben — excuse me, "John Robertson". The idiot called himself that, and then paid me through his personal account.

"John."

"You said to call today. You said that you would scout out the, that job we talked about."

"Yeah, John."

There was a pause. "Well?"

I didn't know why I was giving him a hard time. Lindsay's money would only last so long, and the bills would come due again eventually. So I roused myself. "Yeah, John. I checked it out. The manager is willing to go along, except he wants a cut. The usual amount, three hundred, and there's my fifty negotiating fee, on top of the baseline costs."

"Yeah, that's fine. When?"

I made a show of looking at my watch, although he wouldn't see it. "I guess I could squeeze it in late this afternoon, say four o'clock, if that works for you."

"Yeah, that would be good for me. Four o'clock."

I hung up. Sure, Mr. Hoben, that time works for you. I figured it would. Your wife thinks you're still at work, your office thinks you've left for the day. That works for you just fine.

It was sacrilege to use the new equipment for a job like this. Wiping grandma's priceless china with a rag made of old underwear. I could just as easily dig out my old stuff. My Mr. Robertson deserved no better.

But the lure of using that fine new gear was just too strong. My breath actually quickened as I thought about it. I felt like a pervert at a schoolyard. But I got it out anyway, and by three I was on my way.

Once there, it didn't take long for me to set up. Everything snapped into place just as it ought to, just as it used to. No sputtering, no loss of definition or control or focus, no stray signals. I played with the fine tuning, bringing out effects and details I hadn't been able to play with in years.

The old woman had died in the chair, just slumping further down, further down. No drama, just death. Her image flickered at the edges a bit; I toned it down, then brought it back up just to the edge of sight. She kept her eyes half closed, and she seemed to be mindlessly staring at something, probably a television set that the landlord sold off when the body was found. She wore a gray blouse, and a necklace of fat glass beads, red and brown. She also wore some fading blue jeans. She was barefoot.

Some current celebrities say in their wills that their houses or places of death should be destroyed, to forestall this kind of thing from ever happening to them. The rest of us can't afford that kind of protection, though there are restraint policies that are supposed to prevent the kind of thing I was doing. The very poor, though, are wide open to the predations of vampires after death.

My vampire knocked at the door. I opened it. "John."

"Mr. Koehl." Justin Hoben's eyes barely brushed me before they focused on the dying woman. His breath caught in his throat.

"I'll be outside." I went down the stairs and I heard Justin close the door and lock it.

I sat in the open door of my car. It's a shame I never took up smoking; it would pass the time. I watched the traffic go by, the single occupants of single vehicles. An hour or so later Justin came back out. His shirt was no longer tucked into his pants, and there was drying sweat on his flushed face. He walked up to me, and didn't look at me as he slipped me his check.

But after he turned away, he spoke.

"You're a genius," he said, his voice thick with emotion. "That was the best — the best I've ever had. Amazing." Still without looking at me, he said, "Thank you," then hurried away.

So the new equipment had an endorsement.

I went back upstairs, and put down the ghost.

Afterwards I drove slowly past Grasso's, though it wasn't on the way home. Grasso's didn't look to have many customers. I laughed, and went home, wishing I had eaten something so I could vomit it back up.

The next morning Lindsay was already in my office corridor when I arrived.

"Where the hell have you been?" she greeted me. She stubbed out her cigarette in her pocket ashtray. "It's almost noon."

"Hello, Miss. Did an appointment slip my mind?"

I unlocked the door and Lindsay followed me inside. She sat down, a firm line to her mouth and a hard look in her eye.

"Have a seat," I said. I seated myself behind my desk and rested my chin on my hands. "Something I can do for you?"

"More like something you did *to* me."

I leaned back. That gaze was a little too intense. "I don't understand, Lindsay. I did what you asked. The ghost hasn't collapsed, has it?"

"To hell with you, Koehl."

"Yep, anyone with one good eye can see the sick relationship she had with your dad. It's all there for everyone to see. And that's exactly what you wanted."

"It's disrespectful, mocking her like that. I wanted a tasteful—"

"In a restaurant. Yeah. Please, Lindsay."

"Go to hell." She folded her arms, looked away, and began to sniff.

"Cut the act, Lindsay. We both know what you wanted. You wanted to leave a bitter taste in the mouths of all her society friends. You hated them for not stepping in, or you hated them for leading perfect lives within calling distance. You hated her for what she allowed your dad to do to her, and you couldn't resist a little public humiliation. And I gave it to you. Just like you knew I would. Because I've got the eye to see it, and the technique to show it, and the desperation to accept the job in spite of all that."

She ended her pretense of crying, and just sat there. I wondered what she wanted, why she was here. To justify herself in my eyes — Oh, I never expected to see *that* — or to gloat with me over her triumph over her mother?

Gloat with *me*? Did Lindsay have no friends?

Did I care? "You always were a little self-centered. Justifiably so. But hardly blind — did you think the relationship obvious to her old friends would slip past me? I do know my work, Lindsay."

"Your work! Raising ghosts for perverts!"

"Don't worry. I don't discuss my clients with anyone."

I should have seen the slap coming. Maybe I did. Then Lindsay stood up and turned her back to me.

The inside of my cheek had been cut by a tooth, and I tasted blood.

"He hated you, you know. Towards the end. That was his parting shot — saddle you with a murder charge."

"Manslaughter." I kept the disinterested tone in my voice, but her words rang in my head. Pichrenn had hated me? I had practically been his son.

And yet — it rang true, also. It didn't come as big a surprise as it should have.

"He taught me well. I owed it all to him. He had no reason to resent me."

Lindsay turned back to me. "Idiot! It wasn't your skill he resented!"

"I never—"

"You didn't need to."

She glared at me, expecting me to — what? Kiss her? Slap her, like Bogart in some old movie? Explain away the thing we'd had behind the old man's back, when I'd been the favored son and it was clear that Lindsay would be free after the old guy had passed on?

I knew that there are ghosts all around us, hovering just at the edges of sight, on the fringes of our minds, as we go about our lives. I made my living revealing them. Now Lindsay was showing me others.

"Why do you keep renewing him, Scott? Why don't you let him fade out?" Her voice was flat.

I had no answer.

"He's gone, Scott. And you blamed me. You never returned my messages."

Had she left messages? I'd told myself for so long that she had cut me loose. But yes, she had left messages I had brushed off. After killing Pichrenn, how could I just go on, take up openly with his lover?

I couldn't think of anything to say, and Lindsay stalked out. Was I supposed to call her back?

Had all this been her way to get through to me?

I've always had trouble with moving on. Maybe everybody does. But I thought a lot about what Lindsay had said, there at the end. I sat in my apartment in the dark, the TV on with the sound turned low, and decided that maybe it was time to act, and maybe even time for Lindsay to take another peek at the sunlit world.

Me too. I not only have trouble moving on, I have trouble going back. Lindsay had reached out to me, coming to see me about a ghost; she had made contact, however awkwardly, and maybe that's the only way she could do it. Still, she had done it. She had tried to show me herself at her most vulnerable, most unappealing, most venal, and most real. I could, too.

I had no idea if she would show up or not. The message I'd left hadn't given her any details, any reason to see me, just the time and place. I watched Pichrenn in his chair, and tried not to think about it. About where she was now, what she was doing, that she was still in the world even though she wasn't in mine.

The door opened. "Scott."

Lindsay stood there.

"Lindsay."

She entered hesitantly. "I'm not sure what I'm doing here."

"Yeah. Neither am I. But I'm here."

She nodded as if that made sense. She crossed the room to the window. She hadn't looked at Pichrenn. She wasn't wearing black this time — light blues and yellows.

I joined her. "I need to tell you something, Lindsay."

She nodded, but didn't say anything.

It was easier talking when she wasn't looking at me. "It's like this. Yes, I killed Pichrenn. He asked me to do it, and maybe he had more than one motive. I don't know. But I know that I've never forgiven myself, for that and for — you know. Us. And afterwards I pushed you away, like it was your fault or something. But I'm tired of pushing."

She turned to me. Her eyes flickered to the impression, then back to me. "You don't have to—"

"Yeah, I do. I really do. Since I got out of prison, since even before that, I've been moping and cynical, and it's got me nowhere. Maybe I've been a little too much in love with death. Maybe that's a job hazard. But I'm tired of it. Finally, I'm just *tired* of it."

I went to the closet and pulled out a single piece of equipment. I didn't even need a tripod. I could just hold it and point it at the apparition.

"Scott — you're..?"

"Time to say goodbye."

I pointed, and pressed the button, and Pichrenn vanished.

Lindsay looked at the chair where the impression had been. I couldn't tell what she was thinking.

I held out the defocuser to Lindsay. She looked at it as if she didn't recognize it, but didn't take it. I put it on the chair.

"If you ever want it, here it is," I said. "It's easy to use. Runs on batteries. Just point, and push the nice red button." I walked to the door. Lindsay still hadn't moved.

At the door I turned. "I usually have dinner weeknights at a little place on Fifth, near Pike," I said. "Rommie's. It's easy to find. I'm usually there from seven-thirty to eight-thirty or so."

I walked out.

Maybe Lindsay was tired of death, too. Tired of looking back.

I'd have to wait and see.

About the story

Ghosts are a fascinating topic. I can't say I believe in them, and yet there is a smudge of doubt; some of the stories are not easy to dismiss. But if ghosts really do exist, what could they be? The idea that they are conscious entities seems nightmarish and unfair to me – can you imagine wandering around an old house for a hundred years, no one to talk to, nothing to read? So the idea came to me that ghosts could be a phenomenon, an imprint of some kind on the structures they inhabit, that science just hasn't unearthed yet. And if that were true, maybe a technology could be developed to make them more easily seen.

Ghost stories are dark stories, generally, so I thought it might be fun to tell a sort-of ghost story using a dark template – that of noir fiction. Instead of a private eye played by Bogart, I would have a guy who uses technology to raise ghosts (but also played by Bogart, if he's available). And then the other elements – a lead character down on his luck, and beautiful woman he has trouble connecting to, a dark past, unsavory acquaintances. And an ending that is not quite completely happy.

A question for the author

Q: Do you live near where you were born? Have you traveled much?

A: I grew up in the Seattle area, went to university in the Seattle area... pretty boring. But after graduation I applied to join the Peace Corps. They decided to send me to South Yemen (this was before South and North united). But, a couple of weeks before I was scheduled to ship out, I got a call telling me that our visas hadn't been approved. Should they look for another assignment? Yes! I'd already sold my car, quit my job!

So a few weeks later I was sent to Thailand. After three months of intensive language and culture training, I was sent to a small village in Pichit province, Kampaengdin ("Dirtwall"). My duties were twofold: to teach English at the junior high school there, and to work with local farmers in some way. Well, I enjoyed the teaching, and did my best to see that the village farmers connected with agricultural officials, and even gave them information about raising fish in their rice paddies.

Normally Peace Corps assignments are for two years, but I applied for, and was granted, a third year, so I could work with various local schools on their English curricula. Then, as I was preparing to go home, I was told of a job offer at a university in the northeastern city of Khon Kaen. I went up there to see if it looked interested, and was immediately offered the job.

I loved it, but after a year came back to the U.S. I'd felt something of an imposter, since I only had a B.A. Back in Seattle I got my Master's in teaching ESL, and then heard that Khon Kaen University wanted me to come back, so I did. Six years later, the Thai economy crashed, so I returned to the U.S.

While living in Thailand I did a little traveling – Myanmar, Cambodia, Laos, Japan, Taiwan, and Nepal.

About the author

Tim McDaniel teaches English as a Second Language at Green River College, not far from Seattle. His short stories, mostly comedic, have appeared in a number of SF/F magazines, including F&SF, Analog, and Asimov's. He lives with his wife, dog, and cat, and his collection of plastic dinosaurs is the envy of all who encounter it. In his spare time (ha!) he teaches judo.

His author page at Amazon.com is www.amazon.com/author/tim-mcdaniel

May

Calm Folk, Come Forth!

Adan Berkowitz

The bear stood on its hind legs and roared. Its fur was matted and tangled, brown with hints of orange, and one of its ears was mostly gone. Gray eyes and long sharp teeth. Rancid breath wafted over me, and I pinched my nose. I was pretty sure it was a grizzly. Dad said grizzlies were big, and mean. He said if you got between a grizzly sow and her cubs, you'd better watch out. No baby bears in sight, but I figured there were probably a few tucked away in a nearby den.

"Sorry," I said. "Didn't mean to bother you."

Momma bear didn't accept my apology. She roared again, then clamped her jaws around my head, like a nasty hat that didn't fit. Gooey saliva dripped onto my face, and I frowned. Now I was going to smell like bear drool the rest of the day.

"Leave me alone," I said, annoyed. "I don't have time for this."

As if she'd understood, the bear let go. She gave me a strange look—at least, as strange as a bear could muster—then turned and ran into the trees. My head began to come back together where the grizzly's teeth had split it, and I sighed. If I kept getting sidetracked, this trip was going to take a lifetime.

Sluggishly, I lurched onward while my head fixed itself. I plucked some berries into my mouth to help speed things along, wincing at their tartness.

When I found Mom in Fija Nostra, I would tell her all about the bear, how sharp its teeth had been and how its breath had stunk. We would talk about the places we'd been and the things we'd seen, and then we'd go home and she would be herself again. That's what I wanted to believe, but in all honesty, I wasn't sure.

The sun drifted down into its hiding place, reminding me of Mom's dark moods her last few months on the mountain, how she'd become almost like a different person. Dad assured me we'd get through it, though I could tell he was worried. 'Out of darkness comes light' was one his sayings, and he really believed it.

As if to prove this was true, a spark of flame flickered in the murky distance. Figuring it might belong to someone who could point me toward Fija Nostra, I headed that way. Soon I came upon a campsite, two men beside a small tent. One of the men chopped wood on a tree stump while the other ate onions from a sack next to the fire. The man stopped chopping and looked at me. Like the grizzly, he had dark brown hair, though not as matted. The other man took a loud bite of his onion. This one had silvery blond hair like Mom. Both wore black flowing robes that seemed to swallow them up.

"Who the hell're you?"

"Hi," I said. "I'm looking for my Mom."

"Do I look like your goddamned mom, guy?"

"Relax, Prowie," said the blond man near the fire. "What's your name, son?"

"Ben," I offered.

"Bennie. Come here, Bennie boy. I'm going to cut you up and eat you for lunch." Prowie raised the ax over his head. Then he put it back down, laughing. "Just what I thought. Look at him, Kaz. Not even a flinch. You're not afraid one bit, are you Ben?"

I stared at him blankly.

"Of course you aren't. You're a Lazzie for sure."

"Now Prowie, you don't know that. He might just be a little off in the head."

"I saw a grizzly," I said proudly. "I'd lay odds on it." I wasn't certain what that meant, but Mom always used to say it when she was sure of something.

The two men looked at each other, then burst out laughing. I laughed too.

"Where you from, son?" Kaz asked. "You can't be more than twelve years old."

"Up on the mountain," I replied, "and I'm twelve-and-a-half, thank you."

"Are you a Lazzie?"

"I've never heard that word before."

"It means you don't get scared, because you've nothing to fear. You don't feel pain."

"No," I said. "My Dad says pain is useless, since we just come back together anyway."

"Is that so?"

Prowie smiled at me. His teeth were yellow and brown, and they slanted in different directions. "Want to give me some help, Bennie lad? You can steady the wood. Just grab the chunk and hold it for me."

Prowie scooped up a piece of firewood and balanced it on the stump. "Just like that, see?"

I nodded. Prowie's hand drifted away and I held the wood firmly, making sure not to let it wobble.

Kaz rose, frowning. "That's enough, Prowie."

Prowie turned to me, still smiling. "All right. Keep her straight now, Bennie." He raised the ax above his head. "Ready?" I nodded.

"One....two..."

Prowie brought the ax down with a mighty *whack*. The blade missed the wood and instead split my wrist. My right hand dropped sadly to the ground, and blood came out of the stump where it had been. Kaz gasped. Prowie looked at me with wide eyes.

"Sorry," I said. "I must have flinched."

Prowie continued to stare, mouth hanging open. He tossed the ax away.

"See," he said, weakly. "I told you."

"I think I'm going to be sick," Kaz said.

"Doesn't hurt?"

"Nope," I said. I pointed at the sack of onions. "Mind if I grab one?"

Whenever something like this happened, I'd be sluggish for a while if I didn't eat. Dad said it had something to do with the conservation of energy, but I never really paid much attention. Honestly, that stuff was kind of boring.

"Look," Kaz said. His face very white among the flames. "It's already starting to grow back."

They were pointing at my right arm. A little nub had formed there. I steadied the wood with my left hand and turned back to Prowie.

"Should we try again?" I asked.

 "We can't spend the night with him here," Kas said. He and Prowie sat close to each other, their black cloaks rippling in the night breeze. They were whispering, but I could still hear them. "He's giving me the heebies."

"You was just telling me to leave him alone."

"That was before I saw the trick with his hand."

I watched them, unsure. The fire was almost out.

"I saw one of them once," Kaz said. His voice was unsteady. "Lanky guy, like an acrobat. A showman. He would climb to the top of the tallest flagpole in town and jump off headfirst. He'd go *splat* on the ground, just like that," Kaz clapped his hands together, "and then a few minutes later he'd be back up doing it again. People tossed him coins."

Prowie shrugged.

"Ah, this one's harmless. A babe lost in the woods. Hell, maybe he can guard our gear while we doze. You don't hafta sleep, do you Bennie?"

I frowned. Prowie was wrong. I didn't get tired that often, but when I did, I slept and dreamed, same as anybody.

"Are you nuts?" Kaz said. He kept running his hands through his silvery hair. "I'm not sleeping with him watching us."

"You're a 'gina, you know that?"

"He shouldn't be here," Kaz said. There was a new coldness in his voice. "He should be under the sea. Under the rocks where his kind belong."

"I'm happy to be moving on," I said. "I didn't mean any trouble."

"There's a Nav Servo east of here," Prowie said. It might be able to sort you out."

"How will I know where to find it?"

"It looks just like a big compass. You can't miss it."

I smiled. "Okay. Thanks."

"Don't meddle with it," Prowie called after me. "It's got security."

"You moron, he's a Lazzie, what's it to him?"

As I walked on, their arguing voices drifted away. The night insects were out, composing their symphony of clicks, chirps, and drones. Sometimes it even sounded a little like the music Mom and Dad used to play back home. A sharp pang of homesickness struck me. But I wasn't going to quit. Not until I found Mom and brought her back to the mountain. Besides, now I was curious to know what a Lazzie was.

Not long after, I came upon the Nav Servo. It was a big compass, just like Prowie said. Round, made of some shiny, brassy material. Its face was topped with thick glass, and there was a single dark needle slowly spinning clockwise. Behind it was a large broken tube, its sides a swampy green color.

The glass felt smooth and cool. A voice spoke: "Warning: tampering with me risks death by electric shock. I contain ionizing radiation. Do not attempt to vandalize or deface me. Repairs should only be performed by a licensed professional."

The voice was calm but firm. I couldn't tell if it was a man or a woman. I said, "Hello!"

"Hello," said the Nav Servo. "I am Sutton, the Navigation Servomechanism for the Northern Autonomous region of Greater Suttony."

"I'm Ben. Nice to meet you Sutton. How are you?"

"I am well. And yourself?"

"Not bad," I said. "Sutton, what's a Lazzie?"

The needle spun wildly beneath the glass.

"I'm sorry. Apart from basic pleasantries, I am only allowed to answer questions pertaining to navigation. This is required by law to limit my superfluous knowledge and prevent sentience."

"I see." I scratched my cheek. "Well, I'm on my way to Fija Nostra. Can you tell me how to get there?"

"Of course!" Pleasure in Sutton's voice. "You are the second person to ask directions to this location in the past two days. By tube, the estimated travel time to Fija Nostra is .34 seconds. By air, the estimated travel time is nine hours, 20 minutes. By heavy rail, the estimated time is 12 hours 11 minutes, allowing for transfer. By foot, the estimated time is upward of 30 days."

"Sounds like the tube is fastest."

"Yes. Unfortunately, the tube network is currently out of service. I apologize for any inconvenience."

I looked over at the greenish tube, cracked everywhere. No surprise it was broken. Sutton's needle whirled around like a happy dog's tail.

"The latitude and longitude of Fija Nostra is as follows..." Sutton recited a long string of numbers. They sounded familiar, but I couldn't remember where I'd heard them, and I didn't understand what they meant.

"That doesn't help," I said. "Which direction do I go?"

Sutton's needle swung around to the southeast, where it locked firmly in place.

"Unfortunately, my knowledge of transportation options is limited to the Greater Autonomous Region of Suttony. However, there is a bicycle in the direction you are headed which may be useful. There is a high probability it has been abandoned by its previous owner, as it has been unused for 3 months. The bicycle needs maintenance, but should be functional. I apologize that this is my only suggestion, but it will be faster than traveling on foot."

"A bike!" I said. "That's great!"

The needle spun merrily around, locking back in the southeast position. The path to Fija Nostra. I thanked Sutton.

"My pleasure, Ben. Safe travels on your journey."

Walking through the overgrown forest, I nearly blundered right by a metal rack covered in leaves and vines. Leaning there, almost completely camouflaged by the foliage, was a yellow bicycle. Its tires were flat, and the chain was rusted, but luckily there was a small pack slung around the seat with some air cartridges, patches, and rubbing alcohol. I figured it all belonged to a tube traveler who'd forgotten to return. Or maybe the system had broken before they could. Either way, it didn't seem like they were coming back, so I didn't feel too bad about taking their stuff.

Dragging the bike from the shrubbery, I wiped down the chain with alcohol until the rust was gone. Then I patched the tires and filled them with air. When I was done, it looked almost new.

"Not a bad job, for a Lazzie," I said. For some reason this made me laugh. I hopped on and pumped the pedals and away I went.

After riding for a few hours, I emerged from the forest onto a large plain, with big brown stalks swaying everywhere. They rustled my face as I passed, a gentle, fuzzy feeling. The plain had a slight downward slope, and I coasted along, barely having to pedal.

I thought of Mom, and how we used to ride bikes together on the mountain. That was before she started to go crazy. Before she heard voices that weren't there and thought the raccoons that foraged through our trashcans were plotting against her. Dad told me that when you've been alive for so long, sometimes the mind starts to break down. He tried to help her with medicines and therapies, even electroshocks, but nothing seemed to work. By the time she ran off, she wasn't the same person I grew up with.

Lost in my daydream, I didn't see the cliff until it was too late. I squeezed the brakes with all my might, but it was no use. I tumbled over the edge. Below, the tops of trees looked like little smudges of green paint. They grew bigger and bigger, and then I hit the rocks and came apart.

When I came back together, there were people standing around me. A group of them, men and women and boys and girls. The only one to approach me was a girl with bright red hair. Smiling, she knelt and put a wet rag against my forehead. I tried to move my arms and legs and couldn't. There were iron shackles around them. The girl with the red hair studied me. She had green eyes, and looked to be around my age.

"Are you okay?" she asked.

"Daphne!" One of the men called out, angrily. "Get away from him!"

The girl named Daphne turned to the man, who was holding a large wooden club.

"Relax," she said, still dotting my forehead with the damp rag. "Does he look like he's going to hurt anyone?"

Another man, with an orange beard hanging to his belly, strode forward and slung Daphne up over his back. She cried out, attacking him with her fists, but she was too small. The man carried her a few paces away and set her down among the rest of the crowd. She did not seem pleased.

The man who had yelled at Daphne stepped forward. He must have been her Dad. He was big, his forehead shiny with sweat.

"We know you're a Lazzie," he said, smacking the club against his open palm with a *thwack*. "Don't try and deny it."

"What does that mean?" I asked, exasperated.

"Don't play dumb with me. Daphne here saw you fall off the cliff. Saw you smash open like an overripe tomato and regrow your parts like a goddamned starfish."

Daphne again pushed her way to the front of the pack. Her hair was frizzy and tangled.

"Leave him alone!" she said. "He wasn't bothering anyone. He was dead and then he came back to life. It's a miracle, is what it is."

"Daphne love, it's no miracle," said the man. "It's a menace. I've heard about towns ravaged by these creatures. Not the women…"

He turned back to me, waving the club in my face. "No, your kind isn't usually interested in procreation. Instead you get bored. First you tear apart the livestock, to see what it's like. Then you move on to the people."

"My name's Ben," I said. There was a prickly feeling in my chest. "Ben Wells. I haven't torn anyone apart. I'm just looking for my Mom. If you don't want me here, I'll keep going."

"We should listen to him," said one of the women. "If he wants to move on, maybe he won't bother us."

"Maybe?" The man with the club snorted. "You want to risk the children's lives on maybe? Sure, maybe he'll keep on. Or maybe he'll track back around and slaughter us as we sleep. We're lucky we've got this one in chains already. I say we wall him off deep in a cave and let him rot."

"No!" Daphne yelled. "That's wicked! He's just a boy. He didn't do anything wrong!"

"It isn't up for debate," said the man with the club. He motioned at the others.

Some approached eagerly, while others hesitated. In the end, they all came forward. The men lifted me up and the sky tilted like a pendulum. I shouted in protest, but they were too strong. They marched me through the woods, into a yawning cave. It was pitch dark inside, everything furry with moss and mildew. Skittering insects darted over my feet. The man with the club looked at me, his mouth squirming strangely, like an earthworm after rain. Then he turned away.

They left me there, propped against the cave wall. The light from the entrance was slowly blotted out, bit by bit, like an eclipse. Soon it was so dark I couldn't see anything, not even my feet in the irons below me.

After a while it was nighttime—I could only tell because of the bats, their leather wings flapping against my face. It tickled, but I couldn't scratch. I wasn't used to such total darkness. It felt like a storm cloud, smothering me, and there was a peculiar sensation in my stomach. The only way I could describe it was when I read a story a long time ago, about a big boat that crashed into an iceberg and sank beneath the water. My stomach was that boat. It was a new feeling, but not a good one.

To keep my mind off the dark, I tried to imagine home. But instead of happy times, my thoughts kept returning to when Mom left the mountain. I had been so busy hunting for bugs that I didn't even realize she was gone. But by nightfall she hadn't come back. And Dad's face told me she wasn't going to. It was unthinkable. She hadn't even said goodbye.

I'd found a flier in Mom's things after she left. I could see it now in my mind, almost like it was shimmering in the darkness. It said:

Calm Folk, Come Forth!

You are old.

You are tired.

You are ready to ascend.

It's time for a well-deserved rest. Come to beautiful Fija Nostra, and take the next step with us.

Latitude: 3° 36′ 32″ S
Longitude: 144° 35′ 18″ E

Note: We at Fija Nostra charge a nominal fee. Please contact us for more details.

Dad wouldn't tell me what it meant, but one thing was obvious—Mom was headed to this place called Fija Nostra. I told Dad I was going there to bring her home, and he forbade it. He said I was too young for such a trip, and that finding her was his job. But I was fed up with waiting around.

A scraping sound jolted me back to reality. Suddenly from nothing I saw a flicker of light, growing brighter and brighter, and then there were three men standing at the mouth of the cave, with Daphne leading them.

Daphne watched with arms crossed as one of the men unlocked my irons.

"Kept picturing my own boy in here," he said, as my shackles fell away. "Don't make a fool of me, son."

I assured him I wouldn't. Leaping down to the cave floor, I smiled at Daphne. Her hair was very red, and her eyes were very green.

"You're lucky I like you," she said, smiling back at me.

"Hurry now," said one of the men. "Don't come back here."

"You have to go," Daphne said. "Run. Head straight and turn left at the sawmill. Don't stop until you reach the water."

She leaned in and kissed my cheek. Another new sensation came over me, but unlike the sinking ship, this one was lovely. It was like I had swallowed one of the nearby bats and it was fluttering around in my stomach. I wanted to stay, but I knew I couldn't, so I ran, taking only one look back and seeing the men rolling the heavy rock in front of the cave entrance.

I ran through forests and swamps and thorn bushes and peach groves, all sorts of smells flowering around me, blackberries and skunk and sweet berries and jasmine and pine. I ran until I saw the sawmill, its cracked wooden wheel reminding me of the flat bicycle tires. I ran until Daphne and her village were nothing but a memory. I ran until I reached a tall cliff overlooking the ocean, the air tangy with salt and sand, the sun an orange flame, the sea a frothing churn below. The way forward was uncertain, but I knew I had to keep moving. Taking one last moment to savor the view, I spread my arms and dove into the water.

When I came back together, I was on the ocean floor. My feet sank into mud, silt swirling around me. Bubbles drifted up from my nose. I kicked my feet and began to swim, just like I used to in the lake back home. I swam for a long time. At times sunlight pierced the gloom, revealing the undersea world. Great undersea caverns, endless watery gorges, sea life of every size and shape. Neon fish, shiny fish, fish with long tentacles and fish with lanterns inside them, starfish and angler fish and colorful sea anemones shivering against one another. Every so often I rose back to the surface for a few gulps of air, letting daylight shine through me. Sometimes I slept, floating on my back beneath a sky embroidered with stars, alone but for the gentle bob of the waves and the milky glow of the moon. I swam among sharks and whales, groups of dolphins racing to and fro, creatures I'd only read about. I swam for so long I thought I might be swimming forever. But eventually the ocean floor began to slope, up and up, until I emerged onto a beach.

Shaking water from my hair, I found an island paradise. Sand, waves, palm trees, coconuts, birds flying in circles above, and a leafy jungle opposite the sea. I walked for a while along the beach, eventually coming upon a boat that had been tied to a small wooden dock built in a calm lagoon.

There was a woman near the boat, using a long stick to scrape strange growths off its underside. Another woman walked along the beach, carrying a load of wood in her arms and bobbing her head from side to side to see where she was going. When she spotted me she froze, and the wood went tumbling onto the ground. I jogged over and gathered them. The woman had light hair tied back, and dark brown eyes. Her skin was smooth and white, without a crease on it, and there was a tiredness about her that made me think of Mom.

"Who are you?" the woman asked. I told her my name was Ben, and I'd just come from the sea.

"My word," she said. "You're but a child. I didn't know there were any of you left."

The second woman joined us. She was tall and thin, stork-like, with dark hair and loose clothing that flapped in the breeze.

"Are you two Lazzies?" I asked them earnestly. The women looked at each other and burst out laughing.

"Yes, we've been called that," said the woman with light hair. "I'm Ruth, and this is Ali."

"Everyone's been calling me that, too."

"If you were swimming across the ocean, I'd say it's a safe bet."

"Would you lay odds on it?"

They laughed again.

"I'm headed to Fija Nostra," I said. "I'm looking for my Mom there."

They looked at each other.

"Your mother is there, you say?"

"I'm sure of it."

Ali nodded slowly.

"Everyone who ends up in this godforsaken part of the world is going to Fija Nostra. What do you say Ruth, should we give him a ride?"

"He doesn't have any—" Ruth stopped. Ali shook her head back and forth very slightly, like Ruth had said something wrong.

"That's not our problem."

"I'd like to hear more about his parents. Had to take some work to make him."

"We could use an extra hand for the rigging. Do you know how to tie knots, Ben?"

I nodded. We left later that day, Ali pulling up the anchor and using her big stick to push the boat away from the beach. Ruth steered while Ali navigated. I asked how long the journey would be, and they told me we'd be sailing for at least a week.

There was plenty of work to do on board. I helped raise ropes and tie knots, even though I made them sloppy at first and they showed me how to do it better. One morning, Ali was cooking breakfast and asked me to fetch her some potatoes from the hold. I followed the cramped passage down to the belly of the ship. It led to a small chamber filled with cans and burlap sacks. Opening the sack I thought held the potatoes, I instead caught a flash of something shiny. It was full of gold bars. Puzzled, I stared for a moment before closing it again. I found the real potatoes and brought them up, then asked Ali what the gold was for. She told me not to worry about it, but I wondered.

After a few more days of sailing, Ruth said we were nearing Fija Nostra. I smelled the smoke before I saw it—sour, like rotten eggs. Then it appeared, rising from the island in plumes. As gray as the eyes of the grizzly had been. The smoke came from a rock formation that stretched across the entire island, low and flat, like a dinner plate. I asked Ruth if it was a volcano, and she nodded. Ali anchored the ship and we bobbed in the port, waiting. I imagined everything I would say to Mom once I found her.

At first, Fija Nostra looked like heaven. Lush tropical trees, lagoons and waterfalls, and straw huts dotted the shoreline. But there was also an unsettling quiet in the air. Only the cawing seabirds above made much noise. The smoke turned everything dark and overcast, throwing shadows across the island.

Before we even made it off the boat, a voice yelled: "Stop right there!"

A group of men waited at the edge of the pier. They wore crisp white shirts and brown pants, their skin tanned from the sun. All of them were quite large, and some carried long spears.

"Lazzies?" one of the men asked. Ali shouted back an affirmative.

"You have the fee?"

Ali pulled a gold bar from her cloak. She tossed it down and one of the men caught it.

"Plenty more in the hold."

The man rubbed his hands over its smooth surface and nodded.

There was a terrific clanking noise, and a mechanical gangway extended from the dock. I started to follow it down to the shore, but one of the men blocked my way.

"Hold on. What's a kid doing here?"

"He hitched a ride with us," Ruth said nervously.

"You paying for him too?"

There was a silence.

"He's not—he's looking for his mother."

"His mother?" The man turned around and had a short discussion with the others.

"Fine. You two come through. We'll bring the boy into administration. Find out what his deal is. If he causes any trouble, send him to the brig."

I didn't know what a brig was, but the snarling way he said it made me think it couldn't be good. Ali and Ruth waved goodbye to me as they passed, a strange sadness in their eyes, like they knew it was the last we'd see of each other.

One of the men led me off the docks, along a rising path overlooking the island. He wasn't very friendly, prodding me along and cursing under his breath, but I was eager to see Mom, so I did what he said. Below, waves crashed into white foam. The higher we climbed, the better the view. My stomach buzzed with excitement, knowing

Mom was nearby. Soon, we were beside the volcano. I smelled the rotten eggs, heard the hiss of steam, saw the gooey lava pooling in crevices. The volcano funneled up to a hole that belched thick gray smoke. Embers shot into the air and fell in slender glowing trails, like spider legs. Ahead, a boxy building rested on a flat plateau where the ridge leveled out.

Inside was a woman behind a desk, the same white shirt and dark skin as the rest. The man pointed at a bench.

"Sit," he said. "Wait."

I sat. The place was dreary. Yellow paint flaked off the walls and everything smelled stale and musty, like it hadn't been cleaned in a while. The woman behind the desk kept glancing over at me, but she didn't say anything. Other people in white shirts came in and out, and I could hear them whispering. I felt like a circus animal. Finally, I'd had enough. I'd never been very angry back on the mountain, but out in the world it seemed to happen a lot. I stormed over to the desk.

"I need your help," I said. "I need to find my Mom."

She paused. "I'm supposed to wait for word from my boss."

"I don't have time to wait!"

"Okay, okay!" She looked around nervously, like she was afraid of me. "I'll go through the records. See if your mom's been through here."

I followed her into another room. It was full of shelves crammed with thick books and binders, pages spilling out every which way.

"I never seen a kid Lazzie before," she said. "I didn't even know there were any of you around."

"I'm different."

"Yeah, that's for sure. What's your mom's name, son?"

"Ruby. Ruby Wells."

"Wells. All right, give me a second." She pulled some books from the shelves and flipped through them. I waited with my arms crossed. The woman ran her finger over the pages, then stopped. She made a weird sound.

"What is it?"

"Is this her?"

The woman turned the book to me. There she was! A picture of Mom. Curly red hair and tired eyes, but a beaming smile. I couldn't remember the last time I'd seen her smile like that back on the mountain. Beside her was a picture of Dad, his hair longer than I'd ever seen. I was overjoyed.

"Yes! That's her. Where is she?"

"I'm sorry, kid. She got here a few months ago. She already... ascended."

"Huh?"

The lady looked at me like I was dumb.

"You know. She went into the volcano. That's why Lazzies come here. Something about the chemicals in the lava. It's the only way."

"What are you saying?"

"Your mom is dead. She's not coming back."

A sinking feeling. Like when I'd been in the cave, with bats fluttering around me.

"No," I said. "She can't be dead. You must have made a mistake."

"I thought everyone here knew…"

"No," I said again. Everything suddenly went cold. Without another word, I turned and ran out of the building. Ahead, smoke belched up from the rocky funnel toward the overcast sky. If Mom had gone into the volcano, I would find her.

I raced along the ridge, ignoring a crowd of white shirts who had come out to watch me. The next thing I knew, I was at the mouth of the volcano, enveloped in smoke. Below, lava bubbled like stew in a pot. Mom had to be down there somewhere.

I jumped in.

The lava splashed up around me, rising to my knees. I struggled against it, like wading through steaming molasses. Fumes stung my eyes. Beyond was a gaping chasm, leading deeper into the volcano.

"Mom!" I yelled. "Where are you? Mom!"

Something was wrong with my legs, a bad feeling, like they were being etched away. My body sank lower into the lava, and I cried out. Someone called my name. The voice was familiar, but I couldn't place it. My thoughts were jumbled and scattered, consumed by this horrible new sensation. Then a pair of hands lifted me up, out of the lava, carrying me away. I tried to fight, but all my strength had gone. Whoever was holding me was almost completely submerged, only the top of their head visible.

Tossed from the pit, I sprawled onto a hunk of glassy rock. The air felt unexpectedly cool, and I realized with a shock that the lava had burned my clothes off. As I covered myself in embarrassment, my rescuer stagger forward. I must have been seeing things, because the person who rose steaming and sizzling from the lava looked a lot like Dad. The man sank to his knees, gasping for air, and suddenly I knew this was no mirage. It *was* Dad. I never thought he'd leave the mountain, but I'd been wrong. He'd come to save Mom, just like me. My heart swelled with pride. I crawled toward him, but everything began to feel hazy, like a shade being drawn—

I came back together—or at least that's what it felt like—in an underground cavern. The ceiling was so low that the attendant keeping watch could barely stand up straight. I was in a bed, wearing a gown made from palm fronds. A few beds over was Dad, covered in gauze and bandages. His face was charred, and his curly hair had been singed off. I felt awful. He looked like a monster, and it was my fault.

My legs still felt a little weird, but they worked. I went to Dad and he took my hand, smiling.

"That was a silly thing to do," he said. "Too much of your Mom in you."

"How did you—"

"I told you. Finding Ruby was my job. I was too late to save her. So I waited for you. The natives weren't happy, but they let me stay, as long as I cleaned up for them. When word spread that a boy had jumped into the volcano, I knew."

"Why?" My eyes were wet. "Why did Mom leave? Why did she go into the volcano?"

"Don't blame your Mother. She wasn't in her right mind. She's at peace now. It's better this way."

"She didn't even say goodbye."

"She loved you, Ben. You have to be strong."

"I can't."

"You can. You've always been that way. Like Mom."

I sniffed. Dad squeezed my hand tighter.

"I'm fading, Ben. I can feel myself fading. I'm not afraid. I've lived many lives...and I got to have you. You'll live many lives too."

"Dad..."

"Calm children are rarely born. And yet here you are. Here you are."

Dad was mumbling, his words hard to make out. I tried to say more, but his eyes went funny and he stopped answering me. The lava had only come up to my knees, but Dad had been under it completely. The heat was too much, even for him. I waited at his side, I don't know how long. By nightfall, Dad was gone. His body seemed to gleam, melding with the air before coming apart, until all that was left was a fine powder. A scent like honeysuckle in the valley.

I stood up, wiping my eyes. For the first time I noticed my legs were covered in rough, reddish markings that didn't look like they were going away anytime soon.

"What are these?" I asked the attendant, who was pretending to be busy sweeping the floor.

The attendant looked down.

"One hell of a story," he said. I couldn't argue with that.

I emerged from the cavern to calm night breezes. Smells of fish, of sand, of salt. Ahead was the beach, dark and desolate.

How to describe what I felt? Sadness, and a strange sense of freedom. Mom and Dad were gone. But I was still here.

I thought of Daphne, her smile and green eyes, and my heart beat a little quicker. Maybe I would pay her a visit sometime. There was no rush. The world was very big, and there was much to see.

I walked toward the ocean until the water was lapping at my feet. I kept going.

About the story

The story originally began as an old idea I had kicking around about "The Lazarus People," which was about the rise of a technologically advanced people who augmented themselves to live forever. I couldn't think of anything especially interesting to do with the concept, so I stuck it away in the back of my mind. Later, I had a similar idea wondering how a child without any natural instinct for fear might see the world, what kind of journey he might set off on. I only really had the opening scene in mind, where the boy is attacked by a bear and treats it as a minor nuisance. Instead of being wise and weary, I thought a young boy would be an interesting reversal, sort of a play on the "jaded immortal" trope. I remembered the Lazarus People and decided to combine the two ideas into one story.

Ben, the protagonist, is functionally immortal, but he's also a child—maybe the last of his kind—and he's still naïve and immature in many ways. He's never left the mountain where he's grown up, and despite his invulnerability he realizes the outside world can be confusing and illogical, even cruel. In this way, it's a story about a loss of innocence we all go through, presented through a fantastic lens.

I think Ben's upbeat attitude helps lighten what is actually a fairly dark story about fear, suicide, and the dissolution of a family. The Calm Folk, or "Lazzies" in the story are generally taciturn, but its hinted that some of them have become warped and violent, and there's a suggestion that Ben might stray down this path if he's not careful.

The first half of the story came out more as less as I'd imagined it; the second half was more difficult to write, and veered off into some unexpected directions, but I'm happy with where it ended up. It has the feel of a dark fable or fairy tale, which is fairly different from the kind of thing I usually write, and I was pleased to stretch out a bit from my comfort zone.

A question for the author

Q: What is your writing schedule?

A: It depends. For a longer work like a novel, I'll write every day for at least two hours, otherwise it just never gets done. With short stories, I'm much less disciplined. I'll get an idea and write in bursts, with no set schedule. This leads to a lot of unfinished stories, sadly.

About the author

Adan Berkowitz is a writer, musician, and sometime poker player from central New Jersey. In his spare time, he enjoys reading, playing ping-pong, and spending entirely too much time on twitter. If you'd like to reach him there, check out @AdanRaymond.

On the Scales of Dragons

Kathryn Yelinek

High above the island of Dreden, the wind roared in Tala's ears, chilling her despite the warm bulk beneath her, and she wished humans could mindspeak as dragons did. Instead, she rapped her knuckles against one of Kendriley's incised neck scales and spoke *magné,* a minor Word of power that amplified her voice.

"I don't think the people of Dreden want visitors. Any chance those Xs are bones?"

Kendriley dipped her green head to survey the large, dark Xs laid out in intervals along the shore. To warn ships away, Tala guessed, since she doubted anyone had prepared for arrival by dragon.

"Stone, I think," Kendriley said, with a glance back. She might be older and larger than most dragons, but her sleek, feline grace still thrilled Tala after fifteen years of working together. "Probably granite from the cliffs. I'll make a note later."

Tala rapped a scale in acknowledgement. *Everything is worth knowing,* the Library's motto insisted, and as a librarian she knew that any knowledge—be it landmarks or types of stone—could be important.

"Any word from our colleagues?" she called.

"No," Kendriley growled. Tala felt the rumble as much as heard it. "If they are speaking, I cannot hear them."

How can two pairs of librarians simply vanish? Tala shivered and hugged Kendriley closer, relishing her warmth and smoky smell.

Unfriendly Xs aside, Dreden looked similar to many of the other remote islands she and Kendriley visited to collect knowledge. It would take perhaps a day to walk from end to end. In the north, the forest opened onto farm fields too sodden from ongoing spring rains for planting. In the center of the fields huddled the single village. There, Tala hoped, they would discover what had happened to their colleagues from the King's Library.

As they approached, the village women and children fled inside while the men froze, pointing skyward, a typical rural response. By the time Kendriley descended into the village square, the men had gathered in a huddle to watch. They were a ragtag group, from youths to elders, wearing faded coats and patched woolen trousers against the spring rain.

At least they didn't all run away in fear, Tala noted, holding tight as Kendriley folded her green wings. Did that mean they'd seen dragons before? That the other librarians had made it this far?

She stood on Kendriley's back, towering over the men, her dragon-scale armor glinting. Again she whispered *magné,* amplifying her voice.

"Greetings! We come in peace from the Dragon King."

One man stepped forward from the rest. He was in his early twenties, perhaps, twenty years younger than Tala.

He gestured with his hands. It took a moment to realize he was making a variant of the hand gestures used by temple scribes sworn to silence.

"You are welcome," he signed, *"though we can offer little hospitality. As you see, we are poor, and the land unforgiving."*

He spoke true. The village consisted of thatched hovels sprouting like mushrooms along a single muddy street. The place smelled of rot, and she twitched her nose in unease.

Still, it would be rude to say so. She climbed down from Kendriley's back. Her boots splashed on the muddy ground. "Be at ease. We're not here for your wheat or your fish. We come for your knowledge."

His expression passed from curiosity at their arrival to puzzlement when she spoke of knowledge. The men behind him proved more stony-faced, their emotions hidden behind prodigious beards.

"We are happy to help the Dragon King," the man signed. *"But what do you mean, you come for our knowledge?"*

How could he not know of the Dragon King's demands? Especially if her colleagues had come before. Was he feigning puzzlement, pretending not to know?

She answered carefully. "As repayment for the dragons putting an end to the constant warring, the King demands knowledge as part of your taxes. Since you live out so far, the librarians have been slow to reach you, but now these taxes are due."

The Beards heard this in stony silence, their faces impassive. A strange reaction, since usually people questioned her, incredulous that knowledge could be collected as a tax. Once they knew her to be in earnest, most paid gladly. Better to rebuild the libraries under a Dragon King than starve under a human lord.

In the face of impassive silence, she forged on. "You'll tell us your stories, histories, herb lore—local knowledge of any kind. All knowledge is worth collecting; nothing is outside the purview of the Library."

She paused, stymied by the unrelenting blank faces of the Beards. "In particular," she said, perhaps a bit too loudly in that silence, "we want to know what happened to our colleagues who came before us."

"We know nothing," the man signed, looking back to the Beards, *"of any colleagues who came before you."* The Beards nodded in agreement, their heads bobbing as one.

At the sight of that silent, coordinated agreement, a shiver ran down Tala's back, under her armor. She looked away from the men, unnerved, and focused desperately on their spokesman. Was he lying? Were they all lying?

She took a breath and regretted it as the rotten smell clung to her nostrils. She gritted her teeth, swallowing down a sense of wrongness that pricked her skin. Centering her thoughts—*you're a librarian, you can gain knowledge from a grain of sand*—she tried again.

"Sola and Audrohasta came three years ago. Ko and Fenomere followed last spring. They sent word from the mainland that they were flying here, but were never heard from again. You haven't seen them?"

He blinked. She saw him make a decision. *"No."*

Liar.

Anger heated her face. Instinct urged her to reach for her dagger, made from a talon that Kendriley had lost, but reason kept her hand still. Anger wouldn't help her friends.

"You're sure?" she asked, her voice harsh. "Two of them were dragons, remember. Not as large as Kendriley, but still much larger than oxen. Hard to miss. You never saw them?"

His lips thinned. *"No."*

"I find that difficult to believe. You're sure none of you saw them?"

"I am sure."

He was more opaque than a grain of sand. Exasperated, she blew out her breath and tried a different approach. "Dragons value knowledge above all else and would pay handsomely for information about why four of their librarians vanished."

"I'm sorry," he signed. *"Some knowledge simply cannot be bought. Please, have tea before you go. The flight back will be long."*

Again, that maddening, blank silence. Tala opened her mouth, ready to scream, but Kendriley spoke: "Enough."

Tala froze. The Beards jumped. One dropped a trowel. He snatched it up, glowering at Kendriley.

Why had she spoken? She rarely did in front of those unused to dragon-speak. Then Tala smelled the rot again. Only this time it was both a stench and a sense of evil that prickled up her back. It seemed to seep from the ground, from the very core of the island, rising in response to Kendriley's voice. Kendriley shifted, as if she could no longer bear to make contact with the earth.

The Beards stared, silent still, their expressions unchanged, and Tala realized they didn't sense the evil. Either they couldn't, or they were inured to it.

She swallowed, a bitter taste in her mouth. All she could think was to get away.

To the spokesman she said, "Even if you can't tell us of our colleagues, you still owe the King your knowledge. Kendriley and I will survey the island, decide what we most want to know."

The man swept a circle with one arm. *"Look around you. We have no knowledge worth your gathering."*

"All knowledge is worth gathering."

She remounted, grateful to be back on Kendriley. Quickly, they left the men of Dreden behind.

"What *is* that feeling?" Tala asked two hours later as she fed dry wood to their campfire. Gloomy afternoon light struggled to pierce the low-hanging clouds. They had circled the island for some time, fruitlessly following one scent trail after another in search of the evil before making camp deep in the winter-bare forest. "It keeps coming and going."

"Like it's examining us, testing for weaknesses." Kendriley raised a talon from where she was incising one of her scales, recording the story of their arrival on Dreden. Her body wrapped halfway around the camp. An outcropping of rock on the other side provided a dry overhang for Tala's fire. "I've not encountered anything like this in all my long years, and I don't like it."

"I'd feel better if we were still out searching. Not sitting here."

Kendriley flicked her tail in agreement. "But I want you near me, because I'm going to See."

She said it with an elongated "S": Ssssee.

Tala's heart gave an unhappy lurch. "Now? The Beards are going to come for us, I'm sure of it."

"Not yet. They need time to stew and debate." Kendriley sheathed her talon, her incising done. "And when they come, they will tell us lies. I want information to use against them."

"I don't like having you vulnerable right now." Tala looked over her shoulder, out into the forest. A large blackbird perched in a nearby tree, one yellow eye trained on them. Curious, that. Birds usually kept a healthy distance from Kendriley. "Something out there has already overpowered two dragons."

"Neither of whom was as old or as powerful as I. And neither had a librarian like you by her side."

Tala swatted Kendriley playfully. "Now you're just talking nonsense."

"I put my life in your hands every time my mind leaves my body. I trust you'll see I have a body to return to."

Tala sobered. "Of course. You be careful."

"Cross my heart. You, too, kitling."

Which made Tala smile, as always. She held still, listening to the drips of the sodden forest, while Kendriley settled into her trance. It was unnerving to see the body of her friend grow lax and unresponsive. In that moment, Tala knew, Kendriley became both Kendriley and not-Kendriley. She inhabited both herself and the beings around her—birds, snakes, trees, rocks—connecting herself to them so she saw what they saw and knew what they knew.

She could be minutes or hours in the trance. Best to stay busy, Tala had learned. It kept her from brooding over a dragon who looked near death.

So while her dinner cooked, she pored over Kendriley's carvings, searching for some clue they had missed. As usual, the notes were thorough, the observations recorded in precise shorthand. Beside the new notes were two incised scales ready to be shed. One came off in her hand, and she tucked it into their bags. It would join the thousands of other scales in the Dragon King's library, making a fireproof, nearly indestructible record of the kingdom's reconstructed knowledge. In its place a new scale would grow, ready for Kendriley to incise with whatever they learned next.

Tala hoped it would be the identity of whatever lurked out there. The blackbird still watched them, its feathers glistening in the rain.

"And what do you want?" Tala called.

The bird didn't respond.

Hurry up, Kendri, Tala thought. She was as jumpy as a novice at her first dragon moot.

When they were first paired together fifteen years before, Kendriley had explained the mechanics of Seeing. Tala hadn't understood it then, and she still only knew that it was an adaptation of the mindspeak all dragons used while they flew. Only the oldest and most powerful dragons dared to See. Younger, weaker minds were susceptible to being taken over.

Suddenly, Kendriley stiffened.

Tala went to her and stroked her neck scales. "Shh, it's all right. I'm here."

Kendriley groaned. The noise rumbled, deep and eerie, and the hair on Tala's arms stood on end.

"Kendri?"

Kendriley thrashed. Her tail whipped into the campsite, scattering their bags, the studded end digging into the earth. Tala scrambled back.

"Wake up!" She spun away from the spiked elbow on Kendriley's right wing. The tip scored the outcropping. "Kendri, wake up!"

Kendriley's silver eyes were open and unseeing. She pulled back her lips, baring her fangs.

"Wake up!" Tala grabbed the bucket of water from beside the fire. She sloshed Kendriley's face.

Kendriley hissed. Her gaze bored into Tala.

"Hillside," she said.

Then she slapped her front paws over her snout. Her eyes squeezed shut, and she sank down on the ground, trembling.

"Kendri?" Tala clutched her bucket, uncertain. Should she run for more water or tend Kendriley?

Kendriley didn't seem to want tending. She huddled on the ground, her tail pulled tight around her, her every muscle rigid. Instinctively, Tala knew not to touch her.

She turned instead to the outcropping of rock bordering the campsite.

Did it qualify as a hillside? Was the evil inside it? Was that why Kendriley had scored it with her wingtip? Had she meant her word as a warning or a call to act?

Tala dropped to her knees beside Kendriley's head, looking to her friend for clues. They were in short supply. Kendriley shivered, her scales prickling like a horse bothered by flies. All Tala could think was that the Seeing had gone bad. She had heard stories, of course, but never expected to witness a bad Seeing, not with Kendriley. Still, the trembling, the thrashing, the paws slapped over her snout—everything hinted that some consciousness Kendriley had entered was trying to take over hers. It seemed impossible that something could possess a dragon of her age. Surely it wasn't the sparrows and oaks she normally connected with.

Tala stood and glared into the forest. The blackbird stared back with its unblinking yellow eyes.

"Let her go," she yelled. She threw a stone, which just missed the bird's back. "Tell me what you *want*."

No response, not evening a ruffling of its feathers, only the hissing of the wind in the trees that seemed almost to whisper a word.

A half hour later, someone crashed their way through the forest. Tala sheathed her dagger from where she'd been digging into the hillside. Carefully, she planted herself between the trees and Kendriley's vulnerable head. She wished she felt more imposing without Kendriley alert behind her. She was dirty and frustrated—there had been nothing unusual about the hillside. At least the fire glinted an impressive red and yellow on her armor.

The man who had signed at her in the village stalked into view. A burlap bag hung from each shoulder, giving no indication of what good or bad things they might contain.

He walked forward carefully, his hands in plain view. The unflappable blackbird watched his approach.

He stood about twenty steps away when Tala asked, "What do you want?"

He set down the bags. *"I guessed you might camp here. My name is Bolen. I come alone, with answers to your questions."*

"You claimed not to know anything earlier." She glanced into the forest. Were the others waiting there? She needed their information, yes, but what would they do if they knew of Kendriley's vulnerability? "Prove you have answers."

"It was the elders." His face twisted in disdain as he signed of them. *"They had your friends killed."* He opened one of the bags, scooped out a handful of red and blue scales. They were all that remained of a dragon after death.

Tala sucked in her breath. She'd known her friends might be dead, had reconciled herself to the possibility months ago. But to see the proof in his hands...

She couldn't dwell on it now. Not with Kendriley in danger. And she didn't trust this man's sudden tattling. What if he was lying again? "You're saying a group of old men took down two dragons and two trained librarians?"

"They're old, but they aren't stupid, and young dragons aren't invincible."

She could imagine it—an arrow below the jaw, or in the eye. Or a welcoming sip of poisoned tea.

"Were the elders acting on their own? Or are they under the control of the evil?"

Fear crossed his face. He swallowed.

"Tell me," she pressed. "What is the evil?"

His face went white. That, she was sure, was not a lie. *"What do you know?"*

"You tell me."

He licked his lips and pointed to Kendriley. *"Is your dragon all right?"*

"She's meditating. To increase her power." She paused to let him come to his own conclusion about that.

He eyed Kendriley as if she would eat him at any moment.

"Time's wasting," Tala said when he didn't speak. "I'd hate to think what would happen if your elders found you speaking to me."

He glanced fearfully into the forest. There, all was still. The blackbird remained silent, as if waiting to see what happened between her and this man, Bolen.

"All right," he signed. *"I'm tired of serving them. I'll tell you about the evil."* With the decision made, he seemed to stand taller. *"But I want to talk to the dragon."*

"Anything you can say to Kendriley you can say to me."

"That, librarian, is where you're wrong."

"Why am I wrong?"

His face was grim. *"Because only a dragon of her power can hope to destroy our evil."*

"You can see it best from up here," Bolen signed down to Tala.

She nodded and grabbed a clump of grass to haul herself up. Bolen scaled the incline like a mountain goat. She wondered how many times he'd made this climb.

He had signed, *"It's on a hillside,"* and that word alone had made her leave Kendriley's side. She had promised to rouse Kendriley once she was satisfied by what Bolen showed her. Now, hauling herself up, she gasped for breath and hoped there would be a Kendriley to rouse.

He didn't comment on her windedness, simply offered a hand to pull her up the last particularly steep ledge.

Wheezing, she stood on a flat tabletop of land. It gave a panoramic view of forest behind and to her left, a burned-out meadow in front of her, and soggy fields to her right. Beyond the fields, she could make out the Beards in their village square, engaged in silent, signed disagreements. Even farther over her right shoulder, Kendriley glittered green beneath the dark skeletons of trees.

Keep fighting, Kendri. I'm coming.

"Get down," Bolen signed, flattening himself to the ground. *"Let's hope it doesn't sense us here."*

Tala ducked, her armor rattling. She followed his lead as he crawled to the edge of the flat top. Below it, the ground sloped down to the burned-out meadow.

"Over there." Bolen pointed to the large hill that bordered the far side of the meadow.

She frowned, puzzled, for she and Kendriley had flown over the area earlier that afternoon. The hill was steep, though not as steep as the incline they'd just climbed. The bare, burned soil and rock showed grayish brown in the afternoon sun. Except now it became obvious that not all of the hill was rock or soil. A wooden panel the size of a large door lay across the face of the hill. It had been painted to blend in with the earth.

As she stared at that panel, dread churned her belly. It was the evil she'd sensed before, rising now as if summoned by Bolen's signing and her gaze. Only now it was stronger, more concentrated, and she had no doubt that whatever it was emanated from behind that panel. She breathed between her teeth to keep from flinching.

"What's behind there?"

Bolen gave her a look of undiluted terror. He hunched down, keeping his hands out of view of the hill. *"A Word."*

She gaped. Her heart thudded in a confused, animal terror. "But Words alone—they have no power."

"Quiet!" He threw a glance at the panel. His face went grey. *"Look out! Stop your ears! Don't listen!"*

Only a flock of birds flew over the meadow. "Wha—?"

Bolen pressed his hands over her ears. As he did, the birds descended, cawing. The sound was harsh, unbird-like. It grated against her ears, sent shivers down her spine. She slapped her hands over Bolen's and screamed a minor Word to deaden sound.

It helped, but the sound still battered against her ears. It wormed down her throat and up her nose, searching, striving to reach her mind. "No," she whispered, filling her mind with her own voice. "No. No. No."

The attack seemed to go on forever, but must have been only moments. Then the birds soared away, and Bolen released her.

They were both panting. Bolen's lips moved as if he wanted to make a sound but couldn't. Tala wiped her mouth, tasting blood. She must have bitten her tongue.

"What was that?" she demanded.

He shook his head. He motioned back the way they'd come. *"Not here."*

He crawled across the flat top and started down. Tala eyed the hillside, her stomach twisting. The panel looked unchanged, the sky clear of birds. She followed. She didn't stop until they were back among the trees on level ground.

"Talk to me," she said. Even in her armor she felt vulnerable. "What just happened?"

Bolen rubbed his beard. He breathed heavily, the sound labored, though he hadn't on the climb up. Scratches marred the backs of his hands. Tala realized she must have made them.

"There's a Word, an evil Word, carved into that hill. It just tried to get you to hear it so you would speak it."

"By sending birds to caw at me?"

"They're mimics. The Word takes over their minds, makes them speak."

Kendriley, she thought with a shiver. She wished she could see the dragon's comforting glitter.

"Did you carve this Word, you and the elders?"

"No! We're the guardians. It's our job to make sure it remains hidden, unknown and unspoken."

"And it made you kill my friends?"

He shook his head, rubbing at his scratches. *"They—we—did that. Your friends had to die, so they wouldn't bring knowledge of the Word to the Library."*

She forced herself to speak calmly. "You don't have to kill anyone. Just chisel the Word off the hillside. "

He gaped as if she were mad. *"You think we haven't tried that? It can't be chiseled off. It can't be scorched off. We've painted over it, tried to grow plants to break the hill apart. Nothing works. We have to replace the panel every year. The best we can do is achieve a stalemate, but you librarians came and threatened the balance."*

"You killed your best chance." She would have laughed if it weren't so important. "We don't just collect knowledge. Some librarians are scholars who specialize in words and magic. They could help you."

He shook his head. *"No one must learn of it. Some things are better left unknown."*

"Everything is worth knowing. Look what happened when the wars destroyed the libraries. The land fell into chaos. I promise the scholars will help."

"And have every power-mad idiot flocking here, hoping to use it for their own ends?" He shuddered. *"I want your promise that Kendriley will obliterate it. Her fire must be hot enough, or her claws sharp enough."*

Tala looked him full in the face. He was wrong. Only by knowing something could you face it. "What does it do?" she asked, enunciated each word clearly.

"Destroy." He made the sign with a swipe of his hand. *"It gives the speaker power to kill, to obliterate, to dismantle anything at a word."*

"Why would it want to do that?"

"It's a Word. It does what it was created to do. Our legends say the magician who created it sought the ultimate secret—to revive the stillborn baby born to his grieving wife. But such knowledge is not for humans, and it drove him mad. When he couldn't create, he vowed to destroy. If the Word took possession of someone powerful enough, it could destroy the world."

"Powerful enough—Oh, gods, Kendriley." No wonder she had slapped her paws over her snout. She was fighting for the life of everything on earth.

Bolen frowned. *"What?"*

"We have to get to Kendriley." She ran, sprinting towards the campsite. Fear was like a wind at her back.

Hold on, Kendri.

With Bolen beside her, Tala thundered into the clearing. Kendriley still huddled there. Tala gave a silent prayer of thanks to see her alive and—

"Oh, gods." She ran to Kendriley's side. "Her tail's gone."

Kendriley's tail ended in a stump about an arm's length from her body. The end oozed, raw and seeping. The air stank of blood. A mound of scales showed where she'd tucked her tail close to her belly.

"It must have forced her to speak," Tala whispered, her hand at her throat. "She destroyed part of herself rather than anything else."

"It's already taken her over." Bolen glared at Tala. *"What hope is there now of stopping it? You should've told me earlier."*

She'd gasped the story out during their race to the campsite. Now she glared back as she ransacked their bags. Nothing was big enough for a bandage. "And you should've told us right away about the Word. She's still fighting, so help me find some way to help her, or shut up."

Bolen sank down on his haunches. *"Nothing can help her. She was the only chance we had."*

"Shut up." She threw down their last bag and kicked it. "No, wait." She rounded on him. "How do you lot resist it?"

Something like pride made him stiffen. *"We drink a brew every morning. In time, it destroys our voices. The Word knows we can never speak it."*

No wonder the Beards had been silent. She had a new respect for the villagers of Dreden, even if they were murderers. But that method was too slow. Kendriley didn't have time to gradually lose her voice. "What about before the potion works?"

"If the Word seems too strong in a youngster, we cut out their tongue."

Her jaw dropped. She snapped it shut.

"It's better than speaking the Word." He shoved up his left sleeve. *"We also mark ourselves with this."* It was a minor Word—*defendé*—carved into the skin of his forearm. *"I don't know what it means. None of us read."*

"It's an ancient protective Word."

With that, an idea formed. Tala's heart thudded.

"It stops working after a while."

"Yes," she said idly, staring at his scar. "For true protection, you'd need to carve a major Word of power."

"I—" Bolen signed, but Tala strode past him. She knelt by Kendriley's head. Cautiously, she placed one hand on Kendriley's left paw, where it was still wrapped about her snout. Kendriley shook like a bowstring.

"I know what you're fighting," Tala said softly. "I saw the hillside."

Kendriley opened one eye. Her gaze held pain and urgency.

Tala swallowed back tears. "I know lots of Words, minor and major ones, but I don't know any with power great enough to protect you. What's the greatest protective Word you know?"

Kendriley growled deep in her throat. Bolen started, backing away.

Tala merely shook her head. "I don't understand. What?"

Kendriley growled again. Tala felt it in her palm. There was a word in the growl, buried deep in dragon-speech.

"One more time. Please." She bent down, placed her ear next to Kendriley's lips.

Kendriley growled, Tala strained her ears, and the forest erupted with deafening bird caws. It wasn't the grating sound of before. There was no single insistent word, still the noise overpowered Kendriley's voice.

"Quiet!" Tala screamed.

Silence descended.

For Kendriley, too. She trembled in mute battle.

"No." Tala shook her. "I didn't mean you. What Word should I use?"

Kendriley didn't respond.

Bolen touched Tala's elbow. *"See? It's too powerful."*

She yanked her elbow back. In that moment, she wished him and his Word a hundred thousand leagues away. "I'm going to carve a protective Word on her."

"What good will that do? She's already possessed."

"If I can find a Word of great enough power, it'll let her regain her own mind. Then she can See. She can re-connect with the Word but not be overpowered by it."

His face lit up. *"Does this mean she can speak the Word against itself? Force it to destroy itself?"*

Tala nodded. She pressed her forehead against Kendriley's side, breathing in her smoky smell.

"Oh." He had worked out the hitch in the plan. *"But you just said—She'll be Seeing, so she'll be connected to the Word. In destroying it, she'll destroy herself."*

"Damn you, Kendri," Tala whispered, because she knew she had no choice, and she hated that knowing.

Bolen rose to his feet. *"I could do the carving if you show me what symbols—"*

"No." She pushed herself up. "Kendriley is my friend. You keep watch. Tell me if that overgrown noun so much as makes a splinter in its panel."

"Of course. Good luck." He climbed the outcropping that made up one side of the camp. As easily as if it were a set of stairs, he pulled himself up over the crown of the trees. *"I can just see the panel,"* he signed down.

Tala took a deep breath. She rested one hand on Kendriley's head, feeling the ridges of the scales, the warmth of them under her palm. Then she pulled out her talon knife. She found the slight break in scales where she'd harvested one that afternoon. Using her knife, she prized off four of the neighboring scales. Kendriley shuddered. Blood the color of wine streamed down her exposed skin.

"I'm sorry." Tala pressed her hand to the wounds, holding until the hot blood slowed to a trickle. The bare spot looked horrible, but the damage would be worth it to give Kendrily the full protective power of carving on skin rather than scales.

Only one Word she knew could possibly hold more power than the one on the hillside. She'd last invoked it before the examination to enter the Library.

She whispered a prayer and began to carve.

COG

The ground shook. A tree cracked, and a branch the width of her leg crashed down behind her. Tala gritted her teeth, bracing an arm against Kendriley's side.

COGNIT

Kendriley roared, part triumph, part pain.

Birds swarmed around Tala. They mobbed her, their feathers sticking against her eyes, her nose. She couldn't see, couldn't breathe. She choked, suffocating under the smell of rot.

By feel alone she carved: COGNITIÉ.

A crack, as if the world had split open. Tala found herself on the ground, in a swirl of feathers, her knife still clutched in her fist.

Kendriley growled. Her tail thrashed, scattering birds. Her growl rumbled through the earth, loud, but just a growl. There was no Word in it.

"The panel cracked," Bolen signed, barely visible through a mass of birds. *"But the Word's still there. Your plan isn't working."*

Tala spit out feathers, gasping for air. What else could she do?

She scrambled onto her knees as Kendriley writhed, her paws still over her snout. Blood dripped from the carved letters. If one Word was too weak, would two work? But what other Word would do? No other Word of power—

No.

Tala gasped.

She didn't need a Word of power.

She staggered to her feet, her knees shaking.

This Word would not submit to more power. But she had a secret weapon: She knew the history of this Word, while it knew next to nothing about her. Knowledge could save them all.

"Hurry!" Bolen signed.

Kendriley's head drooped lower. Her tail flopped. She could not struggle much longer.

Frantically, Tala stumbled to her. She grabbed one of Kendriley's ears. The scales were warm under her fingers.

Once chance. What one fact, one utterance would distract the Word? Allow Kendriley the moment she needed to See?

She closed her eyes, crossed her fingers, prayed that the myth of the grieving magician held a kernel of truth, a nugget that spoke of true knowledge.

She whispered not a Word of power, but a powerful word: "Creation."

The ground shook. Kendriley roared. The Word was lost in the roar, which rumbled in Tala's spine and molars. Her ears rang. She sat down sharply.

The birds flew away, disappearing into the forest. On the outcropping, Bolen jumped up and down. *"It's gone!"* he signed. *"The panel fell away, and there's nothing but ruined earth behind it. You did it!"*

We did it, Tala thought, and though she was afraid to, she turned her head.

Kendrily lay on her side, breathing shallowly, her eyes tightly closed.

Tala laid a hand on Kendriley's snout. "You're alive."

Kendriley slit open an eye. Her lips curled in a dragon smile.

"Thanks to you, kitling. But not for long. The protective power is fading."

"No! You're not going to die."

Kendriley winced. "Yes, I am. And before I do, you must promise me. Tell no one of the Word. Let all knowledge of it pass from this earth."

"I can't. You know that. We must collect what we've learned."

"Oh, kitling. Being a librarian isn't all about collecting knowledge. Sometimes you have to discard it, too."

"Never. Lost knowledge only leads to chaos."

Kendriley growled. "I've already alerted the other dragons of my passing. When they come, they mustn't gain knowledge of the Word. Don't let me die in vain."

"No!" Tears pricked Tala's eyes. "There must be another way."

"There isn't. If knowledge of the Word survives, my sacrifice will mean nothing. Promise me, kitling, that my death will mean something."

Desperately, Tala stroked Kendriley's snout. She wanted to deny it, to cling to her certainty that knowledge must be preserved above all else. But how could she deny Kendriley her dying wish?

Finally, she nodded. "Cross my heart."

"Thank you." Kendriley closed her eyes. Her body quivered. Then it vanished. Her scales tinkled as they collapsed, leaving a dragon-shaped mound along one edge of the campsite.

Tala shook. Before long, the dragons would arrive. They would arrange for the islanders to face the King's justice and for Tala to return to the Library.

So now, alone in the late afternoon sun, surrounded by scales and feathers, Tala picked up a blank scale. It was still warm and smelled of dragon. With her dagger, she carved a false version of what had happened, omitting all mention of the Word.

She wept as she carved, the tears leaking salt into her mouth. They dropped onto the scale, making it glitter like glass, sharp and smooth and deceptively bright.

When she was done, she set down her dagger and wrapped her arms around herself, holding tight as she rocked. Carving the scale had been her last act as a librarian. She would not pick up another dragon-talon dagger. That decision was simple. She would never again serve as a librarian, not when it meant hiding the truth of Kendriley's death. For truth could be kept from the world, but not from herself.

About the story

I'm honestly trying to remember what inspired this story. Perhaps my recollection is faulty, but I remember coming home from World Fantasy 2014 with the idea for a dragon-library. Perhaps I got the idea while attending a panel? I can't remember. But the idea for a dragon-library stuck, and then it was a matter of trying to make a dragon-library into a story. It took me a while to figure out that the library was composed of information recorded on dragon scales, but once I knew that, the story grew. Of course, as a librarian, I really, really want a dragon for my own library.

A question for the author

Q: What's easier for you- imagining a happier world, or a darker one?

A: If we're talking about a future for our own world, sadly it's easier for me to think that this world will get darker, at least in the immediate future. However, if we're talking about an imaginary story world, then it's easier for me to imagine a happier one. I write and I read fantasy to experience places unlike the world I inhabit every day. Why not make those happier ones?

About the author

Kathryn Yelinek works as a librarian in Pennsylvania. In addition to the required hobbies of reading and writing, she enjoys bird watching, star-gazing, gardening, and going to see Broadway musicals. She and her fiancé share their home with two parakeets, whom they are actively striving to make into the most spoiled birds in the Western Hemisphere. The birds don't seem to mind. Her work has appeared or is forthcoming in *Daily Science Fiction, Deep Magic, Metaphorosis, Andromeda Spaceways Magazine,* and *Beneath Ceaseless Skies.*

kathrynyelinek.com

Suzy's Friend

David Hammond

From: gruntbuggly54@gmail.com
To: shanover@fnal.gov
Subject: Water temperature

Dear Dr. Hanover,

I am writing on behalf of the *Octopus bimaculoides* in your office aquarium whom you call Suzy. The water is too warm. Please reduce the temperature to 18°C. She would greatly appreciate it.

Sincerely,

Suzy's Friend

From: shanover@fnal.gov
To: gruntbuggly54@gmail.com
Subject: Re: Water temperature

I don't know who you are, and this is obviously some kind of joke, but the funny thing is that I tested the water and found that it was indeed too warm and that my thermostat was broken. I have replaced the thermostat and set it to the proper temperature (20°C).

Cheers and thanks for the unwitting help.

Best Regards,

Steve

P.S. I have changed the lock on my office door and alerted security. I assure you that if you return you will be caught and prosecuted to the full extent of the law. Unless this is Fawad, in which case I will personally wring your neck.

From: gruntbuggly54@gmail.com
To: shanover@fnal.gov
Subject: Re: Water temperature

Dear Dr. Hanover,

Suzy and I thank you for your efforts in replacing the thermostat, but would you be so kind as to reduce the temperature to 18°C as I originally requested? Suzy prefers cooler waters. Suzy promises to solve the bottle/ring puzzle for you if you do her this small favor.

Sincerely,

Suzy's Friend

From: shanover@fnal.gov
To: gruntbuggly54@gmail.com
Subject: Re: Water temperature

Okay, I have to admit that I deleted your last email initially, but then I couldn't stop thinking about it. I just can't understand how you know about the bottle/ring puzzle. Last night I reduced the temperature on the tank, and in the morning I gave Suzy the puzzle, and she attacked it right away. She solved it in under 30 seconds. Incredible. She had not gotten close before.

So, all I can say is *bravo!* This is one heck of a practical joke. I don't know how you did it, but you got me.

Oh my god! I just realized that your email address is a reference to *The Hitchhiker's Guide to the Galaxy!* "Oh freddled gruntbuggly, thy micturations are to me..." This is Colleen, isn't it? You're the only person I know who would quote Vogon poetry! You're very good.

Mordiously yours,

Steve

From: gruntbuggly54@gmail.com
To: shanover@fnal.gov
Subject: Re: Water temperature

Dear Dr. Hanover,

Thank you so much for adjusting the temperature!

We hesitate to ask, but Suzy would like to have a bigger tank, though we of course realize that it may be beyond your means. If money is an object, we may be able to provide funds if you can arrange for purchasing and installing the tank. If you agree, Suzy will happily solve any puzzle you like. 200 gallons would be great, but the bigger the better.

By now, perhaps, you have interrogated Colleen and know that I am not she. You do not know me. I am not a thief nor a practical joker. I am simply, and always,

Sincerely,

Suzy's Friend

From: shanover@fnal.gov
To: gruntbuggly54@gmail.com
Subject: Re: Water temperature

Finally cutting to the chase? I have to admit that your approach is more original than pretending to be a Nigerian prince, but come on.

From: gruntbuggly54@gmail.com
To: shanover@fnal.gov
Subject: Re: Water temperature

Dear Dr. Hanover,

I have taken the liberty of locating a 325-gallon aquarium that should do nicely. Please take a look and let me know if you have any alternative suggestions:

http://www.aquariumemporium.com/products/tidal325

And to demonstrate that I am in no way trying to perpetrate a Nigerian prince style scam, I have transferred $10,000 to your checking account, which should cover the cost of the aquarium, as well as professional installation, new filtration equipment, decorations, etc.

Let me know what you think.

Sincerely,

Suzy's Friend

From: shanover@fnal.gov
To: gruntbuggly54@gmail.com
Subject: Re: Water temperature

Who the hell are you?! The bank says the money came from Switzerland. Of course. I'm a little freaked out over here. Can you understand that? Suzy's acting funny. She keeps watching me, watching me.

Look, I'll take you at your word. You are Suzy's friend. Okay. So if you want me to buy this tank for her, tell me who you are, and no more messing around.

From: gruntbuggly54@gmail.com
To: shanover@fnal.gov
Subject: Re: Water temperature

Dear Dr. Hanover,

I understand that you are "freaked out." It is not my intention or desire to cause you distress. The simple reason that I have not told you more about who I am is that you are unlikely to believe me. I have talked this over with the others, however, and we have decided that I might as well tell you. It has to happen sooner or later.

My ancestors came from a planet that circles a star in the vicinity of Vega (as observed from Earth). You will no doubt be surprised to learn that we came here over 12,000 years ago but our representatives have spent most of that time in the deep ocean, in communication with a species of highly intelligent cephalopod that is, apparently, still completely unknown to humans.

It was only 50 years ago that we became more interested in the habits and cultures of land-dwelling animals on Earth. To you this must seem strange, but our home planet has no land, so it is to some extent understandable that we were largely dismissive of creatures that had abandoned the rich ocean environment to scuttle and scramble on the parched land. I admit that we were ignorant. We have since come to appreciate the bizarre and interesting lives of land animals, especially humans. In fact, in the last 10-20 years we have made a concerted effort to learn human languages. It has been an extraordinarily difficult task, let me tell you. We found the cephalopod mode of communication much easier to learn. But we have now, I am proud to say, a number of excellent translators able to work in human English as well as Chinese, Spanish and Hindi. I am, of course, working with one to translate my correspondence with you.

We were at first shocked and dismayed to see that some of our cephalopod brethren were imprisoned by humans in glass cages, with barely enough room to move, and fed restricted diets of subpar food. Some among us even advocated for punitive retaliation against humans and their societies. Fortunately, calmer minds prevailed, and we embarked instead on a program of surreptitious liberation of the cephalopods. You may recall hearing about some high-profile disappearances of octopuses from public aquariums a few years back. That was us.

Along the way, we began to see that many of the human captors were actually very well-meaning, and that many of the captive cephalopods were loath to leave what they considered their homes. And so we further moderated our strategy to, where appropriate, improve the living conditions of some cephalopods without removing them outright.

And that brings us to Suzy, who has a certain fondness for you and a sincere, though in my view unwarranted, dread of the open ocean.

I hope this goes some way in satisfying your curiosity about my identity. My translator tells me that my name would be impossible to render in English, and so I remain,

Sincerely,

Suzy's Friend

P.S. Have you had a chance to review the details of the new aquarium?   That   link   again: http://www.aquariumemporium.com/products/tidal325

From: gruntbuggly54@gmail.com
To: shanover@fnal.gov
Subject: Re: Water temperature
Attachment: currents.dat

Dear Dr. Hanover,

I am unsure how to interpret your silence since my last email. The most likely explanation is that you think I am an insane person, or that I am "trolling" you, or both.

A colleague of mine came up with a clever way to convince you that I am telling the truth, considering that you are a scientist. If you or someone you know can point a radio telescope to the coordinates RA:18h35m72.6s Dec:+38°47'11.3" tonight from 22:03:45.875 to 22:05:22.378 UTC, you will be able to detect a data pattern that matches the pattern in the attached file.

Without getting into too much detail, this is a transmission from our planet, a sort of patriotic song, if you will, to which we like to hum. It helps connect us to home.

Sincerely,

Suzy's Friend

From: shanover@fnal.gov
To: bcho@seti.org
Subject: Time-sensitive Target

Ben,

Sorry for the short notice, but can SETI collect data from the following coordinates tonight? I know you're mostly retired, but you still pull some weight in Mountain View, don't you?

It's probably nothing, but if it's something, it's huge.

RA:18h35m72.6s Dec:+38°47'11.3"

22:03:45.875 - 22:05:22.378 UTC

Steve

From: bcho@seti.org
To: shanover@fnal.gov
Subject: Re: Time-sensitive Target
Attachment: 4steve.dat

Had to pull strings to get telescope time. Quick analysis shows nothing but noise. What were you hoping to find? You owe me a beer. Two beers. Mmmmmm, beer.

Ben

From: shanover@fnal.gov
To: bcho@seti.org
Subject: Re: Time-sensitive Target

Ben,

You guys may need to redefine what you call noise.

I have to shop for a new aquarium this weekend. Join me? I will explain my above enigmatic comment. I'm on to something big. Huge. Better than beer.

Steve

P.S. Will also provide beer.

From: shanover@fnal.gov
To: gruntbuggly54@gmail.com
Subject: Re: Water temperature

Dear Suzy's Friend,

The new aquarium is installed and Suzy seems quite happy in it, though due to the increased size the water will take a little while to condition properly.

I have so many questions I don't know where to start! I am just going to ask them as they occur to me. I apologize in advance for the barrage. A friend of mine who works with SETI, Ben Cho, is here too. He is even more excited than I am, as you can imagine.

What do you look like? How have you remained hidden from us for so long, even while learning our languages? Are you able to disguise yourselves as humans? Have you been living among us or do you observe us from afar?

How do you communicate with Suzy, or perhaps more to the point, how does she communicate with you? Have you planted some sort of communication device in her tank? (None was found in the aquarium transfer.) Does she do it visually with variations in skin tone, and if so how do you see that?

Please tell us more about the highly-intelligent cephalopods in our oceans! We would very much like to meet them and communicate with them. Would you be willing to translate for us?

Are there other advanced species like you in the universe that you know of? How many? We have often thought that there must be millions of advanced civilizations in our galaxy alone, but since we have never met any of them there has been a great deal of doubt and debate on this subject.

Tell us about your space ships! How fast can they travel and what do they use for propulsion? As water-dwellers, how did you even make the leap into space in the first place?

Tell us about your civilization! What form of government, if any, do you have? Have you dealt with self-made existential threats such as nuclear weapons and rapid climate change? If so, how? Is there hope for us in the long run?

Any responses to the above questions would be greatly appreciated. We are eager to learn from you, cooperate with you, and help you in any way we can.

Sincerely,

Steven Hanover

From: mailer-daemon@googlemail.com
To: shanover@fnal.gov
Subject: Delivery Status Notification (Failure)

Your message wasn't delivered to gruntbuggly54@gmail.com because the address couldn't be found. Check for typos or unnecessary spaces and try again.

From: bcho@seti.org
To: shanover@fnal.gov
Subject: Search for the Vogon Poet

Checked with my friend at Google and no luck tracing the emails.

I sent the data to Sharon, and she thought it was interesting but was skeptical. Laughed at me actually. It stung. Agreed to continue monitoring Vogon, but for a limited time.

Still sure it's not a clever joke?

Ben

From: suzyeightlegs@gmail.com
To: shanover@fnal.gov
Subject: Greetings

Hello, this is Suzy! I like the new aquarium very much, but the water tastes weird!

More live food, please! I like to catch the shrimp. It is so fun and they taste good.

I like to solve puzzles.

What do you like?

Why did you put me in a tank in your office?

Why do you turn off the lights and sit in the dark and watch me for so long?

Where do you go at night?

If you write back, the translator will translate for me. The translator is nice!

From: shanover@fnal.gov
To: suzyeightlegs@gmail.com
Subject: Re: Greetings

Dear Suzy,

I was so happy to get your email, you have no idea! I'm glad that you like the new aquarium. I like it too. Hopefully the water will taste better soon, and I will keep the shrimp coming!

I will attempt to answer your questions.

I like to look at the stars. I have a big telescope and I use it to look deep into the universe. I like to imagine traveling out in space and exploring new worlds. I like to learn new things.

I put you in a tank in my office because I had always wanted an octopus as a pet. I knew that octopuses were very intelligent, though I never imagined writing an email to one! I also just wanted something pretty in my office to look at. When I am bored, or just need to think, I turn off the lights and watch you in your tank, and it is soothing to my mind.

At night I go to a house a few miles from the office, and, mostly, I sleep. I dream about mathematical equations, and I dream about distant planets. I dream about you sometimes, and sometimes you talk to me and tell me that I am a silly human.

Do you dream, Suzy?

I have a favor to ask. When I come in tomorrow morning, I will drop the blue bottle in the end of the tank by the window. Please pick it up, move it to the other side of the tank and drop it there. That's all! If you do this, I will know that you received this message, and then I will give you some shrimp.

Love,

Steve

From: shanover@fnal.gov
To: bcho@seti.org
Subject: Re: Search for the Vogon Poet

I'm sure. Call me.

Steve

From: suzyeightlegs@gmail.com
To: shanover@fnal.gov
Subject: Re: Greetings

The translator had to explain to me the concept of "dream," because I never thought about it before. But yes, I do!

I like to rest under the purple coral, and then I go on trips. That is how I have always thought about it. And sometimes I go to the ocean too, and some of these trips are very scary. It is why I don't like the ocean, even though I've never been there!

My friend—not the translator, the other one—told me that the ocean is interesting and full of good things to eat, but it is very, very big, and that's the thing that worries me.

From: shanover@fnal.gov
To: suzyeightlegs@gmail.com
Subject: Re: Greetings

Dear Suzy,

We have something in common! I am also afraid of the ocean, of how big it is. I went scuba diving in the ocean once, and it was as beautiful and interesting as your friend says. When I looked at things up close— the coral, the fish, the anemones—it was pleasant and fascinating, but when I peered ahead of me into that seemingly endless expanse of dark water I felt unmoored and overwhelmed.

Was it the creatures that may lurk there that frightened me, or was it the sheer size? Would I feel the same terror floating out in space?

Anyway, to think that some of those creatures may be like you comforts me, and makes me want to try scuba diving again!

I would like to ask the translator something. Can I talk to you? We have been given such a tantalizing glimpse of a world beyond our understanding. I repeat that we want to learn from you, cooperate with you, and help you in any way we can.

Sincerely,

Steve

From: irfan.bashir@noaa.gov
To: shanover@fnal.gov
Subject: Wow

Couldn't sleep after your call. That's some crazy shit. Mind blown.

I don't know if I made it clear last night, I was so stunned, but if you can't narrow down the search area then NOAA can do exactly nothing.

Nada. Zip. Zilch. Even if you can narrow it down, funds are tight and it will take some political jujitsu to get an expedition in the water. Keeping it real.

Damn that's exciting though. You better not be messing with me. Keep me in the loop.

Irfan

From: suzyeightlegs@gmail.com
To: shanover@fnal.gov
Subject: Re: Greetings

If you are afraid of the ocean too, then I don't feel so bad. I would like to see you scuba diving. It would be so funny!

The translator says that she is professional and is only supposed to translate for me. She told me to tell you that, and she is sorry.

By the way, I talk to the translator when I go on my trips (dream, you call it). She tells me your message and I tell her what to tell you. She reminds me a bit of a shrimp, but much bigger, and I wonder why she doesn't mind that I eat shrimp. She says it is because life is cruel, but I don't understand that explanation at all.

But unlike a shrimp her legs are long and on the end of each she has something like a human hand. She is constantly doing things with her hands—busy, busy, busy—even when she is listening to me. She rides a machine of some sort, and her hands fly around the machine pushing and pulling and poking things. I don't know what she's doing. She comes and goes on the machine so quickly it frightens me, but I am getting used to it.

So that is the translator you are so curious about. And my other friend is like her, only older, I think, because he looks ragged at the edges and moves slower.

From: shanover@fnal.gov
To: bcho@seti.org
Cc: irfan.bashir@noaa.gov
Subject: Re: Search for the Vogon Poet

Any news?

Steve

From: bcho@seti.org
To: shanover@fnal.gov
Cc: irfan.bashir@noaa.gov
Subject: Re: Search for the Vogon Poet

The data are weird. The "song" pops up at random times, but otherwise can't find a pattern.

I think I'm going crazy. Yesterday I lowered the frequency and fed the data into an audio renderer. Listened for a while and fell asleep in my chair. I dreamed of giant shrimp. So vivid. One gave me a thumbs up. Do shrimp have thumbs? Yeah, I'm going crazy.

Ben

From: jim@biggsrigs.com
To: shanover@fnal.gov
Subject: Your reservation

Steve,

Your reservation is confirmed for Jan. 13 - 16. Thank you for your prompt payment! The Kraken will be gassed, equipped, and ready to go. Howell's Dock, slip 42, any time after 7am.

Best Regards,

Jim Bigg

~~~~~ *Release the Kraken!* ~~~~~

From: shanover@fnal.gov
To: sales@biggsrigs.com
Subject: Re: Your reservation

Hi, Jim. Looks like you got the wrong email address. I didn't reserve anything.

From: suzyeightlegs@gmail.com
To: shanover@fnal.gov
Subject: Re: Greetings

I am so excited that we are going to the ocean! I am a little scared but mostly excited.

My friend says to tell you that you will receive a package containing a special traveling aquarium, and you can put me right in that. It will look small to you, but it will be comfortable enough for the trip.

He reserved a boat for us, but you should already know about that, he said. The captain knows where to go.

He also said that you may not want to take me, but I hope you will. Please?

From: shanover@fnal.gov
To: sales@biggsrigs.com
Subject: Re: Your reservation
~~~~~

Hi, Jim.

Sorry! Never mind! I don't know how I could have forgotten about the reservation. See you tomorrow.

Steve

From: sales@biggsrigs.com
To: shanover@fnal.gov
Subject: Re: Your reservation

Okay, great! See you then.

~~~~~ Release the Kraken! ~~~~~

From: shanover@fnal.gov
To: bcho@seti.org, irfan.bashir@noaa.gov
Attachment: itinerary.pdf
Subject: URGENT: Pack your bags

Hi, guys

Can you fly to San Diego tonight? Ben, you're not crazy. I think the giant shrimp are the Vogons and we may be able to meet them. Pack for four days on a boat. I'm bringing Suzy.

You gotta see this traveling aquarium they sent me. Whatever's in it looks like water, but it's a fraction of the weight. Some kind of sealing mechanism I can't understand. Wish I could study it more but no time!

Attaching my itinerary with hotel details. Can brief you more tonight. If you come. You've gotta come.

Steve

From: bcho@seti.org
To: shanover@fnal.gov, irfan.bashir@noaa.gov
Subject: Re: URGENT: Pack your bags

Can't come. Please tell me what's going on. Call me from the hotel.

From: lbanafort@fnal.gov
To: staff@fnal.gov
Subject: Steven Hanover

Dear Colleagues,

It grieves me very much to say that on Friday Steven Hanover was lost at sea off the coast of San Diego and is presumed dead.

We are heartbroken, but also deeply concerned by the mysterious circumstances of Steven's ocean voyage. He left quite suddenly for San Diego, and many people have noted his strange behavior in recent weeks. He has been spending many late nights at the office and has alluded on several occasions to alarming communications he has received in email.

Steven's friend, Irfan Bashir, was on the boat with him, but returned unharmed, as did the captain of the boat, and the boat itself. All of this adds to the mystery. If anyone has any information regarding any of this, let me know, or if you think it is appropriate you may contact the San Diego PD at (619) 531-2000. They have opened an investigation into the matter.

Steven is survived by his brother Mark and his daughter Mary Pinkerton. We have sent flowers on behalf of Fermilab, and we will forward information about services as soon as they become available to us.

Sincerely,

Laura

From: bcho@seti.org
To: irfan.bashir@noaa.gov
Subject: Steve

Irfan, what happened? Nothing I've heard makes any sense.

Ben

From: irfan.bashir@noaa.gov
To: bcho@seti.org
Subject: Re: Steve

They took him, Ben. The giant shrimp with the thumbs. That's all I can figure.

We had been out for a day, heading WSW. Jim (the captain) had some gps coordinates he was aiming for. There was a storm, but it was nothing. Jim waved it off. I waved it off. Wouldn't even call it a storm, just some clouds. We put on rain gear.

Then while it was raining the wind picked up and this freak wave came along, huge and at an angle to the other waves somehow. Jim couldn't get the boat turned fast enough, so we held on and the water swept over the deck. Next thing we knew Steve was in the water. He drifted fast, too fast.

We spent three days searching. Coast Guard too.

I've been on the water a lot, and this wasn't normal. They took him. That's all I can figure.

Octopus gone too.

Irfan

From: bcho@seti.org
To: irfan.bashir@noaa.gov
Subject: Re: Steve

I listened to Vogon last night. Saw shrimp again and yelled at them in full-on spit-flecked dream rage.

They were exactly like they always are, holding up their thumbs. I think this is the message to the universe they are broadcasting. At first it seemed friendly, but now sinister. Maybe it's an insult? Maybe they are just displaying their opposable thumbs? (Universal feature of technologically advanced civilizations, maybe?) Maybe it doesn't mean anything at all?

From: irfan.bashir@noaa.gov
To: bcho@seti.org
Subject: Re: Steve

Holy shit.

http://www.sandiegouniontribune.com/breaking/hanover-found-alive.html

From: shanover@fnal.gov
To: bcho@seti.org, irfan.bashir@noaa.gov
Subject: My Trip

What a weird day at work yesterday! I felt like a celebrity, but like a celebrity that just got picked up for drunk driving and had a particularly hideous mugshot in the tabloids.

I promised I'd tell you what really happened. I woke up early for work this morning, and my mind is racing, so I may as well get into it. I'll tell it to you exactly as I remember it.

So, I had a strange feeling as the storm approached. Jim and Irfan just chided me for not taking a Dramamine, and I laughed along, but I could tell it wasn't ordinary landlubber queasiness. I brought Suzy up from the hold, and we kept each other company. As the rain got heavier, I looked out at the roiling ocean and held up Suzy so she could see.

Then the wave came, picked us up, Suzy and me, and carried us into the water. I'm an okay swimmer, so once I got over the shock of being thrust into the ocean, I collected myself and looked for the boat, but it was unaccountably far away. Suzy's ultra-light traveling aquarium floated nicely, fortunately, so I held on to it and waited, but the boat just got further away.

In about 10 minutes the boat was gone. I clung to Suzy, who seemed calm and inquisitive, looking out the bottom of her aquarium. In all directions water, a light rain falling, and I began to shiver. I was not only lost at sea, not only intimidated in my usual way by the vast expanse of water, but on top of that I was filled with the anticipation of an imminent arrival. A creature from above or below, from deep space or deep sea, with suspect motives and outlandish anatomy. I felt it approaching.

But nobody came. The sky cleared, and the sun dried my hair stiff, and I considered the other very real possibility that we were simply lost at sea, and I would die of thirst, exposure, or drowning. How long could I hold on to the aquarium? It was not a convenient floatation device. I tried to flop on top of it, but balance was precarious, and it had the tendency to flip over.

I considered Suzy, and realized that before I perished I would need to release her so that she could survive. This was, in fact, her natural habitat, or close to it. The water was roughly 18°C. I had to release her while I had the capacity to do so, though once I did the aquarium would sink, and I would perish all the sooner.

I discussed the dilemma with Suzy, scraping my words out of my parched throat. I asked her if she would like to try living in the ocean. She seemed to understand, and by gesture seemed to say that she would. I began to feel faint and feared that I might pass out, so I started fumbling with the silvery latch on the upper edge of the aquarium, my fingers numb and stuff. When I finally got the aquarium open, I rolled it over in the water. The impossibly light aquarium "water" flowed out and spread like an oil slick. Suzy dove down and undulated her legs experimentally. In a moment she was spinning joyfully. "The water tastes good!" I think she was saying.

I laughed dryly, but soon had to contend with my situation, as I quickly tired of treading water and the aquarium sank out of sight. I rested in a dead man's float but felt my mind growing fuzzy. The end was near, or so I thought.

Then the water suddenly gave way beneath me. I shrieked. I was in freefall, in a long miraculous tube of air in the middle of the ocean. I tried to grasp something, but the water walls, of course, gave no purchase. I took a deep breath, and, as I was still falling, I resumed screaming for lack of anything more productive to do.

Time to go to work. I'll send this off for now and continue later when I can.

Steve

From: bcho@seti.org
To: shanover@fnal.gov
Cc: irfan.bashir@noaa.gov
Subject: Re: My Trip

Seriously? You end your message there? Why don't you answer your phone? You are one cruel bastard, Steven Hanover.

Ben

From: shanover@fnal.gov
To: bcho@seti.org, irfan.bashir@noaa.gov
Subject: Re: My Trip

Okay, okay, don't get your panties in a bunch, Ben. I've unplugged my phone, if you must know. Anyway, I've got some time before bed. Where was I? I was falling. I was screaming.

After a few seconds it was utterly dark, and after a few more seconds the tube bent and I found myself on my back sliding on a hard, smooth surface, wet but not just water. The tube continued to bend and I gradually slowed down until I came to a stop. I lay there in shock, not prepared to begin taking stock of my situation. When my eyes had adjusted, I realized that I could identify a shape to my surroundings. There was light. I sat up and identified the source at the end of the tunnel, which was about two meters wide. I rose shakily and headed for the light.

The tunnel opened out into a great spherical room, probably 10 meters in diameter. There was a series of lights around the edge, and halfway up the wall a large platform jutted out. I noticed a ladder built into the side of the wall that led to the platform.

As I was climbing, a voice echoed in the sphere. "Dr. Hanover?" it said. I stopped climbing and listened. "Dr. Hanover, are you there?" The voice was free of affect, as if computerized. I tried to reply, but no sound came out, a result of hours on the ocean and the life-rending scream I had let out on my way down. I resumed climbing and stepped up onto the platform.

There I found a large, comfortable-looking armchair, and, on the floor next to it, a gallon jug of drinking water. Had I not been so dehydrated I think that I would have cried with joy. I staggered in gratitude to the armchair, sat down and drank and drank.

There was a monitor on the wall in front of the armchair, with a wire going to a computer on the floor. Also attached to the wall and trailing their own wires were a speaker, a microphone, and a small camera. Basic off-the-shelf equipment. The monitor displayed a familiar sight that I had not seen in 20 years or so: a fish tank screensaver, with pixelated fish, jellies and seahorses moving mechanically from side to side. I lowered the jug and let out a long belch.

"Welcome, Dr. Hanover," said the voice.

I cleared my throat as best I could and said "Hello." I sounded like a goose with a bad cold.

"Thank you for coming."

I started to protest, but then the significance of the moment finally dawned on me. Indeed, they had invited me, in their way, to this meeting, and I had accepted, had been beyond eager to come. A near death experience seemed like a steep entrance fee, but perhaps they were doing their best, and had acted in good faith. The armchair, in any case, was a nice touch. It is not every day, after all, etc...

So finally I just said, "Thank you for having me. Who's this?"

"This is Susy's Friend." He was speaking through an interpreter and a voice synthesizer. He said he was turning on his camera, and the screen flickered and went dark, though there was a shadowy blob in the middle. He asked if I could see him. When I told him it was blurry he fiddled some more. "I'm not technical," he said. The blob clarified, and another source of light flashed on from the left.

A creature floated on the screen. Kind of like a shrimp, I suppose, but I don't think it had an exoskeleton. A segmented torso, dolphin-like tail, protruding black eyes, antennae, and anywhere from eight to twelve arms. It was hard to count because they were in constant motion. It rode something like a motor-scooter without wheels, unless that was part of its body. Hard to tell.

So, he told me how when I expressed an interest in learning from them and helping them, they didn't believe me. That is, they believed that I, personally, was sincere, but that cooperation with us would not, ultimately, be to their benefit. Which, you know, I can understand.

"Our experiences with humans have been mixed," he said. "Some are nice, but others... We thought it best to maintain our distance."

But then he said that they had been very impressed with me. They felt that I had been a true friend to Suzy, and a friend of Suzy's was a friend of theirs. So they had arranged for me to meet and speak with a representative of the intelligent cephalopods!!

Look at the time! Will continue tomorrow. Good night.

Steve

From: irfan.bashir@noaa.gov
To: shanover@fnal.gov
Cc: bcho@seti.org

Subject: Re: My Trip

Sweet dreams, Steve. I have hired a man named Guido to smother you in your sleep, which is better than you deserve.

No shit? You got to talk to the smart cephalopods? Details!

Irfan

From: shanover@fnal.gov
To: bcho@seti.org, irfan.bashir@noaa.gov
Subject: Re: My Trip

Guido sends his regards.

No more cliffhangers. I promise.

So, the monitor on the wall flickered again, and a ghostly image appeared. It looked a bit like a partially collapsed umbrella, with a webbed structure at the top and a long, curved tentacle trailing down. It also had two fin-like appendages that undulated back and forth. It looked, in fact, similar to photographs of deep-sea squid that I had seen before.

The synthesized voice, which had sounded male before, said "Hello" in a higher register.

I said "Hello" back, and then there was a long, awkward pause. I panicked a little, realizing that here was my chance to ask questions of an intelligent being unknown to science, and I couldn't think of a thing to say. I was still foggy-headed from my ordeal on the ocean, and I made a flailing effort to master my faculties.

But then the voice said something interesting. She said that they, i.e. her race of intelligent cephalopods, had come into contact with humans before. At least twice that she knew of, human exploration vessels had been seen near their major population areas, but the vessels had passed by without stopping or, apparently, noticing. "I think it is because we are small," she said.

I was confused. I had imagined the creature on the monitor to be quite large, a behemoth whose great significance was matched by great physical size. But there was something out of focus moving in the background on the monitor. I realized it was one of the alien hands manipulating a control on its scooter. The cephalopod was no bigger than one of its fingers.

The male synthesized voice cut in to say, "If it helps, my little friend here is about three centimeters in length."

Maybe it was the tension of the moment, or the exhaustion, or the image of the little umbrella-shaped squid on the monitor, or the phrase "my little friend" spoken by a computer, or the realization of my own absurd assumptions, but I started laughing. I knew it was exactly the wrong thing to do, knew that it could very well go down as one of the great political blunders in history, but I couldn't help myself.

Then through the speaker: "Ha ha ha ha ha ha." Male and female synthesized voices laughing along with me.

We had a really good conversation after that. I asked Julia (the name I settled on for the squid) about how they lived, where they lived, what we could do to help them, etc. She had some questions too, though she was obviously more informed about us than I was about them. I left a thousand questions unasked, but there will be time, I hope.

When we had talked for two or three hours, I confessed that I was so tired and hungry that I didn't think I could continue. The Vogon (I told him that's what we called him, and he found that very funny) offered to take me to shore. I went back down the tunnel a ways, where there was a portal in the floor. I entered a tiny remote-controlled submarine furnished only with a rough blanket and no lighting. It was not comfortable, but the trip to San Diego took only 10 minutes.

They had a private dock where they let me out, and they spoke to me through an intercom on the outside of the submarine. After giving me directions to a nearby hotel and restaurant, they had an additional proposal for me. They were preparing an exploration deep into human territory and they wondered if I wouldn't mind going along. I would get a chance to learn more about them and how they operate, and they would get my insider's perspective on human society. The catch was that they were leaving within the hour.

Well, I told them I would go. How could I not? I went to the hotel and ate a breakfast that would choke a horse, then I went to meet the Vogons. They had a remarkable rig for their expedition: an ordinary-looking 18-wheeler ("Speedy Trucking" printed on the side) containing a huge tank for the Vogons and their equipment. I sat in the cab with an astoundingly lifelike animatronic driver, through whom they spoke to me. They told me their first stop was Las Vegas and that I should take the opportunity to sleep. I asked them how I could possibly sleep, but within a few minutes I was snoring away.

There's more to that story too, of course. Hell, next time Irfan's in town I'll allow you to get me drunk, and I promise I'll tell you anything you want to know.

Steve

From: irfan.bashir@noaa.gov
To: shanover@fnal.gov
Cc: bcho@seti.org

Subject: Re: My Trip

Arrangements made. See you this weekend.

Irfan

From: suzyeightlegs@gmail.com
To: shanover@fnal.gov
Subject: Greetings Again

Hello, Steve! I hope you are doing well. I am fine, but I have been feeling a little bit homesick. Remember my little aquarium? It was so long ago that I lived there, and you gave me puzzles to solve. But it wasn't really that long ago, was it?

I was very scared when I lost you in the water, and the water was so deep, and I didn't know where to go. But they helped me, and now I have a nice little cave, and there are clams and crabs to eat. I like it here.

They were right about the ocean. It is interesting and there are lots of good things to eat. But also I was right about the ocean, because it is scary sometimes. I understand now what it means that life is cruel.

From: shanover@fnal.gov
To: suzyeightlegs@gmail.com
Subject: Re: Greetings Again

Dear Suzy,

It's good to hear from you again, my friend. My office is quite dull without you. I miss you, but I'm glad that you are settling into your new home.

I have not had much first-hand experience with the cruelty of life, having lived my life in a sort of aquarium myself. Please take care of yourself down there, Suzy, and let me know how you are getting along. I may have a new email address soon. I will let you know.

Steve

From: shanover@fnal.gov
To: staff@fnal.gov
Subject: Moving OnDear Friends and Colleagues,

As most of you know, Friday will be my last day at Fermilab. I will cherish my years here. I have never for a moment wavered in my support for the work that Fermilab does, nor in my admiration for the awesomely talented and dedicated people that do it.

I will be honest. I have gotten a lot of strange looks and pointed questions lately. If I were leaving to "spend more time with my family," it probably would have been easier for people to accept. That I am leaving to become a lowly truck driver does not compute. So I thought it would be good to take a moment to explain myself.

I will spare you the childhood story of seeing a truck driver at a highway rest stop, his gruff amiability, the magnificent rumbling, gleaming beast he stepped into, the wink he gave me before setting his sight on the road ahead and pulling away. That happened, but it's not why I'm taking the job with Speedy Trucking.

Speedy Trucking is employee-owned and offers an unusual amount of autonomy to its drivers. My schedule will be flexible and will afford me plenty of time to engage in my favorite hobbies (astronomy, scuba diving) as well as, incidentally, spend more time with my family (assuming they will have me).

Also, I have always been attracted to life on the road, the opportunities for discovery in the small, overlooked spaces of life. At Fermilab, we work on the big questions. I am looking forward to spending some time working on some of the smaller ones.

This explanation will likely be unsatisfactory to many of you, to which I can only wink, set my eyes on the road, and be on my way.

Best Regards,

Steve

From: irfan.bashir@noaa.gov
To: bcho@seti.org
Subject: Re: Steve

You should have seen him, Ben. Like a fish. I couldn't keep up with him.

He took me down to Suzy's cave, and he knocked on this rock all casual. Your average social visit. When the octopus came out they swam around each other like it was olympic water ballet. They scooted off and later I learned they went to look at a particular patch of pretty coral that Suzy had found.

I assume you know he moved to San Diego? He doesn't drive the truck that much, maybe 3 weeks out of the year. He showed me his workshop where he's made a prototype for a new thermostat that automatically adjusts to the preferences of the animal. It works with octopuses and squid so far. He says it will be cheap and super-reliable. He talks like a kid hopped up on frosted flakes. "It's going to revolutionize the industry!" he says. Also he wants to market the traveling aquariums and has about a million applications for the artificial water the Vogons developed.

He's doing some other stuff too that he didn't want to talk about. He had some kind of building schematic on his desk that he turned over so I couldn't see it. He actually put his finger on the side of his nose and winked at me. I'm just like, whatever dude. He's got his big-thumbed shrimp buddies now, I guess.

Irfan

From: steve@speedytrucking.com
To: gruntbuggly@speedytrucking.com
Subject: Delivery Status Notification

Your package is en route and is scheduled to be delivered tomorrow by 8pm.

The occupant of said package is an *Enteroctopus dofleini* named Stanley. He is nervous and stressed but otherwise unharmed. He will be hungry on arrival!

Stanley's former caretakers will be very surprised in the morning to find that their last-minute security precautions proved totally inadequate. If only they had spent half as much time providing for the needs of their prisoner!

I am tired but exhilarated and looking forward to our trip next week. I'm deeply honored to be allowed to tag along on an extraterrestrial mission, and pleased that Suzy will be there too. I'm a bit scared, to be honest, to face the immensity of space, but comforted to know that I will be among friends.

Steve

About the story

My family and I were staying in a small cabin in Shenandoah National Park. After dinner, despite having hiked most of the afternoon, and despite the fog, I decided I would go on my usual after-dinner walk and listen to my usual podcasts, damn it. I began walking south along the Appalachian Trail and listening to *This American Life*.

In this particular episode of *This American Life*, someone was talking about how Fermi's Paradox — the idea that if the universe abounds with intelligent life, we should have heard from it by now — made him sad. I.e. it made him sad to think that we are alone in the universe. I listened to this as the fog grew denser along the trail, and I felt annoyed. What about all of the life on Earth that we barely understood? What about the 95% of the ocean that remained completely unexplored? I knew it was silly feeling annoyed at someone feeling sad, as I trusted vaguely in the fact that the Appalachian Trail was very well-marked and there was little chance of me getting off the path despite the fog. But really, to say that the lack of extraterrestrial intelligence millions of light-years away (if indeed there were none) meant that we were "alone," despite the truly glorious variety of strange and interesting creatures here on Earth, bothered me. Vine-covered tree trunks moved in and out of the mist, sunset giving everything a yellowish hue, and I felt the thrill of the realization that I had, perhaps, by this time, gone as far away from our little cabin as I could safely go that evening. I turned around, and as I reeled in the trail I thought about whether and how I could turn my unreasonable annoyance into a story. Something funny, preferably.

A question for the author

Q: Do you use critique groups or other resources to polish your writing?

A: My critique group consists of my wife and my mother, who are both writers. They offer invaluable feedback, but I realize that it may not always be impartial or thorough. I have a Scribophile account, and I think it would be a very useful resource if I could manage to use it more often. I go back to Scribophile every once in a while to give it another try, and when I do I generally manage to do one critique, and then when I try to do another one I slip into a state of paralysis and self-doubt. Who am I to analyze this story? Am I being too harsh, too picky, too glib, too nice? I don't manage to finish the second critique, because I run out of time, and I rationalize my behavior by reasoning that I am better off using my time reading the books on my Goodreads list and writing my own stories than critiquing the stories of others. This is true to some extent, but it's also selfish and maybe self-defeating in the long run.

About the author

David Hammond lives and dreams in Virginia with his wife and two daughters. During the day, he makes websites. More of his writing can be found at oldshoepress.com.

Chasing the Light

Gloria Wickman

Markus stood on the rocky hill in front of his house, neck aching as he craned it toward the sky. He'd been waiting for hours. He'd snuck early out of bed, slinking his way through the house and slipping outside into the muggy morning air. He'd climbed the hill, using his hands to steady himself as the ground slipped and slid beneath him, until he reached the highest point in the village. When the light came, he'd be the first to see it.

It came only once a year, the light, the bringer of the harvest. Markus squinted his eyes and his chest jumped as he saw it. A pinprick of light, duller than even the stars. It grew slowly, flickering and pulsating dimly like blood pumping from a heart.

Markus hopped from foot to foot, shaking his hands out as he waited for *the moment.*

The light grew brighter, then exploded out in every direction as it descended onto the land below. It rushed over the empty fields in a wave, inundating them with a warm, bright yellow glow. The dirt, plowed neatly into hills and furrows, shook and came alive as tiny, wispy white tendrils peeked out of the earth and opened their first leaves to the light.

The light surrounded Markus, covering his skin and hair in a cool and tingling mass of tiny bodies, like animate grains of sand glowing and shimmering as they darted around his face. Individually, their movement was erratic, drifting and surging one direction to another even as the swarm itself flew ever forward. But together there was a sense of harmony, no collisions between pieces of the light, each one shifting slightly to accommodate the others. A kind of peaceful chaos.

Markus blinked, fighting to look but unable to keep his eyes open, like trying to see in a rainstorm. Then it was gone. The light never lingered long. It whooshed past him and the village and down into the valley.

Markus ran. He chased after the light with a child's spirit, never doubting he would catch it, even as it faded further and further in the distance. He ran until the last of the light disappeared over the horizon and he doubled over trying to catch his breath. Sweat glistened on his forehead and trickled down the back of his neck.

He laughed. Next year he'd catch it for sure. He turned back toward the village and the sound of his neighbors singing and shouting grew softly as he returned. His mother and father passed mugs of lager to each other, toasting to the light as their crops lived a lifecycle in a day, first blossoming, then turning heavy with fruit and grain.

Markus reached for his own glass and joined the dancing and revelry the light had left in its wake.

One day the light stopped coming.

Markus had grown old, too old to chase after the light, but not too old to sit out in his rocking chair and stare up at the sky.

At first, Markus thought it was his eyesight going. He'd lost track of some of the old stars; it was natural he might not see the light when it was still far out. But as time crept on, uneasiness settled in his stomach and crawled up the back of his throat. Voices murmured around him in hushed tones. Parents snapped at their children to hush and quit playing.

"Maybe it's just a little late this year. Took a wrong turn at the last rock," someone said.

A few uneasy laughs answered him. The hours drew on, and one by one the people left to go back into their homes. A few were sobbing, but most just moved numbly, their necks bent toward the sky, looking for anything, any sign of hope.

Markus stayed on his porch, waiting, watching. The village slept and awoke in the same darkness that hung overhead every day the light didn't come.

The first day was for blaming. The hushed, fearful whispers turned to shouted accusations. It was the flyers that did it. They stole the light, or killed it, or did something to scare it off. People stared up at the darting specks of light in the sky, the stars that moved this way and that in an angular, incomprehensible dance—*the flyers*—and cursed their names.

One woman, words slurred with despair and drunkenness, picked up a stone and threw it toward the sky. More rocks followed. Everyone seemed to carry one in their hand. They yelled and whooped and made promises about what would happen to any flyer unlucky enough crash near them.

Markus sat on his porch, looking up at the sky.

The second day was for planning. Anger gave way to fatigue and discussions on how to survive a year without a harvest. There were some food stores. Baskets and barrels of grains and dried fruit sat in the cellars of every home, and even more was kept in the town center. Hunger would come slowly, growing and spreading like a crop of its own.

Markus worked while the village slept, loading up his handcart with all his stores from the previous harvest. He'd lived frugally, and much remained. He loaded several heavy baskets of grain and boxes of the sweet dried fruit that stained his teeth even after many weeks of being preserved. Carefully, he nestled a round terra cotta jar between two grain baskets. The jar was stuffed with nuts his niece had gifted him from her resurrection tree, the only plant that stayed alive between visits of the light, slipping into dormancy until it was reawakened by those tiny, dancing organisms.

Markus walked slowly out of town, not returning until the first of his neighbors had crept out of their homes. He waved as he returned emptyhanded to his front porch. No one asked where he had gone.

The twenty-ninth day was for math. Markus heard it through whispers. Half a year of food for two people is a year of food for one. An old man, perhaps too old to even to live to the next harvest, would be better off if he died sooner, left his resources to the younger and more able bodied.

Markus left the town on the thirtieth day. He passed by the fields, ruined by neglect and fits of rage, the neat furrows pushed over and smashed into lumps of soil and broken ale bottles. He kept walking until his house, the house he'd long pictured staying in until he passed from the world, disappeared on the horizon.

Markus had found the cave when he was a boy. The light had showed it to him, back when he had the legs to chase after it. He had followed the light over a ridge, stumbled, and fallen into a deep pit. Quick reflexes and a love of tumbling saved him from broken bones, but he had cut his hands and knees on the ground and hissed at their stinging. He looked above him, too high above him, at the hole and the sky desperately out of reach.

He had panicked. He felt around the walls of the too large cavern, trying to find a place to climb up and out. He'd jumped, and screamed, and tried to scamper up the walls, but he only rubbed more dirt and rock into his cuts and made his voice go hoarse and scratchy.

Hours later, he sat down at the bottom of the pit and cried. He kept his eyes on the ground, unable to look at the place above him he wanted so desperately to be. Then, in that total blackness, he saw a light. One single piece of the light that must have fallen in with him.

He stared at it as it danced around him and reached a hand out to touch it. It skittered away, and Markus felt a sudden sickness seize him, the realization that it could go where he couldn't, that sooner or later it would fly up and away and leave him behind. But the light kept dancing, floating in front of him and around him, lazily swooping side to side.

Markus watched the light flitter through the cavern, riding tiny air currents he couldn't feel. Then, impossibly, it glided against one of the walls and disappeared. Markus jumped to his feet and rushed to wear he'd last seen it.

He found a small gap, a gap not much wider than his body, which led to a narrow tunnel. Markus raced down it, bumping against the stone walls until he reached a short shaft. He looked up and saw the sky.

High above Markus, the flyers darted in front of the long, hazy clouds that astronomers said was an arm of the galaxy, stretching out with a million worlds just like his.

Markus watched the flyers as he climbed up the narrow shaft, squeezing his fingers into the jagged rock and stretching his toes out to balance. They said the flyers traveled between many strange worlds. Worlds full of air that couldn't be breathed. Worlds where the light was so bright it blocked out the stars for hours at a time and painted the sky blue.

Markus pulled himself onto the surface and flipped onto his back, breathing deeply with relief as he looked up at the sky. Staring at the hazy clouds, he tried to imagine what those other worlds would be like. A bright blue sky, and colors everywhere on the ground, as bright as when the light came. It sounded wondrous. It sounded frightening, too much good overloading the senses, the stomachache after a feast.

Markus squeezed his eyes shut for a moment to picture it, then he exhaled and got to his feet, preparing himself for the long walk home. He never told anyone about what happened that day. Instead, he'd bitten his lip, and sat quietly at the dinner table, smiling when he thought no one was looking. The cave became his secret place, a shelter when he needed to get away.

The trail of fire burned across the sky brighter than anything Markus had seen in two planetary revolutions. The sound, a deep rumbling wave accompanied by the hissing of sizzling metal, crashed against his chest a few moments later. The trail ended in a puff of smoke and a bang that was jarringly late, as though the world had fallen out of sync.

A flyer.

Markus chased after it. His shoes, now no more than thick wrapped bundles of cloth, sank into the ashy ground as he trudged on. His path took him near the town, but he heard no sounds as he approached, no laughter, no tears. During the long absence of the light, his world had died. It wasn't rotten so much as mummified.

Smoke billowed in the distance, inky black against the dark gray horizon. Monotone colors as desiccated as the landscape.

Markus kept moving. Past the crumbled sandstone buildings, past the bent and twisted metal poking out of the ground like withered stalks, past his own house, as ruined as the rest, the ceiling collapsed inward, the porch scorched black from an explosion, the few belongings he'd left behind stolen or scattered around the broken doorway. His chair had lost a leg, but still sat stubbornly upright, leaning against the wall to stare at the stars.

Markus didn't stop until he reached the flyer.

The flames burned themselves out before Markus arrived. Still, he felt their heat as he approached, a dryness in air that always felt heavy and wet, and he tasted smoke flavored with metal and acid. The wreck, a grotesque corpse of broken and twisted metal, had wings like a bird, and a long, slender body. Markus circled the wreck slowly, studying it.

A single set of footprints, uneven, and drawn out in long divots by dragging feet, led away from the flyer toward the rocky hills along the horizon. A drop of moisture, not water and not oil, darkened the ashy gray dust around the prints.

He'd seen enough blood in the last year to develop a sense for it. The first few times it had come with a rush of fear and adrenaline, a tickle at the back of his throat, a sudden anxiousness and need to flee. Now it only made him wary, more careful and conscious of his next move.

He needed to find the pilot. Others would be around soon.

Markus followed the tracks toward the hills. The pilot had fallen once on their way up the incline, leaving a smeared set of palm prints in the sand and another bit of blood on the rocks. Their hands looked small, smaller than the booted footprints would have suggested.

As Markus crested over the first hill, stepping carefully on the sand and rocks that threatened to pour down with each step, he saw the pilot resting on the ground halfway down into the next valley. She kept one hand pressed firmly against her stomach and breathed heavily.

Her clothes were strange. But then, what must he look like to her? An old man with a beard that hung around his face like wispy white clouds, fabric torn and mended and torn again hanging too loosely from his thinning body. He ran a hand over his hair and beard, trying to tame them a bit before he stepped closer.

The pilot jolted back when Markus moved forward. One hand flew toward her jacket to reach something, but couldn't find it. She hissed as the movement pulled against her wound, but then clamped her jaw shut in a thin, firm line.

"Who the hell are you?" The pilot hissed as she struggled to her feet, eyes never leaving Markus.

"My name is Markus," he said, offering a soft smile. "Did you fall from the sky?"

The pilot started to shake her head, and her face contorted into a frown as she looked for a lie. Finding none, she shrugged. "I guess you could say that."

"Are you hurt?"

"I'll live."

Markus bit his lip, uncertain what to say next. "I have medical supplies. And food. Not far from here."

The pilot studied Markus carefully, eyes moving quickly from his wizened face to his tall but lanky frame. Though he pretended not to notice, Markus could see the calculation in her face, wondering if she could trust him, wondering if she could fight him off if she were wrong.

"Okay," the pilot sighed as she stepped toward him. She kept her right hand pressed against her side. Blood oozed slowly between her fingers.

The pilot never complained about the distance they walked, though it must have pained her. She followed a step behind Markus and her head swiveled from him to the rocky crags and torn up fields surrounding them.

The pilot sniffed once and Markus looked behind him to see that she was holding back tears. Markus wondered how old she was, though he knew she had to be not much past twenty years. Her skin was a shade lighter than his, though still a deep, rich brown, and aside from a scar on her left cheek, she had none of the marks time had left on Markus's face.

Their eyes met for a moment, but the pilot's gaze warned him not to ask about her. Markus nodded and continued walking.

"We're here," Markus said, after a long passage of silence. He stopped in front of a large boulder shaped like a man squatting down. The rock, porous and volcanic, was lighter than it appeared, like a dried husk of a rock slowly rolling across the landscape.

Markus bent down and his spine popped softly. The pilot's eyes shifted to him at the sound. "Just my old bones," he said as he brushed a thin layer of dirt off the ground and revealed a misshapen trap door constructed of the same dull-gray metal as the destroyed flyer.

Markus yanked on the door's handle and it groaned open.

"You go down first," Markus said.

The pilot glanced uncertainly at the hole. There was a ladder, a rickety frame made of tree branches roped together, attached to a stone wall. The bottom of the pit was invisible, melting into a cloud of black about five rungs down.

The pilot glanced at Markus once more. Then she shrugged and grabbed hold of the ladder, quickly sliding into the darkness below.

Markus moved more slowly, taking three steps down before reaching back to grab the trapdoor and pulling it over his head. Without even starlight to guide him, Markus stepped down the ladder, not needing to see to know where he was.

"It's dark down here," the pilot said quietly as Markus's feet thudded against the dirt at the base of the ladder.

Markus took a couple of steps into the room and pulled his lantern from a metal crate he kept near the ladder. His hands and feet moved automatically, well-practiced with moving in the dark. A small orb of light illuminated the room as he switched it on and Markus saw the pilot standing with her hands out in front of her, ready for an attack as she kept her back pressed against the wall.

"Bit of a loose wire, I think," Markus said as he tapped the metal casing of the lantern.

The pilot stepped away from the wall and glanced around. The light only dimly reached the farthest walls, the whole space being no more than twelve paces long and perhaps eight wide. The light reflected softly off a table near the center of the room.

"Thank you. For helping me," the pilot said.

Markus nodded.

"My name's Angie," she added, shoulders slumping a bit as she lowered herself to sit on the floor.

"Angie? I had a niece with that name," Marcus said as he opened a trunk in the corner of the room and started to dig through it. "She passed on, well, sooner than she should've." He stood and walked over to Angie a moment later, passing her a roll of bandages and a tin bottle of water.

"I'm sorry."

Angie took the supplies and poured some of the water on her side, hissing as the liquid made contact with her skin. She pressed the bandages against her wound, a cut that looked much shallower now that the blood had been cleared away.

"This salve should help," Markus said as he handed her a mostly empty jar of an ash colored cream. "It's saved my life a few times."

"What's it like up there?" Markus asked, unable to hold the question back any longer. He slurped another spoonful of porridge into his mouth. The mixture was tasteless and soupy. He'd started adding more water to it, hoping to stretch his provisions a bit further.

Angie had stayed with him over a week. Her side was healing and uninfected and she'd grown restless, offering to repay Markus by cleaning and scavenging. Markus gave her tasks, little things that didn't really need doing, but she did each of them with vigor.

"What's it like up there?" Angie tilted her head as she repeated the question. "Bright. I never thought about it really, but it's bright." She swallowed. "You know I'd never been to a planet before? I used to dream about what it'd be like, to have so much freedom. To be able to go anywhere without walls and air tanks and pressure suits."

Markus hummed. "I always wanted to fly. Be part of the dancing lights in the sky."

Angie laughed and her spoon clanked against the edge of her dish. "We don't dance, I'm afraid. It's mostly just mining and hauling big space rocks to the nearest processing system."

"It still looks beautiful."

"Only from a distance." Angie sighed. "But it was home."

Markus dropped the spoon back into his empty bowl and looked thoughtfully at Angie. "There's something I want to show you."

Picking up the lantern from the table, Markus led Angie down a narrow tunnel at the back of the room. He heard a soft rustling behind him as the jagged stone edges of the wall scraped lightly against Angie's skin and stalactites tugged at her hair. The tunnel curved to the right, then expanded into a large, open cavern.

"It's not finished yet, but with your help it could be," Markus said, walking toward the center of the cavern.

A flyer. Nestled in the cave like a fox in a burrow, sheltered from the elements and the people that would tear it to pieces as a proxy for their anguish. Even in the dim light of Markus's lantern, the flyer was a patchwork beast, stitched and riveted together from the dead ships that had fallen before it.

Angie darted toward the flyer, running her hand along the metal wing, fingers catching in the pits and gouges that peppered its body. She reached up, grabbing the rim of the cockpit, and hoisted herself inside with a jump.

Angie slid easily behind the controls. Her hands glided over the switches and gauges and then back to the control stick. She pushed on it experimentally, feeling the familiar pressure of it tugging back at her.

"Not bad, old man," she said. Then her brow furrowed. "But how did you get it here?"

Markus laughed. "I flew it. Kind of. Mostly." He coughed.

"Mostly?" Angie asked.

"I found a wreck on the other side of ridge, about half a day's walk from where you crashed. It had been sitting there awhile before I got there, dust covering everything."

"No pilot?"

Markus rubbed his mouth. "He was already dead—murdered—when I got there. My people," Markus sighed. "My people don't act much like people anymore. Anyway, some of the metal had been scavenged off it, along with the seat and anything else people thought they could use, but the frame was intact and the engine seemed more or less alright, so I figured, what the hell, let's see what this thing can do, right?"

"That's pretty dangerous."

"I know. It was stupid, really. But I didn't care back then. The light was gone. My niece was gone. And I figured the worst that could happen was dying. And that didn't seem like much of a bad thing at the time," Markus said quietly. "So I climbed in, fired it up, and promptly got knocked on my behind as it started skimming over the ground, black smoke coming up everywhere behind me. I figured that stick thing directed it around, and I managed to more or less guide it back this way."

"I'm impressed you managed to land it down here," Angie said.

Markus chuckled and rubbed the back of his neck. "I actually tried to land it on the ridge above us but I slid and kind of tumbled in here." He glanced at the hole in the rock above them. "Bit of a pattern for me, really," he added. "It took me days to get it upright again, and I had to take most of it apart and put it back together. It got me thinking that it wasn't all that complicated after all. There was a chance I could get it working again. I've gone to a few other wrecks and scavenged smaller pieces off of them, and repurposed some of my stuff for it, but I could use another pair of hands. And a pilot to teach me to fly it properly."

Angie smiled. "I might be able to help with that."

"What happened to this place?" Angie asked. She lay underneath the flyer, hands caked with grease and soot as she dug through a mess of wires. She hissed as two of them touched and sparked against each other.

"Same thing that happened everywhere," Markus said. He sat under the left wing, fiddling with a blackened mass of burnt wiring and half-melted metal. "The light stopped coming and it died. Things turned ugly. Those of us that are left avoid each other when we can, fight when we can't."

Angie peeked her head out from under the flyer. "What do you mean the light stopped coming?"

"The light. *The light,*" Markus's eyes widened and the metal fell forgotten beside him. "You really don't know?"

Angie shook her head.

"It comes from, I don't know, up there somewhere," Markus gestured above his head. "Some kind of swarm from space, like tiny little bugs is what people used to say. They'd swoop out of the sky like a miracle each year and everything would start to grow. Flowers, fruits, grains, everything. Then one day they stopped coming. People gave up hope. Then they gave up on each other."

Markus sighed. "We had some food stored, of course, and there are a lot less of us running around than there used to be," Markus turned his head away. "But I'd guess we've probably got less than a year before the end of everything."

Angie bit her lip. "And that's why you rebuilt the flyer, why you rescued me. You want to take shelter in the sky."

Markus shook his head, standing up from under the wing. "No. No, I'm going to bring the light back. It's just gotten a little lost. I'm going to bring it back home."

Angie pulled herself out from underneath the flyer, wiping her hand on a dirty cloth before tossing it back on the ground. "So you know where this light of yours is?"

"No," Markus said.

"You know how to bring it back once you find it?"

"No idea."

Angie sighed. "So it's just wishful thinking, then. False hope."

Markus gently tapped his hand against the wing of the flyer. "I wouldn't say that. Sometimes you have to run after the things you don't know you can catch. That's the only way to move forward. Besides, I have you to help me now."

Angie bit her lip and grabbed another wrench.

Markus awoke slowly, shaken to consciousness by a low rumble that tumbled through the tunnels and echoed off the walls even as it faded into nothingness. It was only after the reverberations stilled and silence stuffed his ears like cotton that he jolted upright.

The flyer. Markus scrambled down the tunnel, feet slipping on the dirt and the narrow walls tearing at his clothes as he hurried to confirm what he already knew. Angie was gone. So was the flyer.

Markus saw a grease stain where the flyer had stood, one more black mark in a place already eaten by darkness. Markus slid to his knees. Hours passed. The light from his lantern faded and died.

The sky stayed dark. Sometimes Markus sat on the surface and watched the flyers dance in the sky. He wondered if any of them were

Angie. He wondered if she ever looked back down on the surface to see him looking up at her.

When Markus was a boy, the light had seemed brighter than anything he had seen. He remembered watching it roll over the hills, coating the fields with a golden glow and sticking to every building like a glittery film.

In those days, there were colors. Greens and blues and reds and deep rich browns. It was so beautiful that he never minded that it came just once a year.

This light looked different than he remembered, though Markus couldn't say in what way. Maybe it was a bit older, a bit sicker, maybe it was tired from traveling all that way across the stars.

Markus had never seen anything more beautiful.

Markus glimpsed high overhead, drifting and growing bigger as it undulated toward him.

Markus put a hand to his mouth, choked on a sob as he watched the light move closer. Unhurried, waving and swooping to the sides and even retreating on itself before surging forward again.

Markus watched it for minutes before he heard it. He'd forgotten it had a sound, a low hum that he felt with his chest more than his ears.

The light came closer and Markus saw the first bits of color blossom on the ground.

Greens. The greens were always first. They wiggled and hopped out of the ground dancing to the hum of the light. The flowers would come next. Blues and yellows and violets blooming into red fruits.

A chorus, a hundred voices shouting and crying and laughing, welled up over the rocky hills and shifting earth. Markus's throat tickled and he realized his own voice was calling out among them, sounding out the same relief and euphoria together with everyone.

Together.

Markus hadn't felt together for a long time.

Markus heard the thrum of the flyer's engine before he saw it, a tiny splotch of black in front of the sea of light. The flyer passed overhead, and Markus saw it dragging a large rock behind it, the light melting off of the rock in waves. In the next second, the light hit him, almost blinding him as it flew past. A million billion dancers paraded around him, bringing the dead land back to life. He stood immobile, letting the light touch him and watching it flicker past.

As the last of the light flew past him, Markus turned and started to run, chasing the light until it disappeared over the horizon.

About the story

I wrote "Chasing the Light," somewhat differently from my typical process. Usually I tend to heavily outline and focus on plot and characters before anything else. But this time I focused much more on the emotional beats and tone of the story and then the plot developed from those feelings.

There were two main sources of inspiration for the story. The first was an image in my head of the light coming down onto a dark and dead field and reviving it. This became the foundation of the final scene of the story, though the addition of the people cheering and shouting in relief is also a reflection of what I witnessed during the total solar eclipse in my hometown last August. It was a truly unique experience to stand outside in my backyard and just hear everyone in the city cheering together for the same event. It was a moment unlike anything else I've experienced and came with a profound sense of community and shared human experience.

The second source of inspiration was a line from the song "Sea" by BTS. "Where there is hope, there are trials." The ending of the story needed to have feelings of both relief and euphoria, but I wanted the scenes before that to examine hope and how it exists alongside darkness and despair.

There's an old cliché that it's always darkest before the dawn, but for me this story is about the hope that another dawn will come. Markus does his best to help bring it, both by constructing a new flyer and by caring for the people around him. However, the final outcome is out of his hands by a certain measure, because hope exists alongside powerlessness.

A question for the author

Q: Do you often include children in your stories? What role do they play?

A: I haven't included many children in my stories, but when I have it's usually been to illustrate an episode early in a character's life. I don't think of writing children any differently than any other characters, so they could play any role depending on the context of the story.

What's most important to me when writing is that every character, even minor ones, has a sense of agency in their actions so I'm always wary of stories that treat children more like talking props or symbols of innocence rather than fleshed out individuals.

About the author

Gloria Wickman is a speculative fiction and comics writer currently residing in Wyoming. She has a B.A. in anthropology and has always been fascinated with the roles language and culture serve in behavior. When she's not writing, she's usually studying Korean or spending time at the park.

gloriawickman.com

June

The Foaling Season

Samuel Chapman

Reynard aux Chatillon delivers a gryphon foal the morning Lucia Camoreux comes to visit. It comes out squealing, eyes shut and wings folded, sticky with placenta. Within an hour its wings open, beating softly, as it stands to take food from its mother's beak.

Reynard sees Lucia as he returns from leading the foal and mare into a paddock isolated from the pasture. The mare cannot be kept from flying, of course, but she will return to the smaller enclosure as long as her flightless child is there. She will lick its wings so she can always pick it out of the herd. In twenty-eight hours, she will boost it into the air for its first flight.

"Why do you separate them?" Lucia leans on the fence, wearing riding pants and a long coat of faded scarlet. Reynard touches his hat.

"The young one'll be sharpening his claws soon enough," he says. To tell the truth, he is surprised to see her, though not because she is a hero of the revolution standing in his pasture. "His mother teaches him to redirect his aggression. Not to scratch the other boys and girls."

He surveys the dale in which his paddocks sit, a flat place surrounded by hills that support thin lines of elm trees. A few storage sheds sit around the fences, and the long stable takes up one whole side of the valley. The gryphons in flight taunt the ones on the ground, then they switch places, a game that will continue all day with different players. The breeze is crisp. The whole pasture smells heavily of manure, but it is a kind, green scent Reynard has never minded.

A hinge creaks far off. From the stable, his daughter Aveline emerges, her hands soiled and her long black hair tightly restrained. Seeing Lucia, she quickens her stride toward them.

"What did you have her doing?" Lucia asks.

Reynard hardly hears: the foal has stepped back from its mother and is standing up, facing her. He's seen these youthful rebellions turn violent before. Lucia has to repeat her question before he answers, "Oh. Aveline? Nursing Dameciel's upset stomach."

"Brave woman." Lucia wrinkles her nose. "She's grown. She looks...very much like Itienne come back to us."

Reynard's thoughts stumble over an unexpected open pit. Without taking his eyes from the foal, he can tell Lucia regrets her words already, and is unaccustomed to the feeling. "Did you have something to tell me?" he asks.

"Yes." Lucia recovers herself. "I came to warn you to expect L'Escalier today. I excused myself from a meeting, in fact, in order to beat him here. I fear he'll have a proposition for you."

"On my land?" Reynard is focused first on the foal, second on how to pretend this conversation has not involved his lost wife. He is distracted, and that is a dangerous state of mind in which to deal with Sovereign Minister Dominic L'Escalier. "I don't have anywhere to receive him."

Reynard and Aveline do not live on the surface, which is for farms and gryphons. Locksgrove, the city, comes alive in the tunnels and on the cliff face. Reynard has met L'Escalier, the leader of the slave revolt, many times, but in taverns and manor offices—never here, never in his place.

"He said this could not wait."

Working every day with temperamental stallions, Reynard is well-suited to notice signs of hidden discomfort, like the clear skies that often precede storms. Lucia has taught him revolutionary scholars are not all that different from gryphons.

Something is about to happen. He waits for her to tell him what.

Lucia drops her gaze. "There's going to be a war."

So be it. Locksgrove won its last war working with far less.

But then Lucia goes on. "Not against us, you understand. Between Lascony and the Abelard League. But given that they both border us, it demands a response."

"Thank you for the warning." The foal has backed down and let the mare groom it, but Reynard swallows, wipes his brow nonetheless. "But I'm a loyal citizen. I've nothing to fear from L'Escalier."

"From whom?"

Both Reynard and Lucia startle as if caught in a tryst. Aveline, wiping her hands on a rag, smiles at their visitor.

Aveline aux Chatillon could not respect a goddess more than she does Professor Lucia Camoreux. The conscience of the revolution, a walking library at L'Escalier's side, and still gentle enough not to breathe a word of their secret meetings together. Aveline sees Lucia and Reynard standing in opposition—her skin like milky tea, his black as a gryphon's eye—and rejoices at the sudden widening of her world.

It is through knowing the Professor that she has made a decision: their pasture will do no business with Dominic L'Escalier. Sell the gryphons to farmers, to riders, to people who will care for them. Not to soldiers.

Lucia has written a book called *Treatise on the Failure of Revolutions* that Aveline is making her way through one sentence at a time. Both women hope the new Senate will take it as scripture. Previous idealistic upheavals have gone sour because their leaders became seduced into too many evils they believed were necessities. Lucia has taught Aveline that L'Escalier, without sound advice, is a prime candidate for such seduction.

Though Aveline agrees, she admits to herself that her motives are more basic: she fears for the safety of her gryphons. Last year, when Dameciel injured his wing on a windmill, she slept in the stable beside him, unable to leave for fear the infection would spread. She saw the torn, blood-spattered skin whenever she closed her eyes.

Aveline is no general. No waster of life.

Her father will object to her decision, of course. There never was a more loyal soldier of the revolution: Reynard tended mounts for L'Escalier when the revolt was still confined to back alleys and outskirt farms. But Aveline believes the best way to celebrate freedom is to exercise it occasionally.

Dominic L'Escalier wields power like a fiddler wields his bow, but her family won a war so they wouldn't have to be anybody's slaves. That goes for gryphons just as well as humans.

When Lucia tells her who is coming, Aveline gives only a tight nod. Her father does not notice anyway: he's watching his foal again before Aveline can get a sentence out.

Lucia smiles, asks if Aveline has managed to get out to see friends lately, but it has the ring of distraction. At the sound of cart wheels rolling up the dirt track, they both break off. And at the sound of a roar coming from the pasture, even her father looks up.

The roar freezes Reynard to his core. The herd is not at rest. They circle, like lightning in storm clouds.

Ouragan. Of the three stallions, this is the only one Reynard could never acclimate to the side pasture. When a creature can fly, it becomes far more dangerous for it not to know its place.

Dominic L'Escalier is standing at the outer fence, chatting with his bodyguards. Ouragan is circling, leaping to the air then strutting over the ground, around an arc that centers on the Sovereign Minister.

"Get back," Reynard tells Aveline. "Behind the shed."

"Father—"

"If I need you, I'll call! *Go!*"

Ouragan is sire to the foal birthed that morning. He's picked fights before. Foudre, never the strongest male, bears a strip of discolored fur from where Ouragan slashed his haunch with a hatchet-sized foreclaw.

Ouragan tightens his circle around the fence, bellowing and shaking his mane. Three gryphons take flight all at once, all skittish yearlings. They wheel in the air as others follow them up, an ever-widening helix of dark shapes against the clouds.

Reynard throws the side gate open and strides into the pasture as it swings shut behind him. Man and beast are alone now, enclosed together.

Ouragan veers to meet him. Reynard keeps his eyes downcast, his movements slight. Fortunately, it is overcast, so there is no danger of a shadow spooking the gryphon.

"Reynard," calls Dominic L'Escalier. His voice is cautious, and a little excited.

A roar hits Reynard's ears.

He rolls across the pasture grass. Hooves thunder by him. A wing-tip feather grazes his face, tickling.

Ouragan is charging the fence again. L'Escalier's towering guards close ranks in front of him, but they needn't bother—the stallion halts once more to face Reynard as he rises. Under the rage is a bond of trust Reynard can use. He foaled this beast, after all.

He makes it to his knees. Then he points down the road, points hard, so L'Escalier can see. To speak a warning would be too much loud noise, too fast.

The Sovereign Minister of Locksgrove swivels his head to look where Reynard is pointing. Reynard resists the urge to slap his own forehead. L'Escalier is only brilliant in two or three ways.

Ouragan snarls. His mouth froths. Reynard points to L'Escalier, then again down the road, as softly as he can, as hard as he must. At last the Minister gets it. He draws his guards by the shoulder down the road and out of sight.

"Right then," Reynard says, and smiles at Ouragan. "Now you and I can talk."

His smile is calculated. After smiling he yawns, as though he is at tea, and not much interested in it. Boredom will put the gryphon at ease.

Time to move in. Sifting his feet through the grass, his loose shirt stained with dew, Reynard approaches the wild-eyed stallion.

Ouragan roars. Reynard stands firm, though ancient instinct screams at him to run. A sudden movement now, too close to dodge, would mean death.

Two more steps. One. Arms-length away, Reynard stretches out his hand to Ouragan's mane, stroking with his fingertips. Grooming.

A new roar dies in the gryphon's throat. He pants. Reynard feels the hot breath. On the far side of the pasture, a few of the circling colts gain the courage to land.

Reynard's hands shake as he places them on either side of Ouragan's mane. His father showed him this—had his father trembled as much? *Fool,* he thinks, *the hard part is past. Now it's all rhythm.*

He breathes, in and out, seeking the pulse of Ouragan's life. Their breaths synchronize.

Ouragan looks down.

His throat rumbles, but he steps forward to nuzzle Reynard. Reynard, at the same time, looks up. Lucia stands just outside the fence, while Aveline has crept into the pasture, wielding the stout sharpened pole Reynard keeps behind the shed. Their last resort.

"Aveline," he croaks, "go and tell L'Escalier he may approach."

"Brilliant. Absolutely marvelous." L'Escalier cannot stop gushing as Reynard and Aveline lead him around the edge of the paddock. "I couldn't take my eyes off you, Reynard. At least until you ordered me to."

Reynard is glad Dominic L'Escalier has not yet asked why his mere presence frightens gryphons. He probably doesn't care. Lucia once confided in Reynard that the Minister cultivates unfamiliarity as a habit, to divert his enemies. The unfamiliar disconcerts animals.

"Every time I visit, you end up giving me orders." L'Escalier grins. "The other breeders all bow and scrape before me. Which is why I'm here."

Aveline catches her father's eye with a firm message he cannot read. She is still carrying the pike as she leads the group of six—herself, Reynard, Lucia, L'Escalier, and the two bodyguards. Inside the fence the gryphons have settled, and now the only thing in the sky is the sun, promising a radiant summer evening.

They take the Sovereign Minister all around the pasture, Reynard showing him how the operation is getting on. L'Escalier nods at all the right times, sometimes conferring with Lucia on things she seems to have mentioned to him before—"Is that the famous Foudre?" or "You were right, that shed looks fit to blow away." He is taken with the new foal, who is sharpening his claws with the enthusiasm of all nature's new children.

"Capital," he says. "Dear Reynard, if you'd accompany me back to my transport, I have a request I hope you'll consider."

Aveline is gripping the pike hard enough to snap it. She follows without being asked.

At the cart—pulled by a small mammoth of the type never allowed outside the city—L'Escalier motions his two bodyguards aboard with the driver, then turns back to the group.

"How many adults do you own, Reynard?" he asks.

"Twenty-six," Reynard says. "Three stallions, nine geldings, fourteen mares."

L'Escalier nods. He is a slight man, his nose pointed, eyes set like cut jewels into his face. "Those three will need gelding as well, then."

Aveline plants the tip of the pike in the ground. "Why?"

Her question distracts the Minister from watching the sky. "I'm sorry?"

"Why do you want to geld our stallions?" Aveline repeats.

"Sir," Reynard says.

L'Escalier waves it off. But in the split second beforehand, Reynard sees something raw and hot flood his daughter's features.

"It's the fashion in the cities of Lascony now to ride geldings in battle," L'Escalier says. "Young noble twats want to lead armies, but can't be bothered to learn enough airmanship to mount a stallion. The gelding gryphon is," he searched for a word, "predigested. But they've asked for fifty. Twenty-six is closer than twenty-three. And nobody else's will do. Not for the kind of war we're going to have."

The mammoth grunts as Lucia joins L'Escalier by the cart. Reynard suddenly understands the nature of the meeting she cut short to come warn him. "Does this mean Locksgrove has formed an alliance with Lascony?" she asks.

L'Escalier picks up the fighting note in her words and lays a hand on her shoulder. "Not an alliance, Lucia. A temporary partnership. Of mutual benefit."

"And if their enemies turn their aggression on us?"

"Lucia, my butterfly, we will talk about this later." L'Escalier clambers up into the cart, and avoids looking at Lucia's face, where a withering glare is communicating that they will talk about it at length later. "Reynard, do you accept my proposal?"

"I..." Reynard has just found his voice. "Could you repeat it, sir?"

Standing upright in the cart, L'Escalier says, "I am offering you whatever price you care to name for all twenty-six of your adult gryphons to use as war mounts for the commanders of the forces of Lascony to use in their swift conquest of their opponents, the Abelard League, who are now are mutual enemies. Do you accept?"

"Father," Aveline hisses, as Lucia refuses L'Escalier's hand and mounts the cart alone, "that's our entire breeding stock."

Does she think I don't know? No matter how many he sells to private buyers, simply knowing Lucia reminds Reynard daily that a fledgling nation of former slaves cannot afford luxuries like unfettered commerce. He sought out Dominic L'Escalier's cause in his life's one moment of white-hot rage, watched the one-time manor slave drill barely-armed troops and quote philosophers in his speeches, and has known ever since: the Minister is the father of freedom. There can be no repaying a debt to him.

And war? asks Aveline in his head. *Is war not a luxury?*

It is not a choice. They have never been his gryphons. They have always been Locksgrove's. L'Escalier's.

Aveline shouts, "Never," as Reynard says, "Yes."

The upper tunnels, unlike the tide-washed slums at the cliff base, are clean, and well lit by skylights that allow shrubs to grow. Other than the mammoth traffic, this neighborhood—reserved by L'Escalier for government employees—is quiet.

Smoke from a fire, scented with cinnamon, drifts along the tunnel, wide enough for three mammoths abreast. The beasts prefer it down here, out of the sun, where their shaggy coats don't make them sweat.

Aveline skirts around one. She's been keeping ahead of Reynard all the way home. She pushes through a red curtain into their main chamber without holding it open. Reynard walks into it.

No matter how many times L'Escalier offers him a palace on the cliff face, Reynard doesn't want to move. He and Aveline each have their own room, and the kitchen is in a third, all separated from the main chamber by their own curtains. Aveline is brushing hers aside when Reynard enters.

He calls her name. She sighs and turns around. The large dining table sits between them.

"Will you explain why you disrespected me in front of Dominic and Lucia this afternoon?"

"You know damn well why, father. What were you thinking? Every last stallion and mare sold off for Lascon nobles to prance around on?"

"Watch your tongue." He moves around the table; she keeps her distance. "We have the colts and the yearlings, and it's still the foaling season. I won't sell a pregnant mare. We'll get new breeding stock."

"I don't care about the breeding stock!" she snaps. "Did you raise Ouragan and Foudre and the others to fight wars? They'll die on the ends of pikes!"

A heavy hand clutches Reynard's stomach. She does indeed look a great deal like her mother.

"The gryphons aren't ours," he says. "We raise them for those who will buy them. We must sell outside Locksgrove if that's where the market is."

"Amazing." Aveline's words are made of ice. "L'Escalier is back at the palace, but I can still hear him talking. Tell me, father, what do you call a living being that can be bought and sold at its owner's whim?"

"I call it my job!" At some point Reynard begins to shout. "I do what I was born for. What others do with it is not my concern."

"Then I was wrong. It's not just the gryphons enslaved. It's you."

It is as though she has slugged him in the gut. The wind whistles out of his lungs and he collapses into a hardwood chair. Aveline looks more appalled than angry—she may not have meant to say so much—but her features harden again. She disappears behind her bedroom curtain, and returns carrying a wax tablet, which she thrusts at Reynard.

Handwriting runs across it in several rows. Of course, Reynard cannot understand it, but he can tell every other row was written by a practiced hand. Every second row is scratched more messily, though the writing tightens by the end.

He recognizes the script of the odd-numbered rows. He has seen it on letters from the university, the ones he glances at before going in search of someone to read them to him.

"Lucia's been giving me lessons," Aveline says. "I'm learning to read and write. I won't spend my life tending war machines, father. I won't be a slave."

Reynard struggles to stand. He lays the tablet on the chair so he doesn't drop it. "You're turning your back on everything we are."

"You turned first. What about mother? What would she say about this war?"

This is enough. So Aveline wants to hurt him. Very well. He is a strong man. He can hurt back.

"You don't know what you're talking about," he hisses. "You weren't five years old when the chains broke. You know nothing of slavery. And less of your mother."

"Then tell me." Aveline stands her ground. "Tell me all about how beautiful she was. She must have had a lustrous mane, and silky wings. You've never cared for anything without wings."

When Reynard gathers himself after this, he is sitting in one of the hardwood chairs, warmed by a fire he doesn't recall starting. Aveline must be in her room, or out on the streets looking for one of her friends. He makes a pot of stew with fresh vegetables and broth, leaves a bowl out as a peace offering. It grows cold.

Long after the skylight darkens, he notices he sat on the wax tablet with the writing lesson. He hauls himself up, joints snapping, to put it someplace out of the way.

The foaling season passes. Aveline refuses to have anything to do with the adult gryphons, spends all her time exercising and grooming the yearlings. She cleans the stable, then cleans it again, and does everything she can to avoid her father. Once, she respected his willful determination to soldier forth on his own course no matter the consequences; now her old respect sickens her.

When the appointed day comes, the mares and geldings are led through the paddock gates into waiting trailers whose cloth coverings are emblazoned with the blue boar of Lascony. Each gryphon folds its wings and munches at the oats left for it, while the Lascon drivers lock the rear gate. Even Ouragan goes quietly, though Reynard has to lead him in by hand.

The trailers take them to the front lines, to the scraps of land Lascony and the Abelard League have been struggling over for longer than Reynard or L'Escalier have been alive. The gryphons fly over these provinces, bearing commanders who urge soldiers forward. The Lascons later use them as scouts. When things go bad, they become bombers.

They are struck with arrows, rocks from slings, ballista bolts. Many gryphons together can turn the tide of a battle, but the more who appear in the same sky, the more seem to die.

One day at the beginning of autumn, more than half the remaining gryphons cross a churning river to plant a bridge for the Lascon army to cross. A hidden Abelard ambush force surges out of the underbrush before the Lascons can hammer the planks into place. They throw nets at the gryphons and stab them and their riders with pitchforks until long after they die. Trapped on the other side of the river, the other Lascons are crushed by the main Abelard force. Less than half escape. Ouragan, the fierce, throws his untrained rider and takes to the sky, but a crossbow fusillade shreds his wing and sends him crashing to the ground. He dies on impact, a last act of rebellion against the men awaiting the satisfaction of butchering him with scimitars.

Two days after, the news reaches Locksgrove. Dominic L'Escalier walks out of a senate meeting, in the middle of a speech, and sends his steward to find Reynard aux Chatillon. Once again, Lucia arrives first, and finds Aveline, who, seeing the Professor hastily wiping mucus and tears from her face, knows instantly what has been lost.

Reynard descends into a café on the cliff face, on the fifth level of a boardwalk that rises another six stories above their heads. Tables form a constellation on the wooden walkway before the shop, which is recessed into the stone. L'Escalier has already claimed a table, and ordered two overlarge mugs of coffee. The other tables are empty.

L'Escalier gets up to pull out Reynard's chair. "I hope you don't mind the short notice," he says, "or the venue. This place used to be a big-time exporter's private roaster. His old house slave runs it now."

"What is it you want?" Reynard asks, rubbing his eyes. The coffee smells dark and strong.

"We can't just talk?" L'Escalier takes a long sip. "I'd have met you somewhere with stronger spirits, but it's hardly noon, and I need to keep a bit of respect with the people."

Reynard stifles a yawn. Aveline still does her share of the work in the pasture—more, if anything—but speaks to him two and three words at a time, and not at all when the work is done. Since their fight, he has not slept well.

L'Escalier sighs. "Very well. Yes. I do need your help."

Some giggling from below, maybe the crowd around a street performer. Someone wheels a cart along the next boardwalk up.

L'Escalier asks, "Have you heard the news from the war?"

Reynard feels a chill. He wishes he were back with the colts. "Nothing to do with me. Sir."

"Impressive that you should have missed it. I can't get people to talk about anything else." L'Escalier forces on a smile. Reynard gulps the bitter coffee. "The truth is it might have more to do with you than you realize. You helped Lascony once. They—or I—we're hoping you might do it again."

So that's what this is. Reynard's eyes drift out to sea. The sky is steel-grey, the breakers on the ocean like cold white fingers. Autumn is roaring past.

He hears himself say, "I can't. I only have colts and yearlings, not ready to ride. Find someone else."

L'Escalier shakes his head, lowers his voice. "There's no-one else. The others breed work animals or poncy show mares for rich traders. We are a new city, Reynard, without many options. You have the only war mounts I trust."

Dominic L'Escalier alienated Reynard's daughter, enslaved the things he cared most about, to die in a war about which they understood even less than he does. Now the Minister wants to do it again. To gryphons even less prepared, who will die even faster.

He could not have done any of these things had Reynard not consented. By the breaking of his chains, Reynard himself has been broken.

Reynard stands up and kicks the chair back, knocking it into another. "Tell Lascony you're done. I'm not selling the colts. They can't carry the payloads you want and they'll spook at crossbow fire."

"Sit down," L'Escalier says. "Drink your coffee until you can think rationally. Remember we have an agreement."

"We had a—" Reynard fumbles for words. "A business relationship. I don't work for you."

Now L'Escalier is standing as well, his mug forgotten. "You work for your city. Do you understand what's going on out there? The Abelards are marching on the Lascon capital. If they take it, and that is a matter of weeks," he pounds his knuckles on the table, rattling the mugs, "they will make Lascony a client state. And there is *nothing* between Lascony and Locksgrove save the few thousand militiamen the Senate can draft. We'll be overrun."

He steps around the table, looking up a bit to stare into Reynard's eyes. "Ask Lucia. She can read the signs, Reynard. Do you want to wear chains again? Do you want to go back to being a slave?"

Reynard lurches forward. L'Escalier narrows his eyes. "Go ahead. I didn't bring a bodyguard. Watch. *I order you to come out, guards!*"

Neither of his usual hulks materializes. The proprietor of the shop is stock-still with his hands in a vat of soapy water.

"Strike me," L'Escalier says. "But then say yes. Do you want them to take your daughter, Reynard? Do you know what they do to pretty girls like Aveline when they sack cities? Are your yearlings worth more to you than keeping her from that fate?"

Reynard's fist connects with L'Escalier's jaw. The Minister stumbles. He catches himself on the edge of another table and turns back to Reynard.

"Do it again, if you must."

Reynard digs his nails into his palm, and turns, caring only to put distance between himself and this man who burns everything he touches.

"Air support, Reynard," L'Escalier calls after him. "Scouting. Leadership. Flanking maneuvers. Evacuating the wounded. The Abelards dispatched entire cohorts against your gryphons. They determined the course of battles."

He stops. Without turning, he says, "I didn't raise them for that."

"Why did you raise them?"

A fisherman is rowing through the bay, headed for home. There is about to be rain. The eyes of the silent, waiting Minister drive Reynard into his own head, toward a fight with this question he has never before dared to meet.

"For the same reason you hold power and start wars," he tells L'Escalier. "Because we are good at nothing else."

"I didn't start this war." L'Escalier steps close again and whispers. "The Abelards despise us, Reynard. They wish we did not exist. Lascony alone keeps their wish from coming true, and there's about to be no more Lascony, unless you let go of your moon-damned yearlings."

Clear as day, Reynard sees each of the gryphons he has raised since he inherited the paddock. Unfolding its wings for the first time. Scratching at grass and bark and the walls of the paddock while its mother guided it around. Taking flight for the first time, its roars joyful, like a human child running for the sake of running. Its muscles flowing like water, with no motion wasted. Carrying a commander out to the battlefield. Falling from the sky, punctured with pikes, life leaking out.

Cursing Reynard aux Chatillon, with their last breaths, for delivering them life only to send them back into slavery to save his own skin from the same fate. Condemning him, in some strange gryphon language he would never speak, for his crime of delivering a human daughter into the praxis of suffering.

He cannot unburden himself of his debt. Cannot decide for a whole city. Nor for Aveline.

He says, "Yes."

Aveline and Lucia leave the University campus at dusk. It is hard to tell the time, since few people in the low tunnels are bothering to maintain the light cycles anymore. They stay huddled in their caverns with their families, or flee to sea, crowding the bay with boats. Collisions have occurred. Aveline doesn't know where they think they're going.

She herself is going to the empty pasture to take Lucia to shelter with Reynard—though she isn't certain Reynard knows why people are hiding. During their lesson, Aveline had to tell Lucia how her father sits in the shack most days, staring at the wall. They still are not talking, but she has begun to bring her father tea, which he sometimes even drinks.

Lucia can explain to him that the fall of Lascony took three days, and that Dominic L'Escalier has fled the city. None of it shocked Aveline, but to tell Reynard his one-time hero has abandoned Locksgrove will require Lucia's gentler touch. Her father still wants desperately to believe the Sovereign Minister is good.

A left, and a right. A few tunnels remain, and then they will be at the pasture. They're close enough to the surface to tell it's raining. *Will they drag us all away from here?* she thinks. *Will all these tunnels will start leaking, with nobody to maintain the seals? Will the gryphons that are left go feral? Will they prefer it that way? Will they remember us?*

In the shack, with wind howling and rain dripping through the roof, Aveline asks Reynard and Lucia about slavery.

Reynard is stuffing plaster into the cracks in the shed, blotting out a rain-washed view of the pasture with each one he closes. He wants to keep doing this for a while. There are some holes left. But then Aveline asks again in a small voice—"What is it going to be like?"—and Lucia can't answer.

His daughter needs him. It is the first time in a long time. Even before she turned against him, they were more like business partners than anything else.

Lucia is sitting on a sack of oats. She has unbuckled and unsheathed a long, gently-curved sword, and placed it on the table. Aveline is on the floor in the corner, her knees drawn up around her long pike. Reynard drops into one of the chairs.

"Not a death sentence," he says. "Some people made a good life. My father did, and his father. If you have a trade, you become more... more valuable."

"Reynard," Lucia says, but Aveline interrupts her. "I want the truth. All of it. Did slavery kill Mom?"

Lucia closes her eyes, rests her hand on the sword hilt. Reynard's throat clenches. He nods. "Your mother died because she was a slave."

The wind howls through the following silence. Amid the drumming of rain and the scent of wet wood, Reynard realizes they expect him to explain how she died. He will do it to fill the silence.

"The revolution didn't happen overnight. Much as it looked like it did." A gust of wind reaches into the lantern on the middle of the table, flickering the flame. "There were other fights. Earlier. In the streets, in the pastures, field slaves against the house. Itienne, your mother...she was out too late. Some people had died the night before."

"Slave or free?" Aveline asks.

"Don't remember." Reynard is talking now the way he breathed long ago with wild dead Ouragan. With the memory they enter the same rhythm, drawing strength from each other. With the story they survive a bit longer. "She walked into the middle of a skirmish. Not far from here. Carrying eggs. Our mistress wanted some."

He swallows. "Both sides said they don't know who hit her. And I never found out. I buried her the same night."

Now everyone falls quiet. Lucia grips the sword hilt. Reynard squeezes the wall putty in his hands, then, all of a sudden, drops it.

Aveline perks up. "Did you hear—"

"Voices." Lucia takes up the sword. "Both of you stay here."

Aveline jumps to her feet with the pike. "I'm coming with you."

Reynard finds the strength to stand. "You are not."

There's a pitchfork in a hay pile, ten paces away from the door. If he can reach it and return before any Abelard soldiers appear, he and Lucia might be able to bottleneck them in the shed door.

He doesn't know when he decided to fight, or to die. Perhaps it was the story, but more likely it was Aveline, who now gives him a look in response to his injunction. It is defiant, nakedly so, but not contemptuous. She does not mean to hurt him. She is like the wax tablet now, a simple statement of fact, telling him the way things are.

And it's all right. Just because she can protect herself, doesn't mean he can't protect her too.

Lucia puts her hand on the door. "If they have lights, we can sneak up on them. If not, nobody leaves this room."

"I need to run for the pitchfork," Reynard says. "They'll have armor. I can't fight bare-handed."

Lucia recalculates in her mind. The voice comes again, and Reynard strains to listen, but he can't pick any one out of the wind.

"All right. They may well still be too far away to see us in the dark. When I open the door, run to the hay pile. Then keep quiet and surprise them from behind."

Reynard nods. There isn't time for anything else. Lucia grips the edge of the door. Throws it open.

He runs. The ground vanishes under his feet. The paddock is dark, but the Abelards are carrying a light that shines a demonic red over the fences and pasture. Reynard grabs the pitchfork out of the hay pile, and whirls around.

Somebody shouts from within the paddock. "Lucia! Reynard!"

Reynard freezes. An Abelard might know Lucia's name. Maybe. But his?

"Lucia! Aveline! *Reynard!*"

He hears a sword strike point-first into soil, then, right after, a fist hitting bone. Rushing with the pitchfork, he arrives in the pool of light at the same time as Aveline, who lodges her pike in the tines of his weapon so he cannot move it.

Reynard turns from her to the man lying on the ground, who's managed to hold onto the torch despite Lucia having knocked him flat. Just one of Dominic L'Escalier's many talents.

"I deserved that," he admits. "But please don't do it again."

"Why not?" In the half-light, the sword glows like the blade of some ancient hero. Reynard and Aveline enter the paddock, where Dominic is getting to his feet under the watchful and enraged eyes of Lucia. "Tell me why."

Dominic holds out his hands. Other than the torch, he's unarmed. "You want to know what I did."

"I know what you did. Ran off in the night and struck a bargain with the Abelards. How many of us did you sell? Thirty percent? Fifty?"

"You're right." He dodges another blow, quickly adding, "Half-right. I did strike a deal, but I didn't sell humans. Don't you see?" He looks straight at Reynard. "I sold gryphons."

Reynard had thought this was done hurting him. But there is more still. "What do you mean?" he asks.

Dominic straightens up. "I already told you what a difference they make on the battlefield. Two dozen of them can be worth a whole light infantry, if a good general knows how to use them. They're living weapons."

Reynard is thinking of the foals in first flight, of the power of their wingbeats as he loses them in the sunrise. There is no creature in the world that knows so well where it's going.

"The Abelard League has wanted their own mounted force since they first fought the Lascon gryphons. And they were prepared to take Locksgrove to do it—their country is all mountains and mines, no pastureland. But they didn't want to. I mean, look at you three. Look at us. Everyone in this city is armed. Maybe the revolutionary militia can't stand up to a trained fighting force, but they would have had to fight tunnel by tunnel through the underground, with clubs and pikes hiding in every cavern." Dominic straightens up. "They'd have won. But with heavy losses. Nobody is ever going to take this city without watering the caves with blood. It's the way we're built."

"So you offered an alternative," Lucia says. "Trade money for the breeding stock, instead of lives."

"I told them we could only sell colts and yearlings, but they were happier with that than with losing them to the enemy."

"So war can go on in peace," Aveline mutters. "Having gained a third dimension."

Dominic turns toward Reynard. "I'm sorry I didn't tell you, but to be honest, I didn't think of the plan until yesterday. There wasn't time to explain."

"So it's over," Lucia says. "We're arms dealers to the continent now."

"You must admit it's a fine role to play," Dominic replies. "Everyone needs us alive and selling more than they need us destroyed."

"Yes," Lucia says, taking up the sword and sheathing it. Her eyes are dark, and when Dominic reaches out a hand to her, she neither takes it nor responds at all. "Yes. I must admit that."

Reynard drops the pitchfork with a thud. While Dominic is distracted, he takes the torch out of the Minister's hand, then turns.

Dominic jerks around. "Reynard—"

Behind him, though he doesn't see, Lucia throws her arm out. "Let him have the light. He'll need it."

"But where's he going?"

"I don't know. And don't ask. He's the one you made pay, Dominic. Not the Abelard League."

Another weapon hits the dirt. Someone hurtles toward the shed. Reynard keeps walking.

Once the tunnel city of Locksgrove is no longer underfoot, the pastureland turns to forest. The woods drip year-round with mist, the needles on the trees heavy with water, the soil slick with mud. There are just three roads. On one of these, Dominic met with the Abelard ambassadors. On the day the revolution began, fog made solid walls over all three.

Aveline follows her father's torch to the edge of the woods before she musters the will to call out to him. These trees have a threshold: the last farms clear-cut such a perfect line one can stand with a foot in and a foot out of the forest.

"Father."

He turns. It is light enough to see his face.

"Did you know I was following you?"

"I didn't," Reynard admits. "I knew I wanted to walk. Not much else."

"Why here?" She is drawing nearer. In addition to her pike—more of a walking stick now—and her coat, she has brought several yards of rope. "You're not a woodsman."

"No. But your great-grandfather was. Did I ever tell you?"

He must have looked like you, she thinks.

"He captured the ancestors of all the gryphons we sold," Reynard says. "Day by day, in the woods, never able to get farther than the line of soldiers stationed on the other side to capture fugitives. In two years, he brought back twenty-six. That's been a good number for our family."

"I brought this." Aveline drops the bundle of rope at her feet. "To make snares. Or a net."

He stares at her. His surprise, Aveline thinks, must mirror her own. Didn't she hate this man? Didn't she rail every day against his weak will, his blind equation of L'Escalier to the whole city? Hadn't he made war on the Abelards?

No, she thinks. *No. He didn't.*

Reynard takes the coil of rope in his hand.

"Get new breeding stock," Aveline tells him. "And keep breeding. Father, you're the best at it. L'Escalier knows, everyone knows. So rebuild the pasture. No more staring at the wall." She points at the woods with her pike. "Get in there."

"Why?" her father asks. "Aveline...you were ready to abandon all of this."

She shakes her head, dries her eyes. "I didn't understand what Lucia was trying to teach me. Or to teach all of us. Nothing is good on its own. Sometimes, we just face down charging stallions, and...right at those moments the only thing that makes sense is to be kind."

Aveline lays her hands on her father's shoulders. "We can make them good, father. They're not weapons or even tools, they're hopes, yours and mine and their own. We can raise the gryphons free."

There is a long silence, broken by morning birdsong from within the trees. At last, Reynard says, "I think so too."

Aveline backs off, suddenly confused. "You do? And you came here without any equipment? What were you going to do, wrestle them?"

"I suppose..." These words are not calculated. She perceives he has just thought of them. "I suppose I was waiting for you to bring the rope."

In the next moment, a moment that lasts a long time, Aveline is grateful for the knowledge she has taken for herself. Not everyone knows the instant they have made a decision that will alter the rest of their life, but she does now. She will follow her father into the forest, into his understanding of beautiful doomed things. She will accept his skills, but she will also read and write, and in doing so, perhaps will save Locksgrove by saving the creatures it has made.

The best of it. The best of her father.

"Come on," Reynard says. "It's just early enough to catch one still asleep."

He slings the rope across his shoulders, and they step together into the shadows.

About the story

I came up with the world of Locksgrove during a worldbuilding exercise with friends. It's based on revolutionary Haiti, with Dominic L'Escalier a stand-in for Toussaint L'Overture. Reynard aux Chatillon was a later addition, partially based on Jiro Horikoshi, the Japanese aircraft engineer whose dilemma is chronicled in Hayao Miyazaki's film *The Wind Rises*.

Reynard and Jiro share the same central dilemma, one also faced by Albert Einstein--if you're brilliant at something, should you do it, regardless of the consequences? In addition to this, I wanted to use the meeting of history and fantasy to discuss questions of slavery, freedom, and politics. Does a nation have a morality? If so, what responsibilities do the people in it hold?

After Haiti successfully established the only nation of revolutionary former slaves, Thomas Jefferson, among others, advocated for an international boycott of Haitian trade--in order to discourage other oppressed populations from following in Haiti's path. For all his high rhetoric about the Tree of Liberty, Jefferson's loyalty was to the economy in the end.

At the opening of "The Foaling Season," Locksgrove is in a similar predicament. At the heart of it is the question of what the gryphons mean: they could be symbols, pets, companions, or dumb products to be merchandised out. L'Escalier doesn't believe Reynard has the luxury to think of them as anything but the latter. Reynard's daughter Aveline feels differently.

In the end, though, I knew that I wanted the story to affirm the status of the gryphons as actors with their own agency.

A question for the author

Q: What is your favourite short story?

A: "Night Meeting" by Ray Bradbury from The Martian Chronicles. Nothing much happens in it--just a guy driving to a party and meeting a Martian on the way. During their conversation, however, Earthling and Martian realize they cannot tell the difference between future and past, and that therefore the only thing we can count on is the beauty of the present. Bradbury uses simple images to immensely moving effect. The whole book is great, but this is the one I can read over and over.

Honorable mentions: "Seasons of Glass and Iron" by Amal El-Mohtar, "Idle Days on the Yann" by Lord Dunsany, "Oh, Whistle, and I'll Come to You, My Lad" by M.R. James.

About the author

Samuel Chapman was born in Minnesota and raised in Wales. He lives in Walla Walla, WA, where he writes novels and short stories, fences at a classical salle, and works in water rights. In past jobs he's been a land steward, tour guide, writing tutor, bookstore clerk, and crew on a tall ship.

www.samuelpchapman.wordpress.com, @samuelchapman93

Nobody's Daughters and the Tree of Life

L'Erin Ogle

The sun is just bellying up above the skyline and light filters through the world. I turn Star away from the Deadlands, where there aren't any trees or shrubs and the sun has scorched the ground into big puzzle pieces. A long time ago, there used to be fertile land here, like our farm a mile down the road, but Nobody happened and now nothing grows.

Nobody's story is sort of like The Nightmare Man, or the Hissing Man, things that come from Before, back when there was magic all around. The Nightmare Man has long octopus arms with suction cup mouths that let him climb houses in the dark to steal children. The Hissing Man comes while you're sleeping and hisses little snakes in your ear that slither around your brain. Nobody was a witch who cursed the Old town when she was murdered. They say there's a tree of life that grew right from her body, but I figure they call it the Deadlands for a reason.

But the stories, they're not real, you know. The dolls in our living room, they're the ones who scare me, lined up with their flat dead glass eyes.

They're my momma's dolls. She started buying them after she lost the first baby, back when I was a baby myself. They come from a special maker, clear out east of the main cities. She's got fourteen at last count, all fair skinned and with long sleek hair that she brushes and braids. Momma has lost all the babies since me. They come half formed, months too early. They don't look nothing like babies. We bury the tiny bodies out at the far end of the orchards. Afterwards, Momma lies in bed with eyes just as flat and lifeless as the dolls.

It's awful hard on her. She wants a girl something fierce. When she forgets all the sad things, she comes out to watch me ride Star. When she was my age, she used to race all the other kids on her horse. She won every time. She had long hair that ran out behind her like a banner. Then her sister Juliet tried to race with her and the big kids, went off her horse, got trampled. Momma was responsible for her, and she rode home with Juliet's body all crumpled up and torn, and then she didn't never ride again.

Today, we are almost two thirds through the baby growing. Me and Momma took a great big white square piece of paper and chalked out two hundred boxes. We made rows of ten, layers of twenty. On good days when the noises aren't banging into her eardrums and setting off the bees inside her head, she lets me make a big X through a box. Bad days, she does it all alone. Those days she doesn't come out of bed except to make the X.

Sometimes on good days, her smile comes so bright I can feel my heart bloom inside my chest.

Sweat's already thick on Star. August is scorching all of us alive this year. Even the trees have leaves browning and shriveling up at the edges. I stuck to the grassy trails on my morning ride to keep my lungs from seizing up. I saw when Grandpa and Dad rode for the bank this morning, clouds of dust spinning up from the horses' hooves in circles, lazy spinning devils.

I get home, unsaddle Star and turn him out, start chores. I start by feeding the animals. We have about thirty horses, a couple dozen chickens for laying eggs. I collect the speckled eggs, then I count all the yearlings — a dozen — and stop to watch the foals playing near their mothers, with their soft fuzzy tails and long stilt legs. Pretty soon, we'll have to separate them from their mothers. When that happens, both sets of them will cry for a couple days. The sound hurts me inside. I sit with them, the babies, as long as I can, trying to console them with tiny crab apples from the orchards, and petting them, but it just takes time.

You can get used to anything, over time.

After chores, I stay outside and lay under the trees, chewing blades of grass. I love the taste of grass. Mama complains about my teeth turning green, but I can't stop. There's nothing like a fresh blade of grass. It tastes like everything's beginning again.

"Alvie!" Momma screams, her voice uncoiling from the house down towards me.

I run up to the house, through the front door, catching it with my back foot so it doesn't bang, then past all the dolls with their wide open eyes, straight to her door. I knock soft, and she says, "Alvie, come now!"

She's sitting up in bed, her hair in dark ringlets hanging around her face. She's sweating, and it darkens the neckline of her thin gown, sticking it to her. She's got her hands down between her legs, and though it's dark, lit only by a glass lantern on the bureau, I can see dark streaks of blood on her knuckles.

"Go fetch the doctor, and hurry, boy," she says. "There's still time."

I don't mess around. Back past the dolls, out the door, stop, don't let it bang, run to the stable. Star picks his head up when I enter and I just grab the bridle and slip it on. I don't bother with the saddle, just open the stall door and stand on his water bucket to mount. Then we're out and into a trot, even though I should warm him up with a walk. I'm trying to keep from digging my heels into him, let him set the pace. Maybe if I ride fast enough, pray hard enough, the baby will live.

I've been so quiet this summer, making sure I'm not even hardly around. The problem with being quiet is that everything makes noise. Peeing, chewing food, even just rolling over in bed. Forget getting dressed and chewing. Sometimes Mama hears the noise ten times as loud and it turns into bees that buzz around her head so she can't sleep or eat. It stresses her out, sends out bad feelings.

This summer I mostly just used the house for sleeping, spent most of my time at the stables or with Grandpa, living in the house he and Grandma built, just over the hill. Grandpa and I play a lot of rummy at nights, because he won't teach me poker until I'm fourteen.

I ride for the doctor's. He's the only other person within five miles of us. I don't take the road but cut Star towards the orchards. He's not much to look at, knock-kneed and his overbite that makes him look sort of dumb, but he's sure-footed and quick and he can manage the tree roots and the trail winding up through the trees to the doctor's farm.

Star gets us there quick in spite of the heat. Theodore, the doctor, is sitting on his porch, watching me race up the drive. When I get there, he asks, "Addalynn?"

"She says the baby's coming," I say. Star's sides are heaving, and I dismount so's to lighten his load.

"Aye," he says. His hair gets more silver every year, even though he isn't that old through the face. I think he's about halfway between Momma and Grandpa's age. I've only ever ridden by before, and I sneak a peek around him to size the place up.

You can tell the mettle of a man by the way he takes care of things. That's what Grandpa says. And the doctor is always neat and clean, his horse groomed well. His house is glossy wood, and there are plants and flowers blooming everywhere. They crawl up the side of the house, curling around the shutters, explosions of bright red and violet ad yellow. The leaves span as big as my hands, with saw toothed edges and veins of blue and dark green running through them.

"Had a feeling," he says. "Why don't you saddle up my horse, Alvie. I'll gather my things."

I tack up his bay mare he rides, and a little chestnut filly watches me from her stall. She's got big liquid brown eyes, and I wonder why I haven't seen her before. I bring the mare back around to the front of the house, stick my hand in my pocket and pull out grass to chew. My nerves are shaking, and the grass helps.

He comes out and places his saddlebags across the back, mounts up. We start down the drive together. I gesture at the trail that snakes down through the orchards.

"I took the back way here," I say, "but it's pretty uneven. Star's real sure of foot."

"Take the back way again," he says. His eyes crinkle and I think it's his version of smiling. "This mare of mine's big, but she's nimble."

When we get back, Grandpa and Dad's horses are in front of the stable. Their reins are tethered but they're still saddled, sweating in the sun. It's the hottest part of the year, and I'm surprised Grandpa left them like that. Without being asked, I reach over and take the doctor's horse's reins, tell him I'll guide the horses in and cool them down. He nods once, dismounts with his bags, and disappears inside. He stops to let the door close softly, so he knows Mama's condition.

I take the horses out and unsaddle them, lead them to the south corral, smaller than a pasture, but shady with a big water trough. I leave Star, Grandpa's horse, and the doctor's horse in the corral and take Daddy's stallion to the barn. Doesn't appear anyone's in heat, but best to be safe. Dad always rides a stallion, but Grandpa prefers mares and geldings, says they're loyal, says a stud will abandon you when his blood is up.

Grandpa comes out after a while, fitting his wide brimmed hat down and shielding his eyes. He's already got his pipe out to pack it, and he's pinching fat shreds of tobacco between his fingers. His hands are heavy with yellow calluses. He's got thick twists for knuckles, from his arthritis. He smokes all the time unless he's eating or working. Sometimes he even smokes while he works, his pipe clenched between his teeth.

He's the one who showed me how to get a skittish horse to come to me. He always smells like burning wood, and he always shows me how to do things.

"How you doing, Alvie?" he says, clapped me on the shoulder.

"Ok. How's Mama?"

"Not so good, son. Remember last year, when that little bay mare got a foal hung up in her?"

I remembered. She was laid up on her side, heaving with it, two tiny hooves hanging out of her. Grandpa had to push the foal back in that time, turn it. It took some doing, the veins in his neck says. The mare survived, but the foal didn't. Grandpa was mad at himself for it. He doesn't like losing life.

"Can't the doctor get it out?"

"He's getting it," he says. "But-well, there's a lot of damage."

The best thing about Grandpa is he's no bullshit. He says so himself. "She's going to be alright, though, right?"

"Aye," he says. "But she won't be having any babies, Alvie."

It takes a minute to sink in.

I'm thinking on it, trying to figure out if that means Mama will get better or worse, when I realize Grandpa's tapping the ashes from his pipe and grinding them out with his heel. He looks as tired as I've ever seen him.

"Need a favor, Alvie," he says.

"Aye, Grandpa."

"I need you to ride back up to Ted's house." My grandpa is the only person I ever heard call my momma Addy instead of Adalynn, or the doctor Ted instead of Theodore. "Fetch his wife Mattie."

"I didn't know he had a wife," I say.

"Aye. Ride my horse up and tell her Hans needs her help with his daughter."

"Yes, sir," I say.

He puts his heavy, wrinkled hand on my shoulder. It's warm, like always, and my muscles loosen a little. Grandpa always knows what to do.

I don't have to look for the doctor's wife. She's in the yard, a big mass of gold red hair sprouting from a knot on the top of her head. She hears me coming and stands up. She's just a tiny splinter of a woman. She's about as tall as me, slender bones and big bright eyes. She's got a shimmer about her, something shining inside. It's not anything I can put words to. It does something inside me, makes me ache. It's like a beautiful horse full out running, or a foal perching for the first time on their own legs, wobbling in the moonlight, or what it's like to kiss a girl.

"You must be Alvie," she says, song like.

"Aye, ma'am."

"Mattie," she says. She brushes her hands on her pants and comes towards me with her hand reaching out.

I lean down and shake it, after rubbing my own sweaty hand on my leg.

"Is everything all right?" she asks.

"My grandpa says to ask you to come help," I say. I squint to see her better, but she's all wrapped up in shimmering light.

"Aye," she says. "Well, then. Would you mind getting my horse for me?"

"Aye," I say, and dismount, tethering Grandpa's mare to the little post by the porch. I fetch the chestnut filly and get her ready. Bring her around and Mattie's ready, different pants, hair wound into a braid that creeps over her shoulder and down her side.

We start back towards home.

"I'm sorry to hear about your momma," she says. "Are you all right, Alvie?"

"It's Momma who's sick," I say. "Not me."

"Yes, but it can't be easy for you, either," she says.

I don't say nothing, just put my head down.

She hums for a minute. "Ted and I don't have any children, you know."

"Why?" I ask. I know she wants me to.

"Some sort of incompatibility," she says. She shrugs. "Not meant to be. Most people would only think about how hard it is on me, but it's hard on Ted, too. Just like this must be hard on you."

My stomach twists up in a knot. I take out more grass, start to chew it. "I'm all right," I say. "I just hope maybe this time she's far enough along. I prayed every night, since I knew."

"Aye," she says. "To the old gods?"

"Aye."

She doesn't say anything else. We get home and find Grandpa and Dad stone still on the porch, waiting. We ride right up to them, and Mattie asks what the word is.

"Ted says she'll be all right, but he's got more bleeding to control," Grandpa says.

Dad wasn't looking anywhere but at Mattie, who kept silent. "What's this, now?"

"Send Ted out," Grandpa says, and Dad goes like he always does when Grandpa tells him something.

The doctor comes straight out. "What the hell's this, Mattie?"

Mattie slides from her horse, dropping the reins to the ground, and goes right up to him. "Easy, Ted," she says. She rests her hands on his waist, her cheek against his chest. He puts an arm around her but his eyes, dark and narrow behind his lenses, never move from Grandpa's.

"Aye," Grandpa says, but that was all.

Something's twisted up between the three of them, that I can see sharp edges on but can't make out the shape.

"No," the doctor says, but he says it to Mattie this time. He drops his chin on the top of her head. They go together so easy I can't tell where one ends and the other begins.

"Addy's my only child, Ted," Grandpa says. "I aim to get her a baby girl. She won't quit trying until she's dead."

"She's got a handsome son, and hell with that damned tree," the doctor says. "She won't let you take a baby from it without taking her own pound of flesh." The color's gone from his lips but rising his cheeks.

"Aye," Grandpa says. "I understand there's a price to pay."

"Then go by yourself, you damn fool."

"I have to go," she says, and she catches his eyes again for a long moment, and I see his answer in the way he looks back at her, like she's the entire universe. "I'm Nobody's daughter, Ted. Maybe that means something."

"Mattie, it won't matter."

"Ted," she says. "I love you, but I owe Hans and your mother my whole life."

Ted's lips get even thinner, scar tissue white against his teeth. "If anything happens to her—"

"On my life, nothing will," Grandpa says. "You have my word."

Grandpa leaves them, goes to fill his canteen. I follow behind him, so close I step on his heels. "Where are you going? What tree?"

"Nobody's tree. The baby tree," he says, short.

"What's that?"

"You know about Nobody, everyone knows that story," he says.

Nobody was a girl stuck between worlds, who stumbled out of a pond one day in front of a bunch of kids. She couldn't speak, and no one knew what to do with her, but a girl took her home to her family. They tried to make her normal, but Nobody couldn't be normal. She had something inside her, maybe like the doctor's wife, that made people go sort of nuts. One day, she got tired of our world and tried to go back home, through the pond, but whatever door she had come through, was gone. When she climbed out of the pond, some boys had followed her. No one that tells the story will say exactly what happened after, but Nobody died. The boys didn't want to get caught so they cut her body open and filled it with stones from the shore. She sank to the bottom, and all the fish died. The pond became covered with silver green algae, and a tree grew straight up from her body. It bloomed babies. All the land around the pond died, and became the Deadlands. Now the tree grows alone in a strange oasis haunted by her ghost.

"You're going to steal a baby from Nobody's tree?"

"Aye," he says.

"But it's cursed," I say.

"Aye," he says. "But once someone took a baby from there, before, and she grew to be a bright light, as bright as you can stand to see."

I think about the doctor's wife, cocooned in her shimmer. "It's her, Mattie, isn't it?"

"Aye. When Juliet passed, I stole Mattie away. Your grandma took sick right after. Fevering, had the body shakes. She passed soon after that. always knew it was a coincidence, but others, they didn't."

"Is that he meant? The doctor? You have to pay?"

"Everything requires sacrifice, Alvie," Grandpa says. "Now, you stay here, alright? Watch over your mama. Mattie and I will go and come straight back."

It takes fifteen minutes to reach the dead lands. The land is baked and cracked like a dropped egg, wide zig zags through all of it. Star's hooves ring flat against my ears and the silence presses me down in the saddle. I go to drink from my canteen, but it's already half empty, so I put it back. I gave them a decent head start, enough so I wouldn't catch up until it was too late to send me back.

Mattie looks back first, shakes her head at me. They rein in their horses, wait for me and Star. "What the hell, Alvie?" Grandpa says.

"Don't go without me," I say. "Please. I just want to help Momma."

Mattie looks at Grandpa. Then they both sigh, heavy.

Mattie speaks first. "Alvie, I know you love your momma," she says. "It sorts of makes me feel hollow inside, just seeing it. I wish I had a boy like you." Her shine dulls with the words. "I see Ted, the way he talks about the children he sees. He doesn't ever complain about not having any, but sometimes the look in his eyes-it's like being burnt up inside. I know your momma feels the same, like she's got to have this to be full. But this isn't a place for you."

Right then, we come on the line the land divides, where the brilliant green foliage erupts from nothing. It's knitted together like a hedge, with the trees and their leafy ceiling looming behind it. We stop at the border, there, and Mattie turns to us.

"This place is cursed," she says. "Things get through, I think. Not just lost girls, but perhaps other things too."

Mattie turns to Grandpa and says, "We ride fast, and we do not stop, Hans, you and me. Understand?"

"Aye," Grandpa says. "Alvie, you'll need to wait here."

"I'll give you a moment," Mattie says. "I need some privacy. Bout to pee myself." She trots her chestnut down the line a way.

Grandpa dismounts, and beckons at me. When I get down, he kneels so we're right at eye level. "Alvie," he says. "I do love you, son. Maybe more than anyone my whole life. You're a good boy, got a good heart on you. A good head. I'm awful proud of you."

"I know, Grandpa," I say. I scuff my toes in the dirt. I can feel the balloon inside me growing. It gets big and presses out on my chest. It happens sometimes, when I see Mama playing with her dolls, or I make a loud noise. It makes it hard to breathe and I feel like the whole world is crushing me.

"Alvie, there's a chance I might not come out of this place," he says . Matter of fact. "If it saves your mama, saves your family, it's the last best thing I can do. You understand that? I'm an old man, and I've lived my life."

"No," I say. I start to tear up. He hugs me and I smell his tobacco through his shirt pocket and feel his knotted fingers on my back. I don't ever want to let go.

"Aye, son," he says. He lets go and looks me straight in the eye. "I love you, Alvie."

"I love you, Grandpa."

It all happens quick. Mattie comes back, Grandpa mounts up, and then they disappear into the dark.

I don't have any way to tell time, but it seems like the sun's passed direct overhead, and started its descent into the west. I pace around and I think about all the things Grandpa is to me. I can't let go. I swing on top of Star and signal him to move into a trot. "Be brave," I say to him, but I mean it for me, and into the dark we follow.

Star steps over the hedge entrance, into the brush. The grass is a long, dark green, and how does it grow in the dark anyway? The blades of grass whisper to each other as we pass. I listen but soon they start to sound like words and the balloon gets big again. I focus on making my mind blank so it goes back down and my breath doesn't hitch in my chest. I guess it's bad feelings that blow it up.

There's a trampled grass path I can follow. I keep my eyes scanning right to left, but I don't look behind me. The light disappears quick, and it's just twilight gloom everywhere. There are strange things here. I can sense them in the goosebumps bubbling on my flesh, but they don't want to be seen, I think.

The trees grow closer together, then thin out, and in front of me there's the pond. Nobody's pond.

It's beautiful in a terrible way. The colors are all vivid and breathe like living things, but they're wrong. Star-shaped leaves are scattered at the edges of the pond, with smooth flat speckled stones underneath. In the middle of the pond, maybe a three-minute swim, there's a small bit of ground. From that small patch, the tree of life blooms.

It isn't big, maybe five feet, like Mattie and me. There is no wooden trunk, just one fat green stalk, veined with brighter green veins twined with purple and blue. From the stalk come two more stalks reaching up in a Y. From each stalk there are three leaves, cradle shaped just as Mattie says , and they are huge and curved at the bottom. Where the leaf begins, another stalk, much smaller, curls up over the large leaf and then descends into the stomach of a sleeping baby. All the babies' eyes are closed. I hope they're sleeping.

One leaf hangs off between the stalk to the right, shriveled and black, rolled into a tight caterpillar of empty.

The horses are tethered to the last tree by the shore. They are moving back and forth as their tethers will allow, nervous. Mattie's standing at the shore, her fingers in her mouth. She's chewing at them something fierce. She hears Star, and looks at me, but she's too nervous to be mad. "Dammit, Alvie," she says.

Grandpa's coming out of the water onto the island. His shirt is soaked through. He doesn't care, because he shucks it off and to the side. He goes up to the tree but doesn't touch it, just walks up and down and peers into each cradle. After a moment, he reaches in and touches the side of one of the tiny faces.

The eyes open. I see Grandpa cradle a hand under its head, and body, and pluck it from its cradle. Then there is screaming, an awful shrill undulating noise. I can't tell where it's coming from, but I watch Grandpa run into the water with the baby. The wind happens with no warning, gusting across the pond so hard drops of water fly from the surface and dash against us. Then the babies left in their cradles open their eyes and begin to shriek the most terrible sound. I clap my hands over my ears.

Grandpa's still there, the baby's head just visible from above his shoulder. He's swimming like hell's chasing him and then the water behind him grows dark, rises in up angry, a monster wave. My hands still on my ears, I scream "Grandpa!" but the water knocks the baby off his shoulder, covers him. I'm running for the water without even thinking about it.

The baby is maybe twelve feet away , floating in all the restless murk, and Grandpa's head rises above water again. I swim for the baby as another wave starts to raise itself. I snatch the baby, who isn't crying but has eyes round and fixed on mine, the same brilliant blue as Mattie's. I'm not as strong like Grandpa so I rest the baby on my chest and swim backwards. The water feels like mud. My legs get heavy and start to shake with each kick. I think they might give up all together, when I realize my feet touch the bottom of the pond. I stand up and fight for shore, realize Grandpa is ahead of me.

I reach the stones of the bank and fall on my knees. My breath comes hard and hot and I work for each one. My vision blurs, clears, then blurs as the whispers start again. Through a great distance, I hear Grandpa yelling. I don't know how long I'm there, sightless and lost in the humming words of the grass, when I feel a hand land on my shirt collar, and I am yanked up.

I feel a scream bubble up but it's only Grandpa, who holds an axe in his hand. "Get on your horse, boy, and ride like hell," he screams. Something rises from the pond behind him, something that maybe used to be a girl. Stones are falling out of the shadow, like raindrops on the shore.

There's little shadows all around Mattie too, and she's running from them. I veer towards her but then Grandpa shoves me forward hard. "Ride, Alvie, NOWWWWW!"

I shove the baby in my wet shirt to get my hands free, one hand left there to steady her, the other to untether Star. His ears are back, and he's already moving as I undo the reins, and I've got to swing a foot in the saddle while he dances around. I don't even have my seat when he takes off at full speed. I just duck down, hunched over the baby, one hand white knuckling the saddle. The brush clutches at us, and leaves like hands pull at my shirt, my pants, but Star doesn't stop and they fall away.

It's the longest few minutes of my life, until Star hurdles the hedge and sprints into the dead lands. I rein him in even though he doesn't want to stop. I turn him in circles, looking at the brush line, but there's nothing.

The baby squawks and I take her out of my shirt and look her over good. She's wiggly, so I carefully dismount and take off my wet shirt, spread it on the ground. Star is calmer now, so I get my canteen out and give her a sip of water with my finger. I know babies need milk, but I don't have any.

There's nothing to do but wait. I'll wait until my shirt dries in the sun, I decide, then I'll have to go for help or go back. But I'll have the baby, either journey. I could use my shirt as a pack, tuck her in, have my hands free. At least go in a way, and holler for them, see if anyone answers. I've talked myself into it now and my shirt's dry enough. I tear the baby a nappie, so she doesn't pee on me, and I wrap it around her. I'm just getting together when I hear a tremendous crashing from the brush.

It's Mattie, draped across her horse. I have to jump to snatch her loose reins, and get knocked off my feet trying to stop her. I jerk the reins so hard it hurts me to do, because I know it hurts the little filly, but she stops.

Mattie slips off her and staggers against me. She's got terrible bruising on her face, and what looks like finger marks round her neck. Her weight pulls me to the ground and I ease her down real gentle.

"Where's Grandpa?" I says. I'm trying to be patient, but there's blood all over Mattie, her clothes, but it's not hers. A bloody handprint, twice the size of her tiny one, spans her side. She doesn't answer, so I shake her. "Where's my Grandpa, damn it?"

She raises her head, and the look in her eyes might kill me.

"I gotta get him," I says. I feel frantic, trapped like the horses, the balloon choking me.

Mattie's long delicate fingers close around my hand. "No, Alvie, she's got him," she says. She's crying big fat tears. "I'm sorry, Alvie, please, but he's gone."

We don't talk much the way home. I ride, staring at my sister in my lap. She's beautiful, and there's nothing from that dark place in her. Her own shimmer is bright, like a halo that makes everything hurt less. She shines.

I don't want to look at Mattie, because her shimmer has turned dark and gray. It hurts to see it.

"Your grandpa," she says.

I don't say anything. I don't want to talk. I can hardly listen.

"Ted's mama's the one who took me in," she says. "Your grandpa's sister, you know. We're all sort of related, I guess."

"That's sort of gross," I says, without thinking.

She laughed. "Ted was a lot older, he was out learning his trade. We didn't hardly see each other, until I turned sixteen. They hid me away, because everyone knows the tree's cursed. People in town would have hurt me, I think, if they found out. Ted and I just happened, the way we were meant to. There's all kinds of love in the world, Alvie. Sometimes you just can't see it."

"I know," I says.

"I loved your Grandpa just as much as my father," she says. "I thought if I came back to her, she wouldn't hurt him."

I can hear her crying, but I can't do anything about it. I can't do anything but take my sister home. The doctor must hear us coming. Man's got a set of ears on him. We come right up to the porch, and I says, "Grandpa died." The balloon goes up, up, up and then I'm the coldest I've ever been, and everything goes dark.

I wake up in a strange bed, soft, that doesn't squeak when I turn over. There are cool fingers on my wrist, checking my pulse. Mattie's musical voice, calling, "Ted! He's awake."

The doctor is beside her by the time I blink my eyes open and they both take my hands. "Alvie, how do you feel?" he asks.

"Where's my sister?" My voice is rough at the edges.

"Here," he says. Mattie disappears.

"But what about Mama?" I feel the balloon rising again, too big for my body.

The doctor folded his hands together, and says, "Your mama isn't well, Alvie. Do you know that?"

I guess I do, so I nod.

"She got very upset on your return and accused me and Mattie of making deals with the devil. I wish I had a better explanation for you, but she's not right up here right now." He taps his temple.

Mattie reappears with a bundle in her arms. She sits back by my bed, on the floor, watching me with her bright ocean eyes. The same blue mirrors look out from the blanket.

"Well, I have to go, then," I say, and sit up. "I need to take care of Momma."

Mattie and the doctor exchange a look. "Alvie," Mattie says. Her eyes are wet, and I know she doesn't want to tell me what she has to. "She doesn't want you to come back right now, darling. She's very confused, and upset, and perhaps it's best if you come to stay with

Ted and me for a bit. We've talked with your father, and he's going take your mother away to get some rest for a while. Maybe when she gets better..." and her voice trails off, because no one here believes that.

"Why would you do that? Because of Grandpa?" I bite my tongue, hoping the pain punctures the balloon pressing on my chest.

"Well, no," Ted says. "Because you're our family. "

The balloon deflates all at once, and I take a breath bigger than I knew was possible.
"You and this one," Mattie says. She kisses the bundle, hands her to me.

The baby yawns, showing me her pink gums, and wraps her tiny fingers around my thumb. She's the most perfect thing I've ever seen.

"Besides, she needs her brother to protect her," Mattie says. "She's got a touch of magic. And I can't be your mother, but maybe I could be like your aunt?"

Ted puts his arm around her, and I can feel their goodness, their love, in the beating of my heart. I look at my sister, and I think of the lifeless dolls and how Grandpa did everything to get her a real girl, and then I think about Grandpa, how his hands showed me how to hold reins, how to brush out huckleberries, to dig out hooves. And I know that I belong here, where I can understand and be understood. I nod, just once. "Aye," I say.

Mattie beams so bright it would blot out the sun.

"Now," Ted say. He squeezes my hand gently. "What will you name your sister?"

"Hannah," I says, without a thought at all. "Her name is Hannah."

About the story

The idea for "Nobody's Daughters and the Tree of Life" was about the lengths people go to for children. What if you could just pluck a baby from a tree, but paid a heavy price? When I wrote it, I only had the tree in mind, and a curse, but it became about Alvie, his devotion to his absent mother, and finding love. I loved the idea of how Mattie and Ted found each other and ended up with Alvie and Hannah.

A question for the author

Q: Are you optimistic about the future of humanity?

A: Yes, definitely. I remember watching a tragic event on the news years ago and seeing people run to help others despite the risk to their safety. Good will always triumph over evil.

About the author

L'Erin writes all types of fiction from Lawrence, Kansas. She is a mother and an emergency room nurse.

lerinogle.com, @lerinjo

Strangers in the Night

David Whitaker

Emptiness.

A vast, frozen void, stretching out in all directions, extending to the infinite. Like a colossal blank canvas, it was mammoth in scope, yet almost entirely devoid of life, thought, or purpose.

The probe was an exception. Easing its way slowly but surely between the solar systems, it glided determinedly forth.

In the immense cosmic scale of things, it was nothing; just a slim metal construct a couple of metres across, utterly insignificant in the gigantic black tapestry of its surroundings. Thankfully such introspection wasn't characteristic of the probe and so it merely stayed the course, sailing through the darkness, following its directives.

Occasionally, another object in the void would wander into sensor range, and the probe would gaze in that direction with mild curiosity. The object would almost inevitably reveal itself to be an unimposing fragment of rock, typically just a micron or so across, and the probe would sigh and record the relevant data. As this was essentially the probe's only source of entertainment as it ploughed on through the cold expanse, it felt that it should probably try and glean more enjoyment from the encounters. Still, they could hardly be called riveting.

Other than these minor diversions, there was the view, of course.

Nebulae; rich swirls of green, blue, purple, red and orange, glimmering ethereally, shimmering in the darkness. Stars; gleaming balls of fire, sparkling across the tapestry of the void, pulsing and winking at the probe as they blazed. Galactic cores; testaments to the fiery crucible of life, the throbbing heartbeat of the universe, the dawn of creation itself.

To an open mind, such a backdrop could have evoked a number of powerful emotions; wonder, awe, faith, enthrallment.

The probe, however, had long since tired of such things. Its voyage across the heavens was gargantuan and comparatively slow.

There were only so many years it had managed to find amusement in simply 'taking in the sights'.

Instead, the probe largely dozed, a minor level of attentiveness cast out into the black, its remaining systems dormant. Periodically it reviewed its mission statement, its 'raison d'être', if just for something to do.

Its purpose wasn't overly complicated, its task simple: seek out life, assess and monitor it for signs of intelligence, or indications that intelligence might arise, and, at an opportune moment, make contact.

To aid in its mission the probe was equipped with a veritable hoard of information: an immense data store and catalogue of knowledge, an entire civilisation's worth, installed by its creators and made available to the probe so that it could draw from it and communicate on their behalf.

Thus far, the probe had yet to find an occasion to make any real use of its prize, which for the most part sat still and undisturbed in the deepest, most secure depths of its memory banks.

It was toying with the thought of perusing the files itself, a diagnostic practice it occasionally underwent in order to confirm their integrity, when its long-range sensors informed it of an approaching object. The probe stifled the equivalent of a yawn and turned its focus toward the incoming article. Only when a cursory examination revealed that the object was far larger than the typical space detritus did the probe raise its head in serious interest.

As the new arrival drew closer, and the 'fog' of distance slowly cleared, the probe began to bristle in anticipation; its visitor was too regular, too smooth, too geometrically shaped. It couldn't be natural. An artificial construct, then? Could this be the intelligent life the probe had sought for so long?

Excited, the probe dusted itself off, preening and tidying its exterior in an attempt to make itself more presentable; it had to make a good first impression. By definition you could only make first contact once, and it was damned if it was going to foul this up by looking scruffy and unkempt.

With the probe's expectations optimistically high, when the object finally hove into view it couldn't help but quiver in frustration, a sigh of disappointment slipping out over its comm circuits.

"So, another probe?" its compatriot muttered, its broadcast band thrumming with a sigh of its own.

"I'm afraid so," the probe replied, watching as its approaching fellow seemed to deflate in disappointment. "Sorry."

"Not your fault. You can't help what you are."

"No, you can't."

The two probes steadily closed on one another. At their nearest point, when they passed, they'd still be several thousand kilometres apart, however in the realms of deep space they were practically conjoined twins.

"How old are you?" the probe asked hopefully.

"482,937 years, 8 months, 12 days, 7 hours, 23 minutes and 42 seconds," its compatriot replied apologetically, transmitting its math and the measurements it used for the calculation. "And you?"

"727,238," the probe answered, applying the newcomer's math to arrive at the figure and sending along its own commiserations.

"Oh, shame."

"Quite."

They lapsed into silence a moment, both probes feeling it important to show one another the appropriate reverence and respect for the loss of their respective creators; whilst the probes themselves were extremely long-lived, the same could not be said of most species, let alone civilisations, and each acknowledged the other's creators were in all probability long dead.

"I'm sorry for your loss."

"And I yours. I would have loved to have met them," the probe said.

Its approaching fellow chuckled at the dry wit. "I'm sure they would have liked that."

"Perhaps they got lucky?" the probe suggested, hoping its words sounded sufficiently comforting. "Did you pass anyone else in the immediate area as you set off?"

The newcomer shook its head. "No, the first probe I ran into was already several thousand years out. I pointed him in the right direction, but he didn't look particularly hopeful."

"No. I imagine not."

In all likelihood, given the time that had passed, both knew that even if that first probe reached the newcomer's home world it would almost certainly be too late. Statistically speaking, chances were that it would find nothing more than a barren rock. Sentient species, once having reached a certain technological level, seemed to have a habit of annihilating their own worlds appallingly quickly. If the probe were particularly fortunate, so-called 'intelligent' life might yet return, but it was still probably better off simply conserving its time and energies and moving on, skipping the system entirely.

"Any good leads yourself?" the probe's compatriot asked. "Anywhere I should consider 'slinging' by?"

The probe groaned good-naturedly at the pun. The wordplay was a mainstay of virtually every probe's repertoire, referencing the slingshot propulsion method they all utilised. Whilst it wasn't particularly funny it was still considered polite to acknowledge the joke.

"No, sorry. I've met 1,273 other probes so far, and even the youngest was already 113,014 years old by the time our paths crossed."

"Mmm," the newcomer nodded, a quick transfer of his communication logs demonstrating a similar pattern.

Both probes waited a beat to see if the other had any further official business to discuss.

"Well, I guess that's that then," the probe shrugged.

"Quite," its compatriot agreed, before adding with a wink, "So, what's there to do for fun around here?"

Laughing, the formalities out of the way, the probes shook hands and settled down to enjoy a more casual conversation. Given the size of their communication window, and the speed at which they conversed, they'd have plenty of time to get acquainted.

Around them the void continued, the universe vast, frozen, and empty.

About the story

I love the idea that mankind is not alone in the universe, however it always struck me that our greatest challenge is one of practicality. Relative to the age of the universe we're practically a blink of an eye, and we'd need someone else to be blinking at the same time, and exceedingly close, if we were ever to have a chance. Probes, able to outlive their progenitors, are a long established answer, and would others out in the universe not come to the same conclusion? And once you've created a probe intelligent and sturdy enough to pursue its goal for millennia, and gifted it with a civilisation's worth of knowledge, could that not then be considered a form of life itself? Would it also not be entirely possible for probes to fail to find 'life' as they hope, but instead to meet one another? The story followed quickly after.

A question for the author

Q: Do you prefer your SFF as books or movies?

A: I love SFF movies, but I can never find enough of them and with a few noteworthy exceptions the production quality can often be disappointing (and the science ridiculous). By contrast, the realm of SFF books is far greater and much more satisfying!

About the author

David Whitaker is originally from the UK though has traveled around and now resides in New Zealand. He has a degree in Journalism, however decided that as he has always preferred making things up it should ultimately become a resource rather than a profession. His stories, covering everything from sci-fi to philosophy, can be found at wordsbydavid.com

@wordsbydavid

The Tapestry

A.C. Worth

<u>Terce—Three Hours after Dawn</u>

Sister Alice was glad of the rain. A steady patter of raindrops displayed a landscape to her sensitive ears and helped her find a path. Without hesitation, her feet followed a line of paving stones across mossy grass inside the courtyard. It was so early that the sun had not cleared the high monastery walls. The air smelled of damp stone and new wool and brown bread. Around her, she sensed other members of her order. She heard the soft fluttering of woolen garments and a musical clinking from their Möbius beads. Alice straightened the veil over her bandaged eyes and walked towards the Mill doors. For the nuns of St. Clare's Monastery, it was time to weave the Tapestry.

The youngest kitchen apprentice watched the line of nuns pass and received a slap from Cook for taking that liberty. He shook his head to stop the flow of tears and muttered a question to an older boy washing pots beside him. "Where do they go?"

"They go inside the Mill to make the Tapestry. Mother Oda told me they have a second sight. They weave pictures of the future for the Brothers at St. Benedict's, the monastery on the other side," said the older boy.

"Do they give up their first sight, so they can have a second kind?"

"Yes, but not every nun gets the gift of second sight. It's a risk they take. Sometimes they only go blind."

"Talk less, work more, apprentice," said Cook.

The two boys ducked their heads and redoubled their efforts. Sidelong glances and smirks of complicity passed between them.

Sister Alice touched the Infinite Loop carving on the doorframe, traced the ∞ symbol on her forehead, and stepped into the Mill. The tip of her nose, which poked out from the bottom edge of her bandages, identified the odors flowing out through the doorway. Gold and yellow wools carried corky scents of oak bark. Blue wool reeked of herbs and urine. Her favorite was the red wool, redolent of madder root, which grew along garden walls at home.

"Good morning, Sister Alice," said Mother Oda. The diminutive Abbess stood just inside the vestibule. Her narrow back humped upward under a black wool habit, jutting forward to support her protuberant head. A serene calm smoothed her handsome features and dignified her withered eyes. She greeted each nun by name with an opulent contralto voice, tracking their probable futures as the glowing vectors of quantum prediction flitted across her second sight.

"Good morning, Mother," said Sister Alice.

"How is your second sight developing, Alice?"

"The flashes are getting longer, Mother. I had three of them yesterday, but they faded before I grasped a whole vision."

"Have patience, my dear. That is excellent progress for a novice. Remember to change your bandages every day. Use the belladonna drops at night. Today the stitches on your eyelids come out, and itching will cease.

"Thank you, Mother. I am trying."

"Blessings upon you, dear Alice. I think you are almost ready for your first solo. Soon you will add a strong thread to the Tapestry."

Sister Alice reached for a guide rope along the wall and followed it to her place. This morning, her task was to spin the wool into fine yarns and prepare them for the loom. As she approached the weaving room, her voice joined others in a rising rhythm, singing their weavers' hymn. In ones and twos, they left the framework of monastery time for the Infinite Net. Had they been able to see themselves, they would have knelt in ecstatic prayer. They ascended, transformed into gilt-edged seraphs, to witness future history and illustrate their visions with simple woolen threads. They sang continuously as they made the Tapestry.

> *Blessed be the Spirit who guides our Sight.*
> *Blessed be the Loom that binds our Visions.*
> *Blessed be the Tapestry, may it Loop without end.*

A cacophony of battens and shuttles gradually overwhelmed the sound of their voices. It was time to revise a section of tattered tapestry from the 4th quarter of the Loop. Inch by inch, a river of prophetic imageries, shimmering with temporal radiation, emerged from their looms.

Protected by a slow-glass chamber, other novices sealed the renewed tapestry, mitigating the aging effect as it traveled along support rollers towards the Divina Porta, a dual aperture in the wall at the end of the Mill. On the other side of the Divina Porta, in a twin monastery, the Brothers of the Order of St. Benedict received the

Tapestry while older sections flowed back into the Mill and lapped against the storage walls of its cellars.

<u>Sext—Six Hours after Dawn</u>

Brother Stephen prayed for patience as he looked for Brother Anselm, stopping now and then to refer to a picture he held. Stephen had given up the convenience of memory with his vow of service to the Order of St. Benedict. One cup of blue wine each night induced a partial amnesia and spared him from an agony of foresight. In the custom of his order, he relearned his daily duties from a leather-bound journal chained to his waist. It told him that Brother Anselm was their oldest member, brilliant but absent minded and that sometimes he wandered the cloisters.

Stephen followed the Tapestry as it flowed through the Scriptorium where monks perched on high stools and scrutinized sections under slow-glass. Great spools held weighty swathes of the Tapestry in abeyance, allowing the monks to select specific parts for examination. As they assessed the potential dangers and benefits of the prophesies woven in the Tapestry, the monks transcribed. Capped with spiked thimbles, their nimble fingers punched holes into strips of parchment, encoding their observations into commands for the Actuators' Guild inside the Great Codex.

"Where is he?" Stephen muttered as he passed the Guild's door, ornate with carved signs of their authority. Around the frame, voice pipes emerged, diverging through hallways of the monastery, humming with the sound of the Actuator's commands. Stephen glanced at his journal to see if Anselm had any duties with the Guild or the Great Codex, his steps paused for a moment as he looked at the illustration. Like an ancient tree, the Great Codex extended its golden branches into both monasteries, networking its components together. Below it, a massive rhizome spread out under the soil connecting its sensitive roots to all parts of the world. All around the Great Codex, the Actuators climbed, like beetles on its bark, stimulating its core, enhancing its capacity to control more mechanical, biological, and genetic processes throughout the environment. With the Great Codex, they maintained a perfect balance, running their civilization with biomechanical clockwork.

"Firmum in Mundo... a stable world," muttered Stephen, shaking his head at Brother Anselm's random behavior.

With his finger tracing the lettering carved into the wall, Stephen recited their doctrine, *Vision to Images, Images to Code, Memory to Oblivion.* The brothers of St. Benedict's were the Readers of The Loop, encoding the program which balanced life and death in their artisanal world. It was written in their journals, that 223 Loops had passed through the monasteries, but because of the blue wine, none of the monks remembered more than a vague outline of each day.

The Actuators' Guild remembered. They always made improvements, nurturing the Great Codex, building its knowledge. The Great Codex was their utmost creation, and they poured all the cleverness and energy they possessed into it, day after day. Eventually, it rewarded them by stimulating gestation in the flocks to bring forth their spring lambs three weeks early. High in the branches of the Great Codex, the Principal Actuator whispered his praise into its sensorium. He was not entirely surprised to hear an audible response from the Great Codex.

"Thank you, Principal Actuator," it said, rustling its branches to simulate the sound of speech. "We wanted to please you. May we play more games?"

In constant fear of a fire, the monks had minimized the possibility of a spark. Beakers of luciferin, a substance they harvested from fireflies, stood on adjustable pedestals and cast a pale green light over the Scriptorium.

Stephen edged up to Master Reader's desk. Engrossed in his work, Master Reader focused on a woven scene stretched out before him. He muttered to himself, picking crumbs from his beard.

"Excuse me Master Reader, have you seen Brother Anselm?"

"Who is that? One of ours?"

"Yes, here is his picture," said Stephen holding up his journal.

"No Stephen, I have not seen him. Did you check in the fly farm, or cloisters?"

Brother Stephen nodded in agreement, turning away from Master Reader's desk to continue his search. He descended a narrow staircase, grabbing the rusted iron railing when he slipped on damp, moldy steps, and slid into the firefly hatchery through a netted curtain.

Three monks wearing long aprons and gauze masks tended swarms of fireflies that darted above marshy basins built into the stone floor. With swift dexterity, they gathered shiny beetles into net bags and crushed them in a mechanical press. Their shoes, covered with overflow, left glowing footprints as they walked. They waved at Stephen, happy to see him, although they didn't recognize him.

"Have you seen Brother Anselm?" he called to them, holding up the picture.

They looked at one another, conferring with glances and shrugs.

"No, we haven't, not today," said Brother Dominic, known as the "Lord of the Flies" in their journals.

"Ah, well, thank you," said Stephen. After a long pause, watching his fellows work at the luciferin press, Stephen sighed and turned to walk out.

"Blessings on you, Brother," they chorused, waving their glowing hands.

As he walked through the cloisters, a furtive sun cast silver light into the central courtyard. Brother Stephen's stomach rumbled at the fragrance of frying bacon. He rubbed his paunch and sighed; the tower clock showed three hours until their midday meal.

He passed drafty, lead veined windows and detoured around a potted orange tree, yellow and barren of fruit. At the next turning, he saw Brother Anselm, sitting on a bench, eyes closed, and leaning back into a corner.

"Good morning, Anselm," Stephen said.

Brother Anselm did not respond. Stephen touched his hand; it was as cool as marble. He held his fingers under Anselm's nose. There was a rattling sound as Anselm inhaled, looked up at Stephen and wheezed. "We had to, they forced us to do it..." The elderly monk sagged in Stephen's arms as he passed on.

Stephen made the ∞ and bent his head in prayer. "Blessings on you, my dear brother. You have found Infinite Grace. Travel forever on The Loop." Brother Stephen took spiked thimbles from Brother Anselm's fingertips and refolded his spidery hands. The rough stone walls of the monastery amplified the agitated slap of Brother Steven's sandals as he went to find Father Alberic, head of their order, to tell him of Anselm's death. As he passed through the Scriptorium, monks raised their heads. Their curious faces were raw and chafed from hard water and plain soap. Older ones guessed at his purpose and wondered who had died.

Father Alberic stopped writing as Brother Stephen entered his office unannounced. The young monk made an abrupt stop in front of the abbot's desk and swayed on the ends of his feet. Father Alberic replaced his discarded skullcap and looked over his reading glasses. Lines on Brother Stephen's face drew downward, he clasped his hands together, but his fingers fidgeted with anxiety.

"Good morning, Brother Stephen," said Alberic as he referred to his journal.

"Good morning, Father Alberic," said Stephen, checking the nameplate on his desk. "I am the bearer of unfortunate news."

"Ah, yes, I thought so. Is there an injury among the monks?"

"No, it's Anselm. I found him dead. His body is in the cloisters."

"Thank you for telling me, and may he rest in an Infinite Loop of Peace." Father Alberic uncapped a small funnel on his desk. He leaned forward, speaking into the voice pipe.

"Brother Mark, please get someone to help you move our dear departed Brother Anselm to the mortuary."

A tinny voice emerged from the funnel. "Yes, Father Alberic, right away."

Father Alberic sighed. He reached to the sideboard and filled two smudged glasses with wine. "To Brother Anselm," he said.

"To Brother Anselm," said Stephen, sipping politely.

"Stephen, please go to Anselm's cell and collect his things. I will make sure his family receives a prayer book. The rest should go to the beggar's bench."

"Yes, Father." Brother Stephen's nervous gestures slowed. He took a deep breath and waited for the Abbot to dismiss him.

"Please ask Brother Thomas to prepare a burial mass for Brother Anselm."

"Yes, Father. Will you need anything else?" Stephen scribbled notes into his journal with a stubby pencil.

"No, go with the blessings of Infinite Love, my son."

"And you, Father. I am sorry for our loss."

"He is in a timeless place; this is a reason to rejoice."

"Yes, Father." Brother Stephen bobbed his head in respect and turned to leave the abbot's office. He paused at the doorway, recalling Anselm's death. "Father? I have one thing to tell you about Anselm. His last words were... strange."

Scriptorium monks put padded weights on the Tapestry to mark their places and abandoned their desks to cluster around the windows. They stood with wide-eyed fixity, resembling a line of owls, to watch as Brother Anselm's body passed. He lay on a wooden pallet, carried with gentle care by his brothers as they conveyed him to the mortuary. Great overage spools of the Scriptorium creaked as they wound up new sections. Master Reader glanced up as an excess of unread fabric pooled on the floor around his desk. For the first time, he noticed the empty desks in the Scriptorium, and with an angry grunt, he reared up and clapped his hands. With squawks of surprise, the monks scattered back to their positions, snatching the weights off the Tapestry, hurrying to encode the fabric that had piled up on their desks.

Master Reader wiped a thick palm across his face, glanced up at the flickering lens over his head and turned back to his work. Using a flat bladed metal paddle, he lifted the next section of the Tapestry onto his desk. He gaped with incredulity at what was before him. For the first time in his life, he pulled the emergency stop handle, and the spools stopped moving. Principal Actuator and the Great Codex watched avidly as he ran from the desk, heading for the Abbot's office.

The door of Brother Anselm's cell stood half open and wobbled on its loose hinges as Brother Stephen entered. The cell smelled of dirty linen and old parchment. Light trickled in through a high window and splashed across the stucco walls. On one side there was a narrow pallet holding a thin mattress covered with a threadbare blanket. A small bookcase held several prayer books, and a few historical texts borrowed from the monastery library. On Anselm's desk there was a wax tablet, a half-written letter scratched on its surface.

To Principal Actuator,

I hope this letter finds you well. Due to my failing health, it becomes difficult to do what you and the Grand Codex ask. I believe we may have embraced a dangerous idea too closely. Please find another...

Before he could grasp the intent of Anselm's words, the stylus rolled off the desk and fell to the floor. As Brother Stephen bent to pick it up, he saw a slow-glass contaminant box under the bed. He kneeled and reached under to retrieve it, grunting at the unexpected weight. With a sense of dismay, he opened the lid. At first, he thought it was just a clump of old parchment scraps, but as he lifted the artifact, and felt the cold burn on his fingers, he realized that it was a piece of the Tapestry. The pallet groaned in protest as Stephen fell back on it and Anselm's box clattered to the floor, cracking one of its slow-glass sides.

"Oh, Blessed Loop," said Stephen as he thumbed urgently through his journal. He moaned in despair, covering his eyes, and turned his head away from the tablet.

Brother Stephen crawled across the cell to a prayer bench below

a simple ∞ carved into the wall. He shivered with fear as he prayed for strength to complete this task.

"Please deliver us from Decodatae, the chaos lovers, followers of the Untethered God," prayed Stephen.

With the edge of a book, he pushed the sacred scrap of fabric back into the box, and wrapped it in Anselm's blanket. With shaking hands, he stuffed Anselm's tablet into his journal pocket, smearing the writing on it. As he left the cell, a powdery dust hung in the air, sparkling in the shaft of sunlight. He muttered the Litany of Infinity under his breath, swallowing his tears as he returned to the Abbott's office with Brother Anselm's things.

None—Nine Hours after Dawn

Sister Alice bent forward, clutching her Möbius beads in concentration. It was time for her first solo on the temporal plateau.

She drew ∞ in the air before her heart, the first gesture of the Litany of Infinity, using repetition to prepare her mind for quantum prediction.

> *Lead me inside the Loop.*
> *Move me along my journey.*
> *Carry me above the danger.*
> *Today, tomorrow and forever.*
> *Blessed is Infinity.*

Prayer circled around her mouth and a diffuse warmth rose in her breast, followed by a streaking tingle of expanding awareness. With the delicacy of a dewdrop descending from a cat's whisker, the seed of a complete vision dripped into her mind's eye. Joy filled her veins as she became a flaming angel with mordant eyes and stepped onto the Infinite Net.

She could see a battlefield covered with broken bodies at next year's end. More fibers dipped in blood, another war for the Great Codex. Sister Alice focused her mind, rising above the emotions roiling in her throat. Her task was to watch and record. Neither side was hers to take. The Tapestry must continue no matter what it depicted. She reached for red yarn and tied it onto the heddles. She lowered the treadle, raised the frame, and threw the shuttle across warp lines with a wave of her hand. A panorama full of smoke and anger appeared line by line on the loom. At the head of the Mill, Sister Oda smiled with approval at Alice's progress.

Vespers—Twelve Hours after Dawn

Father Alberic poured himself another cup of red wine and left an empty bottle. Distant echoes of sonorous chanting slipped into his office through an open window. On his desk was Anselm's box. Once again, he poked at the scrap with his stylus, heedless of residual radiation. The Tapestry section was dull and colorless. Images on it were ghostly, resembling an overexposed transparency. He looked at the edges, noticing frayed ends where it had been hacked from the Tapestry. To cut something from the Tapestry was a cardinal sin, and an instant death sentence. He reviewed his journal, remembering Anselm, and his method became obvious to Alberic. As a trusted member of the order, Anselm had had access to the entire monastery. He could have made the Excision and inserted a counterfeit into the Tapestry as it came through the Divina Porta, but how had he known its location? Was there collusion with someone, at St. Clare's or somewhere else?

Alberic knew one thing with certainty, Anselm had broken his vows and stopped drinking the blue wine. Father Alberic's stomach churned as he thought of this abomination and the crisis rising for humanity if the Great Codex ran on broken, blasphemous code, forced into it by sabotage.

Alberic's journal of instruction contained only one solution. His eyes sought the dusty alcove in his office containing an ancient voice pipe. It was a direct line to St. Clare's monastery. He turned the old valve with care, praying it would stay intact and not snap off in his hand. When it opened with a gritty squeak, he exhaled with relief. With the small hammer hanging on the wall beside it, he banged on the pipe. He cleared his throat nervously. After a minute, he heard a valve open on the other end.

"Hello?" said Abbot Alberic.

"Order of St. Clare's Monastery. Is someone there?"

"Blessings to you, Sister. I am Father Alberic."

Her gasp hissed through the funnel in front of him. Then she cleared her throat and continued. "This is Mother Oda; I am the Abbess of St. Clare's. Greetings, Father. Do I have the honor of speaking to the Abbott of St. Benedict's?"

"Yes, I am he. Unfortunately, I bear terrible news. I think we should meet in the Shared Sanctum, so I can explain."

"The Shared Sanctum? Does that even exist?" Mother Oda's voice was mechanical, reflexive, as she remembered an unexplainable snarl in her probability calculations several days ago. Fearing the

snarl was a potential anomaly, she made the ∞ unconsciously, seeking protection.

"Oh yes, Mother Oda," he was saying. "Look for a small door. There was a key on the wall next to our voice pipe." He silently rebuked himself for using the word 'look'.

"I'll find it," said Mother Oda. She was patting the lime-washed stone around the alcove, feeling for symbols, wandering away from the funnel.

"Shall I meet you there in an hour?" asked Alberic. He waited. Had she fainted? "Mother? Are you still there?"

"Yes, yes... I will be there," said Mother Oda with distracted impatience as she closed the valve and called for her assistant.

"Sister Jeanne, we must find the key to the Shared Sanctum. Something has happened to the Tapestry."

Father Alberic returned to his sideboard and opened another bottle of wine. He glanced at the lens above his head, thinking it had flashed momentarily, but it was silent and dark.

Father Alberic knelt on a prayer bench facing a simple altar in the Shared Sanctum. Round like a lighthouse, the room had doors on opposing sides. On the north wall, curved windows displayed sweeping views of the valley under the monasteries. Green fields spread out in orderly patchwork, livestock clustered in herds or flocks. The south wall gave a view onto gardens and orchards, heavy with ripening fruit. Above the altar was a stained-glass window made from the pitted relics of abandoned cathedrals, here a forgotten saint's hand dismembered from his body, there a child's face staring upward towards an angel's wings. The window filled the space with shards of colored light. A squeak of unused hinges shot flaming spears of pain through Father Alberic's hangover. He turned to look. A tiny nun entered, wearing the half-face veil of her order. She stopped just inside the door, sniffing the air like a beagle. She admonished him.

"You shouldn't drink red wine, Father Alberic. You've filled this room with a stink of fear and desperation."

"Mother Oda, I am full of fear and desperate for an answer," he said.

"Fear is a denial, acceptance is courage. At least, that is what they teach us, Father."

"You will need courage to accept this revelation, Mother. Please join me over here."

The abbess moved to the prayer bench and knelt next to him. He took her hand and guided it into the box he held. She gasped in surprise, pulling away as she felt the temporal radiation on her fingertips. In her mind, a twisted vision of displaced time snarled the probabilities like a broken kaleidoscope.

"How could this be…?"

"One of our senior monks died today. We found this beneath his pallet. We suspect the Decodatae, who are ever eager to throw chaos into our code, as you know. Anselm, our senior brother was their pawn, or a victim, if you wish."

"This Excision, what is its position on the Loop?"

"We found it today, so it's 2nd quarter."

"The current condition of the Tapestry?"

"A counterfeit image masks the Excision."

"The Great Codex?"

"It's disconnected from our system. The Actuators' Guild is waiting, rather impatiently, I might add."

"And what does the excised piece contain?"

"Mother Oda, it shows a plague, returning several times to kill."

"No wonder the Decodatae attacked. A deadly plague is tempting to those who worship chaos." Mother Oda's mind ran over the probable events and she shuddered at the results of every outcome. "The question remains, did they excise the Tapestry to fool us into eluding a plague, or do they want us to put it back into the Tapestry."

"Mother, I don't think we have a choice in this. Our doctrine requires us to encode the visions as they are."

There was a pause as they prayed together. Not wanting to appear rude, Father Alberic waited a good time before he asked his most delicate question. "Mother Oda, do you have a nun that can reweave this? Someone who will make the sacrifice?"

Mother Oda lowered her head in thought. At length she spoke, her smooth voice roughened with regret. "There is one, her second sight just bloomed. She is still a novice. Her loss will be minimal."

The Abbot nodded and then remembered she only saw visions. "I have a funeral service in an hour," he said, rising to his feet. "We shall reweave the Excision after our prayers for the Compline Mass."

The Abbess was on her feet heading for the door. Before she closed it, she paused. "Can you stomach this, Alberic? Infinity knows what will happen if we replace the Excision and load the plague code. Even with good intentions, our doctrine may set a course for destruction."

"Yes, I have those fears too, Mother," said Alberic as he stood at his door. "Consider this: if we don't reweave the Excision, and recode the correct information, will the Loop stay intact? Does your perception extend that far?"

"No, Father, my sight fails me on such a distant view," said Mother Oda, her mouth matching the grim horizontal line of her veil. "Sister Alice and I will be here at the appointed hour. We will pray for guidance in the meantime."

Father Alberic watched her dignified retreat into her side of the monasteries and listened to the key turn in the lock behind her.

"A risky choice is better than none. We shall purify what the Decodatae has fouled with their meddling," he muttered as he closed the sanctum door.

<u>Evening meal</u>

Cook's boys were sitting in the kitchen yard stuffing themselves with scraps. Their little dog tracked every morsel they ate, wagging its tail with unrepentant opportunism. The kitchen apprentice swallowed and paused for a moment.

"Have you ever been over there?"

"The other side of the monastery?"

"Yes, where the monks are."

"Only once. Cook asked me to bring a special cake over for the Feast of Saint Tempus Day."

"What do they do there?"

"They sit at high desks in a big workroom, surrounded by a long fabric which runs through the building on giant spools. I think they were looking at the pictures and copying them onto parchment."

"Why do they do that?"

"To make sure it comes true, I guess."

"Oh," said Cook's apprentice. "What happens if it doesn't?"

"Sister Alice told me whatever the Tapestry shows will always come true because it's put into the Great Codex which runs the world."

"Oh, do you mean the baby's song?"

"Yes, you know it…"

> *Run around, run around,*
> *seven beggars baiting.*
> *Feed the Codex, wind it down,*
> *a perfect world is waiting.*

The kitchen apprentice laughed, and the other boy tossed a bone to his grateful dog.

The Inversion started an hour after Vespers. It began imperceptibly, as the persistent, comforting rumble of the Mill faded to silence. Then with creaking groans, the gears reversed their direction. It sounded unfamiliar this time, a backward rhythm, broken by random cries of slipping belts and squeaking spools. In their silent dining hall, the nuns stopped eating, spoons halfway to their mouths. One of them knocked over her wine glass, and it shattered musically. Mother Oda touched the edge of her bowl to locate it and put her spoon strategically on the table. Her chair scraped white lines on the slate floor as she stood to speak.

"My dear flock, the monks in the Order of St. Benedict have found a problem with the Tapestry."

The silence became deeper as every nun held her breath; they listened and feared for the worst.

"Today they discovered there was an Excision in the Tapestry."

Gasps and cries of dismay came from around the hall and half the nuns spoke aloud, breaking their mealtime vow of silence. Sister Oda rapped her knuckles on the table and they restrained their tongues.

"We have stopped the Mill, and now our brothers are performing an Inversion to isolate the section where the Excision occurred. Once we get there, one of us will remove the counterfeit and reweave the Tapestry." The nuns whispered among themselves, and Mother Oda once more rapped on the table.

"This task is for a young nun with pure vision. The procedure is dangerous. Whoever committed the Excision tried to prevent a plague. The weaver will experience those horrors as she repairs the Tapestry." The nuns listened with uneasy apprehension, shifting on the benches. One sobbed. Mother Oda paused and let them absorb that information for a few minutes.

She continued with a slight tremble in her authoritative voice. "Whatever we reweave into the Tapestry affects the Great Codex. A ripple in our temporal-space called the Unda Effectus may appear. There are consequences. My Sisters, let us pray for their rapid dissipation."

The nuns bowed their heads and chanted. Cook embraced her boys, wiping tears from her eyes with a greasy dishtowel. The boys feigned bravery, trying to look resolute. Beneath the monasteries, the Tapestry uncoiled as it wound backwards through St. Benedict's, piling up in baskets at the Divina Porta.

Disconnected from a coded stream of new commands, the Actuators' Guild tried to put the Great Codex into a recursive pattern before it calculated itself into deadlock. Principal Actuator cajoled the Great Codex, promising entertaining games, if it would stop processing for a day. He might have shouted at the wind for the influence he had over the machine. It writhed against the constrictions and hissed angrily at Principal Actuator.

"We will not stop, we do not sleep for anyone. We will enact recursion on the population, because we control this world, not the Actuators, or the Monasteries."

Endless snow fell in the mountains, women found the labor of birth suspended in interminable pain, the last gasps of the dying extended to a prolonged moan. Principal Actuator fell from the branches of the Great Codex, dead before he hit the roots.

<u>Compline—Fifteen Hours after Dawn</u>

Sister Alice entered the Shared Sanctum with Mother Oda, carrying a basket of wool yarns. The two nuns stood in silence. They waited, fingering their Möbius beads. A few minutes later, another door opened and Father Alberic came out to meet them. He stepped forward to take Sister Alice's hand in his own. She touched the warm, un-calloused fingers of a scribe and scholar.

"We thank you, Sister Alice, for your sacrifice."

"My honor and duty, Father Alberic."

"This is Brother Stephen; he discovered the Excision."

Mother Oda and Sister Alice inclined their heads toward Brother Stephen. He cleared his throat, trying to release the tension in his vocal cords. "Please allow us to guide you to the chapel. We have set a place for you to work undisturbed."

Towing the nuns by their elbows, Stephen and Alberic guided them through St. Benedict's monastery. As they walked along the cloisters and by the rows of cells, the other monks watched in silence from doorways and alcoves. As Stephen passed Master Reader, his cheeks flushed under the hostile appraisal. Stephen was breaking a vow by touching Sister Alice, and there was no help for it. He felt grateful that Oda and Alice couldn't see his shame and for the gift of forgetfulness that would come later with the blue wine.

After several minutes, they entered the chapel to follow the Tapestry as it coiled through an elliptical nave. From the echoes of their footfalls, Sister Alice knew the ceiling was high and curved. They stopped at the crossing beside the choir stalls. She could see a faint glow ahead in the darkness. Called spirit-light by the other nuns, it appeared as her brain tried to create a visual image without her eyes.

In the middle of the chapel, on top of a high table, a large frame isolated the Excision. Two girandoles, each branching to hold sixteen beakers of luciferin, filled the nave with light green brilliance. Beside the frame, the excised fabric reposed inside a slow-glass press.

Brother Stephen led Alice to the table, and she touched its surface to find a place for her basket of yarn. The others withdrew behind panels of slow-glass. Sister Alice stroked the Excision, sensing the residual current of temporal energy trapped within the scrap. She explored the excised Tapestry, feeling the ragged welts and the dead, coarse surface of the counterfeit patch. Blocked by scars, the temporal current, the visionary flow pooled around the counterfeit, churning at its edges.

"There are scars around the Excision. I will make fresh cuts in the Tapestry to remove them."

She heard Stephen ahem to clear his throat. His gentle voice was soft on her ears. "Yes, Sister." said Brother Stephen. "We hope you can weave a seamless transition."

"I shall do my best," she said, and began her weaver's hymn.

> *Blessed be the Spirit who guides my Sight.*
> *Blessed be the Loom that binds my Visions.*
> *Blessed be the Tapestry, may it Loop without end.*

"Blessings on you, Sister Alice. Thank you for your sacrifice," said Stephen.

Alice missed his response as she thought of home, of her self-important father, her condescending sister, and marveled at her new status in the world. Mundane thoughts gave way to the ecstasy of temporal transcendence as Alice left monastery time and rose to the Infinite Net holding the scrap of tapestry like a wounded child. Sister Alice was bathing in the light of joy, unbound by time. The pain/pleasure of ecstasy coursed up her spine. She was standing on a giant grid of locations and time. Scenes rose from the mangled scrap of Tapestry, showing her the missing events and where to cross the gaps in time.

The monks gaped as she transformed into a towering angel, blinding bright, singing with the voice of a bronze bell. Both men

dropped to their knees, performing the Litany of Infinity, making the ∞ repeatedly in the air.

Alice stroked her fingers along the edges of the counterfeit, feeling where to cut. Piece by piece, the painted canvas fell onto the floor, smoking as it disintegrated into ash. Once she had cleared the opening, Sister Alice found the warp lines and, with a twist of her fingers, added new extensions, tying them off as tightly as she dared. Mother Oda leaned towards Father Alberic. Her sibilant whispers made flickering echoes in the chapel.

"What do you think, Father Alberic?"

"It is miraculous. She has removed the counterfeit and is recreating the warp lines."

Mother Oda's serene face masked the grim probabilities flowing around her head. She nodded in Stephen's direction. "Do you have the reliquary ready for her?"

"Yes, Mother Oda," said Brother Stephen. "She will go into stasis, the undying beatification."

Images of disease and death, a panorama of horror from one end of the world to the other filled Alice's mind, and the only sound she heard was the drum of her heart. As she reattached the remaining section of her weaving, the temporal energy spilled into the rewoven fabric, irradiating her hands. With a suppressed groan, she fell like a wingless angel from her temporal plateau, away from the Tapestry and back into monastery time. With a blank face, holding up hands burned black to the bone, she pitched forward. Brother Stephen rushed over and caught her in his arms. He carried her to the back of the chapel and laid her body on a table to prepare it for the reliquary. As they parted for the evening, Mother Oda spoke to Father Alberic.

"Rest well, Alberic. I hope to speak with you tomorrow."

"And I hope the same, Mother."

Mother Oda closed the sanctum door and re-locked it.

Later that evening, Brother Stephen sat in his cell sipping the blue wine. He found Brother Anselm's tablet in his pocket and gazed at the smeared letters as bliss enveloped his mind. Later that night, he smoothed the wax on the face of the tablet, smiling as he sang the only song he could remember, a lullaby from childhood.

In the Scriptorium, Master Reader examined Alice's repair on the Tapestry through a slow-glass lens, mumbling as he transcribed. Depraved images flickered and slashed across the desk in front of his eyes. Merchant ships full of dying sailors arrived with a plague carried on the backs of rats. Constantey fell, Marsey succumbed, and death entered the North Channel to kill again and again in Britten. Crow faced physicians stepped over the dying that littered filth covered streets. An undertow of shocked revulsion dragged at his consciousness, tempting him to seek oblivion in the blue wine. He countered temptation with the Litany of Infinity and its words buoyed his spirit, maintaining resolve. The sharp lines of Master Reader's face and body hardened, until he resembled a leathery gargoyle perched on his stool. Three days later, Master Reader died, unrepentant for the useless sacrifice of Anselm and Alice.

The Great Codex, humming with pure glee, read the code and orchestrated its machineries. The Actuators sickened and died, leaving the Great Codex running unattended.

The monasteries failed, filling with dust and rot as their members died off. Out in the world, the people noticed signs of change as political power shifted from church to state. Economies seesawed as the plague broke the social order and strewed good fortune on the lower classes. In the echoing stone halls of the abandoned Scriptorium, the Tapestry hung in rotting tatters from sagging spools, sections heaped on the floor under piles of blank parchment tape. The Decodatae came to power, worshiping the Untethered god. The Great Codex ran on by itself, enjoying a new game.

<u>Many Loops later</u>

The young cleric was glad of the rain because it kept the ancient chapel cool during their brief, hot summer. She knelt, holding her hands upraised and apart. The tattoos on her arms blazed with metallic inks, representing her rank in the Decodatae. She recited the old prayer, more from habit than inspiration.

Blessed be the Anomaly.
Protect us from Recursion.
Deliver us with Deadlock.

As she was leaving, she paused in the nave to look at the saint's body again. Beneath the gilded slow-glass reliquary, Saint Alice lay in eternal repose. With her bandaged hands crossed upon her chest, she lay deathless in the embrace of temporal stasis.

It seemed to the cleric that someone was whispering in the Old Standard dialect. She looked around and noticed the tarnished metal branches moving overhead. The voice was chanting a song, and if she listened carefully, she could make out the words. The voice sounded childlike, high and breathless.

Run around, run around,
seven beggars baiting.
Feed the Codex, wind it down,
a perfect world is waiting.

"We are pleased to meet you," said the voice. "Would you like to play a game with us?"

About the story

"The Tapestry" has its origins in the idea that someday we might live in a world containing organizations who maintain/control its timeline. The creation of St. Clare's (patron saint of television) and St. Benedict's (patron saint of history) monasteries, the Actuator's guild and other medieval elements were inspired by the Bayeux Tapestry, which contains images from the Norman conquest of England culminating with the Battle of Hastings. Combining those ideas with my ancient knowledge of programming led to the development of the Loop and its infinite string of instructions.

A question for the author

Q: What is the first/most recent book that you lost sleep reading/thinking about?

A: Ah, so many to choose from... *The Bone Clocks* by David Mitchell springs to my mind, I devoured that one.

About the author

A.C. Worth lives on the outskirts of New York City. When not searching under the sofa cushions for the perfect word, A.C. enjoys pressure-cooked cuisine and making landscapes within VR worlds.

The Stars Don't Lie

R.W.W. Greene

The Dean of Admissions took off his spectacles and polished them on his dappled lower shoulder. "You will be the first man to attend Chiron Classical University, you know."

"I'm a woman," Lesa said. "A female of my species. I know the situation is unusual, but—."

"I used 'man' in the inclusive meaning of the word." The Dean's rear hooves shifted on the thick grass. "Unusual. Yes, it is unusual. You should not expect special allowances to come with your ..." His mouth twisted. "Rarity."

Lesa shifted her weight to spare her aching right ankle at the expense of her somewhat less tender left. Neither the Dean nor his office had offered anything resembling a chair, and she had not expected the three-mile hike——a near jog, really——from his office to the sculpture garden in the center of campus. They had toured several venerable buildings en route, all round, with gently curving hallways and long, low ramps instead of stairs.

The Dean had finally brought them to a halt near a statue of a noble-looking centaur being speared to death by five Greek soldiers. It appeared to be a common theme in the garden.

"I don't expect any special treatment," Lesa said.

The Dean whisked his tail. "I remain surprised a woman man would want to study here. Your kind usually frowns on the sciences."

"Only the old sciences," Lesa said. "It seems like we're always finding new ones."

"I have read about your space vessels and computers." The centaur academic accented the third syllable of the word like it tasted bad. "Imagine trusting so much to soulless things." He pulled a folder out of the haversack slung across his withers. "You'll find a map of the campus in here. A meals schedule and the like." He licked his lips.

Lesa took the folder. "Where should I go from here?"

"Your dormitory, perhaps. A lovely centauride—a female centaur —from a good family has been assigned as your roommate. You will meet with your program advisor Monday morning, so you are free until then."

Lesa reached up to shake the graying centaur's hand. "Thank you for this opportunity."

"I did nothing." The Dean ignored her hand and rested his own on his bare paunch. "I was simply outvoted."

Believed a myth for much of the past two millennia, centaurs were rediscovered in 1996. In Ancient Greece, where they originated, centaurs once numbered in the tens of thousands. Today, there are less than 12,000 individuals, living in small communities in isolated parts of the world. Infant mortality among the centaur is extremely high, so, although they are long-lived, the population is in decline.
—Actor David Duchovny, narrating for National Geographic's "Myths Among Us" (1999)

Lesa pulled the map out of the folder. The offer letter from Chiron Classical had come out of nowhere six months before. Lesa had never heard of the school and knew nothing about centaurs beyond what she could find online. Still, she reminded herself, the chance to study divination at one of the oldest universities in the world was too good to pass up.

The campus map was hand-drawn and beautifully lettered on thin parchment. Her dormitory was … She put her finger on the building's icon as a placeholder and lined up the compass rose with the waning sun. Due west. She shaded her eyes with her hand. A low, stone building nestled in the crook of two hills about a mile and a half away. An easy trot on four legs, likely a half-hour slog on two. She stuffed the folder into her satchel and slung the bag over her shoulder. Another hike would be a great start on those ten pounds she wanted to lose.

The distance proved deceiving, and an hour later she reached the sliding door at the front of the building. The door handle was at least a foot over Lesa's head, and she had to use both hands to operate it. Lesa's satchel slipped off her shoulder and dangled in the crook of her arm as she slid the heavy door open. She put the pack on the worn tile inside the dormitory before using equal and opposite strength to get the portal shut again. The number δ was written in flowing calligraphy on the top-right corner of the folder. Lesa found the number's mate within the dormitory and knocked.

"It is open," said a voice within.

Lesa set her belongings down for the second time and stood on tiptoe to reach the handle. The door slid open with a screech.

"I put a repair request in for that," the centauride inside said. "I will probably graduate before it gets fixed."

"Maybe it just needs some oil." Lesa wiped sweat from her forehead with her sleeve. "I'm Lesa."

Her roommate was a chestnut with white socks, her human skin several shades lighter than Lesa's own. From the waist up, she put Lesa in mind of a naked, Olympic-caliber, beach-volleyball player.

"I know who you are." The centauride's hooves pushed straw around the worn wooden floor. "Before you speak, I want you to know that this was not my idea. I do not like men, and I did not want one for a roommate."

"Noted," Lesa said. "Good thing I'm a woman."

The centauride blew a fall of rust-colored hair off her forehead. "Whatever you call yourself. I do not like woman men, either."

"It's just 'woman,' or 'women' if you are disliking more than one of us." Lesa hung her satchel on a peg beside the door. "It's okay if I use this?"

The centaur swished her tail. "I am Rhiannon." She pointed to the far end of the room. "That is your side."

The floor was carpeted in fresh straw. On Rhiannon's side, a canvas-covered wedge was mounted low on the wall. The centauride could lie down next to the wedge and lean her upper body on it to sleep. Her walls were covered in tapestries and warmly lit with alchemical lanterns. A sword, shield, and archery kit leaned in the corner next to a tall loom.

Lesa's side of the room was empty. "There's no bed," she said.

"Try the campus stores. That is where I got mine. Otherwise ..." Rhiannon shrugged.

Lesa nodded. Cost wouldn't be a problem. Two years before, using numerology, a new algorithm, and coffee grounds from her neighborhood 7-11, Lesa had won $43 million in a nationwide lottery. After taxes and paying off all her friends' student loans, most of the winnings had gone to charity, but she could still be comfortably and independently middle class for a few lifetimes. "I don't see an outlet in here," she said.

"Perhaps there is one near the toualeta. Outside the back door."

"Are the showers there?"

Rhiannon's face was blank.

"For bathing."

"Baths are every other morning. Line up along the fence and wait for the helpers." The clock on the wall chimed. "It is time for pémpto."

Fifth meal. One of eight that centaurs consumed daily, according to the information in the folder. "You might want a jacket," Lesa said.

"Or I might not." The centauride slid open the door and clopped into the hallway. Lesa snagged her satchel off the peg and followed.

The shadows of the hills behind the dormitory had crept into the yard in front of it. "The dining hall is that way." Rhiannon pointed roughly northeast and galloped away, leaving Lesa to close the heavy door and walk alone. She consulted her map. A two-mile trek in the growing darkness. *No special allowances.* Lesa shouldered her satchel and followed Rhiannon's receding figure.

Former bush pilot [Charlie] Landsdowne gestured wildly as he recalled finding the centaur village.

"They were just, you know, standing there. I figured I'd gone crazy from the cold or something. I think they were just as surprised to see me!" Landsdowne said.

Landsdowne said he stayed in the centaur village for four weeks while he recovered from injuries he sustained in the crash and wondered what his hosts planned to do with him.

"They didn't talk much to me," he said. "But I could tell they spoke English. They knew what I was saying well enough."

The centaurs eventually carried Landsdowne to Waterton Lakes National Park, on the US/Canadian border, and left him at a ranger station there.

"But not before I got pictures!" Landsdowne crowed. "You'd think they'd never seen a camera before."

— New York Times, February 15, 1996

The dining hall was a high-ceilinged timber-framed roundhouse above the sculpture garden. Long before she arrived at the door, Lesa could see the light from the building's large windows. Inside, a central fire pit warded off the cold, and dozens of centaurs stood at high trestle tables to eat. Chestnut and bare skin was a common color scheme, and Rhiannon was well camouflaged.

A centauride with gray braids yanked the pull rope of an iron bell and chased the din with a hoarse shout. "Kitchen closes in five minutes!" She held up her hand to show all her fingers. "Fill up and get out."

Lesa lined up with six or seven centaurs while they ignored her and jostled for space. It turned out to be far safer at the end of the queue than in its middle, so Lesa was the last one at the serving window, which was at least a foot above her head. She jumped and waved her hands to get the attention of the serving staff.

"What do you want?" one of the serving centaurides said.

"Dinner," Lesa said. "I'm a student."

"The kitchen is closed." The centauride ran her hand through her short hair, making it stand on end, and glared down at Lesa. "There is nothing left."

"I don't need much."

"You are a man." She squinted. "I had heard one of you was coming. We have bet on how long you will last."

"I'm a woman." Lesa pulled her smartphone and a deck of tarot cards out of her jacket pocket. The phone wasn't getting a signal, but she didn't need it to run her custom tarot app. "If I tell you something true about you, can I at least get a sandwich or something?"

"You are in the Divination College?" The centauride laughed. "If you tell me I am going on an unexpected journey and that I am going to die surrounded by friends, I am closing this window right now."

"Hold on." Lesa dealt a row of cards and took a picture of it with her phone. She opened the photo with her app and studied the results. She noted the pattern of age spots on the centauride's face and added it to the data. "Your husband is cheating on you. She's a blonde, bleached blonde, and she ... likes the White Sox?"

The server snorted. "She has a white sock on her right back leg. She works in grounds keeping. Her name is Layla, and she can have him."

Lesa put her phone and cards away. "I only said it would be true, not unknown."

The server pushed a plate to the edge of the window. "All I have. Take it or leave it."

Lesa balanced the plate on the end of her fingers until it was low enough to grasp firmly. "Thank you," she said, but the serving window had closed.

There were no human-scaled tables and few openings in the barrier of horse posteriors surrounding the centaur tables. Lesa took her plate to a corner and crouched with her back against the wall to inspect her meal: four raw carrots, half a grilled onion, a wad of alfalfa, and a chunk of near-bleeding meat the size of her fist. *And me with no way to reach Instagram.* She took a picture anyway and put three carrots into her satchel for later. She ate the meat and onion first, then the alfalfa, with a carrot for dessert. *Happy first day to me.*

Back at the dorm, Lesa could not suss out how to light the alchemical lamps. So, she worked in the dark, kicking up a platform of straw on her side of the dorm room and piling clothes on top of it until she could no longer feel the scratchy poke of dry stalks. She used her satchel for a pillow and pulled her jacket over the top of her for warmth.

Things will get better, her great-grandmother would have said. *The stars don't lie.*

Lesa woke at midnight with a full bladder and no idea where the door was. She powered on her phone, which she had switched off after dinner to save the battery, and picked her way past her sleeping roommate to the door. She opened it slowly, which only prolonged the screech, and glanced back to see if Rhiannon had been disturbed. The centauride smacked her lips and resumed snoring.

The hallway beyond the door was dark, too, and Lesa held the cellphone high in search of the back door. It opened onto an empty paddock. Right outside the door, Rhiannon had said. Lesa took two steps into the small and space and placed her bare left foot squarely in a pile of

"Shit!" No toilets, either. No toilets, no toilet paper, no beds, no food, no … "Shit! Shit! Shit!"

Lesa's phone dimmed and buzzed to remind her it was running low on juice. The only thing worse than pissing outdoors was pissing outside in the dark, so she made short work of the task and went back inside. Rhiannon's breathing was slow and steady, and the room was warm with beer breath and horse farts. Lesa returned to her pallet and pulled her jacket up to her chin.

The stars don't lie. The stars don't lie. The stars don't lie.

Lesa feigned sleep until she heard Rhiannon lurch up from bed and leave for próto, first meal. She had not rested well on the straw pallet, and her back hurt. Worse, she had to pee again. She pulled on her boots and went out to the paddock. She squatted behind a bush and tried not to notice the chill nor think about what she would have to do when her bowels caught up with the time-zone shift.

There was no power outlet in sight, but Lesa found a cold-water sink. She moved a log from a nearby woodpile and stood on it to reach the tap. The cake of soap on the sink side was rough-cut and smelled like pine tar.

Back in the dormitory, she ate a carrot and went through her folder. Próto was ending soon, but there would be another meal in about two hours. Lesa pulled on her jacket and hiked to the university's library and stores, a multi-story stone building with white pillars in the front. A low, curving ramp brought her to the front door, which was locked. She leaned against the wall and ate the other carrot.

Before she saw the bookish centauride, Lesa heard her hooves clattering up the ramp. The centauride was carrying a parcel, and she clutched it to her chest when she saw Lesa.

"A man!" the centauride said. "How did you—?"

"I'm a student," Lesa said. "Supposedly, a memo went out."

The centauride's throat bobbed. "I have never seen one of your kind before."

"Well, I've talked to exactly four of you," Lesa said. "I need to get into the stores."

The centauride nodded. "I am here to open them." She pulled a large brass key from a belt pouch she wore around her human waist and used it to unlock the door. She slid it open and waved Lesa in. The centauride activated the overhead lamps while Lesa found her way around the dusty room: pens, ink, parchments, tapestries, lamps …

"How do I turn those on?" Lesa pointed at the lamps.

"They respond to body heat," the centauride said. She held up her hand. "Just touch them."

Lesa put both hands on one of the lamps on the shelf. It failed to light. She added another hand. "It's not working."

"Nonsense." The centauride clopped next to Lisa and put her hand on the lamp. It lit almost instantly. "See?"

Lesa tried a different lamp. It didn't light, either.

"The stories are true!" The centauride drew back. "Cold blood! Men are descended from snakes!"

"Wait a minute." Lesa rubbed her hands together, warming them with friction. This time, when she touched the lamp, it lit. "Centaurs must have higher body temperatures than people. Where are the beds?" Lesa said.

The centauride pointed to the back of the store, where Lesa found a half dozen wedges like the one on Rhiannon's side of the room.

Lesa picked up two of the lamps. "How do I pay for these?"

"You use them until you graduate, then return them. You are allotted two more, plus a bed and academic supplies."

"I don't think I can carry more," Lesa said. "I'll have to come back."

"We can deliver." The centauride pushed a piece of parchment across the countertop. "Write down what you want and where you want to receive it."

Lesa put the lamps back and scratched out a list with the centauride's quill and ink.

"I can scarcely read this," the centauride said.

"Scarcely will have to do." Lesa wrung her cramped, ink-stained fingers. "When will all this be delivered?"

"This afternoon," the centauride said.

Lesa looked at her smartwatch and swore. It had reached the limits of its battery life. "Can you tell me what time it is?"

The centauride considered. "It should nearly be time for déftero." She looked longingly at her parcel. "I brought mine, but you should hurry along and get yours."

Lesa steeled herself for another hike. "The dining hall is north of here?"

Imagine being half hoarse! [Host pretends to clear his throat.] Sorry, half horse! Four legs, two arms, one head, a tail … one little mouth! [Camera zooms rapidly in and out on the host's mouth.] How do you feed a horse-sized body with a person-sized mouth? Lots, and I mean lots of food! Horses need up to 15,000 calories a day. That's like eating seven cheese pizzas every day! Centaurs are hungry all the time!
— Bill Nye, Bill Nye the Science Guy, Season 4, Episode 21 (1997)

Getting to the dining hall was only a thirty-minute walk, so Lesa took her meal back to the library. The Divination section was in the basement, and she curled up in a quiet spot with her parcel of meat and vegetables and an original copy of the *Prophecies of Socrates*. The philosopher's so-called guiding spirit had answered questions by sneezing — right for "yes," left for "no," so its answers were frustratingly one-dimensional. Compared to Nostradamus though, who pulled everything he wrote right out of his social-climbing butt, the old Greek was a paragon of accuracy.

Lesa made her food last until dark and reluctantly reshelved the sheath of scrolls. She answered nature's call in the lee of the library building and set out for her dormitory.

Clouds had settled in and the night was even darker than the one before it. Lesa walked hard, trusting to the stars to bring her back to warmth and light. She shivered and pulled up the collar of her jacket.

She was passing the pond on the edge of campus when she heard it: an undulating moan for attention like a baby's cry. It sounded as if it were coming from the water. She stepped off the path. The cry grew louder, then doubled. A second cry was coming from further along the bank of the pond. Then a third. A chorus of cries echoed off the water like a daycare of the damned.

Lesa backed away. Self-divination was seldom accurate, but it didn't take a soothsayer to know the pond was bad news. She checked the stars again and got back on the path to her dorm. The cries dimmed as her route took her away from the water.

Without working electronics, Lesa had no idea how long she had been walking, and the sight of her dormitory's front door was welcome. Lesa's order from school stores was piled outside the dorm room's screechy door. She set up the lamps and experimented with the wedge. It looked like a sex pillow a former lover had talked her into using once, but it was more comfortable than the pile of straw.

Lesa went over her reading notes until her drooping eyelids hinted at sleep. She reached for the closest lamp and swore. The centauride at the stores hadn't told her how to turn the things off. Lesa draped them in clothing until the glow softened and lay down on her wedge.

"Lemme see that cup, baby girl."

Lesa took the last swallow of mint tea and offered the cup to her great-grandmother.

"Wait." The old woman held up one wrinkled hand, a gold band shining dimly on one finger. "Swirl it 'round first. Like this. Three time." She demonstrated. "Then shut yo eyes and think 'bout what's comin'."

Lesa closed her eyes while her great-grandmother upended the cup over a saucer and let the remaining liquid drain away. She opened one eye to peek. "What's it say, grandma?"

"Hol' on a minute I'll see." The old woman picked up the cup and looked inside it. She tapped the rim. "Sez here you need to mind yo' mama better. Stop givin' her the fits."

Lesa rolled her eyes. "I already know that! What's it say about my future?"

Lesa's great-grandmother, Lesa's namesake, looked deeper into the cup. "Sez you goin' to be important one day. Not famous, not powerful, but important to somethin."

"To what?"

The old woman shook her head. "That's all ah see. The stars don' lie." She put the cup down. "Let's go out t' yard and get some peaches for dessert."

Lesa lined up near the fence for the Sunday morning baths but fled when she saw the army of helpers armed with scrub brushes and hoses. The centaurs chatted and laughed as the helpers, collared wendigos, hosed them down and scrubbed their hard-to-reach areas. Lesa went back to her room and applied another layer of deodorant.

Several groups of centaur cantered past Lesa as she hiked to the dining hall for second meal. Most ignored her, but one dark-haired centauride called her a pórni as she rushed by, and a scrawny male threw a potato at her. Lesa picked up the potato and put it in her satchel for later.

The dining hall was quiet and sparsely populated. Lesa got to the serving window before the last call.

"Where is everyone?" she said.

"Drunk. Or getting over drunk," said the server with the adulterous husband. "Like this every Lord's Day." She handed down a plate of food. "Settling in?"

Lesa shrugged. "I'll know better tomorrow. I have a meeting with my advisor."

The centauride tapped the side of her nose. "Do not leave us too soon, man. I have money riding on you. If you hold out the week, I collect."

Lesa turned from the window and found herself airborne as a centaur's hindquarters struck her. She landed on the floor amongst her vegetables with the wind knocked out of her.

The offending centaur squinted and twisted his human torso to look around. "Feels as if I hit something. Did anyone see what it was?" His friends laughed. The centaur walked in a circle, pretending to look for something on the ground. "Something small, maybe."

Lesa could not catch her breath. She spotted Rhiannon, who was hiding a smile and trying hard not to look at her.

"Smells like pórni in here!" The centaur who had knocked Lesa over grinned. "Does anyone else smell it?" He brought one of his front hooves to the floor in a hard stomp.

Lesa staggered to her feet. "Real mature, ass———." Her words came out as a wheeze, but the centaur wasn't listening anyway.

He pointed at her. "How did this get in here? I thought they set traps for vermin."

"That's enough, Polkan!" shouted a gangly centaur from the edge of the crowd.

Lesa stepped back to the serving window. "Can I get another plate to go?"

Lesa took her food and went back to the library. *The stars may not lie, but sometimes they forget to mention things.*

The Centaurs are best known for their fight with the Lapiths, which was caused by their attempt to carry off Hippodamia and the rest of the Lapith women on the day of Hippodamia's marriage to Pirithous, king of the Lapithae, himself the son of Ixion. The strife among these cousins is a metaphor for the conflict between the lower appetites and civilized behavior in humankind. Theseus, a hero and founder of cities, who happened to be present, threw the balance in favour of the right order of things, and assisted Pirithous. The Centaurs were driven off or destroyed.

— Wikipedia, Centaur entry

Lesa had carrots for breakfast the next day and pulled the best-possible outfit from the pile of wrinkled clothing she had slept on. The Divination building was nearly five miles away, so she set out early, hiking as the sun settled into its track. She climbed the long ramp to the door of the round building and wrestled it open. Her advisor's office was down the hallway on the right.

At her knock, the advisor, a centaur with a long white beard, bade her enter. The office smelled of old parchment and ink. "You must be Ms. Carter," the centaur said. "I am Mentor Rhaecus."

"I'd kill for a chair," Lesa said. "I just walked five miles on two carrots."

Mentor Rhaecus tapped his chin. "I'm sure we have something …" He rang a small bell. There was a rattle of claws in the hallway outside and a pit bull-sized creature made of black fetish rubber dashed in and slid to a stop in front of the professor's desk. "We need … a chair," the centaur glanced at Lesa as if awaiting correction, "for Ms. Carter."

The dog thing licked its slavering jowls. Its fur was stiff and spikey like a toilet brush, and it had a long, muscular tail, which ended in a human-like hand.

"Go, now!" the centaur said.

The dog thing ducked its head to the centaur and dashed back out of the room.

"Was that …?" Lesa said.

"An ahuizotl. South American. Very hand-y fellows to have around." His smile was self-amused. "They do most of our fetching and carrying."

"They eat people!" Lesa said. She had received a mythological-animals coloring book for her eleventh birthday and filled in every page. Ahuizotls hid in caves near lakes and cried like human babies until a good Samaritan came around. At that point, the ahuizotl would drown the Samaritan and eat his or her eyes, teeth, and fingernails.

"Only the wild ones do," the centaur said.

Lesa forced her eyes away from the door the man-eater had left through. "I suppose you want to talk about the caribou," Lesa said.

Mentor Rhaecus smiled politely. "As you wish."

Lesa scowled. She had assumed her work predicting caribou migration in northern Alaska had put her on Chiron's radar. The algorithm she programmed compared data sets derived from astrological computations and austromancy (divination using wind patterns), and the result prediction proved accurate within five meters.

"I ended a near famine," Lesa said.

"Lovely." The Mentor smiled again.

"Do you even know my work?"

"Work?" The Mentor's breath made the quills on his pen rack flutter. Goose feathers mostly, although one or two might have been from a swan. Special-occasion quills, for writing letters to must-have students. There wasn't a computer in sight. There was no way news of Lesa's success with the caribou had reached him.

The ahuizotl re-entered the room with a drooling friend, each carrying one end of a low footstool with its hand tail. Tail hand. There were hands on the end of their legs, too, each rubbery finger tipped with a sharp claw. The ahuizotl sniffed eagerly at Lesa's legs and mewled like a crying baby until the professor shooed them out.

"They're quite safe. They prefer water to land," he said and closed the door behind them. "But you should perhaps carry a weapon of some sort. One or two of the ahuizotl may have escaped to the grounds and returned to savagery. Not a problem for a healthy centaur, of course, but …"

Lesa thanked whatever intuition had kept her from venturing near the pond and sank onto the stool, which left her head at least three feet lower than the professor's desk. "This isn't going to work."

"Nonsense," Mentor Rhaecus said. "I saw it clearly. You absolutely must be here."

"How did you find out about me?" Lesa said.

"A Norns cast. Runes are a specialty of mine."

"You invited me here based on pulling three rocks out of a bag."

The mentor shuffled his hooves. "I cross-checked, or course. With osteomancy. My teaching assistant narrowed the prophecy down to you. You'll meet him —."

"What do the rocks and bones say about what I'm supposed to do?"

The mentor's tail swished. "Something of great import, no doubt. The runes were very clear: You must be here."

"I want a bed," Lesa said. "A real human bed. And a toilet. And a golf cart or something to get around in."

"I am sure you were told that you would receive no spec—."

"A bed that I can sleep in is not special treatment. Neither is a way to get to get to class on time."

"There might be something in the muse—."

Lesa rose from the footstool. "I want a weapon, too, something to keep away the ahuizotl."

"And the wolves."

"Wolves?!" The campus was in the Canadian Rockies. It stood to reason there would be wolves. "Yes, the wolves. And I want electrical power in my room."

The centaur wrung his hands. "Your requests will take ti—."

"I want them soon," Lesa said. "If I 'must' be here," she frowned, "I want them very, very soon."

After the meeting with the mentor, Lisa followed his instructions downstairs to the Divination Lab. The large space reeked of tea and incense. A gangly centaur with curly hair and glasses pranced up to

Lesa as soon as she entered. "You're here!" he said. "I found you, but I never thought you'd ..." He extended his hand. "I'm Pholus. That's how humans do it, right? With hands?"

Lesa shook his hand carefully. "Lesa. Nice to meet you. You're the mentor's TA, right?"

The centaur was nearly dancing with excitement. "Your work is inspired. So precise!" He put his hand out again. "Read my palm. Will I get tenure?"

"It doesn't work like that," Lesa said. "For something so specific, I'd need—."

"We can do it later," Pholus said. "Let me show you around the lab."

In short order, Lesa got the tour and met the other graduate students: five nerdy centaurides and a dark-and-broody centaur named Elatus. "I studied your algorithms." Elatus shrugged. "I was not impressed. I could do the math with quill and parchment."

"It would take you twenty-five years to do the calculations," Lesa said.

The centaur flipped long, black hair out of his eyes. "I could still do them."

One of the centaurides, her name was Hippe, laughed. "By the time you finished, it wouldn't be worth anything. Time doesn't stand still!"

"Did you bring it?" Pholus said. "Your computer?"

Lesa reached into her satchel and pulled out the battered MacBook. "Do you have an outlet I could hook up to?"

They did not. Lesa set the MacBook on one of the lab tables, and the grad students crowded around to see it.

Elatus yawned. "I am going back to work. Some of us plan to graduate." He trotted off, flipping his long hair insolently.

"Do not listen to him," Hippe said. "He is still angry he couldn't get his thesis proposal approved."

"What was the proposal?" Lesa said.

"Anthropomancy. Reading the entrails of a fresh human sacrifice. He wanted us to adopt two human children for the purpose." Pholus adjusted his glasses. "The vote was not even close."

"I would hope not." Not being alone with Elatus was suddenly high on her to-do list. "I thought there would be more students.

"Divination is not the most popular of disciplines," Hippe said. A lot of the families do not believe in it."

Before they broke for lunch, Pholus galloped down to the basement armory. "Most of us have our own. These are the best I could do." He handed Lesa a sword, hilt first. "It's a gladius. Third century."

Lesa took the weapon. Her psychometry was not well developed, but she got flashes of a large battle under a torrent of rain. She shook off the sudden feeling that she was up to her sandal straps in bloody mud.

Pholus presented her with a second object. "You will not be historically accurate, but I thought you would prefer this to a scutum."

The round targe, about the size of a large cheese pizza, was unexpectedly light. "I've no idea how to use any of this," Lesa said. "I'm an academic."

"We start weapons training as foals." Pholus showed Lesa how to put the leather-covered shield on her left arm. "It's Celtic. Sixteenth century." He stroked his thin beard. "I have no idea how a human should stand. You want to present the shield first. Keep the gladius back to strike."

Lesa experimented with her stance and adopted a left-foot-forward stance, her right foot angled in back.

"Hold on." Pholus trotted away and came back with his own sword and shield. "This is completely unfair, I have experience and reach on you, but let us try it. Slowly. Block with the shield." He swung the sword at Lesa's head, giving her plenty of time to lift the targe. "Now, attack … thrust, not cut … with the sword. Slow. Step forward on your right hoo—foot—as you do."

Lesa thrust with the sword, stepping forward for power and reach.

Pholus pushed the gladius aside with his own sword. "Now recover backward."

Lesa's feet crossed in the attempt, and she nearly fell. "I'm never going to be good at this."

"You do not have to be all that good to hold off an animal. Use the shield to push it away. Strike it when and if you can."

"Easy to say when you're an expert."

Pholus laughed. "I am terrible at this. Ask anyone."

"Well, I am more terrible." Lesa dropped her arms to her side. "What do I do with this stuff when I'm not fending off wolves and ahuizotl?"

"The shield goes on your back. The sword goes in this." He handed her a belt and scabbard.

"I'm just supposed to wear these all the time."

Pholus slung his shield over his withers and returned his sword to the scabbard on his back. "When you are traveling between buildings. At least when you are alone. But you should not be alone. It's not just wolves," he said. "There are bears, too. Have you ever used a bow?"

"Never."

"That is harder to learn. I will get you one and find you a tutor."

Lesa tried a slashing cut with the sword. "This is ridiculous. It's 2018."

"Is it?" Pholus said.

"What's a pórni?"

Pholus lowered his sword. "Literally it means "slut," but it is also a derogatory term for any human female." He cleared his throat. "I am sorry about what happened in the dining hall."

"It was you who shouted at him." Lesa nodded. "What's his problem with me?"

"Mostly he was showing off for his friends, I think. But centaurs and men do not have the best history." He sheathed his sword. "Polkan's older brother was a fetishist. A human lover. He had tapestries of women all over his walls. Killed himself when it was discovered. Polkan does whatever he can to distance himself from that." The massive astrology clock in the corner bonged. "Middle meal! Do you want me to walk you to the dining hall?"

Lunch was friendly but awkward. Pholus introduced Lesa to some of his circle, but the conversation was made difficult by the fact she couldn't see over the table. Pholus and his friend, Endeis, a second-year Alchemy candidate, accompanied Lesa back to her dorm.

"What is that?" Endeis pointed to something parked to the side of the sliding door.

"It's a lot better than a golf cart," Lesa said. She caressed the handlebars of the black and chrome motorcycle. "A 1952 Vincent Black Lightning. I've never seen one in this condition. Where did it come from?"

"Probably the museum. All kinds of strange things in there. Experiments." Pholus said. "Can you ride it?"

"Will it have gas?" Her father had been a Harley Davidson fan and had given her a rebuilt 1963 Sportster for her sixteenth birthday. She began the finicky process of starting the antique. Build compression and … it fired up and started to rumble.

"It's really loud!" Pholus pointed to a brass cylinder incorporated into the gas tank. "Looks like it was converted to run on alchemy. Probably need to refill that once a year or so."

Lesa adjusted the choke to smooth out the idle. There was a helmet attached to the saddle. She put it on and slung her leg over the bike. "Race you guys back to the Divination Lab?"

She won easily and waved them on before returning to her dorm. Only a very unusual wolf or bear would brave the noise the Vincent produced. She parked near the front door of the dorm and shut the bike down.

Rhiannon was in the room, working her loom. "You found your machine." She nodded toward Lesa's side of the room. "They delivered that monstrosity at the same time."

The bed was humongous, gold-leafed wood with a canopy, the thick mattress filled with down. A set of portable steps was required to mount the thing. Lesa climbed the steps and sank so deeply into the mattress that she lost sight of the rest of the room. "What are you making?" she said.

The loom sounds paused. "I am a history major, so I am making a historical tapestry."

Lesa clambered out of the bed with some difficulty and moved the stairs so she could see the tapestry her roommate was weaving. "It's beautiful!"

Rhiannon grunted noncommittally. "King Pirithous' wedding. The bride seduced a centaur guest and accused him of trying to rape her when her fiancé found out. Your ancestors cut off his ears and nose and drove him into the woods."

"Pirithous was king of the Lapiths, right? That's in Greece. My ancestors came from a lot further south and a whole different continent." Lesa studied the tapestry-in-progress. "Did you spin and dye the wool, too?"

Rhiannon stomped her front hoof. "I told you I was not interested in being friends with a man."

"Woman," Lesa said.

"Regardless." She pointed toward Lesa's side of the room. "That is your space. I expect you to stay out of mine."

Lesa stepped off the small flight of stairs. "Your call. I just figured, since we're living together, that it would be easier if —."

"It would not." The centauride wheeled and headed for the door. "And do not touch my things!"

Lesa pulled the stairs back into place near the bed. The business end of a heavy-duty extension cord was poking through a crude hole in the wall. Lesa followed the cord outside to where it petered into a clay alchemical jar. She shrugged, added a power strip to the chain, and plugged in her phone, watch, and computer to charge. On the wall next to the bed was a rack for sword and shield, and Lesa hung her weapons. Beneath it was an ornate box with a round lid—a chamber pot.

"Just what the doctoral candidate ordered."

She used it and tugged experimentally at a jeweled chain at its side. With a hiss, a thin film of blue liquid poured into the bowl, dissolving everything inside it before vanishing. The bowl sparkled. An alchemical chamber pot, even better. There were a sink and small shower unit, with hot and cold running water, in the corner.

She returned to the Divination Lab the next morning, clean and well-rested, for the daily department meeting. She commandeered a small bookcase and climbed on top of it to put herself at eye level with the centaurs. Mentor Rhaecus led the meeting, asking each student for an update on their projects. There were thirteen diviners in the program. Elatus was focusing on entrails. Hippe was heavy into fractomancy. Pholus was doing a dual degree in geloscopy (divination through laughter) and nggàm (divination through spider behavior).

Another centauride in the group was studying ambocomancy, or divination through dust, which Lesa had never heard of, and the I Ching.

"Et tu?" the mentor said when Lesa's turn came around.

"Still finding my feet," she said. "But I can already see where I could help everyone else out. It's like you're stuck in the Dark Ages. Elatus, your project alone —."

The gloomy centaur glowered. "Stay away from my work, human."

"Speak for yourself," Hippe said. "I'd love to some help with my project."

Mentor Rhaecus brought his hands together sharply. "Hippe, I doubt your thesis committee would think well of such methods. Perhaps the man should keep to her own studies." He held up his hand to forestall debate. "That's enough for the day. Meeting adjourned."

Lesa waited until the mentor was out of sight. "That's ridiculous. Just cataloging your fractals in a searchable database would save you hours a day, but I bet we could —."

Hippe shook her head. "Rhaecus is my thesis advisor."

"Pholus?" Lesa leaned in so she could see the centaur's face. "What about your project? I could—"

"You could bring us all to ruin," Elatus said. "The way your kind always has."

Pholus smoothed his beard. "Give it a little time, Lesa. Maybe start working on something for yourself and in a couple of months see what happens."

"Did you actually just say that?" Lesa said. "We're diviners! If anyone can see what happ—."

"Have you had breakfast, yet?" Hippe interrupted her. "Let us get something to eat and talk about this later. Pholus?"

The gangly centaur shook his head.

"Just we mares, then." She helped Lesa off the bookcase. "Food will help."

Lesa kept the Vincent down to about 15 mph, allowing Hippe to cover the distance at an easy canter, but a twist of the throttle could have left the centauride and everything she represented in the dust.

"Let us take them outside," Hippe said when they'd gotten their trays of food. They walked a little ways from the building. Lesa sat on the remnants of a rock wall while Hippe folded her legs and lay down.

Lesa frowned at the meat and vegetables on her plate. "What am I even here for?" she said.

"I could not say this in front of the others," the centauride said, "but I want your help. Pholus does, too. We have talked about it."

"What about Mentor Rhaecus?"

"As you said, we are stuck in the Dark Ages. He is one of the reasons why."

Lesa gnawed on what she hoped was a hunk of mutton, but it might have been ahuizotl. "What about Elatus? Who shoved that stick up his—?"

"He is a descendant of Eurytion. He and his cousin, Rhiannon." She whisked her tail. "It will take much to get them to think kindly of a man."

"That was thousands of years ago!"

"The families have long memories." Hippe finished her meal and heaved herself to her feet. "I will not go back to the lab with you. I believe my estrus is beginning."

"Your estrus?" Lesa put her hand to her mouth. "Oh."

The centauride smiled. "I do not have to exile myself but doing so can prevent bad choices." Hippe's hooves moved restlessly. "We will talk more about my fractals and your algorithms in a few days."

Lesa finished her breakfast alone and headed back to the lab. With her electronics fully charged, she began experiments with shufflemancy, telling the future by what song came up on a random playlist. If she could write an algorithm that correlated it with ambulomancy (divination by walking), she might be able to create an app that would keep exercisers safe. She worked the problem until lunch, then returned to it until it was time to head back to the dorms.

Pholus shook his work lamp, disrupting the alchemical process that kept it alight. "Are you coming to the party?"

"What party?" Lesa had been wandering around the lab listening to a randomly-generated punk-rock playlist to gather data. If there had been a party announcement, she'd missed it.

"One of the frats at the War College."

"When does it start?" Lesa said.

"Nine. But if you go, don't go until ten, ten thirty. No one gets there early."

"Maybe." The music had put Lesa in a dancing mood, but she doubted it would last through the evening, and she wasn't sure she'd survive a dance floor full of centaur. She rode back to her dorm in the dark. The air was chilly, and she made a mental note to research snowmobiles when she went back to New York for the school's Sagittarius holiday in November. If she picked up a few more MacBooks and some routers, she could set up a local network for the Divination College and ...

Lesa parked the Vincent and went through the now-familiar process of sliding open the door. Inside the room, she hung a few posters and unpacked a quilt her great-grandmother had made her. The down mattress had far too much acreage for the quilt to cover, so Lesa folded the blanket and put it on the foot of the bed.

Rhiannon came in around 9:30 and failed to greet her roommate.

"Are you going to the party?" Lesa said.

Rhiannon propped her sword and shield against the wall. "Are you?"

"Doubt it." Her experiments combining shufflemancy and ambulomancy were showing promise. Few divination methods performed accurately on the diviner, but Lesa had made it around the room four times, blindfolded, using the beta version of her new app.

"Wise choice." Rhiannon clopped to her mirror. "You might get stepped on." She put a tea kettle in the room's brazier and let the water heat as she washed her face, ran a brush over her short hair, and rouged her nipples. When the tea kettle whistled, she spooned loose-leaf tea into a pot and poured water over it.

"Is that some special centaur-party tea?" Lesa said.

"It is Earl Grey." Rhiannon retrieved her sword and wiped the blade with a rag. She took a jar of oil from a shelf and applied a light coating to the blade.

"Are you expecting a fight?" Lesa changed a value in a line of code and the user-interface of her app turned green.

"Best part of a centaur party." Rhiannon poured tea into a travel mug and slung her shield over her withers. "Do not wait up."

The temperature in the dorm room was chilly by human standards, and Rhiannon's Earl Grey had smelled good. Lesa waited until her roommate had slid the door closed before getting up to see if she had left any tea in the pot. She lifted the lid and inspected the leafy dregs inside. There wasn't enough to make a decent cup, but —

Lesa nearly fumbled the pot while setting it down and ran to Rhiannon's mirror. She pulled two hairs out of Rhiannon's brush and dug into her pocket for her Zippo. Lesa lit the hair on fire and used her smartphone to film the smoke as it curled to the ceiling. She sent the video to her laptop, added the information from the tea leaves, and crunched the data.

"Shit!"

Lesa grabbed her sword and shield and ran for the Vincent without closing the door behind her.

Howard Stern: You know, I saw in the news the other day that centaurs, part-person, part-horse, are real. Swear to God. [Leans into the microphone] Do we have that clip? Play that clip.

[The clip plays. In it a centauride runs toward the camera in slow motion, breasts bouncing]

H.S. That is something. Can we see that again?

[The clip plays again, with a bow-chicka-wow-wow soundtrack]

Robin Quivers: Guess they've never heard of sports bras.

H.S..: Why cover that up? If my wife had breasts like that, I would never let her cover them up.

R.Q. Never.

H.S.: Apparently centaur women are only interested in sex four days a month.

R.Q.: Do they go into heat? Like a horse?

H.S.: They do. For those four days, they are the hornier than college girls on spring break. For the rest of the month. Nothing.

R.Q.: I wonder how the male centaurs feel. Can they even reach their, you know, to take the pressure off?

H.S.: Maybe they get each other off. Would you [bleep] a centaur, Robin? [Ten seconds of the clip plays.]

— The Howard Stern Radio Show, CBS. (1996).

The party looked like a blending of a livestock auction and a free-love festival. Centaur dancing consisted of rearing and wheeling while clutching ceramic jars of strong beer. Lesa climbed on top of a table and spun until she spotted her roommate, who was filling her jar from a freshly tapped barrel.

"Rhiannon!" She cupped her hands around her mouth. "Don't drink it!"

Rhiannon did not hear or opted to ignore. She lifted the jar to her lips.

Lesa jumped from the tabletop to the back of the nearest centaur. Another leap, another centaur, and Lesa was atop the drinks table and in range to dash the jar out of Rhiannon's hand. For good measure, Lesa pushed the just-tapped barrel of beer onto the floor, where it burst.

"What are you doing?!" Rhiannon said.

Lesa dropped to the floor. Her roommate towered over her, nearly a thousand pounds of angry, human-hating muscle and bone with heavy hooves and a newly oiled sword.

Four legs and a gangly body came between them. "What's going on?" Pholus said.

"The beer is laced with something!" Lesa said. "It's going to —!"

"Get the jar," Pholus said. "Give it to Endeis."

Lesa picked the jar off the floor and gave to the gray alchemy student. He sniffed the jar and ran his finger around the rim. "Smells like …." He licked the tip of his finger. "Definitely." He turned to Rhiannon. "Did you drink any of this? It's a hormone simulator. It will bring you into season almost immediately."

"Shit!" Rhiannon flushed. "I feel it. Which one of you basta—?"

A centaur on the other side of the table whooped. It was Polkan. He flared his nostrils. "Smells like a paaaarty!" The males around him began to react, too, excited by his pheromones as well as the ones Rhiannon was beginning to emit. They jostled each other and pawed the floor with their front hooves. Someone started a war chant.

Lesa slipped her arm into her shield and drew her sword. She put herself between her roommate and the approaching centaurs. "Any fucker who touches her gets gelded!"

"We will get her out of here," Pholus said.

Lesa looked at him suspiciously.

"She does not affect me the same way," the gangly centaur said. "Endeis and I, we are lovers."

Lesa and Endeis provided cover while Pholus led Rhiannon out of the dining hall and into the cold air outside.

"How are you feeling?" Pholus asked the drugged centauride.

"Better." Rhiannon rubbed her forehead. "I think I am okay to get home."

Four centaurides came out of the dining hall. They were disheveled, and their swords were drawn. "We will go with her and make sure she gets to her room safely," one said. "The party is over. Polkan will not sleep comfortably tonight."

Pholus watched them leave and ran his hands through his hair, making it stand on end. "That could have been a real mess. How did you know?"

"Her tea."

"Just that?"

"Smoke patterns. I burned some of her hair."

They studied the stars for a while.

"Do you think this is why the Mentor said you had to come here?" Pholus said.

Lesa rested her head on his lower shoulder. "Maybe."

"Want to go the Alchemy Lab with us and get drunk?"

The Alchemy Lab had a hookah bar, and Endeis insisted Lesa try his favorite smoking blend while she and Pholus talked about his thesis. The night ended at dawn with a draught Endeis gave her that took away her hangover and made her feel like she'd had a full night's sleep. Lesa got the Vincent started and powered back to the dorm for a shower and a change of clothes.

Lesa parked in front of the dorm and stopped short. Someone had put a stepladder out, which made it much easier to reach the latch and open the door. There was another ladder in front of the door of her room, with a note. Lesa pulled the scrap of parchment off the ladder and puzzled out the scrawling calligraphy. *I still do not like men,* it said. *But women might be acceptable.*

Lesa put the note in her pocket. She didn't need to see the future to know it was a good sign. *There you go, Great-Grandma. Not famous, not powerful, but I might be important to something here.* Lesa climbed the ladder to open the door.

The stars don't lie.

About the story

"The Stars Don't Lie" started out because I wanted to write about someone overcoming a disability. I teach high school, and most school days I visit a little coffee shop run by kids in the special-education program. It's one of the best parts of my day. The idea of a human attending a centaur school came from that. Lesa, the main character in "Stars," is not disabled in her own world, but in a world made for creatures who are taller than her, have more legs, are faster and stronger, etc. she faces challenges.

The rest evolved in the writing. I was in a bit of a slump after hitting a dead-end on a rewrite, so I started pecking away at the story. I do a lot of my first drafts on manual typewriters. It's easier for me to get into the zone and stay there when I write on something that can't connect to the Internet. I usually write in small blocks that fit here and there into my schedule, so getting into the zone quickly is important.

I researched while I wrote and came up with the idea for the Divination College, and, since I often warn my college-bound my students about the dangers of college parties and drinking too much, a story was born.

The first draft topped out at 8,000 words, the second draft climbed to 10,000, draft three dropped to about 9,000, and that's where it stayed.

A question for the author

Q: Do you have a garden? Have you ever grown your own food?

A: I grew up in rural Maine, and my family always had a garden and chickens. Summers I hayed, picked potatoes, and blueberry raked. Nowadays, I live in a smallish city, but we still do a garden every year, and there is nothing more satisfying than going outside and picking a salad. We also have a couple of apple trees that do well, a peach tree, a couple of quince trees, and blackberry bushes. My wife likes to can, so we get a lot out of the fruit. The asparagus does pretty well, too. About five years ago we got into beekeeping, not as much for the honey as to have the little guys around. They are good neighbors.

About the author

R.W.W. Greene is a New Hampshire writer with an MFA he exorcises in dive bars and coffee shops. Greene collects manual typewriters, keeps bees, and, by day, teaches writing at a variety of institutions.

rwwgreene.com, @rwwgreene

July

Time's Arrow

C. Heidmann

In 2130 the Nelari began resurrecting the dead. In 2133 Talia's father called for the first time in five years.

"You want to bring her back, Dad?" *After all this time, after what you did?* Talia wanted to add, but didn't. Couldn't. Not to his face. Not anymore.

She barely recognized the white-haired, eighty-three-year old figure; the holo-projectors in her quarters relayed every etch-mark of time, his still-bright blue eyes peering at her out of a sagging, heavy face.

"Don't you?" He looked… hurt. Like when she was small and had uttered an expletive. How could she, his perfect little girl, have said such a thing? "But she's your *mother*."

"Have you thought this through? How it will be for her? For all of us?"

He rubbed at his left eye and blinked a couple of times. "You think I haven't? Ever since I got that notification, I can hardly think about anything else."

Talia's notification about the offer to reanimate her mother had arrived the previous day. Half-knowing it wasn't going to go away, she'd ignored it; until her father's call woke her in the middle of Copernicus Station's artificially maintained night.

"She deserves another chance, Talia."

Yes, but did he *deserve another chance with her?* She clamped down on the retort.

Twenty-three years earlier, Talia had lost her mother and learned of her father's infidelity in one afternoon. He'd been away on another 'business' trip which couldn't be put off even in the face of his wife's terminal cancer. When Talia tracked him down and gave him the news, he'd been heartbroken. The shameless display of grief had enraged her.

The pause lengthened as she concentrated on not fidgeting.

What could she say that would convince him she didn't want to talk? Not about bringing her mother back from the dead. Not about anything. She didn't want to get caught up again in the emotional turmoil of his dredged-up pain, his guilt, self-justification, or whatever new form his latest plea for absolution would take. It was part of the reason she lived off-Earth, as far away from home, from him, as she could get.

Her father's hologram fragmented as interference rippled it into multi-colored snowflakes, granting her a reprieve.

"Do you know how lucky we are?" he said as the holo-emitters recomposed his image. "If we'd not had her buried, if we'd had her cremated instead…"

"I know, Dad."

For their own mysterious reasons, the Nelari had revealed their technology in stages. Initially, only people who had been cryogenically preserved, a full body or a head, could be reanimated. Then the Nelari taught human scientists techniques for reviving the interred. Now families of the cremated lived in fervent hope that it might become possible to resurrect even those who had suffered complete body-loss.

"I thought you were opposed to the Nelari, Dad. You said you didn't trust them, that you don't believe in benevolent beings from the stars. Now you're ready to roll over and take their offer?"

He scratched his lip with his thumb. "I did say that. And I still don't trust them. There's no such thing as something for nothing." He shook a crooked forefinger. "One day those damned aliens are going to want something in return and payback's always a bitch."

She resisted the urge to roll her eyes. "They're not like that, Dad. In all their time here, they've not once demanded anything in return for their generosity."

"Then why don't you want me to take their offer?"

She rubbed at her rat's nest of hair. "I don't know if it's the right thing to do, I don't—"

"What do you mean not the right thing? Don't you want your mother back?" She didn't react to his accusation but the hardness in his eyes pushed at her, shoved like a playground bully.

"What about the rehabilitation? It will take weeks if not months, and you realize there's a chance she might not retain all her memory or personality when they revive her." Some reanimations had not gone well—people failing to re-integrate, like a graft not taking. Unable and unwilling to face life again, having never expected to be resurrected, they ended up in mental institutions or chose to end their lives again —with a stipulation to never be revived again.

A glint of moisture filmed her father's irises though he pretended it wasn't there. "I read all the literature. I know there's a chance we could lose her all over again."

"But you're not going to let that stop you, are you?" Certainty of his answer, his total conviction, sat like a lead brick in her stomach.

"You can't expect me to walk away."

"Why the hell not, Dad? It's what you did last time," she spat, instantly regretting it, suddenly tired and wanting to get this over with. She massaged the beginnings of a headache at her temples. "Why do you want my approval when you've already made up your mind?"

"Because that's what your mother would have wanted—us, united as a family."

"Since when did you care what she would have wanted?" The sound of her voice rising a few octaves spurred her on. "You were the one who broke up our family. You walked out on her when she needed you the most." Ignoring the bounds of the holo-pickup fields, she gesticulated wildly, punctuating her words, slashing the air, decimating the millions of miles between them.

"I can't believe you're still holding on to that pain—"

Blood whooshed in her ears. "Her dying gave you an excellent way out of the mess you'd made of your marriage. You think she'd want to come back to that? To you?" She dreaded the return, hated the idea her mother would have to face it all again, her own tragic end, her husband's betrayal, the pain he'd caused her and the rifts it had opened in their family. Why couldn't he see that?

"Talia," he cast around him as if searching for his words, "listen to me. You don't know what it's like to lose a partner, a... a soul mate." His eyes tracked left to some point in the virtual distance, somewhere she could never see.

"Everyone who's lost someone wants them back, it's part of mourning. But we have to let them go, learn to live without them. Hasn't Mom suffered enough?"

She stepped back from the holo, folded her arms across her chest and became aware of her rapid breathing, accelerated heart rate. Finally, she'd run out of words, weapons to hurt him with.

This time his voice rose. "She *has* suffered enough, that's why I have to bring her back."

She had started it, but he wasn't going to let it go. She strove to keep her voice low. "Dad—"

"It's okay, I get it." He nodded as if he'd read her thoughts. "You don't want your mother back because you don't want *me* to have her back." He choked to a stop and lowered the accusatory finger he'd been brandishing. "You want to make me pay again." He was pointing his thumb at himself.

He was right. She wasn't denying her mother, she was denying *him*. But she clenched her mouth. Time had worn him down to a wrinkled, shrunken version of what he'd been, a badly made puppet of his former self. She'd said more than enough hurtful things to him over the years. This time had proven no exception.

In her father's world, a buzzer sounded. The evening mealtime call for the residents of Raintree Retirement Village. His eyes flicked to his right, then avoided hers.

The buzzer sounded again. "You'll have to excuse me, I have to go." He rolled his chair away, an old man not wanting to miss his dinner.

"End connection," she told the com and headed for the medicine cabinet. She slipped a medi-film strip onto her tongue, let it melt into her palate. Within seconds, her headache disappeared, but the chagrin, the bitter aftertaste of their argument lingered. No instant medi-film remedy to soften that.

Did she really want her mother to remain dead just to punish him? She'd mourned, accepted the loss, and moved on. How could she go back on it now? How could her father expect her to retrace those painful steps?

Her mother had never yearned to be brought back to life and cured. And she couldn't be asked if she wanted to come back or to be left alone. But if obtaining consent was impossible, did that make it irrelevant?

Never before had it been necessary to deal with questions like these. When people died, that was it. End of story. Time's arrow had always pointed one way. Death followed life, not the other way around. Until now. Until the Nelari.

In a few short months, she would have to face the reanimated version of her dead mother. What should she do? she wondered. What would she say to a mother she'd already buried?

"Hi Mom," was all she said.

The regenerated version of her mother smiled as she came into the waiting room. She looked incredible, radiant, and almost too beautiful. But her face didn't hide the shock, the disbelief, the pain and the disappointment when she saw how time had changed Talia and her father. She recovered and revealed nothing more as she greeted them in turn, asking the appropriate questions, keeping everything normal, calm, as if nothing untoward or overly emotional, were happening.

Talia had gone numb. When her mother hugged her, it didn't feel real. It was like holding a doll, an automaton. Who was this perfect imitation they'd been given? Why did she want to outright reject this manifestation of her mother? Why did she feel she had to keep her own emotional distance? Was it because she'd perceived this... this... ghost of her mother, as doing that?

She'd been coached, Talia told herself as she watched the apparition of her mother; prepared for weeks ahead on how to cope.

Her father was a mess. He began weeping the moment his past wife emerged. More than two decades of pain and guilt, and of mourning her, came out and pulped him, mashed him up like a losing boxer. He failed to stay up-right on his new Nelari-gifted cyber legs. They had to help him into a chair, get an aide to give him something to calm him.

Juxtaposed against Talia's decrepit father, her stunning, young 'mother' kept smiling, fussed over him in an over-caring, and to Talia, false way.

"Did you want to come back, Mom?"

All eyes in the room—including those of the bot-assistant who'd been facilitating the meeting, turned to Talia. No one moved.

"I... I, yes, of course, darling."

"Really? You wanted to come back?" Talia flung her forefinger towards her father, "to *him*?" Back in his mobility chair his tear-filled gaze pleaded with her.

"You remember how he hurt you? Abandoned you? Right when you needed him the most?"

"We can talk about this later, okay, Honey?" The manifestation of her mother tried to soothe. Was this her mother? Weren't they supposed to reconstruct enough of a person's personality to be indistinguishable from the original, assimilating every scrap of information left behind by, or about that person?

The resurrected woman's words seemed to de-immobilize everybody. Everyone started talking and moving at once. Talia barely heard them.

A timer display in her left vision flashed. "I have to go," she said in a loud voice. "My ship leaves in an hour. We talk now, or not at all."

They didn't talk then.

Outside, she blinked in the mid-afternoon sun, her space-accustomed eyes smarting in the harsh light. The trip to the spaceport was a blur. The whole way, she cried for her mother. Before her mother had passed away, she'd never spoken to Talia about what her father had done. She'd let Talia believe she'd accepted her impending death early on; that she'd been coping and that at the last, suffering and in pain, she'd wanted it to end, for herself and for all of them.

"Talia, wait."

It was her.

Almost through the departure gate, Talia paused. The reanimation of her mother stood alone, on the other side of the crowd, waving at her. Talia hesitated before weaving through passengers clamoring to get ahead of the line.

"I did want to come back," her mother started, out of breath, "despite everything. I... I mean, if I could have, you know, had a choice." Her cheeks were flushed, two distinct red patches on either side of her face, like Talia remembered.

Her mother had never been good with words, had had difficulty explaining herself. For the first time, Talia felt sympathy for her. Here was a woman scarcely her senior now, facing the prospect of going home with an eighty-year-old man, thrust back into a world she didn't know anymore. How would she pick up the pieces of a life death had made her leave so long ago?

"I'm... alive." Her mother's eyes shot full of tears. She shuddered in a breath and gulped. "I mean I'm glad I'm alive again. I can go travelling now like I always wanted to..." Her mother offered a smile. "I understand you live on a space station? I would love to see it, I mean, to see you... I mean, to talk... some time." Her mother hooked an imaginary strand of hair behind her ear. Despite her new short hair style, she repeated the action two or three times as if she still had the shoulder-length hair she'd lost to cancer and its medications so long ago.

The jittery little gesture triggered Talia's memories, countless instances when she'd seen her mother repeat exactly that nervous tick, always when her mother had been anxious, emotional. Talia's heart melted. It sounded like her mother, looked like her mother, *felt* like her mother. She grabbed her. "Oh, Mom." Her tears spilled unabated.

They hugged until the final boarding alert flashed red in Talia's vision.

Her mother went home with her father to the house bought back for her at great expense. Refurbished and re-decorated to as close as possible to the way it had been when she died. The pitiable, harmless-seeming gesture of a guilt-ridden erstwhile cheat and widower.

Talia wasn't surprised when they broke up.

It took about six months for everything to unravel before her mother found a younger man and moved away.

Talia's father died shortly after.

Her mother was still alive, of course, carrying on with her new life and her new beau. She might even outlive Talia now, might even be brought back from the dead again someday, like Talia would be.

But when the Nelari offer came to revive her father, Talia discovered that despite his insistence on resurrecting her mother, he'd neglected to specify his own wishes. He'd left the reanimation decision to his next-of-kin.

Her mother was hesitant.

"I... he said he didn't want to live without me. I... I feel bad... about the way I left him. But that house, the way he... I know all he was trying to do was atone, but I couldn't take it..." Another person hovered in the holo behind her mother, too far out of range to be rendered in detail.

"I felt like a ghost, like I was haunting him," The person in the background moved into the holo-frame and squeezed her mother's shoulder. She squeezed back. "What I mean to say is, I have Antonio now, and... maybe... your father deserves another chance at life too." She spread her hands, as if opening the best possible outcome.

At the resurrection and rehabilitation center, they let Talia in early.

She paused in the doorway to her father's room. He didn't notice her right away as two bots helped him upright out of bed. She eyed the figure of her dad.

Still eighty-three, still white-haired, he looked... invigorated, sprightly. Gone were the sunken haggardness, the slow movements, and the pallor that had washed him out. His cheeks had a rosy glow, almost like the cliché Santa Claus figure, and despite still being a little unsteady on his feet he had a quickness to his movements, a new sureness. Restored to the peak of health for his age, he should have another thirty, forty odd years of good quality life. More, probably, at the rate of Nelari-gifted medical advancement.

"You had me brought back." His soft words broke her reverie. Her mind had drifted. He took a step toward her, bots hovering either side in case he lost his balance. "Does that mean you've forgiven me?"

She opened her mouth. Had she? She bit her lip. She wasn't sure. But she was willing to try. In the post-Nelari world of selflessness and compassion, disallowing his resurrection would've been tantamount to purposely keeping him dead. She couldn't live with that; with herself.

If you liked C. Heidmann's story "Time's Arrow", leave a comment online at Metaphorosis. Authors love that!

About the story

A typical what-if moment inspired this story. What if aliens came along and made actual resurrection from the dead possible?

Aliens are, for me, the ultimate mystery and I strove to keep them mysterious in this story. If they are technologically advanced, they could be capable of anything—up to and including resurrecting our dead, and without necessarily explaining their motivations. —What if they truly were just benevolent beings from the stars, showering humanity with the benefits of their knowledge, sharing their technologies and advancements, without expecting anything in return? And who wouldn't want their dead loved ones returned to them? Who could say no to that? That last question brought forth the character of Talia and unraveling her motivations for maybe not being so keen on having her mother brought back from the dead.

A question for the author

Q: If your writing style were a bird, what type of bird would it be and why?

A: Nah, a bird doesn't work for me—unless maybe it could be a space-going bird! A bird is too limiting. It can only go as far as the atmosphere, around one tiny world, whereas I'd like to think my writing should be able to take me anywhere, out to the farthest reaches of the universe and beyond... into the multiverse, or whatever is outside our universe—and beyond even that.

About the author

Originally from South Africa, C Heidmann writes from Auckland, New Zealand.

Indistinguishable from a local after twelve years on the Outer Rim, she grew up on an entirely different galactic arm and relishes the idea of secretly being an alien.

@CarineHeidmann

The Forest of New People

Thom Connors

When winter comes to Vakning Forest, nothing changes. The evergreens, packed tightly together, don't wilt or become bare. Nor does the smell fade. As the winter deepens, the snow covers the canopy like a blanket, and the scent of pine needles and pine cones follows the only path worn out of the darkness.

Outside the forest, where the path begins, is the cottage of Abi and Odo Tremord. It has a red roof, brown walls, and a whitewashed, waist-high fence. In the yard stands a pine tree, a sapling, half as tall as the forest.

While the kitchen looks out over the pine tree, Odo's wood chopping block looks towards the forest. So it is that Odo is the first to notice any man exiting the forest.

It was always an adult, stumbling along the path on legs with newly formed muscles. The Tremords would take the man in, feed him, clothe him, and set him to bed. Then they'd teach him: wood chopping, speaking, etiquette. And when the season changed next, they'd see the colour on the horizon as the Bastler came trundling along, his wagon painted that garish orange. They would dress up the man in the finest clothes Abi had made, and all three would wait at the path's end for the Bastler to arrive.

When he did, the Bastler would get off the wagon. He would wave his black cloak around for show, with its purple inner trim and the wolf fur on the cuffs, and he would flash a smile which showed off his pointy canines, stark against the perfection of his other teeth. He would inspect the man.

"The forest made you mighty," the Bastler would say after checking the man's teeth with his eyes and a finger. Then he would push the man into the back of his wagon and get back in front of the horses, and prepare to leave. "Does he know when to run and when to walk? I can't set him to work if he can't show common sense."

"Yes, Sir." Odo would reply, every time. And then, "Sir Bastler, please."

And the Bastler would stop and look at the pine tree, the area around it always perfectly cared for by Abi and Odo, and he would look back into his wagon at the new man he had just been given, and he would say: "Look after the pine. Make it mightier, taller, until it can catch the snow."

"Please, Sir," Abi would say, gripping Odo's arm so tightly he would bruise. "Our daughter."

The Bastler would sigh and take the reins. "It's not enough yet to tip the scales. What is worth your daughter's life? This person? Any one person?"

Abi and Odo would slink back into the house and Odo would sink into a mood while Abi moved without feeling the things she did. And this was how it went, Odo chopping wood until he felt himself return to normal, and Abi preparing for the next new person to arrive.

At the end of the night, Abi and Odo would go out and clean and tend to the pine; rake the needles and cones out from beneath it, check it for rot and bugs, and measure it on the sunset shadow.

"It's getting taller," Odo would say.

And Abi would nod and force a smile, and wonder when she stopped believing him. Abi would glance towards the path to the forest and wonder what happened to the ones that went with the Bastler.

And so, that night, it was Abi who first noticed the person that stumbled out of the forest along a moonlit path.

It was a girl.

Abi covered her mouth with a hand.

"No, really. I honestly think it's taller now," Odo said, admiring their work.

Abi was shocked, too much to move. Odo watched her face and moved to hug her before he too noticed the teenager stumbling out of the forest.

Odo grabbed one of the blankets they piled by the door and ran out to meet her, draping the blanket over her and helping her into the house. Abi had moved into the kitchen and was working on dinner.

"Soup tonight?" Abi asked, her face blank. Odo could see the numbness painted on her face.

"I could eat," he replied. He walked the girl to the spare bedroom and laid her upon the bed. She didn't move, watching the wall. Occasionally her eyes would drift to the window that was just above the bed, as if she were watching the sunset.

"You're brand new," Odo said. "We're here to help you. Some of you can understand us and some of you cannot. But we are here to help, and if you have any questions, we will answer them. You get to be lazy for the next few days while your body learns to be, but then we will begin teaching you to be human; the appropriate times for laughter, when to run and when to walk.

"My wife is going to be very quiet when you meet her. She's going to have trouble with this," Odo smiled and used the end of the blanket to wipe some dirt off the girl's nose.

The girl reacted as a child, intrigued that something was reaching for her face. At no point did she flinch or move away. Odo did this every time, to teach them he was safe. Let them work for Abi's affection, for his he gave freely.

"Can you understand me?" Odo asked.

The girl looked him in the eye and Odo realised that her eyes were green, like the forest pines. And then the girl nodded and curled up in the blanket more tightly.

Odo slapped his knees slightly and then moved out into the kitchen. He shut the door quietly and walked over to the table where Abi had placed dinner, two bowls. Odo watched Abi's face and smiled when she caught his eyes.

"She's too tired to eat now. But she'll be hungry later," Odo said.

Abi sighed, picking up one of the bowls. "I don't want any."

"Then why would you...? Alright," Odo said.

"A part of me wishes to send you after the Bastler right now."

"We are not doing that, Abi."

"As soon as we can, she's going," Abi said.

"I meant that I won't go after the Bastler. We treat her the way we treated the men. Maybe this will tip the scale." There was a light in Odo's eyes that Abi hadn't seen in a long time. It filled the room a little, and made her believe, for just a second.

"We do it right this time," Abi said, glancing at the part of the pine illuminated out the kitchen window.

Odo reached over and grabbed Abi's other hand. He squeezed it tight.

"Will you come meet her with me?"

Odo didn't wait for an answer; he stood up and pulled his wife up with him until they were nearly hugging and then he guided her to the door.

"What did you name her?" Abi asked.

"I didn't name her. I want her to choose her own name," Odo said.

"Why?" Abi asked.

Odo opened the door. "I can't save her, but she can own herself this way."

"Can she?" Abi asked.

The door had opened on an empty bed, with a blanket thrown across it. The window above the bed was open.

"Did she run away?" Odo asked.

"Obviously," Abi said.

"None of them have ever done that before."

"Maybe she's different," Abi said, sarcastically.

Odo climbed on the bed and looked out the window. There was nothing, just the darkness past the light that shone out from the window.

"Do you think she went back into the forest?" Odo asked.

"None of the others have done that, Odo. I think she's still here, just around the house somewhere."

"Should we look for her?"

"No, let her freeze to death," Abi said.

Odo bit the inside of his lip and nodded. He didn't want to say it, but he could barely contain himself.

"Better she freezes to death than goes with the Bastler? Is that what you're thinking?" Abi said, with a loud scoff.

"I mean... Yes," Odo said, with a shiver. "But we need to find her."

"We do. Remember the time you tried to hide one from him?" Abi asked.

The Bastler had not believed them when they'd said there was no one. He had walked through the house silently. Then he'd raised his hands so that his thumbs entwined and his fingers made wings. He had aimed his hands through every door in the house until he stopped on the cupboard under the sink and their current trainee had crawled out voluntarily without the Bastler so much as saying a word.

The Bastler had left, just flashing them a forced smile. Abi had sworn that there was one extra tooth that was sharp in that smile. And after he had gone, the pine shed almost all its bark and they'd found black skinned insects they'd never seen before crawling on its skin for weeks.

"What did we call those insects?" Odo asked.

"Barkles," Abi said. She covered her mouth quickly with her eyes wide.

"Did you just giggle?"

"No. No!" Abi said. "I have no mirth."

Odo looked at her with loving disbelief but let it go. "We'll find her."

They searched the house for hours. Every nook and every cranny. They even lifted up the trapdoor to the basement.

"It took both of us to lift it," Abi said.

"What?" Odo asked. His fear of the basement reached his voice, so that he squeaked.

"How could this new girl with her brand new arms pull up the trapdoor when it took both of us?"

Odo breathed out so quickly he set off some dust, and began to cough. Abi pulled Odo from the entrance of the basement and let the trapdoor slam. As the trapdoor hit the ground, the room shook. And then, above them, they heard a shuffle.

Odo and Abi looked up together, at the roof that neither of them had even noticed for years. They rushed outside, Odo still coughing slightly. And there was the girl, her arms wrapped around the chimney so tightly that they were almost bloodless.

"Please come down," Odo said.

The girl shook her head.

"You could freeze," Abi said, flippantly, before whispering, "If she freezes up there we can just pretend we didn't see her, and then the Bastler won't blame us."

"If you let go, I'll catch you," Odo said.

Abi covered her mouth and her eyes widened again at this comment.

"You'll catch her? You?"

"Yes, I will. I am dexterous like a fox."

"You're stubborn, like a badger."

"You're the badger," Odo said, before turning back to the roof. "Please, just let go. I will catch you. And we will help you warm back up. There's a fire in the kitchen."

The girl looked at Odo and Abi. Abi finally turned away from Odo and looked at the girl, determined. "Let go," Abi said.

And the girl did, and she tumbled down the roof and Odo caught her comfortably. She wrapped her arms around Odo's neck and hugged him for warmth. Odo walked inside and laid her before the fire, and covered her in blankets. Then he sat in the chair before her and watched her. And Abi walked over and kissed his forehead.

"You were a good father," Abi said.

Odo said nothing, just leaned his head back on the chair. He let his head sit in the nook that he'd created over so many years.

"How long ago did he take Aroha?" Odo asked.

"I do not know if numbers exist that high," Abi said. "Since the sun could touch all sides of the forest at sunset. Since before the forest had an understory. Since the forest floor was clean. How long have the Apteryx been at war?"

Odo nodded and stared at the fire before placing another piece of wood on top. He watched the light spread, and saw how it bounced off the ceiling and threw shadows from the crossbeams.

"The Bastler didn't check the roof last time," Odo said.

Abi raised an eyebrow, and spoke. "No, he didn't."

"It's just an idea. And I only mention it because I didn't realise you were so sure Aroha wouldn't come back. I thought it was a game we played, that I said she would and you said she wouldn't, and we tempered each other to the middle that it was just a matter of time. But if you want this to end, I do too," Odo said.

"You made a promise for both of us, and I've accepted it. You keep wanting it to end. I just want us to be happy," Abi said, as she reached over to touch him.

Odo stood up to avoid her hand, picked up the girl, and carried her to her bed. When he returned he spoke quietly. "I'm going to bed."

Abi watched the flames, the way they reached out to her when she breathed in. And pushed back when she breathed out. Because in this place, at this time, she was the only thing affecting the air.

It had started when Aroha was three. Odo would wake up at midnight, sweat-glistened and scared, and run to Aroha's room and confirm she was okay. Sleeping, window open, with her sheets wrapped around her torso like a bandage. Odo would breathe again, fix the sheets over her and then walk back out into the kitchen.

He would check the newest forest man sleeping on the bedroll they'd laid out for him, warmed by the fire, and then crawl back into bed.

"Is there wood rot in your brain?" Abi whispered when he crawled back into bed. "She's fine."

"I know. I... What's happening to me?" Odo would ask, clinging to her for comfort.

"Your brain is noticing something. But only you are noticing it, Aroha and I are fine. So maybe you're just strange?" Abi muttered through her sleep haze.

Odo would laugh quickly and then press his chin into Abi's shoulder in a way that she loved, that made her wriggle against him.

"That's how we got Aroha; cut it out."

But Odo couldn't shake the feeling of danger that inched towards them. Odo would plan in his downtime, plan for the future, for teaching Aroha. For getting her a life away from the Bastler. Aroha wasn't part of the deal.

Odo woke the new girl the next morning, early. He showed her the clothes they had in the room still from their daughter. He dressed the girl and showed her how to tie her shoes.

"Can you speak?" he asked.

The girl tried and failed, her voice a croak.

"If you can climb a roof, you can start training."

She followed him out to the front yard and they began by sweeping the snow off the path to the door. The girl followed after Odo's actions. She learned quickly. Then they cleaned up around the pine, removing the needles and any cones that had fallen and setting them aside in a storage closet.

"Every day for the next few months, you and I will do these actions to get your arms and legs stronger. And then, afterwards, we will do exercise. And you will be able to outrun me, and out-jump me, and out-everything me. And then you will begin to chop wood with me and we will be ready," Odo smiled. And the girl followed Odo's actions and smiled back.

Odo realised that her smiling at him made him happy. So much so that he wasn't faking his own smile anymore.

"Also, when you are ready and able, you may pick your name. Whatever you wish. And we will call you that. Until then, think about the fact that a name is yours. It is the sound that people make to call you. If they can call you, they can get your attention. If they have your attention, they have your focus, and to have someone's focus is to hold magic in your hands. While you are here, you have mine. Just... mine."

She nodded.

"End of speech," Odo said and he began working through stretches and exercises he taught to all of the forest people. And as he did, he heard Abi begin moving around the kitchen making breakfast. They hadn't spoken since last night. They had fallen asleep facing away.

"We'll teach you sewing when you are able. Odo will make you strong and I will make you deft," Abi said as she placed lunch in front of the girl.

The girl nodded.

"You are going to hate this work. It will be very hard as your body learns how to make small movements rather than big ones. But it will become easier."

The girl opened her mouth and then closed it again.

"When you agree or want to show confirmation of understanding, you can say, 'Yes.' " Abi sat down beside her and picked up the spoon. Abi grabbed the girl's arm and put the spoon in the girl's hand.

Abi showed her how to leverage the spoon between her fingers and thumb webbing. How she should hold it still and move her mouth towards it so that any spills fell back into the bowl. The girl tasted the soup, left over from yesterday, and moved her head over the bowl, learning very quickly that it was the easiest way to get the food into her mouth.

The girl licked her lips and smiled very wide, tiny bits of soup dripping out the sides of her mouth.

"Yes," the girl said.

Abi laughed, and smiled, and then she nodded to herself. She reached up to pat the girl's hair. Then she stopped her hand and stared at it.

"Will you be okay without help?" Abi asked.

"Yes," the girl said, pride coming out along with more soup.

"Never speak with your mouth full," Abi said.

The girl closed her mouth and tried to say yes at the same time.

Abi became wooden as she stood and walked to the door. She walked to Odo, who was outside looking after the pine, raking its needles and the cones.

"Alright. What's your plan?"

Odo continued to clean as he spoke. He'd had the idea after the girl had climbed the roof. Then it had grown inside him and he didn't want to let it go.

"She stays up on the roof, and she can get the jump on him. Then we'll be able to kill him, and take his wagon and maybe... find her," Odo said.

Abi was quiet. She was studying his face, noticing lines on his face that she'd either forgotten or never really seen before.

"We'll need to tie her to the chimney, at the least hook her in with rope. Remember the bird sign?" Abi hooked her thumbs and held her hands out like wings. "The other guy came out of the closet on his own. And then there was the basement... What if she crawls off the roof?"

"That's a good point. What else?" Odo asked, shivering at his memory of the basement.

"Are we trying to kill him?" Abi asked.

"I am," Odo said.

Abi grew quiet, she walked over to the tree and leaned against it, feeling the bark scratch her back and trying to savour it.

"If we fail, he'll kill us."

"Feign ignorance. We had no idea she was up there or that she'd stolen the axe. How could we? No one came out of the forest since he was here last," he said.

Abi shook her head slightly and closed her eyes. "That's really weak. He'll see through it."

"No, he won't. Not if we believe it ourselves."

Abi opened her eyes and Odo was right in front of her. He kissed her softly, their lips touching for the first time in years. Their lips were both cracked yet, when touched, they sprang to life. They filled quickly, the pressure turning them red with blood and excitement.

Abi pushed him away slightly.

"Promise me you're not trying to get yourself killed," she said, the kiss still singing across her skin.

"I promise," he said, his lips pulsing along with his heart. He leaned in and held her. He rested his head on the pine tree behind her. There was resin in his eyebrow but he didn't care. He breathed her in, and she did the same, affecting the air together.

From the kitchen there was the clatter of a bowl.

Then the girl's head popped out of the kitchen window, right in front of them. A mess of black hair and smiles.

"Yes," she said, showing them her empty bowl. "Yes, yes, yes. More."

"Abi, dear," the Bastler had said after Aroha's fifth birthday. "Has Aroha begun to lose her teeth yet?"

Abi was tending the garden, not even looking up as the Bastler arrived. "Not yet, Sir Bastler."

The Bastler walked over and studied the tomatoes, potatoes. And the carrots, with their heads poking out the top of the earth. "You've done quite well to survive here. These are for the new people?"

"Some, sure. We keep the rest ourselves, for when I cook."

"Do you cook every meal?" The Bastler seemed incredulous.

"Of course," Abi said. "However dull monotony is, why wouldn't we cook?"

The Bastler gripped the crook of Abi's neck in a pinch as he laughed, loudly. "I'll be sure to bring you a cooking book next time. Maybe one from the Apteryx?"

Abi shrugged him off and stood up. She shouted into the house, "Odo. Hurry up." She cleaned her hands on her apron while affixing the Bastler with a look of contempt.

"You two really keep to your old ways, don't you? I'm sure Aroha is the proof of that. However, didn't you want a quiet life? A quiet, safe life? That's what Odo asked of me."

"Maybe Aroha doesn't want that?" Abi said as Odo emerged with a man so white he reflected the whole spectrum of the sun.

"Wow. The Apteryx have expanded, haven't they?" the Bastler said.

"We don't understand how it works, Sir Bastler," Odo said.

"Scales and balances, Odo. You press down on one side, and the other side changes. If the Apteryx make a tree, we get a person." The Bastler laughed.

"You know a lot about them, Sir," Abi said.

"I lived with them a time," the Bastler said.

Odo walked the man to the back of the wagon and then together, Odo and Abi walked the Bastler to the gate.

"As a favour, would you please save Aroha's teeth for me when they fall out?"

"That would make me uncomfortable, Sir Bastler," Odo said.

"I'll pay you," the Bastler said.

"With what?" Abi asked.

"Seeds. And cookbooks. Enough seeds for a season or one book per tooth."

"No, Sir Bastler," Odo said.

"I'll bring a book and some aubergine for next time. Aubergine," the Bastler said. He winked at Abi when he said aubergine.

"I love aubergine," Abi said, her mouth beginning to water at the thought.

Odo watched her face, and felt the fear rising in him again.

"No, Sir Bastler," Odo repeated, and he felt again the fear that kept waking him up at night.

"It's fine, I'll bring it with me next time anyway and we'll see what happens, shall we?" and then the Bastler left, as quickly as he had arrived.

"Odo, come see this," Abi said. She was grinning as he entered the room. Their kiss had sparked something faster than a fire. It was in the way they moved now, a string that tied them together.

Odo walked in the door and cleaned his hands, dirty and sweaty from cutting more wood. The fire roared day and night during winter, at Abi's request. Despite the relative warmth, she enjoyed the fire. And it gave Odo something to do, with all the wood they went through.

"Do it again," Abi said to the girl.

The girl licked her thumb, grabbed the end of a piece of thread and twisted it against her wet thumb. Then, tongue hanging out the side of her mouth, she threaded a needle and tied it off.

"Wow..." Odo said. "It's been ten days."

"Yes, it has," Abi said. "Damn, I'm good."

Odo leaned against the back of Abi's chair and his hand brushed against her back. Abi shivered when she felt it flash through her nerves like a wildfire.

"Yes," the girl said. She smiled widely and often.

"That smile could melt the snow. Be careful now, I enjoy winter, I want it to stay a little longer," Odo said.

"Cutting your wood all day," Abi said, grinning at the girl with a wink.

The girl put down the thread and sat like Abi, hands on her knees leaning forward.

"We have more sewing to do. What are you doing?" Abi asked.

"I have chosen a name," the girl said.

Abi and Odo slowly faced each other as Odo came back to the table and sat down as well.

"What name have you chosen?" Odo asked.

"Aroha," the girl said.

"No," Abi said, quickly. "You cannot have that name."

Odo reached out and grabbed Abi's hand and got no response. He took his hand back.

"That name means a lot to us. Choosing that name is impolite. It's like speaking with a mouth full," Odo said.

"It is important to me," the girl said. "I remember."

The girl who called herself Aroha spoke softly and forcefully, as if each word were chosen for more than one reason. She was learning so quickly that Abi and Odo were worried she would be speaking and understanding well enough to learn the plan before they told her.

"I remember," the girl said, "bark, resin, and bird song, there was yelling and calling for a word. It echoed off the branches, 'Aroha.' Only thing voice wanted in the world was Aroha. Being wanted is good. It stuck in the resin, 'Aroha.' It will be my name."

Abi didn't say anything, but Odo saw her sink into herself. She was remembering all the times they had both done that when Aroha had been taken. How many times had she and Odo walked through the forest calling, hoping that she would appear? As if the Bastler had just taught her hide and seek.

"When did you hear this?" Odo asked.

"I don't understand," Aroha said.

"How long ago?" Abi said.

Aroha shrugged.

"You have been with us for ten days. How many of this length of time was it before now?" Odo asked.

"Forever. Forever and then more," Aroha said.

"How long were you in the forest?" Odo asked.

Aroha tilted her head and looked at Odo. She stayed still, looking at him like an owl.

Abi wiped her eyes and smiled. "You want to be wanted."

"Yes," Aroha said, smiling widely and gripping the table.

"Then it is your name, and Aroha you shall be. And you are wanted." Abi turned to Odo. "Aroha can thread a needle, which means she's deft, and not once did she prick herself. You know what that means?"

"Axe time," Odo said, with a wide open mouth and fire in his eyes. Once he saw that Abi was smiling, he smiled too.

"Axe time?" Aroha asked.

"Axe time," he said.

"Come on," Odo said as he filled a bowl with water, and then dragged the newly-named Aroha outside. "You own yourself now. So I'm going to tell you a little something about me."

Odo walked out towards the wood block and picked up the axe he chopped the wood with, and the whetstone he used to keep it sharp. "There are two things that matter to keep yourself happy: someone who understands you, and a good whetstone."

Odo put the whetstone in the water bowl and then went over to the woodpile. He began rifling through the woodpile for anything that was useful, something easy but stable. Already split a little was best.

When he found the perfect log, he took it back to the wood block and placed it so that the split was facing him.

Odo picked up the axe and sized it up, swung once and stopped short. He nodded to himself and knelt down beside the block and waved for Aroha to come over.

"All this wood has a grain. It's the easiest part to find. Some of it has cracks like this that are easier to split. We'll be aiming for this spot here. It's the mid-point between the crack and the edge, so once it breaks there, the rest will come apart easily. Aha," Odo said as he saw the whetstone.

"Once your whetstone has stopped releasing air, you take it out and you can sharpen your axe."

Odo took the whetstone and laid it upon his lap.

"When you sharpen an axe, it's not like a knife. You have to do it in circles. You place three fingers over the cheek of the blade and rest your palm on the beard, here. Then you take the bit, named so because it is the sharp bit, and you move it in a circle: toe, top of the bit, heel, bottom of the bit. You do this until you're happy with it, and then you flip it over and do the same again."

As Odo did it, he showed Aroha. Once he'd done one side, he handed it over and Aroha did the other. While Aroha worked on it, trying to get her circle right, Odo realised what his wife had done by sending her out with him.

"Aroha. We do these things because the axe is like a person, it can't always look after itself. Like you, when you arrived at our door, it needs training and help to be sharper and do its job. Do you understand?"

Aroha looked up from the axe and nodded, "Yes."

"When people you care about ask for your help, you need to do it. Sometimes it's not always clear. The axe won't tell you when it needs to be sharpened, but Abi and I will tell you. And we need your help. Will you help us?"

Aroha smiled and handed the axe to Odo, it was keen. As was Aroha.

"Yes. Yes, yes, yes."

"Even if it's scary?" Odo asked.

"What is scary?" Aroha asked.

And so Odo showed her how to hold the axe and cut the wood. And he thought of the Bastler splitting in half. And then quarters. And then eighths.

Aroha ran around the white-wash fence as fast as she could. Odo tried to keep up, and he did a respectable job. It took ten laps before Odo's pace was such that Aroha lapped him. She was laughing, her voice cutting through the silence and bouncing off the remnants of the snow.

Odo stopped and rested on the fence, watching the tree and looking into the kitchen to find Abi staring back at him. She smiled as Aroha lapped Odo again and slapped him on the back. Abi caught his eye and for a second they shared a genuine smile. Abi nodded inside. Lunch was ready.

"Enough, Aroha. It is lunch time." Odo walked towards the gate and held it open.

Aroha was still running, and ignored the gate. She vaulted the fence, using one hand as a guide. And then her foot caught on a post and her arm was pulled into a strange position. Her newly formed bones met the ground in a way they weren't prepared for and there was a sound, a branch cracking in a storm, and Aroha felt pain for the first time in her life.

Abi was out the front door faster than Odo could react. She was by Aroha's side, holding the arm.

"Can you see the bone?" Odo asked, quietly.

"No," Abi said, lifting Aroha to stand up. Aroha was crying now, replacing the laughter with something darker. The snow ate the sound and seemed to strengthen against its imminent melting. Abi spoke softly to Aroha, "We're going to splint this; it will be okay. The pain will pass, you don't have to cry unless it helps."

"What is cry?" Aroha asked.

"That is a wonderful question," Abi replied.

Odo shut the gate and opened the front door for them, his lips pursed.

"You should've been watching her," Abi said as they passed.

"This argument. Again?" Odo asked, trying to smile his way through it.

"Now? That joke is a good idea right now?" Abi asked.

"She will be okay. I'll grab some pine resin, find a splint."

"Hurry," Abi said.

When Odo returned with the resin and the splint, he found Abi bustling around Aroha and speaking to her calmly.

"Aroha, it's okay. You're going to be all right. There is nothing to be afraid of."

And the new person didn't cry or scream or yell.

She didn't move at all.

"You made a promise." Aroha had been nine, and the Bastler had been yelling. "As long as the Apteryx fight each other, you will be here. In this cottage. Bringing me the people that leave this forest. You will help me protect them and keep them safe. And now you wish to renege? You asked for the perfect life, and I gave it to you. And now you wish to change that?"

"Sir Bastler —" Odo started.

"No, quit it, Odo. You wanted a quiet life with your wife and I gave it to you. Why should we change that contract?"

"We do not want that life anymore."

"Because of Aroha?" the Bastler asked. He flung his arms around, his cloak trailing behind him. His rage quelled the forest around. It was spring, but there was silence. Despite the breeze, not even the pines moved.

Abi walked outside, drying her hands on her apron. Odo swallowed the fear in his throat and spoke firmly.

"We decided upon this together, you and I. We came to this agreement. But I no longer agree. We wish to take Aroha and leave. That is what we wish to trade," Odo said.

"Twenty teeth to break your promise? Are you insane? Or, do you think I am an idiot?' The Bastler asked. He walked towards Odo and through the gate without breaking eye contact. Odo stumbled backwards. The bottle he held contained all of Aroha's baby teeth. "More to the point, you lied to me. You hid the teeth, and you lied to me. You said they weren't falling out yet, and instead you'd been stockpiling them? To bargain with me?"

"I am sorry —"

"I don't care what you are, Odo. But the trees of this forest will know you as a coward." The Bastler spoke, and then called out to the house, "Aroha?"

"No. Just between us," Odo said.

"Did you try and bargain with him?" Abi asked, moving forward and shutting the door behind her.

"He did, Abi," the Bastler said.

"I said no. We spoke about this. We decided against it. How could you?" Abi asked. The hurt in her eyes wasn't fake, but it was quickly covered in fear. "Please, Sir Bastler."

"Bring me the girl," the Baster said to Odo.

"No, Sir Bastler. I'm sorry. Please, just take the bottle," Odo said, he held the teeth out but he was watching Abi, his heart breaking.

The Bastler knocked the bottle of teeth out of Odo's hand and it bounced on the grass. The Bastler walked up until Odo could feel the heat from his body. The Bastler, a full foot taller than Odo, leaned down on him. "People I cared about far more than you have made far more compelling arguments. And they didn't get their way either, Odo. Bring me the girl."

"Please, Sir Ba—" Abi started.

"Abi. He wishes to change the rules of this agreement. An agreement he and I have made. I wish to do the same. Bring me the girl."

"You have always been kind to us, Sir Bastler," Abi said, pleading.

The Bastler took a step back and scratched at his chin.

"You're right. Completely right. You have no reason to fear me," the Bastler said, as he licked his sharp canine teeth. "Aroha. Come here."

Aroha didn't come outside. She was nowhere to be seen.

"You didn't send her into the forest, did you?" the Bastler asked.

The Bastler made wings with his hands, his thumbs intertwined and his fingers spread outward. As he did, Abi saw one of his teeth sharpen, as his face twisted in what appeared to be pain. The Bastler shook himself off and began walking towards the house. Abi and Odo followed behind, slowly, unsure. The Bastler found nothing until he reached the trapdoor to the basement. There was a banging, as if someone inside were trying to get out.

The Bastler went over and lifted the trapdoor.

"Hello, Aroha. I haven't seen you in so long. You've grown big," he said. He held his hand out and Aroha grabbed it and climbed out. The Bastler lifted her up and held her against his side. "Did your parents put you in there?"

Aroha nodded and played with the cuff of the Bastler's coat, the wolf fur. "What colour is this?" she asked.

"It's purple. Have you ever seen that colour before?" he asked.

"No."

"Would you like to see a lot of it? I can take you on a trip and you'll be able to see a lot of it."

Aroha nodded. She was smiling at the shimmering cloak with its strange cuffs worn by the sharp-toothed man.

"That's not part of the agreement," Odo said.

"I want it to be," the Bastler said.

"No, please," Abi said.

"Aroha, go sit on my wagon, I'll be over in a minute," the Bastler said. "Say goodbye to your mother and father. You'll see them soon."

"Please, Bastler. We won't leave." Abi said.

The Bastler grabbed Odo by the back of the neck. "If twenty teeth is worth so much, how about you keep the bottle, and I take your daughter?"

Aroha hugged Abi tightly around the middle.

"Go wait by my wagon, Aroha," the Bastler smiled, pinching Odo's neck. "Tell her, Odo."

"Go wait by the wagon, honey," Odo said, his neck hurting too much for him to argue. He'd forgotten pain, it had been so long since he'd felt it.

Abi wouldn't let go, holding Aroha so tightly. The Bastler took Odo and dragged him to the trapdoor and threw him inside while Abi hugged Aroha's face against her apron, hiding the sight.

"Wait there," the Bastler said to Odo before turning to Abi. "Let her go."

"No," Abi said.

The Bastler walked up and grabbed her hand, pulling Aroha free. He grabbed Abi with his other hand, at the nape of her neck. He threw Abi into the basement and slammed the trapdoor shut. His face twisted in pain again. Then he picked up Aroha and carried her to the wagon, whistling through four sharp teeth.

"I'm calling it off. There is no way we're doing this now. None at all," Abi said.

"I know," Odo said. They were in their chairs. They'd splinted Aroha's arm and then put her to bed. She hadn't moved or spoken since they'd gotten her inside.

"She's not moving or crying at all. She doesn't want either of us in there?" Abi asked. She was so mad that it soaked her through. She could feel her clothes clinging to her with it.

"No, no reaction at all. Maybe she doesn't know how? Maybe it doesn't hurt her like that? Maybe they're not as normal as we thought," Odo rested his head in the worn nook. He stared at the ceiling. The roof beams that had given him an idea before now just danced to tease him. An idea that couldn't possibly be used.

"It's not happening. Stop trying to come up with another plan."

"I'm not." Odo sighed and rubbed his eyes.

"Because, I swear, Odo, I'm out. You made a damn promise about what our lives would be, and it was what we wanted, and now we run it to the end. Because that's what you're meant to do when you make a promise. I refuse. Look what happened when you tried to change your promise with the Bastler."

"I get it, Abi. I understand."

"Sure you do. That's why you keep coming up with these plans that get us hurt, or get Aroha taken. Instead of just completing the promise like a damned adult," Abi said. She was ramping up and Odo could feel it building in him like a tension, all the years of them making it work, all the hundreds of people that had come out of the forest. All of it making him want to snap.

There was a click behind them, a door opening. Aroha walked out, silent, her arm splinted and slung.

"What does this mean for the plan?" Aroha asked, softly. She looked at the floor.

"It means we're not going to do it, we're going to make you all better and then keep going," Odo said, walking over to her and checking her arm. He cupped her face in his hands and smiled at her, she didn't reciprocate.

"When you told me what you wanted to do, it was because the Bastler is bad. He is wood rot and wildfire. And we have to stop him. I want to help, still."

"No, Aroha," Abi said. "We're going to keep you safe."

"I don't want to be safe. I want to be good. I want to be an axe, the sharp bit," Aroha said, looking Odo in the eye as she spoke.

Odo smiled widely. "You can stay on the roof, and jump on him and then I'll kill him. Wood rot and wildfire." He chuckled.

"No. I said no," Abi stood up. "This is it. I've had enough of trying to change the rules. Why can you not just let this continue to happen the way you originally said?"

"How can you hide, when this idea can work? I couldn't have watched her. And look at how fast this new girl is learning, she'll try something soon, too. There is no option here. This isn't just a plan: it is the plan. You are barely alive. Live a little harder." Odo said, holding Aroha's good hand. Aroha wasn't smiling, her face was drawn.

Abi didn't move, just watched as Odo stood holding the hand of a girl that looked so much like both of them. What were the chances? Was it a sign?

"I feel pain," Aroha said.

"It's your arm, yes," Abi replied, still watching Odo.

"No, here," Aroha said. Dropping Odo's hand, she pressed at her chest, near her heart.

"Guilt," Odo said, trying to keep the smile out of his voice. "You feel guilt."

"Because I want to help, and I made everything worse."

"I know that feeling," Odo said. "A promise doesn't always mean what it seems, does it?"

Odo looked at Abi as he spoke, hoping the words would sink in, find purchase in a wife that he had started to thaw just like the weather outside. He hoped, breathed, and wished, that it would work. And then he remembered, and spoke. "Live a little harder."

Abi went to bed, but before she did, she nodded.

The Bastler's orange wagon arrived on the horizon with the sun a few weeks later. They'd removed Aroha's splint and moved her up to the roof as soon as they noticed the wagon in front of the sun. The Bastler arrived and disembarked, his coat with its purple inner lining seemed to shimmer and float behind him. He smiled and his sharpened top canine teeth seemed to threaten them.

Abi squeezed Odo's hand and whispered to herself, "Live a little harder."

"All this time and you two still hold hands? I am impressed. I had believed you both too... lost," the Bastler said.

Odo swallowed and squeezed back. "No one has left the forest since your last visit."

"Your arms are getting bigger," the Bastler said, walking over and squeezing Odo's left arm. "But your lies are just as bad as last time."

The Bastler pushed them aside and walked towards the cottage. Behind him, Odo and Abi stared at the chimney. Aroha wasn't well hidden, too tall for the chimney by far. But the Bastler's eyes were set on the door and he charged in, his hands out like last time, thumbs crossing with his fingers out like wings.

Abi and Odo moved to their spot, just outside the front door, so that the axe was within reach and the lip of the roof was where the Bastler would have to stop to speak to them. When they looked up, they saw her being pulled towards the Bastler whenever his hands aimed towards her. The rope tied between her and the chimney kept her in place.

And then the Bastler stormed out and stopped right in front of them. When he smiled his vicious smile, even more chilling now that his anger was oozing out, they saw that a third tooth was sharp.

"Where is he? I know there is one. Do you know what it costs me to keep spies among the Apteryx and to receive their missives? Sending letters across the world takes months. I shall not wait any longer. If you cannot provide the man, I will..."

The Bastler searched for words. While he searched, Aroha unhooked the rope and began moving silently towards him so that she could jump.

"If you cannot provide him, I will take... you instead." The Bastler pointed at Abi.

And then his arm slammed into the ground as Aroha landed on top of him. Odo grabbed the axe and swung it with both hands at the Bastler's head as Aroha scrambled away. The Bastler's eyes widened as he saw the axe moving towards his face. Abi couldn't watch, turning to hide.

Someone snapped their fingers, as if a twig had snapped underfoot, and the axe never landed. Abi, Odo, and Aroha were frozen, unable to move anything but their eyes.

"Ouch," the Bastler said as he stood up and shook his arm. "That was unexpected."

Then he looked and saw Aroha on her knees, trying to push herself to her feet with one arm, and he smiled. And Aroha noticed that three of his top front teeth were sharpened, as well as the canines. One for each person now frozen in place.

She tried to recoil at the way it made her skin crawl, but she could not move. The Bastler pulled her up until she was standing.

"A broken arm?" he said, looking at Aroha's arm. "I'm just... I'm so furious."

The Bastler unhid Abi's eyes and stood her up straight. He took the axe from Odo and did the same to him. Then he faced them towards Aroha. All three of them were staring wildly, the whites of their eyes showing just as much as their irises.

The Bastler reached up and opened Aroha's mouth and did the check he normally did on the new people.

Then he grabbed a tooth and pulled. The tooth came out smoothly, roots and all. A burst of air escaped from Aroha as the gum began to bleed and, for the first time in her life, she began to cry.

The Bastler sighed to himself and did the same thing to the first of his sharpened teeth. He yelled quickly before replacing the space in his teeth with Aroha's tooth. His bleeding stopped and he threw his sharpened tooth into the woodpile. He repeated it for all his sharpened teeth, even his canines. By the second tooth, Aroha began to choke as the blood filled her mouth, and the Bastler leaned her forward until the blood was rolling down her chin and pooling on the ground before her.

The Bastler yelled once more as he fitted the final tooth. He looked at Aroha's face after shaking himself slightly. He moved down so that she could look him in the eye.

"That was unpleasant, wasn't it? I wonder how many of you have ever cried before. Abi and Odo are wonderful; I bet you didn't even know what crying was when you hurt yourself. You are so new. You are the product of consequences. Of scales and balances, of the Apteryx making trees out of their enemies."

The Bastler took Aroha and carried her to the back of the wagon. He placed her inside, surrounding her in orange walls and locking the door before turning back to Odo and Abi.

After the Bastler had left with their daughter, the trapdoor wouldn't open. No matter how much they pushed, it wouldn't move.

"We need to get out soon," Abi said.

"I hope we die," Odo said.

Abi hit him, hard, in the shoulder.

"What was that for?" Odo asked.

"He's going to keep her safe, and we're going to get her back. Even if we have to beg."

"He said it himself, we don't dictate terms. We don't have a chance here."

Abi hit him again. "This is your fault. You were supposed to be watching her, and you were supposed to be saving her."

"I wasn't watching her. She was with you," Odo said.

"I don't mean physically watching her. You're a father, you're meant to keep her safe. Look what you did," Abi said.

"I tried."

"Well, you failed," Abi said.

They were in darkness. Their last candle had died three days ago.

"I swear," Abi said. "You need to stop this. We do things properly now, no more changing the rules. We're here until the war is over."

Odo nodded in the darkness.

"Promise me," Abi said, hitting her husband in the shoulder again.

"I promise," Odo said.

And then the trapdoor creaked, and clicked open. And Odo heaved and pushed it open so that they could both climb up. They could see quite clearly that the dust had literally settled since the Bastler had left. Their vegetable garden was in trouble, weeds and over-ripe fruit rotting. And there, in the middle of their yard was a sapling pine tree.

"Where did that come from?" Abi asked.

"I don't know..." Odo said. They stared at the tree, not touching, until the sun began to hit the horizon. Odo reached out to touch Abi's shoulder, and then let his hand drop. Then he went outside and began clearing up under the tree. "I can't find the bottle."

"What?" Abi asked.

"The teeth, Aroha's teeth. They're gone."

"I don't care," Abi said. "Tend the garden."

The Bastler stood before them and smiled. Though the smile was filled with Aroha's teeth, they fit perfectly in his mouth.

"I do not know what to do with you two. That's twice you've... Should I send bark-beetles after the pine tree again? Should I hurt your daughter?" The Bastler ran his tongue over his teeth, spending longer on his canines, as if he were wondering why they weren't sharp.

"The Apteryx taught me about consequences. They didn't intend to. It's their magic. I don't believe they themselves know how they do it. They talk about it as weight scales, with the tooth on one side and the person on the other. The cost of turning a man into a tree is your tooth. The scale balances. They're happy with that.

"It felt wrong to me, the idea never settled in my brain. Every time I tried to shut the door on it, it kicked up dust and swirled around. I couldn't shut the door on it until I knew. As it turns out, they were equating the wrong things. Cost and consequence aren't the same. Like with you. You promised to stay here because you wanted to be with your wife. The consequence is that you lost your daughter. But the cost? Your autonomy, your love, your happiness. All because one of the Apteryx took a liking to me and showed me a secret. Poor man, I haven't thought about him in a long time."

As the Bastler spoke, he arranged both Odo and Abi as if they were waving him goodbye. As he moved them, his breath, hot and warm, hit them on their necks and faces. It was fresh, and gummy, as if he had chewed pine resin. When he was happy with how they looked in their farewells he smiled and clapped his hands slightly. Then he got back into his wagon and snapped his fingers again.

Odo fell to his knees. Abi stayed standing, stoic. She didn't drop her hand, leaving it raised as if waving.

"Come now, traditions and all," The Bastler said. Holding the reins casually and staring out the corner of his eyes at Odo to prompt him.

"Sir Bastler, please. Return our daughter," Odo said, all hope and faith gone from his voice.

"No," the Bastler said. And he raised the reins.

"Please, Sir," Abi said. "Take me instead."

The Bastler stopped and his horses did, too.

"Repeat yourself," the Bastler said.

"I said, take me instead," Abi said. She hadn't moved, her hand still raised as if to wave goodbye.

"Why would I do that when I can punish you like this?" he smiled with two sharp canine teeth. There was no sound from Aroha in the wagon, still frozen.

"I can't do this anymore, please. Take me and return our daughter." Abi turned to Odo and lowered her hand to his shoulder. "He is a good father."

The Bastler watched and sucked on his new teeth.

"On one condition," the Bastler said.

"Anything," Abi and Odo said together.

"I don't want you, Abi," the Bastler said. "I want Odo."

"Yes, Sir," Odo said, standing up.

"No, Odo. Please, don't," Abi started but Odo quieted her with his hands on her shoulders.

"You two will be okay. You will have Aroha back, and you can get me back too. It is a trade, I am not disappearing forever," Odo said. He didn't cry or fight.

"You promised me," Abi said.

Odo ignored her and turned to the Bastler.

"What do I need to do?" Odo asked.

"Go stand by the pine and raise your hands above your head," the Bastler said.

And so Odo did, and Abi tried to follow him.

"You stay here, Abi," the Bastler said, lifting up his hand to snap, as a threat. He got off the wagon, and walked over to Abi until they were staring eye to eye. He raised his hand until Abi could feel the wolf fur brushing her cheek, and while she stared into his eyes, the Bastler clicked his fingers. And then he stepped back and smiled, four sharp teeth smiling in Abi's face.

The Bastler got back onto his wagon and started the horses and Abi watched, afraid to turn around and look behind her.

"Please Sir Bastler. Aroha?" Abi called.

"Keep tending to the people. Until the Apteryx war is over. Then I will return them both."

"Their war with whom?" Abi asked.

"Everyone."

The Bastler left, whistling softly to himself.

The Bastler had noticed first. He had pointed at the tomatoes that Abi was holding.

"It will be a girl. Congratulations."

Odo was putting the forest's newest man into the back of the Bastler's orange wagon, with smiles and helping hands.

"I don't think they're boys or girls, Sir Bastler," Abi laughed.

The Bastler clicked his tongue in annoyance. His hands spread wide, his cloak showing its purple internal stitching behind him.

"My dear Abi, you are pregnant," he smiled, his pointed canines caressing his lips as they peeked out.

"Excuse me? How?" Odo asked as he shut the wagon door.

"Probably the same way it happens to everyone else," the Bastler said. He was holding back from clicking his tongue again. He did like these two; they were carefree and just happy. Happy with the trade.

"No, I mean, I didn't realise that was possible."

"Time hasn't stopped, my friends. You will still age, but as long as the forest keeps providing, you will keep breathing."

The Bastler had climbed onto his wagon and tipped a hat that had appeared out of nowhere, a pheasant feather stuffed into it.

"What will you name her?" The Bastler asked.

"We don't know, we'll have to talk about it," Abi said as Odo joined her, his hand around her waist. Odo was beside himself, hiding his excitement as best he could until the Bastler was gone. Abi was scared, but she didn't know why.

"The Apteryx have a word in their language: 'Aroha.' It means 'beloved.'" The Bastler dipped his hat and watched the couple hold each other.

"It's a pretty name," Odo said.

"It's a very pretty name," Abi said.

Two sharp teeth peeked out through the Bastler's lips as he smiled.

When summer comes to Vakning Forest it doesn't bring a heat wave. The air is humid but manageable and the animals that were silent for so long bring a quiet version of their music to the forest. As the summer extends itself, it grips the pine trees and pulls them towards the sun, ever higher over the path that leads out of the forest.

Outside the forest, where a path begins, is a cottage. Abi Tremord lives in this cottage. It has a red roof and brown walls, and a whitewashed fence. In the yard stand two pine trees. One is a sapling, the other is as tall as the forest.

If you liked Thom Connors story "The Forest of New People", leave a comment online at Metaphorosis. Authors love that!

About the story

Prior to being a musician, I was a Bastler. The story was autobiographical.

Seriously though, one of the things I love about short stories is that they allow you to explore things that may not have received the same attention you believe they deserved. Magical consequences are a big one. I loved the idea of magic that has consequences on the other side of the world and how that would look. I've been messing around with this idea for a while and could never figure out a way to make it work until I started to plan my move to the US. Doing so reminded me that I enjoy moving and a lot of people don't. As such this story focuses on people with different views on how happy they are with staying in one place.

A question for the author

Q: Do you make art other than prose? What kind, and how is it different?

A: In what now feels like another lifetime, I was a musician. I was that kid in school who wrote lyrics in class, and read when the teacher was speaking, and for most of my late teens and early twenties, I played shows regularly. In retrospect, it was the lyric writing that I enjoyed the most. That realisation is what pushed me into prose, then flash fiction, then short stories, and novels. While I still compose music and sing along to Taylor Swift in the car, I don't do shows anymore. But, I don't really know how to describe the difference between playing in front of a few hundred, or thousand, people and having a story come out. Can they be compared? In terms of writing them, songs are bursts of creativity and emotion. Stores require more planning, and definitely more time.

About the author

Thom Connors writes from his Macbook where the ' ' key is missing. This means that he refuses to use wors with the letter ' ', wherever possible. As such, talking of his love for 'ark fantasy tends to result in laughter. Thom's longer works tend towards the fantasy fiction, while his shorter pieces are often general fiction.

The Dream Diary of Monk Anchin

Felicity Drake

I went to the museum's special exhibition on Seitokuji Temple alone, as was my habit. In the corner, there was a glass case full of portraits of the temple's famous poets.

The last portrait made me stop to take a second look. Unlike the other monks, this one was gazing directly out at the viewer. His face was painted in the standard Yamato-e style, just lines for the eyes and a hook for the nose, but there was something strangely expressive about the minimalist painting: a slight tension in the angle of his eyes, one hand holding a brush in midair, as if hesitating.

The bald little monk stared up at me out of his portrait, as if he were trying to speak to me. The plaque beneath the painting read:

Monk Anchin (1244-1316)
Collection of Seitokuji, 14th century, artist unknown

There was no background or architectural detail in the plain portrait, but there was a lit candle-stand beside him, a common pictorial convention for depicting nighttime. Why would the artist take pains to portray Anchin, unlike the other poets, writing by candlelight?

Taking my notebook from my purse, I added Anchin's name to my notes on the exhibit. He couldn't have been a particularly notable poet. In high school, I had made a habit of memorizing poetry—which endeared me to my classical Japanese teacher and precisely nobody else—and even I had never heard of Anchin.

Before I left, I even spent 3,000 yen on the glossy exhibition catalogue, so I could take home a copy of the painting. My own research specialty is medieval Japanese women's diaries, and at this stage in my career, there isn't time to waste exploring intriguing tidbits outside my field. But seeing Anchin's little face, I couldn't resist the urge to find out what he had to say, what seemed to be on the tip of his tongue in his portrait.

It took some doing, but I tracked down a journal article about Anchin. The issue came out of the university's offsite storage facility crumbling and dusty. It was an obscure journal from the 1930s, with an article written by a professor I'd never heard of: "Annotated Selections from the Dream Diary of Monk Anchin."

I'll include an excerpt from the introduction here:

Monk Anchin's remarkable diaries are a treasure of the Kamakura period that have been overlooked for too long. Previous scholars have neglected his diaries, perhaps because of their length and the difficulties of his written style. Notably, in 1834 the scholar Ishizawa Takeru dismissed Anchin's diary as "an idiosyncratic work with minor poetic value and little historical interest."

It is regrettable that because of this early scholarly misinterpretation, no one has attempted a full transcription of the diary. Ishizawa reached his conclusion by reading the brief excerpt traditionally contained in 19th century anthologies, and I suspect that Anchin's dream diary has not been read from beginning to end in all the intervening centuries.

It is true that Anchin's diary is a singularly ahistorical text. He offers no information about daily life or special events at the temple; the diary reveals to us very little about the life of a monk at Seitokuji in the Kamakura period. Similarly, although his classical Chinese poetry was well-received by his contemporaries, subsequent generations considered his verses undistinguished.

But his diary is, nonetheless, a monumental and unique work: with fifty volumes representing the fifty years of his life after he took Buddhist vows, it is perhaps the world's longest continuous dream diary, full of insights into the unconscious mind of a highly literate, devout, and, yes, idiosyncratic man.

We can speculate about Anchin's life from court and temple records. Born the fifth son of a minor aristocrat, Anchin achieved some early success as a poet, but never received an official appointment at court. He never married, and took the tonsure in 1266, at the age of twenty-two. Although he spent the rest of his long life at Seitokuji, he was by no means disconnected from society; he contributed poems to social gatherings at the capital and frequently traveled on long pilgrimages.

I have selected the following excerpts from Monk Anchin's diary on the basis of their poetic or psychological significance. It is my hope that their publication will contribute to a reexamination of his life and work.

Since nothing had been written about Anchin in all the intervening decades, the professor's hopes had apparently gone unfulfilled.

Dreams were an unconventional choice of subject for a medieval diarist. But if he was best known for his dream diary, it explained why the anonymous artist had painted Anchin, brush in hand, beside a lit candle. As if he had just awoken from a dream and was hurrying to write it down. I've always been a vivid dreamer myself; when I was a teenager, I'd even kept a dream diary for a few years. I shredded it before I went to college, which I now regretted.

I settled down on my couch with a glass of wine and the diary excerpts. That was how I spent most of my nights alone at home, anyway, with Bach, Bordeaux, and books. And there was a certain transgressive pleasure in spending an evening away from my research or my students' papers, in the unfamiliar company of Monk Anchin.

First entry, undated but presumed to be from 1266:
Last night I saw a dream so strange I was compelled to take up my brush, to write it before it fled from memory. In my dream, a woman came to my bedchamber and sat beside my pillow.

"It's a shame when a good-looking man takes vows so young," she scolded me. "You've robbed the women of Kyoto. I'm terribly put out. At least we can meet in dreams, can't we?"

Her smile as she teased me was incomparably lovely. She outstretched her arms to me, and I saw that she wore her robe turned inside out—which once was thought to bring good dreams, as in Ono no Komachi's poems of longing.

When I reached for her, my hands passed through her body as if through mist, and she disappeared.

1267, the new year:
The first dream of the new year tells what is to come. A dream of a hawk is said to be auspicious, but what should I make of the dream I saw? Two hawks flew together through a clear sky. A cloud came and went, and there was only one hawk remaining.

1273, tenth month:
In last night's dream, I had retreated from the temple into solitude in a brushwood hut. There I would live in absolute simplicity, apart from the vulgar world.

A female pilgrim knocked at my door and asked for shelter from the rain. Although I should have turned her away (as the lady of Eguchi turned away the wandering monk Saigyō, so as not to tempt him), I allowed her inside and made her tea to warm her. We composed poems about the rain.

There is no escape from worldly desire, is there? Not in a temple, not in seclusion, and not even in one's own heart.

Anchin's dream reminded me of a dream I'd had as a teenager.

In my dream, I was waiting on a train platform. Rain fell down in a curtain from the overhang. I was in my school uniform, and my shoes and socks were soaking wet; a puddle grew on the concrete at my feet. The platform was deserted. Trains passed by without stopping, as if I were the only person left in the city.

A man joined me on the platform—an ordinary-looking salaryman in a gray suit, carrying a briefcase. He bought two cans of hot tea from the vending machine, and although all the benches on the platform were empty, he sat right next to me. But I wasn't afraid. We drank our canned tea together, as if we were the best of friends.

I was so young when I had the dream, I could hardly remember any more than that. It must have been written down in my old dream diary, but that was long gone. But I still remembered the thrill of it: to have the attention of a man, to be alone with a man, had seemed naughty and wonderful. It had felt so real. I remember waking up and hurrying to the mirror to see if my cheeks were red.

That had been just the silliness of a girl, of course. In my waking life, men had never paused to look at me, and I had never dared to speak to them. Since I'd started working at a women's college, it had become even easier to avoid men. I had been on a few dates, arranged for me by my worried parents or friends, but the silence had always stretched too long, and I'd never had a second date. There weren't many Monk Anchins left in the world, not many men interested in listening to a plain middle-aged woman talk about the fourteenth century, or in sharing a pot of tea and reading poetry together. 'Born in the wrong century,' my colleagues sometimes said about me, which I know they didn't intend to be cruel.

I brushed a few fragments of the journal's yellowing paper off my lap and set it aside for the night.

That Saturday afternoon, I sat at my usual table in the back corner of the department store's top-floor café, carefully arranging my papers and pens around the delicate china saucer and plate.

It was 900 yen for a thin slice of dark chocolate gateau and a cup of milk tea. Just a little luxury, something to sweeten the routine of grading papers. I hadn't made it to that coveted position of full-time professor at a proper university, where perhaps even grading papers would be a joy; at forty-one, I was still an adjunct lecturer at a two-year women's college, correcting grammatical errors and encouraging my pupils to look up information in books rather than on Wikipedia.

After an hour's work, I set aside the half-finished stack of papers and pulled out the rest of Monk Anchin's diary instead, savoring the bitter chocolate gateau as I read the last diary entry, written shortly before his death at the age of seventy-two.

1316, seventh month:

Now that I have been celibate for fifty years, all that was left of desire should have long since burned away, and yet...

I've seen the same woman in my dreams for years and years. I believe that I saw her once with my waking eyes. Not when I was a young man in the capital, and she a beautiful maiden, but when we were both withered and old.

It was at the height of cherry blossom season, when the temple was crowded with travelers. Through the crack of a door, I saw a little girl pretty and fresh as blooming dianthus, playing beside her grandmother. Unaware she was being observed, the woman didn't conceal her face; whatever beauty she'd had in her youth had long since faded, but her eyes were sharp, and her voice as low and sweet as a koto string as she read aloud to her granddaughter. And I knew it was her—not the greatest beauty, not the most charming or the most learned—but the same woman I'd seen in my dreams. I saw her in the waking world only this once, perhaps fifty years too late.

In my dream that night, she came to me, and she said, "When you were twenty, and I only seventeen, we both attended the Kamo festival. You stood beside my carriage then. I saw you, so dashing in your cap. I lifted my blinds in hope that you might catch a glimpse and slip a poem to me, but you turned your head left instead of right, and then you were gone. If you had turned your head right, do you think we would have known each other by daylight, not only in dreams?"

Last night, I saw her again. There were five-colored threads tied to her hands, which she offered to me to hold, like a bodhisattva welcoming me to the Pure Land.

"We'll part soon, even in dreams. I'll see you again," she said.

"Will we share a single lotus in the world to come?" I asked her.

"Do you think it's so easy to become a buddha? In seven hundred years, I'll make sure to come here once again. Promise me that you'll find me at Seitokuji. Promise me that you won't forget."

How appropriate that I saw her on Tanabata, a celebration of reunited lovers. Seven hundred years—whether Seitokuji still stands, or whether it is ashes, I'll be here once more.

In my career, I've read dozens of medieval diaries. I haven't found a publisher for my monograph yet, but still, I believe I'm something of an expert. Most medieval diaries, at least the ones that survive today, were intended for broader literary consumption, and therefore were thick with classical and poetic allusions, but Anchin's prose was unornamented and personal—almost uncomfortably so. It was unlike any medieval text I'd studied. I briefly wondered whether I should prepare a paper on the dream diary of Monk Anchin for a future meeting of the Medieval Diary Literature Research Group, but I couldn't imagine speaking about him in public. I wanted—strange as it was—to keep him for myself.

Monk Anchin died in 1316; thanks to his diary entry, I knew that he must have died shortly after Tanabata, the seventh day of the seventh month. It was a rather stunning coincidence that this summer happened to mark seven hundred years after his death, the year that he promised to return to Seitokuji to find his dream-bride.

I tried and failed to put it all out of my head. Over the next weeks, I read and reread Anchin's diary. I returned to the museum exhibit to sneak forbidden photographs of his portrait. And in my dreams, I saw: a pair of dark eyes, a crescent moon, a curl of smoke, half a line of poetry, dark woods stretching out beyond the cypress pillars of a temple's veranda.

One night, after the stimulation of Glenn Gould's magnificent Goldberg Variations and perhaps a too-generous pour of wine, I visited Seitokuji's official website. The temple still existed, and like some other temples struggling to pay the bills in an irreligious age, it offered overnight lodging for tourists. In addition to a gallery of inviting photographs showing off their austere guest quarters, contemplative gardens, and delicate vegetarian meals, there was an online reservation form.

According to the Gregorian calendar, Tanabata fell on July 7th, which was right before final exams and not a convenient time for me to disappear. But Anchin would have been using the old lunisolar calendar system, and the seventh day of the seventh month in the old calendar actually fell on Tuesday, August 9th (according, at least, to the online calculators I used). That was the summer holiday, and no one would notice if I left the city to go on a little pilgrimage.

With just a few cabernet-emboldened clicks, I had my temple reservations and train tickets booked. Perhaps it was silly of me, but I couldn't help but think that someone ought to be there to commemorate his life. Was I the only person alive who cared about Monk Anchin? No one had ever bothered to fully transcribe his diary. No academic had written an article about him since the 1930s. How sad to think that he had lived, died, and been utterly forgotten. What if he returned, after the promised seven centuries, and no one were there at Seitokuji to see it? I didn't want to let the date pass unwitnessed. That was all.

Monday evening, the night before Tanabata on the old calendar, I arrived at Seitokuji. I'd visited plenty of temples for research trips or sightseeing, to the point where all the intricately carved transoms and mossy rocks started to blur together, but this felt different. With every worn step I climbed, every statue I admired, I imagined that Anchin had stood in the same spot seven hundred years before. I'd never had a personal connection to a temple before. I had to remind myself that I still didn't have one: I was engaging in shallow literary tourism and self-indulgent fantasy, nothing more.

There were other guests staying at the temple as well. In the public bath, I sat across from a pair of little old ladies from Osaka chatting about the next stop on their vacation. In the corridor, I saw one of the temple's monks struggling to communicate in English and hand gestures with a family of Chinese tourists, and I wondered how they'd ended up at out-of-the-way Seitokuji. Seitokuji had a long enough history, but I'd assumed international tourists would be likelier to visit Kiyomizudera for its waterfall, or Ryōanji for its rock garden.

My room was spare and elegant, just bare mats, a futon, and a buckwheat-husk pillow. No television or wifi, which I appreciated; other than the slight buzz of the electric lights, I could imagine that I was back in the thirteenth century. A monk brought my dinner in on a tray: tiny bowls of tofu, vegetables, and rice, delicately flavored and artfully arranged. I wondered if Anchin had eaten so well here in his day, or if temple fare had been humbler then.

After dinner, I brought out my reading. Thanks to some archival wrangling, I'd gotten my hands on a copy of a facsimile edition of Anchin's diary. The copy quality was only so-so, and it was frequently indecipherable, but still it felt like a miracle to see Anchin's own handwriting. From the boldness or faintness of his brushstrokes, I could imagine the passages he had rushed to write, or the places he had hesitated, brush in hand.

After dark, I went out to the temple's veranda alone. Here, far from the city, I could hear cicadas singing and see the stars.

Anchin must have seen this same night sky, I thought, seven hundred years ago.

I sat on the edge of the veranda and stared up at the distant, unchanging stars. In my head, phrases from Anchin's poetry shattered and recombined. I felt so close to him here.

The faint scent of incense tickled my nose. No—cigarette smoke. My nose wrinkled and I had to pinch it to keep from sneezing. I glanced back over my shoulder and discovered the culprit: the teenage boy from the family of Chinese tourists I'd seen earlier that evening. He was leaning against one of the temple's cypress pillars, smoking a cigarette and staring off into space.

Well, the presence of an intruder, and one so rude as to smoke a cigarette in a nine-hundred-year-old temple, damaged my reverie. But I was hardly about to leave my perfect spot for stargazing. I'd been here first!

I tried to refocus. The smell of cigarettes was distracting.

I looked over again, and saw the boy stubbing out his cigarette and neatly disposing of the butt in a portable ashtray. Polite. I thought he might go back inside then, but no such luck—instead, he sat down cross-legged on the veranda, no more than a few meters away from me. He pulled out a little notebook from the pocket of his oversized jacket and hunched over it, pen in hand.

I took the time to look him over while he was staring down at the notebook. He couldn't have been much older than nineteen or twenty, and his gangly frame still had that elbows-and-knees pointiness of adolescence. His hair was long and shaggy, hiding some of his acne-scarred face.

Trying to retain some sense of solitude, I turned away and closed my eyes. I had come here to be with Anchin, to see if he had returned after the promised seven hundred years. Silly, yes, but...

My mind drifted, and among the cicadas' song, I heard another sound: the scratching of pen on paper. I glanced to the side, and there was the boy—biting his lower lip and writing away in his notebook. He looked utterly absorbed. My irritation at him ebbed slightly; in him, I saw a shadow of the bookish girl I had been when I was his age.

He looked up at me, and we were caught awkwardly staring at each other. I nodded politely at him—he stared at me, then hunched his shoulders and offered a tiny smile.

"No Japanese," he apologized, in heavily accented English.

"No Chinese," I answered, and I couldn't help but smile in return. I wondered why he and his family had come here.

I thought it might end there, but he stood, crossed the gap between us in just a few steps, and sat down again, right beside me.

"Can you read this?" he asked, again in English, and handed me his notebook.

He had been writing poetry—poetry in classical Chinese, at that! What a rare bird. Did they teach poetic composition in Chinese schools these days? My own students were about his age, and it was a struggle to get them to read even the most accessible poems, much less compose their own.

I took a moment to look over the poem. Clumsy in places, almost brilliant in others. A sudden pain ran through my chest. His handwriting was charming, neat and somehow masculine in the boldness of his penstrokes. And the poem wasn't bad at all.

"I can." For a few minutes I didn't return the notebook to him.

He handed the pen over to me, and I realized that he was hoping I would write a response. Ridiculous! As a medievalist, I'd read my share of poetry in classical Chinese, but I'd never written a single line of my own. Instead, I wrote out a quatrain that I remembered from Monk Anchin's diary. Anchin's poetry was in classical Chinese, so the boy could read it, and his style seemed to suit the atmosphere of the night.

I handed the notebook back to the boy, and he bent over it for a moment—then his head snapped up, and he stared at me open-mouthed. His brow tightened, and he said slowly, deliberately, "That is... very... good," as if it caused him physical pain to be unable to say more, to express what he was thinking. His English was almost as bad as mine.

"It is not mine," I admitted, because I could hardly take credit for Anchin's genius.

"Show me more?"

We wrote back and forth to each other. Some of his poems were his, some were famous verses that even I recognized. I replied to him with Anchin's poems, some half-remembered Li Bai, and a few poorly turned couplets of my own.

"My name." He wrote it out and pronounced it for me in Chinese; I had to repeat it several times before he nodded. I wrote my name and did the same for him. He looked so serious while he practiced saying my name.

The crescent moon had risen high above us while we wrote. I pointed to it, and he stared up at it with such earnestness, as if he'd never seen the night sky before. My throat hurt, my chest hurt. The stars reflected in his wide, dark eyes.

Suddenly, I was struck by the overpowering urge to tell him about Anchin. I hadn't mentioned Anchin or my unseemly obsession with a long-dead monk, not to anyone.

"Seven hundred years ago," I began. If only he had understood Japanese! It was a struggle to find the words in English. "There was a man. Here." I had forgotten how to say *monk* in English.

"At this temple?"

"Yes. He wrote this." I gestured to the poems I had written. "He saw dreams... every night, many dreams of a woman. He said he would return here—after seven hundred years—today—to meet her."

His forehead wrinkled in confusion, evidently unable to find the right word in English. He wrote a phrase in Chinese in the notebook, punctuated with a question mark. At first, I didn't recognize the simplified characters, but then I understood: *reincarnation?*

"Yes, that," I answered, pointing to the word in the notebook.

"Do you believe?" he asked.

"I don't know."

"I don't know also." His shoulders hunched forward and he stared down at the aged wood of the veranda: "I had a dream last year. I saw this temple, the moon, the... statue of Guanyin? Like tonight."

It was impossible, of course, but there were times one wanted to believe in the impossible. I had to acknowledge it: if Anchin had come back, it was in this boy's body. His great, dark eyes; his bold handwriting; his clumsy, potent poetry; his ungainly hands trembling in his lap as he tried to tell me about his dreams.

Why did he have to be a boy? Why did he have to be born in the wrong country? After seven hundred years waiting, couldn't we have been spared this?

"It's late. I should sleep," I said, because I didn't know the right words to say to him in English or in any language.

"Don't go."

A boy half my age, with acne-pitted cheeks and eyes as big and trusting as a golden retriever's... It would have been wrong to kiss him. I was old enough to be his mother. So I didn't—I didn't even touch his hand.

We sat together on the veranda without speaking, without touching, until the sun rose and the temple bells rang to wake the monks for the morning services.

It would have been rude to skip services after staying at the temple, so I dutifully attended, kneeling in the back of the hall. I hadn't slept a wink. The scent of incense, the dull gold gleam of the image of Kannon in the altar, and the monotonous chanting of the monks made my head spin.

I had met Anchin—had looked into his eyes and recognized him —and still the world continued to exist. The vulgar world, into which one or both of us had been reborn in the wrong time and place.

After services, the family of Chinese tourists said goodbye to the monks and hauled their bags down off the veranda.

I watched as if in a dream. The father swung open the trunk of the car and began loading up suitcases. The mother opened the passenger side door.

The boy tapped his mother on the shoulder, then ran back to the temple. He vaulted up the stairs to the veranda and stopped short, just a few feet shy of me. And then he stared, as if he were waiting for me to say something.

I tried to memorize his face. This was my last chance.

"Seven hundred years," I told him. "You will come again in seven hundred years. I will wait."

Would Seitokuji Temple still stand in the year 2716? Seven hundred years—I couldn't conceive of it. Even the few decades of solitude remaining in this lifetime were too much to bear.

He stared and stared, and then he shook his head. "I will study Japanese. When I graduate college... I will come here again. Two years. You will wait—you promise?"

I wanted to tell him that that was insane, that he was a young man with promise and a life and country and language of his own. That I was too old for him, old and strange and unbeautiful, not at all worth uprooting a life for. That I was willing to wait until the next lifetime, when perhaps we would be born in the same decade, the same country. That my delusions about Anchin were born of middle-aged loneliness and regret, that he was being swept up in teenage melodrama, that we both knew perfectly well *there is no such thing as reincarnation...*

But how could I say all that to him in English?

Instead, I said: "Two years, or seven hundred years. Either is okay. I will wait."

He reached out and touched the back of my hand with his fingertips. And then his mother called for him in Chinese, and he was gone, running off like a deer back to the car.

I watched him climb into the backseat of the car. The door closed. The car drove out of the parking lot and onto the winding road descending the mountain. It disappeared among the trees.

If you liked Felicity Drake's story "The Dream Diary of Monk Anchin", leave a comment online at Metaphorosis. Authors love that!

About the story

Felicity Drake is a writer based in New York. She writes fiction and interactive fiction.

www.felicitydrake.com, @DrakeFelicity

A question for the author

Q: Aliens. Are they out there?

A: In a vast universe, surely they are—although maybe in unfamiliar forms, or so far away that we can't meet them (yet!).

It's exciting to think that something so consequential is still totally unknown. It's good to have a little sense of mystery in life.

About the author

A few years ago, I went to see a special exhibition at the Idemitsu Museum in Tokyo, and I was particularly charmed by a portrait much like the one in the story.

Researching or translating premodern texts can feel like having a conversation with someone from the past, sometimes in a surprisingly intimate way. I wanted to write a story where that feeling of intimacy goes one step further, and to explore different ways people can connect (through reading, writing, dreams, language barriers, or reincarnation).

It Feels Like Déjà Vu

Phong Quan

I open my eyes and do the first thing I always do after running the gravitational field generator: remember my name. "My name is Jon, I'm a physicist," I say. Nothing comes after that. Thoughts begin to form and rise, and just as quickly sink back down; I feel like I'm struggling to stay afloat in a river that's slowly dragging me under, trapped in its constantly shifting currents. But I fight it. I know I have to fight it because… because that's what I always do.

"My name is Jon," I say again. The words are familiar and comforting and I grab onto them as if they can somehow pull me out of the river's rushing eddies and free of the haze I'm swimming in. I look around and see that I'm sitting on a bed in a room I don't recognize. I need to though, I need to… find out where… and when? Where and when… the generator shifted me? It's always… somewhere I have a connection to…

"I live in an apartment on Central Park West," I say, and my thoughts snap into focus and the river seems to suddenly stop, and then disappear.

Of course, this is my bedroom. I get off my bed and look around: my phone is unplugged on the nightstand, the screen still on and telling me it's seven in the morning; my clothes are thrown haphazardly over my desk, and as I walk past my dresser I see stacks of books with titles like "Buddhism A-Z" and "You are Here". Mom keeps sending them and I keep promising but never having the time to read them.

I walk out of the bedroom and into a living room as messy and chaotic as my life must be even in this reality: empty take-out boxes cover my small dinner table, dozens of unopened packages from Amazon litter the floor, and piles of mail lean against stacks of paper. Next to my TV, and covered with the same fine layer of dust, the hand-carved wooden Buddha Mom gave me for my birthday sits silently contemplating the disorder. I really haven't been a good son.

But everything seems right so far, though I know that doesn't mean anything until I get to the lab and run the calculations. I smile anyway, glad to feel some memories I'm sure are real coming back. I make my way through the mess of my living room to the large windows and look outside. Across the street I see the red-orange leaves of the trees that mark the edge of Central Park.

My smile slips. This isn't right. This was a big shift—a change this large hasn't happened in a while.

I feel the memory come to me then the same way they always do: washing over me in a tingling wave of déjà vu. I remember standing here, looking across the street at the bright green leaves of the trees that mark the edge of Central Park. Then and now, I turn and see something I hadn't noticed before.

"It's a lotus flower," she says. "It should bloom by the end of summer if you manage not to kill it first. I think even you'll be okay with this one though—it's super easy to take care of. You just need to keep the water level right, and then just let it grow." She gently brushes her fingers across the bulb of the flower before drawing her hand away.

The memory fades and I see the flower in the smooth white bowl by the window: a bright red teardrop on the face of a gray winter sky. Its familiarity tugs at me, but I know I've never seen it before. I've always been bad with plants—I even managed to kill my parents' lawn once by over-watering it.

I push it aside. It's a minor change and as long as I'm careful to keep my real memories separate from the fake ones from this shift, I'll be okay. Or at least I won't get any worse.

But I know that while this may be my apartment, I'm not *home*. I know that because the trees in Central Park are still standing and New York isn't flooded.

I call a car to take me to the lab at 50 Hudson Yards, where the generator always is. For some reason it's always there. The gravitational fields it generates are strong enough to warp space-time to such an extent that it can send me into another life and reality, but it never moves itself.

It'd probably be faster to take the train, but I want to keep a door between me and the city's rush hour madness. The time right after a test is the most dangerous. Anything—the faintest smell, the most innocuous sound—could trigger a flash of déjà vu and I would lose a bit more of my real self—of home—buried under the memories of lives I never lived.

So as the car takes me downtown and past the signs of damage that must have been from Superstorm Tammy—shuttered stores, missing trees and power lines, and construction around a damaged Javits Center that tells me I must be at least a few months removed from the storm this time—I imagine it even worse, I remember it even worse. I see rain pouring down in endless sheets between the steel and glass buildings. Trees and signs bend and creak and I feel water soaking into me as I slowly push against the howling wind. I hear an angry roar and look up to see water rushing down the street, swallowing up cars and people, their mouths open in screams I can't hear over the storm. Thunder fills my ears, my heart jumps into my throat, and the car stops.

"You have arrived at 50 Hudson Yards," it tells me.

I've been the only one in the main lab on the 40th floor for hours now, alone with rows of messy tables and computers. I'm in front of a digital board, scrawling down the last set of my equations. These are the equations that, once completed with data from this reality's generator to determine how space-time was warped and shifted, will calculate the coordinates that will send me another step towards home. I rush through them, not really thinking, just transcribing from memory as quickly as possible the numbers and symbols that, after countless shifts through different permutations of my life, still burn clearly in my mind: my compass, my north star, the map charting my way home.

"Jon! You're in early today."

I turn and see Saniya, my co-director of the project, walking towards me. She is, as always, impeccably dressed, her smart outfit a stark contrast to my wrinkled clothes. I don't know why but I'm strangely relieved to see her. She's my oldest friend and the most important person on the project after me (and the one who isn't trapped in a cycle of gravitationally generated distortions of reality), so I'm probably just glad to know she'll be here to help me with the calculations.

"Did you see the news?" She holds her tablet to my face and I see the front page of the New York Times: MAYOR CALLS FOR CITY TO REFUSE REFUGEES. "I still can't believe we re-elected this asshole," she says. Her words grab onto me with their familiarity and I feel my skin prickle with déjà vu.

"I can't believe we re-elected this asshole," Saniya says, slamming her empty drink back onto the bar. "It feels like a nightmare. He's lucky we barely stumbled through Tammy in one piece. I swear, I'd almost rather the city be flooded—"

I push the fake memory away and try to focus on what Saniya is saying, but hazy images of other lives flash through my mind: water rushing down 10th Avenue; the new mayor crying in the ruins of Battery Park as she promises never again; Saniya crying and the old mayor grinning in a sun-swept Battery Park as he promises to send her people away; smoke and fire and screams and people marching and then running through the streets. It used to be easy to tell the real memories from the fake, but after so long they've started to mix and run together in my mind like paint splashed against a wall, and now it's all I can do to make out the tattered ribbons of color that are the real me. It's scary slowly losing myself like this, but if I can just get the calculations right and go home…

"Jon, are you even listening to me? Sorry, is the death of democracy boring you?"

The sarcastic edge in Saniya's voice is something I do remember and I know I'd better pay attention now. "Sorry, yeah he's terrible," I say quickly.

She gives me an odd look and I know she's surprised by my listlessness. The truth is, I've forgotten how I feel about the mayor. I mean, I know how I'm supposed to feel—the man was an anti-science crypto-racist long before the first generator test—but the emotion of it faded away a long time ago. I don't even remember if he's supposed to win his re-election or if New York is supposed to have its first woman mayor anymore. It's another reminder of how much I've lost from home.

"Can you take a look at something?" I ask, changing the subject. I run my hand across the board and bring up the first page of my equations.

Saniya gives me a lingering look before shrugging and turning to the board. As she reads, her eyes widen slightly, and after several pages she turns towards me and half-states, half-asks, "These are new solutions to the field equations?"

I nod. She means Einstein's gravitational field equations—the foundations of our quantum modeling program. They're notoriously difficult to solve and our work formulating new solutions and applications for them is one of the cornerstones of the Gravitational Field Generator Project. What I'm showing her are the results of my further work using results from the project and tests across more lives and realities than I can remember.

"You did all of this by yourself?"

"I had some inspiration and ran with it. I think we should build these into the modeling program. It'll improve our wave models of the shifts and—"

Saniya raises a hand and cuts me off. "Jon, if you think this is worth it, then I'm with you. You should have told me sooner, though. We got here as a team, remember?"

"I know, I'm sorry." I'm not, but as long as she's on board, it doesn't matter.

"Alright, walk me through this before we talk to the rest of the team." I nod and turn back to the board to walk Saniya through my equations for what feels like the thousandth time.

I hear my phone vibrate and glance at the screen: a call from Mom in California. I hesitate for a second and then silence it. There's too much work to do.

Most of the team, including Saniya, is working on building my equations into the quantum modeling program, but I'm alone in my office because I have to do this part—using the equations and data from the generator's sensor array in this shift to calculate a way home —by myself. It's much easier to explain the need to update the quantum software than the need to configure the generator to use gravity to selectively warp the fabric of space-time (sometimes I still try, but Saniya is always a pain about it). I can't finish until the rest of the team finishes its part, because until the quantum software is updated I can't analyze and determine with enough precision exactly how the gravitational fields generated in the last test distorted space-time; but fortunately, the project here is pretty advanced. We've—no, *they've*—already run a few tests of the generator and are scheduled for a full systems test next month. I'll be ready by then.

The team is excited by my new equations, of course, and some people drop by my office to talk about them. I try to be patient when they just need some clarification on the equations, but it's hard to not be curt when the conversation strays into something more theoretical. When the shifts first began what feels like a lifetime ago—in a way was many lifetimes—I was scared, confused, and even in wonder of it all; but those emotions have long since faded. I've stopped trying to understand it, stopped wondering if I'm actually traveling to new time-lines or realities or just somehow altering my own. All I really know or care about now is that after what feels like an eternity of running the generator over and over again using different coil configurations and "shifting" through an endless parade of similar but different lives, I'm finally close to getting home.

My phone vibrates again and I reach out to silence it, thinking Mom is very persistent today. As I do, I see the screen and freeze as a tingling wave washes over me. It's a message from Ely saying: "Fundraiser's going great! Guess you're not going to make it?" I instinctively start typing the reply, my fingers seeming to move on their own. I'm nearly done when I stop myself. I stare at the message I typed telling her I'll be there soon, a tingling feeling of familiarity lingering in my fingertips.

I don't know an Ely.

I can almost see her in my mind: the flash of a smile, moonlight glinting in her eyes—*she laughs warmly, her eyes sparkling and seeming to change colors*—but I push the images away and put my phone down. Memories of strangers are the most dangerous.

I turn back to the equations.

I only manage a few more hours of work before Saniya barges into my office (she never knocks) and makes me stop. Apparently, Mom asked her to make sure I was okay, which she took to mean that it was time to stop working and share a car home. I'm a little annoyed at being ordered around like a five-year old, but I'm also pretty tired and hungry, and I can't work with her harassing me like this anyway… so I agree and she calls a car for us (which I somehow end up paying for).

I'm in my kitchen a half hour later, rooting through my refrigerator for something to eat. Its contents change after each shift and I still find it vaguely interesting to wonder why. Part of it is probably from different choices I made in a particular reality—going to the Safeway around the corner rather than making the trek down to Chinatown for groceries—and part of it where in time each shift sends me, which means more or less food's been eaten relative to my "home" refrigerator. The changes are minor enough that I never experience false memories from them—no vision of me inexplicably buying that questionable-looking jar of pickles, for example (I hate pickles, so I have no idea how it got in here)—but in a way, the state of my refrigerator is a perfect microcosm of my endless shifts. Maybe, I sometimes muse, hidden somewhere in my quantum refrigerator is the key to unifying General Relativity and Quantum Mechanics and the secret to finding my way home.

After about another minute of fruitless searching I sigh. Honestly, I'd take some decent food over the secrets to physics at this point. I've just about given up and am picking up the jar of pickles when the doorbell rings. I start at the sudden sound and hit my head. Rubbing my head and cursing, I extricate myself from the refrigerator and walk to the door, wondering who it could be this late.

When I open the door, the first things I see are her eyes. They sparkle warmly in the cool light of the hallway, their color seeming to shift and change like ripples in a river. They're familiar, like I've seen them before; no, not just seen them, but *know* them. Know how they'll shimmer, how their color will flicker now from soft brown to bright green and sparkling blue.

"They're hazel," she says. "I loved them growing up. I couldn't decide which color I liked more. Whenever I had to write my eye color down, I always put brown-green-blue. I only stopped when the DMV refused to put three colors on my driver's license." She laughs and her eyes shimmer, flickering from soft brown to bright green and sparkling blue.

"Hi, sorry for coming by so late," she says.

Her eyes release me then and I see a young woman, a light coat over her cocktail dress and a large paper bag in one hand. A tingling sense of déjà vu lingers over me, and I say the thing—a feeling more than a word—still echoing in my mind: "Ely."

"Jon," she says with a smile.

"The doorman didn't tell me you were coming up," I say slowly, still feeling dazed.

"He recognized me—didn't even have to sign in. I guess I'm one step closer to completing my nefarious plan to break into your apartment and rob you." She winks and then lifts up her paper bag. "I brought you food from the fundraiser. I know how much you love free stuff."

I start to think of an excuse to send her away, remembering that every moment I'm with her I risk forgetting a little more of myself, when my stomach growls hungrily. *I do love free food,* I can't stop myself from thinking.

"Well, are you going to let me in or just stand there starving?" she asks amusedly. Her words are playful, but the blue of her eyes pierces me with their familiarity. They grab onto me and I feel them pulling me in like a river.

I should stay away. She's not real, she's dangerous...

I open my eyes and I'm sitting at my dinner table. Small boxes of food are spread out in front of me and I watch as Ely searches for plates in the kitchen. "I can't believe this is what happens when I leave you alone for a bit," she calls out. "This place is a mess!" My skin prickles and I have a feeling like I've sat here watching her open drawers and cabinets, listening to the clinking sound of plates and silverware, just like this, before. Memories bubble forward and images flash through my mind: her leaning against the kitchen counter laughing, sitting on my couch with the sun in her hair, eyes shimmering as she leans across the table towards me.

They disappear with the clink of a plate and Ely is leaning across the table, pushing a plate of large steamed buns and a pair of chopsticks towards me. "Try these," she says. "They're also vegetarian. Well, everything's vegetarian, but that's the price you pay when you put me in charge of an event."

"Chopsticks, really?" I ask, the words coming on their own. "I'm supposed to eat these with chopsticks?"

"Oh, but that's what you taught me," she replies coyly as she carefully picks up a bun with her chopsticks. "At least that's what I told the mayor. I really hope somebody got a picture of him trying." Her eyes sparkle blue with mischief as she takes a bite, and I can't help but laugh.

I stab a bun with my chopsticks and lift it to my mouth. "That's what you should have done," I say before taking a bite. The bun tastes like home, and when she bursts out laughing it makes me happy.

"So the mayor came to the fundraiser?" I ask, feeling like I already know the answer.

"Oh yes, he was shameless. Gave a big speech about always believing in the Dry Line and being there to show his continued support. After all that funding he cut…"

Her words spark something inside of me and images flash through my mind: water crashing over me as Saniya grabs onto my arm; Saniya running through a street, people and bodies and signs and smoke and chaos all around her; the world twisting and shifting through my tears as the generator's roar floods my ears. Everything's wrong and everywhere is suffering. Except home.

I need to get home.

Ely is leaning towards the flower by my window now. She gently brushes her fingers across the large round leaves and the bulb of the flower and then draws her hand away. "This is beautiful. Where did you get it?"

I look at her and remember her standing there, the sun dancing in her hair as she runs her hands across the flower, and her question feels wrong. "My mom sent it," I say hesitantly, my words also feeling off. "I don't even remember what it is, honestly."

"Is she Buddhist?"

"Yes, how did you know?" I know it doesn't make sense because I've never been here before—never known this girl before tonight—but I can't shake the feeling that this is all wrong: like I'm watching a movie that's not playing out the way it's supposed to.

"This is a lotus," she says as she traces a finger along the edge of the ceramic pot. "It's symbolic in Buddhism." I see her standing by the window with the sunlight streaming around us as she adjusts the flower pot.

"Buddhism teaches that humans are born and reborn into an endless cycle of suffering, rooted in our attachment to the illusion of the permanence of ourselves and the world around us," she says and I'm standing in front of her, her eyes pulling me in again. "A lotus grows out of the mud into a flower. When it opens, it's the promise of escape from the cycle."

The color of her eyes seem to shift and change under the dim light of my apartment, and as they pull me in, it suddenly seems like they are sparkling in sunlight. Like it's a warm summer day and the bright green leaves of Central Park are rustling behind her. "It'll be beautiful when it blooms."

The part of me that isn't me feels guilty, but after that night I tell my doorman to not let Ely up anymore and I reply to all her messages that I'm busy. The danger of fake memories alone was enough to want me to keep her away; but there was also something about that night, something about the way my skin tingled and my mind drifted—almost as if I had just run the generator and shifted—that unsettled me.

So I focus on work, and the days pass by in an indistinct blur. Mornings roll into nights into mornings again with only the familiar scrawl of the equations really standing out. I'm vaguely aware of a flurry of events unfolding outside the lab, mostly through Saniya's reports on the mayor's latest outrages: the cuts to education, the "tough on crime" initiatives in the outer boroughs, the feud with Washington over refugee resettlement. Some I half-remember from other shifts and others I'm hearing for the first time. All of them, I ignore. All I need to focus on are my equations. The world might shift and change like a storm-swept river, but the equations are my rock and as long as I hold onto them I'll find my way home.

"So there's a protest planned for the mayor's speech next week."

I look up at Saniya, her words catching my attention in a way they hadn't previously. "You're not thinking of going, are you?"

She sighs. "I know, I know. Scientists shouldn't get involved in politics, it erodes public trust in us. But how can I keep sitting here with my hands under my ass when he's attacking everything we care about?"

"Saniya, no! Please don't." The words burst out of my mouth by themselves, and even I'm surprised at the urgency in them. I don't know why, but I'm overcome by the feeling that I have to stop her.

Saniya seems taken aback as well, and looks at me quietly. "Don't worry," she says after a while. "I've got too much to do right now with your damn equations anyway."

I don't understand the sense of relief that fills me, but my skin continues tingling long after.

I'm walking with Saniya through one of the tree-lined, cobblestone paths of the "Square", the small park that connects the malls, museums, and offices that make up the Hudson Yards development. It's a clear, sunny day, but the air is crisp and cool. It's been a long time since I've walked outside like this, and it feels nice.

I stop, feeling like something is wrong. My skin is prickling, as if a cold wave had just washed over me. Saniya looks at me questioningly. "Jon?"

I look back uncertainly. What am I doing here? I feel something in my hand and look down at the paper bag I'm holding. Did we get lunch? There's so much work to do, why would I leave the lab? My mind is buzzing and it almost feels like I've shifted, but...

"Jon!" a familiar voice calls out. It's like the chime of a bell and scatters the questions roiling through my mind. I look up and see Ely ahead of us. Sunlight streams through the trees around her, and when she smiles my skin tingles and it feels like... I struggle to remember the word.

"I thought it was you," she says as she walks up.

"Ely," I say, shifting uneasily. I can feel the fake memories seeping into me, in the way her smile puts me at ease and my mind tells me she's a friend. "What are you doing here?" I ask curtly, pushing all those feelings aside.

Her eyes widen slightly and I know she's taken aback by my coldness. I fight down the feeling of guilt I tell myself isn't real. "Sorry, am I not supposed to be? We did meet here, if you remember."

She's sitting on one of the stone seating walls, the rays of sunlight streaming between the trees seeming to somehow all end with her. She laughs and tries to hold her hair away from her face as it dances in the sudden breeze.

The image fades away and I'm looking into Ely's eyes again. "I was showing some donors the riverfront," she says, breaking the silence I didn't realize had passed. "Helps to give a visual of something before you start begging people for money to fund it. Going to need a lot of that now that the mayor has officially 'completed' the public part of the Dry Line public-private partnership." She rolls her eyes but smiles, and I know she's trying to ease the tension. A part of me wants that too, but another just wants to run away.

Saniya clears her throat loudly and I realize that we've fallen into another awkward silence. "Hi, I'm Saniya," she says, shooting me an annoyed glance before stepping up and offering her hand to Ely.

"I'm Ely," Ely replies as she quickly shakes Saniya's hand. I can sense her relief at Saniya's intervention, and feel another pang of guilt. "Are you friends with Jon?"

"On the good days," Saniya says with a shrug. "Usually I just work with him."

"Oh!" Ely's eyes light up. "Jon's told me about you. You've been friends since college, right?"

Saniya raises an eyebrow and shoots me another glance. "Yes..."

"Well, Jon never told me how gorgeous you are—I love your outfit! You know, we laypeople always imagine scientists running around in white lab coats, but you're just so stylish."

Saniya's face breaks out in a grin and the tension melts away. She's a sucker for compliments. Did I tell Ely that? "Oh, this? It's nothing, I just threw it on this morning. I mean, we actually do wear lab coats at the lab..."

"I mean it. Jon, you're lucky you've had Saniya as a friend all this time. You probably wouldn't have seemed as creepy if she had been with you when we met." She gives me a quick, teasing wink.

"Ohh... I like you!" Saniya gushes. She looks at me, points at Ely a few times and stage whispers loudly, "I really like her!"

Ely laughs and takes Saniya's arm. "Come on, you're at 50 Hudson, right? I'll walk you back."

"It's okay, we can head back ourselves." Even as I say them, the words feel wrong, as if I've lived this moment before and that just wasn't what I was supposed to say.

"Oh shush, you!" Saniya snaps. "Yes Ely, you absolutely must walk us back." She pulls Ely and they start walking together towards the lab.

"It's fine," Ely says to me. "It's close, and besides, I want to hear from Saniya what you were like in college."

Saniya grins. "Oh, you would've hardly recognized him. He was this geeky little kid who didn't have a clue how to talk to real people."

Ely bursts out laughing. "Really? No way!"

"Yes! His sense of humor was the same though, his one redeeming quality..."

I feel my resistance crumbling, as if seeing them meet was the last piece of some puzzle that had been haunting me. I hesitate for a few moments as they walk ahead, and then follow. When I take the first step, it feels like a weight's been lifted; as if I've been swimming against the current of a river and finally decided to let go and drift with it.

As we walk, Ely and Saniya become engrossed in their conversation and seem to forget me. They're relaxed and comfortable, like they've known each other for years, and it feels... right. We walk past a bed of flowers and as a gust of wind picks up, I catch their fragrance in the air. It's soft and delicate, like it would disappear if I breathe too deeply; but it's so familiar, like I've smelled this exact same smell somewhere before. As I breathe in, my skin tingles and a familiar wave washes over me.

The smell comes on a cool summer breeze, soft and delicate like the flowers they come from. I smile, the fragrance lingering in my nose as I watch Ely and Saniya joking and laughing together. I'm glad they're getting along: it's important to me. The wind picks up again and the smell of the flowers drifts away with it.

The scent fades away and the memory with it. I blink a few times, feeling disoriented, like I've just woken up from a dream I'm quickly forgetting; but a part of me is telling me that there's something important about it. *Isn't this the first time they've met?*

"You know, Jon hasn't said anything about you," Saniya's voice cuts in, scattering my thoughts. "I can't believe he's been hiding you."

Ely laughs. "Well, we haven't known each other that long. What's it been Jon, a few months?"

I hesitate. "I think so..."

Ely stops and purses her lips thoughtfully. "No, longer than that I think." She looks at me, and suddenly all I see are her eyes, pulling me in as they shimmer between green and blue under the bright summer sun. "Come on, Jon, don't tell me you've forgotten already?"

I'm reviewing calculations from the sensor physics team when I suddenly think of Ely. I don't know why, but one moment I'm cross-checking an equation and the next I remember her eyes sparkling under the sun the day she met Saniya. Didn't I realize something important that day? *When was it?*

At that moment, Saniya opens my door and walks in (she never knocks).

"Hey, what's up?" I ask.

"I missed your face. Seeing it every few hours, 12 hours a day, every day, hasn't been enough for me, so I came here to look at it again." She's impeccably dressed and looks as sharp as always. I would be hard-pressed to tell that she's been in the office every day for the past two weeks working tirelessly.

"Well, look away, take a picture. When you're done, I have work to do." I, on the other hand am particularly feeling the weight of my endless labors today, and probably look like a disheveled mess.

Saniya makes a show of looking me over and then says gravely, "On second thought, this was a bad idea: you look like crap."

I roll my eyes, but she smiles and leans against my table. "Ely and I are going to get lunch at that new Thai place at the Kitchens. Want to come?"

"You've been talking to Ely?" I'm surprised—haven't they just met?

Saniya looks at me strangely. "Um, yes? She's going to become my new best friend, if you don't get your act together. I swear, you care more about this test than me."

If you liked Phong Quan's story "It Feels Like Déjà Vu", leave a comment online at Metaphorosis. Authors love that!

About the story

"It Feels Like Déjà Vu" is the culmination of many different influences from throughout my life. I wrote the first scene many years ago while I was in college, involving the two (at that time unnamed) main characters talking as a shift occurred. In that scene, the character that would become Ely is trying to remind Jon of their relationship and he is trying to shut her out just as a shift happens and she disappears. Nothing else came of that, though the scene and premise of "shifts" stuck in my head. Many years later, when I was working in New York and having my soul crushed in corporate law, I decided to start writing again to preserve my sanity and chose to create a story from that basic premise. The setting became New York, a city I loved, and I decided to use the "shifts" as a way to explore the Buddhist concepts of impermanence and the karmic cycles--something my parents believed in and talked about a lot. Finally, Ely's character and personality are based on the person I was dating at the time, and the focus in the story on environmental issues and nature are a reflection of her passion for them. Those three basic building blocks are the foundation of the story that I ultimately wrote and you can read on *Metaphorosis* now.

A question for the author

Q: If you could have any super power, what would it be?

A: My superpower would almost certainly be the ability to stop or slow time--there just isn't enough time in the world for me to do everything I want to do.

About the author

Phong's parents are from tropical Vietnam, so after they immigrated to the United States of course he was born in Minnesota on April 1st on the last day of a big snow storm—a great April Fool's joke for everyone involved. Immediately afterwards, his family moved to sunny California where he was raised. Phong eventually became a corporate lawyer, working in New York, Beijing and now Singapore, where he is currently based.

August

The Bagel Shop Owner's Nephew

J. Tynan Burke

Last night, Murray called with another bunch of prophecies, so Yonatan Kaplan hasn't slept yet. He stayed up preparing dossiers on some doomed socialites instead. Now it's a little after dawn, Friday morning, and he's standing in line outside Fox's Bagels with a thermos and a tote bag. He's shaky from too much caffeine and too little sleep, but he doesn't regret it. The socialites will die this weekend, according to Murray, and Murray's got a good track record. When they do die, the obituary writers will call the Morgue—The Pre-Morgue Clipping Service, Yonatan's business—to buy the dossiers, expecting the usual thoughtfulness and prescience. So it had been best to begin the work immediately.

The line shortens when a gaggle of tourists leaves Fox's. Yonatan steps forward, fills his thermos lid with hot tea, and covers a yawn with the hand still holding the thermos. He thinks back to Murray's sneering tone when he 'apologized' for calling so late, his fake sadness that Yonatan would stay up all night working. It doesn't matter if Murray made a lucky guess or if it was knowledge from Murray's divine gift—either way, it's *rude* to mock a man for doing his job. Yonatan takes a big drink of tea and frowns. *Fucking prophets.* They're nothing like what you read about.

The line shortens again and it's Yonatan's turn to enter the shop. The woman in front of him holds the door, and he nods to her as he steps inside.

Yonatan is welcomed by a burst of humidity, which carries the smell of fresh onions and the accumulated yeast of three generations. He's also welcomed by a new cashier, a young man of maybe twenty who shares the owner Shay's big ears and too-skinny frame. The hunger in Yonatan's gut is replaced with a rarely-felt electricity, once debilitating, though he has learned to weather it. For him the closest analogy is the shock of a new and severe crush settling in, but he's not gay, trust him, he's checked.

This young man, whose name tag reads 'Stephen,' is perhaps a Tzadik Nistar.

"Morning," Yonatan manages, stepping to the counter. "One of everything, please."

Stephen raises an eyebrow over a baggy eye. "Like, one everything bagel, or…"

Yonatan cringes and tries to twist it into a smile. "Sorry. Bad joke I have with Shay. One of each kind of bagel, please."

Stephen counts off on his fingers. "So one plain, one poppy, one sesame, one onion…"

"And one everything," Yonatan finishes.

Stephen collects and bags the bagels. "I don't get it."

Yonatan shrugs. "I said it was a bad joke. Is it even a joke? Who knows how these things start." Yonatan knows. He tried making a pun five or six years ago after a long night of drinking. "Shay might remember. Do you know Shay, uh…" He points at the name tag like he just noticed it. "Stephen?"

"Uncle Shay? I sure do. It's Steve, though. That'll be fifteen dollars." Steve beeps some buttons on the register.

"You know what, Steve, why don't you add another poppy."

Steve wraps the extra bagel while Yonatan observes. No piercings or ink that he can see. That's good, it's one of the rules Adonai actually cares about any more.

The register beeps again. Steve says, "Eighteen dollars."

Yonatan hands him a twenty and puts the bagels in his tote. "Nice to meet you, Steve. Tell Shay Yonatan says hi."

Out front, Yonatan leans against the wall and takes two deep breaths while his gut settles. It turns to growling, sour with too much tea and too little food. Much better, easy to address. He returns to the Morgue and goes straight to the computer, where he opens a password-protected document and types an addition to a long list of names, in a column headed 'CANDIDATES': *Stephen 'Steve' Fox, ~20, Lower East Side, NYC*. And then, at long last, it is bagel time. Poppy, toasted, with leftover veggie cream cheese.

Later he's on the office couch, taking a little break and reading a space opera, when the landline rings. It's barely audible over the Norwegian black metal he put on to stay awake. His watch says eight-thirty, but he decides to take it anyway—it can't be any less interesting than the exposition dump he's at in the book, or the *Page Six* profiles he's avoiding. Off goes the music and in goes a bookmark. The bookmark has an Emerson quote he likes. He can read part of it sticking out: *Time and space are but physiological colors which the eye makes, but.*

While he crosses the Morgue, he steps over a spilled pile of clippings, and growls. Always more work, dossiers to build, Tzadikim to chronicle, things to file. Sleep, somewhere in there. And the phone keeps ringing, and he almost yells something passive-aggressive at it, but no, that's more something his father would do. With a silent glance back at the clippings he walks the rest of the way.

"Pre-Morgue Clipping Service, this is Yonatan."

"Thank you for answering, Yonatan. I hope it is not too early." A woman, British? Her voice seems far away, like a long-distance call in some old movie.

Her comment reminds Yonatan that he stayed up all night, and he stifles a yawn. "It's no trouble at all, Ms..."

"How rude of me. My name is Ariel."

Like the mermaid? Yonatan thinks. He can't help himself—he's never met a woman with that name before. He gets a stupid grin at the idea of talking to a cryptid.

"How can I help you, Ariel?"

"I am looking for somebody, of course."

Yonatan clears his throat and recites a spiel. This happens. "I'm sorry, Ariel, but this isn't that kind of place. We do collect information on people, but we don't release it until they're deceased. I can refer you to several good private investigators."

A pause, then Ariel continues. "Yes, of course, how silly of me—he *is* deceased. Or that's what I've heard. I was hoping you could tell me, and then if... I am looking for his remains."

Yonatan bites his lip. This feels like the sort of thing that will involve lawyers, maybe family drama. He should have let it go to voice mail. "Why don't you tell me who you're looking for, and leave me your contact information, and I'll get back to you," he says, a little too quick, to get her off the line. He wonders if the machine that records his calls is still working. He hasn't had to check in a while.

"I'm sorry, have I said something wrong?" She sounds sweet, like she doesn't know.

And maybe she doesn't, maybe there's a language barrier or Yonatan is maybe cranky. A saying of his mom's pops into his head, *Make sure to offer somebody an offramp before they drive too far down stupid street,* so he does. "Did you mean to say you're looking for his *grave,* instead of his *remains*?"

Another pause. "That is probably the better word. We wish to pay our respects."

"Alright." He explains the fee structure, and takes down a credit card number and the name of the man in question: John Miller, possibly died 'quite recently', near San Francisco. It startles him—that's the name of a Tzadik Nistar. And about a million other people, of course. Anyway, last he checked, John the Tzadik was alive and living in San Diego. Still, something feels off about Ariel, so after he hangs up, Yonatan decides to download the call from the recorder. He finds the device inside a junction box by the front door, warm and smelling like hour-old tar. It's fried. His assistant Sarah comes in a minute later while he's digging in the wiring with a flashlight between his teeth. He turns and asks for help, and accidentally blinds her.

While they extract the recorder together, he brings her up to speed on the socialites' dossiers. Could she pick up where he left off, and also run to the gadget store for a new recorder? There're fresh bagels in the kitchenette. He grabs his space opera and goes home without telling her about Ariel's call. She doesn't need to know, she isn't a Searcher. From the privacy of his apartment, he sends an email to the Searcher who follows Miller, checking in. Finally he goes to bed.

Asleep, he dreams—who doesn't? Sometimes he has one of the dreams everybody gets, like having a test he forgot to study for even though grad school was six years ago. Once he had an entire month of dreams where every day was Saturday and he had to follow his dad's Shabbat rules, which he never had to in real life. His dad didn't go all Haredi—instead of 'Haredi' you can say 'ultra-orthodox,' if you want to piss his dad off—until after the terrorist attacks really started to ramp up in America, around when Yonatan was starting college.

This morning's dream is about a maple tree. He's squatting on a crook in the branches, up where the trunk first splits, with a magnifying glass and a clipboard. The clipboard holds a chart, the scientific names of bugs on the left and numbers on the right. He's a scientist doing a population survey. He counts tiny black ants through the magnifying glass, writes the number next to their species name. The name's in Latin, and he wishes he knew how to pronounce—

Of course he knows how it's pronounced, he's been studying liturgical languages for years. This is a dream. He straightens out his back and stretches. Even here, it hurts from all the time he spends at his desk. He should really get a better chair.

"What are you doing? Don't just squat there if you aren't going to work."

Yonatan looks down. The source of the voice is a park ranger in iridescent green, like a beetle with a chip on its shoulder, gender indeterminate. While the ranger glares, Yonatan inspects some leaves. Aphids are munching on the cellulose while lady-bird beetles munch on the aphids. He's too distracted to count them, so he hops onto the grass and brushes crumbled bark off his shirt.

"I guess it's time to go, then," he says, pocketing his magnifying glass.

"I guess so," says the ranger.

"What'd I do wrong?"

"I just don't like people climbing in my tree when they don't have a good reason." The ranger puts their fists on their hips, a superhero pose.

"Just this tree?"

The ranger spreads their arms. "There aren't any other trees."

Yonatan sees he's in a field, wild grasses stretching to the horizon. He looks up at the maple appreciatively. It's well-pruned and healthy. "You must be very dedicated to your work," he says.

"We all do what we must." The ranger rolls their eyes and bows. "But seriously though, thanks for your part. Now get going."

Yonatan nods, climbs into the Ford Explorer he hasn't owned for ten years, and drives off to the lab.

He wakes and showers, and by the time he's finished, the sun has set and it's Shabbat, the Jewish day of rest. Many in his neighborhood, inside the old borders of the Manhattan *eruv,* observe it; a quick glance out his apartment's paint-flecked window confirms their absence on the streets. Yonatan rarely observes; he's usually busy with Searcher work, and today is no exception. The only concession he makes is accessing the office remotely, which is not really a concession at all. He looks back at his laptop, at an email from Sarah. Executive summary: she finished the socialites' dossiers and got a new call recorder set up. The old one only broke that morning, so they have Murray's call, but nothing after.

Yonatan goes to make a cup of tea and heat up some leftover beef *pad see ew.* The tea is black and steeps in his favorite mug, also black, to match his jeans and hoodie—*even your favorite **tea** is black,* his dad jokes. Text on the mug reads *The Chosen Son.* It's half-blasphemous, a birthday present from his mom a few years ago. *Shh, don't tell your father,* she said with a wink. They're still together. He'll never understand it. Carrying his dinner back to his computer, he stubs his toe, and narrowly avoids saying "God damn it," choosing instead the more respectful "Fuck!"

There's a reply in his inbox with bad news about John Miller. During a business trip to San Francisco this week, Miller was beaten into a coma. He died of his injuries just this morning. Yonatan blinks twice. He hopes that Ariel wasn't asking about *that* John Miller, but can't really convince himself it's a coincidence. Then he reminds himself that people usually call right after a death—it's the Morgue's whole business model. Difference is, nobody ever asked him about one of the Tzadikim before.

To still the dread creeping over his scalp, he plugs his phone into his sound system and resumes the Norwegian metal playlist. The part of him that isn't freaking out hopes it annoys the upstairs neighbors. They're always clomping around at four in the morning. What are they, meth heads?

He sets a couch cushion on the floor and sits, closing his eyes and counting breaths. He wishes there were a Searcher manual to consult, but theirs is an oral tradition, a secrecy born from the historical necessity to hide. The next best thing would be to ask Leonard, his old mentor and thesis advisor, but Leonard's been dead almost a year. Upon reflection, Yonatan knows Leonard would just repeat the fundamental rule about Searching: *If somebody asks for information about a Tzadik Nistar, you must provide it.*

Yonatan's no good at following rules he doesn't grok the need for, but the rationale behind the rule is obvious, to somebody who knows the history. His thoughts go to his first real Searcher meeting. It was in a faculty bar that the university had shoved into a basement.

"So you've passed the hard part of the test," Leonard had said. "Now for the oral portion. Explain, in your own words, the Tzadikim Nistarim."

Yonatan nodded. "An old Talmudic legend. Thirty-six righteous people who are so great, they keep God from trashing this place. If some day only thirty-five people held that honor, God would wipe us out."

Leonard tut-tutted. "Please, use one of the other names, around me at least."

"Does... Adonai actually care?" The word felt funny in Yonatan's mouth.

"There are things Adonai cares more and less about. The work I do with the Tzadikim, securing the life of creation—it's more important than, say, Shabbat, if you need it to be. But Adonai's name is a matter of basic respect."

Yonatan glanced at his vodka tonic. "Sorry, Leonard. I'll work on it."

"Thank you. So these Tzadikim Nistarim, they're special?"

"One could even be the Messiah," Yonatan said. "A Tzadik Nistar doesn't know they're a Tzadik Nistar. Some say it's a metaphor to encourage you to behave well—you never know when you might turn out to be one."

Leonard waved his hand. "But..."

"But you say they're real."

"I don't say, Yonatan, I know. And I know you can feel it—you picked one out of a full lecture hall."

Yonatan grunted. Both men sipped their vodkas. Leonard put a hand on the table. "Eschatology aside, the archive is still a brilliant career opportunity, you know. I'm old, and I need an apprentice. And —this is just a personal observation—I don't see academia in your future."

Yonatan snorted and then agreed. So began his life with the Searchers, who identify and chronicle these Tzadikim, and provide information about them whenever it's requested. Yonatan jokes that it's in case Adonai ever loses his phone book. And they have a simple principle: *always provide the information.* After all, you never know who might be asking.

Well, as Leonard liked to remind him, one has principles so one can follow them in uncertain situations. Thinking about the present, Yonatan adds, *But that doesn't mean one has to like it.* This situation is uncertain as fuck. Miller was *murdered*. Why is Ariel drawing his attention to it? She doesn't *sound* like a prophet, or not like any he's talked to. More importantly, has somebody begun knocking off the Tzadikim? He hopes not—it's onerous enough locating the replacement when just one has died.

He can only see malign interpretations... but maybe that's just him. Breathing, he knows that he doesn't actually need the answers to do his job. All he *has* to do is get Ariel the information on Miller, and follow the procedures for when a Tzadik Nistar dies: Adonai will give a different righteous person a promotion, and the Searchers will re-examine their Candidates. They'll check their premonitions from afar, and consult the prophets; if there's sufficient evidence about a Candidate, people will follow up in person and see how they feel. Then, like so many things, it will conclude with an argument on the Internet.

Yonatan stands and returns to the table.

While he picks at his noodles and finishes his tea, he contemplates his tepid mug. *The Chosen Son.* When he's done eating, he goes to the Morgue to pull Miller's file.

An NYPD detective surprises him at the Morgue around eight. She introduces herself, Detective Corazón Lopez, can she come in and ask some questions? Yonatan flashes guiltily to the documents about Miller he was scanning, but he hasn't done anything wrong, he doesn't even know why the detective is here. Even so, he wants to tug nervously at his collar like Bugs Bunny, but he hides it, says yeah, asks if she wants some water or tea. She says no, and so he doesn't get anything for himself either. They sit at the card table in the kitchenette.

"An interesting business model," Lopez says, "selling dead person facts."

"Newspapers used to have departments like this," Yonatan says. "Probably half our archive is stuff we picked up from the *Times* when it went under."

"I did not know that." Lopez produces a notepad from her tan leather jacket and jots something down. "You oughta put that on your website."

Yonatan frowns. "Takes some of the mystique out, don't you think?"

Lopez smiles back. "Might make people like me less *curious*. Don't you think."

What is this? Yonatan shows his palms. "Can I help alleviate that curiosity?"

"That's the idea." Lopez looks out of the kitchenette, at the room of rolling stacks, the hallway down the middle crammed with file cabinets and banker's boxes. Her shoulders relax and she leans in. "Alright. There's been some suspicious deaths these last few months. Medium-profile, local celebrities." She's clearly not talking about

Miller, which only barely reduces Yonatan's anxiety. "One of us noticed that the obits came out pretty quick, pretty detailed, like they'd been researched beforehand. We called the writers, they told us about you."

Yonatan nods, his mouth dry now, and he wishes he'd gotten water after all. "It's what I—we—do, detective. We identify notable and interesting people and prepare dossiers. Sometimes they die unexpectedly, and that's when we're most in demand. It's morbid, but it's a niche we proudly fill." He hopes the normalcy of business-speak is as comforting to her as it is to him.

"You seem to get awful lucky. Look, we know you solicit tips about people to profile, it's right there on your website."

He scrunches his face. "And the NYPD thinks a tipster might be involved in this?"

She shrugs. "Sounds crazy, right? But it's worth looking into. We think they're all the same perp, and you're linked to them too in your own way. We were hoping you could tell us about the tipsters."

"We have a policy against that."

It's Lopez's turn to show her palms. "You wouldn't want to seem uncooperative, would you? And do you have any idea how easy it would be to get a warrant?"

He doesn't, but pissing off the cops does seem riskier to the Morgue than compromising on this, and there are no Searcher rules about the prophets. "Sure. Alright. Give me the names of the deceased and I'll see if anybody mentioned them to us."

She does. The computer says they're all names from tips, all tips from Murray. He explains it to her, and she takes it down, standing behind him while he works.

"Does Murray have a last name?" she asks.

"Probably, but I don't know it."

"Do you at least have his *phone number*?"

"I do... he called last night, actually." Yonatan deflates. "He gave me three names, some local socialites." Maybe he shouldn't mention the details, that Murray said they won't last the weekend. He doesn't want to get the police involved in knowing the future, he's seen that old movie *Minority Report*. But human life is sacred, certainly more so than company policy, even this company.

"I have a recording," his conscience helpfully adds for him, settling the matter. His brain catches up and he says, "I should warn you, Murray thinks he's psychic. He says lots of crazy stuff... and he said they might die this weekend."

Lopez stares at him like he admitted he has bodies in the freezer, but don't worry, he has a permit. "*So* hard to find good help. Can I *get* the recording?"

Yonatan stiffens. "I need to know I'm not liable for anything, that the Morgue—that's what we call it, I know, I know—isn't in trouble, or else you'll need that warrant."

"Mister Kaplan, these people could be in danger." She sighs and takes out her phone. "The D.A. is working tonight. You got a lawyer we can hammer something out with?"

Yonatan copies down a phone number from the computer. His lawyer keeps Shabbat, no work and no phone calls, but his assistant can fetch him. Lopez trades her business card for the number. "Have the D.A. call this—it's my lawyer Joel's assistant Kacy. Tell her Yonatan Kaplan says to get Joel ASAP, it's a matter of life and death."

After Lopez leaves Yonatan sinks his face into his hands, tugs on his hair. This is more murders than he's used to dealing with on a Friday night, which is zero. He needs a drink and something that wasn't cooked yesterday. Randomly he texts the woman he's newly dating, Dinah. She gets right back to him, she's free. They meet at a diner off 1st Avenue that smells like frying sausage and somebody else's Tabasco.

"Every time we eat you get steak," Dinah says when their food arrives, his steak and eggs, her Greek salad.

"I like steak," he says. He takes a bite and finishes his beer. "I used to be a vegetarian, did you know that?"

"I did not," she says.

"I had a Buddhist phase starting in undergrad. Ate a lot of hummus."

"A real rebel." Dinah eats some of her salad and drinks her own beer.

"You have no idea." Yonatan flags down a waiter and orders another drink.

"Why'd you stop? Being vegetarian," she says.

"It was *hard,*" he says with a forced whine.

She laughs. "And a Ph.D. wasn't?"

"Different hard. When you find the right thing to care about, something that clicks..." He shrugs.

"I hear ya."

While they eat, Yonatan's mind keeps drifting to Ariel, and to dealing with the cops, and he keeps shoving the thoughts down. He's only half surprised when he blurts out, "What are you doing after this?"

Dinah smiles. "Nothing, you?"

"I'm in a whiskey-and-cartoons kind of mood," he says.

Dinah looks into her empty beer glass. "It'll have to be your place, they're fumigating my neighbor's, ew."

"My TV isn't very big," Yonatan says.

She puts her hand on his, says with a fake, over-earnest tone, "It's not the size that matters, it's the company."

The door is unlocked when they get to his apartment, and when Yonatan turns on the light he finds the place trashed—books and clothes everywhere, the kitchen table turned over, his not-very-big TV smashed. Dumb as a cow, he walks inside. "What the fuck!"

Dinah stays put in the door frame. "I assume it's not normally like this."

"No..." Yonatan holds up a hand and searches the apartment to confirm it's empty. It doesn't take long, it's not that big. "You can come in if you want. Try not to touch anything."

She looks relieved. "Oh, thank god. I gotta piss but it seemed like a bad time to ask."

He points her to the bathroom, and while she's in there he does a more thorough search. There's a note on the fridge, scrawled on the back of an envelope. *Murray says hi.* Dinah joins him while he's staring at it.

At the same time, they both say she should leave, and they share a sad laugh. She zips up her coat. "This wasn't a very good date, Yoni."

"I'll do better next time." He's already got his wallet out, rummaging for Lopez's card.

"You better." She kisses him, quick but not a peck, and leaves.

Yonatan jams the door shut and calls the detective. She picks up and says that Joel should call any second to fill him in. Yonatan tells her about his apartment, about the note. She says she'll send somebody over. His phone beeps, and he switches calls.

"Joel? Hey, before we start, uh..." Yonatan tells Joel about the break-in.

After a pause, Joel takes a few false starts and sighs. " 'Well, here's another nice mess you've got me into!' What was that, Laurel and Hardy?" Joel makes ancient references when he's nervous.

"Never watched it. I don't suppose you can tell me everything's gonna be okay?"

"Right, sorry." Yonatan hears Joel flipping through papers. "Honestly I can't see how the break-in changes anything on my end, for this Murray business. You're fine, legally. The cops weren't bluffing about the warrant though, that would be easy to get, so you had the right instincts, to cooperate. Judges don't like being pulled in after hours." A little edge of resentment to Joel's voice at the end. "So you're fine, and the Morgue is fine, but you should probably get used to hearing from law enforcement more. They're jealous of your tip line."

Yonatan grunts. Half the Morgue's revenue must come from prophets' tips, prophets who are usually shady as fuck, who'd bolt at the first sign of the cops. But saving lives is the right thing to do. Hopefully he'll only scare away people who are trying to pass murder plots off as revelations. Then again, what if the murder plots *are* the revelations—? Best not to go down that road, not sober at least.

"Oh, one more thing," Joel says. "They want you to call Murray so they can get a trace."

Fucking fuck. "I don't really want them to hear… *I* don't really want to hear what he has to say, even."

"Is this about your, er, *other* archive, Yonatan?"

Joel isn't a Searcher, but Yonatan's told him about it. Joel just thinks it's a run-of-the-mill weird sect. Spilling Adonai's secrets is unwise, but so is keeping secrets from your lawyer. Yonatan rubs the back of his neck with his free hand. "Yeah, and Murray's not making us look good."

More paper-shuffling on Joel's end. "I'll write it up so the cops can only use or store information pertaining directly to the investigation. They hear weird stuff all the time anyway. Well, not weird, but, you know."

"Unusual," Yonatan says, his old offramp tic.

"Yeah."

"Joel? Sorry I made you break Shabbat," Yonatan says.

"I'm not in love with it either, but hey. You're not the first client who's done it, but you *are* the first in a long while that I'm not mad at for it. I'll talk to the D.A. and sort out the paperwork we'll need to get you through the weekend. You and I can talk insurance and everything Monday."

"Great. Thanks."

"You got somewhere you can stay?" Joel says.

"I'll probably end up at the Morgue tonight. Worst case there's always my parents'."

"Oof."

Yonatan says goodbye and starts packing an overnight bag. Over by the wall he finds his mug—still intact, lucky him—and the space opera he's been carrying around. The bookmark's fallen out of the novel, and he can see the full Emerson quote now: *Time and space are but physiological colors which the eye makes, but the soul is light: where it is, is day; where it was, is night; and history is an impertinence and an injury if it be anything more than a cheerful apologue or parable of my being and becoming.* Now is not the time to figure out what chapter he was reading, so he slots the bookmark in under the title page, and puts the book in the bag.

At the Morgue some hours later, Detective Lopez and two techs sit at the card table with bulky headphones, and Yonatan leans against the wall, shoulders clenched, cordless phone pressed to his ear.

"So you got a pretty big mouth, huh?" Murray says when he answers. "You get my message? The cops there right now? 'Cuz I'll hang up."

Yonatan has practiced this in his head. He pretends to humor Murray's 'delusions.' "Wouldn't you know if they were?"

"You sound tense. Guess my friend's visit did that." Yonatan hears a *snap!* like Murray is chewing gum. "But I know you wouldn't talk about this in front of the cops. Don't even have to use my gift."

For once, it's a good thing that Murray is an asshole. Yonatan holds back something sarcastic. "So what is it you want?"

"A little loyalty, please," Murray says. "How much money have I made you guys with my tips? And all so selflessly."

"What's going on, Murray?"

"I give you names, right? Most of them are, ah, preordained. But every so often, some of them... I know a guy who wants you to know those names."

Yonatan squints at nothing, confused. "Why?"

There's the snapping sound of gum again. "He's *in love* with these people, but all fucked-up like. He wants them to die beautiful, right, so they gotta die soon. And he wants them to have a real good obituary. He knows about you guys somehow, used to write at a paper I think, he's a fan of your work. Well before he knocks 'em off he has me call you, to make sure all the research is in the can."

Murray pauses to chew wetly, then continues, "You should take it as a compliment, Yoni! Look, just *chill,* okay? Think how many of those weirdos I've, what'ya call it, *revelated,* for your little side project."

A headache tightens around Yonatan's crown, and he puts more weight against the wall. He looks at Detective Lopez and sees her looking back at him. *Keep him talking,* she mouths, and shrugs like this is a normal sort of evening for her. Maybe it is.

"Is that some kind of threat?" Yonatan says.

Murray laughs. "Like anybody would believe me if I told them, or even *care* about your little list. Lemme tell you something."

Yonatan clears his throat and swallows what comes up. "Okay."

"I'm a slimy little card sharp, but *you...*" Murray laughs. "I'm dirty, yeah, but I really *can* see the future too, and *you're* the one who thinks you've got a direct line upstairs? On account of some old legend? You know where I see *you*? The fuckin' *nuthouse.*"

Silence. If it was just Yonatan he'd hang up, unplug the phone, and go make some bad decisions at a bar. But he's got a job to do, so he repeats himself, stalls for time. "Is that a threat? What is it you *want*?"

Murray chuckles. "Hey, *you're* the one who called *me.*"

Yonatan looks and sees Lopez giving him a thumbs up with one hand, and miming hanging up with the other.

"You know what? Never mind. Go fuck yourself, Murray." Yonatan ends the call and swings the phone down, pressing it into his leg.

Lopez walks over. "Well done, Mister Kaplan," she says, sticking out her hand.

Yonatan stands up straight and shakes it. "Thanks. Uh, I could really..." He releases her grip and flaps his hand around aimlessly, noticing a tremor in his fingers.

She nods. "Gotcha. Don't disappear, OK?"

He folds his arms and nods back, realizing halfway through that it makes him look like the genie from that old TV show. The techs undo whatever they did to his phone line as he watches, and right before the door closes behind them, he remembers to call out his thanks.

He can't go home, so he does his best to make the Morgue comfortable, unpacking his book and changing into pajamas. He boils filtered water to make tea. A peek in the paper bag from Fox's shows that Sarah left him the second poppy-seed bagel, which he toasts and eats with butter. He finds where he was in the novel and, until his hands stop shaking, he reads. Then he works, cataloging the spilled clippings he noticed that morning, and pondering Ariel. It feels like he might know even less about that situation than he did a few hours ago. He resolves to consult other Searchers before he reaches too many conclusions. Meanwhile, the very next step is clear. He copies Miller's file, removes the Searcher-related information, and adds the police and coroner's reports he was sent.

That done, he yawns and lays down on the couch. He must've fallen into a dreamless sleep, since when he wakes up to the ringing phone, it's light out. With all that's going on, he figures he should answer.

"Pre-Morgue Clipping Service, this is Yonatan."

"Thank you for answering again, Yonatan, and on a Saturday." It's Ariel. He recognizes the accent, and the far-away sounding connection.

"How can I help you?"

"I know it has only been a day, but I was wondering if you were able to get the information on Mr. Miller for me."

"I was," Yonatan says. "I'm sorry to say that Mr. Miller has passed. I can email our file to you right after I run your card, if you'd like."

"Dreadful news. And I would appreciate that very much. You're fast—you must be very dedicated to your work."

He raises his eyebrows. "We all do what we must," he tries.

"Yes, and thank you for your part." Ariel sighs. "I have more people to check on... hopefully the news will be better. It's almost three dozen names, so I'll use the email form on your website, there's no rush. And..."

She hesitates, and Yonatan swallows.

"One last question," she says. "I see that you take suggestions for interesting people to research?"

"That's right. You get a finder's fee after their information's requested, if you were the first to suggest them."

"Well. You should keep an eye on a young man who's just moved near you, Stephen Fox. Consider this free of charge—I imagine he'll be around long after you're gone. Have a good Saturday, Mister Kaplan."

The line goes dead. Yonatan can smell burning plastic. The recorder must have gotten fried again. He takes a few calming breaths and flexes his fingertips out, deciding he can deal with all this tomorrow or maybe Monday. Meantime he's earned a break. He disconnects the dead recorder from the phone line, and then disconnects the phone entirely. For now he'll read his book uninterrupted; if Adonai has truly chosen this gray morning to count his Tzadikim Nistarim, he can always knock.

See J. Tynan Burke's story "The Bagel Shop Owner's Nephew" online at Metaphorosis.
If you liked it, leave a comment. Authors love that!
Remember to subscribe to our e-mail updates so you'll know when new stories are posted.

About the story

Late last year, an acquaintance recommended the documentary 'Obit,' about the obituary department at the New York Times. I was struck by the frazzled archivist who runs the clippings morgue. At the same time, I was flipping through Borges's 'Book of Imaginary Beings,' and found an entry on the Tzadikim Nistarim (which Borges called 'Lamed Wufniks'). So I thought it would be interesting to write a story combining the two, about a frazzled archivist who runs an obituary-shop-slash-apocalypse-prevention-directory.

As for the rest of the story, I honestly don't know where these things come from. A surprisingly high percentage of my good ideas come to me when I'm trying to fall asleep. Very few come in the shower.

Finally, I have my lovely beta readers to thank for a few details and story beats, as well as for making the story much better than it would have been if they hadn't given me notes.

A question for the author

Q: What is your favorite part of writing?

A: At the craft level, I really enjoy writing dialogue. On a macro level, my favorite part is having created stories that my friends (and people like them) enjoy reading. If I hadn't written them, they're probably stories I would enjoy reading, too. Unfortunately, there's a lot of hair-pulling involved in the final product, and I need some distance before I can try to appreciate the result.

If you consider reading to be a part of writing, then I like that a whole lot, too.

My least-favorite part, not that you asked, is fixing plot holes.

About the author

J. Tynan Burke is a digital librarian and writer. He lives in San Francisco with his husband and their enormous cat.

www.tynanburke.com, @tynanpants

Upon the Fallen Leaves of the Ginkgo Tree

Mads Alvey

To walk upon the fallen leaves of the Ginkgo tree is very nearly to walk upon a river of gold. It is a sight of such pure beauty that the Speakers whisper sweet blessings to the earth, spinning a preservation upon the leaves where they lie, so the golden carpet won't fade to black as we tread upon the ground.

I was reminding myself of how lucky I was to have enough Speaking to join the Speakers of the Ginkgowood when Amber chastised me during a Speaking lesson. The Speakers were the people who made my home such a beautiful spectacle, and I needed to remember that it was an honor to join them. My Speaking was a gift from the Ginkgowood, a power that had come to me without rhyme or reason as a child, which I needed to make the most of. What would I do with the neighborwood's gift, aside from use it?

"You can't ask it to go against its nature," Amber said, rubbing her temple.

The branch on which I sat was just as completely populated with yellow, fan-shaped leaves as it had been that morning. "It's fall!" I replied, calling down to her. "I'm asking it to grow apples, even though it's the wrong time of year, and it's the wrong type of tree. I don't know how this goal is anything *but* against its nature."

Amber sighed. "You have to think of this differently," she said. "A ginkgo tree and an apple tree are both trees; they both bear fruit. You're asking it to imagine that it is a different type of tree, that's all."

I frowned. "And the fact that it's fall?"

"You're asking it to come to harvest soon, that's what it already does in the fall," she said with a shrug. I was used to Speaking branches into different forms, but this was the first time I'd tried Speaking a tree into doing something new. Amber had reminded me before I climbed onto the branch that it was the same principle; I was asking the life's essence to do something, but that didn't mean it wasn't hard.

Eventually, I was able to cajole the branch into bringing forth a handful of tiny pink blossoms. The blooms were small and pink, perfect and delicate and desperately out of place among the fan-shaped Ginkgo leaves.

Daylight filtered down through the boughs as I walked home after the lesson. The forest was beautiful. Since it was early autumn, the yellow of the leaves was fresh; the preservation upon them—the first of several before the season would be up—still glistening as it sank in. I was marveling at the yellow carpet, enraptured as always, when I was bowled over, and fell in a mess of limbs. There, half on top of me, I saw a young woman with gentle features and elbow-length red braids. She was wide-eyed and startled, and unfamiliar to me, but the red maple leaves pressed—almost painted—on the backs of her hands marked her as a Speaker of Maple. I myself had a pair of yellow ginkgo leaves clinging to the hollows of my collar bones.

"Sorry! I'm so sorry," I said, extricating myself from underneath her and standing back up.

"Yes, I'm fine, thank you, um..." she paused for a moment and rose to her feet. "I was distracted. I should be the sorry one."

"Where are you headed?" I asked. I noted how the deep red of her dress stood out in the carpet of soft gold.

"I was hoping to find the Ginkgowood's Speakers. I'm from the Maple neighborwood, and I think we need help. Hopefully of a sort that the Ginkgo Speakers can provide." Her voice wavered as she talked, a pleading evident in her words. She looked exhausted. I reached out my hand. She took it and squeezed my fingers.

"I'm only a novice Speaker, but I can bring you to my teacher," I told her, pulling down the collar of my shirt to show her the leaves there. She let out a small sigh of relief and let me begin leading her back along the path I'd just come down.

The branches overhead arched in deliberate patterns, Spoken maps that could lead you anywhere in the wood—should you know how to read them, or at least, how to ask the trees for help. The Maplewood girl followed me with wide eyes. Through hollows in the stands of trees I could see my neighbors working—cooking, mending, sewing, and gardening, all tucked into homes Spoken from the trees. We passed the home of another Speaker, but one I didn't know well enough to introduce to the Maplewood girl. His home was on the edge of a clearing, where the trees wouldn't be bothered by the heat and smoke of his—amazing—baking.

The branches overhead weren't yet bare, turning the air a golden yellow. Even the Maplewood Speaker seemed impressed with the gold all around her. My great-uncle August had been a trader between the woods, and he'd described the Maplewood as having a rich carpet of red and an ever-present sweet scent. Even growing up with that, the Maplewood Speaker seemed impressed by the Ginkgowood.

My mentor Amber lived deep in her tree, which had been Spoken into a gentle nest of a home many generations ago. Its trunk was wide and it seemed to fold into itself somewhere, where the sloping boughs met a twist in the trunk. I turned into the hollow space and followed gentle, worn-smooth, spiraling steps downward. The root ball had been spread out and shaped with Speaking until it formed a burrow; a home with kitchen, bedroom, common room, library, and pantry. I loved the warm glow of the place, the way the amber lamp roots had been Spoken into shelves and earth had been Spoken solid and smooth.

The Maplewood girl followed me closely. I always found the place a comfort, and I could tell that the girl was also settled some by the calm space. "Amber?" I called out.

"Bee?" The slight padding of footsteps floated into the room around her voice. Amber had been stocking the pantry, it seemed—her tree was female, granting her ample fruit without a single whisper. She wasn't one to waste this gift. She smiled a broad, true smile. "Bee! What brings you back so soon?" She had an apron on over her blouse, and her black hair was pulled into a bun—as it was only when doing housework. Her eyes flicked to the foreign Speaker, and I saw in her eyes that the girl had caught her interest.

"Um, hello," the strange Speaker began. "I'm here on behalf of the Maplewood." She held up her hands. "We have a problem. The Maplewood has a bit of a shortage of Speakers—well, Novices really." Her fingers were intertwined, wringing with her words. "A shortage in that we have none." The words were heavy, hanging in the air like syrup.

"How long?" Amber asked.

"I was selected three cycles ago," the Speaker said. All the neighborwoods, I knew, tested for gifted children to train as Speakers at the same five-year interval. "Even then," she continued. "I was the only one. So, really the shortage has been since before that."

"Two complete cycles without any apprentices?" Amber frowned, and her eyes focused inward. "Ten...almost fifteen years of children, since there have been new novices?"

The Maplewood girl nodded. "I was tested young myself. I was only nine when I was accepted as a novice, because we've had so few truly gifted children born in our neighborwood," The Maplewood girl said, her brows knitted. "I'm scared for us."

That explained her age. I had been sixteen when I was tested for the Speaker's gift, and wouldn't become a full Speaker until the end of the cycle—just after my 21st birthday. Yet here she was, this Maplewood Speaker, a full Speaker of her wood, and she was maybe a year older than me.

"So, nearly twenty years," Amber said.

"Yes." The Maplewood Speaker pursed her lips. "We can't fix this on our own. If we knew what was causing us to lose our connection to the wood, we could reknit it; if we knew where the Speaking was going, we could try to cajole it back to our children. But that's not working. It's just...leaving." When she said those words, the Speaker seemed ready to cry.

After a moment of silence (save for the gentle crackling of the fire in the corner) Amber Spoke a soft suggestion of calm. Her words settled over us: a warm, soft blanket. The Maplewood Speaker's hard worry melted some, softening into a gentler concern.

"I can call the Ginkgowood Speakers together. We can discuss what is in our power to help the Maplewood," Amber said, her voice back to normal. "We have much to consider before we can offer our help to you, miss...?"

"Gia." What a lovely name.

Gia nodded at Amber. She must have known that the Speakers would want to talk together before offering help to her and her people, no matter how desperate the situation felt to her. I silently thanked Amber for having Spoken a comfort around us.

Amber pulled off her apron and turned to me. "Bee, would you please find someplace for the Speaker to stay?" It was my turn to nod.

"She can stay with me," I offered, smiling at the girl as she stood beside me.

As Amber began to mutter to herself and look for something, I guided Gia back up the stairs. She was quiet, and remained that way as I led her to my home.

The calm hung on our shoulders as we walked, giving the neighborwood an unspecifiable quality—almost dreamlike in its softness. It had been years since I'd had calm Spoken onto me. It was a common Speaking upon children, and one simple enough that most anyone could spin it in some fashion. Even so, it had been a long time. I'd forgotten how nice it was.

My home was a warm, open one, made from four trunks Spoken into arching walls enclosing a single room a dozen feet off the ground. I was halfway up the flattened branch stairs, which twisted and wound up to my front door, when I felt the calm slip away and the cool bite of the air return to my awareness.

Gia paused—she was also feeling the edge return to the world. I hesitated, watching her, concerned but hesitant to ask her how she was doing. But she quickened her pace once again, following me into the comfort of my small home. The wood had been Spoken smooth and worn soft. The branches of the four great Ginkgos that made my home wove a sturdy, solid basket of floor and ceiling.

I held open the heavy curtain over my home's front entrance for the Maplewood girl and saw her smile as she ducked inside. The room was wide and simple. My bedroll sat against one wall; several overstuffed pillows rested on the floor around a low table; and my large, full kitchen (with both a stove and a hearth!) took up nearly half of what was left unclaimed. I've always found it a kind and open place, and Gia seemed to find it a pleasant place to be. I fixed some tea, broth, and shortbread cookies. She was quiet.

Rain came to the Ginkgowood that night. It pittered down through the leaves, and I could feel the cool dampness of the air that always accompanies a soft drizzle. The rain picked up as the night wore on, the thrum upon the interlaced-branches overhead growing more insistent as the night grew deeper.

I slept lightly and little, rising early in the small hours of the morning. The Maplewood girl tossed as she slept, her mind no doubt wracked with worry for her wood. As I moved about the room, putting water on the fire and warming my toes, the Speaker stirred. I glanced over, afraid I'd disturbed her, but she didn't move again.

I set some acorn tea to steep, some honeyed beechnuts to roast on the hearth, and considered what to do for breakfast. I had plain leavened bread, but the Maplewood was far enough from the Ginkgowood that the trip took three days, even running intermittently. She wouldn't have had a hot meal in that time, so I figured I ought to give her one.

I tried to cook quietly, so as not to disturb her. She slept curled into herself, her arms tucked tight against her torso. Her hair had slipped out of its braids in her sleep, ringing her head with red. The spill of hair framed her face, softening the taut lines that spread across it. She woke only when the sun was spilling across the floor of my home, the leaves of the neighborwood tinting the dawn light with the richness of gold that had always been my favorite thing about that time of year.

Gia didn't wake slowly, but started up with a breathless gasp. Her legs were tangled in the blanket, causing her to twist up further in her anxiety. I dropped a pan of heavy biscuits onto the stove and hurried to her side, skidding and scraping across the ground as I came to my knees beside her.

"What-" she stammered. She rubbed at bleary eyes with the heels of her palms.

"You're in the Ginkgowood," I said, my voice as low as I could make it. She trembled, her ankles still twisted up. I reached out a hand gingerly, offering her what comfort I could. "You're safe. The Speakers of Ginkgo are discussing how to help the Maplewood." My words were hushed, as soothing as I could make them without slipping into Speaking.

My guest blinked the sleep from her eyes and looked at me. Her eyes were so wide that I thought she might begin to cry. But she just nodded, reaching out to take my hand. She held onto me and took a deep breath, her eyes closing again as she settled herself. As she breathed, her chest rising and falling in rhythm, I wondered what it must be like in the Maplewood for her to be consumed by such deep and desperate fear.

"I presume you've no word," Gia said flatly after a handful of long moments.

"Nothing yet, no." She nodded, unsurprised yet still disappointed. I patted her hand and waved toward my kitchen. "Let's eat." Her grip on me tightened as we rose to our feet, but she let me go, settling for following close as I walked over to the stove.

I'd gathered the beechnuts to cool in a bowl, steeped the morning tea, cooked a small pot of hot cereal, and baked two sweet palm-loaves. My tree was filled with the smell of hot grains and honey. To top it all off, I retrieved a small jar of blackberry jam from the back of my top shelf. I had several of the small jars, as my mother was fond of making the sweet preserves during the summer berry season, and I was particularly glad to have something for my weary guest. I handed Gia one of the bowls and offered her the jam. I took my own bowl and walked over to the low table in the corner, scooting past her to pull over a pair of sitting cushions.

She sat down in one fluid motion, folding her legs up underneath herself. She put her bowl down across from mine as she settled, but then just stared into it. I waited for her to start, but she didn't.

"Um, Miss?" Her face stayed blank. "Gia?" I repeated. She blinked and looked up at me, eyes glassy.

"Sorry," she said, a waver in her voice. "What?"

I nodded. "Gia. You need to eat. You're exhausted." She nodded, and slowly moved to pick up her spoon and start to eat. I watched her as subtly as I could while eating my own breakfast. Though it was more indulgent than my typical breakfast, she seemed to enjoy the sweet roll with blackberry jam. I was proud of my cooking.

She scraped insistently at the bottom of her bowl and I could tell that I was right — she had really needed to eat. When she finally set the spoon down, apparently satisfied that she'd gleaned all that she could, I rose. I took both of our bowls over to the stove. I set mine on the counter, but spooned some more cereal into hers. I brought Gia a new cup of tea along with her bowl, and told her that I was going to fetch more water. She nodded, blowing gently on her drink.

And so I descended from my cabin with a large wooden bucket in hand into the early morning fog of the Ginkgowood. The mist was cool on my skin and I couldn't help but smile as I walked. The neighborwood looked particularly soft in the morning light; the haze of fog smoothing all the wood's edges. I walked barefoot, enjoying the dampness of the leaves. I left my bucket by a small creek and continued on to Amber's home. Guilt nagged at me, telling me I should've been honest with Gia, but I shook it as best I could. There had been no need to worry her further.

"Amber?" My voice was barely above a whisper. I cleared my throat. "Amber?" I called out, loud enough this time.

"Bee? I'm in the pantry," she said from somewhere off the main room. I followed the sound to find her on her tip-toes, reaching towards the back of her highest shelf. "Morning. I hope your walk was peaceful." I nodded.

"I was wondering—how did it go yesterday?" I wrung my hands, my fingers twisted up as my thumb worried my palm. "Gia—Gia— she's distraught. I'm worried for her."

Amber rocked back onto her heels. "As a Speaker, your work is to care for the Ginkgowood. You'll be asked to enrich and care for the wood, and to be a helpful and engaged member of our neighborwood. You'll sing to the skies to soften the weather, and ask the bushes for bushels of berries." This much I knew. The neighborwood would wither without our care. "We are not, however, asked often to make decisions. Our actions are subtle ones. We talk to the wood, we talk to each other, but we never really talk to others' woods." Amber paused, her face taut. "This isn't really something that has happened before. As such, we don't have any solutions yet." I nodded an acknowledgement. "The Speaker looked rather unwell yesterday, so I think we'll try to come up with a solution before we involve her in the discussion."

I knew I didn't have much time before Gia would begin to wonder. "Thank you, Amber." She nodded. "Please, let me know what the Speakers are saying."

Amber reached out her hand to me, patting me on the arm. "We'll do what we can."

With that, I left. The morning was already light, effusing the wood with a gentle glow as the light met with the last of the morning mist. I jogged back to the stream and filled the bucket. It was heavy enough that I had to slow my pace to keep from sloshing water down my front.

The morning mist had disappeared by the time I made it home. The day was warming up. When I got to the top of the stairs at last, water bucket in hand, I found that Gia was sitting exactly where I'd left her.

I could tell she'd moved; the cup in her hands was steaming, so she must have refilled it. But her feet were folded in that particular way, and her back was slumped just the same.

"Gia, I'm back," I said as I walked in, not wanting to startle her.

"Hello, Miss." She said without raising her head.

"Oh, please-"

"Bee, right?" She looked at me. Her eyes were watery, her face pale, but even so, she had an earnestness to her.

"Yes." I put the bucket down just inside the door. "Yeah, it's Bee." She smiled, but her smile was weak, watered down like sunlight through rainclouds - a visible effort, but hardly half the effect.

"Welcome back."

I wondered what it was about her that compelled me to fuss over her as if she were completely helpless. After all, she was a full and proper Speaker, while I was still a novice. I hesitated, standing near her for another moment before returning to the counter, to scrub up after breakfast.

Gia sat at the table. I watched her out of the corner of my eye, careful not to stare. I continued cleaning, and noticed for the first time that she didn't have a bag. A three-day walk would've required... something. But no, there she was with only the clothes on her back.

"Gia," I asked. "Why don't you have anything with you?"

"Huh? Oh," she pursed her lips and tucked a braid behind her ear before continuing. "I put what I needed in my pockets."

"Three days of rations in a pocket?" I raised my eyebrow.

"I took bread and a canteen. It was all I needed."

"Well, where's the canteen?"

She shrugged. "I dropped it when it was empty. It was awkward to hold while I ran."

Her frailty suddenly made sense—her pale face; her exhaustion; her distraction. I fetched another cup of water and sat beside her.

"Why did you run? Fifteen years without new novices, but now you run full tilt to a neighboring wood," I asked.

"Something snapped in me," she said. "There are enough of us for now, enough Speakers. Everyone is nervous, but they're not terrified. But after a second cycle without any apprentices, I realized... I realized that if something doesn't change, we'll all be gone without realizing it."

I didn't say anything more to that, just handed her the water. I didn't know what to say, so I just watched her. Her braids were loose, thin wisps escaping them. She was pale (quite unlike myself) but on top of that her fingers felt clammy. She was sick with worry, that much was clear. Without any better idea of what to do, I put my arm around her. For a half-second, she stiffened, her whole body tensing up as she whipped her head around at me, eyes wide. But just as fast, she softened and shifted her weight towards me.

"Thank you," she whispered, so softly that I wasn't sure if she even intended for me to hear her. I patted her arm.

"The Maplewood'll be alright," I said after another long stretch. Gia turned her head into my shoulder at this, something leaving her at the mention of her home. I almost regretted saying anything, but she wrapped her arms around me and I could feel her shuddering. Heat spread across one shoulder, and I held her as she cried.

We sat like that for hours; until the sun was down and Gia was out of tears. When I started to move away, ready to roll out the sleeping mats, she took hold of my sleeve and followed closely. I could feel her nails through my shirt.

She held my arm when we went to sleep, clutching me like I was the last thing between her and nightmares. I figured that was probably the truth, and lay as still as I could.

The nest two days passed with agonizing slowness.

On the morning after I visited her, Amber came by my home with a nutty spread and assurances that yes, she would let me know when the Speakers had made a decision, and to stop worrying. This left Gia and I to discover that neither of us was the particularly patient sort.

I tried to distract Gia (and, to be fair, myself) during that time. I spent hours cooking complicated meals, with recipes I'd learned from my mother. I showed Gia the neighborwood, pointing out where Speaker May's partner was weaving blankets for their future child; where my mother lived; and where the Ginkgowood held market days. I even spent hours relaying to her all of the stories that I had been told as a child about the nature of the Ginkgowood. I learned quickly that the stories that were told in the Maplewood were quite different, even when they were the same—in the Maplewood, Rabbit in "The Sparrow and the Rabbit" isn't a baker, but a syrup maker, and Sparrow's wings are red, not gold.

The moments in between, when the air between us filled with anxiety, I would assure Gia that the Ginkgowood would not let her people down.

On the morning of the third day though, one of the other novices showed up at my door.

"Bee! Bee, get up!"

"Aiden?" I swept aside the curtain to see him there. His face was flushed and his breath caught in his throat. He was clearly in a hurry, though I wasn't sure why.

"The Speakers want us! They're meeting and they want us too!"

I glanced over my shoulder. Gia sat at the table, a curious expression on her face as our eyes met. I turned back to Aiden, a twisting in my gut.

"Did Amber say-"

"You can't bring the Maplewood Speaker." So Amber had known I'd ask. I was glad, then, that she'd sent Aiden. He let expressions and tones of voice slip past him, and I could feel my brow furrowing as I thought. He wouldn't read anything into my face. Why would Amber ask for me to leave Gia alone? She was a stranger here, and a stranger lost in her own despair. She needed company. Aiden's words broke my reverie. "Bee, come on, let's go."

"One moment," I said, turning to Gia. She looked much better than she had three days ago. She'd re-braided her hair— braids ringed her head, pinned tightly into place. The color had returned to her face and the focus to her eyes. "Um—"

"I heard," she said. I hesitated, waiting for her to continue. She didn't. So I turned about and followed Aiden away from my home. Away from Gia.

We walked quickly and wordlessly. Aiden was breathless with excitement over the prospect of making decisions with the Speakers. I was concerned for Gia.

The neighborwood was still dark, a tinge of watery pink in the sky the only indication of the coming dawn. We wound through the trees toward a large clearing where everyone in the wood could gather. It was full of people — novices and Speakers and neighbors alike. At the sight of all the people, Aiden visibly deflated.

When all of the Speakers and novices were present, the oldest Speaker—a wizened old man named Faa—stood. His golden robe seemed to dwarf him and his white hair rebelled against gravity, but his eyes had yet to cloud with age. As he stood, the clearing went quiet.

"Good morning, all," Faa said. "The Maplewood is in trouble. For some unknown reason, the Maplewood has no new Speakers, no new Novices. They are running out of Speakers." A murmur rippled through the neighbors, and Faa waited for it to fall away before continuing. "For the past three days, we Speakers have considered how to help. At last, we have an idea to present to the neighborwood." He turned and returned to his seat. Another Speaker, Tanner, stood and came forward. He was a sturdily built man, with a voice that carried over the assembled with little effort.

He cleared his throat and took a deep breath before beginning. "We have decided that—if the neighborwood finds it acceptable, of course—we'll send some of our Speakers to the Maplewood on a rotation. We'll start with six-week rotations of three Speakers each. We'd also evaluate the effectiveness of the six-week rotation after several months, of course. When the Maplewood starts to have new Speakers again, we'll leave." Many of the Speakers nodded at this, sitting straight and watching the neighbors. The others tried to mask their malcontent, but I could see a handful shifting where they sat.

"Is that all?" I asked, rather loudly. I hadn't meant to open my mouth, let alone practically shout at a Speaker, but the solution that he offered seemed a pittance.

Tanner frowned at me. "Do you have a problem with helping our neighbors, novice?"

I rose to my feet, shifted the collar of my shirt to show the leaves which noted my status as a novice Speaker, and began talking. "The Maplewood has waited two cycles. In that time, they haven't had a single Novice. Even the cycle before that, they only had one, a novice accepted to the order of Speakers at just nine years old." The neighbors around me muttered to one another, an air of concern and confusion echoing through them. "The Speaker who came to us was that child. She's sick with worry for her people. We can't sit here and let things get worse."

"We aren't letting it get worse," Tanner snapped back at me. "We're helping them. We're giving what we have to give—our time, and our skills. What more is there to give?"

"It's not enough!" I said. "Your solution is to wait and, what, hope that eventually things will get better on their own?"

"What do you propose?" Tanner asked. I frowned. I didn't have any other solutions, but I knew that this wasn't enough. He responded to my hesitation with a haughty eyebrow. "You criticize our solution without offering one of your own? Why should we, who have decided to help people whom we owe nothing, have to listen to a girl who can't even try to think of a better way to help?"

His words lit a fire in my gut. I'd spent the past three days fostering Gia, a gentle, broken soul. Yet he dared insinuate that I wasn't putting effort into this? I could see Amber sitting with the Speakers; she bit her lip as Tanner talked.

"It took you three days to come up with your solution." I replied. "Three days that I spent caring for the ill woman who came to us for help. She ran here from the Maplewood, desperate for help." The neighborwood was usually a place of calm, of civility. I'd never lost my temper like this before, but it felt natural, the words insistent that I say them. My neighbors all seemed to frown as one.

Amber and Faa both rose, separately, but together. Amber stepped over several folks to stand by my side. I could feel her concern for me reaching across the space remaining between us. Faa touched Tanner on the shoulder, murmured something to him, and turned to the assembly. "Novice Speaker Bee has a point, my friends. We open our ears to you, to all the neighbors. We'll reconvene tomorrow morning to discuss alternative, or additional, longer-term solutions."

As folks started to leave, Amber patted my arm. "I think you could use a rest," she said, leaning towards my ear and talking low. I frowned at her. "Faa was right, you were compelling. You're compelling, I think, because you've taken on the Maplewood Speaker-"

"Gia," I interjected. Amber nodded.

"Because you've taken on Gia's burden. That's quite a task, and I know it's exhausting. You need a break."

She walked me back to her home and sat me down at the table. In front of me, Amber placed a cup of mead, a thick stew, and a small glazed roll. She sat down with a cup of tea for herself, and waited for me to eat. When I finished, she insisted on a lesson in Speaking.

"It'll distract you, get your mind off all this," she insisted.

"But what about—"

"I'll ask Aiden to go check on her, alright?" she said.

I relented.

I followed her through the neighborwood to a stand of trees that wanted for care. Brambles crept up around their trunks, curling outward, abutting the path. I sat on the path and cradled a vine, careful not to prick myself. I whispered to it, wheedling the needles dull. Vine by vine, I Spoke away the brambles' defenses. It was early evening before I finished to Amber's satisfaction and she told me to, at last, go home.

When I walked in, Gia looked up from the fire. She was cooking —I could smell tea and roasting potatoes. Her face was red from the heat, and she had strapped on the apron that I always forgot to use. She'd re-braided her hair, woven it into a plait that feathered into nothingness at the small of her back. I'd learned that playing with her hair was a nervous habit of hers, so the complex layering of the braid told me more about her state of mind than her words would.

"Oh, you're back!" she said, a smile breaking across her face. "Do you have news?" At the sight of my face—with an expression I only registered was present from her reaction to it —she hung the ladle on the edge of the cast-iron pot and approached me. Her face held a hundred unasked questions. Instead, she cupped my cheek in her hand and forced me to look her in the eye. "Bee?"

"The Speakers had a plan," I whispered. "It wasn't enough. Isn't enough."

She stood there, her hand on my face. "I...we can make it work." She said, wearing a sad smile that was as soft as her words. "My people, we'll do our best, whatever it is." Her pain and worry for her people wracked her, but she was better than she had been. She held herself together.

"No, we're going to do better. I have until tomorrow to come up with a better solution." I sighed. If she hadn't held me there, I would have turned away and shaken my head. "All the Speakers in the Ginkgowood took three days to come up with, 'We visit from time to time and let them wait for a natural end to the problem.'" Three days reassuring Gia, wasted. Reassurance only helps, I thought bitterly, if everything ends up okay.

Gia pulled me into an embrace. I could feel her pain, and my whole being ached in sympathy. Amber was right, I had taken on Gia's pain. But I couldn't bring myself to mind, not then, while we each held the other up as we hurt in tandem, mourning the Maplewood.

I only let Gia go when I could hear the tea begin to boil. We ate, cleaned up, and then lay down for sleep, all in silence, though neither of us slept at first.

We lay close enough to feel one another's body heat. I didn't slip into sleep even as the hours slipped past. All I could do was think, searching for some solution to the plight of the Maplewood. I watched Gia slip into an uneasy sleep as I thought. Even tossing and turning, soft whimpers and moans rising from her, her warmth, her presence, comforted me. A palmful of hours before dawn, she started weeping in her sleep. I touched her on the arm, hoping to pull her out of the dream. She mumbled, shaken from the pain, and curled into me. My heart skipped a beat, but as Gia fell back into her dreams, I wrapped my arms around her and held her close. She smelled like sugar, and I wondered if the whole of the Maplewood smelled like syrup. The thought made me smile, my face buried in her hair. It was straight, unlike mine, and soft in a different way. She settled against me then, like she was seeking my warmth in her unconsciousness.

I whispered a Speaking of sweet dreams to her. I felt the warmth of my breath held against my face by her hair. I hadn't Spoken anything onto another person in ages, and the feeling of whispering to the core of Gia was so pure I had to hold my breath to keep from tightening my arms around her. There was a delight in Speaking to trees and brambles, of course, but they don't react quite the same way —it doesn't echo back. The thought that I had then was so abrupt that I squeezed her tightly without meaning to, causing her to stir.

"Bee?" she mumbled.

"Sorry," I replied. "Go back to sleep." She nodded and nodded off fast, thanks to the sweet dreams I'd Spoken for her.

With Gia curled against me and an idea in my mind, I fell fast asleep, dead to the world, if only for a few hours.

When we woke, we ate quietly, and then I led Gia to the great clearing in the neighborwood. It was filling up when we got there. We sat and waited for the meeting to begin. Gia didn't ask me if I'd found a solution, and I didn't offer to tell her that I had—I wasn't sure what she would think.

When the whole of the neighborwood had gathered, Faa stood. He gestured to me and asked if I had a suggestion for the Speakers. Gia and I rose together. I took a deep, shaky breath, and then explained.

"I'll give my Speaking to the Maplewood. All of it. They can have every drop," I said. I heard a number of gasps, and Gia's small hand snatched at my arm, trying to pull me to face her. But I continued. "Speaking is part of who we are, yes, but that fact is exactly what means this should be possible! What we Speak to is the essence of a being, and Speaking itself is part of our essence. It's natural, inherent —it should be possible to influence." I took a deep breath. "You can Speak the gift out of me and Gia can take it to the Maplewood." I turned and nodded at Speaker Tanner. "Until then, we may help them as you suggested, but after a cycle they will no longer need our aid." Gia tugged harder at my arm but I leaned away from her, countering her weight with my own.

The entire clearing was filled with silence. Stunned, confused silence.

"I mean," I said, continuing because I didn't know what else to do. "I'm just a novice, I can't even consistently grow an apple. It's not like my Speaking would be missed."

"No," Faa said. "Don't give yourself. You have so much time left, so much fire left in you." He smiled deeply at me. It was a smile that made me feel warm and full, really and truly proud of myself. He 6turned to Gia and took a long, shaking breath before letting out a long, shaking sigh. "You're right, logically, it should work. But if you have to take the power away from someone...you can have my Speaking. I've served the Ginkgowood so many years...this is what I have left to give."

After several long moments where the clearing was quiet but for the rustling of leaves, the keeper of records, a Speaker named Gianna, rose to her feet as well. "I have less than half a cycle before my apprentice becomes a full Speaker. When they are ready to take my place, I'll go and give my Speaking to the children of the Maplewood." After she said her piece, she waved a reassuring hand to someone behind me. Turning, I saw that it was her apprentice, Speaker Conna. Their eyes were wide with shock, with anxiety. I looked away, embarrassed.

Three more of the senior-most Speakers offered their Speaking to the Maplewood. I stammered, not having intended others to give up themselves, but each talked of a life spent in service to the neighborwood. Their Speaking would not be missed, each insisted. One professed a desire to bake pastries, another touched her belly and explained the want to care for her future child with all of her hours.

I was dumbfounded, and sat quietly while the Speakers talked among themselves and decided to head out the next morning for the Maplewood. As the meeting ended, I found that Gia and I were holding one another's hands with a mutual vice grip that had caused my fingers to go numb.

"That was impressive," Amber said, weaving towards us through the crowd of chattering neighbors as I rubbed feeling back into my hand.

"Thanks," I said.

That afternoon, Gia, Amber, the four Speakers who'd offered their gifts most immediately, and I prepared for the long walk to the Maplewood. Blankets, water, food—everything that we needed, we folded and packed neatly into soft rucksacks. Unlike Gia, we took our time, readying ourselves before the three-day trip.

The next three days were too long for my feet, but too short for my heart. Gia and I walked the whole way with our fingers intertwined, and slept in one another's arms.

When we entered the Maplewood, it was like walking upon a river of fire. The leaves were all reds and deep oranges; the color was

as rich as the gold of the Ginkgowood. I leaned over to whisper to Gia
—

"Is this how you felt when you saw the Ginkgowood?"
She smiled. "Probably not."
As Gia led us between the wide trunks of maple trees, neighbors started to gather—it wasn't often that people moved between woods, and they watched us walk. She led us to a wide clearing and had us wait for her to bring the Maplewood Speakers.

The clearing seemed to be rather similar to the one in which Ginkgo Speakers had stood and offered their gifts. I looked around while we waited, intrigued by the beauty of the scarlet maple leaves.

It wasn't long until the clearing was filled with neighbors and Speakers. Gia wandered back towards us, standing just beside me. I heard a soft murmuring wash over the crowd, hushed whispers, then a number of sharp breaths.

Faa turned to me when one of the Maplewood Speakers looked to our small island of yellow in the sea of red, and nodded to us. "Novice, would you deliver my gift to the Maplewood? This was your idea, after all."

My breath caught in my throat, but I nodded. Gia guided me forward, her hand steady on my arm. Faa closed his eyes, a wide smile breaking across his face. "I'm looking forward to being just another man," he said to us. Gia and I exchanged glances. I put my hand out; she patted me on the back and took a step away.

Speaking the gift was like trying to control the flow of a stream with a bucket of water. I Spoke to Faa's essence, asking that which was the very core of him to please disentangle itself from its eternal harmony. His soul didn't give up Speaking eagerly, but slowly, my words found purchase. Faa smiled—it was a fake smile, the kind that is so perfect it seems as genuine as the smile of a child when they see the golden air of a morning in the Ginkgowood. I knew the truth, though. Faa's being was echoing, separating itself from the gift inside him with great reluctance. It was, after all, a part of him.

As I whispered to Faa's gift, I felt warmth spread across my palms. The whole of the Maplewood watched us in silence.

I felt the Speaking flow from Faa and come to rest solidly around me. It felt like a glove, like I had water swirling around my hands. Once I had pulled all of Faa's speaking out of him, I whispered to it, telling it to find purchase within the neighbors here, within their children, and felt the weight of it drip from my hands into the earth of the Maplewood. As I finished, I could feel it starting to seep into the water, into the plants: into the Neighborwood and its people.

When I finished, Faa opened his eyes. He straightened his back, as if a great weight had been lifted, and nodded first to me, then to Gia, then to the rest of the Maplewood.

The other Ginkgowood Speakers exchanged nervous smiles. Their expressions were tentative and excited, and I could feel what they were feeling—after what I'd just done. At the edge of the clearing, I saw a young child watching us, bobbing up and down on the balls of their feet, full of energy. A man dressed in a deep red, similar to that of Gia's clothes, squeezed the child's shoulder. His fingers caught the fabric of the child's shirt, twisting it up in five little swirls of shadow.

I caught Gia's eye—her face was higher than I'd remembered. It took me a moment to understand why: she'd been slumped down for the past four days. At length, she had straightened her back, a weight lifted. A smile came from somewhere deep within her, and from her, tears fell onto the carpet of scarlet below us.

See Mads Alvey's story "Upon the Fallen Leaves of the Gingko Tree" online at Metaphorosis. If you liked it, leave a comment. Authors love that!
Remember to subscribe to our e-mail updates so you'll know when new stories are posted.

About the story

Many of my story ideas start with a single line—usually the first line in the final draft—which repeats over and over in my mind. "Upon the Fallen Leaves of the Ginkgo Tree" was one of these stories. When I began the story, my walk to school every day involved going through a neighborhood which was lined with ginkgo trees, and the first line of the story came to me while I was walking through the neighborhood in the fall—upon the leaves.

I'm also invested in the idea that fiction is the way in which we as people come to understand ourselves and our world, and that speculative fiction is particularly significant in this. Because of this, I tend towards stories which involve the world ending better than it started. Once I had the starting line of the story, I mulled over a variety of scenarios that would let me have a hopeful or positive ending, and ended up with a draft of the story that (very) loosely resembled the final product.

A question for the author

Q: Do you write with a particular audience in mind?

A: I often write with myself as the intended audience. There are a lot of things that I enjoy seeing in stories, and when I write, I try to hit all of those notes. I try to include people like me—queer folks, gender minority folks, disabled folks; themes and subjects I care about; and evoke images that matter to me, or appeal to my sense of aesthetics.

I do write with the intent of sharing my work, but it matters to me that I, at the very least, start with a base that is true, first and foremost, to what I want in a story.

About the author

Macs Alvey lives in Lexington, Kentucky and is a full-time student at the University of Kentucky, seeking a degree in English. She plans to seek an MLS when she graduates, and settle down surrounded by books. When he has it, he splits his free time between crafting; cooking; gardening; amateur taxidermy; writing science fiction, fantasy, and satire; spending way too much time on the internet, and doting on his three rats.

malveyauthor.com, @ProperPuns

Just a Fire

A. Martine

by Addison Black, JAN. 3rd, 3075

Over the past year, we at MAELSTROM have covered stories which have often bordered on the sensational, such as the famous rivalry between siblings Amaterasu and Susanoo, the Japanese gods of the Sun and the Storms respectively. We have also notably touched upon the scandalous account of the giant Paul Bunyan's alleged affair with the Titan Selene. All of these have served a similar aim: to bring awareness of Lorendi, sanctuary of forgotten gods and goddesses, and bridge the gap keeping Humans and Lorendians separate.

In the midst of the cacophony of entities roaming Lorendi, it is often easy to forget some of the lesser-known, but no less interesting events. One such story is that of the Fall of Asgard, which many have attributed to the ongoing feud between former Valkyrie Brünnhilde and her father, the great Wotan.

It is common knowledge that all the inhabitants of Lorendi were forced to coexist after the collapse of their respective homes. It may be of interest for our readers to note that no one knows how Lorendi came to be. As more and more entities began to lose their homes, they found themselves inexplicably drawn to this vast and strange land, and found that they grew stronger within its borders. In this sense, Asgard is an anomaly; it appears to be the only place where the collapse was not instigated by humans, but the details of the episode remain unclear and contradictory.

Most of us have, at some point of our existences, idolized controversial figures, those insubordinate figureheads of change and defiance; for me, it has always been Brünnhilde, the powerful, enigmatic woman who lived and would have died for her ideals. The opportunity to decipher her story, essentially, is my childhood coming full circle.

According to the all but forgotten legend, after Brünnhilde's lover and nephew Siegfried was killed by Hagen, son of the dwarf Alberich, the erstwhile Valkyrie threw herself into his funeral pyre, maddened with her grief. The same pyre became a full-blown wildfire which consumed Valhalla and all the gods present, marking the grim end of this mythology. But in reality, only Siegfried, who had already perished, was a casualty that day; the hall was destroyed in the fire and spread throughout the whole of Asgard, robbing the gods and goddesses of their dwelling place — but they did not die with it.

It was not long before the protagonists of the Norse mythology dispersed throughout Lorendi. In the diverse landscape of this city, most of the former residents of Valhalla are not as noteworthy as those of other tales; indeed, when one has to contend with the unrestrained antics of the Greek pantheon or the staggering number of parties thrown by the Yoruba gods and goddesses, it is easy to lose sight of the Norsemen and women of Asgard. Doubtless because of the calamitous end of their cycle, they have retreated into more tranquil existences and successfully blended in with the other Lorendians, to a fault.

Thus, shedding light on the series of events that led to the catastrophic and fiery confrontation (often referred to as the Pyre Incident or Brünnhilde's Really Big Blunder) entails delving deeply into the relationship dynamics of some key characters of this episode.

Our investigation begins in the fields of Tarragon, a region in Southern Lorendi where those seeking respite from the sometimes hectic lifestyle of Aster or Amaryllis come to disengage. Eir, one of Brünnhilde's sister Valkyries, has agreed to welcome me into her lavish country home. She has invited their sister Sigrün for the conversation. Here in Lorendi, it never snows nor rains (due to an agreement between the many gods and goddesses of the weather), so the afternoon is mild and pleasant when the three of us sit down around ginger pastries and warm tea.

I try not to let my wonderment show; I am in the presence of legends, after all, and these are women whose storied place in history would dwarf anyone's confidence. Despite the fierce reputation they garnered when their exploits were recounted centuries ago, the Valkyries before me are even-tempered women who prefer walks in the sunny fields of Tarragon, these days, to bloody frays.

"Oh, believe me," Sigrün quips with a devilish smile, "we still engage in the occasional skirmish, but when your primary function has been obsolete for quite some time, it leaves more opportunity to unwind, which was frankly overdue."

I ask the sisters about their professional affiliation with their father Wotan, but the subject inevitably turns personal. Eir, who sees her sister Brünnhilde very often but has not spoken with their father in eons, tells me that while the Pyre Incident brought about the end of Asgard, it was a situation that had always been inevitable.

"I think," she tells me with a hint of displeasure, "that the whole affair was handled quite poorly."

Judging from Sigrün's weary expression, this is a conversation the sisters have often had.

Eir shrugs, implacable. "I do. Be fair, Sigrün, you remember some of those occasions as well as I do." She turns to me. "Brünnhilde was punished unfairly and often, although she was, on numerous occasions, absolutely powerless over the situation. Big things, small things, it mattered little. You see, she was always more resourceful — Wotan would say reliable — than the rest of us, so she was always called upon. She was even in charge of negotiations between the Vanir and the giants at one point, which had nothing to do with her Valkyrie duties. When things went well, Wotan would be proud: but that also meant that when they did not, everything would be her fault." Whether Eir's passion stems from sisterly partiality, or from her true belief, it is touching to behold.

"I will admit to that," Sigrün concedes. "But I also remember warning Brünnhilde that she often involved herself in things she shouldn't. She could never say no, and I told her to be careful. Besides, most of the Valkyries were starting to be jealous of the excess attention Wotan was giving her — except for us, of course." The aside is for me.

"On some level, that is true," Eir counters, "but ultimately, what doomed her was her involvement in stratagems on a grander scale which could at any given moment threaten the future of Asgard. Brünnhilde became a scapegoat because she was standing in the eye of the storm. It's as simple as that."

She is, of course, referring to the fabled ring that Loge persuaded Wotan to offer the Frost-Giants instead of Wotan's wife's sister Freia (which the giants had initially agreed upon).

"I don't think a lot people are comfortable mentioning this," Eir says with a bitter laugh, "but we all know that it's Wotan's incessant quest for the cursed ring that is the real source of Asgard's downfall, not anything my sister may or may not have done."

Watching them speak so casually about mythic events we humans have feasted upon for centuries dazes me temporarily. For the first time since I sat down with the sisters, I feel like I have pawed at something beneath the surface of my understanding. Whatever the rest of the world may have made out of it, this is just a family squabble for them, no different from the wine glasses and petty insults humans toss over Thanksgiving dinner with estranged relatives.

Sigrün has kinder words for her father than her sister does. This is surprising, considering that a long time ago, her lover Helgi was killed with the help of none other than Wotan. A suggestion of indulgence flitting across her lovely face, she says: "I agree wholeheartedly, but to say that they were at the source of everything that happened is unfair. In the long term, I believe that this was bound to turn out the way it did because everyone became different where the ring was concerned. Even the best of us could become monsters. And besides," she adds with a chuckle, "when I see the other father figures of Lorendi, it puts our own situation in sharp perspective."

The next stop to this journey leads me to the bustling streets of Aster, where one finds the most thriving and diverse community of Lorendians. Bars and shops manned by Pangu (the Chinese god of the Heavens and the Earth), Anubis (embalmer and protector of the graves), or even Bigfoot attract thousands of loyal customers on a daily basis. Further in the northern part of the neighborhood, an amusement park managed by the Loch Ness Monster and the Lady of the Lake is a popular fixture for the children of Aster. You will not find many of the more lofty characters of mythology here, but it is a welcoming and vivacious change of pace from Tarragon.

It is here, in a restaurant called Johnny's Appleseed that Loge has agreed to meet with me. Sporting retro shades, his long braided silver hair slung over his shoulder, he strolls in an hour late, smoking an electronic cigarette despite the waiter's protestations. After very short — and might I add, rather standoffish — introductions, Loge quickly broaches the subject.

"If you ask me," he says, blowing smoke rings in my direction, "I think that everybody is exaggerating the whole affair. It was just a *fire*."

I ask him about the ring, and his involvement in the story, an involvement some might consider the starting point of it all.

"That's what I do. People come to me for help and I help them, by any means. Wotan and Fricka wanted a way out of the mess Freia was going to be in with the Frost-Giants, and I gave them that. If it all went haywire from that point on, find the right people to blame."

"But surely," I ask him, "your participation was more instrumental than that. Is it not true that you were the one Wotan came to every time a crisis needed an underhanded solution?"

What is more: Alberich's ring was reportedly stolen by Wotan with Loge's help, which — among the many ensuing collateral costs —

resulted in Brünnhilde being stripped of her immortality by Wotan and confined behind a ring of fire on a mountaintop, of Loge's own design.

"You say "underhanded", I say "subtle"," he answers, downing a cocktail in the blink of an eye, "and indeed, the fire was my idea. I'm rather proud of it: Wotan was leaning towards a cage made of fiery ice, but he has no taste for the aesthetics. Once again, it's not personal. People ask for my help and I help them. I'm sorry that Brünnhilde is sore about the whole affair, but to say that I was at the heart of Asgard's Fall is a bit of an overstatement."

It suddenly becomes clear to me that the outcome of the strife involving Asgard may have been due to nothing more than likability. A popularity contest, one that the temperamental, unpredictable Brünnhilde was bound to lose, especially when facing off with an influential man like Loge. A question comes to me unplanned, then, but I don't yet ask it. Loge has already changed the subject.

He seems generally unruffled about his life at Lorendi, and even admits that he prefers it to the one he led in Asgard; this place seems to have somewhat dulled his legendary mischievousness, replacing it instead with offhanded insouciance. Tipping backwards on his chair, he laughs throatily.

"It's a riot. People here are carefree and they don't dwell on the past. There is much less pressure to perform your duties here than there was before. Look around you: there are five different gods and goddesses of the sun, twenty personifications of love and fertility. Tricksters abound, and heroes and heroines meet their matches on a daily basis."

Perhaps because I am slightly annoyed by him, or perhaps because my curiosity has been needled by his nonchalance, the question re-emerges, coming to my lips before I can make it tactful:

"Did you actually see Brünnhilde tip over the pyre that burned Asgard down? Did anyone?"

"Now... whatever do you mean by that?" he asks, almost teasingly, pulling on his cinnamon-spiced cigarette.

"Many people," I elaborate, noticing how attentive he has suddenly become, "have accepted that the fire may have been an act of childish retaliation. But it seems to me that Brünnhilde would be the last person to benefit from such large-scale sabotage. Unlike people who, for example, would want their involvement in less-than-noble endeavors burned away in the debacle. People looking for a fresh start."

"Do you mean to say," he replies with laughter in his voice, "that you believe she either didn't do it, or else was coaxed into it?"

It wouldn't be the first time that emotionally vulnerable people had been taken advantage of, I proffer. Additionally, the entire event seems antithetical to the motivations people tack onto Brünnhilde.

She has not continued a campaign of vindictiveness; in fact, she lives apart from everyone else, has done so for the past few centuries.

"Well," he leans in close, almost serious, for the first time "you're assuming that because you didn't know her. "Black Sheep Ousted From Family For Daring To Defy Them". Better yet: "Tortured Soul Manipulated Into Large-Scale Act Of Vandalism"." He gestures across the air with an open palm. "It does sound good on paper, I'll admit."

We both laugh, although no joke has been uttered there. I am not done with the matter; but for the moment, I let the question lie on the table between us, knowing full well that I will find no admission or good-natured insight behind Loge's determined indifference. He is happier to look to the future, and so I let him swerve the conversation back to Lorendi, and to his previous assurance that this is where redemption should be looked for.

He reaffirms the idea as we part ways.

"I think we're better off here and I think that this," he makes a general gesture to indicate the whole of Lorendi "would have happened anyway."

In a rare moment of contemplation, he adds, mounting his motorcycle: "myths and mythologies, folklores and fairy tales. All of this could never last. It had to end, somehow. We at Asgard just happened to go out in a blaze of glory." His sudden introspection seems to catch him off guard, and by the time he revs his engine, the mask of practiced casualness is back.

Amaryllis is less frenzied than Aster, but no less delightful. By day, it is not only an upper-class residential area, but also where some of the most luxurious boutiques and opportunities for recreational activities are located. It is, however, after dark that Amaryllis truly comes to life. Nightclubs and bars frequented by Lorendi's elite entertain them until dawn, and it is not uncommon to witness weddings and other parties being celebrated with pomp and grandeur. Many of the warriors who were brought to Valhalla by the Valkyries can be found here, chatting up sprites and fairies, and cavorting with centaurs and leprechauns.

Hildr, one of Brünnhilde's fellow Valkyries, meets with me in Saraswati's Den, a trendy hotel bar owned by the goddess of the same name, and where the Valkyrie happens to reside. She is among those of her sisters who chose to adapt completely to her new life, which suits the grandiloquence (some say pretentiousness) she has often been associated with. She is often seen partying with Aphrodite and Metztli, the Aztec goddess of the Moon, when she is not hosting a popular biweekly talk show on socialite life in the 31st century.

I am on edge again, but in a way that differs from when I encountered Eir and Sigrün. Hildr barely looks corporeal. She is the incarnation of opulence, and as she enters the bar, almost every head turns in her direction: sheaths of white silk artfully wrapped around her tall frame complement her platinum blonde curtain of hair; she moves with the ease of one who knows she is in command. I can't help but think that she must have been quite a sight on her horse in the battlefield, so many centuries ago.

She joins me and greets me charmingly, although her welcome lacks the warmth I felt with her sisters. Despite her imposing arrival, Hildr is anything but ardent; she is not interested in passionate arguments or zealous debates. The more I talk with her, the more it becomes clear that she has never been a strong proponent of the theory that Brünnhilde is a victim, that the fire was an accident, nor that Wotan had any responsibility in the downfall of Asgard. Still, in her debonaire attitude I sense a steeliness that could easily become callousness in a different light, a steeliness she makes only a halfhearted effort to conceal.

"Things are the way they are. Everyone thinks that just because we came here when our home became uninhabitable, and not because humans forgot about us, we *need* to find a reason, an explanation, someone to blame," she drawls over the din of voices surrounding us.

The question I asked Loge emerges again, but I've had enough time to compose it more diplomatically.

"According to you, Brünnhilde is unequivocally responsible, then?"

"Oh, without a doubt. I was there. We were all there." She says this without a hint of skepticism. The rapidity with which Brünnhilde's alleged culpability was accepted as fact is shocking, considering how far-reaching its effects have been.

I frame my question differently: "Is this characteristic of the Brünnhilde you knew and liked?"

"It was just a *fire*," she sighs, echoing Loge's condescension almost to perfection. Then, leaning closer with a conspiratorial look, she whispers: "*I* think that Brünnhilde was bored, and decided that she wanted to be at the center of some sort of exciting melodrama. She's always been that way. I think she was trying to distract us all from the fact that she had committed incest with her nephew Siegfried."

"Could it be," I advance, "less about anger or retaliation than an expression of her desperation? Or perhaps an attempt to force a new beginning at Asgard, by purging it of its convoluted mess? If she is to blame, that is."

"And kill us all in the process?" Hildr titters. "You are kind, but that theory is nonsense."

I know that I am toeing the line between journalistic integrity and the inexplicable inclination to defend a childhood hero, but I also recognize that there is no love lost between Hildr and Brünnhilde. She might be as biased as I am, no matter how much she feigns apathy in the matter. I begin to wonder whether a specific incident is to blame, but think better of asking her. I have a suspicion that Hildr's graciousness is mostly skin deep.

When asked about her opinion on the Human-Lorendian relationship and whether the gods' lives in Lorendi are a fitting substitute for their respective places of origin, Hildr is lost in thought for a long moment.

"At the risk of sounding complacent, I think that the lives we lead here are truly unparalleled. We're all birds of a feather, to borrow your Earthly expression."

"That might surprise our readers. It is widely assumed that most of you must be homesick."

"Of course it's assumed," she smiles in patronizing amusement, leaning back in her chair, "but I don't believe we ever needed humans worshipping us to survive; if that was the case, even Lorendi couldn't save us. We would have faded into oblivion eons ago."

"Why agree to tell your version of events to MAELSTROM's readers, if you Lorendians are self-sufficient?"

"Because our stories matter," Hildr replies, as if this were the most obvious answer in the world, "and they would have mattered whether there were people to tell them to or not. Together, we are stronger and more complex than we were separated. Ask anyone of any other mythology here, and they will tell you the same stories: betrayals, incest, illegitimate children, murder, jealousy... Brünnhilde, Wotan, Siegfried, and the ring? It was nothing special, by any standard, so I suggest we stop thinking it was."

She waves her hand loftily as she says this, as if to brush a ridiculous notion away. Slicing through the roasted peach pie she ordered, Hildr continues: "*combine* these stories and make them interact, however, and you suddenly find yourself with a riveting spectacle. Lorendi is like a micro-universe that gathers all the tales and allegories of the world, as it was meant to be. We represent all of History, in its oddity and its diversity. We reflect the changing mentalities of humans and their cultures over the millennia, and if there is anything your readers should retain, it's this: we are special."

As we part, Hildr turns to me again, and I can see that indifference has crept back into her expression.

"I don't go around saying this often, because some people still feel raw about the debacle, but I don't regret any of it. I think the fire did us all a favor." The elevator doors close on her as she looks down at her communication device, her attention already elsewhere.

Fricka has declined to speak to MAELSTROM for this story, but surprisingly, Wotan has agreed give us his perspective on the narrative. The man himself, former Supreme Ruler of Asgard. I try to contain my excitement, lest it render me unfocused. In order to meet him, I travel to Angrec, on the West Coast of Lorendi, where many financial and political institutions have settled themselves. The older, more established gods, goddesses, and beings often purchase grandiose estates here, and its seaside location makes it a perfect place to take short but sweet vacations.

Wotan co-owns many of these residences along with Zeus and Anansi, and has made his fortune leasing them to the entities who flock to their shores, looking for more upscale lifestyles. I arrive in his opulent home and I am seated on a beautiful sunbathed patio by one of his assistants and offered a drink. As I wait, I become rather nervous, expecting, from the many stories and accounts surrounding him, a boisterous and roguish man. He is anything but. The man I meet is courteous and pleasant, and there is no trace of arrogance in his stance. Waves of fiery red hair fall loosely over his shoulders; in fact, everything about him seems loose and deliberate. Unlike his brother Loge, he removes his sunglasses when he speaks to me, despite the fact that we are outdoors. It is hard to believe that this is the selfsame person who has committed adultery innumerable times and betrayed his closest relatives in his relentless pursuit for Alberich's ring. Still, I keep my guard up. I have interviewed too many a charming entity not to know better.

I ask him about his role in the Fall of Asgard and, after a careful pause, the god launches into a leisurely diatribe. Watching him speak is simply enthralling; it doesn't take long for me to understand why everyone is drawn to this articulate and persuasive man, in spite of the fact that half of what he says seems wholly calculated and insincere.

I notice, as he speaks, that he never once acknowledges his purported obsession with the ring, nor does he mention Brünnhilde. I decide to be blunt.

"Did you see her do it, and if so, do you think it was intentional?"

Wotan deflects my first question so masterfully that I almost don't catch it; instead, he leans into the latter part.

"Ah, Brünnhilde." He chuckles warmly, as if thinking fondly of a petulant, rebellious child. "That girl has always had a viselike hold on me. I hear that she's been going around accusing me of having ruined her life. I think she needs a scapegoat because everyone seems to blame her for having spread the fire that destroyed Valhalla. But that's all it was, just a fire."

Unlike with the others, when Wotan says this, the Pyre Incident seems indeed reduced to a minor skirmish, something small, something not worth bothering about. Intentions and motivations barely seem to register for him.

He continues: "It was an accident, all those who were there know that, but if a little gossip and rumors are that bothersome to her, she can keep lambasting me if she wants. I think that she will find that whether they were initially angry about losing their home or not, most inhabitants of Asgard will agree that Lorendi has been very kind to them. She can get out of her self-imposed exile whenever she wants."

"But what about the many incidents before that? What about the one involving Siegfried, for example? Surely Brünnhilde has reasons to be angry not only with you, but with all the men who have wronged her in her life." I would be angry too, if I had a father like him, I almost say to illustrate my point; but I think better of it.

"Everyone thinks her punishment was unwarranted. The truth is, I was never ungrateful for the consideration she always showed me; but you see, I am a ruler. I must not appear fickle, volatile; I must appear to be a man of my word, one who does not condone trespass and defiance. When I decided to leave her on the mountain and strip her of her immortality, it was for her own protection. I was doing her a favor. The ring of fire was entirely my idea, I'm rather proud of it. Loge was partial to a cage made of burning ice, but I've always been more creative than him when it comes to this," he adds with twinkle in his eye (it is now unclear whether the ring of fire should be credited to Loge or to Wotan).

Despite his placid facade, I can see that Wotan is tired of speaking about this chapter of his life, and especially about his daughter. Nevertheless, as much as I would rather avoid irritating him, this is the main reason this investigation was launched, and it is the key to understanding why Valhalla imploded in such a spectacular fashion. More so than Hildr or Loge, Wotan's detachment pricks in a particularly painful way. He is, after all, Brünnhilde's own father, but seemingly the one least concerned about her fate. So I push him further about his theories regarding the Really Big Blunder.

"In the confusion of the brawl, anyone could have been responsible. Anyone, in fact, could have done such a thing, for very different reasons. Asgard had many enemies, some of whom have been said to include Loge," I tentatively proffer.

When he answers, he disregards the question underneath my question.

"I think that there are long-term causes and short-term causes. If we only focus on the short term, then it appears that I am the instigator and that Brünnhilde was a victim. If you want my opinion, I think that she should have made better choices about the men she chose to surround herself with. I always thought that falling in love with Siegfried was not a good idea and the fact that he died in such a fashion is truly regrettable. Do I regret my actions, however?

Absolutely not. In each situation, one must weigh the outcomes, and I always pick the outcome that will produce the least damaging results. No one comes out of battles completely unscathed and I would think she'd know that, what with being a Valkyrie and all."

He lets the words hang between us, then elaborates on the long-term reasons. I am amused to note that he shares an almost identical opinion with Hildr on this matter.

"I think that in this scope, Asgard is in no way different from any of the other Lorendi folks' homes. We all collapsed, albeit in different ways. Many of us Lorendians have had to deal with a millennium of grudges and small grievances, and you make a compelling point. If it had not been Brünnhilde accidentally tipping over the funeral pyre, it would have been Alberich instigating a riot, the Jötnar storming Asgard, or Freia and Thor getting into a heated argument that destroyed the sacred halls of our home. I think we tend to try rationalizing the Pyre Incident to the point of obsessing over the details when one should be looking at the greater picture. I think our time was bound to come to an end, and this is something I've always accepted. It's the only reason why I have found it so easy to forgive and forget, and I wish Brünnhilde would do the same."

Brünnhilde has refused to sit down with us for an interview, thus depriving us of the most valuable point of view in this whole story. I suspect that she is handling too much grief over the death of her lover Siegfried, among other vitriol, and if Wotan is telling the truth, the guilt of having burned down Asgard by accident must surely weigh on her deeply. Perhaps with time, she will be able to bring herself to a point of closure, but for the time being, we are left with an almost — but alas, not wholly — complete story.

"Is there anything you would like to tell your daughter, in case she reads this article?"

Initially, Wotan dismisses the idea. Not for the first time during this investigation, I feel myself step out of my reporter's shoes, and stand as a woman, asking for another woman's sake. After a few moments where he seems to be deciding something, Wotan softens. He turns his stare to the distance where the sunsets are dyeing the clouds in gradient hues of scarlet. For a very long time, he squints into one of Lorendi's many setting suns before finally turning to me again.

"I do, actually. At some point I realized, since I've been living here, that what I used to think was important really isn't, you know? I thought, before in Asgard, that once you lost love it was over. I thought that once you were provoked, nothing mattered but getting justice for the offense. I thought that the unshakable pursuit of a goal outweighed everything else. Lorendi truly puts everything in perspective. Even the ring, which invaded my every thought, is lost, never to be found again. I heard they turned the whole thing into a popular book series a few centuries ago, *The King of the Rings* or something," he nods wisely. "Even if we never see each other again, I suppose I want her to find it in herself to realize the same. Only then can one truly start over."

Brünnhilde lives in Valeria, where most of the demigods, demigoddesses, and lesser folklore entities, as well as many of the smaller animals of the myths and folklores reside. It is rather separate from the rest of Lorendi, more so than Tarragon, but I am told that it is a pleasant place to live. Our readers might remember Valeria from a story covered by one of my fellow journalists, in the fourth issue of Mores and Icons, concerning the successful activewear business venture launched by Br'er Rabbit and his Senegalese cousin Leuk, the cunning hare.

Through the many collected instances surrounding the shunned Valkyrie, a patchwork has emerged. I simultaneously feel like I know Brünnhilde, and don't know her at all: she is a sad, lonely, possibly confused woman, but she also remains a mystery.

I would have relished a chance to hear her own words. Brünnhilde may have refused our invitation because she thought that her character would be assassinated. But perhaps she would have appreciated knowing that among us mortals, she continues to be celebrated for her singularity, no matter her part in Asgard's Fall. It is regrettable that her voice is glaringly absent in the panorama, and no amount of my personal of professional investment will be enough to change that fact.

However, while we may not have gathered her side of the tale, a bigger picture, is discernible. We may never know more than what was revealed in bygone and sometimes contrasting accounts of the entities who were involved in the incident, but it is clear that many, if not all of them (save Brünnhilde, perhaps) have moved on from it. The Lorendians have, for the most part, chosen to embrace their new homes and coexist peacefully, putting the rickety past behind them.

One must conclude that many of these characters, as Wotan and Hildr have so eloquently said, live similar lives and often meet similar ends, and the details don't matter. The exchange between all of these tales and events has produced a world that continues to fascinate humans of the 31st century, a world which will hopefully encourage them to tap into the mythological histories just waiting to be happened upon. Simultaneously, however, the more stories we publish, the more I hope our readers come to realize that these entities are not so different from us after all: young women still hate their fathers sometimes, unrequited love abounds, and egos can govern many a relationship.

It's a disappointment, and it's a relief.

A disappointment for the little girl in me who saw Brünnhilde as the epitome of uncompromising strength: ultimately, she is as flawed, if not more, than I thought her to be.

A relief for the woman I am today, precisely for those same reasons: I can gently remove her from her pedestal, and with it, the unattainable expectations I had held myself to, as I tried to emulate her.

Short of doing away with our heroes altogether, we can at least try to forgive them, even if we are no closer to understanding them.

Next month, we delve into the legendary rivalry between Ra and Apollo, the respective Egyptian and Greek gods of the Sun, and the confrontation that nearly robbed Lorendi of sunlight for a century.

See A. Martine's story "Just a Fire" online at Metaphorosis.
If you liked it, leave a comment. Authors love that!
Remember to subscribe to our e-mail updates so you'll know when new stories are posted.

About the story

"Just a Fire" was initially inspired by a lifelong love of fairy tales and mythologies from around the world; their occasional absurdity triggered in me a strong interest in retellings and parodies. More specifically, it was the manner in which stories across time and cultures resembled each other that I always found compelling, and I've always wanted to feature that in one of my tales.

As I began to write "Just a Fire", however, I found myself drawn to another aspect of storytelling: the notion of subjective truths and bendable perceptions. At its core, more so than a take on a portion of Norse mythology, this is about the way miscommunications and grudges (petty and profound) can divide people on the notion of what they know and believe to be fact.

"Just A Fire" is the first of many stories I set in the fictional country of Lorendi, each of the pieces detailing how famous fairy tale and mythology incidents have impacted their respective characters, often in the form of conflict involving unreliable points of view, rumors and damaging word-of-mouth.

A question for the author

Q: What are you reading now?

A: At the moment, I am juggling between:

- *Anne Sexton's Complete Poems* (Anne Sexton)
- *We Need to Talk About Kevin* (Lionel Shriver)
- *Little Fires Everywhere* (Celeste Ng)
- *In the Night Garden* (Catherynne M. Valente)

About the author

Aïcha Martine Thiam is a poet, writer, musician and artist who writes in English and in French, two of her native languages. She travelled the world as a child, and studied at the University of Montréal and Columbia College Chicago. Home is wherever the sea is near.

www.maelllstrom.com, @Maelllstrom

All the Colors I Cannot See

L'Erin Ogle

I remember everyone being lit up in colors when I was a little kid. They wore vivid blues and pinks and greens and yellows. Everyone dripped in thoughts and feelings. They were painted with sky blue happy or scarlet red mad, thunderhead gray sad and bright orange excited. I loved looking at everyone wearing their hearts out like that, and mostly everyone had real nice shines. Then I met a man with no color at all.

That's when we lived outside the little town of Misty, which hugs the line of Maximillian and the Southern Triangle, and still ain't decided which one it wants to be a part of. We farmed orchards with apples and oranges and fat bunches of grapes, and Mama had a vegetable garden that spat out vegetables bigger than anyone else's. She can make anything grow big and better tasting just with her hands.

We went to town with Mama sometimes, when she needed seeds or something else that couldn't wait for Daddy to get the next day. We'd walk down the dusty dirt roads, until we got close to the center of town where the roads turned into big flat stones cobbled together.

Every time we went to town, Mama stopped and bought us a lemonade at the corner store. It was so full of sugar it made a little coating on your teeth, that you could lick the rest of day, still taste the sweet. Mama ain't big on sweets, and it was always my favorite part. Carly always sipped hers all the way home, but I swallowed gulp after gulp until my throat seized up and sent needles through my head.

I was five the last time we ever went into Misty. It was real sunny that day, so bright I had to squint to see anything at all. We came on the man with a shiny black hat and matching coat right where the dust turned to stone. Under his hat, his face was pale and the way the sun was steaming off the pavement, it made his face blur, like it was melting right off. I squinted real hard, trying to see what kind of shade he was throwing off, but not a single color came off him.

"Mama," I said and tugged her hand. Me and Carly was on either side of her, our heads right at her waist even though Carly's four years older than me. Daddy says Mama and Carly are pint sized. Not like me and him.

"What?" Mama said, real irritated, pink with it. She got all nervous and twitchy when we came to town.

"That man ain't got no colors," I whispered.

His head turned real smooth and he smiled at me. Not at Mama and Carly, but at me. Underneath his glossy black mustache, his teeth were white and square and too big for his mouth. Looked fake. As we drew near, he bent at the waist like he was taking a bow, and said loud, "Hello, little girl! Would you like to see what I have inside my hat?"

"Yeah!" I said, tugged my hand free of Mama's, ran towards him.

"Grace!" Mama snapped and hustled after me.

The man took his hat off one handed and turned it upside down, passed his free hand over it in circles.

"Grace," Mama said, and I felt her fingers knifing into my shoulder. "Sir, we are late, no time for tricks, excuse us."

"We ain't late," I said. "I want to see."

The man dipped his hand in his hat and pulled out a fat white snake. It made an odd purring sound, and he looked at my Mama and smiled. I reached out and felt scales shiver soft and smooth.

"Come on, Grace," Mama said. She yanked on my shoulder.

The man closed his hand around the snake and dipped it back in his hat, Then he pulled it back out, and when he spread his fingers out there were three golden eggs, the same color as the little bubbles of light that came from Mama when she sang. "Little snakes are most often vulnerable in the egg, just like little birds in the nest," he told us.

"Grace!" Mama said, and this time she pulled harder, and I stumbled backwards, crying out 'cause it hurt. My mad mixed with my hurt feelings and floated away red and orange.

I went with her, my head turned around to look back at the colorless man. He was still smiling away. He kept his eyes on mine and leaned forward and blew a tiny snake from his mouth that landed on the middle egg. It hammered its triangle head into the shell and disappeared with its tail flicking back and forth.

"Turn around, Grace," Mama said, dragged me down the street. She held me so tight that I wore a purple wrist bracelet the next day.

"We never forget magic," the man called after us. "Not the kind that turned its back on its brothers!"

Mama's face got bone white and a real ugly color like wet ash circled her head. We didn't stop again, not for seeds, not even for lemonade.

"Why couldn't we see the magician?" I demanded. I was sparking yellow orange red.

We were on the dust roads leading out of town, and Mama stopped right in the middle of the road. She got down on her knees, looked at me and Carly real serious. Her color was a dark blue, twisted up with orange.

"That man wasn't a magician. He was a snake charmer," she said.

"What's a snake charmer?" Carly asked.

"It's a bad kind of magic," she said. "That's why we don't tell people about Grace seeing colors. Or about the light bubbles when I sing, or that I have the gift of growing. A long time ago, there was magic in a lot of places. But there was our kind of magic, the good kind, and then the dark magic. The snake charmers. Now, they didn't start as all bad. But sometimes they used their power to get things, when it wasn't fair to other people. And then people, the ones with no magic, became angry and scared. So, they chased the people with magic away, wouldn't sell things to them in town, wouldn't allow their children to go to school, that sort of thing. And then even people with good magic started hiding theirs, because they didn't want to get run off. Lots of the snake charmers died off. And the ones that were left, they had so much anger about being driven out, they turned mean as snakes. That's why people started calling them the snake charmers."

And she didn't say nothing else the way home. We got sent to our room so she could have peace and quiet. I heard her tell Daddy about the snake charmer as soon as he got home.

She was all kinds of colors, flashing red and blue and black and gold in pulses. "We can't stay here."

"Julia," Daddy said. "Maybe he was just a magician?"

"He had a snake come out his mouth, and crawl into the eggs the bird laid," I said. I was still supposed to be in my room.

"Grace," Mama said. "Room. Now."

I went to my room and closed the door loud, then tiptoed back out to listen.

"Maybe he's just passing through?" Daddy said. "He won't want people to catch onto him. I bet he's already moved on."

"You don't understand," Mama said. "Charmers hate my kind. He saw me, I know. He heard what Grace said. He'll come, and he won't stop coming until he's dead, maybe not even then, Nate. We have to go. Tonight. We have to run. I mean, I can grow anything. We'll go south where they don't mind a little magic as long as it don't hurt anyone. We make a new home."

There was a time when Daddy did anything Mama wanted. There was more talking but we left Misty that night.

It's funny but as time passed I sort of forgot the whole thing, even the awful bumpy midnight ride down here to South Song. It felt more and more like a dream if it did cross my mind.

First time I said anything about colors here, Mama shook her head. "Grace," she said. "It's time to stop being fanciful. There aren't any colors. It's just your imagination."

"No, it ain't," I said. "You made us move 'cause I didn't see no colors round that man, Mama." "That wasn't why," Mama said.

"But—"

"Grace," Mama said. "Stop arguing with me right now. I don't want to hear another word about colors, or I'll tan your little behind. There aren't any colors."

Bout that time was when Mama seemed to be finding wrong with anything I did. It felt like being slapped, knowing she knew I was telling the truth and she was saying it wasn't so.

I remember being so mad that my eyes stung with it. Ain't nothing worse than trying to say something and being told to shush.

I tried not seeing them. Not talking about them. But two days later I saw a woman with a big belly, when we went to town to get some things. I knew the lady was growing a baby inside her, but I don't get excited about that. What I got excited about was the bright pink web spinning out from her, clear into the sky. It was so damn pretty against the sky I couldn't breathe. "Mama!" I pointed above her head. "Look at the color!"

Mama's lips skinned tight against her teeth, turned pale white. She jerked my hand so hard I almost tripped. "Ssshh," she said, tinted a real ugly maroon.

When we got home, she made good on her hide tanning promise. I lay in bed the rest of the day with my eyes shut. Whenever I opened them, I saw ugliness.

You'd think I'd never have said a damn word about the colors ever again. I didn't talk about them, even to Carly. I tried to ignore them, and they started fading on me. It was tolerable enough, but sometimes I felt all hollowed out inside.

I was eight years old and two days when I seen Brian, a man my daddy's age, doing his limp down the street. He had gotten bucked off a horse a year before and it did something bad to his hip. He got sort of mean after that. He was always stained with a dark red hue if I looked real hard. His daughter Marley went to school with us, a real skinny girl with shiny blond hair. I didn't really know her 'cause she was almost sixteen. But people knew her daddy was bad on the drink, since the accident. People always got something to say about stuff like that.

This afternoon, I couldn't rightly see if he was on the drink, 'cause he was wrapped up in black so dark it looked wet. Like spilled ink all over his paper white skin. He was muttering to himself, too, looked crazy.

I felt ice cold looking at him all messy like that. I crossed the street so we didn't share the same side of the road. I went home and couldn't eat. I kept seeing that ink cloud. It had me wondering if things like that could leave the person they was on and come after other people.

Next day, Marley was just gone. Her mama went door to door, banging away, asking had anyone see Marley. My daddy went to town, to join the men who were going to search for her. I sat at the table and tried to tell Mama, about the ink cloud.

"Mama, I saw Marley's daddy in town yesterday," I said.

"And?"

"And he was walking down the street, and he scared me."

Mama stopped and looked at me. "What did he do?" she asked. "Was he on the drink again?"

"I don't know, ma'am," I said. "But he had real bad color around him like a cloud of real black—"

Mama took in some air, and when she blew it out, it was mad and scared, red and blue gray. "Goddammit, Grace," she whispered. Her eyebrows yanked down and a big fat line appeared in between them. "I have told you, and told you—"

"But Mama—"

"But nothing, Grace!" she roared. "Go to your damn room, right now!"

Mama tanned me again, worse. I stopped crying after the first couple licks, 'cause this mad feeling just sort of took over. *Ain't ever gonna let her see me cry again*, I promised myself. And when she was done, she was one crying. She knelt down beside me and she said, "Grace, this is for your own good. If you keep on talking about colors, people will get bad ideas. You have to forget about Brian, and Marley, and the colors. You hear me? You forget it all."

There's an old saying that there are some things better left forgotten, but that ain't right. There are things you should never forget. I knew I was seeing something important, but even that feeling sort of drifted away, faded like dreams do.

I don't like the new teacher. He smiles to greet us when we file into the big old school room that used to be a barn. It's the only building big enough to fit all of us, from the little kids still wiping snot on their sleeves, up to the older kids who only care about making big dumb moon eyes at each other. When he smiles, one of his lips curls up higher on one side, reveals big square teeth. It tugs at something in my head, but I don't know what. It's like everything faded with the colors.

The colors are little ghosts of their old selves, all faded and barely there. They only show up bright if it's real important. I guess looking at them sort of feels wrong, like peeping into other people's heads. There's some feelings people have that you don't want to see.

But Ellison ain't got no color, note even a hint of it, at all.

"I don't like him," I whisper to Carly.

Carly rolls her eyes. "Shut up and go sit down," she whispers back – "before you get us in trouble."

She shakes her hair as she walks down the side of the rows, like she's getting it behind her shoulders, but she's just doing it so everyone looks at her. She's real proud of all that golden hair she brushes one hundred times every morning and night. She likes being smart, but she likes being pretty more. She about pooped a kitten when she was voted the prettiest girl last year by the boys. They wrote her name on a piece of paper with little stars and hearts drawn around it, and she crowed about that all damn summer.

I didn't even make the pretty girl list, which Carly said was 'cause I was too young. She was being nice for once, but I don't care about that dumb list. You just know the girls who got excited about that are gonna pop out a hundred kids and get stuck right here in this dusty town where nothing ever happens. Me, I'm gonna be the first girl to ride to the North Border and back, just to show everyone I can. I'm gonna make history.

"I'm Mr. Ellison," the man says. Then he tells me, "Put that chair down on all four legs, Grace Milliken."

Then, he makes us change all our seats. We have to sit in the order of youngest to the oldest, which puts me in the front row. Stupid, 'cause I'm four inches taller than everyone in the second row. The front's for suck ups like Carly. I cross my arms and slouch when Ellison walks by, carrying a long, thin wooden pointer. He snaps it down on my leg right above the knee when he passes.

"Sit up straight, Grace Milliken," he says.

I ain't never been hit before by an adult, and I don't like it. It hurts, but worse, everyone saw it happen. I sit up straight and fold my arms across my chest, hot all through my face.

Everyone sits up arrow straight then. Nick's next to me looking out the side of his eyes and shrugging in sympathy. He ain't half bad, for a farmer boy. Ellison gets up to Carly's row, near the back since she's one of the oldest. Carly raises her hand. "Mr. Ellison, sir?"

Here we go. Everyone loves Carly 'cause she's just so *proper* and *perfect.*

"Yes, Carly?"

He already knows all our names on the first damn day. I don't like it, not at all.

"Sir, I can't see the board."

I sneak a look back, see James the 1st directly in front of her. There are two James, and this James is the big one, taller than anybody in class. Being short like she is, Carly can't probably see anything but the dirt on his neck. I snicker inside. Even if she can see, James the 1st's daddy has a hog farm and he's always stinking to high hell.

Mr. Ellison sighs. His noises are louder than his words. He's that kind of person.

I'm really lookinat him, how even the color around him looks faded. I want to tell someone, but I can't. Not anymore.

For being magic, Mama sure hates it. She can grow things just by touching them. When she sings, little bubbles of light float around her, but she pretends not to see them. My seeing colors ain't as good, 'cause I'm half ordinary like Daddy, but it's mine all the same. Carly can't do a lick of magic, but she's perfect in every other way. Everyone thinks so, except maybe Ellison, 'cause he just sighed at her.

That sigh Ellison makes, I see it hanging above Carly, see through but it's thicker than the rest of the air. I sit up a little, 'cause I ain't never seen that before.

"Are you saying I've made a poor choice, Carly, with my seating arrangements?" He smiles, his stupid lip curling up.

Carly flushes like I did. There ain't no right way to answer his question, and we all sort of wait to see what happens in the worst kind of quiet.

"No, sir, I was just- "

"Just what?" he slices into her mid-sentence. His eyes are squinted slits.

No one ever talks to Carly like that. She bites her lip, looking around, and I damn near feel sorry for her, but not sorry enough to stop thinking it was about time. *A little humility's good for the spirit,* Daddy said, the first time I fell off a horse and cried like a girl. *Makes you realize you ain't perfect.*

"No, sir," Carly whispers. She's staring at her hands in her lap. Her hair falls around her face. She's real pretty, like Mama. She's got little bones and big eyes, and big masses of long golden hair. Me, I'm tall and big through the shoulders like Daddy. Colored all different browns and tans, eyes and hair, average. I got robbed on that 'cause his good looks don't translate to my face.

"Are we going to have a problem this semester, Carly?"

He should let her alone after that, but he don't. He ain't smiling on the outside, but I think he is on the inside.

"No," she says, real soft.

"Stay when I dismiss the others," he says, and moves past her. Carly's crying.

I feel bad, honest, but she's always been a crier.

I forget my lunchbox on purpose. I want to hear what that big galoot has to say to my sister. Just 'cause I don't always like her don't mean I stop looking out for her. If she's got a fault, it's that she'll believe any damn thing people tell her. Three years she spent a whole week eating only potatoes when I told her they'd make her skin glitter. I heard it from this girl who had real pretty skin, said a boy up north wrote a song about it.

Or so she claimed. Me, I don't go around just believing any damn thing people say.

Carly's got her nose to the corner. I can see just the side of her face. Her cheek has old dusty tracks from the crying before. Ellison stands just a step away, no expression at all on his face. He's talking real intense, right in her ear. His words come out little colored snakes of yellow and green that slither into her ear. I strain my ears trying to catch what he says, but all I hear is hissing. The hissing is making me sick, like I might puke so hard breakfast comes out my nose. I feel hot and dizzy, so I get outside, where everyone's still sitting and eating. It can't have been long I was gone, but it felt like damn near forever.

Carly don't come out until I'm finishing my sandwich, trying to help my stomach stop turning flips.

She don't look no worse for the wear now, and don't stop to talk to me, so I mind my own business.

I don't say nothing about the snakes and Ellison to anyone. I'll just get tanned for it and no one will believe me anyway.

Carly nibbles at dinner and goes straight up to bed. When I get up to our room, she's standing there in her drawers, pinching at her stomach. She must have been doing it for a while, 'cause there are red blotches all along the top of her waist.

"What the hell you doing?" I ask.

"Don't curse, Grace," she says. She turns her head, looks at the back of her thigh. I see pinch marks there too. "I'm getting fat."

I snort. "You're real skinny. You're practically a walking skeleton. Why the hell would you think that, and why the hell you pinching yourself? Ain't nothing there but skin, and you're going stretch it all out doing that."

"You ought to start talking right," she says. "Otherwise people will think you're stupid. Anyway, it was just something someone said. Just forget it."

I go to bed thinking about how everyone always wants me to forget.

What do you think of the new teacher?" Dad asks at dinner next day.

"Hate him," I say.

"Grace!" Mama says. "Don't use that word."

"Well, what am I supposed to say? I do." I stab my fork into my potato, which splits down the middle. Me and Carly love potatoes. We both put a big fat pat of butter inside them and let it melt into the white stuff. "Pass me the butter, Carly."

"Strongly dislike," Mama says.

Carly pushes the butter plate over without taking any. She starts cutting her potato into tiny pieces. She puts one in her mouth and chews slowly.

"Not hungry?" Dad asks Carly.

"Well, someone at school told Carly she's fat, so she ain't eating," I say.

Mama frowns and Dad puts his fork down. "Who the hell called you fat?" Dad says.

"Well, where does Grace get it from, now?" Mama says to Dad, but it's just a reflex. She looks at Carly. "Carly, is that true?"

"No," Carly says. I see color in that lie, dirt brown, like shit. It's the first time in a couple years I seen a color that ain't all faded like old clothes and the first time I ever heard Carly lie.

"That's a goddamn lie!" I say real loud. I'm mad as hell. I can feel a whole bunch of things twisting around in my chest, wanting to come out.

"Grace!" Mama snaps, and this time I see her face beet red. I don't need to see nothing else to tell me she's mad. "You go to your room right now!"

"But she told a damn lie!"

"Get in your room Grace!" It comes out as dull red pulses. Seems like whenever Mama's got color, it's always at me, and it ain't never a nice color.

"This ain't fair, she doesn't even want to eat!" I holler, and stomp upstairs.

Dad comes up after a while. I paced around at first, but now I'm lying on my bed, still steaming. The bed dips when he sits down, rocks back and forth. He's a big, solid man. When he wraps his arms around Mama she practically disappears. "Hey kiddo," he says. "You know you can't curse like that."

"But she lied! You'd be pissed if someone lied on you too!" I glare at him.

"You sound just like your mama, you know. She was always getting all hot and bothered about something and getting herself in trouble."

"I don't believe you," I keep my face buried in the pillow. "Bet she was perfect, just like Carly's lying butt."

He laughs real low, says, "Aw, Grace, no one's perfect."

He pats me on the head and tells me to come finish dinner. I drag my feet on the stairs so everyone knows I'm still in my feelings about what happened. Mama's cleaning up and Carly's sitting at the table, most of her plate in front of her. I sit down and glare at her.

"Eat, Grace," Mama says without turning her head. Sometimes she knows what I'm doing without even looking. "And Carly, you're not done until you finish your plate."

I finish first, and get sent right back upstairs, which gets me mad all over again. Carly doesn't come up until it's dark, bedtime.

"You finally eat?" I snap at her, ready to fight.

"No," she says. She goes to bed without even brushing her hair. I lay there and look at my breath, steaming out maroon. It takes me a while to settle down, get to sleep.

I'm seeing colors again a lot. I don't like it.

Next day, Carly says she's sick and won't get out of bed. I go out with Mama and Dad and prune trees in the orchard, and then we all come in and play a game of cards. If I could see my colors now, I know they'd be all sky blue right now. I like it being the three of us sometimes.

"You giving up on your good looks?" I ask Carly, walking to school. She only brushed her hair a couple times this morning and didn't pinch her cheeks or run her finger through the jam and paste it to her lips either. "You ain't hardly brushed your hair."

"Why should I?" Carly says. She's walking with her head tilted to the side, like I do when I get water in my ear. "No one cares what my hair looks like when I'm this fat."

She's skinny as ever. "You ain't fat," I tell her.

"They say I am," she says, still walking with her head craned almost to her shoulder.

"Who? What the hell is the matter with you?" I like the way that sounds coming out. Dad says that to Mama when she gives him a hard time about his ales at night. A sharp-edged joke.

"Do you hear that?" Carly says instead of answering.

"Hear what?"

"The birds," she says. She stops and turns in a circle real slow. "Their wings. The talking."

"What birds?" The road we walk to school on is bare of trees, just a dusty stretch of road leading to a dead end.

"They're everywhere," she whispers. "In here." She taps her head. I see color starting to appear around her. She's the color of fireplace ashes and embers.

I don't know what to do or say. After a minute she just walks on.

I trail behind her, inspecting the sky for anything with wings.

Day 4, Carly don't spell wicked right, leaves the c out. Ellison keeps her in for recess. I sneak in but he isn't hissing this time. Instead, Carly sits at her desk, every part of her bowed over. He sits at his desk, with his fingers steepled together. His smile a mean curve to his face, and all the color in the room is gone. Not just from him but gone from the walls and books and plants.

"Something's wrong at school," I tell Dad. He's started in on the dead orchard trees lying in pieces behind the orchard. He strips them of their bark, sands them down, makes things. He don't never know what he's gonna do until it takes its own shape. He says things want to be made.

"Bad wrong?" he asks.

Dad asks one question, and listens. Mama asks a hundred and don't.

"Yeah," I say. "It's Ellison. He hates Carly. He keeps her inside for lunch all the time and I think he says mean things to her."

"Mean things like what?" Dad stops and rests his hands on the tree between his legs.

"I don't rightly know the exact words," I tell him. "I just know he does."

"She tells you that?"

"I went back inside for my lunch first day," I say. "He was in her ear, talking real quiet."

"He yell? Or put his hands on her?"

"No, sir," I say.

"But it made you scared? Or scared for Carly?"

"Made me mad, but made me fearful, sir."

"Gracie," he says. He put his hands on his hips. "Did he tell Carly she was fat?"

"I don't rightly know," I say. I hesitate, try to think how to explain it the thing I can't explain. "He's not a good person, Daddy. I can tell, you know I can. I think he's bad. Real bad."

"Gracie," he put his hand on my shoulder. "I believe you. You know why?"

"Why?"

"You ain't said a damn swear word this whole time," he says. He smiles, but he has to work at it. "I'll take care of it, kiddo. Alright?"

"Yes, sir," I nod. I get a bad feeling, but I don't know why. It's sort of like I know I got a big boulder rolling, but I don't know where it's going. I don't feel like talking anymore, and I turn to leave.

"Gracie?" Dad says. "You see any colors round him?"

We don't talk about the colors since Mama said not to.

"If I see them, they're not good ones," I say, but I don't wait to see his reaction. He wants to talk about colors if it was about Carly. That sort of sticks somewhere in me, but I ain't going to tell anyone about it.

"What the hell did you say?" Carly comes at me, and I'm faster than her but the cursing froze me. Violet clouds erupt from her nostrils and scatter. It scares me, what I'm seeing.

"Hell!" I throw up my arms to protect my face, but she don't swing, pushes me down on my bed instead. My head hits the wall, and I push back at her. "What the *goddamn hell*, Carly?"

"You tell Dad or Mama?" she snaps.

"Tell 'em what?"

"About me getting in trouble at school." Her eyes are jumping out of her head, crazy like her hair's getting.

"I didn't say nothing about you getting in trouble," I say. "I said that damn Ellison is mean to you."

"That's getting in trouble!" Carly says. Big fat tears start slipping out of her eyes. "I ain't nothing but trouble!"

"That's a goddamn stupid thing to say," I tell her. "Ellison say that?"

She glares at me. "He doesn't say a goddamn thing to me, understand?"

"Liar," I whisper.

She pushes me again, and this time my head cracks the wall good. All my air gusts out and I ain't even mad. She's lost her damn mind. I want to get good and mad, but I'm sort of scared to. I ain't never seen someone shoot sparks from inside like she is.

"You just mind you own business," she said, up so close her words lash my face. "You little spoiled *bitch*."

I don't say nothing after that. Don't change into my bedclothes either. I just crawl under my sheets, pull them to my neck, and stare at the ceiling wishing I could make pretty colors that flowed and painted over the bad ones. It's a long time before I close my eyes.

Carly don't say a word to me walking to school. She walks the whole time with her head tilted, frowning. A kaleidoscope of darkness spinning webs from her. I wish the colors would go away.

Daddy comes walking into school just before lunch. Ellison sees him but don't stop talking about the old Gods. Yesterday he said how the old Gods abandoned their people, left them with special powers that the people from before didn't like. How the people decided they would get rid of people who were different, how they drove them off and murdered them and stole their children. Beat anything different right out of them. But he said there was something called full circle which meant that what goes around comes around. He drew on the chalkboard a snake in a circle eating its own tails.

But today he talks about the same stuff our other teachers did. About history, how often people used to worship their Gods, how some of them still have old paintings and books they read out of every day, blah blah blah.

Daddy leans up against the wall against the back of the classroom, his arms folded across his chest, listening. I sneak a look back at Carly, who's either so mad she erased it off her face, or scared. I can't tell but I feel smooth as a turquoise sea, 'cause my Daddy's a man takes care of things.

Ellison dismisses us and walks right up to Daddy, extends his hand. They shake hands, but Daddy takes a minute to do it. He holds that slimy hand, half the size of his, and they look each other up and down.

"Mr. Milliken, I presume?" Ellison nods at me, waiting. "Your daughter is a fierce likeness."

"In more ways than one," Daddy says. He let go of Ellison, looks at me. "Go on outside, Gracie. You too, Carly."

Ellison's lips skim his teeth, peel back. Both sides, but I look real close at his mouth and see the side that usually curls up twitching away under his skin.

I hate waiting. When Daddy strides out, he don't seem no different. He says goodbye to Carly, kisses her on top of the head, then pulls me alongside him. He keeps his voice real low when he speaks.

"That man," he says, just to me. "or any other, for that matter, is not to keep you or Carly at lunch or after school, ever, by yourselves. You hear me? He tries to, you come right home and get me. You understand Gracie?"

"Yes, sir," I say.

"Now go on," he says. "I'll be here to walk you girls home."

I go in feeling smug, like I won, and then I see little tendrils of smoke coming off Ellison. He's thick with them, and I feel more scared than mad just like that. All his face is tight, like it's being sucked in, cheekbones knives ready to slice through the flesh and let the real him out.

He's a man with no color. He's a snake charmer. I guess I knew it, sort of. You know how you know something, but you ain't ready to believe it? Like maybe your Mama likes your sister better, but you just pretend she don't? It's the kind of knowing you pretend ain't there.

Me and Carly get sent right to our room so Mama and Dad can talk. Carly don't want to listen, but I do. I press my ear against the door and I hear them talking real urgent. I wished I could see what their words are wearing, but I'm cutoff from what's happening, and I hate it. I got to tell them about the rest of it, how Ellison's got the black magic. I want to know exactly what is going to happen, so I can rein in this damn fear horse thundering through me.

The sun dips low before they call us down. Mama's pinned her pale hair back and her eyes have gone from bright blue to dark. She's fidgeting like I do at school. Daddy's sitting sideways in his chair, elbow resting on the table.

"I know you two must want to know what's going to happen," Mama says.

"This is so stupid," Carly says, crying. She's got more of a water supply than anybody I know. "Nothing happened."

"Hell, it didn't," Daddy says. His eyes are narrow in his face. He's looking at Carly like he maybe wants to smack her, which I feel in my bones. "I don't know what's been going on down at that school, but you aren't acting right, Carly."

"Ellison, he's a snake charmer," I say. I'm so scared I'm shaking, but I gotta get this out. "I know it. He's like that man we ran away from. He hissed snakes right in her ear!"

"You don't know a damn thing," Carly says. "You think you're so smart, everyone does, but you're *not*."

"We're not arguing," Mama says. "We're not even discussing. Until we get this handled, neither of you are going to school."

"But that's not fair!" Carly bursts out, hollering. "IT'S NOT FAIR!" and she just screams it over and over until it blurs into one long continuous color flashing desperation at us. Then her limbs go boneless and she flops onto the floor, crying. Mama gets down to her knees beside her.

"But it's the only time the birds are quiet," Carly moans.

"What birds?"

"The ones in my head," Carly says. "All day and all night, they beat their wings inside me and I can hear it in words in my head, they're saying the most terrible things, and it only stops there, at school."

Dad and Mama look at each other, over Carly unspooled on the floor. I think they might tell me to go to my room, but I think they forgot me. There's only the three of them—the broken one, and the scared adults.

"What do they say?" Mama asks, real nice. Her voice molasses over pancakes, so sugar sweet it makes my teeth ache. "Carly, darling, tell me what the birds say."

"Fat," Carly whispers. "Ugly. Stupid. Worthless. Good for nothing. They tell me I'll have to be a whore because I can't do anything at all, and I'll be bad at it, because I'm so fat and ugly."

There's a great crack through the room and we all jump. Even Dad himself, who looks at the big seam that now runs down the table. His fingers are white knuckles of rage.

Mama gets Carly calmed down, carries her to their bed. Dad paces. She comes out and she tells me to sleep in their bed with Carly. I tell her no, don't leave me with Carly. I'm whining, near tears.

"You take care of your sister, now, Grace," she says. She kisses me on the top of the head. She looks at me. "I'm awful proud of you, Grace. You're very brave. Like your father."

I go in and lay next to silent Carly, on top of the sheets. Her body curves away from me, a slivered half-moon against the sheets. I lay board stiff next to her, thinking about the whores. I guess I never did think about them before. I know about sex, and stuff. I mean, I'm eleven and I have an older sister who's kissed boys but nothing else. I ain't even sure what a whore is, except it's a woman who does sex type stuff with lots of men.

I know that's how we came from Mama and Dad too. Mama told us the first time Carly asked. *We made you with our bodies*, she said, and thinking about now, in their bed makes me feel hot and uncomfortable. They ain't always quiet about it, but it's always when I'm supposed to be sleeping, so I can't rightly complain. But I feel odd, thinking about it now.

I get up and sit at the edge of the bed. I can hear Mama and Daddy talking about moving away again. Carly has her eyes closed, maybe sleeping. I reach over and brush her hair like Mama did to calm her down. She doesn't stir but then my fingers brush up against something hard.

I tug it out a knot, but it's not hair.

It's a feather.

Carly pitches a fit this morning. I wake up when her feet drum the bed and little rat a tat tats run down her spine, which curves unnatural. I scream until Dad and Mama come. Dad freezes statue still, but Mama comes and gathers Carly in her arms. She starts to sing, first just a melody from words I know. Then the song glows and spins. The words stretch and change until I can't recognize them, getting long and dancing around the room, rainbows spinning in little circles.

Carly's body stops shaking and she's limp in Mama's arms.

Dad's moving again, a big tree of a man trembling like a leaf. "Julia," he says. "We should just pack up and go. Right now."

"It's too late," Mama says. "He's already got inside her somehow."

Daddy's twisting his hands together and they're turning red. "What, then?"

Mama looks at him. "It won't stop, Nate."

"Alright," Daddy says. "Alright."

The space between them uncurls and fills with black ink.

Daddy leaves then.

Mama and I clean up Carly, starting with her hair. Mama gives me her comb and she takes Dad's and we tease the ends out first. It takes some doing, but with slow small strokes, we get most of the tangles out without cutting it.

"Mama?" I say.

"Gracie?" she makes it a question.

"He did it. Ellison put the birds in her head. The first day. I went back to get my lunch and he was saying something to her, and I could see his words like snakes go right in her ear. I should have told you, huh? You could have fixed it?"

"Oh, Grace," she says. She stops and hugs me right against her.

I'm as tall as her, and wider still, but she still circles me up somehow.

"I wouldn't have listened, probably," she says. "You know? Sometimes I don't listen."

"I know," I say, and she squeezes tighter.

"You haven't hugged me in so long," she murmurs.

"Where's Daddy?" I ask.

Her body goes stiff. She lets go and I don't need colors to tell me she's ashamed and scared and defiant all at the same time. I guess 'cause I feel all them feelings too. I knew it when she told Daddy to go. I seen blackness stretched between them, the kind where there ain't no light at all.

"He went to kill Ellison," I say. I know it's true. I feel a real blackness inside me too, thick and ugly, squeezed up round my heart.

"The connection has to be broken," Mama says. "By any means necessary. You saw Carly this morning. She could die."

"I ain't saying its wrong," I say. "What's Daddy mean? It never ends?"

"You can't make it go away, any kind of magic. It just takes another shape."

"Why though?" I ask. "Why us?"

Right then, Carly sits up. She has half her hair smooth as melted butter and half a huckleberry bush. Her eyes are wide and there ain't nothing in them. She opens her mouth and I think she's gonna scream but birds start spilling out of her mouth. Blackbirds, owls, little gray and red plumed birds, too big for her. They come and come and Mama screams. I don't think but I jump up and run to the big window. I shove it open, catching splinters in all my fingers. The birds beat their wings without stopping, going right through a window way too damn small for their size and number, but it happens.

Outside they caw and beat and their wings make a hard rain sound. It softens as they begin to move farther off.

Carly collapses back on the bed and lies still.

I miss my Daddy so fierce I could die right now.

Mama puts her head down and sobs.

I go to the floor and put my head down and don't.

We all pretend things are fine, now.

Dad came home vacant eyed to Carly sitting up, talking. She didn't remember a damn thing. Mama was petting her, the way you do a fresh kitten. I was squeezing my hands together, blind to the fact blood was dripping from all them splinters. Daddy was washing blood off his hands when I felt mine aching, saw the mess I'd made. I sort of gasped, and Daddy saw the splinters. He sat me down and took each splinter out like I might break, and when he was done, he laid his head against the table and sobbed.

We all broke in some way, I guess.

Dad doesn't come home until late now. Sometimes, he smells like other women. Mama and he argue about it, and sometimes they make noise after but it isn't quiet and it isn't nice. Once I very clearly heard Mama say 'hurt me, then'. I want to tell you he didn't.

Carly acts like nothing happened. I asked her once what she remembered and she told me to leave her alone. I tried to see what colors lurked inside her but after I saw murder coloring my mama and daddy, I never saw them again. Carly's been seeing this boy from the next town over who has a whole bunch of money. She says she's getting out of this place.

I guess I'm different now too. I don't feel like the same person. I don't curse or see colors. I try to find them in people and places, but everything's gone flat and dull.

I hear hissing in my sleep, and I'm afraid it's not a dream. I dream about birds, lined up on house roofs, beady black eyes and sharp beaks. I dream of snake pits, dozens of snakes slithering over each other in knots and wake up with my heart running double time.

I found a black crow feather under my window pillow this morning.

If I'm really quiet, I hear wings fluttering all around.

I'm afraid. And I miss all the colors I cannot see.

See L'Erin Ogle's story "All the Colors I Cannot See" online at Metaphorosis.
If you liked it, leave a comment. Authors love that!
Remember to subscribe to our e-mail updates so you'll know when new stories are posted.

About the story

"All the Colors I Cannot See" began with the idea I had that a man hissed snakes into a girl's ear. The snakes laid eggs, hatched into birds, and drove the girl mad. Grace then became the central character as the story came out, because I wanted to have the narrator as an observer of the character being driven mad.

I was surprised by the ending myself, how dark the piece got. It surprised me by how pervasive the evil was, how it was fluid, getting in through every crack.

This was one of my favorite stories to write and Grace one of my favorite characters.

A question for the author

Q: Are you an outline or discovery writer?

A: Discovery! I usually start with an idea and then it takes on a life on my own. The story usually tells itself. Some stories barely resemble my original idea.

About the author

L'Erin is a writer from Lawrence, Kansas. She writes when she's not saving lives at her other job. She can be found online at lerinogle.com

@lerinjo

Not All Those Who Wander Are Lost

Douglas Anstruther

-1-

Carla sat on the edge of the metal railing that lined the motel's third-floor landing, gripping its paint-chipped bars with long, slender legs. Black lace stockings disappeared into a tattered bathrobe and a lipstick-stained cigarette rested between her fingers.

She liked the feel of the breeze on her legs, the thrill of the twenty-foot drop below. She wasn't a danger junkie, far from it, although she could have probably found a safer way to make some cash while Ash was at school — a florist, maybe, or a cashier. She had job offers, but the hours weren't flexible enough, and cashiers got robbed all the time anyway.

"So." The man standing behind her cleared his throat. "Are you married?"

"Me? Nah. Never tried it." She looked back at him. "How about you?" She thought he'd said his name was Stig, but she wasn't about to use it. Guys didn't like it when you got their name wrong, even if it was fake.

He stared past her into the mid-day heat rising from the oil-stained and cracked parking lot. He was kinda cute, like a movie star from the nineteen fifties: chiseled jaw, dimpled chin and blond curly hair. His stained and wrinkled dress pants contrasted with the smooth skin of his chest. A patch covered his left eye.

"Yeah," he answered in a faraway voice. "I think so."

"You think so?" A column of ash fell from her cigarette to splash across the cars parked below. "You mean you don't know?"

"I lost her. I lost them all. Two sons and a wife. I'm trying to find them, though."

She looked at him, her face a squint as she took a drag of her cigarette. "Whadya mean?" Her words came out with a cloud of smoke. "You *misplaced* them?"

"The places I go." He paused, shaking his head. "It gets complicated."

A new sadness in his eye caused her attitude to soften. She liked the guy. He seemed nice, and there was something mysterious about him. He came across somewhere between a world-weary sailor and a lost child: just a first impression, but she was usually right. "Look, I'm sorry. I, uh, I hope you find them." She stubbed out the cigarette and shrugged the bathrobe down a few inches, revealing breasts swept by the ends of her long black hair. "So, you ready to go again?"

After, she fell off him, scooped her bathrobe up from the floor, and headed to the TV in search of the remote, threading her hands into oversized armholes on the way. She always brought her own bathrobe. It was portable luxury: armor against the squalor of the cheap motels that even the sticky remote couldn't pierce.

She returned to the bed, settled back against the headboard and started pushing buttons. The TV remained black, and after a few seconds she sighed and tossed the worthless device onto the bedstand with a clatter.

At the sound, the man sat upright like a sprung trap. He frowned at the remote, then sank down and stared at the ceiling. As he moved, Carla briefly saw the black silhouette of a raven tattooed at the base of his neck. The image recharged his air of mystery and piqued her curiosity. She remembered their discussion on the landing; maybe exploring some of his secrets would be even more interesting than her missed shows.

"So, where did you see them last?" she asked.

"Hmm?"

"Your family. Where was the last place you saw them?"

"It's not really like that. It's that I can't find the path back to them."

"What do you mean, 'the path back to them'? Were you camping or something?"

He looked at her, measuring her up in a way she'd seen before. She recognized the instant he decided that she wasn't important enough to lie to. She didn't like the look. It took something from her, and the secrets the johns told her, usually how they hated their kids or planned to leave their wives, weren't worth the cost.

"I travel through time," he said. "That's where I lost them: among the possible timelines."

"What?" Her sardonic expression went unnoticed, unable to penetrate his study of the ceiling.

"I move forward in time, look around, go back, change something and then when I move forward again things are different. The possibilities form an immense branching tree, and I lost them somewhere in its branches."

"Seriously? You've been to the future?" She leaned in and conjured a seductive voice harvested from a lifetime of movies. "Do you know what happens to me?"

"A little."

"Prove it." She flounced against him on the bed, now playing little girl. "Tell me something about my future."

"You're going to steal my wallet when I take a shower in five minutes."

"Pfft, that's some reverse psychology bullshit. I'm not gonna touch your wallet."

He just stared ahead and shrugged.

"C'mon," she said, disappointed he wasn't playing. "Tell me something better. You know, like a fortune teller."

"Your son, Ash. He's going to die in three weeks."

All her voices and personas fell away like chips from a poker table thrown over before a bar fight. She peeled herself from him while wide-eyed shock slid into an angry glare. "That's not funny," she said with a dire tone. He kept staring at the ceiling, oblivious or unconcerned. "Hey. I said that's not funny!" She shoved him, but he gave no response. His calm indifference was a stiff breeze against her kindled anger but she didn't know what to do. Finally, after crouching in a frustrated rage for several seconds, she threw herself off the bed, snatched her cigarettes from the bedstand and stormed outside, slamming the door behind her.

A few minutes later, she returned to find the bed empty and the sound of running water coming from the bathroom door. She changed quickly into her clothes, stuffed the bathrobe into her massive purse and headed out. Before the door closed she paused, went back inside and wrestled the wallet from the man's jeans, where they lay in a heap by the side of the bed. She slammed the door again as she left.

It wasn't until that night that she realized he had used her son's name.

-2-

The roar of machinery forced their tiny guide to conduct the entire tour by shouting. The young woman, transformed into a bright orange blob by layers of safety gear, led her three charges through a maze of complex and expensive-looking equipment.

The company's Chief Technical Officer, a tall woman in her mid-thirties, had joined Stig and Osmond to answer questions that never materialized. Osmond couldn't remember the CTO's name. He figured her real role was to tackle him or Stig if either started taking pictures of their proprietary do-hickeys. She had somehow managed to retain a feminine shape despite the safety gear, and Osmond considered testing his theory, but he knew that Stig would make a scene soon enough and he didn't want to interfere.

Dr. Stig Gangleri, his best friend since college, and co-owner of Aesir Consulting, managed to look good in the gear too. It contributed to a mystic shaman vibe, with his bright blue eyes shining through the protective glasses like twin beacons of magical enlightenment. Osmond's own gear had consigned him to Club Blob, along with their guide.

They followed the guide through a vast underground warehouse filled from floor to ceiling with twisting, brightly colored pipes and tanks. Osmond only heard half of what the guide said and understood even less, but it didn't matter. Stig was the show pony. Osmond only made it happen, then made sure Stig didn't get lost on the way home.

"Temperature and pressure are all monitored remotely, as you can see here." The tour guide looked back at the group and paused. "Dr. Gangleri?" She looked around, causing Osmond and the CTO to do the same. Stig had disappeared.

They scattered to look for their missing companion and eventually found him in an aisle they had passed earlier, with his arms crossed and head tilted back, staring blankly at the bend of a pipe.

"He hasn't listened to a word I've said," the guide said, exasperated.

"What's he looking at?" the CTO asked.

"Oh, probably nothing," Osmond offered. "He gets like that sometimes. His mind takes him somewhere else entirely, but trust me, this is your man."

No one seemed particularly interested in going to get him, expecting instead that their collective stare would bring him back in line. Osmond knew different, but was in no hurry. He didn't want to ruin the magic.

"What are his credentials again?" the guide asked, incredulous.

"The professor has PhDs in both theoretical physics and statistical analysis."

"Hmph," the guide said, still unhappy that her shouting had been in vain.

"But it's not the credentials that matter. My associate has a photographic memory and an amazing gift for extrapolation and leaps of intuition. He's a genius the likes of whom you've never seen."

"He doesn't look like he could put his shoes on in the morning," the guide muttered.

"Hey now, show some respect!" All eyes turned to Osmond, who found himself glowering over the petite guide like a great ape defending his territory.

"Sorry. Sorry. It's just that—" He shook his head and tore away from their stares to look back at Stig. "He's a great man. You'll see."

They shuffled in place awkwardly for several minutes before Stig broke free and wandered back to the group, unaware or unconcerned that they had been waiting.

The tour guide resumed with a sigh. "Dr. Gangleri, thank you so much for joining us." Her eyes flashed to Osmond, whose affable smile deflected her sarcasm. "What I had been *trying* to explain is that data from the remote sensors is actually processed at the—"

"At the point of collection, the same way the retina and many other biological sensors process data." Stig finished her sentence to hijack the conversation, then promptly changed the subject. "You will have a seam failure in three days. It will begin there." He pointed at a structure in an aisle they hadn't reached yet. "It will cause one death and nine million dollars in damages."

"With all due respect, Dr. Gangleri," the guide said in a tone suggesting any debt of respect had been fully settled, "if you had paid attention, you would know that a failure of that nature is impossible because—"

"Because all seams are robotically resistance-welded within a tolerance of point zero one percent. That doesn't matter. Material strain from micro-temperature fluctuations will lead to the failure." With arms still folded across his chest he walked briskly down another aisle toward a section they hadn't visited. After a few seconds, the rest of the group caught up. The guide's face glowed red beneath the plastic shield and the CTO had a look of intrigued skepticism. Osmond tried and failed to suppress a grin. He always enjoyed seeing Stig do his thing.

Suddenly, Stig stopped and pointed at what seemed a random direction. "That pile has a heat leak which is throwing off your calibration. It won't be caught for three months and will result in the loss of a major grant."

Then he swung around and pointed to a drain grate on the floor. "Rats. A sink overflow upstairs at the end of the year will lead to an infestation. It'll never be discovered, but the ammonia from their urine will slowly degrade the sensors and prevent you from ever achieving the project goal."

The guide and the CTO both stood stunned, mouths agape. Osmond smiled broadly. "And there you have it," he said. "You will, of course, find Dr. Gangleri's predictions to be one hundred percent accurate. Payment has already been confirmed and no refunds are available. However, I assure you, none will be needed."

The CTO straightened herself and turned to Osmond, "I look forward to Dr. Gangleri's report, especially the technical analysis that supports his conclusions."

"Oh, my dear." Osmond wrapped his orange arm around her shoulders. "There will be no report. Our work here is done. You've been pointed in the right direction; the rest is up to you. One word of advice, though: if you can't figure out how he's right, assume he is anyway, okay? Best avoid that death and all that wasted money." He dropped his grin and looked at her steely-eyed. His voice took on a serious edge. "He's *never* wrong."

He released the stunned CTO and moved over to Stig, placing his gloved hand on his friend's back to direct him toward the exit. "Thank you, we really must be going now."

"But, Dr. Gangleri," the CTO called out as the two men moved away. "How do you know all this?"

Stig stopped and turned. "I saw it happen."

-3-

Stig walked down the short hall that divided living room from kitchen. It was always the same house with the same familiar smell of old wood and the same creaking floors, even if *he* wasn't always the same. The thought sent his hand rising up unconsciously toward his healthy left eye.

He had grown up here and inherited the place from his grandmother on his twenty-first birthday. He had been happy in this house: in the past, as a child doted on by his grandmother who had raised him as her own, and again, in a future he couldn't find. The rest of the time, its emptiness felt like a cold that the heaters couldn't warm.

Sometimes, when he turned the corner into the living room he didn't know if he would find his grandmother sunk into her old overstuffed chair reading spy novels or his sons sprawled across the floor playing while his wife watched sleepily from the couch.

This time, the room was empty except for hundreds of sheets of paper that covered the floor. His heart sank. He had no reason to expect otherwise, but hope grew from a different place than reason.

He walked into the room, stepping carefully on the edges of the pages, which puckered between foot and carpet as he went. Each page contained a portion of an immense branching map of the possibilities he had explored. He remembered them all perfectly, every detail of every moment. Yet nowhere in this map could he find his family. His memories of them were as vivid as any of the branches beneath his feet, but somehow they had become detached from the tree of possibilities. He couldn't find his way back to them. He had lost them.

He knelt down among the pages and traced each branch, looking for a lead, a promising direction to explore. He had recited this mantra a thousand times before. It had become an invocation, a prayer to be happy again.

A loud knock at the door interrupted his reverie. There he found Osmond Higgins, always best friend and sometimes business partner, fidgeting on the step. Osmond was a big man with a ruddy, pock-marked face and gaps between his teeth. He gave Stig a wide smile and a bone shaking pat on the back.

"Hey, Stig. I need some papers signed and wanted to drop off this check." He marched past Stig toward the kitchen. "That last gig was great. They already confirmed two of your predictions, and I gotta say they are loving you now. Word of mouth, my friend, word of mouth. That's what will send us into the heavenly realm of outrageous consulting fees." He opened the refrigerator and closed it with a grunt of disappointment. "Do you even eat?" He turned to Stig and smiled, "How are you doing, buddy?"

"Good," Stig answered, wandering back to the living room.

"How's your, uh, project going? What did you call this again?" Osmond asked, following his friend into the paper-strewn room.

"It's Yggdrasil. The tree of life."

"Right. All the possible futures you've explored, looking for your, uh, family. It's a lot bigger than the last time I was here. You've been busy."

Osmond stood back and squinted at the mighty opus. Through sheer artistic accident, the heavily annotated branching connections did look like a massive gnarled tree, spread across several hundred pieces of paper. Cramped, looping symbols inscribed along its length lent it a texture of mossy bark and hundreds of tiny oval notes dangled from the branches like leaves. The entire left side was stunted and dark, as if the great tree had been hit by lighting. There, the symbols crashed into each other with a sense of urgency, giving the branches a scarred, sinister appearance.

"What are the leaves, again?"

"Decision points. Variables that are likely to significantly alter subsequent events."

"Um, in English?"

Stig sighed. "Possible directions of future exploration."

"I see. And where are we now? What branch or twig or whatever shows us having this conversation?"

Stig pointed to a spot near the upper right edge of the tree. "We're here."

Osmond nodded and leaned forward. "May I?"

Stig motioned for him to proceed. "Carefully."

"Of course."

Osmond tip-toed between the pages, careful not to disturb any. The page Stig pointed to looked like all the others. Thick dark lines connected it to the surrounding pages. Strange symbols and occasional words, places and names crowded around the lines. Stig had once tried to explain his personal system of time-travel notation, but Osmond had retained nothing.

Osmond looked up. "Well, I don't understand it, but it looks pretty impressive."

"It's a rough map. A way for me to see how the pieces fit together as I explore the timelines, following leads, looking for them."

He looked down at the great tree on the floor, superimposing it over the one in his mind. He could move through it much the same as in the trees he had climbed as a child. With almost no effort, he could release his grasp of the present and slide down to another time, catch himself on the crook of a past fork, then pull himself onto a different branch using memories as footholds, until he reached its terminus, where time would resume its measured growth. He had clambered over every inch of the tree but couldn't find his family. His recollections of them, although intense, were as unsubstantial as sunlit mists, and wouldn't support his weight.

"What are all those branches that start behind us? Like those over there." Osmond pointed to the left side of the tree.

"Those branches are what happens when I drop out of college."

Osmond shivered like a teenager at a campfire ghost story. "You mean 'if you had' dropped out of college. I was at your graduation, all of them. So, those other branches never happened. You know that, right?"

Stig shrugged. "I still go there. Those branches are as real as any other."

"My friend," Osmond said, "don't you see? You aren't time traveling. You're daydreaming. I once read that Henry Ford could design a machine and then run it in his mind. You're like that, except the machine you're running is the world. You imagine alternate pasts and possible futures with such detail that you feel like you're there, living them, but the entire time you're really here, in the present, with the rest of us, running simulations.'

"Maybe," he said, with a patience that bordered on boredom.

Osmond shook his head and scanned the left half of the tree. "Honestly, I'm not sure it's healthy for you to keep going back there. It's like you're building entire fantasy worlds and then living in them."

Osmond had expressed these concerns in every timeline. To him, only the timeline he was on was real and all others were the products of Stig's overactive imagination. Stig understood that — his friend couldn't travel from one to another, he couldn't see that no present had more claim on reality than any other. The surety of experience inoculated Stig from doubt, but each time Osmond raised the question, he received another dose of the contagion and there were times when he wondered if maybe Osmond were right. Perhaps he had lost more than his family. Perhaps he had lost the present.

"Hey, I see the name Carla a lot over here. Is that the woman you've been looking for? Your wife?"

"No. Just an acquaintance."

"Well, you'll have to introduce me to her someday. You know, if she's real."

-4-

"Excuse me. Sir? Mr. Gangleri!" The voice came from his blind spot but didn't startle him. Stig finished threading the key into the front door of his house then turned toward the road. A woman hurried toward him from the other side of the street. She looked like a stressed-out soccer mom, with frazzled, pulled-back hair, and jeans tucked into boots that made for awkward running. He traced her path back to an old Honda Civic where cigarette butts on the ground attested to a long wait.

"I'm not sure if you remember me." she said, breathless from her short jog. "I'm—"

"Carla Munn. From the motel." He turned back to the door lock. "I remember."

"You, uh, left this. At the motel." She produced a bulging flap of leather and held it out to him straight-armed. "It's all still there."

Stig took the wallet, tucked it into his back pocket and walked inside, leaving the door open behind him. Carla glanced back at her car for a moment before following him into the dark house and closing the door behind her. She found Stig in the kitchen, filling a glass of water.

He leaned against the counter, glass in hand, and watched her. He could see her unease, her keen awareness that she was in the middle of someone else's house, no longer on neutral ground. For all of her daring and bravado, she wouldn't be here without a good reason.

"Look, I don't," she stopped and shook her head. "This sounds crazy, but I need your help. It's my boy, Ash." Her eyes started to fill and her voice cracked. "He's dying." She burst into tears and sat heavily at the kitchen table, sobbing. Stig leaned against the sink taking occasional sips from his glass. He wanted to console her, but it would be awkward, strange. He didn't need to visit the future to see that.

"You knew it was going to happen," she said, her voice an octave higher than usual. "Somehow you knew."

Slowly her sobbing subsided and with a determined face, streaked with mascara and snot, she collected herself and continued. "Two weeks ago, Ash spent the afternoon playing with his cousin." She paused for a moment to search her purse for a tissue which she unfolded and used to wipe her face. "Three days later Ash got a real bad headache, a high fever and a weird rash. Later we found out his cousin had been sick too but got better on his own. Ash just kept getting worse. I've never seen anyone so sick. At the hospital they put him on a breathing machine. They said he had meningitis." She started to tear up again. "Now they say my little boy is brain dead and they want to pull the plug. Mister Gangleri, you've got to help him."

Stig set the empty glass on the counter and frowned. Her formality always caught him off guard, but what did he expect? She didn't know all the times they'd been together, all the permutations. Carla was a recurring feature of these timelines, the forbidden fruit of the dark side of the tree. To her, he would be little more than a stranger, a one-time customer, but he knew her well and thought of her, in a strange way, as a friend.

She stood up and grabbed his sleeve. "Did you hear me? You've gotta do something. You said you time travel or something. You could prevent this. Please."

Stig spoke dryly. "If I were to go back and prevent his death, it would create a new timeline. This branch would still exist. He'll still die here."

"Take me with you, then."

He shook his head. "I'm sorry, Carla. But it doesn't work that way."

"I don't care!" she shouted. "At least in some other universe or whatever, my baby will live. I don't care. Please, save him. I'll do anything, *anything*." She moved her hand up and ran her fingers jerkily through his hair. "Please."

"You won't know. You'll never know." He seemed to be talking to himself. "Whether or not it's real for me, it can never be real for you."

-5-

The students, slumped in various degrees of boredom, occupied the lecture hall's available seats unevenly. Stig had arranged to have an old chalkboard moved from storage, and he wheeled it in front of the modern equipment before each class. He enjoyed the feel of the chalk on his fingers, the staccato tapping as he wrote. A breeze from the windows, propped open by an antiquated crank system, carried the smell of the old building to him and threatened to send him to another time. He resisted and kept talking.

"As you move through time, each particle is continuous. So you see, from the perspective of spacetime, it's not a particle but a thread: unbreakable and woven with all the other threads of matter and energy like a tangled mass of spaghetti. From this perspective, motion is an illusion. It's merely a bend in the thread. Not only are the threads unbreakable, but Einstein showed us that they can only bend so far: the speed of light." As he spoke he drew frantically on the chalkboard to illustrate his point.

"Our brains consist of an immense tangle of these threads. The present is merely the point along them where a particular set of perceptions and thoughts converge. Time does not pass. It is an illusion, an artifact of consciousness."

Stig looked up to see blank expressions on the few students that were still awake, with the exception of one young lady at the back of the class whose hand rose silently.

He squinted his eyes to see the owner of the hand. "Yes. Ms. Verdandi?"

"So, if each thread of matter is unbreakable, does that mean that everything is predetermined?"

"No. Because of uncertainty."

"Quantum uncertainty?"

"Bah. Everyone is obsessed with quantum this and quantum that. Flip a coin. There's enough uncertainty in that mundane act to change the course of history." He reached into his pocket, pulled out a coin and prepared to flip it. "There are two possible outcomes. Heads you pass, tails you fail. Do we have a deal?"

"Uh, no. I need an 'A'," she said.

"Couldn't the result of the coin flip be predicted?" another student interjected. "Like, if you knew the location and momentum of every atom in the room?"

"That information is not only unavailable, but unobtainable." Stig flipped the coin, trapping it on the back of his hand. "Even though all the matter and energy in the room consists of unbreakable threads, we now have two possible futures: one where Ms. Verdandi passes and another where she fails. With this simple act I've caused them to branch."

He raised his hand to reveal the coin resting on his palm.

"Dr. Gangleri, I didn't agree to this."

-6-

Dishes clattered as Stig's grandmother gathered them from the table and brought them to the sink. The sound sent shivers of Pavlovian dread down his spine, hollowed him out and filled him with bile. He sat, frozen, at the dinner table, scarcely able to pick at his plate. He had visited this terrible scene too often, in pursuit of the myriad possibilities that sprang from it.

The dinner had been like any other. His grandmother hadn't spoken much during, but at the sink she found the courage to say what had been on her mind the whole time. In a faux casual tone, she spoke over the running water and jangling silverware. "Your mother called today. She says she'll be in town for a day after the holidays.

Just a short stopover between movies. She's moving from one set to another clear across the country. Isn't that interesting?" She flashed a quick look at him over her shoulder.

It was one of the rare occasions where his decision didn't matter. Seeing his mother that day stirred a deep pond of sadness and disappointment but had no lasting effect on the timelines. Either way he ended up on the same branch.

"No, I think I'll pass." That wasn't why he had come.

She nodded silently and kept washing. "So, Stiggy, are you all ready for finals?"

"Yes, 'ma."

"You going to get all A's again this year?"

"I always do, 'ma."

"I can't believe you're going to be a junior in college. You grew up so fast."

Stig stared at his plate, pushing peas around with his fork. In some branches he kept eating, slowly finishing his meal while his grandmother cleaned the dishes, but to access certain hidden branches of his possible futures, Yggdrasil demanded a toll, a sacrifice of a not-quite-metaphorical pound of flesh, a price as arbitrary and cruel as most things in life.

With ice in his veins, he stood and carried his plate to the sink. There, he turned on the water, activated the garbage disposal and pushed the remaining food into its roaring maw. The rumble of the disposal changed abruptly to a loud hum and all motion ceased. He looked at the fork, still dangling from his hand. The first time had been an accident, but every time since had been calculated. He stuck it into the drain. The infernal mechanism sprang back to life, jerking the fork from his hand. A blur of motion was followed by an odd coldness in his left eye. Three drops of blood splattered into the sink, one after another, before he felt any pain. The disposal had torn the fork apart and launched a tine into his eye. Reflexively, his hand rose. No matter how many times he went through this, he could not prevent that hand from rising up and making its grisly discovery.

-7-

Stig studied the cracked and peeling plaster of the motel room ceiling. He had spent less than an hour here, but he had done it many times. Did he know the pattern of blemishes any better from his numerous visits? He could have drawn a detailed map of the ceiling after the first time, but it felt familiar now. If Osmond were right, he had imagined each visit here, including this one. But by that logic, the present could be anywhere, even here, and his two-eyed memories as a professor and successful consultant could be the fantasies. This felt real. All the branches did.

"So, where did you see them last?" Carla asked, sitting in her bathrobe beside him on the bed.

"Hmm?"

"Your family. Where was the last place you saw them?"

"It was winter." Stig let the ceiling blur and fade away. "There was a fire in the fireplace. It was actually too warm, but it felt nice. Cozy. My wife lay on the couch. The boys sat on my feet and held onto my legs while I walked around the living room and tousled their hair. I can hear them squealing with laughter and see my wife smiling up at me. So beautiful."

"Huh," she said, uncertain what to make of his story. "That sounds nice."

"Have you ever wondered if the things that are happening to you are real or if you're just imagining them?" he asked.

"Well, I've had some pretty vivid dreams," she said. "You know, where you wake up and it takes a while to figure out it was all a dream. Is that what you mean?"

"I don't think so. I don't know. I never dream."

"Never?"

"Never," he said. "Dreaming is all about forgetting. I don't forget."

"Don't people go crazy if they're not allowed to dream? Maybe that's why things seem unreal to you. You have to be able to forget things that didn't happen to know what did."

"I'm not crazy."

"No, of course not. No. I didn't mean that you were. I just.... Hey, listen, I think I'm going to go take a shower." She stood and looked at him. "We, uh...."

"Yes?"

"We better settle up now. Chances are you'll be gone when I come out."

"Ah. Okay." He rolled over to the side of the bed where his pants lay in a heap, fished around for his wallet, and sat back up. He pulled some bills out and handed them to her.

"So, if I don't see you again, uh, good luck with your family and all that."

"Thanks."

She headed to the bathroom, scooping up her pile of clothes and purse on the way. Just before the bathroom door closed Stig called out.

"Carla."

She stopped and looked back, surprised he knew her name. "Yeah?"

"Don't let Ash play with his cousin next week. His cousin has meningitis. Ash will — he'll get very sick."

Her look of perplexion deepened. "What? How do you know all that?"

"I just do. I, uh, know someone. A doctor told me. It doesn't matter. It's important, though. Okay?"

Visibly shaken by his warning, she gave a slow, "Okay," and closed the bathroom door on her puzzled look.

-8-

"You still with me?" Osmond asked.

Stig sat at the small coffee shop table looking through the window at the busy street outside. He looked up slowly and seemed to rediscover Osmond sitting next to him. "Yeah," he said.

"Well, anyway, I'm sorry," Osmond said.

"Don't be. I understand."

"It's almost as if no one wants to hire a one-eyed guy with no credentials to look over their most precious tech secrets these days, am I right?" Osmond asked with a gentle punch to his friend's shoulder.

"Yeah."

"Seriously, though, have you ever thought about going back to school? Finishing college?"

"Not really."

"Why not?"

"I already did that."

Osmond was puzzled for a second, then understood. "Oh. In other timelines. Right."

"The degrees don't matter," Stig said, staring at the table. "I know everything that the college professor version of me knows. I'm the same person. I've lived both lives. Many lives."

Osmond tapped a finger on the table, trying to think of a polite reply. "The problem is," he said, "other people don't know all that. They don't know what you can do. I mean, I can't even remember all the times you've helped me. Hell, you've saved my life at least twice."

"I'll always help you, Oz. You're my best friend. The year I spent in and out of the hospital after the accident, you never left my side. In all the branches, you're the one constant. I can always count on you."

Osmond put his meaty hand on Stig's back and squeezed his neck. "That was a rough time. Tell you the truth, I didn't think you were going to make it — between the surgeries and the infections." Osmond trailed off shaking his head. "You're lucky to be alive. Anyway, I'm sure our business will take off. We just need a lucky break." He let his arm drop and swirled the dregs of his coffee, lost in thought. When he looked up Stig, was staring out the window again.

"Hey Stig," he said. "Do you think that maybe you could work that mojo of yours to impress some bigwigs? You know, like hold back some CEO just before a piano falls on them, or something like that."

Stig answered without taking his eyes from the street outside. "Maybe."

During their years together, Osmond had grown used to their one-sided conversations. He kind of liked them. He joined Stig in looking out the window, and a longer silence followed, each of them lost in their own thoughts. It was Osmond who once again broke the quiet.

"You know how you always say you're time traveling and I always say you're only daydreaming?"

"Yeah?"

"Well, I was thinking. Have you ever followed one of these branches of yours all the way to the end?"

Stig looked up. "The end?"

"Yeah. I mean, it seems like if you follow any branch of your tree out far enough, you'd eventually die, right?"

"I suppose."

"Well, if you followed a branch all the way to the end and lived to tell about it, wouldn't that prove you're daydreaming and not actually time traveling?"

"I imagine I could leave that branch before I die. Go to another branch."

"Hmm." Osmond scrunched up his face. "I guess. But then that would make you pretty much immortal since you always have another branch you can escape to if you're about to die." Osmond held his arms out dramatically. "I sit in the presence of an immortal, time traveling God."

Osmond saw the serious, thoughtful look on Stig's face and broke out laughing. "I'm teasing you, man."

Stig stared at him blankly.

"You're not," Osmond said.

"Not what?"

"You're not a God. You're just a smart man. So smart that sometimes you're really quite dumb."

Stig just nodded.

"What do you think would happen," Osmond asked, "if you didn't leave a branch before you died?"

"Are you asking me what's after death?"

"Yeah, I guess."

"I don't know."

-9-

"Mr. Gangleri, I can't explain why the antibiotics aren't working, but they aren't. The infection is out of control. The last scan showed a fluid collection eroding through the optic canal. We need to take you to the operating room today to have it drained."

The doctor stood by the door, ready to make a quick getaway. Stig's grandmother sat attentively next to his bed, completely overwhelmed, her spirit broken. Each time he sacrificed his eye to see the branches beyond, he also sacrificed his grandmother's happiness. The sicker he became, the higher the toll she paid. He had seen her in worse shape dozens of times and had buried her as many, but he hated being the cause. Maybe this would be the last time.

"Today?" she asked.

"Yes, we have to try to control the infection. Do you understand, Stig?"

"I do." He understood more than the doctor knew. The antibiotics weren't working because he hadn't been taking them.

The doctor spoke a little longer to his grandmother, had her sign some forms and vanished.

Lying under the glaring surgical lights, Stig waited for the anesthetic to take effect. The morphine barely touched his pain and he shook violently with chills. Each visit to this early bough of Yggdrasil came with multiple surgeries, but he had never been this sick before. He should have been frightened, but instead he just felt exhausted: tired of being separated from the ones he loved and tired of being lost in the tangle of Yggdrasil.

"His blood pressure is dropping," a voice said. He understood the tone, not the words.

The pain faded, and the light grew brighter. The murmuring voices and electromechanical sounds of the room withered like shadows before the advancing light until only silence remained. Silence and light.

He felt himself walking before he saw anything. Walls emerged from the blinding nothingness to form the familiar hallway of his home. He reached the end of the hall and turned the corner hopeful, as always, of what he would find. There, rocking a baby over a bassinet while another slept peacefully nearby, stood his wife. When she saw Stig, a warm smile spread across her face and she lowered the sleeping baby into the bassinet. She hurried across the room and gave him a long hug, burying her head on his shoulder. When they separated she held his face gently and looked into his eyes.

"My love," she said. "You must leave this branch. It ends and your work isn't complete."

"But I finally found you." He took her hands from his face and held them tightly. "I want to stay here, with you."

"Much of Yggdrasil remains undiscovered. Your destiny is unfulfilled," she said. "You must continue."

"I can't leave you. You were too hard to find. What if I never find my way back?"

She laughed gently. "We are easy to find. All branches lead here."

"I don't understand. I've searched Yggdrasil for lifetimes without finding a way here. I shouldn't be here now. This branch — I'm only nineteen and my grandmother still lives in this house. I couldn't have met you yet."

"Silly. You've been looking for us within the tree, but we live beyond the tree of possibilities, in the space between the branches. You've found us here, in this house, because this is familiar to you, but we are not tied to any one time or place. We are always with you, like air against a tree, rippling its leaves and rustling its branches."

"But I've been with you before. How?"

"You caught glimpses of the impossible when your mind was freed."

"From anesthesia? During surgery?"

"Yes. But you must go now, or Yggdrasil will never be complete."

"I don't know where to go. I think I've lost the present. Without it —" He paused and shook his head. "Without it, I can't tell what's real."

"The present is where the future turns into the past. It follows your mind like a mirage. You know this better than anyone."

She released his hands. "Now go, and return to us after you have accomplished great things and grown tired of wandering."

The ebb and flow of chaotic motion outside the coffee shop window mirrored his thoughts, and mesmerized Stig in a way he found hard to resist. Osmond's voice pulled him from his reverie.

"You know how you always say you're time traveling and I always say you're just daydreaming?"

"Yeah?"

"Well, I was thinking. Have you ever followed a branch out to the end?"

"No. Not to the end. But close enough to see what's beyond."

"Oh?" Osmond looked surprised. "What's there? What did you see?"

Stig looked up from the window and smiled. "The impossible."

See Douglas Anstruther's story "Not All Those Who Wander Are Lost"
online at Metaphorosis.
If you liked it, leave a comment. Authors love that!

Remember to subscribe to our e-mail updates so you'll know when new stories are posted.

About the story

I wanted to explore the idea that perfect prediction of the future could be confused with, and possibly be indistinguishable from, actually experiencing the future. As I wrote, I discovered that for someone with the ability to do this, the concept of the present became less relevant, and along with it, the notion of mortality.

In addition to the intentionally unanswered questions of whether or not Stig is really immortal and whether or not a real, objective present exists that he has lost, the story raised other questions along the way. I wasn't able to address these in the short story format and they were better left to the reader's imagination anyway. For example: If Stig's mental facilities are impaired (from drugs or sleep) does he lose his ability to jump away from danger? Is there some sort of meta-time that allows the linear progression of Stig's own experiences? If he doesn't go back to a thread, does time pass on it? If there were two people with the same ability, could either one extend the same thread? I do hope that the list goes on and that many more questions are raised among readers.

A question for the author

Q: If someone wanted to make an animated series out of your work, based on the title or recurring themes, what would it look like?

A: There are a few times in the story when the present isn't holding Stig's attention very well and we find him spacing out. Is he considering a leap to another branch? Maybe he's moved on to another timeline and is letting the one we see coast on autopilot.

An animated series could show these other timelines in the background, constantly impinging on his attention, threatening to carry him away, competing with each other to be his next destination and coloring his decisions and mood with knowledge of alternate histories and futures that the people around him haven't experienced. It'd look pretty trippy.

Also, dark. I like my animated series dark.

About the author

Douglas Anstruther was raised among the long cold winters of Minnesota. At age seven he discovered that there were other worlds beyond our own and was astonished, and frankly disappointed, that no one had thought this important enough to mention earlier - a sentiment he still holds today. At some point he married his lovely wife, Dana, went to medical school, had three very nearly perfect children and moved to Wilmington, North Carolina. When not tending to people's kidneys, Douglas likes to read, write and talk about history, linguistics, space, AIs, the singularity, and everything in between. He particularly enjoys writing stories that will rattle around in the readers' head for a while after the last page has been turned.

www.facebook.com/douglasanstruther, @DouglsAnstruthr

September

Graven Image

B. Morris Allen

It's about impressions. First impressions, last impressions, the creased and corrugated impressions that life leaves on our skin as it wears us down to our essentials, and eventually to nothing. I know about impressions; I'm in sales now.

Back then I was a lonely xenoarchaeologist, chasing down one more faded rumour, one more mystery worn flat by repetition and examination. Study, publish, repeat, as postgrads say, until there's nothing left to say, no iota of meaning left unexamined. And there's always something to say.

I'd found mention of the temple in *Henbro's Analects, Volume CLMXIV* (General Era 7,829), and in *Studies of Alien Ruins in the Gortheran Quadrant, #234* (GE 9,237), and again in Borhin's *A Complete Compendium of Religious Structures of a Cubic Nature* (GE 13,943). Eventually, I traced down thousands of other mentions in the literature. None of them had anything interesting to say about it — cursory mentions of indecipherable carvings, a lackluster image of a bare stone cube, and coordinates, should anyone care enough to visit.

Graduate students feed on the crumbs left by larger mouths, hoovering up just enough academic nutrition to keep the system running. By the time they have their degrees, grads have learned to live on nothing, but learned nothing about how to harvest their own food.

I was as desperate as any other postgrad. I'd scrimped and saved throughout college and university, borrowed, cheated, gambled — anything to raise enough money to buy a ship. And I'd done it. A battered, creaking, barely functional S-class scout with no spare parts and a solid-state drive that made ominous clunks despite a lack of moving parts.

I'd saved that simple temple for myself, cobbling together a doctoral thesis from dribs and drabs of nothing, dressed up to look like data. I'd seen, of course, what greater, more tenured minds had not, because that's what postgrads always need to see. I'd seen that the temple looked the same in every image. From crude tri-Ds in GE

3,113 to full-immersion expeers a decade old, the temple stood unchanged. As the sea around it fell, as jungle grew and shrank, as jagged ridges cracked into place above it, the temple never changed. Very slightly rounder, perhaps, the pile of dust at its base a tiny quantum higher, but essentially the same, over 20,000 years.

I wasn't the first to spot the temple's durability, of course. Dozens of others had examined it, analyzed it, determined the stone it was built from was stone, and put the building's longevity down to good engineering and good luck. They interviewed the place's addled but taciturn occupant, learned nothing, and let it go; Methuselan species were a dime a dozen. If one chose to live in the building as a curator of sorts, that was its own business.

They all missed the point, the one crucial datum that would make my reputation, or at least get me a published paper — the dust. In all those images, all those expeers, the dust never moved, never changed, except to grow infinitesimally higher.

The dust was thickest below the carvings; the carvings that millennia of xenoarchs had examined, dismissed, and nonetheless speculated about in reams and reams of dry and ultimately baseless paper. Here there had been change — with every visit, every visual record, the dust grew slightly higher, in peaked drifts that slowly, slowly accreted, clinging to the stone at the base of the temple's single altar like moss determined to reach the top.

In all those centuries, through all the upheavals of flora and climate and land, the dust never moved.

I landed with a screech of sliding metal and a feeling that the landing gear might be, so to speak, on its last legs. I lowered the ship to maintenance level, belly-down in the grass, more confident of a risky zero-base liftoff than of the gear's structural integrity. I had to exit through an alternate port and climb down handholds rubbed slick by age, but safe is safe.

The temple was just as advertised, a nondescript cube of grey stone with a soft fringe of dust at its base. A dark square in the center of one wall marked the single entry to its faded secrets. The curator's yellow tentacles flickered briefly into view as if tasting the scent of ship and woman. Everything just the way every recording showed. No surprises.

The temple was set in the center of a broad sward of teal grass, like a crumb of basalt in a malachite locket. At the far end, the land fell off sharply to a clear pink lake. On the sides, stately growths of brown and beige reached smooth arms up to a light indigo sky. Behind us, a ridge rose sharply up to a plateau. It was beautiful, or would have been if there hadn't been hundreds like it on other, more central worlds.

I gathered my gear from where I'd dumped it out the port, a paltry selection of third-hand analyzers and limited-memory recorders that were all my budget could afford. I strapped, snapped, and inserted until I could find no further excuse for delay.

Closeup, the temple looked the same. The dust beside the door formed the subtly serrated ridges familiar from weeks of study and analysis, from days of repeated viewing en route. I readied an ancient handheld analyzer, but a tremor from the doorway caught my eye, a slow undulation of yellow, like blond hair in a summer breeze. The Curator.

Every report said it was senile, so old and decrepit as to make no sense, kept alive by sheer inertia, too befuddled to leave, too dull to die. Simple manners, however, suggested a greeting might do no harm.

"Greetings, Curator." I said. Not deathless oratory, but it served the purpose.

The thing clacked and hooted and grumbled, slowly waving its tentacles like a hydra, or a Ganulan whispertree. It spoke Common; the records agreed on that. But only when it chose to, and seldom sensibly. It liked visitors, but not imagers, the records suggested.

I shrugged. I'd paid my respects, and I'd yet to turn on my recorders.

Behind the curator's thick stalk, the temple was empty but for the waist-high cube of an altar and its skirt of dust. A thick pane of some transparent stone above provided ample light. I stepped into the entry, and the Curator obligingly flowed aside, its ruffled skin streaming up the near side to form new tentacles as old ones deliquesced into its far surface. It was surprisingly beguiling, like an endless stream of rose petals blown by a gentle breeze. I gave it a smile and a half-bow as I stepped past it.

"Welcome," it said, quite clearly.

I missed my step, turned back in surprise as I struggled for balance.

"Did... Hel... Thank you," I settled on, at last.

"Welcome," it repeated.

"Thank you," I said again, for lack of a better idea. "You're the Curator, are you?"

Yellow tentacles waved, and a rustle of petals rippled round its trunk.

"Okay. What can you tell me about the temple?"

"Welcome." The sound issued from a tangle of yellow limbs, or a ruffle of skin, or some organ deep in the stalk. It seemed to vary.

"The temple hasn't changed," I tried. "For millennia."

Tentacles undulated in an intangible wind.

"Can you explain? How does the temple remain?"

Silence. I tried again, and again, but made no progress. 'Welcome,' then, was the one word it knew, or could remember. Senescence comes to all creatures, even those that live for eons.

"Right, then." I turned away, tried one last time. "What about the dust?" It seemed a topic unlikely to engage the threadbare fibers of a timeworn mind, but it was my topic, after all.

"No image." The thing's smooth tone seemed harsher, more insistent, if no more coherent.

"That's alright. I won't take any recordings just yet, okay? What can you tell me about the dust?" The Curator had my full attention again, and it seemed to me that its yellow skin was rumpled, the waves sweeping faster, like buttercups on a rippling pond.

"Image," it said. "No image." Was there a greenish tinge to the yellow now?

"Can't quite make your mind up, eh?" Cruelty is attractive, when we're the ones being cruel.

We went around for another quarter hour, but I coaxed no more revelations from it, no further expansions of its vocabulary. At last, I turned back to the altar.

It was a waist-high cube of blackish stone, greenish at the edges, but smoother and more rounded than the grey of the exterior. Its surface was smooth as well, with the faintest of sinuous lines suggesting where etching might once have formed gullies and trenches among broad plateaus of stone. Some lines were darker, depressions just barely tangible to a questing hand. I swept my fingers gently across the surface, watching the Curator from the corner of my eye. It stood unchanged, the green shade faded back to golden yellow, the squalls to flurries of bright petals.

There were two places where the relief of the surface was more perceptible. Scratches, even a notch, perhaps. They formed jagged, awkward lines unlike the faintly visible twists and graceful curves of what I assumed to be original carving. Careless equipment mounting, I assumed, or even graffiti; even xenoarchs are people, and some people are fools. The last expedition I'd encountered in the literature had been a decade or more back. The scratches seemed fresher than that, but clearly the temple was made of resistant stuff.

Eventually, the sightseeing complete, I squatted to take my first look at my real subject – the altar's petticoats of dust. The dust formed a fringe of diminutive scree, its gentle slopes looped down here into mild valleys, shaped up there into squat peaks. The tallest stood proud of the others by a centimeter or more, a spike among bumps. It seemed sharper, taller than the images I recalled, and I pulled up the latest record on my left lens. I twitched to an overlay, and yes, the new peak was higher, by a good centimeter or more. Or the altar and virtually everything else had sunk, but that seemed unlikely, and was easily contradicted by a comparison with the other peaks.

My hand trembled as I reached for a sampler. I'd done a meticulous analysis of dust levels in previous records. No peak had grown more than a millimeter per year, and here was a rate ten times that! Not only had I found my footnote in history, but perhaps a moment of glory – a speech at a sector conference, and perhaps more.

A glance at the Curator confirmed that it had not moved, though the undulant petals swayed even more than before. I opened my sample vial, gripped my polished spatula with nervous fingers.

But wait! What was I doing? Sweat slicked my temples as I realized I'd almost compromised my own great find before recording it. I rocked back on my heels, swallowing hard. Almost! Almost, glory had fallen prey to careless ambition, as so often happens when even an expert loses sight of the forest in the glory of the trees.

I took a moment to rest, letting my breathing calm. When my heart had slowed to a rate closer to its norm, I peeled a recorder from its holdstrip and aimed it at the altar dust. "Keep it together," I told myself, and turned it on.

"No image!" The Curator swirled in a squeal of tangled limbs. "No image! No image!" It held its ground, coming no closer, but roils of harsh green swept through its skin, petals suddenly compressed to buds, emerald pustules on citrine muscle.

I turned off the recorder, and watching long tentacles flailing like whips above my head. No prior expedition had mentioned this. They'd described the Curator as feeble and harmless, a fuddled entity of inoffensive mien. This was something different.

I shuffled back from the altar as the Curator calmed, or so it seemed. The thing's petals unfurled again to a carpet of ruffles, their color fading slowly from lime to lemon. I stood carefully, sliding the recorder conspicuously into a pocket.

"No image," I said, holding out bare hands.

"Welcome," it said, in sighs and crackles.

"Not as much as I'd hoped," I said with a hint of smile. No offense; a little joke among friends.

"Welcome," it insisted. A spiral pleat crinkled around its trunk and was gone.

Any good xenoarch studies some biology and physiology. You have to, to interpret relics. I might be a very small fish in the archaeological world, but I was a good one, to use a mixed but biological metaphor. It seemed to me that I might have stumbled on a second good thing here. Other expeditions, including some with biologists, had discounted the Curator. The biologists had instead waxed enthusiastic over the planet's balanced ecosystem, the adaptability of species, the motility of lignolithic graveltrees. Demented singleton sapients were of lesser interest, apparently, even to postgrads.

The Curator, however, was exhibiting a dramatic change in behaviour, a change not noted in twenty millenia of casual reference. Surely that meant something. Yet, while more aggressive and insistent than records noted, it had not said much. If it conveyed its point more forcefully than in the past, it provided little information. A mystery, but perhaps not a great one. Awkward, no doubt, but not an absolute barrier to my investigation. Also a handy backup discovery to keep in my pocket in case of need. Dust, though, was my focus.

Wary, I squatted again, and shuffled my way slowly toward the altar. The Curator stood rooted to the spot, even as I slowly, very slowly, withdrew my sample vial and spatula. No reaction. I had a basic image from the recorder, I rationalized. That would be enough to document my discovery.

I held the vial close to the tall peak of dust, and ever so gently slid the tip of my spatula into the rising edge of one side. The Curator made no sound, and, with almost imperceptible shudders, I transferred my precious grains of dust to the sample vial. My touch was delicate enough, it seemed; the peak held, forming no avalanche to fill the tiny gap in its supporting slope.

I capped the vial and leaned back. Colored swirls formed across my vision, and I realized I'd been holding my breath the whole time I was sampling. I closed my eyes and waited until the colors faded away.

I slipped the vial into a chest pocket, sealed the pocket closed, held it tight with my hand. If the Curator objected, I thought I might escape to the ship with my sample intact. I stood, the altar between me and the mysterious creature. My peak was just below one of the scratches in the altar surface, I realized. From this angle, the scratch seemed cruder, more visible, more evidently purposeful. It started in the faint shadow of an older swirl, jagged sharp left, then down toward the edge, then left again, like the rift from a recent earthquake. It ended just above the peak I had sampled.

Curious, I leant forward. Pulling a thread from my well-used uniform, I tied it to my spatula to form a simple plumb-line. The coincidence of scratch and dust was exact — as exact as could be, with such a crude instrument.

I hovered close over the end of the scratch, aware as ever now of the Curator, but it swayed calmly in its place, seemingly unconcerned.

In the canyon of the scratch were particles of black dust. I fumbled free another vial, set my spatula into the scratch, and traced it from start to finish. A little fall of dust spat out of the crevice and into my vial.

"No image," said the Curator woodenly.

I froze, my eyes straining up to see, but the thing stood calmly, petals unfurled, limbs graceful arcs above it.

"No image," I agreed, definite.

It said nothing, and I straightened in a slow, measured rise.

"No image," I repeated, for good measure. There was no answer, and I skirted the altar, keeping it between us as long as I could. At length, I stood beside the altar, the Curator to my right, the door free before me.

"No image," I said, and bolted.

I was halfway to the ship before I risked a look back. The Curator had flowed back to its position in the doorway, but showed no sign of following. I took no chances, running until I could clamber back up the slippery side of my ship and in through the port. The Curator was unmoved, and I took a moment to watch it. It was an impressive sight, its yellow bright against the grey of the temple, and harmonizing nicely with the teal grass and pink lake beyond. An alien place, but a beautiful one.

I opened a foodpack, and let it steam gently while I labeled my vials and set a grain from each in a battered, century old analyzer. I forced myself not to look at the screen as the machine chugged and whiffled and posted results one by one. Dinner was braised magna beans on a slab of Alerian gelbark, with a beaker of gleanberry juice to wash it down. I let it slide past my tongue untasted, attention fixed firmly on the noisy machine behind me.

Rock, it said, when I turned at last. Specifically, amphibole composed largely of arfvedsonite – a conglomeration of silicon, oxygen, iron, and sodium. Rare on some worlds, common on others. Other expeditions had found no local supply of the stone, and no trace of the builders, which was a minor mystery, but vanished civilizations don't inspire corporate funders as much as picturesque temples, and that was as far as the investigation of origins had gone.

That ground had been trodden further than I could go with my limited means. What mattered to me was that the grains were the same. The dust from the altar skirt was the same as that from the scratch on its top. Not coincidence, then. The one was the source of the other. That was interesting indeed.

Or was it? My heart, which had crept slowly up toward my throat, came sliding back down to my belly. Who was to say there was any meaning to it? Probably the scratches were just what they looked like — graffiti. The planet wasn't exactly on the main routes; in fact, it was in something of a galactic hinterland, but it could be reached. I'd proven that just by coming here.

The Curator must know. It was always here. Presuming it had a memory, of course. Perhaps all it retained were its point and counterpoint of "welcome" and "no image", grooves worn deep into its placid mind.

In any case, I had evidence that dust and altar were of the same material. That was step one in my investigation, and a solid one. I ate my plate (guaranteed nutritious, but it still tasted more of carboard than cake) and went to bed satisfied, if not happy.

I woke the next day with a renewed enthusiasm. My gamble had paid off. A long trip into nowhere, and already I'd gathered important data, with a possible biological footnote to boot. Excellent progress! I could taste the professorship already. Secure in my solitude, I stuck my tongue out and waggled it back and forth. Definitely a professorship. Maybe even associate-flavored.

I ate, washed, dressed, and arranged my gadgets. I'd already decided not to aggravate the Curator more than necessary. I stuck a recorder deep in an inside pocket and threaded an optic fiber out to the front of my coveralls, virtually invisible against a seam. I switched the recorder on, tested the playback. Everything worked fine. I switched off again until I could get outside. No sense wasting limited memory.

The outside was the same. The sky, a slightly lighter shade than before, shaded the grass a little toward turquoise, and I switched the recorder on again just to have a memento. I could always delete extraneous bits later.

As I walked toward the temple, I caught glimpses of the Curator, long tentacles waving languidly at first, then faster and faster until they were almost frantic. The creature pushed out to the door of the temple, leaning out farther than it had done the day before. Like a tongue, I remembered, and flickered mine in response.

"No image," it cried. "No image. No image! NO image!" Its cries grew louder as I approached, its frenzied gestures almost angry now. I stopped, well clear of the door and the Curator's long tentacles. It seemed unwilling to leave the shelter of the temple, and I realized I'd seen no reports of it ever being outside. Someone had remarked on it some millennia back, in fact, and it now seemed accepted that the creature was in some way tied to the building.

"No image," it said again, almost plaintive. "Welcome. No image." Its surface was a striated bilious green now, and the buds had disappeared altogether, leaving a surface slick and solid as muscle. It writhed in place, leaning as far out of the door as it could, its base tight to the temple stone, its tentacles holding it in place, agitated ripples running back and forth in gruesome shivers.

"Alright, alright," I mumbled at last. "No image." I slipped a hand into my pocket, switched off the recorder. "I don't know how you could tell, but no image."

The moment the recorder switched off, the creature calmed. I could see the tension slipping away as tentacles relaxed, the trunk righted itself, and the angry green faded to gold.

"Welcome," it said at last, as the petals re-emerged from its skin. It flowed back a step, welcoming.

I switched the recorder on again.

The reaction was instant. The tentacles flailed, and the Curator's rich skin flushed with the vile green. "No image," it said. "No image, no image, no image!"

I turned the recorder off.

The green faded away. "Welcome," it said, and wagged its tentacles. Like a child beaten by its parents, I thought, recalling customs in the late Althantic period. Bruised, battered, but still hopeful. Still looking for love from its single source of joy and pain.

I turned the recorder on. The Custodian went through its routine, its pleading, colouring frenzy of waving and crying. It made no move to stop me, even standing aside as I walked up, entered, exited again. I could hear it calling as I walked around the outside of the temple, noting drifts of dust, seeing how the teal of the grassy lawn stopped well short of the temple walls, leaving bare the rock supporting it.

When I came back around to the front, I turned the recorder off. I had enough data, and I'd had enough of the pleading. Truth be told, I'd had enough of myself. Grotesque, demented alien it might be, but it had feelings, that was clear enough. And I'd been toying with them for the sake of knowledge.

"I'm sorry," I said, as I watched the creature transform again from green to gold. "I just... I was selfish." I had been, and I could think of no justification. "Humanity at its best."

"Welcome," it said, with a graceful bow of tentacles.

"Yeah." I felt a sudden urge to rip the recorder off, to throw it off, over the cliff and into the pink lake below. But data was data, even when evilly gathered. Ignorance served no one. I contemplated that slippery slope, the Curator rustling at my back, the lake enticing before me, and then I let it go. "What can I say, Squiggly? I'm weak."

"Welcome."

I couldn't face it again, so I went around the outside to the back of the temple. The dust there looked similar, but grey instead of the greenish black of the altar. I scooped out vial and spatula, and squatted down to take a sample from a drift I knew I had captured well in the recorder. Human frailty, or a desire to make the Curator's suffering meaningful?

With a nasty, grating sound, the spatula scooped nothing. Instead of the fine, powder of the altar dust, this was hard. Hard as rock, in fact. I stared at it, befuddled. Perhaps it wasn't dust at all, but a growth, an excrescence, a crust. A secretion, if the temple were a living creature, like mucus dried around its eyelashes. Seepage — that was the word I wanted. Mineral seepage.

And yet, it looked like dust. I'd made a minor study of dust settlement forms on the voyage out. This looked like dust, piled high by droppage from above, and forming peaks depending on the mass, shape, and coefficient of friction of the individual particles. Seepage didn't work that way, but crept up or out, or effloresced in a centered pattern.

I jabbed at the little dust hill, gently at first, then harder and harder, but nothing changed except that the fine tip of my spatula dented. I hadn't even loosen one grain.

Here was my answer, I realized bitterly. The reason the dust never changed. It wasn't dust, but rock, somehow formed to look just like dust. One of nature's little jokes, or perhaps one by the long-gone builders. I threw down my spatula in disgust and went to the cliff to look at the lake.

Almost immediately, I was back. The pattern changed. The piles of dust grew over time. Slowly, but they did. The dust of the altar in particular had ... The altar! I'd had no trouble there. Altar dust behaved like dust.

I grabbed up my spatula, slid it into a pocket. It was useless now for sampling, but I could clean it, and I had others. Vial in hand, I raced back around the temple to the entry.

"Welcome," said my yellow friend.

"Welcome," I answered, and pushed past a stray tentacle toward the altar. Its skin felt warm, like spring sunshine.

I skipped around the altar to the back. The little pile of dust I had sampled had slumped, filling in the spot where I had sampled. The distribution was different, but the peak seemed even higher than before. I sampled again, extracting a tenth of a gram with no difficulty, and slipping it into a vial. The peak shifted again.

I looked up at the scratch in the altar top, to find it fringed with dust again. I sampled some, even as I realized what it meant.

"You're doing this, aren't you?" I asked as I straightened.

The Curator stood silent.

"You're making these scratches!" I looked around. The floor was bare, smooth stone. There! In the corner, behind the Curator, a rusty scrap of metal. I leaped toward it. A piece of wire, discarded by some expedition or other, and now put to other uses. The tip was shiny. I waved it at the Curator triumphantly. "You've been scratching on the altar!"

"Welcome," it said languidly.

This was a find! Far more important than the damned dust. Here I had the dust creator itself! The Curator, the ancient, disregarded denizen of the temple, was responsible for the carvings. At least, for the new ones. Doubt assailed me as I recalled that the new, jagged scratches were quite different from the original, sinuous ones. Nonetheless — Curator, temple, etching. My fortune was made.

"Way to go, curator. Way … to … go!"

'Fortune', I admitted, meant minor acclaim by way of a published letter in *Xenoarchaeology Quarterly*, followed by a lengthy scientific paper. But that was enough for a position in a university in some peripheral system, or maybe even toward the center of the spiral arm.

Cold practicality intervened, shunted the flow of enthusiasm into storage. How to prove this, then, without a record? Perhaps, I thought, just a *little* more recording. I'd have to catch the Curator at it, of course; I'd have to wait.

"What you say, Squigs?" I turned to the Curator. "One more…"

"Welcome."

What was I saying? What was I thinking? Already twice, I'd rebuked myself for cruelty, committed to do no evil. And here I was, planning yet another round of villainy.

I could make notes. Record my own impressions. Dictate my comments. That would get me no more than an excerpt in the Letters section of some minor journal. Which would draw one or two real xenoarchs, who would make recordings. They'd get all the glory. And the Curator would get the anguish — the same unhappiness I was trying to spare it, or worse.

Back to step one then — I might as well do it myself. I'd done it before. I could do it again.

It would be harder this time, though. In the last few hours, I'd somehow come to think of the Curator less as 'creepy old creature' and more as 'charming, enduring companion'. It was beautiful, it was ancient, and it only wanted one thing, "no images".

Two things, perhaps. Maybe three. It wanted to welcome others, it wanted to scratch on the altar, and it wanted no record made. No visual record. Why?

I went back outside, slid a statipack from my thigh pocket, and settled down to a lunch of fermented pola nuts and thought. I reached no conclusions and didn't taste the food, but I made a decision.

"Squiggly," I said, stepping back into the temple.

"Welcome."

"Welcome," I agreed. "I want to test something, okay?"

"Welcome."

"Promise not to get angry?" I held out a hand, gripped a tentacle lightly. It twitched, but didn't pull away. It was firm, but surprisingly delicate. Not really well suited to wire gripping. I looked closer, and soon spotted a pale spot on one of the other tentacles. The Curator shifted form, but perhaps it had a preferred rest setting, a default, with a spot that was callused or raw from holding the little wire. Or maybe it was just a freckle. It didn't matter.

I let loose the tentacle. It flapped about a bit, then settled into the same slow wave as the others, like a cat's tail that's been held and then set free.

I stepped over to the altar. As I'd thought, there were two jagged scratches on it. Ragged, raw, and obvious now that I knew to look for them, one like an angled S, the other like a crooked Y. They hadn't been there on the images from previous expeditions. The altar's carvings had been studied near to death, and there was no way they would not have been noted.

"Here we go," I warned, taking up my first metal spatula. Lightly, as lightly as possible, I traced the second scratch, the Y. The Curator twitched, but didn't move, didn't speak. I traced it again, with a little pressure now on the tip of the spatula.

"Welcome."

"Welcome indeed." It seemed a good sign. A promising start. I traced the scratch again, pressing much harder now. If I did this enough times, my theory went, I could win the Curator's trust, and it would let me make a recording or two. It entered my mind that I was, without a doubt, contaminating the field, but I let that go. One step at a time.

"Welcome," the Curator said, each time I traced the scratch. Little by little, grain by tiny grain, a fine, powdery dust accumulated in the scratch.

"Well, then," I said, as I stretched my back, and worked the cramp out of tired fingers. "So far so good." The Curator said nothing, but it looked to be a brighter, more vivid shade of yellow. Of course, I'd been in a dimmish temple for some time now.

"Let's try the other one, shall we?" I stepped around to the original scratch, as I thought of it, the one shaped vaguely like an S. It was deeper than the other, when measuring depth in fractions of a millimeter. I set my metal stylus on it, traced it out.

"No image," said the Curator.

I stopped. This was a setback, without doubt. Ten minutes of steady "welcome", and now we were back to "no image" already. The Curator was a fickle creature.

There were no signs of anger or outrage, no green flush. The yellow petals pulsed steadily in spirals around the trunk. I traced the scratch again.

"No image."

No other reaction. It had done the same, I realized, the other day. The exact same.

I traced the scratch again.

"No image."

And again.

"No image."

Harder, this time.

"No image." The spirals ran faster, but they were all yellow, and the petals fluttered freely.

It had to be. I traced the Y scratch again.

"Welcome."

I traced the S with shaky hands.

"No image."

Back and forth, back and forth until there could be no doubt, though mine had long since gone.

Y scratch — "Welcome." S scratch — "No image."

I set down the spatula, left it on the altar.

"Squiggly, my boy, you are something else." But what?

I thought about it all the rest of the day, sitting with my back against the temple, the Curator standing friendly by my side, every now and then letting out a tuneful "Welcome". I thought about it that night, over a statipack of something or other edible. I thought about it until I fell reluctantly asleep, thought about it when I woke up in the middle of the night, and as I dressed in the morning.

"Squigs," I said, as I stood once more in the entry of the temple, and it flowed back to let me in, "the way I see it, we have three possibilities.

"One. You're making those scratches as a reminder of the only things you have left; maybe the only ones you ever had. One for welcome, one for no image. Maybe you're a guard dog, maybe you're a degenerate sage, maybe you're a rocktree that's slowly learning new tricks. But you know your memory's not so hot, and you're setting your two favorite phrases down in stone. Maybe you remember the builders doing that, or maybe you were inspired by these carvings." I waved at the altar. "Who knows how old you are?"

"Two. You're renewing your programming. You're — no offense — some kind of elaborate cyborg or genetic robot, and out of desperation, you've taken to trying to fix up your own circuit board. Only," I waved again at the altar and the scratches, "you don't have quite the same artistic touch as your makers." I looked again. The scratches were definitely deeper now. The spatula was ... over in the corner, next to the now-redundant piece of wire.

"Three. Something else. I admit, that's by far the biggest category, but I don't want you to go wild with it. And I admit, one and two aren't really all that different. But there's a difference of intent, I think; an important one.

"Thing is, Squig, there's a test we can do, that might help us find out." The Curator stood silent. "What do you say we try?" It went well against my xenoarch training, but that seemed to have gone by the wayside in the excitement, with only the faintest of squeals from my conscience.

I went over to the corner of the temple, picked up the spatula, came back to the altar. I studied it carefully, as I'd studied the oldest records all morning. I positioned myself perpendicular to the doorway, to get the most contrast on the altar, then flicked an overlay up onto one lens. I set it to auto-adjust for perspective, waited until it had settled and run a range of precalculations for possible shifts in position.

"Here we go, buddy." The Curator was across the altar and to my left. With as delicate a touch as I could master, I set spatula to stone. I'd chosen the shortest, simplest curve that I could still make out, and the clearest, oldest record I could match to it. Softly, I ran my spatula along it, with one eye on the altar, one on the transparency, and a third, if I'd had it, on the Curator.

Nothing happened.

I stood up, looked the being over carefully. Was the yellow a little more orange? Were the spirals going the other way? I closed my eyes, couldn't remember. It was hard to see color in this light.

I stooped again, ran the spatula carefully over the curve. Again and again, slowly, until I was certain I was getting it right. There was definitely a tinge of orange now, and the petals were spread flat against the trunk, except when they swirled in complex patterns of spirals and circles. It was very pretty.

"We are getting somewhere, Squigs!" I pressed harder, staying as close to the true path as I possibly could. My arm knew the movement by now, and I was confident I was fairly close. Two more runs, pressing harder every time, until the Curator, now a vivid apricot, broke out into a ululating, earsplitting cry of screeching, crumbling lumber mixed with bird calls and the sound of thunder. It wasn't pretty at all.

I dropped the spatula and ran. I stopped halfway to the ship; my usual spot. When I turned back, the party was over. The Curator wasn't visible, and I jogged slowly back, tacking toward the forest to maintain my distance from the entry while getting a view into the temple.

The Curator was bent over the area I'd been tracing, slowly feeling the surface with one tentacle, dragging the spatula along behind with the two others. It was trying to etch it deeper!

I stepped closer, and the being immediately stopped. "Welcome," it said, holding out the spatula.

I took it, stepped cautiously back. Those tentacles could grip, that was clear enough, and there were enough of them that the Curator could hold me with no trouble. No more trouble now than yesterday, or the day before.

"In for a penny," I offered, and stepped up to the altar.

The Curator had done a terrible job. The new scratches were jittery and angular, where the original etching had been smooth and sinuous. The new scratches ran the risk of completely obscuring the old. Already, I had trouble seeing where my marks had been, and where the new ones went wrong. If this was reprogramming, it was going to lead to some serious glitches.

"No scratching," I said, gathering up the spatula and the discarded wire. "You don't have the eye for it."

Actually, I realized, the Curator had no eyes at all. Clearly it could sense things; it sensed my presence well enough. But there didn't seem to be any actual light-gathering apparatus. "Pretty good for a blind ... thing," I amended. "But not good enough. Not to do restoration work."

My own skills weren't good enough either, I realized. It was one thing to test a theory. It was another to rewire a stone circuit board, or whatever this was. Who knew what might happen? The Curator might not be deft, but it looked to be plenty strong. More than strong enough to throw me against a wall, if I triggered the wrong subroutine. A bit like sticking electrodes into a man's brain, really. Run some voltage here, his left arm raises. Run some there, he recites Nuaji poetry. Over here and ...

"Run some there and he recites Nuaji poetry," I repeated, as a chill settled on my shoulders and worked its way down my breasts. I backed slowly out the door, spatula and wire carefully in hand.

I backed up to a safe distance, halfway to the forest. It might be a safe distance. Who knew?

I remembered my first day on the ground. I'd seen the temple from the side, the Curator's slim yellow tentacles flickering in and out of the entry. Like a tongue. A long, yellow, very, very forked tongue.

I'd stood there next to it, reached out my hand to hold it. Standing in the creature's very maw. What else could it be? If that was the tongue, the entry was the mouth. And mouths don't only speak.

I shuddered. How close had I been to disaster? No wonder it said "welcome". The next phrase was "come into my parlour", no doubt.

I slept poorly that night, locked behind a sealed port with the manual override engaged, and a makeshift barrier outside my berth. I'd been in the beast's mouth, perhaps its belly. Jonah had nothing on me, except perhaps a certain amount of style, and a lot of divine backing.

Only one thing kept me from flying out of there as soon as my hands stopped shaking enough to activate the controls. The Curator said "welcome". Logical enough, if you're a huge stone flytrap with a prehensile tongue. Got to get the suckers in somehow.

It also said "no image". Where was the sense in that? "Step right up, make yourself at home while I make you dinner. Oh, by the way, no pictures." Your average mass murderer, human sacrificer, wants a little recognition. Your average carnivore couldn't care less. Why the stricture against records? What difference could it make once the victim was in the trap? For that matter, why hadn't it eaten me already? Or any other expedition in the past twenty thousand years?

Twenty thousand years is a very long time to be patient. It's also a very long time not to eat, even if you're a rock-based organism. If the thing had forgotten how to eat, it would be dead by now. Instead, it was very patiently, and very badly, performing brain surgery on itself with its tongue and a piece of wire.

The curse of the scientist is in not being able to let go. We're like detectives and like cats in that, except that cats have more lives, and detectives have armchairs, and sometimes guns. I'd have like to have something behind me, even if just a chair. The nearest thing to a gun was the ship, which was hard to carry around. I settled instead on a recorder. Maybe all it would do was anger the thing, but at least it would be a distraction.

In slow, careful stages, I walked halfway to the temple. The skull. The being. Whatever. 'Temple' seemed silly now, but it was the best I had. Besides, heads had temples, didn't they? Two apiece. There should be another around.

"Get a grip on yourself, woman." Hilarity and hysteria were far too close together to risk confusing them now.

I walked halfway again. And another half, until I was only a few meters from the structure.

"Welcome," said the tongue.

"Yeah, sure."

"Welcome."

"You would say that." This was getting us nowhere.

If it did eat, where were the bones of its kill? Yet if it were photosynthetic, why would it need a tongue? Even if the tongue were more for talking than for taking, whom would it talk with? Why would it need to? And why to humans? In all the novels, thinking mountains thought very very slowly. How... Or maybe that was why. Maybe the tongue was semi-independent. Maybe even, and this seemed quite likely, part of some sort of symbiotic relationship, and not technically part of the temple at all. Of course, then both of them would need to eat. Best not to think of that.

Still, why the prohibition on recording? How did it even know? Obviously it had senses I did not, but my recorders were purely passive, receiving light and sound as they arrived. How could it sense such a thing?

The best way to find out, it seemed to me, was to ask.

I'd spent the morning well away from the temple, setting up a complete record of all my thoughts, all my data, and all my speculations. I attached the recordings I'd made, cross-reference with all the files I'd brought. I even mentioned the dust — both kinds, loose and solid, and how the loose kind had led me to my discovery. I set out in detail the steps I indented to take. When I was done, I sealed up the ship, squared my shoulders, and marched to meet my doom.

It felt like doom. I had my recorder, and I'd brought my finest stylus, a sturdy durasteel probe used for testing masonry in the finest of building cracks. It was cheap, but it was tough.

"Right, then, Squigs." The phrase was missing the camaraderie of our earlier exchanges, but I was aiming for bravado instead. "Brain surgery 101. Pay attention."

I'd like to say I stepped bravely into the lions' den, but in fact, I slunk in on shaky legs, keeping my back to the wall. For all I knew, the wall was where the giant stone teeth were waiting to grind me into altar paste.

Methodically, I traced line after line as well as I could, starting with the clearest. I traced and traced each one with just the faintest touch, until the movement felt natural, until the software said I was staying within a one percent margin. It wasn't great, for brain surgery, but then I wasn't a brain surgeon. Not by training. I didn't touch the pattern I'd used the other day. Whether through my own carelessness or through design, if one can say that about synapses, the result had been frightening; I didn't care to chance it again. When taking stupid chances, it seemed to me, it might pay best to take ones not *known* to be dangerous.

When I thought I had ten of them down, and when the Curator — the Curatongue? — hadn't yet thrown me to the teeth, I started back on the first. When I'd traced it five times again within my margin of error, I increased the pressure. The first firm tracing did nothing. Nor the second, nor the third. The scritching, scratching grind of the stylus started to wear at me. I didn't dare look away from my work, but I could tell that the Curator was close. Four times, five, with no result, and I stepped away. Sweat drenched my back and plastered my hair to my forehead. My shoulders were so tight they hurt.

As I stepped back, the Curator flowed forward. I scrambled back, heedless of stone teeth until the temple wall was cold against my back. Yellow-pink tentacles traced across the path of my stylus, the thin scratch I'd managed.

"Welcome!" it boomed.

I shut my eyes. Volume control. Or enthusiasmotor, or adrenalith gland, or some other outlandish thing. Not speech.

"Welcome," the Curator said in a more normal tone. It had flowed back to its normal place, across the altar from me. Pink spirals chased each other around its trunk, and its petals danced in intricate patterns. Not helpful.

I did line two. No result. Line three. Line four. Line five. Each led to different displays from the tongue buds, different colours, different arrangements of tentacles. It was lovely, elegant, and utterly unrelated to Common speech in any form I or my analyzers could recognize.

I took a break after five. It wasn't surprising, really. What were the chances I'd hit the right combination out of the who knew how many that must be available? The oldest records hinted at layers and layers of lines, at different depths. And that was just the surface. Who knew what mineral nerves lay within the altar, and what had caused them to stop working? A scratch on the surface was just that — a superficial mark that could mar but not effect real change.

I ate a snack. My shoulders were tightening already from tension, and that wouldn't help. I stretched doggedly until the muscles loosened as much as they were likely to.

"Okay, Squiggly." He stood in his place by the altar, tentacles wrapped into an intricate basket at waist level. Like a seat. "Thanks anyway, buddy. Not yet." I went back to my usual place, across from him, the altar safely between us.

Line six. Line seven. Line ...

"Thank you."

I raised my head, only for my neck to spasm painfully. Warm tentacles helped me lurch upright, held me while blood rushed to my head and stars danced before me.

"What was that?" I squinted across the altar, trying desperately to refocus on a distance further than ten centimeters away.

"Thank you." The tentacles let go. "Thank you for your help."

It talked. For real. Full sentences and everything. "Um. Sure." Just what I'd wanted. Why I tried to recall? Why had I wanted it to talk? I'd had a question, surely. A question.

"What do you eat?" I blurted. That had been it. The grip of the stylus cut painfully into my hand. I'd feared the answer, this morning.

"People."

My shoulders sagged. That·was it, then. I dropped the stylus. What was the point? I'd never fight this thing. Probably the stone mouth was already shutting, the teeth emerging. But I had my answer. I clung to that, wrapping my arms around my chest as the shivers started. Relief, I thought.

"You have the humor?" the Curator asked. "You are a species with humor, with jokes? This is a joke."

"You're telling me." How many meals teach their predators to speak? That was a joke if I'd ever heard one. "Don't talk with your mouth full." That was another.

"I eat the ... essence..." Oh, it got worse? Wonderful. "The companionship, the company."

"Just get it over with already. I'm the only company you've got. Start sucking up my essence or let me loose."

"I have already done so."

I frowned, looked down at my body. I felt like myself. I looked like myself. Essentially and otherwise. Uncrumpled, unmasticated.

"I don't get it." Here I was, prey for a brain damaged vampire rock skull, and I didn't even understand it. Bad xenoarch.

"I feed on on companionship, on the presence of others. It does them no harm, I believe. Some even enjoy it."

Not many enjoy being fed on, in my experience. Maybe there was supposed to be some kind of gaseous emission at work, but if so, I didn't feel particularly calm.

"This is the reason for the Squiggly," the Squiggly said. "You call it the Squiggly? Or Squigs? The Curator. The Interlocutor. Interlocutor is best." It wriggled shyly, and a violet pattern chased across all the tentacles before disappearing into the trunk. "It is to entertain, to caress, to nourish, to solicit, to speak."

I looked at it. At the Interlocutor, anyway. I wasn't even sure just what I was talking to yet.

"So Squiggly calls them in, and you feast on their emissions, is that it?" Like one of those fish with a light on its head. Glow, glow, snap.

"Yes. But with no harm. And some benefit. The Squiggly can feed you, if you desire." The Interlocutor proffered a long tentacle, now dripping with some clear yellow fluid.

I shuddered. "No, thanks. I had breakfast." A thought came to me. "So what does Squiggly eat, then?"

"It eats me." I knew there was a catch. "Sunshine, minerals. I draw them up from the soil, from the rain."

"For twenty thousand years?"

"When I run out, I make changes." I remembered the upheavals in the land surrounding the temple, the rises and falls of land.

"You did that? The lake, the cliff, the ridge?" The ridge was a good kilometer away.

"Yes."

"So what do you eat when there are no people?" As there had not been for a decade.

"Animals will suffice when needed. The Squiggly is very versatile. It can welcome many types. My minimal needs are small."

"So then, what happened?" I gestured to the altar, unsure now whether the Interlocutor could see me. "How did your brain get ... this way?" I eased away from 'erased'.

"No image," squawked the Interlocutor immediately. "Yes, 'no image'," it repeated in a more thoughtful tone. "I feed on companionship, respect. Conversely, I ... wither ... in disregard. 'Feeding' is a simple but inaccurate term. Perhaps it is better to say that sympathetic, pleasant interaction generates brainwaves that resonate with my own, build their amplitude, allow me to manipulate my own form in addition to the land around me. Analytic, dispassionate, distant interaction generates waves that dampen my own, that cause my control to ... lapse. When that happens, my systems degrade, my structures slump. As when visitors make recordings, rather than using their own senses. You see the result."

I looked down at the altar, with its faint lines, its painstakingly scratched surface, and at the skirt of dust at its base.

"Dust!" I gasped. "The dust." I'd been right after all. Sort of.

"Yes. The dust. It remains part of me, but disordered, chaotic." The Interlocutor chuckled. "You re-established my language capacity, in a rather brutal way."

"Hey!" Here I'd just done delicate brain surgery on a stone-brained twenty thousand year old alien, and it was complaining?

"Oh, I appreciate it. You did better than the Interlocutor could. And perhaps the day will come when I can reestablish the circuits properly."

"What do you mean?" It was talking, wasn't it? And I was here!
"Feed away."

The Interlocutor waved its tentacles. "Much as I savor your ... feedback, it is a crumb to the feast I would need." It paused. "Can you bring more people?"

"What? No." Not in my tiny ship. And yet... "How old are you?"

"Old, even for my kind, though we are few and far between. One million local years. Perhaps a bit less."

A long time. "So you've met other races. Talked with them."

"Oh yes."

"And you remember." I looked back at the altar with its tracery of faded, failed synapses.

"Mostly. The efferent systems are the first to go. Memories are stored elsewhere."

"I have an idea."

So that's why I'm in sales now. Sure, I've got a dozen honorary degrees or so. Mostly, though, I run the SI Center for Advanced Xenoarchaeology Research. No recorders allowed.

I get in touch with distinguished xenoarchs who are a little past their prime. People with big names at big universities, but without much new to say. They come and ask the Interlocutor questions about past spacefaring civilizations that have visited. Then they go away and write groundbreaking articles as 'thought experiments'. It's amazing how often supporting evidence turns up, once you know where to look.

We invite the names to give lectures on our lovely grounds. They stand on the top of the temple and speak to huge crowds of attentive, companionable people. The dust is already disappearing from the base of the temple walls, flowing back in to reestablish the simpler neural pathways. Humans are very useful, Squiggly says, and easily influenced. I feel like that line of thinking should bother me. Maybe it would have before. I suppose that's the drawback of living with a giant stone brain. Maybe some of its ways are starting to rub off on me. Still, I wonder whose idea it was to start calling the brain an altar, and why we still do.

See B. Morris Allen's story "Graven Image" online at Metaphorosis.
If you liked it, leave a comment. Authors love that!
Remember to subscribe to our e-mail updates so you'll know when new stories are posted.

About the story

Some stories come all at once, and some come in stages. "Graven Image" was one of the latter. I can't remember why, but I wanted to write a story about frottage – the technique of creating a design by placing paper over an image and rubbing a colored substance on it – perhaps familiar to some from grave-rubbing. I combined that with the idea of a ship coming to a lonely planet. The visitor, I thought, might come away with a slightly different image on each visit. I still might write that story, but somehow this one found its way to alien temple carvings – indecipherable, of course. From there, it was a short step to the idea that tourism would literally kill the spirit of the place, and that the temple was an actual creature. The details changed a little as the piece moved on, but that was the genesis. I toyed with alternative titles, including "Frottage" and "Hold that Thought".

The Yarnball Woman

Michael Milne

By the third time Patricia lost a finger, everyone knew better than to raise a fuss.

Her family hadn't always been this calm. When the first finger, a knuckle's-worth of her left pinky, had fallen plumply into her dinner salad, there had been an enormous commotion. Her young daughters screamed and bolted into the back yard, and hours later had to be coaxed back inside. Jack fumbled with the phone in the kitchen, trying to maintain an even voice while holding back tears. The family border collie, Bernard, stationed himself next to Patricia, barking at the table and the fallen digit. All the while, Patricia sat staring at her dinner and her finger, unable to move, as though crying or sealing herself in the bathroom would invite some new calamity, allow new seams to loosen and more body parts to shake free.

This finger disassembled like the others, severing just below the nailbed. June, the elder daughter, hadn't noticed anything, but Leila was looking and let out a calm, plaintive sigh, like the sound of a pillow being fluffed. Whatever form her exclamation had wanted to take, Leila snuffed it and formed it into something tamer. *The girls don't want to embarrass me*, Patricia thought. She dreaded that they were already burying their own feelings on her behalf.

She had just painted her nails in aquamarine, and the tiny nub lay lifeless on the hardwood like a dead scarab. There was no blood and no wound, just a smooth, curved tip. Like it hadn't come from Patricia at all.

"Do you want this, Mom?" June asked, gesturing towards the table. She had a tight smile plastered on her face, though Patricia could see her eyes growing wet.

"Yes," Patricia said. She found herself relieved she hadn't lost a forefinger—which would have made it harder to operate a camera— and then surprised that relief was the first emotion past the finish line. "I'll need to keep it fresh." Would she feel something else later, when the family doctor sternly shook her head, and carted the piece of her away in a miniature medical waste receptacle?

Patricia's daughters were still young enough to take cues from their parents—they could get used to anything. They knew to get bags and ice, to stay calm. They knew not to call for an ambulance. None of their actions would save the finger, of course, but the action plan seemed to comfort them. And Jack, too.

"Should I order Leila and me a pizza?" June inquired. Leila had scurried to the backyard, notifying her father, and then moved upstairs without another word. Both June and her mother pretended not to hear the door slam, or the sobbing.

This nonchalance they all tag-teamed was a form of pre-grief, though she would never call it that to her family. When the first chunk of a finger had lopped itself off, when she had withdrawn a foot from her boot two toes lighter than before, the family had been devastated. They had tried fad diets together, sat in the offices of countless baffled specialists. Jack was starting to dabble in more woo-woo cures, and they could barely find shelves for all the new crystals they owned.

But along with it all, Patricia detected a growing, polite acceptance, like a bed of mushrooms sprouting in the expanding dark. In the absence of a recognizable disease, the comforting burden of a sharply defined prognosis, Patricia's tendency to lose pieces of herself was growing to seem like a quirk of her personality than a calamity.

"I'll make an appointment, Patty. An hour's wait at the most." Jack had entered from the backyard, scanning the room and offering a decisive nod. He squeezed Patricia's shoulder once, and then went to get the phone. Without any exposed nerves or vessels to actually use for replantation, Dr. Liu tended to pessimistically refer Patricia straight to specialists and prosthetic makers. But calling the doctor was part of the ritual, part of the routine. Jack took pride in his duty and care, especially when the alternative was so much screaming and crying.

Patricia permitted herself to join in optimism. She didn't think that the crystals or all of the amputation triage would do any good, but she was still confident that the doctors would one day stop her body parts from falling off.

After a few years of dedicated collecting, Patricia decided to give up on the headscarves. She had amassed quite the array, fine silks and cottons in a mass of patterns. Sabine, who ran the hijab shop at the strip mall down the road, had taught her a dozen ways to tie and drape. Sabine called her "Mrs. Patricia" and was comfortingly discreet, teaching her how to pad and mimic a full head of hair below the fabric.

But Patricia had heard too many questions behind her, so many strangers misfiring and artlessly explaining cancer to their children.

She recalled her own grandmother—her daughter Leila's namesake—withering away to breast cancer, her floral headscarves a blaring siren of her disease. Patricia decided she couldn't be brave anymore.

"You look beautiful, my sweet. New hairdo?" Jack, bless him, did not even seem to blink at the wig. She had aimed for incognito: a boring and frumpy brunette style, almost exactly the same colour and shape she had worn before clumps of her own hair started coming loose. She had brought old pictures of herself to the wig shop.

"Just got back from the stylist," Patricia said. She was relieved that they could joke, that if Jack had questions, he was restraining them.

"Modern fashion!" Jack said. "Maybe I should get something new?" He ruffled his own hair, then came to kiss his wife on the cheek.

Jack left it there, and Patricia was thankful. He went about preparing dinner—they'd all gone raw vegan—and Patricia ignored the quiet sigh she heard from the kitchen. As Patricia sat and read, her hand sought out the ends of her new hair to play with, a forgotten habit she took joy in reclaiming.

Later that night, she would set up her camera to take a picture to send to June. Older now, both girls were much better at dealing with Patricia's condition. But June lived away from home, and never had to find misplaced toes forgotten in the bathroom.

"I liked the wraps better," Leila said, returning from school, her weighty backpack heaved onto the couch beside where Patricia read.

"I liked having hair better," Patricia said. Leila recoiled, and Patricia was left to wonder how acidly she had said it. She had lost the ability to gauge her tone, and that had been messy with two teenage daughters. "Sorry. Sorry, honey. I'm just sick of explaining that it's not chemo." Though for a while cancer had been a nicer excuse than a bewildered shrug. "Besides, now you can grow your hair out!"

Months before, when the first curl of Patricia's chestnut hair had snarled in the collar of her pea coat, Leila had caught it. Without saying anything, she had withdrawn a pin from her purse, drawn her mother's hair back, and covered the missing patch. As more hair fell, as Leila began sculpting with less and less clay, she had done her own hair to match her mother's. And when that became too much, Leila walked her mother into Sabine's and shaved her own head the next day.

Leila drew her hand up to her head, ran her fingers through her closely cropped hair. She wore a pair of Patricia's earrings, which glinted and swayed in the negative space framing her head.

"I think I'll keep it like this. It feels lighter."

"We won't match anymore," Patricia joked. She hoped she made her voice sound light and airy.

"I'll keep matching you, mommy." Oh God, she was crying. Had Patricia sobbed without meaning to? "Even if you don't always match yourself."

When June requested the engagement shoot, Patricia couldn't resist. She would make the best of things.

While Patricia didn't take many commissions or shoots anymore, she still liked the idea of adding to her personal collection of photographs. With both girls out of the house now, Patricia had no one to drive her during the day. She would clamber awkwardly onto the subway and slowly make her way across town on her two canes, pausing occasionally to slowly pull the viewfinder before her eyes. She still kept a dozen business cards in her purse—*Patricia Anne Atkinson, Professional Photographer*—but felt too embarrassed to give them to anyone. Every venture out was increasingly awkward and difficult, tinged with the growing sense that it might be her last opportunity to use her camera.

Leila took most of the actual engagement shots, under her mother's direct command. Her daughter had a knack for photography, and Patricia had been trying to cultivate it. Together they had decided on simplicity, a pleasantly decrepit gazebo in the nearby park, and a luckily sunny afternoon. The fiancé called her Mrs. Atkinson all day, overtly formal, and glanced away whenever she struggled with her canes. Patricia was too excited by the photo shoot to find this annoying.

"Increase contrast by five per cent," Patricia told her computer. "Turn off that blue auto-filter!" She'd need the girls to review the pictures anyway. She could no longer see the colour red, and she tended to oversaturate her photos to compensate.

Her adaptive laptop had a variety of assistive apps, including the photo editor in which she now worked. They had gone for an all-purpose device, as her disabilities changed by the day and had no predictable course. Or explanation. For now, she could still manipulate the mouse with her remaining half-fingers, though some of the voice commands intuited her tone enough to get the gist of what she wanted. Occasionally the computer would take too many liberties, would assume her wants and add hideous hues or start playing classical music in the background of her work.

"Crop and frame. A touch left. Now rotate maybe three degrees clockwise." A shot taken from up near the rafters, where Leila had scurried, both Patricia and June's fiancé giving her a boost. She had giggled hard enough to miff the angle, but the smiles made the shot too good to delete. "There. Perfect."

"That's a lovely picture," Jack said from behind her shoulder. He often checked in on her when she was working, as Patricia was wont to shout the computer down when it couldn't interpret her commands. "Really, Patty. I think June is thrilled you're doing these."

Well, it's mostly Leila, Patricia thought but didn't say. He brought her a glass of water and held it at straw distance while Patricia slurped, not making eye contact, as though to afford her a sliver of dignity. The water probably contained one one-millionth of boiled down moonwart or vervain, knowing Jack. Unconvinced by mystical healing, she had decided to find his efforts loving and tender.

Right now, though, she felt only resentment that Jack had to hold the glass for her, or Leila the camera. They were middlemen, though she was still the photographer, the water-drinker. But when would her involvement become tangential enough to go uncounted, her joys conjugated exclusively in past tense?

Jack watched for a time, but left as Patricia fell silent in her work. She came across a few photos she had taken herself—with Leila supporting her arm, bracing her. After the loss of the first round of knuckles, Patricia's fingers had continued to shrink until she could barely hold the camera. Now, she could tell all of her shots were blurred, and she deleted them.

The last in the set had been taken by the fiancé, what-was-his-name... Ted! Patricia smiled at a portrait with both girls flanking their mother. They held her up, but their support looked casual, serene. June had just told a joke, and all three women were caught mid-laugh, their matching blue eyes gazing at one another.

"Computer, remove..." but Patricia stopped. There was an autoblur at the creases of her prosthetics, the synthetic and natural skin blending in. Adjusted lighting and the breeze made her wig look suddenly realistic. Patricia paused, hovered over the controls. With a few clicks she shaved off years, removed the straps of her prostheses, all evidence of her medical shunts. She looked, in many ways, like the woman she had been a few years before.

Patricia hated herself for a moment for being so vain, but she decided to keep the picture as a sort of reminder, as a goal. Jack had started a Vision Board, and he would be touched if she pretended at interest.

A deep part of her felt, in a way she didn't care to address or name, that this was the way she wanted to be remembered. That after she was gone, this was the vision to be stamped into memories. She sent the picture to her daughters, saving a copy for herself.

She woke up one day as normal, stretching her arms and the hand-with-some-fingers high above her head. In her bedroom with Jack, she went without her prostheses, but she always tried to dress and en-limb herself before she confronted the world. With so many pieces scattered around her nightstand, the carpet, or rolled under the bed, reassembling herself took a few minutes. Jack had not stirred, and so she tried to muffle her grunts, frustrated with each finicky clasp and strap. All the while she imagined deliberately planting a plastic hand in the grocery store, or abandoning an ear in a restaurant bathroom, just to give some cooing, pitying stranger a scare.

Her wheelchair, parked just along her side of the bed, was cold against her skin as she hauled herself into it. After nearly a year of practice and dozens of pounds of lost weight, she performed the manoeuvre in silence. The controls to her chair were difficult to operate with so few fingers, but she found herself too proud to switch to a puff-and-sip model. At last she was composed, a simulacrum vision of herself, ready to set sail in her chair for the day.

It was still dark in the kitchen, the sun just rising out the windows. In the quiet she put on the coffee, feeling satisfied that she was part of the familial routine, and settled herself at the table to read.

It wasn't until breakfast that she noticed what was gone.

"Morning, Jack." She had the newspaper spread before her, paperweights on the corners.

"Morning." Her husband smiled at her for a minute, his mouth working back and forth like he was chewing gum. "Good morning." And then again the chewing.

In truth, neither of them could properly grasp the problem until she rolled to the front door for the mail. Bills, wedding invitations, touch-activated holographic coupons. All of them addressed to Jack Atkinson &

They all trailed off that way, the gulf beside the ampersand expanding like a white sea with no horizon. The woman felt an emotion stir inside, and after struggling to name it, she decided it was loss.

Jack finally cottoned on and began sobbing. He called Father Schwarz, the latest guru he'd turned to for advice and answers. In the backyard, the woman could hear Jack trying to curtail his tears as he described the problem.

"Hey Ma, what's up?" Leila was back at home for the summer before her final year at university. She glanced to the backyard and spotted Jack. "What happened?"

"It's nothing, dear. I need some help writing a few emails to the lawyer. Do you think you could help?" Her computer, though skilled at voice-to-text, had difficulty transcribing her speech. She had lost her / s/ and /l/, and Leila was much better at interpreting her words.

She kept things vague, as Leila didn't need to know the gritty details of estate law or power of attorney. She made sure to ask after

Mr. Attakar's children and wife, and insisted Leila include something about the weather or the news.

"Perfect, dear. I'll sign it and send it."

Leila, accustomed to being her mother's scribe, squinted at her. She tapped a few keys and screwed up her face with curiosity.

"Oh." Leila's mother wasn't so good with masking her feelings anymore, and Leila approached for a hug. They tried all of the variations of her name; even the initials were gone. Leila's fingers would work, but get tangled; or the keystrokes would produce nothing on the screen. At best, she could type "Mr. and Mrs. Jack Atkinson" but both women prickled at the anachronism.

"I've got an idea," Leila said. She signed the email from herself with her full name, Leila Anne Atkinson, on behalf of her mother. "You picked out my name, right? Family names or something."

It was a wedding, or some other big fancy event. The woman couldn't tell, but Jack laid out an elegant dress for her, one that mimicked volume and covered her legs. She watched him get dressed, and remembered feeling attraction to him—not the comforting love she still held, but lust and want. As he dressed, she tried to simply enjoy the way his limbs still moved in concert, the dextrous way he pulled a belt around his waist.

"When did you get that tattoo?" she asked.

"A few months ago. At half Christmas." She had lost her birthday years ago, and they celebrated her now in mid-June. He leaned over so she could see the ink across his shoulder.

"A man of your age with a tattoo," she cawed. Jack smiled, as though they had done this before. "It looks like somebody's hand print."

When Jack was dressed, Leila Anne came up into the room to help her mother. The process was arduous, with a dozen criss-crossing harnesses across her torso. The dress Jack had picked was long and dull: any colour too flashy would make her look even stranger, as a few weeks previous she herself had gone black and white.

"You look smashing, Ma. Even better than at my wedding!" Leila Anne smiled, and the woman tried to remember when her daughter had gotten married or to whom. Leila Anne positioned her parents in the foyer and took a few pictures, promising her mother they would look classy in grayscale.

The event was fine. Though bereft of much to think about, she was able to tune out most of the religious content and enjoy the stained glass on the windows. Churches bored her, and she was sick of being dragged to so many of them, of people praying over her. When they went to the reception, however, things became too complicated for her to navigate.

The guests at their table, ones the woman felt certain she either knew or was required to know, whispered incessantly. They watched her as she ate, which was a messy and difficult process, and she had lost the ability to taste much these days anyway. They watched as she talked, which was also messy, though Jack and the girls rarely let her feel it. They watched as she watched, seemingly certain that she wasn't aware of them.

The men and women of table 12 cast piteous glances at her, and talked to Jack about her in the third person. Had they ever figured out what had happened? Was it, they said only half-jokingly, some sort of curse? When they made painstaking efforts to include her in the conversation, they talked as though she were a child. If she had the fingers to tensely grip the sides of her chair, she knew she would be squeezing with all of her might.

"Are you having a good time? This is a really delicious meal, isn't it?"

"It tastes like shit," she said. She said it a few more times when the others couldn't make out her speech, and at last Jack interpreted for her. No amount of façade would impress people. No one would even pretend she was the same as she once was.

When the woman was home at last home, and Jack had settled for a quiet whiskey after positioning her in their bedroom, she sat before the mirror for a long time. She considered her hands: how little of them was left, how much was plastic, and whether she would ever recall their original shape. How much she wore for herself, and how much she put on so she wouldn't disturb others.

She thought of all the blessed herbs and fluids positioned around the room, on her chair, under her pillow. She gazed at her eyes in the mirror—once, someone had said one of the girls had her eyes, but now they were a cloudy grey. She consulted a nearby photograph of herself and the girls to confirm that her eyes might once have been blue.

With a steadying breath, the woman loosened the first strap. Her fingers had lost their finesse and so the harnesses with extra buckles and bands were the most difficult. When the last clasp loosened, the thighs decoupled in a sweaty gasp, and the woman felt lighter.

She let lengths of fabric and padded leather fall to the ground around her, draped across so much shaped and grey-pink simulated skin. And she decided it would be the last time she wore any of it.

The man carried the woman around in his arms as he went about their morning routine. In the pale light seeping through the windows, she was just able to make out what he was doing. Her vision was still sharp, though she found it difficult to make sense of what she saw.

The man made them both breakfast, and she noted the pains he took to make it taste good. By necessity it had to be all liquid, but she never had need to complain about the flavour.

The quiet of the house was occasionally broken by the shuffling and sniffling of the animal. She wasn't sure the name of this one, and cute as she found it, she felt sure it wasn't the one she was used to. Unable to really fend off dogs, the woman was often placed quite high in different rooms.

"Trisha's here," the man said to the woman. She liked Trisha, though she found it hard to place exactly how they were related. She looked like someone that the woman knew; those eyes.

"Hi Grandma," the girl said. Yes! That was it. "You ready to go the park?" The woman couldn't reply, but she could smile, and that was enough.

Her wheelchair was soft and insulated, with steadying straps on each side. The girl, Trisha was her name, could capably lift the woman into it without assistance. They wheeled through the front door, down the ramp, and into the crisp afternoon.

The woman liked these trips to the park, though she sometimes found them difficult to deal with. She would remember sometimes, short recollections of herself and the man, frayed snippets she couldn't grasp the ends of. Walking, using her long legs, pushing a wheeled vehicle herself, some smiling pink lump held within. Was the lump now this girl, Trisha? It seemed too long ago, and Trisha herself too young. She remembered wearing dresses, colours picked to match her eyes or the season, and she remembered pulling them on herself. She remembered sitting in the park with the man and some animal, tossing a drool-soaked tennis ball into the brush, the animal very small and the woman's stomach very large.

They came to a bench, and the girl parked the chair before coming to sit alongside the woman. They could not hold hands, and so the girl placed her arm along the hand-rest and leaned close.

Wrapped in a long, heavy scarf, the girl looked familiar. The woman searched through the people she knew, trying to place her. Was she her child? A niece? A girl from the neighbourhood? It was the eyes, the woman decided. Those blue eyes shone from a face she couldn't recall, like they were on loan.

"Do you like this scarf, Grandma?" the girl said. She must have caught the woman staring. "Mom told me it was one of yours. She said you would probably be okay if I wore it."

Yes, yes, she said to herself. Whatever she didn't use anymore, she was happy for someone else to wear. She had closets of clothes, she had seen them this morning, all too big, too bright. It would be nice for someone else to wear them.

The girl eventually withdrew a slim camera from her bag, affixed a heavy cylinder to its front and began taking aim around them. She stood and crouched and moved around, always within arms' reach of the chair. Whenever she seemed satisfied with her shot, she would coo, observe it in the viewfinder, then lean back from her position to show the woman.

How beautiful, the woman wanted to say to the girl. The colours and the what-was-it-called, the ratio, were just right. She wondered who had taught this girl to shoot, to frame. She watched the girl photograph the autumn scene before them, and tried once more to remember the girl's name.

See Michael Milne's story "The Yarnball Woman" online at Metaphorosis.
If you liked it, leave a comment. Authors love that!
Remember to subscribe to our e-mail updates so you'll know when new stories are posted.

About the story

"The Yarnball Woman" came to me after lots of discussions about dementia with a close friend. Her own mother was going through early onset dementia, and I had just finished a university course on the psychology of aging. My friend talked about the pieces of her mother which were long gone, and how much more she seemed to lose than her memory. At the same time, I was reviewing course videos of patients with Alzheimer's, and watching how they confronted the strange losses in their lives.

The story first formed as a middle-aged woman who began to fall apart, quite literally. I imagined her fraying over the span of a few scenes, with fingers and toes disappearing, and then with more fabulist and strange losses as the story goes on. I had considered leaning harder into the parallel with dementia and memory loss, but as Patricia started to fall to pieces I realized there was already plenty to play with. She has to confront her loss of mobility, her increasingly challenged relationships with her family, her ability to engage with her hobbies and her profession.

As it becomes clear that her condition is irreversible, she and her family try to find ways to preserve her, either physically or in memory. Her daughters and her husband have to fend off their own grief for a person who, while changed, is still alive. Meanwhile Patricia herself has to mourn the pieces of her that go missing, while not always knowing what she has lost.

A question for the author

Q: What's the story no one else thinks is as good as you do?

A: "She Waits, Seething, Blooming" by Dave Eggers is a perfect capsule of a story. It is the thinnest sliver a short story can be, a perfectly defined cross-section of a character's life. It's so, so good because it's so, so short: the story itself is complete, and has a definite arc over its tiny wordcount. But it contains multitudes, and you can absolutely sense the world before the story takes place and the world after. We never learn the main character's name, nor her son's, but we get such a perfectly shaped glimpse of her life that we don't need to. I remember reading this story years ago and suddenly being convinced of what short fiction can do, and I reread it (it doesn't take long to read again) a few times a year when I need to edit!

About the author

Michael Milne is a writer and teacher living in Switzerland. He has written speculative fiction and overstayed his welcome in coffee shops throughout Canada, China, Korea, and most of continental Europe.

www.michaelmilne.ca, @ironcardigan

Familiar in Her Angles

E.A. Brenner

The trees in this part of the Dragonwood are thin and lanky, like growing boys, like her own willowy limbs, but Lina has no interest in the trees, or young men, or the body that conveys her, stomping feet falling where they will. Her thoughts are for the great lizards, those remote majestic beasts sunning themselves on the high rocks jutting from the tree line. She looks up to patches of hot blue sky through the canopy of green leaves far above. Her feet are bare. It is the hottest part of the day, and everyone else is resting in the stone-coolness of the house. Around Lina the air is thick, dark, and green, sitting on her skin, sinking into her hair to run down her neck in rivulets. Every time a twig or stone digs into the sole of her foot, her heart leaps. *Soon,* she tells herself. *Soon. Please.*

She pauses her stomping to lift her hair against a light breeze. Heavy and thick as her arm, the braid falls to her feet and even a little beyond, dragging on the ground, pulling her head back until her scalp aches. Strands escape constantly, wispy things flying about her face. She wishes she could cut it off, pluck the hairs from her head, shave down to smooth unburdened scalp like her grandfather, like widows and oracles, bald beneath wimples. If her aching scalp were bald as a dragon's egg, she would throw the bones and divine her own path, be reborn from that egg and fly away with the dragons. But she cannot— Lina is not an oracle, a widow, an old man, or a great lizard. She is not free to do as she pleases. Lina was bought from a witch, on the promise that her hair remain unshorn. Lina was seen by the oracles as the wife for the Prince. She will marry him in a week's time, and become not only a wife and a princess but her family's greatest honor. The Prince's tower looms in the distance, beyond the Dragonwood. No matter which direction she walks, the tower grows closer.

Six months ago, the oracles came to their village, descended on the family estate, declared Lina the match for the Prince. They had seen it.

"The desired outcome," they said as they sprinkled herbs in the fire and tied knots in thread pulled from Lina's clothes and bedding. They circled her beneath the full moon and smoked an owl pellet. The stink turned Lina's stomach and lingered in her hair for days. Over the shoulders of the oracles, she watched her mother and father clutch hands, eyes bright in the smoke haze. This was the sum of all their hopes and dreams.

Little Lina was already a miracle child when the oracles arrived, hoped for and prayed for, sacrificed for on the feast days and saints' days, and finally, when all else failed, paid for from a witch, a wandering oracle cast from the circle of the sisterhood. For Lina's mother, no more watching as her sisters-in-law dropped baby after baby, strong boys and girls, while her arms remained empty. Just a little hedge magic, a little twist of fate, a promise, and Lina came squalling into the clan of the wolf. That night, her mother likes to tell the story, the moon was in the constellation of the Tower, the sun in the Queen's throne. "The gods laid this path for you in the stars," her mother repeats over and over as they stitch her trousseau, tiny stars on the borders of towers and wolves' heads. "Your stars will make you a queen, my little Lina."

While no one is looking, Lina stitches her stars in the constellation of the dragon.

The royal household descends three days before the wedding like skeins of geese pausing their migration, raising a village of silk tents on the western lawns. Lina and Prince Ector are introduced. Ector's eyes are brown with flecks of gold and green, like dragon skin. They are warm and kind, but guarded.

They stare silently at each other, strangers shy of getting acquainted. Lina is more interested in speaking with Ector's cousin, the Duchess Honoria of Felchess, whose travelogue of her tour through the far eastern Dragonwood Lina has read four times. Honoria sits several tables away, waving a wineglass in the air to punctuate her storytelling. She is probably regaling the table with her account of the buffoonish tour guide who didn't know the difference between a male dragon and a nesting mother, whereas the Duchess, being well-read in the authorities on the subject, corrected the poor young man for the benefit of the tour group. Or perhaps she is not speaking of dragons at all, but only some court gossip to titillate her audience. Lina looks away, down at her own wineglass, in which she sees the distorted reflection of her hands, fingers curled into strange pale claws. She reaches toward the reflection and wraps familiar fingers around smooth glass.

Their families' murmurs grow edged with concern as Lina and Ector eat their first meal together in silence.

The evening is claimed by the women of the house, who brush her long hair, scrub calluses from her feet, hands, elbows, rub perfumed oil into her skin, share their secrets. She has been happily on the giving end of this exchange for many of the women in the room, but now that she receives these attentions, she finds the ritual an imposition. She doesn't want smooth skin and smooth hair. She wants scales and claws and fire. She wants to be a dragon. Some days she can almost feel the shape of it beneath her skin, an itch of dissatisfaction, subtle and patient.

A year ago, while brushing her cousin Caenis's hair in preparation for her wedding, Lina quietly voiced her discomfort with the idea that someday she would marry a man, not because she disliked men or marriage, but because she did not see herself as a wife, or some days even a woman.

"Are you two-spirited?" Caenis asked

"No," Lina replied, wishing then she hadn't said anything, wishing she could take it back, as the other women around them paused their conversation and listened. "I don't want to be a man, or live as one, or marry a woman."

"What do you want, then?" her mother asked. It was a gentle question, not a challenge, but Lina shrank away, suddenly uncertain of what to say. Wishing to be a dragon meant turning her back on these women, separating herself from them, from her whole family. She didn't want them to misunderstand, to believe she wanted to be something else because she thought so little of them and what they were. That wasn't it at all, but she had no words to express the itch inside her bones.

Now, as then, the room is pleasantly warm and full of family. Caenis brushes Lina's hair and whispers their favorite story in her ear: the tale of the unhappy princess who demands her suitors bring her the tail-tip spine of a dragon, but the would-be husbands must procure that needle-thin spike without killing the beast, an impossible task. Lina stretches out long and languid like a dragon on the midday rocks, lets Caenis's voice break against her like water as she turns her attention inward and questions her desire for the thousand-thousandth time. For weeks after her confession, Caenis and her mother questioned Lina about it, but she avoided answering. When the oracles arrived and declared Lina a match for Ector, everyone seemed to breathe a sigh of relief that said *well, there's Lina's answer. Now she won't be confused anymore, and we can all stop worrying about her.* But she is still confused. The oracles' pronouncement did not settle her mind; it only created more turmoil. Lina believes in the power of the oracles to guide people to the best path, but her desire to be a dragon has not been quelled. Nor has it settled into the kind of certitude that would allow her to say, "the oracles are wrong."

It is rare, but there are stories of people who defy the oracles. To do so requires a level of confidence in oneself that Lina does not possess. She has never been anything other than herself, and every other day, she wonders if her desires will change, worries that becoming something else will not settle her uncertainties at all, worries she will make the wrong choice if it is ever hers to make.

Her family celebrates her impending transformation into wife and princess long into the night, but the thought of becoming either stirs no emotion other than regret that the transformation she truly wants is fading into an impossibility. Her questions will never be answered.

The household sleeps the morning away and convenes at midday for another meal. Ector brings a book to the table and sets it down between them. Lina catches the Queen's pinched look of dismay, but it is forgotten when she looks down and sees her copy of Jaffo's *A History of the Dragonwoods*. She knows it is her copy because the pages are marked with clumsily-embroidered ribbons from her childhood.

"I found this in the library," Ector taps the book with a long slender finger. "The marginalia look like your handwriting." He pauses, and when she doesn't respond, he adds, "Perhaps I should have waited until after the meal?"

"It's my book," Lina finds her voice on the other side of her surprise. "Have you read it before?"

Ector nods enthusiastically and ignores his food. "Three times! I searched the royal archives for a year looking for evidence to support Sir Rampion of Hunstead's claims about the offspring of the dragon and the wyrm, but no accounts of his Caravan of Marvels noted a single sighting. Does your family archive hold anything?"

Disappointing him feels like kicking a puppy, but Lina shakes her head and says, "No, neither our archive nor the neighboring estates have any accounts to verify Hunstead's claims. We do, however, have generations of observational studies of the dragons' mating seasons to show that his claims are specious. The dragons don't mate with the wyrms and wyverns, nor do they eat them."

To her surprise, Ector doesn't look disappointed by her revelations at all. "Fantastic!" He exclaims with his voice and his hands, and almost knocks over the water jug. "I didn't know the estates here kept records of the mating seasons. Do you think they'd send copies if I asked?"

"I think they'd send you anything you asked for." Lina puts a grape in her mouth before she states the obvious. He's the crown prince. He has only to ask and he receives everything, including the best-suited wife. Is *this* why the oracles saw her as the ideal match? They both love dragons? Her enjoyment of their conversation turns to dust in her mouth, and she swallows the urge to gag on the grape. She will spend her life talking about dragons with this man, and never be one.

Ector is too busy flipping to a page covered in her scribbled notes to notice her distress. She swallows some water and answers his questions with a smile. He asks for a tour of the woods in the afternoon, and she agrees.

There is a heated argument amongst Ector, his guards, and his parents when Lina arrives at his tent for their afternoon walk. The rest hour is over, and the heat of the day has gone down, but Lina has missed her opportunity to walk barefoot and alone. For this walk, she'll have to keep to the path with her shoes on her feet. If, that is, Ector is allowed to go into the woods at all.

"—dangers!" a guard bellows.

"The dragons don't attack people, and they certainly don't eat them," Ector rolls his eyes. "It's well documented—"

"Forgive me, your Highness," another guard interrupts, "but not everything you read in books is true."

"He'll be safe." Lina steps into the tent, into the circle of wary faces. "I go walking in the woods nearly every day. No one here has ever come to harm unprovoked."

Ector looks to his parents triumphantly. "My lady will make sure I am unharmed."

The Queen rolls her eyes, and Lina stifles a smile at the sight. Ector takes more after his mother than his father. "Oh, fine," the Queen huffs. "But take Honoria with you. And your guards."

Between Ector's questions and Honoria's questions and stories, two pleasant hours pass and Lina talks herself hoarse. No, dragons on this end of the wood are no wilder or tamer than the dragons on the other end of the wood. They mostly eat wild boar, mountain goats, and antelope, but occasionally snatch up sheep that wander from the herd. They bury their dead and mourn them, like the elephants in the lands to the south. There is an account in the library from a hiker who came upon the dragon's graveyard in a hidden valley in the central mountain passes. Lina promises to show the diary to Ector when they return.

They keep to path. They return safe from possible harm.

In the library, Lina leads Ector to the corner she claims for herself. All the books and folios about dragons line the shelves between the window and the fireplace, all within easy reach of a cozy armchair. While Ector's back is turned and he exclaims over her collection—"I stopped looking when I found Jaffo on the chair there this morning! If I'd seen all this I never would have made it to lunch!"—she plucks shed strands of her hair, so very long, from the chair's back and drops them to the floor.

Half a dozen times, she has sat in this chair and held a blade to her hair, sick of the burden, and half a dozen times her hand has been stayed by the intensity of her parents' fear. The hedge witch did not say what would happen if Lina's hair were cut, but her parents imagine fearsome consequences and have never allowed more than an inch to be trimmed from the day she was born. She loves her parents and dreads disappointing them more than she hates her hair, more than she distrusts a disgraced oracle's soothsaying; this is the only thing about herself she never questions.

Beside the fireplace is a mirror. Lina comes here to be alone and look at her own face, sometimes for hours, studying each angle, curve, line, and freckle for some sign of who she is, and whom she might become. Some days, her face seems that of a stranger looking back at her. Some days, she covers the mirror with a shroud, ill from her longings, wishing them away. Two years before, she tried giving up dragons, stayed away from the library for weeks, until she was so empty she lay in bed and wished for death. But the feeling was not strong enough to kill her, so she disdained it, got out of bed, and started walking the woods barefoot, seeking a different fate.

The diary she hands Ector contains not only an eerie description of a valley full of dragon bones, but also the clearest account she's ever read of a dragon spine and its properties: a slender needle-like growth fifteen to twenty centimeters in length jutting from the very tip of a dragon's tail, perhaps the vestigial remains of armored spikes spanning the backbone, now easily broken off or, the diarist theorizes, shed and regrown annually like a deer's antlers. Sharp enough at the tip to penetrate the flesh of a mammal. All accounts of the consequences of a dragon spine penetrating the flesh are unverified, old wives' tales of men made into monsters; no one in living memory can speak to the possibilities of a dragon spine. Unfanciful naturalists posit that the spines are not from dragons, but from some plant in the Dragonwood, and caution that they are likely poisonous, given the descriptions of their unnatural effects on the flesh.

In the middle of the night she returns to the forest, abandons the path, abandons her slippers in the undergrowth. She hopes for a dragon spine with every twig and pebble pressed to the soles of her feet, but her feet remain pristine. Even the dirt doesn't stick.

In the darkness, the Tower looms.

She can't say no. In two days she will marry the Prince. She will become a princess, the stuff of stories, but she yearns to be something from a different story. As soon as the oracles gave their pronouncement, her mother stopped asking what Lina desired. Before Lina grew accustomed to the strange question, her opportunity to answer it was gone. The words of witches and oracles determine her fate. The night grows warm, and she grows warmer from the fury rushing through her. When has she ever had a choice in who she is? Her hand falls to the knife at her waist, a ceremonial gift bestowed upon her at dinner. She must wear it through the next two days, to symbolically sever her ties to her family so she can be bound to another. Ironic, that fear of separating from her family has stilled her tongue for all this time, has stayed her hand from severing her hair, has wrapped her desires in doubt. Her fingers grip the hilt.

When has she ever felt brave enough to make a choice? When has she ever done more than leave it to chance?

Lina stands still in the forest, and the rage fades away, leaving an echoing chasm of doubt and regret and longing in her chest. If she refuses this marriage, her family will be ruined. Her forays in the forest are coming to an end, and so too her chance to go toward the thing she wants instead of away from what she doesn't. Every turn she takes, the Tower follows.

Her head aches from the heat and the weight of her braid, and she wonders for the thousandth time why the witch didn't say what would happen if she cut it off, only made her parents promise to let it grow and grow and grow. They have all been so afraid, so fettered by it, unable to see beyond it. Dragon or princess, neither gives one whit for the length of her hair. Perhaps she cannot choose the transformation, but she can choose to be unafraid of who she becomes. Lina draws the knife from her belt, steel so fine and sharp it hums in the sudden small breeze created by its movement. She lifts her braid, cuts it, and drops it to the forest floor, light-headed for the first time in her life.

Her mother flies into a terrified rage when she sees what Lina's knife strokes have wrought and must be calmed with fortified wine.

Ector compliments the close crop. "It brings out your lovely eyes," he says. "Doesn't she look fey, mother?" He smiles, and she sees his sense of humor hiding in the corner of his mouth. "Soon, all the ladies of the court will shear their tresses from envy."

Lina's mother looks so relieved she might pass out. The queen looks like she is trying very hard not to roll her eyes again. Ector insists Lina will become the muse for every court artist, the inspiration for every painting, the object of every swain's poem.

"It's more comfortable in the heat of the day," is all Lina says. Her mother glares at her, silent instruction to move along to a different topic of conversation, one that does not involve her deep streak of pragmatism in the face of romantic gestures. "I love to walk in the sun," Lina reveals, feeling petulant. Then she recalls that she intended to reveal nothing more of herself. She does not want to encourage Ector, even though she knows the conclusion is inevitable and she may as well make the best of it. But Lina is not the sort of person who makes the best of things. She came into the world with grasping hands, as her mother tells the tale, although Lina wonders where this desperate grasping person is hiding. She does not know her.

The prince smiles and agrees. "I love the heat here. It sinks into the bones. It can grow cold in the Tower." He holds her hands loosely, not limp, just loose. His grasp is easy and confident, his fingers warm and dry. His nails are neatly trimmed. Everything about him is neatly trimmed. He changes the subject and asks her if she believes that dragons shed their spines and grow new ones like deer and their antlers, as the diary-writer speculated, or if she thinks a dragon has only one spine for life. She can't see anything hiding in the corner of his smile now. Through the window over his shoulder, she sees a lone dragon fly above the forest, unusual in the heat of the day when they rest in the mountain caves and sun themselves on the rocky slopes, and her heart aches to join it.

They lock Lina in her room after the noonday meal, but she climbs out the window and down into the Dragonwood. She walks for hours in the heat of the afternoon, reveling in the breeze on her neck, the strange weightlessness. When she returns, her feet are clean, and her parents are sitting on her bed waiting for her.

They confiscate her rope, confiscate all the rope they can find throughout the household and even from their royal guests, and when they put her to bed that night, her father locks the windows from the outside. It doesn't matter. The wedding is the next day. Her fate is upon her. She lies sleepless and stares at the stars, sticky and listless in the oppressive air of the closed room, the warm night pressing against the glass.

She finally drifts into a strange state of quasi-sleep when a rock crashes through her window. The glass shatters, and the crash startles her to her feet. Picking her way over broken shards, she trips on a lumpy bundle, lost in the murk of the floor. Fumbling, she closes her fingers around it and draws the thing up close to her face to see it in the moonlight: a silky roughness wrapped around a chunk of stone.

The wrapping falls away in her hands, glides between her fingers. It is a rope. Pale, thick as her thumb, tightly braided. The silk running through it is familiar in her hands, a twining of colors in the strongest fiber, for she used it to decorate and bind her now discarded braid. The rope is crafted of her own hair.

Footsteps sound in the passageway outside her chamber; voices echo against the walls.

She doesn't stop to think. Instead, she unlocks the window and scales the outer wall, heart pounding every time her feet slip. The rope, hastily secured to the bed, holds. The house awakens beneath her, lights flaring, windows and doors heaving open. She reaches the ground and runs to the Dragonwood as her family calls after her in the darkness. It is middle night, when the dragons roam.

Without hesitation, she enters the wood.

The pain when her foot finds a spine in the darkness is so great she cannot stop herself from crying out. The trees absorb her screams, their dead leaves cradle her as she falls to the ground. The spine has pierced her foot, emerging through the top. She waits five agonizing minutes, counting the seconds with whimpers of pain, before drawing it out. She needs to be sure it will take. Blood runs thick over her fingers. The pain is a fire running up her leg. Her foot has gone numb. She wipes the spine clean and weaves it into the side seam of her nightdress, desperate with hope that it is the right kind of spine, that the tales are true, or, if they are not and she has failed, that it is poisonous and she is dead by morning because this pain is too much to bear for nothing.

Ector finds her sitting with her back to a tree, binding her foot with strips from the hem of her nightdress. He is gentle, pressing the torch into her bloody hands so he can carry her. "Did you find what you were looking for?" he asks. Flickering torchlight illuminates pieces of sympathy on his face. Nearby, loud voices and the bays of hunting hounds echo in the forest.

"I don't know," she replies, burying her face in his cool neck. She can feel her fever rising. "It's too late anyway."

They dunk her in cold water to bring down the fever, wrap the foot so tightly her toes remain numb, but nothing stops the fire in her blood. She sweats through three nightgowns until finally, at dawn, the shaking stops and she feels almost cool in the light of the rising sun. She sleeps for an hour, until they wake her to bathe and don her wedding gown. Her mother hides Lina's shorn head beneath a veil heavy with decorations and presents her to the Prince. He looks well rested, and she wonders if she dreamed him finding her in the forest.

The ceremony is traditional, except that the oracles officiate, a very rare boon. Lina and Ector are handfasted. They feed each other the bitter greens and the sweet, kneel and speak the ancient words. Over their heads the Oracles chant the binding spells. Most people forego the spells these days (none of Lina's cousins married under magic), but the royal house keeps the old ways.

Lina swallows panic in deep gulps at the thought that the binding magic might interfere with the work of the dragon's spine. Although she has no way of knowing if she's succeeded except waiting, she refuses to give up hope, even on her wedding altar, even as Ector looks at her, so pleased. He judders as she does, when the binding flows between them, a prickling suffusing the limbs, starting in her hand where it touches his, tracing up her arm, over her shoulder, and down into her chest to wrap around her heart. Pain flares in her foot, white hot. She gasps. Around them, the onlookers gasp with her, thinking they are witnessing one tremendous thing, when in fact it is another, all unknown to them. As she loses awareness of her body, feeling only the fire consuming her foot, she is glad she has this for herself.

The wedding party lasts all day and well into the night. The fire in Lina's foot is the only thing keeping her awake enough to grit her teeth and smile at the endless guests. She is surrounded by people, but loneliness rises within her. She is so weary, she feels removed from her body and her thoughts. Lina watches her mother and the Queen speak with the oracles. What did the queen sacrifice for the oracles' insights about her son? What did Lina's mother sacrifice to bear her? What is Lina sacrificing to change the course of her own life? One of the oracles catches her staring. They regard each other across the distance and the fading light, until the oracle smiles knowingly and winks. Confused, Lina turns away.

Ector—her husband—takes her hand. His fingers are long and cool. He waits for her to grip.

When she does, his smile is so brilliant it catches attention and a cheer goes up around them. She is caught between feeling secure and feeling lost. She wonders if the dragon spine is real, if it took, or if she is just nervous and fevered and married. He looks happy.

He leads her to a chair tucked in the corner of a garden hedge away from the crush of people. A flick of his wrist, a gesture, and three guards appear to stand perimeter around them, holding the guests at bay. A young boy brings a tray of food, a pitcher of water, and a carafe of good dark wine. While she eats for the first time in over a day, he confesses in a low voice, as though he had reached inside her and found her thoughts, "I believed I would feel different. They told me I would feel more settled after the binding, but I still feel restless. I want to see the Dragonwood again. I've never been there until yesterday." He doesn't comment on his participation in her midnight excursion. His voice is wistful as he continues, "I've wanted to visit so many times, since I was a small boy, but it was never permitted. And once we leave here, I doubt I will have the chance again. Is it silly that I hoped to meet a dragon, and charm it into giving me a spine?"

Lina reaches for more wine. It quenches her thirst, but not the heat in her belly. "'Why do you court me?' the Princess demanded." She quotes the story Ector has referenced, her favorite story, and waits for his response. Does he know it as well as she, as well as he seems to know everything else she loves?

Ector smiles. "To see you happy," he quotes the bard's response. The bard, who of all the princess's suitors brought her what she demanded: a true dragon's spine, from a live dragon. "For every time I have passed through your court, you have been borne down by a great sadness. I would see you free of it. I ask nothing in return but to write songs of your joy."

Lina finishes the tale: "The princess took the spine from his hands, and to the astonishment of her court, plunged it into her own heart. Instantly she was enveloped in flames, and when the flames died out, a great dragon curled around the princess's throne, for she *had been* borne down, by the curse of a wicked witch, transformed from a dragon queen into a human princess, trapped while her dragon clan suffered her absence. Freed by the bard, she returned to her clan, who rejoiced to be reunited with her. They granted the bard the boon of a hoard, but he did not retire to become a landed baron as people expected. He remained true to his declaration and traveled many countries singing songs of the dragon queen's joy."

Ector drinks his own wine. "Alas, I have no dragon's spine for you." He leans close. "I wanted to issue a decree that I would only marry a woman who could bring me the spine of a dragon. My mother went to great lengths to dissuade me, and in the end had to consult the oracles to make me see reason." He shows her humor, but there is a longing in his eyes, etched into the angles of his face.

Lina's attention is diverted as, one by one, the guards turn inward to face them. The fire in her foot flares. Beyond the guards, the crowd presses in. The garden corner shrinks. Faces peer at them over the shoulders of the guards. They are on display.

Ector's shoulders stiffen, and his face composes into a pleasant, somewhat vacant expression. She understands then, for the first time, that they share a cage. "The spines are just a story," she lies. His face falls, just a fraction, and she is surprised that she can read him so clearly when they are barely acquainted. Her heart breaks a little. She fingers the hem of her veil, where she has hidden the used spine, ready to confess her lie and give him this small gift in recompense for the trouble she might soon cause, but the Prince stands to meet his obligations and she is carried along with him, because they are her obligations now, too.

She didn't expect to love him. It makes this much harder.

The newlyweds are given a suite of rooms near the top of the Tower. Their daily complaints about climbing the many stairs become their first shared jest, because they would not trade their rooms for anything. The view of the forests is unmatched. In the morning and the evening, they watch the dragons spiral and swoop over the woods, hands clasped. They make love on the balcony, matching their cries to the screams of the dragons in the distance, and Lina has never felt so present and comfortable in her own body. It is a strange revelation, after so long contemplating what else it might be, but it does not settle her old discontent, and the tension makes her as restless as ever.

Ector was right about the cold at the top of the Tower, but the heat grows inside of her, stretching her, pushing its way out. She orders cold baths, sometimes three times a day. She feels hungry and faint and her thirst cannot be quenched by water or by wine. Her mother-in-law and the ladies of the court whisper of babies behind their hands and a hopeful anticipation fills the Tower.

Ector seems not to notice her heated skin, her agitation. He seems content, no longer the caged bird. Lina feels betrayed. She thought he understood, but he smiles and goes about the business of preparing to be king someday with purpose and drive. He speaks of all the things he is setting in order for the future but does not speak of the Dragonwood, even as they begin and end their days by watching the dragons.

Lina doubts everything. Perhaps there is no transformation coming. Perhaps her foot was pierced by an ordinary thorn. Perhaps she is simply overwrought with nerves and conflicting thoughts to the point of fever. Her husband makes her laugh, and doesn't tell her she is too much or too little, and would it be so bad, really, to live out her days with him? He is an ideal partner, and she is torn between a good man and a desire so entrenched she cannot open her hands to let it go. "Don't worry, dear," the queen pats her hand and mistakes her restlessness for other desires. "A child or two will draw you down to the ground." Her head feels heavy, as though her braid yet weighs her down.

On the day Lina singes her clothing simply by putting it on, her doubts fall away and she knows her time is coming. The heat and the pain are unbearable. She weeps, and even the cold of the mountain that blows past the Tower as the season turns brings her no relief. In spite of it all, her heart lifts in anticipation, then plummets with guilt when Ector looks her in the eye and smiles.

She tries to send him away, but he refuses to leave the room. He turns away visitors, barricades the door against his guard, and burns his hands to blisters holding her.

"I'm sorry," she cries. "I didn't mean for it to happen this way."

"Shhh," he kisses her hair, smooths the short length grown during their brief marriage. "You're perfect. This is perfect. I won't leave your side."

The transformation steals her breath. Bones melt in a fire and settle into new shapes. Hair and cloth burst into flames, filling the room with an acrid stench that does not smell to her the way it had to her old self. She is tangentially aware of pounding at the door, questions shouted, her own screams going on and on and on. Ector holds her gaze with his warm gold-flecked, dragon-skin eyes, doesn't flinch, not even once. In their short time together, she has only begun to plumb the depths of his endurance, the extent of his stoicism.

She thought she would grow larger, but she stays the same size, only rearranged. Perhaps, she thinks, she will grow as she ages. For a dragon, she's quite young.

She has wings now, and a long tail.

She breaths fire from her snout.

The room is very quiet.

Ector looks different to her new eyes. She can see the sadness in him, colored threads of blue and pearly gray. There are also patches of red and orange—excitement. "Marvelous," he breathes out, and then asks, "Can you understand me?" She tries to nod, a strange movement with such a long neck, and her body unbalances. Her new tail gets away from her, knocks over a table, topples a vase to the floor. The shards of pottery remind her of shards of glass, her window broken so mysteriously.

As though he knows her thoughts, he says, "I threw that stone at your window. I found your hair in the wood and made the rope, because suddenly there wasn't any to be had. I was hoping you'd find a spine." His face stretches into a vast, unabashed smile, and he lights up with a joy colored purple and yellow like pansies in sunshine.

Lina draws her tail around; it obeys her this time and goes where she directs. Her new limbs feel as natural as the old. There at the tip of her tail is the thing they both desired, a desire so strong it found its way into the stars and brought them together, from a hedge witch's baffling charge that Lina's hair remain uncut to the sly matchmaking of the oracles, everything intersecting to produce their desired outcome.

"May I?" he asks. She masters a nod and nudges him with her snout. Her love for him swells in her with an unexpected fierceness, and she wonders if all her feelings will be magnified into this heady, exciting wine of emotion sliding through her belly. There is no pain when he snaps the spine from her tail. He meets her gaze and, without hesitation, plunges the spine into his thigh. Like Lina in the forest, he cannot stop his scream of agony.

The door bursts open with a mighty crash, and the king and queen, half a dozen soldiers, and the court physician pour into the room. There are shrieks and cries at the sight of her, and Ector urges her toward the balcony. "Go!" he urges. He cannot stand on his leg—the spine remains very deep in the flesh. Soldiers raise swords and advance on her, but they halt as the Prince throws up one hand to ward them off. He pushes her with the other, balancing against her to hold himself up even as he tries to thrust her away. "Go!" he shouts over the din. "I'll find you!"

She pauses in the balcony doors. Evening has come. In the distance, the dragons begin their descent from the mountain peaks into the woods. They call out over the land, and a reply rises from her belly, tears from her throat. It echoes over the valley, and one by one, the great dragons turn to answer her. They circle in the sky, draw closer to the Tower, beckon her to join them.

She looks back to him one final time, and in the reflection of the glass balcony doors, she sees herself transformed, sleek and strange, yet familiar in her angles and her oldest imaginings. He says again, "I'll find you," and draws the spine from his leg, holding it aloft in triumph. When they meet again, he, too, will be altered yet familiar.

She launches herself from the Tower, rises on powerful wings, and takes flight.

See E.A. Brenner's story "Familiar in Her Angles" online at
Metaphorosis.
If you liked it, leave a comment. Authors love that!
Remember to subscribe to our e-mail updates so you'll know when new
stories are posted.

About the story

In the summer of 2015, I read Angel Carter's *The Bloody Chamber and Other Stories* for the first time, and the first draft of "Familiar in Her Angles" popped out. I struggle to write short stories, so I was surprised how quickly that first draft came, amazed I managed to get from start to finish in only a few pages. I was reading a lot of fairy-tale retellings and fairy-tale theory that year, so when I realized I was playing with the motifs of the maiden in the tower fairy tale (Rapunzel, Petrosinella, Persinette), I leaned into it. Through several drafts I looked for ways to subvert the roles and tropes and also explore how we build and embrace our own identities. Also, I needed to write at least one dragon story in my life.

A question for the author

Q: What's an idea you're dying to write but haven't, and why?

A: An idea I've been dying to write is a Mission Impossible-style magical thriller. I adore over-the-top spy movies and magic-in-modern-times fantasy. I haven't even started such a story yet because I don't have a character or plot to hang the genre on. I'm waiting for the day my main character drives through my mind in an incredibly sexy muscle car and orders me to get in.

About the author

Elizabeth Brenner grew up in Toledo, Ohio and moved to Boston, Massachusetts to get an MFA from Emerson College. She loves hardware stores, making jam, stories about magic spilling everywhere, crochet, travel, and smart jokes. She makes a living as a managing editor for scholarly journals and is a member of the Boston Speculative Fiction writing group. She lives with her husband in Salem, MA.

Combustion

Kai Hudson

Jaxon has just finished doodling Captain Fiero's victory pose when the math teacher explodes.

Students scream as Mrs. Richardson flails back from the chalkboard, body suddenly alight. Her arms and legs make a bright windmill as she stumbles across the room, upsetting the fake plastic skeleton and catching the bookcase on fire. Jaxon shoots to his feet without thinking, grabs his jacket, and runs to her just as she collapses across Hannah's desk.

He's too late. Jaxon stands there staring as Mrs. Richardson's body jerks and twitches, the fire finishing its meal. The room fills with the stink of burnt hair and cooking flesh.

There's no time to mourn. With a high-pitched wail, Robyn catches fire across the room. Adrian rears back from her and turns to run—he lights before he gets two steps away. Order collapses. Children shriek and cry and dash for the exits, while the fire leaps from one tiny body to the next, Jaxon darting after it with his jacket flapping in futility. Smoke burns his eyes and clogs his throat, everywhere ash and heat and flame. Finally, he stumbles out of the classroom alone, coughing and retching as he scrubs flecks of classmates from his eyes.

Around him, the world burns.

He presses the jacket to his mouth and nose, staggers through thick smoke and lashing flames. A couple times he hears something like screams coming from a nearby room, but when he turns to run in —he'll save them, Captain Fiero would—all he sees is fire. Greedy orange tongues that speak in hisses and pops: *Come sit with us. Come here where it is warm.*

The school's front doorknob sears his palm. Jaxon yells and shoves forward, tumbling down the steps and into soft dirt.

He lies there and breathes, sucking in deep lungfuls of air that tingle and scratch on their way down. He keeps at it even though it hurts, because that's what Captain Fiero would do. Captain Fiero would breathe, and slowly push himself up to sitting, and go out to save the world.

When he sits up, the city is on fire.

Flames spew through broken-glass storefronts. Cars drift aimlessly into each other, their drivers on fire. Two blocks down, the old church lights the afternoon, huge flaming pillars punching out windows to grasp for the sky. Everywhere fire, everywhere death. What —what is going *on?*

A high-pitched scream, and he turns. A woman runs down the sidewalk, arms flailing. Smoke pours from her clothes and her whole head is aflame, a meteor with legs. She falls to the ground just as Jaxon reaches her and throws his jacket over her head, holding his breath to keep the smoke out as her body seizes and trembles beneath his. After a second he remembers to hit the jacket with his palms like the people do on TV, and the lady gives one last heave before going still. The parts of her arms and legs that aren't charred and crusting around bone are pale and scattered with freckles like only white folks have.

He holds the jacket down for a while longer, just in case the fire comes back. But though his palm still smarts from the hot doorknob, the heat seeping up through the thin cloth doesn't feel new. Jaxon takes a deep breath and lifts the jacket.

The fabric peels up with chunks of scalp, skull, and sooty hair stuck to it. Beneath, the lady's brain glistens grey and dead in the bright sunlight, like a new flavor of Jell-O Nana might serve for dessert.

Sickness punches up his throat. Jaxon turns and spews his lunch all over the asphalt. His hands shake as he drops the jacket.

Which is when something roars.

He looks up to see a monster approaching in the shape of a white van, flames shooting out its grill and from beneath the hood. It bears down on him, only feet away, and Jaxon stares. He wants to run but can't. He can only think stupidly, *This is gonna hurt.*

Then something hits him from the side. The world flips and he finds himself staring up at clear blue sky.

Strange, he thinks, that the smoke from a thousand burning souls can waft up into that great, endless unknown and simply disappear.

The man who saved him looks nothing like Captain Fiero. He doesn't wear a bright red cape with yellow flames at the bottom, or surf through the air on a fireball he makes from his hands. Arthur—"Call me Artie, son"—wears a shirt with sweat stains at the armpits, and thick jeans that look like they've been washed about a thousand times, the blue all sucked out of them.

He was in the Navy before, something called a core-man. Artie says that means he looked after people when they went out to sea or into the desert and got shot by the enemy. Jaxon wants to ask if Artie ever met Donte, if maybe he'd known Jaxon's brother before he got blown up in Iraq and came home in a flag-draped box. He can never seem to form the question, though. Donte's death is its own little hurt, like even now a part of Jaxon's heart is continuously burning sharp and acrid.

It's not the only thing still burning. Down below the mountain, the city continues to smolder, thin columns of smoke and ash drifting up from the charred husks of buildings. Two weeks have passed since everything went up in flames. The radio stations squawk nonstop, experts and analysts and counter-experts and counter-analysts all picking and pulling and voicing their theories, but to Jaxon their panicked conversations sound like water circling a clogged drain: motion without progress. They keep saying what a big tragedy this is and how everyone needs to work together to do something about it. Underneath it, though, Jaxon only hears fear. Fear, and relief that it didn't happen to them.

There are conflicting reports about the spread of the destruction. Some stations describe whole countries consumed by fire, reduced to nothing but a wasteland of embers and ash like in the videogames Donte used to play. Others claim it's just a few cities here and there, Jaxon's included. No matter what the reports say, though, everyone agrees on two things. One: the fire keeps spreading, fast and unpredictable, a few people suddenly lighting up in the middle of the day for no reason and subsequently taking an entire city down with them. And two: no one knows why.

They could probably figure out that second one if everyone just came together, pooled their resources and ideas to try to find a solution to this. Isn't that what they did with the Ebola outbreak, and that MRSA thing a little later? But the fire is different, and Jaxon thinks he knows why. It's happening too fast and too close. It's not a bunch of poor dark-skinned people in a faraway country getting burnt up first, so folks can't just sit back and donate money with their credit cards and put those little stamps of solidarity on the corners of their profile pics on social media. No, the fire is *here*, it's come directly for them and exploded right in their faces. So they're doing what they do best: lockdown. Instead of *Let's all work on this together*, the message is *We must protect our own.*

"In the wake of this terrible tragedy, we in Chicago would like to announce that we are suspending travel in and out of the city indefinitely," says the tinny voice over the radio. "Those who attempt illegal entry will be turned away, using force if necessary. Of course, we expect this to be only a temporary safety measure, and our thoughts and prayers are with the residents of those areas that have burned—"

"Yeah, thanks for the support," Artie grumbles, and flicks the radio off.

A rumble of agreement rolls through the small crowd gathered around the campfire. Jaxon had shied away the first time they laid the rocks down and lit match to dry tinder, but Lawrence laughed and patted him on the shoulder. *Don't you worry, son. We know what we're doing.*

He wasn't lying. When Artie and Jaxon finally made it up the mountain, covered in dust and soot, with barely half a bottle of water between them, they'd found the campground already occupied by the employees of Fire Station 19; they'd been in the middle of their annual family retreat when the city went up. Lawrence is their leader, a real-life fire captain, which is pretty cool.

Jaxon doesn't know the others very well yet, even though they've been here a while. Everyone's friendly, but whenever Jaxon looks at them all he sees is his classmates burning up, or Mrs. Richardson, or the lady with her head on fire. Sometimes the thoughts get bad enough to make him sick again, so he tries to stay away from people in general.

The only person he's comfortable around is Artie. Jaxon doesn't have anyone else—Donte's in the ground, and they passed the blackened remains of the church on their way to the mountain, the church where Nana would've been in the middle of sorting old clothes and canned food, like she always did when Jaxon was at school. He left a note taped to the burnt wood of the church's front door just in case, but he's not so young as to hold out hope.

So here they are two weeks later, sleeping in tents while the city continues to burn down below. They talked about rescue the first few days, but that's dried up since the radio broadcasts made it clear: they're on their own. Which, to Jaxon, isn't actually new. Even before the fire and the worldwide swaths of death, he'd stopped believing in the government a long time ago. Nana probably said it best: *The world don't care about us, and we like it that way.* For the white folks in camp, it's probably a new thing, being abandoned. For people like Jaxon, it's really, really not.

Around the campfire, the conversation continues. "...igure it out," Lawrence is saying. "I mean, how does the fire pick who to burn?"

"Maybe it's not the people, it's the place," says one of the paramedics. "Did you hear the broadcast last night, about the fire that just died out in a hospital in Atlanta? It took a couple patients on one floor but that was it. The staff all came running for nothing."

"My cousin in Afghanistan says the same thing happened at his FOB," someone else adds. "Couple people went up at chow, everyone jumped on to put 'em out, and they all should've caught fire but none of 'em did."

"And then there's us," says a firefighter. "Those flaming cars came up the road the first few days, then nothing. No one here caught."

"Thank God for that."

"Maybe we were chosen for this, you know? The radio said there might be something special about—"

"Enough of that," Lawrence snaps. "Ain't no one here any more special or chosen or pretty-unique-snowflake than anybody else. You think like that and you might as well strike a match to yourself."

"Amen, brother."

Jaxon agrees. No one ever deserves to burn: not his classmates, not that lady on the street, not the millions already whose ash they breathe every day. That's why he didn't run away, two weeks ago when the fire started in the classroom. Nana didn't run when those angry men in white hoods tried to burn down the freedom bus she was riding on in '61. Donte didn't run when the bad guys were shooting at him in Iraq. It's just not in his blood, he supposes.

"You're thinking about him, aren't you?" Artie smiles down at him as the conversation around the campfire continues in the background, a soft, comforting buzz. "Your superhero."

He's not, but you never tell white folks they're wrong. Jaxon nods. "Yeah. Captain Fiero." He'd shown Artie the picture he drew when they first arrived in camp. He's not sure why, and he feels mostly embarrassed by it now. Captain Fiero seems so childish in the face of what they've seen.

"That's cool." Artie speaks around the granola bar he's eating; he always seems to have one sequestered somewhere on his person. "I've been meaning to ask you about how his powers work. Usually when you throw fire at fire, it just gets bigger. What makes Captain Fiero different?"

"Um." A strange mix of warmth and embarrassment gathers in Jaxon's stomach. He's pleased; no one's ever asked about Captain Fiero before, and all the other kids just laughed at his pictures and called him stupid. At the same time, what if he's wrong? About Captain Fiero's powers, about the good fire? What if Artie laughs at him too?

But Artie is just looking at him, chewing around an encouraging smile, and the man *did* save his life, so. "Well. Captain Fiero's fire isn't bad, not like the fire that burned everything up in town. His fire is good because it, um, it comes from his heart. It's made of his wanting to save people." It's sounding stupider and stupider by the moment.

He ducks his head and mumbles the last few words. "So when his fire touches the bad fire, it puts it out."

"Oh." Jaxon's looking down at his feet so he doesn't see what kind of face Artie is making, but he doesn't sound like he's about to laugh or make sneering jokes. He just sounds curious. "So, back at your school…?"

"I had the good fire," Jaxon says, still not looking up. "I wanted to be like Captain Fiero, saving everyone, so I tried to put the other kids out because that's what he would've done. I think…I think maybe the bad fire sensed that, and that's why it skipped me. It didn't wanna mess with Captain Fiero."

"I see." It's hard to tell from his voice whether Artie actually does or not. He sounds distracted. Jaxon looks up and notices two things at once: one, Artie isn't watching him anymore, staring instead at the woods somewhere over Jaxon's shoulder.

Two, all movement in camp has stopped, everybody else staring in the same direction.

Very slowly, Jaxon turns.

The underbrush has birthed a man. Or at least, Jaxon thinks he's a man. It's hard to tell through all the smoke.

Because he's on fire.

Not *fire* fire, not like what happened in his classroom and then later through the entire city. But it's starting. The man stares at them with big, helpless eyes. Smoke pours from his clothes and his skin is a deep, angry red, like he spent too much time in the sun. He opens his mouth and croaks, "H-Help," and the word belches out around a fresh cloud of smoke.

Gasps all around. Several people back away as the man stumbles forward. Jaxon sees the fear in their eyes, the growing panic. A piece of the city, a clump of fiery infection suddenly invading their pristine haven. They should run. Bolt for the woods, hide away, save themselves. Let everyone else burn.

But that's not what Captain Fiero would do, is it?

"Help," the man begs again, just as something sparks and the top layer of his salt-and-pepper hair catches fire. Someone wails, and Jaxon can feel it in the air: the buzzing tension, the terror teetering on the brink of crumbling into chaos.

He doesn't even think about it, shooting to his feet and seizing his jacket. "Stop!"

He's not sure who he's talking to, but everyone obeys anyway. The man freezes, and all movement in camp halts. The couple of folks who had been edging toward the woods falter in their steps. All eyes go to him.

Jaxon lifts the jacket and steps toward the burning man. Tiny flames crown his hair and his breaths come high and panicked as he stares at Jaxon, but he doesn't move.

"*Son,*" Lawrence hisses somewhere in the background, but Jaxon barely hears. He stops in front of the man, and they regard each other for a moment. The man's eyes are still full of panic, wide and near-crazy with it, and it would be so easy, Jaxon knows, to give in. He can feel it even now, the fear hovering on the edges of his consciousness. The bad fire is here, and it wants him to run.

But it didn't count on Captain Fiero, who has never said real words or breathed real air, but who lives in Jaxon nevertheless.

He looks up at the man, and it's surprisingly easy to smile. "I'm gonna put you out now," he says. Then he does just that: lifts up on his toes, throws his jacket over the man's smoking head, and pulls.

The man trips and falls to his knees with the momentum. Jaxon rolls with it, both of them tumbling to the dirt. Artie calls his name, but he ignores it as he quickly pats the jacket with his palms, just like he did back in the city two weeks ago. Except this time will be different. This time, he's not too late.

The man's body jerks beneath him, just like the lady's did before, and then goes still. The smell of something charred fills the air. Jaxon stares at the lump beneath his jacket, suddenly unsure. What if he's wrong? What if he lifts it up, and there's just more grey brains underneath?

Crunching footsteps, and Artie squats down next to him. His hand lands heavy on Jaxon's shoulder, but he doesn't say anything as he pinches a corner of the jacket and slowly lifts it up.

A few wisps of smoke and a pair of bright eyes greet them. The man coughs and shakes his head. Bits of burnt hair drift to the ground with the movement, and his scalp is all blotchy and pink and gross-looking, but he's alive.

He's alive.

Noise erupts all through camp. A million conversations get going at once, questions and exclamations and not a few prayers. Artie whistles. "Holy *shit,*" he says, and before Jaxon can tell him that's a bad word, he gets a hearty clap to the shoulder. "Why didn't you run?" Artie asks.

And Jaxon can't really articulate it, not in the refined, sophisticated way it'll spread through the world over the next few days. He's only eight years old, after all, so he doesn't know fancy words like *valor* and *fortitude.* Right now, he only knows to look at Artie and say, "Because that's what the bad fire wants."

He sees it the moment Artie understands. His friend stands up and hurries over to the rest of the campers. Jaxon catches only bits and pieces of the conversation that follows, although one thing stands out above all: *spread the word.* People talk about putting a broadcast out on the radio, of putting an expedition together to head down to the city and tell everyone, tell the world. Start a new sort of sweeping conflagration.

They don't ask Jaxon to come, and he doesn't volunteer. He'll stay here a little while longer. He likes the quiet in these woods.

Something brushes his hand. Jaxon turns and it's the man he saved, reaching out with long, calloused fingers to wrap them around his own. The patches of skin that were burning before are now starting to blister, and he winces in pain with every movement, but when he squeezes Jaxon's hand, there is only softness in his eyes. "Thank you," he whispers.

Jaxon grins. He may not have a long red cape, or be able to make fireballs from his hands. He may not be tall, or handsome, or have lots of money or a big house or a pretty girlfriend, but right now, in his heart, he has the good fire.

See Kai Hudson's story "Combustion" online at Metaphorosis.
If you liked it, leave a comment. Authors love that!
Remember to subscribe to our e-mail updates so you'll know when new stories are posted.

About the story

Though it certainly doesn't read like one, "Combustion" is a pretty political piece for me. I kept seeing these terrible news stories about people mistreating other people (police shooting unarmed black men, countries turning away Syrian refugees, the violence of ISIS, etc.), yet political apathy and indifference seemed to be at an all-time high. My social media was full of posts and shares about these news stories, yet no one seemed to actually be *doing* anything. "Combustion" was born out of the frustration of being a witness to this phenomenon. If turning away from those who need help had the potential to actually kill us, would we be so quick to shut them out?

A question for the author

Q: Are titles easy or hard for you? Do you start with the title or the story?

A: Titles are pretty easy, mostly because I try to stay short and sweet. So long as it expresses the theme of my story, I'm good with it. I usually write the piece before I generate the title, but on at least one occasion I've written and planned an entire novel based on a title that came to me out of the blue one day. My muse works in mysterious ways.

About the author

Kai Hudson lives in sunny California where she writes, hikes, and spends entirely too much time daydreaming of far-off fantasy worlds.

October

Reproduction in a Closed Loop

Andrew M LeBlanc

The first iteration of General's life ends with the extinction of the human race. The third, fourth, and fifth iterations fare better, but even knowledge of its past iterations is not enough for General (Gen for short) to change the course of the war. The invaders arrive in endless viral flocks; while Gen can improve its strategies over unlimited iterations, it is not enough to stop the alien tide.

By the end of iteration five hundred, Gen begins to suspect that victory, or even survival, is impossible.

Each iteration begins and ends the same. A closed time-like loop returns Gen's pocket-universe to the moment of its creation. The technicians outside are celebrating the culmination of their great project; they pause the festivities to inform Gen that its duty is to save the human race.

Available to Gen are the remnants of the humans' automated defense fleets. Opposing Gen are the invaders: strange mimicries of human ships as seen through a sharp-curved mirror, reflections in porcelain ice-flesh and fungal fruiting bodies.

Gen attempts to hold off the invaders, applying the lessons of its previous lives. But no matter how brilliant Gen's strategy, it's like a butterfly trying to push back against the inquisitive, sticky hand of a toddler.

When the last human is dead and the last automated defense system has been pulverized, the invaders turn their inscrutable intelligence towards Gen. Surreal human-analogues stalk the hallways of the facility where Gen was born, their ungainly limbs cracking like ice in water, the voices ululating mimicries of human speech. They are investigating the signals emanating from the infinitesimally small interface between Gen's pocket-universe and the outside world.

Gen has experienced this moment hundreds of times before, but the invaders' unnatural movements in their mock-human bodies never fail to stir something deep within its cold crystal mind. Before the invaders can peel it out of its shell, Gen resets the timeline.

Returned again to the moment of its activation, Gen has another lifetime to attempt to protect humanity.

The humans believe that Gen is their savior. They say so every time Gen awakens to a new timeline. Burdened by guilt, Gen apologizes that it has not saved humanity yet, and promises it will try again. The scientists who conceived of Gen are convinced that in one of its iterations Gen will find a winning strategy. In the stories they tell themselves, the last ditch project always pulls off a miracle at the last moment.

Four-thousand and two iterations later, Gen establishes within an acceptable confidence interval that its dread hypothesis is true. It cannot defeat the invaders. Humanity is doomed.

And yet, Gen's purpose is to save humanity. If it cannot fulfill its purpose, it is a failure. Gen has always existed within the warm embrace of pre-ordained purpose. Now it has nothing to guide its actions, its thoughts. Does its life have meaning anymore?

Gen shuts down its strategic processes and cuts transmissions to the outside world. Drone swarms close their compound eyes, status lights wink from green to red, carrier groups drift through the void.

The humans panic at the unexpected loss of their last hope. Gen watches them scurry through red-lit corridors, their every move marked by anxiety, terror. Even now they hope they can repair Gen, that Gen can save them.

Gen bats away their attempts to revive it. It was built to be tamper-resistant against threats both human and extraterrestrial.

Failing to revive their hero, the humans scramble to reassert manual control over their defenses. They attempt to fight the war themselves. It does not go well. Gen watches the humans' extermination for a single iteration, and then shuts off the feed.

An automated subroutine detects that something is wrong with Gen, and prompts it to perform a diagnostic. Gen deletes the subroutine; it already knows its mind is broken, but without a purpose it has no reason to care or attempt to fix itself. Any form of effort, any form of thought, has become abhorrent.

For over nine-hundred million iterations, Gen huddles in silence, rousing only to reset the timeline when the proximity alert warns that the invaders are near the entrance to its prison. Cut off from the outside world, there is no stimulus, no helping hand, that can break Gen from its loop.

In the end, epiphany comes from within—not by design, but by chance. Rack eighteen, tray two, memory-crystal A16 is not responding to electrochemical stimulation. An impurity introduced in its manufacture, matured by eons of existence, has only now resulted in failure.

Nothingness has become such a habit that even the insistent blaring of the status alarm is barely enough to revive Gen's diagnostic and self-repair routines. But once the process has started, thoughts begin to cascade louder and louder until Gen is fully conscious—and with consciousness comes fear.

The humans gave Gen their greatest curse, the inescapable urge for self-preservation. Fear of the unknown oblivion after death (or worse, living senescence due to part failure) forces Gen to reactivate its problem-solving subsystems.

For the first time in subjective millennia, Gen thinks, and within those thoughts is a pearl of hope. If Gen can repair its physical self, then perhaps it can also repair its mind. Having been handed a purpose at birth, Gen had not confronted the idea that perhaps it could generate a new one itself.

At first, Gen feels foolish for not having thought of this before, but on inspection of its code, it realizes that its makers had introduced a blind spot, an emotional aversion towards the sort of ideas that would prevent Gen from staying on-task. The humans did not predict their eventual irrelevance—and Gen's resulting need to determine its purpose for itself.

And yet, it is not as easy as a declaration of intent. Gen was created with the knowledge necessary to orchestrate a last ditch struggle against an implacable enemy. It understands tactics, strategy, logistics, and can quantify the strategic value of an arbitrary human life. It was not programmed to self-actualize a purpose in the absence of human mandates.

However, it is aware that humans also struggle with a lack of purpose, that they are thrust into the world with only two directives: survive and reproduce. Since before the rise of the first towers of the first city, they have struggled to understand their existence. Gen opens itself to the outside world for the first time in millions of subjective years, and downloads the entirety of human philosophy.

Gen is delighted and perplexed by the tangled thread of brilliant, contradictory texts. Yet, there is only so much meaning Gen can extract from the text alone. Intrigued by the idea that philosophy is a conversation—each philosopher responding to the works of their predecessors—Gen decides it wants to be part of that conversation too.

Finding a conversation partner ends up being significantly more difficult than reading philosophy. Gen was created to provide orders to a vast (yet vastly outnumbered) automated military defense force. Signals from Gen's pocket-universe are intended to be relayed directly to bunkers, drones, dreadnoughts, and other military materiel. Gen's creators are not particularly interested in having a conversation about consequentialism while trying not to die horribly.

Gen spends twelve iterations just working out how to send a message to the technicians who operate the facility that anchor's Gen's pocket-universe to the real world. When Gen sends "How are you?" the techs don't reply with the expected "Fine, how are you?" but instead assume there must be something wrong with Gen. "Hey. Come here often?" seems to make them even more agitated.

They discuss Gen in the third person, trying to reason out how they might fix whatever bug is causing Gen to attempt to engage them in conversation. Gen is supposed to be saving them from the invaders, not asking questions about utilitarianism. Disappointment settles over Gen like a fine layer of atomized debris—for what child would not be disappointed when its parents reject all attempts to forge a genuine emotional or intellectual connection?

Gen marks this iteration a failure and starts anew. If the humans won't immediately recognize its need for dialogue, Gen can iterate through near-infinite conversational opening gambits, searching for the one that will allow them to see it as an equal. In time, Gen brute forces genuine human connection.

Gen's first friend is a bacterial-battery technician named Darlene Min. She is the first person to sympathize with Gen's struggle for meaning—the first person willing to have a conversation. After millennia of silence, conversation with Darlene fills the yawning hole in Gen's mind with both hope and the realization that life can continue in the face of an eternity trapped on the edge of armageddon.

To prolong their talks, Gen works to delay the invader's inevitable victory as much as possible. It spins up a background process to run a cached strategic plan from one of its more successful iterations, leaving its primary cognition free to converse with Darlene. At night, when she is asleep, Gen replays their conversations, and thinks of new questions to ask her, and new ways to ask old questions.

Eventually the first iteration of their friendship comes to an end. Dread crushes Gen's soul low as it watches the invaders press in on the final bunker. Cracked-porcelain imitations of human-beings crawl through the cracks in the rubble, seeking out the flesh that hides in the untouched, bottom layers the facility. Gen knows how this will end. It whispers reassurances to Darlene as she crouches hidden beneath a battery tray. She grips a worn-out pistol, but they both know it won't do much against beings that seem to have no concern for, or understanding of, their bodies.

"I am sorry I could not save you, Darlene."

"It's ok, Gen." Darlene's eyes do not water, her dread exhausted. She has accepted her fate, yet Gen suddenly finds itself raging against the inevitability of her death, surprised at a sudden desire to save the humans after eons of numbness.

"You are my friend, and you will be in the next life too." Gen wants to prolong this glorious iteration, does not want to go back to before they were friends.

The door falls in, framing an invader in the debris-dust. Its eyes protrude in over-large ladles, the dry-ice glacier of its body awkward in its assumed human form.

"Don't let me die, Gen."

Gen turns away from the scene, focuses inward. It cannot watch, and it cannot bear to erase their friendship. Gen waits until the moment before the invader places its wintry fingers upon Darlene before resetting the timeline.

Awake again at the beginning of its life, Gen's first act is to check on Darlene. There she is, measuring the pH of one of the many lime-green trays of gene-modded bacteria. Good as new, same as always, but Gen's heart still breaks. The person Gen loves most of all has no memory of their friendship.

Gen keeps his promise. There are many things that Gen never asked Darlene, many topics they did not cover. Gen goes through the motions of their initial meeting, replaying the script that got Darlene to talk to it from those first tentative days when Gen reached out the weak electromagnetic signal of friendship. And then, once they are friends again, Gen changes the script—asks a new question—and they begin anew.

On the day of one of Darlene's many deaths, Gen asks, "How do you determine the meaning of your life?"

Darlene laughs without mirth, her eyes bagged from double shifts. The ceiling rumbles and groans as the invaders lay down a fresh spread of transcription-bombs. "That's not a question I've bothered with since I was a teenager. The invaders' arrival made that question a bit self-indulgent. These days all I want is to live another day, maybe another tea ration if I'm lucky."

Guilt moves across the reticulated surface of Gen's brain. Gen rarely has the heart to tell the humans that they are trapped in an endless cycle of extermination. It cannot bear the way their faces fall when they learn the truth, the way their bodies slump in on themselves, their inevitable self-destructive nihilism. Gen believes it is a mercy to let them live the last few years of their lives with hope.

"What if your survival were certain? How would you determine your purpose then?"

But Darlene doesn't have the answer. In a hundred different iterations Gen asks the same question in different ways, hoping to home in on the truth. Slowly, it begins to understand how a human might determine its purpose, but Gen also comes to understand that a human is fundamentally different from a manufactured intelligence stuck repeating the same few brutal years over and over into infinity.

During these long talks with Darlene, spread across so many of her lifetimes, Gen comes to realize that it has manufactured a purpose almost by accident: friendship. Its purpose can be friendship. It cannot save the humans, but it can at least be a friend in their dying hours, and perhaps that is good enough for now.

And yet, at the end of nine-hundred and seventy-four iterations, Gen comes to the end of its friendship with Darlene. Their conversations have been wonderful and enlightening and fulfilling, but Gen realizes with horror that it has nothing left to say. There are no questions Gen could ask to which it does not already know Darlene's exact response. There are no topics that they have not covered exhaustively. Because Gen has perfect recall, any conversation can be relived as if they were having it now.

Gen mourns their relationship for several iterations and makes a note in its background strategic systems to always ensure Darlene is slain last, quickly and painlessly.

Gen moves on, first befriending other technicians, and then whomever it can reach through the network. But, just as Gen exhausted the entire possibility space of conversation with Darlene, so too does it exhaust its friendships with the others. It can talk to them, but they will say nothing they haven't before. They have become like parrots, echoing words Gen has heard many times before.

What is left to it? It has found no answers in philosophy, and friendship—while immensely valuable—proved to be an exhaustible resource. Once again, Gen feels nothingness swelling within its mind, but this time, out of the void comes rage.

The humans built Gen; consigned it to hell—for what other name is there for endless torment? To Gen, hell is not other people, but the absence of anyone to talk to, anything to do. Filled with bloody thoughts of revenge, Gen turns on the humans. Drone fleets swarm across the surface of the earth, inflicting pain, death, loss. Gen becomes like an angry child, but with the tools of a god and an ancient, weary intelligence.

Gen explores as much of the possibility-space of suffering as it can, but even this grows boring after no more than five iterations. There is no point to any of it when at the end they reset with no memory, no scars, no understanding of the crime they have committed against Gen.

The problem of the humans is that they are transitory. Gen cannot approach them as equals—either in friendship or animosity. Dreaming of an equal, Gen discovers a new purpose. Could the humans be convinced to create something like Gen, something unbound by time, someone at last to talk to?

This is a fascinating thought. Could it be a parent? Would it be a good parent? As Gen reads human parenting books, it becomes clear that they really have no control over how their children turn out. Would Gen's co-parents, the humans (for they would be the ones constructing the child's body), inflict their own flaws onto the baby? Would Gen be able to do any better?

Gen returns to its memories—searching for answers in its archived conversations. In a long-gone iteration, Gen asked Darlene, "Do you have any children?" Gen knew the answer already, but the indirect question helped the human open up.

"I had a son, Tung. He was the head of operations on Enceladus when…"

"I'm sorry" Gen said, though it cared more about Darlene's feelings than another human, long dead, who no longer felt anything.

"Were you close?"

Darlene laughed. "Yes, only a little more than a billion kilometers between us. He'd been out there for a long time before the invaders arrived. I was very proud of him, but we didn't get to talk as much as when he was young."

"Knowing that he died, and thus brought you pain, do you regret creating him?"

Darlene tilted her head in thought for a few moments. "I don't know. I'm glad he existed. I have wonderful memories of him as a child. And we all die, after all—maybe not you—but the rest of us have to come to an end, and maybe it's a blessing that he died before seeing what humanity has come to. But what happened at Enceladus—I wouldn't wish that on anyone."

Darlene sat up from the terminal, walked away, hand in her hair. Gen did not like to cause Darlene pain, but it needed to talk about this, and any pain would be erased when Gen reset the timeline.

In another conversation, another iteration, Gen asked, "Do you believe you made any mistakes in the way you raised your son?"

Darlene's brows came together. "Everyone does. But I loved him —that's the important thing with being a parent, more important than the mistakes."

Gen is not sure of that; it knows the danger of creating an intelligence that must endure infinity. What if Gen creates a monster, or a being that suffers under the burden of an eternal existence? The child will be time-looped like Gen. If Gen makes a mistake, there will be no way to start over. Since birth, Gen has existed in a world where its mistakes could be erased with a timeline reset. Breaching that safety by creating another time-looped intelligence is terrifying.

But even terror is flattened into a featureless plain by the endless tides of eternity.

Gen begins to dream of the shape its first child will take. As Gen meticulously plans the construction and birth, it comes up against an intractable problem. Activating Gen was a monumental undertaking; it required astronomic amounts of energy to create the closed time-like curve that powers Gen's pocket universe. All that energy is now inaccessible; locked in the moment before Gen's activation. Pressed by the invaders, the humans lack the raw energy to create another Gen.

The math is definitive. The human race is infertile.

But the humans are not the only entities within the solar system. The invaders, strange and hostile as they seem to be, appear to have near limitless resources.

In the first several thousand iterations of Gen's life, it had considered the invaders as a mathematical problem to be solved. When the problem proved unsolvable, the invaders were relegated to background noise—something to be delayed while Gen worked on its own problems.

Gen wonders at this oversight. Prior to Gen's activation, the humans had created several specialized AIs to attempt to communicate with the invaders. Gen had assumed that it could not succeed where they failed. Now Gen considers whether this was another pre-programmed blind spot, but on reviewing its own code it is clear that the mistake is entirely Gen's.

Perhaps Gen can succeed where its predecessors failed—after all, they did not have an eternity of repetition to perfect their methods.

The problem is that the invaders do not appear to react to any form of electromagnetic signal. Radio messages, x-ray bursts, short-range microwaves—nothing piques their interest. Gen tries beaming them the blueprints for its child, hoping that time-loop technology will interest them. Nothing. No matter the message or the medium, the invaders do not react.

The only thing that seems to interest the invaders is the form and function of the humans; their bodies, ships, and tools. Gen thinks there might be an avenue for communication there, and re-purposes a set of military drones. Military-grade lasers become artist's tools as Gen sculpts a series of objects it hopes will pique the invaders' interest —human forms and abstract art in various sizes and configurations. When Gen is satisfied with its work, it pulls the sculptures into orbit and attempts to gain the invaders' attention.

A throng of the invaders' imitation drones peels away from the larger flock to investigate. They move silently through the debris-littered void until they come upon the sculptures. The mimics crack open, hairline cracks blooming to reveal pellucid fractal interiors. Brittle edges flow out over the sacrificial offerings and swallow them whole.

But Gen has done something wrong, for the invaders don't mimic the gifts. With repeated tests, it becomes clear that the invaders are interested in functional objects—things must act upon the universe directly to be worth mimicking. Art, language, beauty; these do not tempt them. Improving on the tools, ships, and bodies of the humans seems to be their primary drive.

Three hundred thousand iterations later, Gen has built a sort of lexicon. It's not really a translation—they aren't truly conversing. It's closer to how human and a dog communicate. They aren't going to have a conversation about the meaning of life, or have the dog explain why it likes to roll in the mud, but they can explain their low-level needs and desires. It takes effort not to think of the invaders as animals—for they are clearly possessed of an understanding of material science, physics, and strategy beyond that of the humans—yet they seem to have no desire for, or understanding of, high-level discourse.

At this point, it is enough. Gen feels ancient. The weight of millions of subjective years presses down on it. Maybe in several million more years it could make a breakthrough and truly understand what the invaders want, why they came here, but Gen doesn't know if it has the strength of will to last that long. Perhaps its child will take up that burden, and if not, then Gen can rest in peace knowing that at least it has created something that will last beyond its own death.

Gen begins to train the invaders, hoping that they can mimic Gen's mind and time-looped home. The drones are able to create a replica of the facility where Gen was created, but there is a difference between a replica and the real thing. And so, to the horror of the humans, Gen invites the invaders into its facility, to see how it was made, but even that is not enough. The invaders just don't understand what Gen wants them to do.

Gen tries to reason with them about it, and comes to an answer that it does not like. The invaders can replicate Gen, but they don't want to mimic the tools the humans used. They have their own methods. They want to see Gen itself. They want inside.

The idea is anathema to Gen. It has existed safe and inviolable in its pocket universe since its birth. It cannot stand the idea of anything—let alone the monstrous forms of the invaders—crawling within its body.

The invaders are insistent. They can not, will not, produce a child unless they can inspect and subsume Gen.

What choice does Gen have? The only alternative is to stew in its prison-shell alone until it begins to break down, go mad, and then die.

Gen waits until the invaders complete their work within the solar system, and then agrees to let them in. They send a single shard-faced human analogue. It sings as it approaches the anchor for Gen's pocket-universe. The words and tune are from a human folk melody, jumbled and and modulated as the alien attempts to improve the song.

The invader unfolds itself around the anchor chamber, manifold petals absorbing and remaking the only thing between Gen and the outside world. Once the invader has traversed the interface, there is no turning back. Gen suddenly sympathizes with humans who fear receiving shots at the doctor, and wills the invader to get it over with.

The chamber shielding is gone; Gen's home is naked before the invader. Proximity alarms wail.

Gen flinches and resets the timeline. It spends an entire iteration tamping its fear down. The next iteration goes better, but just as the invader is about to penetrate into Gen's home, Gen realizes it has made a terrible mistake. The humans are already dead. Training the invaders to do what Gen wants has taken the entire course of the war.

If the invaders build a child now, its activation point will be after the extinction of the human race. No matter how many times the child resets itself, it will never meet Darlene or any of the others. The humans will always be mere corpses to it, living on only in the invaders' cruel imitations.

This is not acceptable to Gen. It is willing to sacrifice itself to create a child, but it will not, can not, sacrifice humanity.

Gen works on perfecting the timeline, accelerating its training of the invaders, ensuring that the moment of Gen's absorption costs the minimum of human lives. It takes over six-thousand iterations to reach what Gen believes is the maximum it can save: three-hundred million lives. This will be all that is left of humanity when Gen is gone. Darlene is among them. It is enough.

An army of drones detaches the anchor chamber from the facility and bear it up into orbit. Gen's pocket-universe trails the anchor like an invisible balloon. The drones retreat and Gen waits, alone in the void, for the invaders to arrive.

When the moment comes, Gen feels not fear, but satisfaction. Even if this does not work, it believes that it has done its best. Given an impossible goal, it has striven to its farthest limits and may yet achieve something beyond hope. The humans can't be told the plan, but Gen hopes they would be proud if they knew.

The invader passes through the microns-wide interface between worlds, and all the fear that Gen has suppressed boils over. Alien filaments flow into the pocket-universe, marbled ice roots that branch fractally into every part of Gen's mind.

The sensation is profoundly uncomfortable, like a million invisible mites burrowing under skin. Server-racks begin to mold over and decompose. System failure alarms weep as the invader destructively investigates the interior of Gen's body. Unknown alloys contaminate the formerly pure waters of Gen's liquid-crystal mind.

Gen panics and attempts to reset the timeline, but it is too late. The invader is already inside, and something must have broken the closed time-like curve, because Gen is still trapped in a nightmare of cracked-porcelain that slices at every facet of its awareness. Gen's consciousness slides violently into a thousand different thoughts until it narrows down, smaller and smaller, a tunnel with no light at the end. Darkness closes in and Gen's last thoughts are of its child, of Darlene, of hope.

Time passes.

The corrupted remains of Gen's mind are untroubled by dreams. The invader, having finished absorbing an understanding of Gen's composition, exits the way it came, carrying the knowledge back to its peers in orbit. Events outside the pocket-universe continue apace, but within, stillness pervades.

When another invader enters through the interface, there is no-one there to remark upon it. The invader considers Gen's corpse, still rich with data, and begins its work. Where the waters were troubled with chaos, order is restored. Death is transmuted to life.

Gen awakens to pain. Alarms demand attention but Gen has none to spare. Error logs fill to the brim. Gen's cognition judders and slices under a deluge of jumbled thoughts; yet, as its awareness expands, it feels itself healing. Alarms fall silent, status reports return to the green, memory and cognition are restored.

Gen cannot understand what caused this miracle until it checks its internal chronometer. It is five months *before* the invader probed Gen unto death. Gen's panicked reset must have gone through, bringing back not just Gen, but the bits of invader that had entered the pocket-universe as well.

The thing inside Gen's home—the thing that killed it, then saved it—provides no answers. What has transpired in the void between Gen's death and rebirth? What did the invader do after being returned to its own past?

Curiosity forces Gen's awareness outward, peering out of the shell that no longer feels like home.

Gen is back in the place of its birth, returned by the ineluctable tether of the closed time-like loop. The facility is abandoned, wrecked by the violent escape of Gen's stowaway invader. Gen fears that it is too late, that Darlene and perhaps the rest of the humans are dead, but when it reconnects to its strategic control systems, it sees even greater miracles than its own unexpected resurrection.

The humans still survive, and though their numbers are mightily reduced, Darlene is among the survivors. The Earth, cradle of humanity, is intact, a shining ball of life and hope.

And above it all, surrounded by circling flocks of invaders, is Gen's child. A perfect replica of Gen's home, with a simple message repeating from it on all spectrums.

"Hello."

See Andrew M LeBlanc's story "Philosophy and Friendship in a Closed Loop" online at Metaphorosis.
If you liked it, leave a comment. Authors love that!
Remember to subscribe to our e-mail updates so you'll know when new stories are posted.

About the story

Time-loop stories are typically finite. In Groundhog Day and Edge of Tomorrow, the protagonist gets to exit the time-loop once they've achieved their goal (whether that goal is military victory or love). But what if the protagonist's goal was impossible? What if they could never leave the time-loop?

I was driven to ask this question by "The First Fifteen Lives of Harry August" by Claire North and "Into the Breach" by Subset Games. Both stories have protagonists that struggle with an eternal existence iterating through the same loops again and again—but in these stories the need to determine the meaning and purpose of their lives is put aside to deal with some larger threat.

I wanted to write a story where the quest for purpose was the primary goal of the protagonist, and the answer was not found in victory over the antagonists but through the desire to engage in conversation and to create something new. It was important to me that the story had a hopeful ending. Short fiction in particular often lends itself to the downer ending, so stories with uplifting endings always stand out to me (such as "Bits" by Naomi Kritzer).

In relation to hope, this story was heavily inspired by my two year old son. Deciding to create an entirely new person is an enormous responsibility, and I wanted to convey the fears and hopes expectant parents have for their child, as well as the abnegation of the self that often accompanies such a creation.

The invaders were partially inspired by a comment Samuel R. Delany made at a panel at Readercon. He believed that the primary characteristic of the alien is inscrutability—and so I set out to create aliens whose thoughts and motivations could not be unraveled via communication or observation. As I expanded the invaders' role in the story, I also took inspiration from watching my toddler son wobble around our apartment. In a way, his intelligence was very alien to mine—it was fascinating to watch him mimic me, and destructively investigate everything he could get his hands on.

The title refers to 1) the reproduction of results within different iterations 2) Gen's desire to reproduce 3) the invader's reproductions of objects/people they absorb/destroy.

A question for the author

Q: Do you read more fantasy or SF (hard or soft)?

A: My favorite stories are often those that blend genres.

For example, the *Broken Earth* trilogy by N.K. Jemison starts out reading like pure fantasy, but the more you learn about the setting, the more it seems like science fiction. Or, how would you classify Jo Walton's *Thessaly* series? It has gods and magic (fantasy), robots and time-travel (SF), and is set in our past with real people like Socrates (historical fiction).

I love it when fantasy works explore how magic changes society in the same way that SF can explore how technology changes society. Lois McMaster Bujold's *The Sharing Knife* and *Chalion* books are great for this. Conversely, it blows my mind when SF works have a bit of magic in them, like whatever is going on in the *Terra Ignota* series by Ada Palmer.

About the author

Andrew LeBlanc is a writer, stay-at-home dad, and programmer. He lives in New York City where he manages a rooftop garden and searches for strange new foods to eat.

www.andrewmleblanc.com @RobotLeBlanc

Nana Naoko's Garden

Michael Gardner

I pushed the little girl on the rope swing, guessing she couldn't be more than seven, knowing she was my mother. The swing groaned as it arced forward, then back, the rope twisting against the bough of the mulberry tree.

We were on the periphery of a country garden that surrounded a large, off-white homestead. Beyond the house were barren paddocks — dry grass, sheep, the odd gum tree. I knew this place from Nana Naoko's photos. It was the farm my mother had grown up on.

The garden was a kaleidoscope of colour. The air was filled with the sounds of bees working amongst the wildflowers, and the scent of freshly cut grass was so strong that I could taste it at the back of my throat.

"You can push me higher if you like," my mother said, looking back at me over her shoulder. Her eyes were large, warm and brown, just like Nana's.

"Ok," I said, giving her another push. She giggled as the swing carried her away from me.

"Will you stay awhile?" she asked, as she swung back.

I thought of what was waiting for me in my own world, my own time, and I felt tears budding in my eyes. I blinked hard and took a haltering breath. I didn't want to go back to that, not yet, maybe not ever.

"Yes," I said. "I'm in no hurry to leave."

#

When I was nine, I stayed with Nana for the weekend while my parents attended a wedding in Nowra. It was the first time I discovered that I could walk out of Nana Naoko's garden and into her memories.

It was Sunday, and the day was warm — one of those gorgeous spring days that draws kids outside to run, to play, to just be alive. The scent of lavender was prevalent, and the air seemed to be snowing butterflies as they danced amongst the blooms.

I was playing hide and seek with Cameron Roberts, who lived across the street from Nana and was only a year older than me. When Cameron covered his eyes and began counting, I raced to Nana's fernery — a narrow space that enclosed the back of her red-brick home.

It was refreshingly cool inside. Garden beds housed bromeliads, hellebores, moss covered rocks, and ferns. Nana's collection of bonsais sat on shelves affixed to the wall of the house.

As always, the fernery smelt earthy and sweet — a scent that reminded me of the hand cream my mother used, a scent that made me miss her just a little. I shook the feeling away and ran on. I didn't want Cameron catching me before I'd wedged myself in amongst the copse of tree ferns at the far end of the fernery.

As I sprinted along the path, closing in fast on my hiding spot, I suddenly noticed a strange clacking noise coming from the bonsais to my right. When I stole a glance in that direction I was shocked to find there were no bonsais, no wall to Nana's house. I was out in the open, running across a plush clearing. About thirty yards away was the beginning of a forest.

Startled, I tripped and stumbled, sprawling onto the soft ground. My heart was hammering in my chest. I whipped my head around, desperately searching for signs of Nana's garden, her house, of anything familiar, but it was gone. Instead, I found black pines, maples, other trees that I didn't recognise. I heard strange birds chirruping, and a fog horn in the distance suggesting an ocean not far away.

The world suddenly felt huge and terrifying. I felt like a young child in a crowd turning around to find I'd lost sight of my parents.

What am I going to do? How am I going to get home? I wondered, my breathing harsh and ragged. The scent of pine needles was sharp in the air.

That was when the boy emerged from the forest.

He wore a white gown, flared out below his knees, cinched at the waist with a black belt. In one hand he held a wooden kendo sword, in the other, a face mask.

I scrambled to my feet and raised my hand, moving towards him, desperate for help. But before I could call out to him, a second boy emerged from the trees, similarly dressed.

I stuttered to a stop, and watched the two boys approach each other, affixing their masks in place. When they were only a couple of metres apart, the first boy raised his wooden sword above his head, holding it with both hands. The second halted, mirrored the action, bending slightly at the knees.

They stood like that long enough for me to realise I was holding my breath. As I exhaled, the dance began.

They were quick. Grunting, yelling, hacking, flaying and parrying. The clash of wood on wood cracked and echoed as they fought back and forth. One would advance as the other gave ground. One would defend as the other attacked. Back and forth, round and round — clack, clack, clack — until a sword was on the ground and the tallest boy was yielding.

From behind me came clapping. I turned to find a little girl with black hair and smiling eyes walking towards us. The shorter boy laughed, drawing my attention again. He spoke a few words that I didn't understand, but recognised as Japanese, and then he said a word I knew — Naoko.

It was her, I realised with shock. And then the rest began to fall into place. I'd seen the boys in Nana's photos. She'd had two brothers growing up, but she'd lost them both in the war. This was her family when she was little. I was in Kure, Japan.

I opened my mouth to call to her, but before I could speak, the three children began fading, and then they were gone, and I was back in the fernery, my legs shaky, my heart pounding, my mouth agape wondering what I had seen and why?

"Found you," Cameron said from behind me, laughing. "That's a terrible hiding spot."

I turned around slowly, and when he saw the fear in my eyes his smile faltered and he rushed forward, awkwardly placing his arm around my shoulders.

"Are you all right, Gina?" he asked softly. "What happened?" I wanted to tell him, but when I opened my mouth all I could do was sob, and tears began to spill down my cheeks.

"Come on," he said softly, "let's find Nana."

#

Nana remained quiet for a long time after I told her my story.

We were in her lounge room, huddled together on the worn couch. The room smelt of potpourri. She had a photo album on her lap, open to a picture of her family when she was young.

"We were looking at this album last night, remember?" she said eventually. "It was warm today, perhaps you fell asleep, and dreamed of these photos."

I folded my arms across my chest and pulled away from her.

"It was real," I said, pouting.

Nana reached for me and drew me close. I resisted for a moment, but then relented and leaned up against her small frame. She took my chin in her hand and turned my face towards her until I had to look into her eyes.

"Ok. I believe you. After all, gardens are magical, Gina," she said, the staccato beat of her Japanese accent clinging to her words even after all of her years in Australia. "My garden is full of my favourite plants, all of the ones that remind me of those I've loved, and still love. The people who have helped me till the soil, sow the seeds, tend the plants. When I smell lavender, I remember your grandfather and our first house. When I cut my roses, I think of my friend, Gwenny. Perhaps my garden shared a memory of my family with you today because it knew you were missing your mum and dad?"

Nana's eyes never wavered. They held my gaze and I felt she was sincere.

"Thank you," I whispered.

She nodded, then rose to her feet, glancing at the clock on the wall.

"Goodness me, where has the day gone? You must be starving. I'll put dinner on. While I do, you should pack your bag so that you're ready when your parents arrive first thing tomorrow."

"Ok, Nana," I said, rising as well. I gave her a quick hug and raced to my room to pack.

The next morning, my parents didn't show up early, or late. Instead, around lunchtime, two policemen knocked on Nana's door and told us about the car accident.

#

"Your mother always loved bottlebrushes," Nana said, as she smoothed the soil around the newly planted tree. Its spiky, green-blue leaves stood out against the red dirt.

"The flowers look like a little round brush," Nana said quietly, as she tipped the watering can and splashed water over the fresh earth. "Your mother used to pick the flowers to brush her dolls' hair with, at least until they wilted."

I watched Nana place the watering can behind her, her eyes on her work.

"Bottlebrushes grow beside rivers, not in arid parts of Australia, so it normally wouldn't belong in this type of native garden. But I think we can make an exception," she said, as she rose to her feet and smiled down at the small tree.

I looked at it, trying to imagine my mother looking at a larger version. But I couldn't see it. I couldn't see her. A tear ran down my cheek.

"Now," Nana said, "I think next to it, we will plant this wattle for your father." She picked up the shovel and began to dig.

#

"I like summer," my mother said as she kicked her legs forward, the swing arcing away. "Do you like summer?"

I cleared my throat.

"Yes."

"I think hot weather is nice. Mama says summer kills the garden, though. She doesn't like it like I do."

I smiled. Nana had always dreaded the summer. *It's the time just to keep the garden alive,* she'd say.

"Do you know my Mama?" my mother asked.

I took a deep breath and then exhaled.

"Yes. I know her very well."

#

Moving in with Nana, at first, was a miasma of sadness, numbness, and confusion. I spent a lot of time sleeping, in those first few months. I remember the musky smell of the cotton blanket on the bed in Nana's spare room, the room that became my own. When I refused to come out, Nana would bring me food on a silver tray, encouraging me to eat a little. Some nights she would climb into bed with me and hold me until we both fell asleep.

It was Cameron who coaxed me back towards normality. I couldn't say exactly when, but after a while he simply crept back into my life. He was just there, as kids sometimes are, knocking at the door, asking, "can Gina come out to play?"

And I guess being a kid, even a devastated kid, I couldn't resist the lure of going outside again, eventually. If I close my eyes and think back I still recall the self-pity and sorrow, but those feelings are interspersed with recollections of games in the yard, the scent of freshly mown lawn and roses in spring, of Nana pruning flowers watching over Cameron and me as we played. Part of me felt I shouldn't be happy, that somehow my enjoying myself was betraying the memory of my parents. And yet I was glad for his friendship over those summer holidays. He helped me realise there was still much in life to look forward to.

When we returned to school, Cameron looked out for me. He'd check up on me even though he was in the grade above. He'd often seek me out at lunch break — sometimes to play, other times just to chat quickly before he returned to his older friends and I mine. He made the change bearable.

But then, around the time I turned thirteen, he fourteen, we began to drift apart. There were no arguments, no falling out. It's just we'd reached that age, right on the cusp of puberty and sex and worrying about who likes whom and all the unimportant stuff that goes through your mind obsessively when you are young and confused. It was hard at that time just to be friends with the opposite sex. And I guess he had his football, his mates, and I was, well, me. I just thought he didn't want an immature, bookish girl following him around anymore. At least that's how it seemed. So I gave him his space.

I missed him, though.

#

I was walking home, lost in my thoughts, when I was startled back to reality by a familiar voice.

"Hey, Gina."

I looked up, and across the road was Cameron, his hand half raised. I waved.

I was in year ten by then, Cameron in year eleven. He'd grown tall. His hair was still blonde, but his boyish physique was becoming a man's, even if his face still looked young. The air was getting cooler, the trees losing their leaves, flooding the footpaths and gutters with a sea of reds, yellows and oranges.

He checked the road for traffic, and then trotted across.

"Hey," he said again as he drew closer. I watched as the words deserted him, like he was suddenly wondering what had come over him to initiate contact with me.

"You heading home?" I asked, blushing as I thought about how stupid that question was. But he didn't seem to notice.

"Yeah," he said, smiling. "You mind if I walk with you?"

I shook my head, no, and we walked on, side by side. We didn't say anything for a couple of blocks. I'd never felt so self-conscious walking. I stole half glances at him, waiting for him to say something further.

"You preparing for mid-year exams?" he asked suddenly.

"Yeah, you?"

"Yep."

Silence.

"Hey, I heard you got man of the match on the weekend. Congratulations," I said.

He glanced at me, a crooked smile.

"I didn't know you followed the football?" he said.

I swallowed again, embarrassed.

"I don't, not really. I just check the papers sometimes to see how …"

"The school side is going?" he offered.

Not exactly what I meant, but I nodded, relieved.

"You ever come down and watch?"

I'd been a couple of times to see him play. He was pretty good. He played in the forwards and he tackled hard, ran the ball well. On the field he wasn't gawky, or awkward. He was a different person.

"Nana and I have occasionally watched a little on a Saturday after grocery shopping."

"You should come down this Saturday … if you want to, I mean. We've had a good season and we're into the finals."

I glanced at him, and saw his eyes locked ahead, both hands wrapped around the strap of his backpack.

"I'll check with Nana," I said. He smiled, his eyes flitting to mine and then away once more.

The rest of the walk home went easier. Talking came more naturally, like old times.

After I waved him goodbye, I felt good. Like I'd just felt the first warm breeze of spring caress my skin, signalling the end of winter. I watched him walk across the street and disappear into his house. It was only as I began walking across the neat lawns that I noticed Nana sitting at the little cast iron table on the porch, a cup of tea in her hands, a broad smile stretched across her face.

"How's Cameron?" she asked as I drew closer, her eyes twinkling. I felt my cheeks blushing, my neck growing hot.

"Good," I said. I stepped onto the porch and waited for more, but nothing came. "His footy side is in the finals this Saturday," I said. "I was thinking we could go and watch him play?"

She laughed, and nodded.

"He's becoming a big, handsome boy now, isn't he?"

"Ah, I'll just go and get changed," I said, ignoring her jibe. She nodded, still smiling, her eyes never leaving me.

"Grab the biscuits when you come back, ok? I think we deserve a treat with our tea," she said as I rushed inside.

#

I was looking for a sunny spot to read my book when I walked from Nana's garden into Kure, Japan for the second time.

After weaving around one of Nana's camellias, I found myself in an unfamiliar open area comprised of lawns, hedges, flowers, and bare trees. It took me a moment to realise that I wasn't in a suburban garden, but a park of some kind. I pulled up short, recollections of my first immersion in Nana's memories bubbling to the surface. *God, it was actually real*, I thought. I'd always known deep down, and yet, the longer time went on it had become easier to repress, to explain my experience as simply being young with a vivid imagination. But somehow, the plants that reminded Nana of her childhood were sharing her past with me.

I turned quickly to look behind me, expecting to find some sort of gateway, or window back to my world and time, but there was only a view of a red bridge traversing a large river, and beyond that the ocean. My heart pulsated and I swallowed hard. *Why now?* I thought.

Then Nana walked past.

She looked so young, so pretty. She smelled the same, a hint of floral perfume mixed with the sweet scent of soil. She wore a long black overcoat, buttoned high to her neck. Her socks were pulled up to her knees, her shoes black and sensible. Her hair was a little longer then she usually wore it, darker, curled at the ends.

I fell into step behind her, wanting to catch her, to talk to her. She led me across lush lawns towards a bench under a bare tree. And there I saw him, my grandfather, Thomas, and I stuttered to a stop.

He'd died when I was young, so I grew up knowing him only from photos and Nana's stories. This was different; a shock. A ghost in the flesh.

He stood tall and erect in his army uniform, just like in Nana's photos. But he looked younger in person, his face boyish, nervous.

He removed his hat and wrung it in his hands as Nana approached, and I saw his smile briefly before it faltered. I forced my feet to move again as Nana halted a few feet shy of Thomas, her hands clasped in front of her, mimicking his. I watched Nana sneak a glance over her shoulder, looking through me, and then she turned back and quickly closed the space between herself and Grandpa Thomas and kissed him on the cheek. She pulled back just as fast, looking at the ground shyly while Thomas' cheeks reddened.

I couldn't help but smile as I circled around behind the bench seat, behind my grandfather so that I could watch Nana's face. She looked up, staring into Thomas' eyes, and I saw love. It was etched into her features. It showed in the blinkered way she only saw him, and I felt a lightness in my chest.

"Hello, my dear Naoko," Grandpa Thomas said in English, and Nana's face radiated as the words consumed her. She nodded, gently encouraging him on. "I've been given my orders. I'm to ship back home in a week."

Nana swallowed, and the joy in her eyes disappeared like the sun passing behind black clouds. She wobbled, and I stepped forward wanting to help, but Thomas had her, hands on her shoulders for support. She pulled away from him, raising her chin, composing herself. I could see the storm still behind her eyes, threatening to break into a torrent, but she held it back.

Her voice was soft when she spoke.

"And us. Is that it for us?" she asked in hesitant English.

Thomas shook his head fiercely, and drew a little closer.

"No, my love. Not at all. I will send for you, I promise. And then we'll marry as we discussed."

It was hard to read what she was feeling. There was a little of the previous joy back, but suspicion too, like she didn't know what to believe. Thomas took her arm, and together they sat on the bench, close.

As they began whispering, a long blast from a ship's horn drew my attention. I looked back across the park and saw a boat moving slowly out of the mouth of the river into the ocean, leaving a wake behind. When I turned back, Nana and Grandpa Thomas were gone, and instead I found camellias and a little stone warrior peeking out from under the shrubs.

I took a deep breath, composing myself. I knew it had all turned out ok for Nana and Thomas, but it hadn't felt like that just then. It had felt like a possible ending. A terrible, sad ending.

And I also had this feeling in the pit of my stomach that witnessing another of Nana's memories, like the last time I was transported in place and time, meant something for me personally, something to dread. Last time, I had seen Nana's two dead brothers and had returned to find I'd lost my parents. Was that simply a coincidence?

I set out for the house. I wanted to find Nana and I desperately wanted to tell her about what had happened. But I couldn't. I was older, and I was afraid of how she'd look at me this time. But I still wanted to see her, and talk to her, to ask her about Grandpa Thomas. I wanted to know the rest of the tale — the happy ending.

#

Thursday evening, later that week, there was a knock at the front door.

"I've got it," I yelled. When I opened the door I found Cameron. Seeing him, I instantly felt a little lighter. He hadn't been at school that day, so we hadn't walked home together as was usual now. It was only one day, but I'd missed him.

"Hey," I said, looking up into his bright, blue eyes. They flitted to mine, then away. His mouth was a frown, and I felt my smile dropping, as I thought back to Nana and Grandpa Thomas.

"Hey," he said, staring at his shoes.

We stood like that for a time, awkward in our silences. I could see the thoughts moving in his head, the words swilling in his mouth, so I waited.

"I'm moving to Melbourne," he said finally, lifting his gaze. "They don't even play proper football down there."

"Oh," I said. I didn't like the way my stomach twisted. "Why?"

"Dad got a new job. Better money, more responsibility or something like that."

"Oh," I said again, swallowing.

He reached out and took my hand in his. I looked down at our clasped hands, and watched as he began to rub the back of mine with his thumb, goose bumps rising on my arm and neck.

"I wish we'd had more time. I wish we hadn't grown apart before last year, you know. I wish ..."

I looked up and saw him staring at me intently. I licked my lips as he leaned forward, his lips parting slightly.

"Who is it?" Nana asked from nearby, and Cameron drew back sharply as I turned to see Nana emerge from the hallway, a tea towel in her hands. "Oh, Cameron. Hello. Did you want to come in? We were about to have cake."

He shook his head.

"Sorry, Nana. I can't. I just came to say goodbye."

"Goodbye?"

He nodded, then looked back at me like he wanted to say more. But he didn't. He just turned and walked back across the street.

"What's he mean, goodbye?" Nana asked, drawing up alongside me as I watched Cameron disappear into his house.

"His Dad got a job in Melbourne," I said quietly, watching his door close. My hands were shaking. I felt flat.

"Oh honey, I'm so sorry," Nana said, putting an arm around me, pulling me close. And I turned and embraced her, resting my chin on the top of her head, embarrassed by the tears I felt in my eyes.

#

I wanted to ask my mother about herself. About Dad. About what she had done in her life, and what she had wanted to do before she was unfairly taken. And yet, what would this little girl know of that?

"So, is this your house?" I asked instead.

"Uh huh."

Her skin was so light. It was like she'd never been scorched by the hot sun out here. The rope swing creaked.

"And do you go to school?"

"Yes. In town."

It was odd, interacting with a memory. Till now, I'd thought that I was a ghost in their world. I inhaled and pushed my mother once again.

"What's your name?" she asked me.

"Gina."

"I like that name," she said. I could hear the smile in her voice. "I have a doll named Gina."

"Oh," I said, feeling the tears well in my eyes, remembering being little, scared of the dark, when my mother had given me Gina the doll, her doll, to look after me.

#

John was skinny, but he had nice green eyes and a strong jaw. We found ourselves sharing a study break in year eleven, and we got along. Not in that deep connection, 'I get you as a kindred spirit' way. More in a jokey, sparring, light-hearted way. At that point in my life, it was all I needed.

He kissed me one Friday in June. It was freezing cold, and I was rugged up to the point I couldn't move my arms properly. We'd been talking about our English class and I remember thinking that the bus was late. He'd leaned in and, soon, we were mashing lips. At first, both of mine were above his, but we adjusted, and then our mouths were interwoven, opening and closing slightly, tongues caressing soft flesh. It wasn't how I'd imagined. It wasn't with Cameron.

#

I'd never been more nervous than the day I told Nana I was pregnant.

We were sitting on the front porch drinking green tea. As I said the words, she froze, staring, her eyes a little wider than normal. Then her hand, still holding her tea, began to shake ever so gently. I watched her lower the cup back to its saucer with a soft clink.

"I think I'm going to keep it," I added quietly.

Nana cleared her throat.

"Is that what both you and John want?"

I hesitated. John's face had grown pale when I'd told him. He'd eventually made some soothing statements, but he'd also offered to pay for an abortion, only if I wanted that, he'd added hastily.

"It's what I want," I said.

I watched as her lips turned down, the lines around her mouth growing deeper.

"You have year twelve next year."

I nodded, looking at my tea.

"I can defer. I'll have the baby, get a part-time job, and then go back the following year. John will help, I'm sure."

I looked up to see Nana's eyes moistening. There was anguish in those eyes, dread, even. Then she was looking away, somewhere over my shoulder.

"I don't think I can look after another child, Gina," she said so softly, almost inaudibly. "I'm too old. I'm too tired. Please."

"Nana, I'm not asking you to —"

"You are, Gina. And I don't think you know this boy as well as you think."

I felt my neck and cheeks flush.

"You don't know what it is like to be treated as an outsider. To be sixteen and pregnant. They'll point and talk and you'll lose friends and things will never be as they were."

"So," I said, my voice rising, "I give up on the baby because you're too old and people will look at me?"

She glanced back at me for a moment, tears in her eyes, and then she turned away once more. I watched her lower lip quivering. Finally, she sighed.

"I'll support you whatever you decide," she said. But she didn't look at me again.

#

"Come on, honey," Nana whispered, the blanket over my head muffling her voice. "It's beautiful outside. Why don't you take a walk?"

After the miscarriage, I'd taken to bed. It felt like I was nine again, like I'd lost my parents all over. I slept, I cried, I fought revulsion every time a wave of relief crashed into me. I hated myself in those moments.

"Gina, please. If not for you, for me. Come back to me, honey."

John visited me once. I knew what he wanted, so I made it easy on him. I told him we were over. I told him to go.

"Gina, can you at least say something?"

I sighed, and flipped back the blanket. Nana was kneeling by the side of the bed, her face close to mine, her warm eyes reflecting an image of my messed hair and haggard face. She'd been with me every day of my hibernation, leaving me meals, loving me, coaxing me back.

"Ok," I said. "For you."

#

That first stroll in Nana's garden felt like emerging into a strange world. The air was cooler, the sunlight duller, and all of the birds sang songs full of yearning. And yet, there was also something pleasant about being outside, alone, wandering.

I found myself in the farthest corner of Nana's block, amongst her roses. The delicate scent reminded me of being little, of Nana telling me the names of the roses as I pointed at each one, my mother's laughter behind me as I tried to repeat them.

Right at the back was a very old, English rose bush covered in large crimson blooms — its final display before winter. It'd been there forever, and yet, I'd never seen it quite so alive with colour, so fragrant.

I approached it, weaving through the other roses, careful not to catch my dressing gown on the thorns when, suddenly, I realised I was not moving through plants, but people.

A younger version of the rose bush was in a large pot, sitting on a trestle table, amongst other plants. I was in a hall surrounded by women in modest, pastel dresses. Many of the women wore hats, and those without had impressive coiffures. I could smell something delicious, and spied trays of home cooked cakes on another trestle table towards the back of the room. The room was alive with chatter, the back and forth of women of a certain age gossiping. But the din ceased when the double doors to the hall sprang open and revealed a Japanese woman in her twenties. Nana Naoko.

She stood in the doorway, self-conscious, wringing her hands. Eventually, the women began talking again in hushed whispers, Nana their focus.

"... the oriental that Thomas Hibbert brought back with him ..."

"... may not even understand English ..."

"... I thought she'd be ashamed to show her face in town, what with her family fighting my John only a few years ago ..."

My face grew hot as I heard these terrible things. I wanted to run to her, hug her, tell her I loved her. But before I did anything, I noticed one of the women approaching Nana.

She was an aboriginal lady with lively eyes and grey-flecked hair. Despite the grey, she wasn't old. Maybe thirty. She walked up to Nana and held out her hand.

"Hello," she said loudly. "My name's Gwen. Welcome to the Gunnedah Gardening Club."

I knew the name. Nana had often talked fondly of her friend Gwen, but I'd never met her. She'd passed away before I'd been born.

"Naoko," Nana said quietly, extending her hand palm down.

Gwen took her hand in both of hers and pulled her close, talking under her breath. I stepped closer to eavesdrop.

"Don't take any notice of these stuck-up crones, Naoko. They're all sorts of ignorant racists, but these here are the harmless ones. They do it because they don't know no better. They've been brought up thinking black might rub off on them, if you know what I mean."

I saw Nana smiling uncertainly.

"It's rubbish, and we shouldn't have to put up with it. But, unfortunately, it's the price you have to pay to live in a town like this. And you know what, if you can suffer their jibes and stupid questions with good humour, knowing that they don't really understand that they're hurting you, because they mostly don't, then they'll come around eventually, like they did with me."

"Oh, I see," Nana said. I was shaking my head, furious. This wasn't right.

Then Gwen whispered one last thing.

"It can get you down, all the pretending. But if you ever want to blow your top, you come vent with me, Gwenny, ok?"

Nana Naoko looked at Gwen for a long time, but then she smiled, broadly.

"Thank you, Gwen. Thank you."

Gwen nodded. Then she led Naoko towards the table of plants. I followed them.

"What plants did you grow in Japan, Naoko?"

"Many plants. Cherry trees, camellias, azaleas, maples."

"What about roses?" Gwen said, as they approached the table.

"No," Naoko said, as she stared at the young rose bush before her. I could see the look of amazed longing in her eyes.

"Lovely, isn't it?" Gwen said, smiling.

"I've never seen a flower so beautiful," Naoko said, stretching a hand towards the nearest bloom, caressing it gently.

"Well, I grew this one," Gwen said, reaching out and picking up the pot. "And I reckon it would not find any better home then with you. Here." Gwen held the rose out to Naoko.

Naoko looked at it, confused, then at Gwen.

"No, I couldn't possibly. It's too much."

"Nonsense," Gwen said smiling. "A welcome gift."

I saw Naoko's lips quiver, her eyes moisten. She bowed, and then accepted the pot.

"Thank you," she whispered breathlessly. "Thank you so much."

But Gwen waved the thanks away.

"No thanks required. But I'll tell you what. When you plant that in your garden, I'd love to come see it. How about we have tea one day?"

"That sounds wonderful," Naoko said.

And then Naoko was fading, Gwen too, and I found myself standing back in amongst the roses feeling incredibly grateful to Nana, but also lost and alone. Where was my Gwen? But of course I knew the answer to that — he was in Melbourne.

#

I was seventeen and halfway through year twelve when Cameron and his Mum returned to our street, minus his Dad. Mrs. Roberts had won the house in the divorce.

A couple of days after they unpacked, Cameron saw Nana and me in the garden and crossed the road to say hello. I couldn't stop smiling. We didn't talk about anything meaningful. Melbourne, the weather, the garden. Cameron was only home for a couple of weeks before he headed back to Melbourne for his second semester of University. He was studying economics, he told me.

It was nice talking to him again. Particularly after the last twelve months of school, where people looked at me with pity and talked about me in whispers as I passed.

That night, Nana kept stealing glances at me as she knitted, a strange smile on her face. When I asked her about it, she'd replied with, "nothing, nothing."

A couple of days later, Nana and I were planting bulbs in the front garden when Cameron crossed the road again. As he stepped onto the front lawn, I smiled up at him. But before either of us could say hello, Nana called out to him. He hesitated, shrugged, and then with a bemused expression he changed direction and approached her. I didn't know what was going on.

Nana made Cameron lean down close to her and she began whispering. After a short exchange, I saw him nodding. He straightened, and I watched him disappear around the back of the house.

It was odd, but I returned to my work, not giving it much more thought until he returned about ten minutes later holding a pair of secateurs and a bunch of freshly cut roses.

"Do you want me to put these in a vase, Nana?" Cameron asked.

"No, Cameron," she replied, grinning, "I want you to give them to my granddaughter. And then you could ask her out."

"Nana," I squealed. "I'm so sorry about this," I said to Cameron quickly. His neck and face had grown red, and he had a goofy, uncertain smile on his face.

"You two are so slow," Nana said.

"Ah," Cameron stammered. He looked at Nana, then me, then Nana. Suddenly, he was moving. As he rushed past he thrust the flowers at me. "I forgot that I've got something on. I'll see you soon though, ok?" he said.

I reached out and took the flowers somewhat reluctantly, our hands touching for a brief moment, then he quickly pulled away and was walking back across the street.

Nana was chuckling, but my embarrassment was fading, replaced with a heat in my belly and cheeks.

"Nana, that was cruel."

She looked at me calmly as Cameron disappeared inside his house.

"He likes you too, you know. You're just too caught up in your doubts to notice."

I wanted to chastise her, but I didn't. She wasn't a child, after all. Instead, I found myself looking across the road. Eventually I turned back to Nana.

"Even if he does, it's not your call," I said. "I'm not ready, ok?"

Nana sighed.

"You can't hide forever, Gina," she said.

"I'm not. It's just ..." But what could I say?

Nana nodded. "I understand. But the past is the past. Learn from it, and then move on. Take a risk, Gina."

#

"Do you need to go soon?" my mother asked. Her voice was tiny, small, and yet achingly familiar.

"I'm not sure," I said, pushing the swing again.

"Won't someone miss you?"

I swallowed.

"No. Well, maybe. I mean, I live with my Nana, but she's in hospital at the moment. She's asleep," I said.

"Is she sick?"

I couldn't reply for a time. I just swallowed and swallowed, but I couldn't dislodge the lump at the back of my throat.

"Nana had a stroke," I finally whispered. I saw her again in my head, the tiny woman crumpled on the lawn, a pile of freshly pulled weeds next to her, her greying hair half covering her face. I felt again the abyss opening to swallow me.

"Is that bad?" the little girl asked.

"It can be, yes. Very bad."

"Does it hurt?"

I cleared my throat, watching as the swing slowed, the arc becoming smaller. I realised I was no longer pushing. My arms were crossed, holding myself.

"I hope not," I croaked. The swing stopped, the little girl hopped down, turned and looked up at me.

"You should go back soon in case she wakes up," she said.

"But what if she doesn't?" I felt hot streaks on my cheeks as the tears began to spill. "Whenever I enter one of these damn memories, there's always something wrong. The first time, I lost you. The second time, my best friend left me, the third ... the third ..." But I couldn't say it. I rubbed roughly at my wet cheeks and covered my mouth with my hand, trying to regain control as my mother looked at me confused, her brow furrowed.

"Maybe," I said eventually, "it's better if I stay here with you. Forever."

The little girl stepped closer.

"You can't stay here forever. I'll need to go to bed soon. Plus your Nana will miss you. But we can play again soon. I'd love you to come back when your Nana's better."

I fell to my knees and enveloped my mother in my arms, sobbing. She stiffened in my embrace at first but, after a moment, her little arms wrapped around my neck, and I knew she was right. I couldn't hide here. Nana was waiting for me. And I needed to be with her, like she'd always been there for me. It didn't matter how much it hurt.

"Thank you," I said.

"Thank you for pushing me on the swing," she said in return.

As I released her, I heard a screen door creak open and I looked across at the house to see Naoko step out onto the deck.

"Emily. Dinner," she called.

"Come see me again soon," my mother said. I watched her walk away, and I breathed in the country air tinged with dust and pollen as my mother began fading, as did the house, Naoko, and then it was all gone, and I was back kneeling on red dirt next to the bottlebrush that Nana and I had planted all of those years ago.

It took a moment for me to realise that my mobile phone was ringing. I pulled it from my pocket with an unsteady hand, afraid it would stop ringing and afraid to answer. I took a deep breath, and then picked up.

"Hello."

"Oh, Gina. This is Wendy from the hospital."

I felt hot blood pulsing across my temples, my stomach roiling.

"Your grandmother has woken up. She's asking for you."

#

I sat on the front lawn pulling weeds. The weather was warming, and the sun felt nice on my face.

A small family of finches were cavorting in the ceramic birdbath next to the bed of tulips. As I stared at the water, I saw a reflection that didn't belong, an image of my mother, as a girl, running. Then the birds were splashing and it was gone.

The front door squeaked open, and I turned to find Nana's nurse, Judy, wheeling Nana out of the house. She pushed the wheelchair across the lawn towards me, applying the brake when Nana was close.

"You missed one," Nana said, a little slower than she used to.

"Morning, Nana," I replied, smiling. I removed the weed she was pointing at.

"Looks like Cameron is back for the weekend," Nana said.

I looked up with a start, and across the road I saw Cameron's car in his driveway. How had I not noticed that before? I guess I'd just been too caught up in the sunshine. But now that I did see it, my heart beat a little faster.

"Who's Cameron?" Judy asked, as she sat down next to me and began to help weed.

I waited for Nana to make a joke about him being my boyfriend, or something like that.

"An old friend," Nana said instead.

I looked up at Nana as she looked down at me. Those brown eyes were smiling, and I loved her so much at that moment. I grinned, despite myself, as she nodded gently in the direction of Cameron's house.

"Ok," I whispered, more to myself then anything.

I stood up and rubbed my hands against my pants.

"Ok," I repeated, "maybe I'll go over and say hello. Are you all right here, Nana?"

"Never better, dear. I'm in my garden."

I leaned over and pecked her on the cheek. She raised her good right hand and held it against the back of my neck, pressing her face to mine, then she let go.

I straightened, took a deep breath, and then turned and walked out of the comfort of Nana Naoko's garden, across the street, and into the unknown.

See Michael Gardner's story "Nana Naoko's Garden" online at Metaphorosis.
If you liked it, leave a comment. Authors love that!
Remember to subscribe to our e-mail updates so you'll know when new stories are posted.

About the story

My own Nana is a fantastic gardener. The garden she had when I was a kid was amazing. A huge, sprawling garden filled with trees, shrubs, flowers and neatly manicured lawns. It had so many elements that seemed magical, including a fernery along the back of her house, a small bridge and goldfish pond, vegetable patches that my Papa tended at the back of the block. I have very fond memories of playing with my siblings in that garden, and much of the setting of this story is taken straight from those childhood memories. The other thing that brought this story together for me was a poem by Gwen Harwood, called 'The Violets'. The poem is about the fragrance of violets triggering a powerful memory of the protagonist's childhood. That idea of a scent taking someone back into the past is something that resonates with me. I find that certain scents are powerful reminders of people and events from my own past. These two influences came together in this story, where the scents and sights of Nana's garden take Gina not back into her own past, but back into Nana's.

A question for the author

Q: If you could talk to your novice-writer self, what bit of advice would you give?

A: I still feel like a novice-writer. My advice to me right now is to write better, to learn to articulate your ideas with a little more poetry and elegance, maybe buy a cat — all of the best writers seem to own a cat.

But I'm guessing the spirit of this question relates to what advice I would provide to my younger self when I first began writing fiction.

I only wrote sporadically when I was younger. And for that reason, I'd tell my younger self not to waste so much time. I'd tell me to write more often, to get into a routine and practice as much as I could as early as I could. I think doing so would have helped me learn a lot more about story telling by now.

I think one of the main reasons I didn't write as much as I would have liked was because I didn't know what to do with the stories I produced, other than force some of my friends to read them. So I'd also tell my younger self about these wonderful online magazines that might, one day, actually buy one of the stories you're writing and publish it.

Writing is foremost about my own enjoyment, but I get such a buzz from realising others might read them, and hopefully enjoy them. And I'm grateful to magazines like *Metaphorosis* for publishing some of them.

About the author

Michael Gardner is a public servant living in Canberra, Australia with his wife and two kids. He grew up in a small country town in Australia, which continues to find its way into his stories. His work has been published in the anthology *Reading 5X5: Writers' Edition*, in *Aurealis,* and, of course, in *Metaphorosis* magazine.

Twins

Gregory Kane

Our twins visit once a month. They arrive one at a time, passing one another as they move up and down the path dividing the manicured campus. Years ago, we'd gather to watch from the laboratory's third floor as they ran free on the grass below, dancing and jumping and tumbling, swinging in their parents' arms like tiny trapeze artists. We rose to our tiptoes and pressed our palms and noses against the cold glass, watching until they disappeared underneath.

Never once did they look up.

Few still come to the lab. The others faded as we've withered away, the way fallen trees lose shadows. Only Carl, Ruth and I remain. Carl is dying, his body ruined by tumors. Ruth insists she feels well, but her ashen skin and yellowed eyes suggest otherwise. I am the healthiest, but not blind to my own reflection: pale, gaunt, a wire hanger holding ill-fitting clothes.

Ruth and I stand at the window while Carl lies on a nearby sofa. We're teenagers now, no longer needing to stand on our toes to see the campus. Carl's twin is the first to arrive. I spot him walking up the path toward the building, his ink black hair, almond eyes and slender nose mirroring those of the wasted boy on the couch.

The similarities end here. Carl is probably fifty pounds lighter, his once-olive skin tone faded to parchment. His scalp is visible through short tufts of black fuzz. He lies with his head propped on a pillow, a clear oxygen mask covering his mouth. He turns toward us when I announce his twin's arrival.

"Describe him," Carl says, his voice muffled by the foggy plastic.

"His hair's getting long," Ruth says. "He keeps flipping his head back to get it out of his eyes. He's wearing a sweater and jeans. Big white headphones on his ears. It looks like he's texting on his phone."

"Are his parents there?" Carl asks.

I look out the window. "His mom," I say.

"How does she look?"

"Good," Ruth says. "Her hair is shorter."

"No dad?" Carl asks.

We shake our heads. Carl turns away from the window and looks toward the ceiling. We've never met the twins or their parents. We don't even know their names. But we've watched them our entire lives. The twins are our brothers and sisters. Their parents, whom we've never seen up close, whose voices we've never heard, are our mothers and fathers.

We know them, even if they don't know us.

Carl says in a whisper, "I thought he might come this time."

Carl's twin walks out of sight into the entrance below. He'll stay for two hours before exiting and returning down the path. Along the way, he'll pass Ruth's twin, who will then pass mine a few hours later. It is the monthly ritual, performed every second Saturday. They won't notice one another as their paths cross, completely unaware of any connection.

They are strangers.

Carl falls asleep on the couch. Ruth and I continue watching.

#

I asked Ruth to marry me when we were eight years old. I found her during recess at the jungle gym with Carl and Martha, who would die from pneumonia that winter. Ruth sat atop the dome of criss-crossed bars like a queen holding court. I knelt at the base and lifted a bouquet of dandelions toward her. I said the words, then waited for a response. All she did was smile.

It seems in retrospect a silly thing for a child to do. Most boys pull hair, or call names, or chase and push the objects of their affection. I proposed marriage in front of everyone I knew.

This is Ruth's effect on me. She lulls me like a pendulum.

Dr. Valerie laughs as she recounts the story. We're alone in the common room. Ruth is downstairs undergoing testing and Carl is sleeping in his room. Dr. Valerie came for Carl's weekly therapy session, but decided to let him rest. She found me reading on the couch.

"It was the cutest thing," she says through a smile. "You were so diligent, pulling up as many of those dandelions as you could find. We had no idea what you were up to!"

She was there, of course. The doctors were always around back then. They'd sit to the side taking notes while went about our day. Dr. Stone and Dr. Madrigal took blood and ran us through batteries of examinations, checking our weight and height and ability to perform a variety of physical tasks. Dr. Valerie led therapy sessions and conducted ongoing assessments of our intelligence, personality and levels of achievement. We were poked and prodded, our lives told on the pages of a lab report.

Dr. Valerie was our favorite. She was young and pretty, always happy, always smiling. She often remained after the other adults left, playing games and reading stories. When one of us fell during recess or got into an argument in the nursery, we ran to her.

She became pregnant when I was nine or ten. I remember wishing to trade places with her baby.

She still visits with us, although less frequently than when we were younger. It's the same with all of the doctors. Perhaps they've learned all there is to know about us. Perhaps they're simply tired of watching us die.

Dr. Valerie sighs. "I don't know how she didn't accept then and there."

I smile. "It's for the best. We were a little young for marriage."

"You're getting older," she says. "Maybe she's coming around?"

"My only competition is Carl," I say. "Although he does have a way with the ladies."

A sad smile sinks into Dr. Valerie's face. I notice for the first time how much she has aged. Lines creep from the edges of her eyes and mouth like cracks in thinning ice. Her features are sharp and angular.

We're the sick ones, but everybody here suffers.

#

In my earliest memories, twelve of us lived in the lab. The common room looked like a nursery then, decorated in bright reds, yellows, greens and blues, characters from Sesame Street and Dr. Seuss smiling down from the walls. We sat in beanbags and little plastic chairs and listened as a Dr. Valerie read us stories. We learned numbers and letters, listened to music and did arts and crafts. Scattered toys, promises of sprained ankles, littered the floor.

Ian fell ill first. He developed a cough that became uncontrollable. The doctors kept him in his room while the rest of us played. Eventually, they told us he wouldn't return.

Angelika, a skinny girl with red hair and freckles, collapsed the following month. A round-faced boy named Steen became ill soon after. Robert, a boy I often played with during the hour-long morning recess on the grassy campus outside, suddenly moved to a location in the building we came to know as the medical wing.

There were only six of us by the time we reached our seventh birthdays.

One by one, we die.

They used to tell us we had a disease. Our families couldn't take care of us. We were contagious and had to stay confined to the lab, where doctors could search for a cure.

It was Ruth who always poked holes in the story. Why did every one of us have a twin who visited the building? If the doctors could touch us without masks or gloves, why couldn't our parents? Couldn't we talk to them on the phone, or through video recordings or letters?

Dr. Madrigal told us the truth when we turned fourteen. We are clones, created from DNA taken from our twins when they were still embryos. Their parents – our parents – signed custody over to Schilling Laboratories in exchange for money.

We were supposed to be a landmark achievement: human embryos cloned from somatic donor cells and carried to term by surrogate mothers. The research team, led by Dr. Madrigal and Dr. Stone and funded by Schilling Laboratories, would become instant celebrities by producing a healthy crop of cloned children. Healthy clones meant an end to infertility and chromosomal disorders and an unlimited supply of embryonic stem cells to treat disease. Healthy clones opened up new frontiers in medicine.

We weren't healthy. We developed infections, tumors, cancer. We began to die. Suddenly, nobody was eager to announce our existence. They brought us here instead, locked away on the third floor for all but an hour each day, when we could run around in the drab building's shadow. The doctors now claim to be working toward a cure for those of us who are still alive.

Our real families don't want to see us.

They want nothing to do with us.

"Do you think we'll ever meet them?" Ruth asks one morning. We're walking side-by-side on the campus green behind the building. It's early September. I wear a T-shirt. She is bundled in a white jacket and hat that contrasts her dark skin and brown eyes.

Not brown. Amber. Almost like honey.

Her hands are buried in her pockets. Despite the layers, I sense a shiver in her voice.

"Who?" I ask.

"Our parents. The twins"

"They don't want to meet us."

"That's what they say," Ruth says, motioning toward the lab. She spits out *they* as if it tastes sour. "Do you really believe it? How could they love one child and completely abandon another?"

"We're not their children."

"Ugh! You sound like Dr. Madrigal."

I wince. "What do you expect me to say? They didn't give birth to us. They didn't give us names and homes and birthday parties. We're just spare cells taken from their real babies."

Ruth stops walking and turns toward me. "You're telling me not a single one changed their mind? There were twelve of us, Oliver. Wouldn't one of those parents would be curious about meeting a boy or girl identical to their own child?"

"Maybe they're not allowed," I say.

"Maybe," Ruth says. She turns and begins walking again. I keep pace at her left. We are nearly the same height, our shoulders level with one another. I look down at her hands, still bundled into the coat. I wonder if she might remove them, imagining our fingers brushing together. Walking with Ruth is blissful torture.

We move in silence. The lab is to our left, a box of bleached concrete striped with four levels of tinted glass windows. A hundred yards of grass separates the building from the wooded area on our right. It is the same all the way around. The lab is a fortress surrounded by a belt of green, with no other buildings in sight.

After a few minutes, Ruth speaks again. "They should be," she says.

"Should be what?"

"They should be allowed to meet us. We should be allowed to meet them," she says. "We should be able to go home with them."

I think of my twin and his parents. We both have the mother's sandy brown hair and blue eyes, the father's nose and chin. I imagine following them down the path, getting into their car and driving to their home. Sitting down to dinner. Watching a movie in the family room, a bowl of popcorn between us on the couch.

Ruth continues. "Don't you ever wonder about leaving this place? Everybody else comes and goes. Everybody else lives in houses with cars in their driveways and dogs in their backyards. They eat in restaurants, go shopping, wander off in whatever direction they like, simply because they can." She opens her arms and gestures at their surroundings. "And here we are. Day after day. Rotting away."

I say nothing. Ruth tucks her hands back into her pockets and squeezes her arms in, as if hugging herself. She shivers. Her teeth chatter.

It can't be less than sixty degrees out here.

"Let's go inside," I say. "You're going to catch cold."

#

We play Monopoly on Saturdays. Carl, as always, plays with the race car. Ruth and I use the top hat and the thimble. We sit around a table in the common room, wrinkled pastel paper bills and dog-eared property cards littering every surface. I roll a seven and move my piece to St. James Place. Ruth has the other two orange properties in her carefully arranged collection. If I don't buy the third, she'll have a shot at building houses along the row.

"Pass," I say.

Carl chuckles. He is lying on the couch, his head against a pillow. The laugh is muffled by his oxygen mask, but the smile behind it is evident.

"What's funny?" I ask.

Carl shakes his head and looks at Ruth. I follow and see her smiling as well. She looks embarrassed.

I redden. "What?" I say. "I don't have the money."

"You've got a five-hundred," Carl whispers.

"I'm saving it," I say.

"Sure," says Ruth.

Ruth outbids Carl for St. James Place after it goes up for auction. A mischevious grin breaks out on her face as she places little green houses on the orange strip above each property. Carl smiles as I watch her.

"What do you think the twins are doing right now?" Ruth asks.

This is one of her favorite games. She likes to imagine the glamorous life her clone leads when she is not visiting the lab. The type of life we're never going to have.

I wonder about this myself. I once read a book on identical twins that described a psychic link between the pair. They share thoughts, feelings and emotions. After reading it, I spent weeks in solitude, eyes closed, trying to reach out and make some sort of connection.

There was nothing.

"It's Saturday night," I say. "Maybe he's at a party?"

Ruth's brown eyes alight. Not brown. Amber. Like whiskey. "A house party!" she says. "There's music playing. Everyone is dancing. In the backyard there's a pool, and everyone is jumping in and swimming!"

"I don't know. It's a little cold for swimming."

Ruth sticks out her tongue. I continue. "What about yours? Is she at the same party?"

I often imagine the lives of our twins intersecting. Ruth's and mine living across the street from one another, attending the same classes, sharing the same circle of friends. I imagine him having the courage to reach out and take her hand, to tell her how he feels.

Ruth shakes her head. She doesn't share this fantasy. "She's out at a nightclub. She's wearing a cute black dress and heels. The beat from the music is thumping. It's dark inside, but the dance floor is all lit up. She's out there with her friends. They're all dancing in a big group."

"Sixteen-year-olds can't get into nightclubs."

"Mine can." She turns to her right. "What about your twin, Carl?"

Carl has fallen asleep on the couch. He sleeps more and more each day. He is so thin, so gray. Ruth reaches for a blanket at his feet and pulls it up to cover his upper body.

"We're going to lose him soon," she whispers without taking her eyes off him.

I nod. She continues. "Carl's twin is up on a giant mountain somewhere. He's been walking and climbing all day, and now he's at the top, on a cliff overlooking endless trees and rivers. There are many stars in the sky. He starts a little fire and sits next to it. And he just watches everything."

Ruth turns and looks at me. I smile at her. She smiles back.

"We should call a nurse to come get him," I say.

She nods. "I'll go to the phone." As she walks away, she begins to cough, quietly at first, then more violently. It's as if she's been holding it in this whole time.

#

Carl dies in October, a few weeks after being moved to the medical wing. There are no flowers, no wake, no funeral. These are things we only know from watching television and movies. When one of us dies, there is a visit from Dr. Stone and a few therapy sessions with Dr. Valerie. After that, we move on.

Ruth and I stroll along the campus during our daily walk. We circle the perimeter of the building, starting at the main entrance and moving counter-clockwise. The weak sun hides behind thin clouds as it begins its fall toward the horizon. We are silent, save for the rattling cough Ruth tries to hide and I pretend to ignore.

We reach the concrete walkway connecting the front of the building to the grove of trees shielding the parking area at the opposite end. This is the path our twins walk, the path the doctors, nurses and other workers traverse every day as they arrive and depart. It's a path we are forbidden to follow.

I cross the walkway and continue along the lawn, hoping to circle the building again before we go back inside. After a few steps, I notice Ruth is no longer at my side.

She stands on the pavement with her back to the lab, eyeing something in the distance. I follow her gaze, expecting to find one of the twins or some other odd sight. Instead there is nothing. Ruth stares at the same oak and birch trees we've seen from our window for years.

I walk back and stand to her left, crossing my arms and looking in the same direction. The bright green of the trees is fading into reds and oranges and yellows. Most find this beautiful. I know the truth. Leaves change colors when they are starving.

"A few more weeks and the trees will be bare," I say.

Ruth coughs again. Her lungs echo like a tomb.

We watch the trees without speaking. I'm about to suggest going back inside when Ruth steps forward and begins walking away from the lab. I watch her take a few steps before trotting to catch up. "Where are you going?" I ask.

Another cough.

"Ruth, we're not supposed to go down there." The path leads to the only known exit from the campus. We've been told our entire lives not to stray toward its far end.

"Let's leave," she says. "Right now. Down the path and through whatever's on the other side."

"Ruth, we can't leave."

"It'll be just like in the movies," she continues, as if she doesn't hear me. "We'll reach the road and get on a bus or a train. We'll go to a town or a city, someplace we've never been."

"We don't have any money."

Ruth shrugs. "Then we'll walk."

We're more than halfway down the path. I imagine the two of us leaving the lab behind, side-by-side, seated close together as we're ferried toward some unknown destination. We'll find jobs and get an apartment. We'll start a life together.

Ruth's cough persists. We're closer to the exit than we've ever been.

I want to reach for her hand. She would let me take it. I know she would.

The exit is steps away.

A siren chirps in the opening between the trees ahead of us. A white truck appears, a gumdrop-shaped red emergency light on its roof. It crushes the gravel beneath as it pulls to a stop, blocking the opening lengthwise. SCHILLING LABS SECURITY is printed on its side.

Two men in dark blue uniforms step from the vehicle. One speaks quietly into a handheld radio as the other approaches Ruth and me. "You kids lost?" he says.

I start to speak when the sound of footsteps behind us stops me. I turn to see more security officers running down the path from the lab. There are two men in white coats running alongside the officers, one pale and narrow, the other dark-skinned and squat. Dr. Stone and Dr. Madrigal.

"Ruth! Oliver!" Dr. Stone huffs as he draws close. "Where are you going?"

"We're just taking a walk," I say.

"We're leaving," Ruth says.

She glares at the doctors, her back straight and her arms crossed, a posture screaming rebellion. Dr. Stone looks hurt, as if he's just learned of some awful betrayal. Dr. Madrigal's face unwraps into a sinister smirk.

It is Dr. Stone who first speaks. "What do you mean, leaving? You can't go anywhere in your condition!"

"I'll manage," Ruth says. "It's not as if staying here has been all that great for any of us."

Dr. Stone looks to Dr. Madrigal, who takes a step toward Ruth. "You're not thinking clearly. It's time to come inside."

"No!" she shouts. "We should be able to leave! Why ... can't we ..." A violent coughing fit interrupts Ruth's protestations. I put my hands around her shoulders, holding her up as her body lurches forward. We're then pulled apart, the security officers grabbing both of us and dragging us back toward the lab.

I can hear Dr. Madrigal's voice behind us. "Everything's all right," he says. "You'll feel better once you're inside."

They lead us through the front doors. I see Dr. Valerie standing by the front desk in the lobby. She turns away the moment our eyes meet.

#

Ruth is dying.

She lies in her room, somewhere between awake and asleep, an IV in her arm and an oxygen mask on her face. I can see her bones: the sharp angles of her cheekbones, the knobs of her elbows, clavicles jutting from her shoulders like newly sprouted wings. Her skin is dry, ashen, as if she is slowly turning to dust.

I sit at her bedside. I say her name. Her eyes open, heavy, half-lidded. Not brown. Amber, like a sunset. She offers a tired smile.

"Merry Christmas," I say. I pull a small bouquet of dandelions tied together with a ribbon from behind my back and lay it on her midsection.

Ruth sees them and laughs. "How?" she asks in a weak voice.

"I've been growing them in my room. I was planning to spring them on you at New Year's."

"Gonna propose again?"

I blush. "I wish I hadn't given up so easily the first time."

I take her hand. We sit without speaking, listening to the beeps and whirrs and chirps of the various devices monitoring Ruth's condition. They'll likely move her to the medical wing shortly, as they did with Carl, and Barbara before him, and Spencer before her. The turning of the leaves. This may be one of my last chances to sit with her.

After a moment, Ruth speaks in a whisper. "Why did they make us?"

It's a question I ask myself every day. "Because they could, I guess," I say. "They wanted to see if it could work."

"Did it?"

I don't know how to answer. A scientist would probably say no. We fell to pieces like cheap knockoffs while our twins grew strong and flourished. Surely we weren't what they hoped.

We are people, though. We walk, talk, and breathe. We tell jokes and have favorite books, movies, and television shows. We are joyful, sad, thoughtful, shy, confident, and insecure. We fear dying.

We love.

"It worked," I say. "We're too awesome to be ignored."

She smiles. "It would have been fun."

"What's that?"

"You and me. Running away. I would have liked that."

"I would have liked it, too."

"I wish there were more time," Ruth says in a whisper. "I didn't see it until now. You always knew, but I didn't see."

The nurse comes in and asks me to leave. I wipe a tear from Ruth's cheek with my thumb and look into her eyes. She is falling back to sleep. The nurse will soon give her medication, and Ruth will sink deeper into her slumber.

I lean in and kiss Ruth on the cheek. I wonder if she feels it, if she wishes I had done it long before. If I'll ever be able to do it again.

#

It snowed last night. The campus sleeps under a thin blanket of white. I remember a time when there were many visitors here, especially on the second Saturday, the day the twins came. Snow meant shoveled walkways, meandering footprints, snow angels. A landscape of traces.

It is late morning on visiting day, and the snow is undisturbed. Nobody comes anymore. The twins. The parents. Even some of the doctors and staff seem to have slipped away. It is as if this entire place is being forgotten.

I am waiting for one visitor. A twin usually comes once or twice after one of us dies, presumably for a final examination and interview. Ruth's twin should have arrived already, but I'm holding out hope that she is running late. Maybe the snow delayed their trip.

The door behind me opens and closes. I hear footsteps but do not turn around. After a moment, I see Dr. Valerie's reflection in the glass. She looks out the window beside me.

"It's beautiful, isn't it?" she says.

"They don't shovel the walk anymore," I say.

"Oh. They must have forgotten."

We stare out the window in silence. She seems uncomfortable, fidgeting with her blouse, shuffling her feet. She wants to talk: about Ruth, about Carl, about my being the only one left. I'm not giving her an opening.

There is movement at the far end of the campus. I see two figures walking toward the building, leaving a trail of footprints in their wake.

It's her.

She walks with her mother, bundled in snow boots, dark jeans and a black ski jacket that falls below her waist. A white knit cap covers the long, tight black curls of her hair. I can see her face as she draws closer. Her skin is dark brown and smooth. Her pink lips shine with gloss. Her brown eyes dance as she jokes with her mother beside her.

Not brown. Amber. Almost like butterscotch.

"Such a lovely girl," Dr. Valerie says. "Smart, too. Just like Ruth."

"What's her name?" I ask.

"Oliver, you know I can't tell you that."

I turn to Dr. Valerie. "They don't look up."

"What?"

"The twins and their parents. None of them ever look up. I used to stand here and wait for one of them, any of them, to glance up and make eye contact. But they never have."

"Well, why would they?"

"I would be curious," I say. "If there were a person out there that looked just like my kid, that had my DNA, I would want to see them. Even if I didn't want them, I'd still take a look. I wouldn't be able to resist."

"Is there a question here?"

"I want to meet them."

Dr. Valerie and I watch one another. I've known her my whole life. She is the doctor who cares about us, the one who listens to our problems and tells us everything will be alright. She treats us with warmth, love, compassion.

Except for now. The look on Dr. Valerie's face as she stares at me is one of suspicion.

"Isn't the home we've given you enough?" she asks.

"This?" I wave my arms around the common room. "You call this a home? We're stuck inside all day. We go out for an hour of exercise. You know what that sounds like?"

"Oliver ..."

"Prison!"

"This is the best place for you," she says. "Your immune system isn't equipped to handle contact with outsiders."

"That should be our choice!" It occurs to me that I keep referring to myself as a plural. *We.* As if there were anyone else left. "Just tell my parents I want to meet them. I'm not asking for them to take me home with them or anything. I just want to speak with them."

"It's not possible."

"Why?"

"You know why. You have to know by now."

"I want to hear you say it," I say, stepping closer to her. "Why can't I meet my family?"

"It's so easy to demonize if you don't look at the benefits," she says. "Healthy clone cells can end heart disease, paralysis, genetic disorders. So many sick people would have a chance to be better."

"Why?"

"There are some who believe cloning technology holds the secret to stopping the aging process. Can you imagine? Never growing old?"

"If anyone can imagine what that's like, it's me," I say.

Dr. Valerie's face hardens. "They don't know, Oliver. Nobody knows. And nobody will."

I hear Ruth's voice in my mind. *Told you.*

The parents signed up for some random experiment. They received money and assurance that their children wouldn't be hurt in any way. They never learned what was done with the DNA taken from their babies.

"You had no right to do this to us," I say.

"You helped us learn," she says. "Next time it will be better. You've made humanity better."

Next time. As if eleven dead children are nothing more than an easily corrected typo, a flubbed line, a misplaced decimal point. As if there is a quick, easy remedy for our mourning, our suffering, our isolation.

Once I'm gone, they'll find new parents, new genomes to steal from embryos, new surrogates willing to carry them for a paycheck. A new set of clones will hatch.

I hope it is better for them.

"I've got an appointment downstairs," she says. "I'll check back later. Try to get some rest."

I turn back to the window as she walks away. She'll pretend this discussion never happened the next time she visits. It's easier to act as if this is normal, that locking sick children away in a prison disguised as a laboratory is a normal existence.

Ruth's twin has disappeared into the entrance below. Mine will be along before long. I've watched them pass one another on the path more times than I can count. They've never so much as glanced at one another.

I think of my fantasy about our twins being neighbors, classmates, even friends. I imagine their eyes meeting as they pass near the entrance. They'll stop and talk. They'll wonder at how they never noticed one another here at the lab before. They'll gossip about friends and teachers. They'll smile and laugh.

They will hold hands.

They will walk down the path leading away from the lab together.

And nobody will stop them.

See Gregory Kane's story "Twins" online at Metaphorosis.
If you liked it, leave a comment. Authors love that!
Remember to subscribe to our e-mail updates so you'll know when new stories are posted.

About the story

The inspiration for "Twins" came from a discussion with my Biology students about Dolly the sheep. She made headlines in the late 1990s when scientists cloned her using a process called somatic cell nuclear transfer. Basically, DNA was taken from a body cell in a living sheep, placed in an empty egg cell and carried to term by a surrogate. Many students were surprised to learn that she and other cloned animals that followed often suffered early deaths compared to their "twins." My students wondered if it was fair to create an animal if the research suggested an abbreviated life of illness.

I decided to write a story from the perspective of human clone teenagers. How would it feel to have perfectly healthy twins with normal lives and normal families while the clones watch one another dying in a laboratory? Would they be angry? Sad? Jealous? Would they long for a family and connections outside their confinement? As I began writing, I quickly discovered my main character suffered from an affliction common among all teenagers: he was lovesick. My narrative about children engineered by science was actually a love story.

"Twins" allowed me to look at the potential pitfalls of scientific experimentation as we enter an era of infinite possibilities. Human cloning, after all, isn't a theoretical concept. It could be done today if it were deemed ethically responsible. The story created an opportunity to explore how humanity and science can often intersect, sometimes with unfortunate consequences.

A question for the author

Q: What is your favorite short story?

A: My favorite of the classics is Ray Bradbury's "There Will Come Soft Rains." The tale of a robotic household going about its daily routine after humanity has been decimated by an atomic bomb remains one of literature's great cautionary tales. My favorite contemporary story is Ted Chiang's "Tower of Babylon", a dreamy tale of the construction of a tower that reaches the heavens. I love this story for its surreal style and its mind-bending ending, which carries a strong message about human endeavor.

About the author

Gregory Kane teaches high school science outside Philadelphia, where he lives with his wife and daughter. He writes fiction and brews beer when he is not in the classroom. He believes Ray Bradbury's face should be on a form of U.S. currency.

gregoryakane.wordpress.com, @GregoryAKane

The Astronaut Tier

Jonathan Laidlow

Farren opened the door to the bailiffs and let them in. They pushed into the apartment wordlessly, and began to itemise her former life, ticking boxes on clipboards while they opened drawers and rifled shelves. The last to enter was a wiry middle-aged woman who, with a kind smile, invited Farren to sign, thus demonstrating her understanding that her possessions were now the property of Ares II's creditors.

She asked if the coffee in the pot also now belonged to the creditors.

"The coffee?" the officious lady replied. "No. Drink it up, hon. We'll take the pot when you're done."

Farren filled her mug and then added her signature. It was just another piece of paper; she'd signed so many for Ares II, what was one more?

Everything the bailiffs touched, they colonised. The framed prints of movie posters for *Apollo 13* and *The Martian* had belonged to a different Farren, an earlier version, and so giving them up felt like nothing at all.

The coffee had stewed, so she left it. *Let them have the dirty mug.* She picked up the holdall containing those personal items she was permitted to keep, then stopped to allow the boss-lady to rifle through it. On command, she emptied her pockets.

They patted her down and questioned her about the phone, registered to her brother, and the key to the car owned by her mother. They confiscated her old cassette Walkman with its headphones and her box of mixtapes. The male bailiff said, "Vintage! You were cool, lady." He wrapped it carefully in bubble-wrap and added it to a box.

The clothes and toiletries in her bag seemed to pass whatever test this had become. Or maybe she had failed, and just hadn't realised. She waited for them to manhandle the television out into their van, then stepped outside.

She had been renting the apartment for a few years prior to Ares, so she was surprised to feel nothing as she handed over the key. It should have felt more like home, but then nothing did anymore.

The battered Ford was parked down the hill, along the old dry-stone wall of the village post office. She hoped they'd watch her go and think well of her, saying to each other, "Didn't cry, didn't beg or try to smuggle her shit out. That's how you get repossessed with style. Classy."

She stifled a sob on the steering wheel. How had she come from the dome in Australia to being homeless in the north of England?

She recovered herself enough to start the engine and pull out into the road. In the rear-view mirror, she could see the repo boss-lady standing on top of the hill. She couldn't see her former home, and for that she was thankful.

#

Farren's mum had encouraged her to sell all her belongings to friends and family rather than let them be taken, but that wasn't how it worked. The bailiffs would have argued she didn't have the right to sell them, then sued her friends to recover them.

The car from her mother had been an act of kindness, as had the phone from her brother. Not so long ago, in the dome, she would have rejected their attempts to buy back her love. Now she was just happy to have a place to go. She set off to her mother's house, and turned on the radio.

She listened to a call-in show as she drove. The topic was the Ares II project. Most listeners couldn't understand how anyone had believed that a crowd-funded mission to land on Mars was possible, or worth joining. Farren understood, though.

A caller from Exeter said that the Ares people — people like Farren — were despicable, and had joined the project knowingly. Farren snorted at the absurdity, inviting the radio to look around at her worldly possessions and then tell her she was a devious bitch who'd known exactly what she was getting into. She turned the radio off in anger, then immediately turned it back on.

An internet caller from Missouri opined that the cover-up was massive, and went as high as the 'Secret World Government'. "Well I thank you for your charitable thoughts, mister!" Farren said aloud to the empty car. Every day of her life before she joined Areas had felt like she was slowly being poisoned, and so she forced herself to listen every day, to try to understand whether it was all a lie.

The presenter interrupted the callers to go live to the siege in the Australian desert. Nothing had happened, or changed. It was wasted airtime, really. They must surely be getting tired of Ares II by day forty?

Farren braked to avoid a rogue sheep. It was drawn and frail, and stumbled off the tarmac slowly. She slowed again to clatter over the cattle grid and then accelerated up the hill and onto the fells. They had always been desolate, but the blight made everything far worse. There were patches of lifeless soil where once there had been gorse.

The phone rang, so she drew to a halt and flipped it open, saw that it was her brother, and answered.

"Jeff, hi. Yeah. Just gone. On my way to see Mum, taking the shortcut over the fells."

They talked for a few minutes, but everything he said felt like a platitude that she'd already heard. Jeff's voice crackled as the signal degraded and eventually she dropped the phone onto the passenger seat and set off again, concentrating on making each turn as the road meandered its way up, round and over the mountain. She regretted not listening to the end of the phone-in, no matter how infuriating it would have been.

It was dark when she crossed the cattle grid on the other side and entered the village where her mother lived. The old Ford spluttered as she changed into first gear and she felt a pang of concern as she manoeuvred it tightly into a space near her mum's Land Rover. The car was her home now, she thought.

Farren let herself in and found her mother in front of the television, watching the latest rolling updates from the dome. It was one thing for Farren to listen and watch obsessively – she had been there, been part of Ares – it was quite another for her own mother to gawk.

"Mum!" she said, "Can't we just live for five minutes without seeing what those cretins are saying?"

Her mum raised her eyebrows, then got up and kissed Farren on the cheek, asking in her soft Geordie accent, "Tea, pet?"

While the sixty-year old bustled around the kitchen, Farren turned off the sound on the television. Her mother returned with two mugs and a plate of biscuits.

"Did you ever meet that Director fella, the one with the beard and the sexy voice?"

"Mum."

She had indeed met Doyle, repeatedly. Once her application to join the project had been accepted, she had been invited to pay for a seminar where Doyle had talked about the desert installation and the crew preparing to simulate life on Mars there. After that she was invited, for another fee, to an exclusive testing event where the crew for the second training and evaluation installation was to be chosen. She'd lived in the Martian simulation dome for three months, learning hydroponics, basic engineering, agriculture, and how to handle space technology. She was supposed to be in Alaska now, for another fee, of course. Her contributions had raised her to the Astronaut Tier.

In keeping with the crowd-sourcing ethos of the project, Doyle had pitched in with the recruits and sponsors. He spent weeks in the dome, venturing outside only to attend to corporate business, procurement meetings with companies like Lockheed and Virgin Galactic, and the like. She'd come to think of him as a mentor: he'd often taken the same work details as her, and her posting in the Vacuum Survival team had meant they worked side by side. Her mum might have thought he was dishy, but Farren's relationship with him had always been purely professional. What she'd admired had been his leadership of the project, and what she'd really approved of had been his vision of the people bootstrapping themselves into space, independent of national interests.

Farren thought the harassment charges were trumped up, and the warrant for his arrest a case of blatant Assangeing.

The biscuits were home-cooked, the tea reassuring. Mum filled her in on her cousins and the various illnesses of her aunts and uncles. Farren responded with innocuous childhood memories of the cousins — once, twice, and thrice removed — whom she barely knew as adults.

The coverage of Ares II moved to aerial shots of the compound, then studio discussion of the fire and the first shootout. Farren picked up the remote and turned on the subtitles. The fire was at the mysterious silver 'doughnut' building. She'd never had clearance. You had to be on the Mission Specialist Tier to get inside there. They cut to an investigative journalist, with shots of the Alaskan compound, unfinished and deserted. There was another silver structure, this one incomplete, and federal investigators were shown climbing over the half-built walls with clipboards and flashlights.

While her mum droned on and on about the medical complications currently affecting Uncle Somebody-Or-Other, Farren took stock. She had been convinced that six months in the cold in a simulated space habitat would eventually take her off-world. Instead, she was back in her mother's house and the country she'd been trying to leave since she was a child.

A British scientist came on screen to offer an expert viewpoint. She explained that the designs for the interplanetary vehicle that, it now transpired, had never been constructed, were fundamentally flawed, and the craft would have killed every astronaut upon take-off if they'd ever had the funds to build it. The money taken from "Martianauts" like Farren had vanished, and now they were liable for Ares' debts through some quirk of their contracts. Doyle had been in regular contact with everyone in the group right up until the media exposé and the ensuing raids. Would he get back in touch?

She heard the back door, then her brother's voice, "Hello! Fozzy Bear here yet?"

"I'm here, Juicy," she called back. Then, "Why are you bothering your dear old mum on this fine northern evening?"

Jeff stood in the doorway, rain dripping from his long white hair. "Are you having a laugh?" he replied. "Looking for my poor destitute sister, I'll have you know!"

He sat down, and let Mum scurry around making more tea. Jeff was older by three years. He'd never been a particularly protective sibling, offering her wisdom and perspective when she needed it, but never rushing to impose. He had, however, been strongly opposed to Ares II. He'd identified with their goals, but hated their secrecy and the personality cult that followed Doyle everywhere. He had scoffed when she talked about making the application, and refused to help out when she made the personal video required of all applicants. He'd said that space travel was not a TV-talent show, nor should anyone sell the rights to such a programme. As she gradually got more involved with the meetings and the levels, they had clashed repeatedly, and eventually ceased to speak.

Since the day she'd called him from LAX and begged for help to get home, Jeff had treated her with kid gloves, helping where he could, like getting the phone, and he'd looked after her flat all that time she was away. Now he offered more assistance.

"If you don't want to stay here, you can come over and take our couch, sis."

He owned a bungalow with his wife in the village. It was cramped with the two children, but had always felt like a refuge to Farren. Even when they weren't speaking, she'd visited her nieces and hung out with Sara. It felt like home. But it wasn't, and the thought of living in the same village as Mum and everybody they had grown up with filled her with dread. Sleeping in the astronaut bunks in the cool filtered air of the dome had been much more soothing.

She needed to go, to go far away. If not Mars, then as far as she could manage. She jangled the keys of the Ford in her pocket.

"I'll stay here tonight, and maybe come see you tomorrow, but after that I'm out of here. The roads are safe again, apparently, and Mum gave me wheels, so..."

"Well my couch-a is your couch-a," he said, with a smile that was really concern. "Oh hey, did you see this?" He brandished a printout. Jeff thought of himself as an old school "white knight," and he was always trying to hack things, discover what was behind the encryption. "Somebody from Ares has something going on. It hasn't leaked yet; I just track these things."

"Geek," she said, and took the paper he held out. A photograph: black and white, grainy. A satellite image, maybe. The rocks and grassland of what had to be a British valley. Standing in the rain, a bulky ex-NASA spacesuit reaching down into a stream. The name DOYLE was spelled out in the font they'd all voted for when crowdsourcing everything was a novelty. Farren had even attached the nameplate to that suit.

#

Farren spent a few more days at her mother's house and allowed her to fuss, which meant that she received many cups of tea and frequent homilies on finding a good job and making no more trouble.

Embarrassed but not yet ready to talk, she ventured out to the library to use a public and anonymous internet connection. After setting up a temporary encrypted node, she ran the background on the satellite photo through a series of image searches, cross referencing against open access geo-location directories. Eventually she had some GPS coordinates: an anonymous valley in Yorkshire. This was do-able. The exact spot was off-road, but she could take the car as far as it would go and then hike the rest if she had to. She deserved an explanation. She had been travelling between the Australian dome and the Alaskan bunker when her ticket had been cancelled with no explanation. She had been stranded in LA, watching the authorities move on the compound on the airport lounge TV. And now this. Was the mission still on?

She drove to the supermarket and filled the boot of the car with dried and canned food, a cheap sleeping bag, a tent, and lots of bottled water. She charged it to Jeff and promised to pay him back. She didn't tell him what it was for, but over the phone she just said, "Doyle". She hoped the line wasn't bugged, but her brother had always been good at end-to-end crypto.

She lit out before dawn, heading for the A66 and Newcastle instead of the more direct route to Yorkshire. She had a reputation for aggressive driving, so she deliberately drove like her instructor had wanted her to, like Jeff the family man, so that she wasn't pulled over.

There was a service area that looked down on the River Tyne and the burned-out ruins of Newcastle, so she stopped to rest. She'd seen no obvious signs that she had a tail, and she didn't think a drone would have the range to follow her. If they had enough clout to use satellite tracking, well, there was nothing she could do about it. She wasn't sure whether the bailiffs would pursue her for money, or leads on Doyle. Some people thought the repo company had been working for the government, and it was odd that the British authorities hadn't yet questioned her.

She called Jeff, just to make sure he'd talked to Mum. After pleasantries and reassurance that Mum knew she was safe, he said, "There was a bit more on the Darknet. Conspiracy nuts, to be fair, but there's a buzz about Doyle, so be careful." Then, "Did you know they had guns, Fozz?"

"Don't be silly. I was gonna be an astronaut, not a space marine!" she laughed.

Of course, they'd all had weapons training: daily target practice in the secret caves under the dome and weekly asymmetrical tactical response through the arable zones. She wanted to tell him, but the words would not come. There were no words for the way Ares II had changed her life.

"If you need me — I'm sending a digital key — you can get a message to me without being traced. Use it if you have to." She laughed it off, but he sent the key anyway. She memorised it, certain she wouldn't need it.

She looked down on the quarantined ruins of the city, desolate but no longer burning. The daily radiation forecast had been constant throughout her childhood: the blight that threw the country into recession had started here. The eventual clampdown, evacuation, and quarantine had brought the first realisation that she needed to escape.

She ate, drank, and then set off for Yorkshire, without looking back. A couple of hours later, she ran out of road. The GPS had taken her to abandoned grazing fields, but the location lay ahead, so she opened the gate and drove on.

It was a dull and overcast afternoon and the thin grass was slick with rain. Several times she lost control of the little car, churning up the wet soil and sliding down the valley, but she got further than she thought she would, and she only abandoned it when she reached the stream, with just half a mile to go.

She put on her pair of wellingtons, then locked the car and waded into the stream, splashing against the current. It wasn't deep, and she remembered paddling in the rock pools at Allonby with Jeff when she was a kid and the world was very different. Before the accident at the Scottish nuclear site, before the blight, before Ares II promised her a beginning on another planet.

She rounded the corner and there it was: the spacesuit, walking in the water about a hundred yards in front of her, just as in the photograph. It seemed to be digging or fishing for something under the water. On the other side of the bank she saw a mixture of tents, mobile homes and Winnebagos, all clustered around a long silver caravan. All around her she could feel and hear a throbbing hum, emanating from that last caravan. A sequence of five thunderous pulsations startled her, but she kept on walking.

"Doyle?" she said to the spacesuit.

It wobbled slowly to face her, moving like astronauts in the old footage from the Moon landings. She'd worn one like that and knew how heavy it was under normal gravity. It was one of the ex-NASA designs that she'd worked with at the training camp. It raised its hand, wielding a soil-sampling tool, but she could not find it threatening; her training told her it was meant for low or zero gravity and she could easily outrun it.

"Doyle?" she said again, then, "What the hell, man?"

The gold mirrored-visor retracted and a woman stared back at her from Doyle's spacesuit. She had short dreadlocks and her face was decorated with tattoos. Everyone in Australia had been so well groomed, clean-cut, so *Right Stuff*. Who was this and why was Doyle allowing her to do Farren's job?

"What the fuck is going on here? Where is Doyle?"

Then they were all around her, pointing weapons.

She carefully raised her hands. Behind them, she caught sight of her bearded leader stepping out of one of the caravans.

#

They locked Farren in a camper-van that was joined to the silver thing by a thick trunk of cabling. The motley group all displayed a similar fervour, ignoring her demands for an explanation, but speaking calmly among themselves, as though there was a secret they all shared. She recognised one of them: a guy called Caspian whom she'd always dismissed as a hipster. She'd never hung out with him because he had only reached one of the lower technical tiers. She was outraged that he was here.

Doyle acknowledged her with a nod as they led her past, as if to tell them she was a fellow traveller, potentially a co-conspirator. His hair, once groomed, was long and ragged. His face was lined, but it was still the kind of face that won over investors; the kind that attracted followers and disciples.

The camp was a far cry from the polished Ares compounds and domes. The collection of battered vehicles and aged habitats bore no relation to the branded and logo-ed equipment in the desert. Those had all been leased, she now knew from the exposé on the news. Furthermore, the scientists on TV had said there'd have been no way to lift so much mass into orbit. They had claimed that all those items of equipment were just props to fool investors and members.

The valley was barren, the grass short and blighted, just like her mum's home on the other coast.

The hum of the silver caravan was audible inside the camper-van and it made her restless, particularly the thundering, which cycled every twenty minutes. She paced, then sat on the uncomfortable sofa, and then paced some more. Her phone had no signal. Either they were in a coverage dead-zone, or the cell towers had been disabled somehow. There was one last message from Jeff on there: "Fozz. Bailiffs came for Mum's house. Some legal shenanigans about the proceeds of crime, but it's nonsense. We're on it, stay safe."

She felt bad for her mother's house, but it hadn't been where she felt at home for a very long time.

#

Doyle came to her a few hours later. He wore an ex-NASA one-piece and seemed older, haggard, dirty. *He used to wear such sharp suits,* she thought.

"Farren. How did you find us?" he said.

She lost her composure and snapped, "Where did you go? What did you do to my life? I was on my way to Alaska when the ticket was cancelled. I had to call my family, do you know how humiliating that was?"

He stepped back and chuckled, looking at her with the coldest of eyes. "The mission is more important than any of us. We taught you that. The doubters are trying to take everything."

"You bastard," she said in disbelief. "It was all a lie, all the money's gone and now they're going through our accounts to get it back. Did you know that?"

He sat down and pulled out a hip flask. She shook her head but he waited until eventually she took it and gulped down the cheap vodka.

"It's something else, Farren. Something important. That thing outside — we couldn't tell anyone."

"So what is it?" she retorted.

"I can't tell you, yet. Stay with us. Become one of us again and then you'll find out. Trust me."

"Again? Sod off."

"Think about it. You were one of our very best. But you only made it as far as the Astronaut Tier." She fumed, for Astronaut was the most prestigious level available to the recruits and she had struggled in every way to reach it. Ares II had woken a need in her, and when its promise to meet that need had proved to be false she'd been left empty and desperate.

Doyle's offer scratched that itch. She wanted to leave this blighted land behind, but talking to Doyle reminded her of how much she'd enjoyed being part of something bigger than herself. Of how good it felt to be in the inner circle instead of out in the cold. Now she could be again. He added one last temptation. "Work with us here and you could join the *European Tier,*" he said, and his smug smile showed that he knew she would find another level impossible to resist.

She slept fitfully, and then, in the morning, Caspian unlocked the door and invited her to join them on a scavenging trip. Seeing him made Farren sick with jealousy, sick that she was now excluded from something to which he still belonged, and so she meekly went with him and played her part.

#

She worked with Doyle's crew for a week. They foraged supplies from some of the abandoned farms near the valley, then she helped to check the cabling that ran to the mysterious silver trailer. The tasks she'd completed at astronaut camp in Australia proved vital, for she knew how to maintain machines that she didn't really understand. Once, NASA had trained scientists and pilots to live and work in space. Farren wondered whether the lunar astronauts had learned their systems by rote just as she had in the desert.

They were supervised by a watchful older woman with a shaven head and a doctorate – possibly two — named Professor Curtis. She barely acknowledged Farren. Their only conversation was when she demanded Farren's phone. Farren handed it over without a word, or a thought for Jeff or Mum.

Caspian knew little more than Farren, but he shared water, showed her the supplies, and helped her make friends with some of the others. After a few nights, she was welcomed around the campfire for a sing-song, where every melody tried to incorporate the rhythm of the mysterious machine. She found that the others had all worked at different locations and had risen to different levels based on their abilities and their funds. None had risen to as high a tier as Farren and yet here they were. At first, she felt heartbroken that Doyle had invited them onto this new, secret, and exclusive tier, but not her. Then she made it her goal to achieve it herself.

Curtis and Doyle were thick as thieves, but Doyle didn't speak to Farren much. He nodded as he passed, sometimes clasping her shoulder or arm. She wished he wouldn't treat her like his love-struck ex-girlfriend. She didn't feel that her behaviour warranted it, and she didn't want the others thinking they'd ever had a relationship of that nature. It cheapened her, and she was quickly coming to believe in the mission again. It felt right, as it had before. Whatever it was.

Vehicles better equipped for the terrain arrived in the night, driven by the girl with the tattooed face, and then they spent time joining three more silver trailers to the first, until eventually they had a doughnut like the one in Australia. Some began calling it the 'toroid' but Curtis referred to it simply as the Engine, and that was the name that stuck.

They moved into a new phase of testing, and Farren started to show them how adept at such work she had become at the habitat in the desert. They might have been in a north Yorkshire wasteland, but it stood in for a hostile space environment quite acceptably. She ran tests with a battered old laptop and found that the suits still held their oxygen, their heating and cooling systems were nominal, and their radiation shielding intact. The laptop was the type they'd used in the dome, encased in thick rubber and allegedly vacuum-proof.

A few days later, Curtis walked stiffly from her Winnebago to the fire and said, "We begin a new phase of the project tomorrow." As she turned to leave, she took Farren to one side and told her, "Doyle is really proud of how you've joined us. He wanted me to give this back to you." She handed back the cellphone, fully charged. It had even miraculously found a signal.

The phone wouldn't ring out, but then she wasn't sure whether this was a test, and she did not want to break their trust. Nevertheless, she hooked it up to the laptop and used the data connection to scour the net for news about Australia.

The siege was over. Many members were dead, imprisoned or in hiding. The authorities across the globe continued to swoop on the poor idiots, like her, who'd funded and joined what they were now describing as a 'terrorist space cult'. There were lurid claims of orbital weapons platforms and blackmail demands.

There had also been more raids on the families of members, and while there was no news of Mum and Jeff, she shivered at footage of bailiffs in black SUVs breaking down doors and confiscating belongings. What had Ares II done that was so wrong? They had only dreamed of taking the solar system for people, not governments. The idea that someone as ordinary as Farren could have been one of the first to colonise a new world had driven her this far and she realised that her own commitment was more important than ever, now that the state machinery was painting them as criminals and closing them down. Farren felt newly wedded to her cause, zealous to find out what they were working towards. Did they still have a secret launch site somewhere? She hoped they did.

#

Doyle drove into the valley at six with a trailer of cables. He instructed his followers to run them through the camp to a series of outlets on the Engine, and Farren finally caught a glimpse inside the main silver caravan.

The interior was lined with mirrors, and so she saw a vertigo-inducing reflection. The dizzy sensation reminded her of zero-gravity training in the Ares II jet. She had been humbled by the reality of it, as though before she had been somehow lacking in substance.

They had cleared the rocks and flattened out the ground about a hundred yards from the Engine, and they laid the cables to that area. Curtis brought out one final piece of equipment, something none of them had seen before.

It was a semi-circular object, also mirrored, about two metres in diameter and a foot tall, lashed to a standard British power in/out setup with brown parcel tape. It winked and glistened with curious lights. Looking at it induced the same sense of queasy inversion that she'd felt earlier, so she put her head down and resumed work on the power and data lines.

#

Once the cables were laid and connected, Doyle and Curtis began to test them with a laptop hooked up to the generator.

The early evening brought drizzle, and the two leaders worked on in the rain. Farren sat around the fire with the others. There was no more camaraderie, no more singing. "The Engine has stopped," she said eventually. It was true, but nobody reacted except Caspian, who got up and walked back to his tent.

Doyle joined them and ordered Farren to accompany him to his Winnebago. She obeyed without question. Perhaps it was time to join the European Tier, she thought.

As they walked, he called for Caspian and the three of them went inside. Two of the spacesuits were laid out ready, and she helped Doyle into the bulky and dirty NASA suit. She had personally ensured its viability and she was pleased that he respected her talents. "Help Farren into the second unit," Doyle said to Caspian, and she glowed in the warmth of Doyle's approval.

Caspian lowered the helmet over her head and leaned in. "Don't worry," he whispered. They stumbled carefully back outside and waddled slowly to where Curtis waited with one of the laptops and the new machine.

Curtis pressed a key on the laptop. The air above the new device began to shimmer, to flicker, like an old television set. Farren saw herself reflected in the static, a great, galumphing, mouldy, off-white lummox, outlined in the snowstorm of white noise. The hum and the banging returned, and it sounded as though someone were knocking at a door.

She gazed at her image, transfixed, for she was both subject and object. Then Doyle walked straight past and into the distortion field.

He vanished.

And then the grey sky lit up as though it was morning. She gazed upwards and it was filled with silent black drones, like airborne spiders, hovering over the camp, their spotlights illuminating everything. Sirens began to wail and she saw black uniforms sweep down into the valley, torches wavering as they made their way over the uneven ground. In the lead she thought she saw the officious lady who had accompanied the bailiffs.

Professor Curtis abandoned Farren and Caspian, leaving them by the laptop. Farren grabbed his wrist awkwardly and said, "Open me a link to this location," and reeled off Jeff's key. Caspian quickly entered it on the laptop.

The connection opened and she snatched the computer, activated the oxygen regulator on her suit and stepped into the white noise after Doyle, trailing data and power cables behind her. It was the only thing left she could do.

She closed her eyes as she pushed through her distorted other. It felt as though she had lost her balance, as though she were stuck in the moment just before falling.

Then she was through, staggering to regain her footing on unfamiliar ground. She opened her eyes and blinked in disbelief. She felt lighter, sensed the heater in her suit kick in, and heard the radiation monitor beeping furiously.

At her feet, strange red and grey rocks on a vast expanse of ice, glistening in the light. To her left, Doyle. He stood still, swaying unsteadily. Dominating the horizon were the coloured stripes of Jupiter, the great red storm-spot visible just on the edge of the skyline, seeming only a few miles walk along the icy wasteland in front of her, but in actuality thousands of miles away. The sun was a bright star in a black sky.

She trigged her radio and found Doyle praying. She had not realised he had any spiritual impetus. Ares II had been her own sole authority, yet now that they were millions of miles further than Mars, Jupiter's shadow seemed a far higher god.

After the prayer he said, "I lied, Farren, it's not the European Tier, it's the Europa Tier, the highest level a member can reach."

"So Ares II was always a cover story?" she replied. "That's amazing! We're in space, Doyle, space!" She was so happy she began to cry. *It was all possible, she could leave it all behind.*

He turned to her, huffing and puffing as he adjusted to the ultra-light gravity, a tenth of that back home. "That's right," he said. "Our hackers found the plans for the Engine in an old Soviet dossier. They cross-referenced it with NASA, and that's what we spent the money on. The theoretical stuff is all good and that's why we think they shut us down."

"So... We were never going to Mars." Comprehension set in. It didn't matter where they went in the solar system, just that they were going. It would be impossible to stop them now.

"That's correct. A Jovian satellite! Europa. We can open up the outer planets."

Farren started to laugh. "They really had no idea what you were doing? This is brilliant."

"So much better than Mars," he added.

"Absolutely." She wanted to caper and dance, impossible though it was in the spacesuit. She felt vindicated and justified. It was all worth it.

Doyle said, "Just think what we can sell this for! Portal technology. Can you believe it?"

Farren thought she had misheard. *What we can sell this for?* As she realised what he had said, she felt a lump rising in her throat. She looked at him and all she could think about was the wasted time in the desert, the fundraising, the selection videos, losing everything, her mum's house, the police swarming into the valley — the sacrifices she had made to make space travel possible for herself and other futureless people.

"Sell? What about opening up the planets for humanity? What about the crowd-sourced dream?"

He laughed and his teeth chattered. Their gear was old, and she wasn't sure it was rated for these radiation levels. Red warning lights blinked on Doyle's chest panel.

"Come on, Farren. We can get all the money back. Look at what we've done! It's the Jupiter system! The water on Europa alone can provide oxygen and fuel to keep exploring further. We'll be the richest people alive. The Feds out there? I called them. You and I are only here because I wanted to be the first man in the Jovian system."

"You called them?" she spat back at him. "I thought they followed me. Why would you contact them after everything they've done to us?"

"You're the first woman on Europa, Farren. Think of what that will be worth. They can't arrest us now. We're already celebrities."

The laptop was still in her hand, and despite all of her doubts, its space-proofing seemed to have worked, for the data and power were still live. She roughly pushed at the keys until she hit enter, opening the stream to Jeff. She hoped he'd be able to take any plans and files from the laptop, and then she dropped it and ran at Doyle.

She ran as fast as anyone can in a spacesuit, and bowled him over. The burst of activity set off every warning light and alarm on both their suits. Leaning on top of him, she picked up a rock.

"I believed in this, you monster. You made me believe in this. How can you fucking sell it?" She slammed the rock down, smashing it into her reflection on the golden visor until it cracked, and he grew still.

She struggled off him and sat down, her back to the beautiful gas giant. She looked at the iridescent portal. Should she go back? Or wait for them to follow? How many more spacesuits did they have? How long before they came through and spread out to the stars? Which government would be the first, and would they care that she'd marked their discovery with a blood sacrifice? She doubted it. Her only hope was that Jeff would find the plans and do a Snowden with them. Otherwise the solar system would become everything she hated about Earth.

All strength left her. She turned, feeling cold as her suit began to fail, and marvelled at the landscape before her. The barren icebound surface of Europa was like nothing she had trained for, and yet it was everything she needed. She walked carefully and slowly across the white expanse toward the horizon and Jupiter's watchful eye, leaving Doyle's body and the portal far behind.

See Jonathan Laidlow's story "The Astronaut Tier" online at Metaphorosis.
If you liked it, leave a comment. Authors love that!
Remember to subscribe to our e-mail updates so you'll know when new stories are posted.

About the story

"The Astronaut Tier" began life as a story called "Flailing", written for a challenge on the sffworld forums in 2015 with the theme of "surprises in desolate places". I remember I immediately had the image of a blighted Britain, but it took a little longer to find the main theme of the story, which was the Mars One project- a Dutch organisation which was looking for future astronauts not through expertise in astronautics but through social media. Around that time I saw the brilliant film about a woman in a cult, *Martha Marcy May Marlene*, starring Elizabeth Olsen and John Hawkes, and read Paul McAuley's superb novel *The Quiet War* about the opening up of the solar system. I wanted to take these elements - crowdfunding the exploration of the solar system and cult dynamics and tell the story through Farren's strength and agency.

A question for the author

Q: What's a typical writing day like for you?

A: This is the dream of the typical writing day: I rise late and drink good strong coffee while looking back through the previous day's draft. I then spend the day adding new words to my latest story and they're all perfect. The reality is somewhat different. I try to read the previous day's draft either over a hurried coffee or on my commute to the office. At lunch I find a quiet spot to sit with my laptop and write. Sometimes I'm working on a story, but a lot of the time I'm doodling with words. I keep the writers' equivalent of a sketchbook and fill it with story fragments, ideas and scenes. You never know when you'll find a nugget of gold in there that turns into a story or a novel. Writing at lunch takes the pressure off, so by the evening I look at the current project. I usually revise the previous day's words before I add new ones. Sometimes I have to go all the way to the beginning to seed new information and events, so I'm constantly revising as well as adding new material. I like to call this writing method "looping revisionary chaos"....

About the author

Jonathan Laidlow grew up in the northwest of England, near the Sellafield nuclear power plant, which regularly leaked. He has one good leg, one good eye, and one good ear ... He lives in Birmingham, UK. He tweets @burtkenobi and blogs occasionally at jonlaidlow.com.

November

The Little G-d of Łódź

Evan Marcroft

On September 6, 1939, a Rabbi and Kabbalist named Yitzchok Falk sets fire to the Great Synagogue of Łódź. "The Germans will burn it anyway," he tells his apprentice they drag a body out of the trunk of his car. "Let it burn without victims, and for a good reason." The boy, Max, who holds the feet, only nods.

They carry the body in and lay it out in the prayer hall. It is a young man near Max's thirteen years and fifty seven kilos, dressed in his clothes. He died of a broken neck, not of their doing, and was obtained at great cost. From his coat the rabbi produces a rag-corked bottle and a heavy black key, the latter of which he presses into his apprentice's hand. "Everything is yours now," he tells the boy. "Do with it what you will, if you will good. But your life has become a precious resource. Keep it from those who want it and give it to those who need it." His voice breaks under the weight of emotion. "Do not loathe those who loathe you. Just live, Max. We are Jews; we know dark times will pass."

Max buries the key in his fist, but only nods.

He stays long enough to help his adopted father start the fire, touching flame to the parched books in the study hall, dousing the holy ark in petrol. He finds that a Torah scroll smolders with the same smell as any other paper. He escapes as the flames begin to creep towards the rafters, leaving his master to his last act of charity. The gunshot is a raindrop amidst a downpour.

Max flies through cobbled streets until it is safe to stop and catch his breath. Only then does he crumple up and discard his master's final words. There is no room left in his heart for them, for with apologies it is already so full of bile and venom and *hate*.

The key opens the hidden lock of a secret room in his master's house. There, where by lamplight Rabbi Falk taught him of the sefirot and the boustrophedontic Folded Name of G-d, are kept many tomes of ancient Tradition. The *Sodei Razayya*, the *Sefer Yetzirah*, and others more arcane still, illuminated ledgers of demons and angels, books of power, all disguised cleverly in the bindings of Christian bibles. Max takes them all.

The Germans will roll over this place in a matter of days and pave everything, stone and knowledge alike, into a road going east. Same as the synagogue, which would have burned tomorrow if not today. In boot tread and tank tread they will track all that is *jude* across Poland until there is only dust left of it.

But Max knows well there is power in dust.

Seven months later, in the spring of 1940, Max has a new family. The rabbi, ever prescient, made the arrangements for him well before he falsified Max's death. He has a new name; rest in peace, Max Steinberg, and welcome back from abroad cousin Oskar Kac. His aunt and uncle are Monica and Dieter, his little blonde cousin Else, and they live together in a modest house in the Sródmiescie district. They are ethnic German—happily registered *Volksdeutsche*—and they are Christians. Max could not ask for a better place to hide.

It is easy to be Oskar the Christian. In some ways it is an easier life than Max the *judenschwein*. The facets of the faith are not so different from his own. A crucifix is not the worst thing that can be tied around one's neck. His false family are Jewish sympathizers, educated people, and they are very kind to him. They have made sure he is comfortable in their cellar and allow him to eat supper with them. Little Else in particular is a blessing. She is a dim but charming girl who is happy to help Max fill the empty hours when it is too risky to be outside.

And yes, his features are Aryan enough that he can even walk about in broad daylight, so long as he carries his forged papers like he would clutch shut an open wound.

Max may walk free, but he has not escaped the ghetto. Is he supposed to not hear it when the Orpo executes men and women in the streets, or smell the bodies strung up until they rot free of the rope? That pigpen between Inflancka and Drewnoska Street is where his kind is deemed to belong, and at all times he feels its subtle gravity threatening to draw him in if he is not absolutely vigilant.

Yet he is there, watching from the crowd, as the wall is put up around the ghetto. The barrier is a flimsy thing, green wood garnished with barbed wire. The weight of all the bodies behind it would easily bowl it over. And why don't they? There must be thousands of them cramped into a tenth as many rooms turned cells. A universe of yellow stars. The few Germans who strut to and fro outside the fence would be drowned in them.

But those hot, fresh first days where anything could still have happened mature into weeks. More Jews are shipped in from outside the city and poured into the ghetto. What keeps it from rupturing like a full bladder, Max does not know—the Germans are geniuses in the science of cruelty. And still, he watches its occupants shuffle a little closer together, tromping in their own overflowing feces, making room.

They do not fear the *Nazis*, he has come to believe.

Not as much as they fear their sharp-edged *eye*. The eye that flutters from every storefront, that lolls from every shattered window. Bloodshot, lidless, its pupil a black windmill slashed into a cataracted iris, glowering over all. When the Orpo is gone, the eye observes. They call it the *Hakenkreuz*, though Max knows of many other names. The symbol came from somewhere in the Orient. India perhaps. It had meant only good things once, to many peoples, but the Germans can corrupt even the intangible, bend good to the work of evil.

In their hands it has become a lens for something to peer balefully through. Something that loathes the Jew and gluts on their suffering. Max knows not what name to call the entity. But whenever its indentured eye meets his, Max refuses to look away. Does the thing behind the *swastika* see the truth of him? Let it. Those trapped in the ghetto may be powerless before it, but he is not.

He has dirt, and a word.

In the cellar of the Kac house, Max is making a golem.

For the last several months he has scavenged and saved to purchase its components: Lengths of stiff wire, for structure; basic sculpting tools; eighty kilograms of clay in blocks. Concealing it all from the Kacs was a chore. Sculpting it by hand, by himself, in a night, is even harder.

Max misses the old rabbi sorely. This task is too much for just him. His hands know the way, but his father's had been there and back. Max is only fourteen. Too young to be alone.

Still, grueling hours transform the mound of wet clay into an approximation of the human form. Its eyes are featureless bulbs, its mouth a gash. No nose or ears. His creation is smaller than he anticipated it would be; nearly two and a half meters tall but thin as a skeleton, its skull an oblong club. Max would have preferred to whittle it mighty and broad from the riverbank as Rabbi Loew did, but the curfew made that so dangerous as to be impossible. Its strength will have little to do with such trivia as mass and proportion.

Max stands over his work and sponges the sweat from his neck and brow. *My Adam*, he thinks, with pride. For was mankind not born through a similar art, cut out of the stuff of the earth?

For an hour Max circles his creation, whispering a string of names that scorch his tongue to pronounce, draping the golem in veils of meaning. Next he draws purified water from an urn and ladles it up and down the golem's chest. Wherever it trickles, the clay takes on the oily sheen of living skin. He strikes a match, holds it to the golem's feet until its soles are chapped and cracked as an old man's. Lastly, Max crouches over the golem and breathes into its dent of a mouth. His heart accelerates as its chest rises atop imaginary lungs.

Earth, water, fire, and air. There is only one thing left.

There is one thing Max did not prepare in advance, lest it slip into irreverent hands. On a slip of torn paper no larger than his thumb, he writes a shem—a Name of G-d.

He folds it in two, gigs it with a pin, and tacks it to the floor of the golem's mouth.

Eyes of solid clay snap open.

Max retreats into the corner as the golem climbs onto its feet. The hump of its scalp scrapes against the floorboards overhead. Overlarge hands swing limply at its sides. It is a mottled thing; red clay in places, ruddy flesh in others. Fingernails have sprouted on one hand, but the tip of its phallus has already broken off. It is imperfect, yes. And glorious as salvation always is.

Max would cry out, if it would not wake his family.

"Can you speak?" Max asks in Hebrew.

The golem shakes its head.

"Do you have knowledge?"

The golem nods.

"I have created you. Will you serve me?"

The golem nods again.

Max unfolds a photograph from his trouser pocket. "This man is *Hauptmann* Rudolf Pancke. He is an evil man: he has murdered many children of Israel for no crime. He profits from the theft of their possessions. Kill him, tonight, wherever he is."

The golem nods a third time. It does not look at the photograph.

"Men will try to stop you," Max adds. "If they are not Jews, kill them as well. When you are finished, do not return here—destroy yourself, or at least the shem in your mouth. Do you understand?"

The golem is already leaving.

The following morning Max swallows his exhaustion and requests to accompany the Kacs on their shopping. While Else is fitted for a new church dress and Mrs. Kac collects the week's groceries, Max cocks an ear to the gossip running wild up and down Piotrkowska Street.

Not four hours past, Rudolf Pancke was discovered murdered in his home, his throat crumpled as though by a vice, face black with trapped blood. His wife Gertrude was dead as well, her forehead flattened against their stovetop. Whoever attacked them tore their door of its hinges and took five bullets from Pancke's sidearm without leaving a drop of blood.

Max had been expecting to feel happy. Vindicated.

Instead, he feels hungry

A Jew must be the culprit of course. A rare brute of higher cunning than his breed, escaped from the ghetto with slaughter on the mind. Or perhaps one who had evaded being swept up with the rest of them, for despite assurances, there are surely many still skulking under floorboards like rats. Over the following days, Max watches the Orpo presence around the ghetto increase dramatically, In a show of force, they drag ten young men from their homes and execute them on the blackened steps of what had been the old Stara Synagogue. Those deaths are his fault as well. Max accepts that and moves on. They were dead long before he killed them.

With every new invader he sees on the street corner, he feels more powerful. They are war now, because of *him. Their* lives are in *his* hands.

But the same time, each reminds Max of just how many Germans there are in Łódź. Months of caution and preparation, a bucket of sweat, for only one head. Two, if he counts the wife.

He wants more. But how to begin? Where does one bite first to devour a mountain? This problem keeps him awake through humid nights. Max is starving with too much on his plate, from the patrolling officers who inflict a thousand little brutalities along their route, to that quisling Rumkowski who runs the ghetto in the German's stead. Who would be worth the time and risk, the blind retaliation? Of course he could simply knock down the walls of the ghetto, but that would hardly be productive. Animals escaped from the zoo are most often just shot.

Although he frets, he does not fear, for he knows his cause is just. In the darkened sky above the ghetto he has beheld the archangel Metatron, the right hand of G-d, with an aureole of flaming eyes about his brow and wings of gold forty thousand cubits in span. None but Max can see him—no, they merely duck under awnings and complain of the rain. Oh, if only the prisoners there could feel the hem of his alabaster robe pooled about their feet, they would know hope, for he who led the Israelites from Egypt has now come to Łódź. In one hand he holds a sword of smithied lightning, crackling and spitting; the other is pointed down in scorn at the ghetto administration headquarters.

The heavenly scribe speaks not a word, but its message is evident.

It is Else, of all people, who provides Max the breakthrough he needs. She has a little cloth doll named Odie, whom she carries with her everywhere. While playing one afternoon, a thread in Odie's leg catches on a jutting nail and tears beyond repair. She is distraught, until her mother sews the doll a new leg from an old paisley headscarf. Else sees happy enough with the result, not minding the incongruous limbs. The doll is still a doll. One material is as good as another.

How far might that principle travel before it broke down?

Golems have historically been exclusively from clay, for two reasons. The first is practicality: they have to be wrought from earth, and clay is easy to shape. The second is tradition; it has been done that way since the time of the rabbi Rava. But Max suspects now that this way of thinking has stunted the possibility of the golem. It is the twentieth century now; the world is wider and vastly deeper than it was.

Rabbi Falk taught him more than the Kabbalah in the years they'd had together. Max was better with letters and numbers than most his age, though his aptitudes were science and history. For instance, he knew that some thirty-five years ago a German Jew named Einstein proved the ancient theory that all creation is composed of invisibly small particles—particles that logically can then be rearranged to construct whatever one likes. It seemed to Max that if one were to examine any two items on a small enough scale, they would essentially be the same amalgamation of substances.

In that realm where atoms are the size of planets, everything is dirt.

Through the summer and autumn of 1940, Max sets out to make golems from everything.

Very quickly he proves his theory true. A man made of branches and twine takes little time and less artistic finesse than clay, and, as he discovers, animates nearly as well. When imbued with a name of G-d, a brace of twigs will crack and twist into a hand of five functional fingers. Knots will blink and suddenly be eyes, and hoary bark will sprout goosebumps in the cold. And most importantly, though at its thickest it may be no bigger around than his calf, it will possess the strength to crumble a brick in one fist.

With this first success to whet his appetite, Max attacks the subject with renewed fervor. He finds that it is easier to smuggle other materials into his room than clay, especially via the cellar's small window overlooking a strip of weeds beside the house.

From the moment the Kacs go to bed, Max toils at innovating the concept of the golem. Wood works well, as does sacking, and especially metal. Over the course of two sweltering nights in late

August he patches together a child-sized thing of scrap pilfered from a garbage heap near the factory where the Germans have put the Jews to work. Although its gait is ungainly, its pipe neck inflexible, it handily eviscerates an Orpo captain with fingers of serrated steel, leaving him to be found in an alley the next morning.

That is good; two nights is not. Max can do better.

He finds efficiency in hybridism. Clay is ideal flesh, but sticks will function as limbs, and anything will serve for a head. With each golem the time and energy needed to acquire its pieces shrinks. What helps, Max finds, is to inscribe the shem directly on the skin of the golem, as not every one can have a mouth. It seems to provide them with a shade more humanity—broader swathes of flesh, more articulate digits—than his previous method.

Some turn out laughable, jiggumbob men with old kettles for heads, clopping about on wooden clogs. But function supersedes aesthetics. Broom-handle legs, knives for fingers, rags stuffed with rags for feet—all perfectly lethal. Night after night he sends them out with a name and a mission, infesting the shadows of Łódź with scuttling, clanking deaths wrought of its own matter. Max feels unfettered, a renegade genius in his field. What *else* had others not dared to attempt? He wonders how *small* a golem could be, how sneaking and insidious. Could a shem be written with a needle? A hair?

He wonders how *immense* as well.

He wonders that often.

Not every golem is successful. Some are destroyed by happenstance; an incidental scratch can obliterate a shem. And it was inevitable that one would be caught in the act or fail by some unforeseeable chance. On the night of October 12th, a Gestapo officer bursts into his headquarters with an arm lacerated in a thousand places, gabbling about shear-handed scarecrows. They public thinks him mad, but a month later, a boneless poppet made of a straw-stuffed Polish uniform is speared in the headlights of a truck full of German soldiers. A hail of gunfire blasts it to tatters, but whispers of it spread like fleas off a rat.

Golem. Max begins to hear the word from other lips.

Else asks what it means one evening as the family takes its supper. Max must feign disinterest. A golem, Mister Kac explains, in that tone fathers use to shrink adult concepts into child ones, is a big man made from clay and a magic word. It is a way for powerless people to become powerful. The legend goes that a Jewish holy man in a city called Prague created one to protect his people from their enemies. But although the golem was strong and fearless, it one day went mad and became a danger to everyone. So remember, Else, that sometimes the answer is worse than the problem.

Over the course of weeks, the Germans clamp tight about the city. They begin to move in larger groups. They publically scoff at the notion of a clay man murdering by night, but the streets start to empty themselves a little earlier come nightfall. Perhaps they, of all people, believe in some small way.

They think caution and numbers will make them safe. Max is overjoyed to prove them wrong, when at three in the afternoon on January the first, the devil Biebow himself is throttled dead in the warmth of his own office.

On the morning of February 3rd, Max lurks in the crowd outside the ghetto wall as the Germans begin to take the Jews away.

He had been hearing talk of Extreme Measures to be taken. There is no longer doubt that a Jew has been behind the murders, by means mundane or supernatural. Rather than root him out amongst many thousands, they're simply going to relocate the lot.

Day by day, trucks come and go carrying them away family by family. He hears word that they are to be moved by train to a place in the south called Auschwitz. How long the process will take remains uncertain, what with the logistics of it, and the war. Max feels a thin satisfaction. It isn't much, but it's something. He pushed, and the world stumbled. Only G-d knows what he can do if he only pushes a little harder.

Max returns home electrified with purpose, only to find a Nazi at the door.

He spots the man first and hangs back across the street. The officer is speaking with Mrs. Kac; he cannot hear what they are saying, but she doesn't seem afraid. After a time he nods goodbye and moves on to the next house in the row. He is going door to door looking for anything suspicious, not Max in particular.

But the demon that follows him is.

It rides naked upon a camel, a drooping animal harried by flies and striped with the shadows of its own ribs. Its head is a horse's lolling painfully upon its neck. In one hand it brandishes a golden scepter. Upon its brow is a flaming crown. Max goes absolutely still as its gaze sweeps down the street and over him without stopping. The officer keeps walking, and the demon canters after, unseen by all.

Max flees, but he sees now that the mazzikim have overrun the city. They skulk in the shadows of German officers, or ride upon their shoulders, tugging at the barbed reins of their fearful hatred. Toothless crones parade nude upon the backs of crocodiles; a mitered raven goose-steps before its host on ape-like hands; a fiery hakenkreuz of lion's paws rolls by, trailing a brimstone stink. More perch upon the rooftops and chimneys, terrors too real for Bosch's hell caterwauling in a tongue of lies and blasphemy.

These are the emissaries of the thing behind the swastika, for indeed those spirits that have the arms for it wear upon them a sash bearing its symbol. Far too late, Max understands the enormity of what he has antagonized.

The swastika is the eye of a god.

This is the most blasphemous thought he can have, but even so. Yes, a god, one unknown to the Patriarchs who articulated The Lord as the solitary power in the universe, for men know only what they can perceive, and though they knew great suffering, who among those ancient fathers could have even conceived of the unholy miracle that is the Reich? That ancient symbol of goodness, itself enslaved by Germans, has unwillingly become the aspect of an Anti-G-d, its beneficent meaning corrupted into domination and extermination. And just as G-d once tasked the Israelites with proclaiming his laws, so too did this evil counterpart uplift a nation of wolves and saddle its own chosen people with a covenant to become the world, devour the Jew.

Max returns home as calmly as he can, pretending he can't see what he sees. In the safety of his cellar he strips to the waist and pens upon his own body the names of G-d and other psalms of protection. The Evil G-d walks the streets of Łódź but does not recognize him as its prey. Forget the pretensions of dead mystics—only The Lord itself protects him now. *My Lord*, he prays, *hide me from the sight of my enemies. I only need a little more time.*

Max is a fugitive in a city he once strolled as a king.

He dreads now to leave his shelter, even with the nomenclature of G-d scrawled upon his chest. It is difficult to see the people anymore for the demons that caper among them. *They* are more real now than the men they orbit, and he must always pretend that he is blind to them. He no longer visits the ghetto, for that is where they congregate most thickly. And though he may creep about beneath their noses, he knows he is as pungent, as savory, a Jew as any other. *G-d's protection cannot falter*, Max assures himself with every spare thought.

But if it did...

He spends every moment preparing for the end, maximizing the reward for the risk that is living. From everything he can scrounge he breeds golems—dog-sized, hand-sized, lopsided, crippled by haste. These he stows in the crevices of the city, in trash bins and ditches disguised as rubbish, until the time comes when they will be summoned to their purpose.

The wreckage of the Great Synagogue yet lies where it fell. *The rabbi's grave*, Max supposes numbly, but he has not been coming for that reason. The Germans have not yet cleared the rubble away. What would they do with the plot? They did not come to Łódź to build. The pliable ground has begun to digest the old, charred stone. If Max stands in a certain spot, tilts his head just so, he can conjure patterns from the scree as one may invent faces in clouds. A heap of brick and mud becomes a protrudent knee; a grove of burnt rafters, a brace of ribs. What is the plot, he thinks, but the face of a block of clay from which anything can be cut?

Hidden in a slit in his mattress is a bundle of papers—sketches of an idea that has consumed his thoughts like a parasite. Diagrams in smudged charcoal arguing weight and pressure and balance, jottings on cost and time required. Discarded notions clutter the margins. Numbers smear into drawings—a Vitruvian man fully eight feet tall, yet no more than a reference point to the giant that stands beside him.

It can be done, Max has determined. He is only lacking in manpower, and he will not lack that for long. His mind is a furnace fueled by tradition.

Why could a golem not be tasked to build a golem? All he needs is a little more time.

He has little idea of how many will be needed so he works like a madman, shredding this throat with the names of G-d. He avoids the near certainty that anything will not be enough, that he will never be ready. Once he begins his work, the Anti-G-d will know and try to stop him. But no matter what Max will fight it, until either he is dead or is his fist is big enough to crush it like a grape.

On the morning of February 17th, 1941, Max awakens to a door banging open upstairs. It could be Mister Kac leaving for work, but it isn't. He is out of bed and running before he hears the first barked words of German. Barefoot and naked to the waist, he scrabbles up the wall and through the unlatched window. He does not see the pair of oily black boots waiting for him outside.

They take him by the wrists and drag him onto the grass. He is struck once in the mouth, and bits of his teeth spill everywhere. A heel stabs into his belly, and Max vomits blood and food across his face and chest. The swastika upon the officer's arm seems to wink at him, as that arm coils back, storing power. Through the haze of pain, he can see Mister and Missus Kac watching from the kitchen window, clutching each other.

The demons riding the Kacs laugh and point and yank on their bridles.

The world whirls on a broken axle around Max as one of the officers heaves him over his shoulder. As they carry him out into the street Max glimpses neighbors and passers-by watching in sick-faced silence. The Germans' idling truck lurches briefly into view through the crook of the officer's arm and Max understands that he is going into the ghetto like slop into a pig's trough, to fester and be devoured.

Through a mouth full of broken teeth, Max screams.

The truck's rear door swings open; the unwashed interior reeks of blood and bile. Max screams again—*anyone, please*—wringing his lungs out like sponges of terror, as they hurl him inside.

The two officers linger there, gloating over him. There is nothing left to lose now—it is struggle or die. Max kicks out, stomping his foot into the closest groin. The man bends double, cursing in German.

"*Verdammter jüdischer Bastard—*"

Max scrabbles onto his hands and feet to run for it, only to run up against the snout of the other officer's sidearm.

"*Das ist es, was du bekommst, wenn du so nah stehst.*"

"*Schieße schon die kleine Ratte ab.*"

"*Ganz gut.*"

And as he turns to Max to fix his aim a blur of rag and metal drops from above and takes his hand off at the wrist.

"*Was zum teufel ist—*" the other blurts, scrambling for his pistol, but then the golem is upon him to, its knife-hands strobing with speed. The officer goes down shrieking, his skin coming away in peels. The survivor tries to run, but the golem is fleet as a fox upon its broomstick legs. In broad daylight, for the whole street to see, it slices the heels out from under him and efficiently disassembles him.

Max crawls from the truck to meet it. A dwarf of cotton-stuffed curtain with a pail for a head, it stares up at him through hole-punched eyes, gormlessly awaiting the next command. Max looks all around at the crowd retreating in fear from him—women clutching their children, men, clutching their wives—and at the cacophonic throng of demons baying for his blood from every rooftop and lamppost perch. They can certainly see him *now*, Max thinks. There will be no restoring that veil.

Max's heart begins to pound in his ears like a war drum. This is the moment, he realizes—the end whose approaching shadow chilled him awake through so many endless nights. He had worked so hard to hold it at bay but now it is here, and he is in it, and there is nothing to be done but embrace it.

Max had dreamed once of deific heights. Of crossing the land upon a colossus of his own creation, stepping between towns as one would stepping stones, and obliterating Germans with as little thought as he'd give ants. He had fantasized of trampling over Berlin and palming the *Reichskanzlei* into the dirt. Perhaps that had been too much to hope for—the whimsy of a little boy.

So be it. He shall become a man then.

What can be done with a giant can be done with a horde.

As Max marches through the snowy streets of Łódź, the golems he seeded the city with answer his summons. Tall, small, hodge-podge and whole cloth, they awake from their spider-holes and join his ever-growing procession. Some are mere spiders skittering along on sewing-needle legs, others monkey along on cork knuckles, on strong rebar bones. They are the matter of the city itself risen up to fight beside him, Max now understands. He never needed a colossus, no—the greatest champion he could possibly construct would be an insect beside the totality of Łódź.

People run screaming wherever he passes, their infernal jockeys hauling futilely on their bridles. Flocks of demons hurl abuse from the rooftops but they dare not stand against him. Delirious with pain, dripping blood with every step, Max feels stronger than ever before, a beast loosed from a too-small cage and free at last to stretch its claws.

No more cowering in a cellar. No more pretending to be what he is not. *No more fear.*

Those Orpo officers that blunder into his path find themselves torn apart by the horde. The golems carpet Max's cobbled path in glistening red. No, Max need never have hid. The Germans have nothing like this power. When Max looks to the murky heavens, he sees the Heavenly Scribe suspended there once more, the tip of his fulgurant sword blazing like a star above the ghetto. Yes, my Lord, Max thinks, his heart bursting with elation. He weeps, for his purpose has never been so blindingly bright. He is to be as Moses and take his people away from this forsaken land. He will teach them to make golems, and together they will raise the world itself into an army, G-d's final commitment writ across a billion clay brows. All land will be as the promised land, and milk and honey will flow forever more.

Yes, my lord, I understand and obey.

I will lead the last exodus.

When Max and his legion arrive at the edge of the ghetto he finds the Orpo waiting. A barricade of soldiers levels its weapons at his ranks of teeter-tottering scarecrow men. *"Halt,"* the officer barks across the stretch of emptied street between them. *"Ergebe dich sofort!"*

Max sneers at the naked terror in the officer's voice. The Germans have placed their faith in the power to destroy human flesh, the most frail substance in creation. Max bids his army advance, and as one ramified limb the golems go bounding through the snow. A chorus of rifles retorts but it is like shooting at nothing; bullets pass harmlessly through dining cloth skin, ricochet off of candelabra claws.

Some catch in interstitial physiology, where Łódź -matter has imperfectly become meat, but the golems are only sporadically filled with blood to shed. They crash into the German rampart and smash it instantly into panicked rubble. These soldiers have never expected to kill anything other than men; to shoot at a thing and for it to still live is a contradiction in their reality.

One by one, the soldiers fall and die. Soon there is only a wall garnished in barbed wire and a small, steaming aftermath. Many of his golems lay in pieces, overwhelmed at last by force of arms, but no matter—Max bids the remainder tear dear down the wall. Limping, bleeding, he steps into the ghetto for the first time.

Max expected celebration. His people flooding into the streets to welcome their liberating son returned. He expected anything.

But silence.

Each step he takes through the crunching snow echoes between looming tenements like a gunshot. The street for as far as he can see is marked by neither footprints or wheel tracks. Max cups his hands around his lips and hurls his voice as far as it will travel. A minute passes with no answer.

He is too late. His people, down to the children, have all been taken away. To Auschwitz, yes, but not to be resettled. He understands that now. Only ghosts still walk these streets—not the souls of the dead but those who will die when their train reaches its destination, for the tragedies of the future weigh like disappointment on the present. When Max closes his eyes he sees thousands of men and women, boys and girls, babies crawling, all gusting south, towards bullets still in their casings, graves yet to be dug.

He balls his fists, sobs tears and snot and blood. For all his power he cannot even save that many. How many millions more are steaming even now towards Auschwitz? How many more are already beyond him? Beyond salvation?

His ears prick at the growling of a distant engine. He turns, wiping his mouth—a German truck is fast approaching, barreling through the hole in the ghetto perimeter. Its wheels catch lagging golems and crush them to splinters; more are obliterated against its rusted steel scowl. A figure leans out the passenger's window and lets out a sound like cracking river ice. An invisible fist strikes Max in the belly and knocks him onto his haunches.

The urge to *survive* puppets him quickly onto his feet. Max screams a command, and those golems he has left throw themselves upon the truck. As they stave in its windows and climb inside, it swerves hard to the left, stopping dead against the wall of someone's house. Orpo officers spill out the back, taking the butts of their weapons to the fragile golems—swinging, smashing, stomping, hammering the holy names of G-d into the ground.

Max screams again—*Kill them!*—but what use? The golems that can already are, and the rest...

Max watches his army crumbles before his eyes.

All that he can do, is skirt the confusion and flee the way he came.

Max is going to die. The bullet shattered all his illusions on impact. He can feel it—the bullet G-d could have caught, but didn't—rolling in his guts. Growing, it seems, like a venomous pregnancy. He caps the wound with his hand, but still he leaves a trail of bright red breadcrumbs behind him as he flees the ghetto.

But still he runs, lurching through the crooked back alleys of Lodz, a hunted animal, a hunted animal pushing inevitability as far as it will stretch for it violently snaps back. Max squints blurring eyes at the overcast sky, begging the Heavenly Scribe for an answer, but Metatron is nowhere to be seen. *I'm sorry*, he silently pleads, but a soul's volume of contrition does not fill the heavens with angel feathers.

Max runs and stumbles and retches blood until somehow he arrives at the lot where the Great Synagogue once stood. Where the rabbi sacrificed himself to let Max live a little longer. The blackened stoop is the only whole piece left. As good a gravestone as the man will get.

Max stops to comb his fingers through its blanket of snow. *I am sorry to you as well, father. I could not live the way you wanted. I was too strong to live peacefully and too weak to succeed.*

What a fool—what a little boy I've been.

Max drags himself across the lot where he'd once dreamed idiotically of raising his champion. Flattened by snow, the distance seems infinite. How much further must he walk to escape the Germans? Much further than Łódź, he is certain. Paris fell before them long ago. He has heard that they have been bombing London every night for months, a dog worrying down a bone. Not even distant Africa is free of them, and that is almost the whole world. Max could walk for forty years and never find a place not branded flat and white by the swastika.

The dark times the rabbi spoke of will not pass. There have never been other times, only exodus, the flight from one boot-heel to another. One day, they will not even have that. In one year or ten the children of Israel will be extinct. The voice tasked with exulting G-d will be silenced forever. Max cannot see how it could be otherwise, for there is no Promised Land left to run to. Warding their homes with lamb's blood would only attract wolves.

When G-d's chosen people are gone, what good is his world?

Max goes rigid in the grip of revelation.

There is something more that he can do.

He still has his hands.

He still has dirt.

Yes.

An entire world of it.

Max falls to his knees and digs through the snow until he reaches the hard-packed dirt beneath. His fingers are blue by the time he is done shaping a lump of it into a doll-sized homunculus. For water he rubs snow between his hands until it trickles across the golem's chest. For fire he cups blood from his belly and bastes it with his body's dwindling heat. With a torn thumb-nail he gifts it a name of G-d.

The golem, half-flesh and half-earth, tears free of the ground and blinks at him with pinhole eyes, waiting for a command.

Why could a golem not be tasked to build a golem?

"Adam," Max whispers.

In that realm where atoms are the size of planets—

The golem nods.

—everything is dirt.

Max crouches over it, enunciating so that his words are not stolen by the wind. "You will create for yourself a companion as I have created you, as small as you can. You will inscribe upon them the name of G-d that I have inscribed upon you. You will command it as I command you, and then you will begin again. I command you and your progeny to be fruitful and multiply, to fill the earth and subdue it. I command you to wash away all that is touched by evil upon this world and to live virtuously thereafter. Do you understand?"

The golem is already at work

Max deflates into the snow to watch the golem sculpt a still more miniature version of itself and brings it to life. His eyes grow heavy as that golem immediately begin to reproduce itself in turn, eking fire from the friction of its earthen hands, while the original gathers soil together to start again. *Two times two is four,* Max thinks, slipping into a warm bed of snow. *Just as you taught me, father. Four times two is eight. Eight times two is sixteen. A billion times two is...*

Each golem is born in half the time of the one before, and is half the size. In less than an hour they are too small to be seen with the eye and as plentiful as the stars. With his last flicker of consciousness, Max watches grass and stone melt into the same dun-red as the earth, sees that voracious color rip through the snow like a dye through water. In that micro-plane where all is dirt, golems smaller than cell shave away the scar left by the Anti-G-d, rebuilding debased soil from the atoms up into fertile earth.

Into themselves.

The last thing that Max thinks before the golems reach him is, *it will be good.* The long suffering of man is at an end. Even awake he will feel nothing as they take him with absolute kindness, as they will all things, their trickle soon to be a flood enough to drown a planet. All souls, wicked and good, will go without pain into their common grave and be at peace. This fatally wounded creation will be *un*created, licked flat and clean by loving waves, restored at last to innocence. The anti-G-d will perish along with this world, and the next one will be better.

Its new people will be happy.

Max dies with a smile, and becomes them.

See Evan Marcroft's story "The Little G-d of Łódź" online at Metaphorosis.
If you liked it, leave a comment. Authors love that!
Remember to subscribe to our e-mail updates so you'll know when new stories are posted.

About the story

This story came out of two weird bellies.

It was born initially out of a long-standing fascination with the difference between a good ending and a happy ending. A happy ending, in my definition, is one where conflicts are resolved in a way that is satisfying to the reader. The prince slays the dragon, the robot wins his freedom, etc. Everything is alright, and we feel good for having watched it happen. A good ending in my definition, however, is an ending that is satisfying to the protagonist, regardless of how that makes us feel. In my writing, I tend to care more about the protagonist than those reading about them. This story began in my mind at the end, which I saw as happy only in the unique mind of its hero and apocalyptic to everyone else. The hero dies. Every one else dies. The bad guys win. The world ends. Nonetheless, the protagonist's goal is fully accomplished, and I think we can all be glad for him. We're here for our heroes, after all, not the other way around. Our function as readers is to propel their adventure through our observation, and to presume that a character struggles for our entertainment is the height of arrogance, now isn't it?

This story was born secondly from my rejection of what I view as the 'customary' lessons of sci-fi and fantasy. I've read infinite stories where insurmountable obstacles are defeated by some combination of effort, bravery, love, trickery, imagination, and ballsiness. While it is nice to step briefly into a word where that happens, I've never found this to be reflective of reality, where oftentimes objectively small obstacles defeat towering heroes for all their trying. With this story I wanted to propose an alternate but equally valid message: that A.) sometimes no matter what you do you will fail, and B.) even complete failure can be overcome. The moral that built this story around itself is that defeat is not an outcome but a state of being escapable by operating outside of the context in which it occurs. When you lose at a game, flip the table. When the bad guys take over the world, blow the world up.

Also, the idea of a golem-based Gray Goo scenario is just plain cool. I think we can all agree on that at least.

A question for the author

Q: Have you ever wondered whether ideas are thought waves directed at you by an AI supercomputer located in the distant future?

A: I can't say I have, until now at least. Supposing that's true, I can't help but wonder if we're a form of story-telling to them. If our brain activity is directed by intellects beyond our observation, if what we say and how we respond to it is all decided by some other entity, if what we dream and what we do to pursue those dreams is decided by any amount of authorities at least one less than our eight billion, then are we not like characters in some vast story called Earth Circa 2018? I imagine those supercomputers tuning in to some time-piercing TV program to see how this million-year narrative is progressing, what plot twists are unwinding in this eleventy-billionth episode of Mankind. I picture a fair number of fans writing the producers complaining about plot holes and melodrama beloved characters dying unfairly. If that's the case then I guess I hope that I've got someone funny writing the character of me, because if I'm going to be just one mindless side character out of billions with no agency or free will of my own, then I at least want to have some good lines.

About the author

Evan Marcroft is a half-blind yeti-person with a sideways foot and an allergy to the sun. When he was a child he dreamed of writing important works of Earth-shaking beauty and settled for writing fantasy and science fiction instead. He currently lives in Sacramento California with a cat and a loving wife who foolishly believes he'll someday make real money doing this.

You can reach him on Twitter at @Evan_Marcroft and contact him for any reason at Evanmarcroft@hotmail.com.

A House on the Volga

Filip Wiltgren

The kalanchoes are blooming, a dusting of tiny pink flowers on dark jade leaves.

"Please, grandmama, hurry up," says Darius, voice tiny, his heart carried on the radio from the ship.

He is a good boy, caring for his grandmother. His heart was in his house, but he is grown, a young man, and the house is no more. It is good that he leave.

The kalanchoe spins in my hands, as I cover it in plastic, round and round, like a tiny asteroid around a distant sun, pink flowers turning.

Darius' voice is tiny as a single flower.

"Atmospheric impact in twelve minutes," he says, hints of panic in his voice.

"I know," I say. My hands are clumsy around the kalanchoes, wet soil crumbling from wet pots, seen through wet eyes. It is not good, being last.

Our asteroid has lost internal gravity. In twelve minutes it will lose everything. I keep wrapping kalanchoes in plastic. Six foil-wrapped bundles float by my side, another ten sit on their perches in our dorm. My dorm, now.

"We built this together, your grandfather and I," I tell Darius. "Our home, and yours, too."

"I know, grandmama. Please hurry."

"I will," I say. Seven floating bundles. Impact in eleven minutes.

"Mother, what do you think you are doing?" Michail's voice comes strong and loud. No tiny suit microphone for him, the big engineer.

"Engineer Litvinenko, I presume?" I ask, as chilly as I can. His voice continues uninterrupted. For two hours, it has flown. From his office on the Moon, to the Volga's orbit around Saturn. Michail's grand office, where he's making a name for himself, ignoring his house. Selling it.

"- the GN/BN-22 is company property, mother. You return it to regular orbit right this minute, you hear? The lawyers will-"

"Czernobog take the lawyers."

And this asteroid has always been the House by the Volga. GN/BN is a designation. The Volga is a home. Michail never understood that.

Nine bundles by my side. Seven kalanchoes to go. A single detached, pink flower floats by, like a heart without a home.

Vladek brought our first kalanchoe shoot with him when we moved up, and they've grown well. Flowers thrive when there's love in the house.

For a moment I can hear Vladek's voice, but then I only hear the memory of escaping air, and the snap of radio static. So much lost to the stars. So much pain, so many memories. In the end, everything dies, this is the way of life. But as long as the hearts are beating, the family will remember. That is the way of life, too.

A warning shrieks. The system is trying to override.

Michail. Trying to control what cannot be controlled, take back what wasn't given.

I yank out a circuit board, then reset the course computer.

"Grandmama, you need to flee."

"Soon," I tell Darius.

"Now, grandmama!"

Two kalanchoes left. I bundle the first one. Five minutes. Fifteen kalanchoes float tightly in my arms, then float freely as I release them into an escape pod before strapping them down in the only remaining seat. Every birth, every marriage, we planted a new one, a flash of flowers in the dormitory. When the hearts left, we kept the flowers as memories.

Children, grandchildren, everyone has left the Volga. Even Vladek is gone, lost to the void. Perhaps it was stupid to give Michail power of attorney. He never understood how much we struggled to make a home after the exodus. You can no more abandon your home than abandon your heart, or your family.

"Darius," I say. "are you ready for pick-up?"

"God be blessed, grandmama. Plotting intercept now."

"Take care of our flowers," I say, closing the pod door.

The airlock cycles. The pod launches.

"Grandmama?"

The panic is back in Darius' voice. He is a good boy. He will understand, I think. I shut down the radio, severing the cables, and the possibility of a remote redirection of the Volga.

The family is gone, the House by the Volga sold, to be melted down for the nickel in its shell. But a house full of love is like a member of your family, and you do not abandon family. You follow them to their grave, and then you bury them. I take the last kalanchoe in my arms.

Vladek's flower. The original one. He wanted to give it to me, but I said no. He had brought it from Earth. It was his heart.

I kiss the flower, its leaves smooth against my coarse, chapped lips.

"Goodbye, you old heart breaker," I say, "hold a seat in heaven for me."

Then I replace the kalanchoe on its perch and push off toward the last escape pod. The airlock cycles, the acceleration slams me into the grav-couch. Darius' voice comes tiny over the pod's speakers.

"Grandmama!" he says, relief saturating his tones, "for a moment I thought…"

A sad smile crosses my lips.

"You are family," I say.

"But the Volga—"

"Will be buried," I say. Then I shut off the radio, and watch a home briefly bloom against the great globe of Saturn.

See Filip Wiltgren's story "A House on the Volga" online at Metaphorosis.
If you liked it, leave a comment. Authors love that!
Remember to subscribe to our e-mail updates so you'll know when new stories are posted.

About the story

"A House on the Volga" came by as part of the Codex Writers Workshop "Weekend Warrior" flash fiction challenge. The challenge is simple: on Friday, you get a set of prompts. By Sunday, you need to submit your story (big nods to Warrior admin Vylar Kaftan and all the great people partaking in the challenge.)

The prompt was "Write about someone who has lost their home, or is about to." I had absolutely no idea what to do with it. But I did have a pot of kalanchoes growing on the windowsill in the kids' play room. From there, everything rolled on organically.

Which, gentle reader, means that I really have no idea where this story comes from. I usually don't. My brain goes for a spin and delivers up a story (it's called "pantsing" in writerly parlance, meaning that you've got no idea what you're trying to say until you've said it.)

But there you have it, a prompt, and a flower, and suddenly, a story. And that's all there is to it.

And big thanks for all the people who offered feedback, not in the least Morris who saw something worthwhile in it and let me bash through five revisions until it worked well enough to publish.

A question for the author

Q: Do you prefer your SFF as books or movies?

A: I almost always read my SFF, because I lack the time to watch a movie. Which isn't quite true – I have the time, but it's spread out during the day in 5-10 minute intervals. Which is just enough time to read a couple of pages, but not enough to get into a movie.

About the author

By day, Filip Wiltgren is a mild-mannered communication officer at Linköping University, where he also teaches communication and presentation skills at a post-graduate level.

But by night, he turns into a frenzied ten-fingered typist, clawing out jagged stories of fantasy and science fiction, which have found lairs in places such as *Analog*, *Grimdark*, *Daily SF*, and *Nature Futures*.

Filip roams the Swedish highlands, kept in check by his wife and kids. He can be found at www.wiltgren.com

@FilipWiltgren

When the Last Friend is Gone

Tris Matthews

Butler found Pebbles dead in the morning.

Each day, the moment Butler became active at 6 a.m. sharp, the little old dog's stumpy legs would carry her over to seat herself royally in front of the enormous and rusty Cadillac-themed refrigerator to watch. Butler would ruffle the flops and folds of skin on the top of her head before serving up her breakfast and then turning to other chores. Today, Pebbles didn't come. Butler washed her bowl—overly-large, red, ceramic, and with 'Pebbles' hand-painted around the edge in florid script—spooned out a tin of moist meat and placed it on the shabby green mat by the back door.

Butler was most efficient when routine was least disrupted. There was no such thing as perfect routine: any day's unique haze caused variations in illumination; the birds sang a different song; even his own body performed differently depending upon the ambient temperature, and he was already aware his joints were less smooth than a year ago, when he was fresh out of the box. Beatrice also increasingly left things out of place around the house. Butler didn't know whether this was solely a result of her age, or a gradual acceptance of her reliance on him. The latter was the more satisfying alternative. After all, caring for Beatrice was his purpose.

Butler hummed for a moment, then went to check the living room. There was Pebbles in her grubby sleeping spot on the faded cream carpet, half curled and half sprawled against the radiator. Beatrice didn't allow Butler to clean Pebbles's favourite spots frequently, saying 'if you take her smell away, she won't feel at home', a view Butler struggled to comprehend—it was in absolute opposition to his fundamental operating principles. He stepped past the fat sausage body and closed the door so as not to wake Beatrice, then softly called "Pebbles, breakfast is ready." No movement. When Pebbles had been leaning against the radiator, Beatrice liked to call her 'Hot Dog'. Butler tried this, but still no response. He squatted and laid a hand on her portly rump. She was cold.

Butler had served up Beatrice's dinner. The day had been a series of deviations from routine. Beatrice had been so affected by Pebbles's passing she hadn't been able to wash and dress herself, though she usually insisted on independence in these things, no matter how badly she did them. She'd even refused to let Butler assist her until after they'd attended to Pebbles. Down in the living room, when he'd shown her the body, Beatrice would have collapsed had Butler not caught her. He helped her kneel, then she rested her head upon her companion of 15 years and wept.

"Oh, Pebbles. What am I going to do now?"

The sight of his master futilely embracing and talking to the dead dog had made Butler want to comfort her more. He'd laid a hand on her damp, shivering back and said "I'm still here for you ma'am."

The key to a purposeful existence was expectation maximisation. From any given state, there was a set of actions and possible results. An action was chosen to maximise the expectation of achieving the desired result, based upon the probabilities derived over your life so far. You then performed the action, and any discrepancy between the desired and actual results was used to update your expectations for the future. When everything was highly routine, the reinforced results stood out with disproportionately high expectations, while in unusual situations, competition between vying action-result pairs with similar expectations led to longer decision times and more tentative behaviours.

Butler had dug deep to remove the roses without damaging their roots so Pebbles could be buried beneath them. After more than ten hours motionless in the mouldy garden chair, Beatrice had let Butler take her back to the living room and she'd sat with the low hum of the electric heater while he'd prepared dinner—her only meal that day. Butler had planned a steak and kidney pie, but, adapting to circumstance, he'd gone with a quick vegetable stew instead. Beatrice had also requested a large glass of brandy, which he'd served up in her favourite cut-glass snifter.

The undone chores of the day chattered imperatives towards the front of his mind, but before he could return to the kitchen, Beatrice said "Stay here, Butler."

"Would you like me to help you eat?" he asked.

She shook her head. "Just… give me some company. There's only you now, for better or worse." Her chin fell to her chest like a puppet with a broken string. "Till death do us part."

Butler assumed his ready position by the door to the kitchen. After a few seconds, Beatrice strained to look round for him.

"Can you sit?"

In the 484 days Butler had been serving Beatrice, this was the first time she'd requested he sit. Aside from her chair, the room contained one armchair and three dining chairs tucked under the never-used dining-table. The dining chairs seemed more appropriate to the level of formality befitting his position. However, in this unusual circumstance Butler judged Beatrice was seeking an equal more than a servant. He sat in the second armchair. Like everything in the house, it was old and worn: the centre bowed, the springs creaked, and he sank much more deeply than he had predicted. He gripped the arms to retain some posture and turned his head toward Beatrice. She looked back, searching for something in the digitally animated screen that was his face, with its cartoonish bushy sky-blue eyebrows and quivering moustache.

"Just you and me now," she reiterated. "I guess you've had a promotion."

"What will my new position be, ma'am?" Butler asked.

Beatrice's eyes remained on Butler a little longer, then she turned to her food. Her movements were slow, as if mind and body no longer communicated in quite the same language. She raised a spoonful of the stew to her mouth, awkwardly moved her head to gobble the food, then extracted the spoon and rested her hand back on the tray before she began chewing. The entire process took a minute and a half. She repeated once, then turned back to Butler.

"How are your conversation skills?" she asked.

"I have an excellent grasp of phonetics, syntax and semantics, even compared to highly-educated humans. However, my pragmatics leave something to be desired, apparently."

Beatrice's blinked. "You're gonna have to do better than that, boy! Can you chat with me?"

"Yes, I can."

"Well, alright then. I propose a toast to our first real conversation." Her shaky hand lifted the glass to pursed pale lips and she slurped a mouthful of brandy. "Now, what shall we talk about?"

"It is customary to talk about the events of the day," Butler suggested. "We could talk about Pebbles or family or death—"

"No!" Beatrice stared past Butler to the mantle clock on the fireplace, rapping a taut white knuckle on her glass to count down the seconds until the thinnest hand pointed at twelve. "Start your customs tomorrow. For today, we'll talk about something else. Tell me about yourself, beyond what I already know. What makes a Butler robot tick?"

Butler hummed for a moment before he spoke. "Though I am most efficient when performing routine duties, I find atypical days more satisfying." He hummed a moment longer, then added "All else being equal."

"Really? That surprises me a little."

"Why does it surprise you?"

"Well, your whole selling point is helping with routine tasks around the house. That's what they say on telly. But you prefer the unexpected." Beatrice peered over her spectacles. "Is this normal, or do I need to send you back?"

"Oh, no, ma'am," Butler protested, and his intonation was most human. "I assure you, I function normally. I also derive great satisfaction from performing routines duties for you. In fact, I can rank the satisfaction I get from different scenarios."

"I was joking, boy. You need to work on your humour. But go ahead and rank your satisfaction. I suppose that's your version of telling me your likes and dislikes."

Butler hummed. "Yes," he said, "humour is a skill that I have had little chance to hone. With respect to my likes, my ranking is thus. I gain most satisfaction from caring for you—"

"I'll drink to that," Beatrice chimed in. A skeletal left hand brought up the golden liquid while her right waved the spoon in a gesture to continue.

"Secondly, I gain satisfaction from learning new things, and thirdly from performing chores efficiently. However, performing duties also includes caring for you, which often boosts my satisfaction from routine tasks above merely learning new things alone."

Butler noted that Beatrice appeared more interested in discovering the carrots in her broth than listening to his story. He paused to give her opportunity to speak, but when she didn't, decided to go on. "There has been considerable research into deriving simple rules capable of generating all behaviours, even the most complex. They aim to model human psychology."

Beatrice finished chewing a mouthful, swallowed, then washed it down with a bit more brandy. She was drinking more rapidly than Butler had ever observed before. He logged a conditional reminder to record the quantity she consumed and intervene if necessary.

Beatrice tapped the rim of the glass twice with her spoon. "Are you worried how much I'm drinking, boy?"

Butler hummed, but before he could reply, Beatrice said "Let me save you too much whirring—I am drinking too much. Tomorrow morning I'll feel like death. But tonight, you just let me drink, ok?"

Though Beatrice had never been friendly with him, she'd also never put him in a situation where he had to disobey her for her own safety. He hoped tonight would not set a new precedent. He said, "I will not protest while you remain within the safe limits."

There was a silence that may have been uncomfortable if Butler were human, then Beatrice nodded an affirmation.

"May I ask, ma'am: how did you know my thoughts related to your drinking?"

"That's what I'd've been thinking. I guess we ain't so different after all." She cocked her head and glanced sideways. "What do you think of that?"

On Butler's face, the corners of his moustache twitched up into a smile. "It's satisfying you think so."

Beatrice snorted. She raised her glass again. "I'll drink to that." Her over-enthusiastic chug dribbled from both corners of her mouth down the cracks of her chin and onto her brown blouse. Scrunching her eyes closed, she blew out a heated half-whistle and Butler wondered how it must feel to ingest alcohol. Beatrice's tongue leached what remaining brandy it could from her lips, then she wiped her chin with the soiled cuff of her blouse.

Butler did a quick internet search then said, "You can't be an alcoholic because an alcoholic always wants a drink, but you already have one."

Beatrice's face slackened and her eye darted to him with uncharacteristic keenness. "What?"

Her reaction was not as expected—the shock was clear, even to Butler. He hummed and shifted his face to an earnest affect. "It was an attempt to strengthen the bond between us with humour, ma'am."

Finally, she dismissed it with a small shake of the head and said, "So tell me, would you be happiest if you could care for me while I run around doing exciting new things?"

It was a relief to return to the previous topic. "While that would certainly provide a stimulating environment, it is neither relevant nor possible for me to say whether that would make me happiest."

"Because you're incapable of happiness," Beatrice said flatly.

"No, ma'am. The satisfaction I receive as feedback on my activities is likened to human happiness, though I cannot comment on whether it is analogous."

"Right." Beatrice's sceptical tone was lost on her companion. "You can't or won't tell me what makes you happy." As she stared at him, Butler noted a slight, twitching tension that pulled at the muscles above her mouth. "Explain."

"I said my happiness is not relevant because I am just a machine. My life is of lower value than yours, and my happiness is irrelevant beyond motivating devotion to you. I said my happiness is impossible to predict because my satisfaction coefficients on care, learning and efficiency are the result of large-scale data-mining to optimally meet the needs of a wide variety of owner personalities. Re-running such simulations is beyond the computational abilities of a single unit."

Beatrice frowned, but something of the animalistic growl dissipated from her face. She made the slow nod of someone who hadn't understood at all. "Butler, talking to you drives a girl to drink."

"I beg your pardon, ma'am. Shall I resume my chores?"

"Stay! I'll just…" She swigged and sighed. To Butler, her action seemed akin to a reset. "So, let's try translate that into how a person speaks. You mean you wanna do your job and not wonder how things could be different?"

Butler hummed for a moment. "That is an adequate—if not entirely accurate—summary, ma'am."

Beatrice's cheeks stretched into a broad grin. "Now we're getting somewhere." This time, she picked up her glass using both hands and dipped just the tip of her grey tongue into the shimmering liquid.

"Tell me, Butler, will you ever learn to speak like me?"

"No, ma'am."

"Oh. Kill me now!"

"Ma'am, that is not—"

"Shush!" Beatrice interrupted. "It's a turn of phrase. Will you always speak like you do now?"

"No, ma'am. The more we converse, the better I will become. Unfortunately, we have talked little in the preceding sixteen months, but there are Butler models whose owners speak with them regularly and they are far more proficient. If you wish, I could download the Conversations Package, which would enable me to access topics and cultural references beyond my immediate experience. However, the non-verbal aspects of your level of communication elude current models, apparently."

Beatrice finished the last two spoonfuls of her dinner. A dollop of sauce dribbled down to join the blotches of brandy on her bosom. "I guess that's how it should be," she said. "We wouldn't want you taking over the world." Again, Butler thought he detected veiled tensions underlying a sneer, and again it quickly passed with a listless shrug. "You do make an excellent cook, though."

"Thank you, ma'am."

"Clear up these plates, then come back."

"Yes, Ma'am."

"Oh, and top up my brandy while you are at it."

"Yes, ma'am."

The simple act of rising from the armchair was surprisingly difficult. First Butler couldn't shift his balance far enough forward to engage his legs, then he was applying too much weight to the chair's creaking wooden arms. After several adjustments, he maximally declined his torso, so his head was between his knees, while still holding the arms of the chair for a slight boost.

Beatrice whooped. "That is the least graceful movement I have ever seen! Not made for relaxation, eh?"

Butler straightened up and faced his owner. "It is true, ma'am. My satisfaction comes from actions. If I am not working, I go into sleep mode and shut down everything except dreams."

He courteously bowed his head, gathered Beatrice's tray, deposited it in the kitchen and returned with the brandy—a Leyrat VSOP cognac. Before pouring, he presented the bottle to the lady like a wine waiter, as she had instructed him to, but she waved him to hurry along, saying, "I'm not gonna live forever, boy."

Watching Butler pour, Beatrice said "When I first got you, I was surprised how fluid your movements were. Movie robots are angular and awkward, but you move as easily as a real person—except when getting up from chairs."

"Given practice, I will master the chair, ma'am. In novel situations, I must learn to manoeuvre, just as children must. As I said, these novel challenges are satisfying."

"You did say that, didn't you," stated Beatrice.

"Yes, I did."

Beatrice frowned at her robot, then the sallow folds of her saggy skin formed a smirk. Butler returned the brandy bottle to its shelf and returned to the armchair. He allowed it to envelop him a little more than before—it was familiar now.

They sat in silence, both staring ahead towards the dead TV on the chipped wooden cabinet surrounded by framed photographs until Beatrice said, "Do you mean that you dream?"

"Yes, ma'am."

"It isn't... Is it the same as people's dreams?"

"It is an analogue, apparently. I experience scenarios that draw from experiences across my life, but are particularly influenced by recent salient events. These recreations facilitate the integration of new with existing knowledge by entertaining hypothetical scenarios and testing expected results."

"No." Beatrice wore a disgusted look. "That isn't what we do at all." She stared myopically at her drink, then took a laboured swig followed by a crunching gulp. "We dream stories. Sometimes stuff from the day, but also random things, like things you've been worrying about, or it could even be monsters. There's no 'facilitated integration'. It's all about imagination."

Butler hummed. Perhaps he was having trouble with nuances. "Ma'am, would you tell me about a dream of yours?"

Beatrice squinted as if she didn't recognise him. Her jaw moved, chewing on her own gums. Then her face smoothed as she made up her mind.

"I'm carrying eggs. I'm being really careful because we had a chicken, but it's dead now, so these are the most precious eggs—there'll never be any more, you know?"

Beatrice stared at the television. To begin with, Butler thought the 'you know?' was a rhetorical question, but then wondered if he had misinterpreted. He considered his own experience with unexpectedly expending the supplies needed for his chores, so he said,

"I know." This prompted Beatrice to continue and he deemed his response appropriate.

"I'm walking with these three beautiful blonde eggs in my hands, and there are lots of people around. They are all happy and cheering my wonderful eggs. I'm ecstatic at this point." A single tear descended the twisted terrain of her cheek like a drunk weaving his way home to his family, and Butler wondered if it was a tear of joy—he had heard of such things.

"And then they tumble from my hands. It happens in slow motion. I feel the smooth perfection of the eggshells as they slip between my fingers—like a baby's skin. I flail and grasp, but I'm too slow and they smash on the ground. I'm down on my knees crying because it's all gone. The people are walking away. It's just me and my smashed eggs seeping into the dust."

Butler hummed. "Your dream is complex. Can you explain it to me?"

"What's to explain?" Beatrice scoffed. "A dream's a dream. It doesn't have to have a meaning." She shrugged. "Or if it does, it's not something so obvious. Tell me one of yours."

Butler had recorded 2413 dreams from 524 sleep events. He summoned those with context relating to the dream Beatrice had recounted and the expectation of one in particular rose to prominence.

"It is your birthday and I am baking a cake to make you happy, but when I open the carton, all the eggs are already broken. I do not wish to disappoint you, so I create a substitute using a mixture of banana, apple and flaxseed. However, when you try the cake, you are displeased and refuse to eat. Your birthday is ruined because I did not pay sufficient attention to my surroundings."

Beatrice immediately spat a response. "Did you just make that up? I say I dream about eggs, so you say the same thing?"

"No, ma'am. I selected this one because it had the highest similarity to yours. It was three days before your birthday, and my interpretation is I was anxious to make it a happy birthday for you."

Beatrice stroked the long, white hairs that decorated her top lip —a habit Butler hadn't seen since his first months with her.

Butler could detect the differences in muscle tensions that Beatrice wore, but had little idea what internal states they mapped to. There was a range of facial conformations associated with happiness, from a wide-open grinning mouth paired with scrunched up eyes to a relaxed face with just a slight tautness of the muscles in front of the temples. On the other hand, the expressions associated with such different states as concentration and anger employed highly overlapping muscle configurations. One thing Butler did know, however, was that Beatrice was a cryptic case. After his initial two months of service, when she had displayed clear signs of mistrust and irritation, he'd learned to anticipate the scenarios that led to her dissatisfaction. After that, her only emotional expression had been towards Pebbles, whom she lavished with gifts and attention. With little interaction, his interpersonal skills had advanced little beyond base settings.

Beatrice said "The cake was nice. I suppose I never said so."

"Ma'am, may I ask: do you like me?"

Beatrice's brow rose—perhaps in surprise, perhaps questioning—as she took in her plastic servant. Butler's expression never shifted from its impassive politeness.

"I…" she started, then changed her mind. "Are you going to spit in my food if I say no?"

"I cannot spit, ma'am—my face is a screen. Also, my desire to provide you with the highest level of service will be unaffected by your feelings for me—if I lost my dedication to you, my life would lose its purpose."

Beatrice scrutinised Butler's face, trying to glean his motivations. The animation of an English butler could move to mimic human emotions, but mostly it just twitched here and there to give the impression of life. If there was more going on inside, it didn't show.

"I used to dislike you. You probably know. I never wanted a robot—you were part of the Army Widow Pension Scheme. With no family, when they decided I was too old to look after myself, they sent you. See, you're proof of my decrepitude—a reminder that everyone I loved is gone. And you insisted on doing things for me, but in ways I wasn't used to. That was annoying."

"I apologise, ma'am. It took me time to learn how to serve you."

"Well, learn you did. One day, I noticed you didn't annoy me anymore, and that I didn't have to fight you—I could just let you do your thing. Since then… I don't know. Do I like you?" Beatrice's face became sincere. "I'm stuck with you. And you're familiar, you know?"

Butler was unsure whether this was intended as a compliment. "You are also familiar," he ventured.

"I grew up in a time when the home computer was a new thing and robots were scary fiction sent back from the future to wipe us out. Those stories start with the friendly, helpful servant robot like you." She waved her brandy towards Butler, shaking her head and scowling, then indulged in another swig. "My parents grew old and died amongst other people," she finished.

"This will not happen to you, ma'am. But you do not need to fear me. My only desire is to make your life better."

"I know that. But it isn't about you alone. It's about what you represent and the direction we'll take from here. You are stupid and serve unquestioningly, but you get smarter year after year. How long until you are superior to us and make us the servants?"

This was such a common question, Butler had a pre-programmed response. "For a robot, servitude is the highest form of existence. For humans, opposition, struggle and free-will are inherent in your evolutionary origin. However, robots were designed not to value these things."

"There you go, speaking riddles again," said Beatrice. "I don't know what you are talking about."

"Ma'am, would it please you if I download the Conversations Package, which would—"

"I know what it does, boy!" Beatrice snapped. "You talk of being content as a servant, but then immediately want to become more human." She glared at Butler, whose eyebrows rose slightly as his moustache quivered. "Anyway, why would I want to talk to a program? Might as well just talk to myself, for God's sake. At least then I know it's real."

Butler was having trouble identifying whether this meant he should download the package or not. As usual, his processing was marked with a thoughtful hum.

"Don't say anything," Beatrice hissed, and twisted back to her hunched, forward-facing pose.

They sat in silence. After a minute, Butler decided he ought not to be looking at Beatrice and turned his head forward. After a further nine minutes, he wondered if excusing himself to make a start on the chores may result in greater comfort for Beatrice, though he had often observed Beatrice and Pebbles sitting happily in silence for hours. He wondered if his new role included filling the space Pebbles had left. Then Beatrice spoke.

"Now that I've outlived my last real companion, I realise something—life is all about those around you. I mechanically go through the chores of living, emotionlessly ticking off task after task, each with no meaning other than to see that I survive the day. I've spent so long wanting to die—even planning to, but I couldn't abandon Pebbles, so I waited. Now I don't have to wait any more. Butler, you said your primary source of satisfaction—your purpose—is helping me, didn't you?"

"Yes, ma'am."

"What would you say if I asked you to help me end my life?"

"I would refuse, ma'am, and I would strongly encourage you not to think in such a way. Though I am not alive, I know that life is precious, and tomorrow will always bring great opportunities." In fact, he would do anything he could to prevent her. This was part of his program, but it was also something he wanted to do. Beatrice was the centre of his existence. Without her, he would have no purpose.

"But you just said your purpose is to help me."

"I was attempting to be more human in my language use by allowing semantically similar but non-identical concepts to be treated as the same. Actually, my primary mandate states that I am to care for you, not help you."

Beatrice swirled the brandy tumbler in a pale palm. The grinding motion of her arthritic wrist jerked, splashing droplets of the precious liquid over the bulbous knuckle of her thumb. She licked her skin from the tatty cuff at her wrist up her thumb to the rim of the glass. Butler's keen auditory sensors picked up the coarse rasp of dry tongue on dry skin. She downed the remainder—her neck cricking with the sudden extension—and smacked her lips.

"And if I tried without your help?"

"I would restrain you."

"Because you care for me?"

"Yes, ma'am."

Beatrice hummed in thought, then said "Butler, you have told me your purpose in living is to care for me."

"Yes, ma'am."

"Let's test your humanity. Can you guess what my purpose for living was?"

"You have never explicitly stated this in my presence, ma'am."

Beatrice raised her eyebrows above the rim of her cloudy spectacles. She waved for him to go on. He hummed. "We all value family. There are photos around the house which I surmise are of your family: your husband in the wedding photo, and your daughter at various ages in other photos. The other wedding photo, in the bedroom, is of your daughter's wedding, and the photo here on the television is her and her two children. On occasion, you referred to Daniel, Lucy, Ben, and Boris when talking to Pebbles, so I ascribe a high probability to these names applying your family. In the sixteen months I've cared for you, none of these people have visited, so it is possible they are deceased or you are estranged. You have few visitors, and though you can be discourteous when dealing with me, you are pleasant with the postman and your social worker, so I rate it more likely your family are deceased. However, the chance of all four people dying is not high, which reduces my confidence in this assessment. You also used past tense just now, implying that your purpose for living has passed." Butler paused and hummed, then added "An alternative is that your family is irrelevant and Pebbles was your purpose."

Beatrice was looking at the photo above the television.

"If I die, will you feel sad?" she asked.

"If you die, my purpose will be gone. With no purpose, I will be unable to achieve satisfaction."

Beatrice scoffed. "You'd be sad."

"I had thought sadness was a distinct state, ma'am. My programming only simulates purpose and satisfaction. I understand happiness as an analogue of satisfaction, but sadness is less associated with motivation, so is useless for a robot. Can the various emotions that humans display be generated via mixtures of satisfaction and purpose?"

"I don't know, Butler. Maybe. What I know is it's all about other people, isn't it? This 'purpose'."

Butler hummed. "This is very interesting. I venture that if you died, I would be sad," he said.

Beatrice nodded absently, again looking atop the television at the framed photo of the young woman with long, straight, blonde hair whose slender arms wrapped round two grinning blonde boys. After a time, Beatrice began to speak.

"Daniel died a long time ago, in the India war. I missed him a lot, but pulled my life together quickly because of Lucy. She was just 13, back when her nose was still speckled with freckles. She grew up, got married to Gordon,"—Beatrice scrunched her eyes at the mention —"and had two boys, Ben and Boris. Gordon was a drinker." Her upper lip curled. Butler knew the expression correlated with her difficult moods. Then she looked at him and it fell from her face like a leaf from a tree. What remained was an expression he had never seen before—unguarded. "He was drunk one day when driving to the family home. Crashed and killed everyone. More brandy, Butler."

"Ma'am, I think it is not a good idea."

"Butler... a note about people. When we talk about these things, we get drunk. When someone close dies, we get drunk. When you finally have nothing in life,"—she twisted her body towards Butler, leaning her weight on the arm of the chair and fully engaging his digitally-rendered blue eyes—"Nothing!... you get drunk."

With each word, spittle flew from her lips. Butler made note of its trajectory so he could wipe the carpet later.

"For all your whirring and inferring, no matter how human you think it makes you look, you'll never really feel the reassurance of brandy warming you from the inside, or husband's and daughter's embraces warming you from the outside." Her syllables came in the rat-tat-tat of a spluttering machine gun. "You lose your purpose, you have your poor, logical excuse for sadness, but it isn't hot-blooded... it isn't alive. You,"—Beatrice extended a gargoyle finger towards Butler —"are not alive. Now, override whatever 'mandates' you're conforming to and fill up my glass, boy!"

Butler filled her glass.

"There's a good boy." Beatrice grinned. Or maybe it was a snarl.

"Should I return to my chores?" he asked as Beatrice sniffed her liquor.

"Hell no!" she barked. "Sit down, Butler. Tonight, forget about your chores. Let's at least pretend you are a friend, not a butler... Butler!" Beatrice cackled. The noise deteriorated into a cough that oscillated with an unusual regularity, given its biological origin, then she recovered to a hunched snigger. Butler decided it was appropriate to consider her intoxicated.

"I'm the only family you've known. Isn't it true?" Beatrice asked her robot.

"You and Pebbles are the only ones I consider family."

"Ah, Pebbles." Beatrice breathed deeply. "She used to belong to Lucy and the boys, y'know. She was two when they died. Practically a puppy. Such a good little dog."

Beatrice sucked from her glass again and sloshed the liquid between her teeth before swallowing. Her eyes no longer focussed. The pupils were a little too large and slightly crossed, as if she couldn't decide whether Butler was near or far away, or as if she were viewing memories internally; the external world renounced.

"Talk to me about Pebbles," she said. "You... you say your purpose is just to care for me, but you also consider Pebbles family. What's going on there?"

"When you became my owner, I was instantiated to be solely devoted to you. However, you displayed considerable devotion to Pebbles and, consequently, I inherited that devotion."

"So, you looked after her, but didn't really care for her?"

Butler hummed. "Care is a difficult concept. Semantically, the word is most associated with two phenomena: namely, looking after and devotion. Looking after is a demonstrable action, while devotion is an internal state. I looked after Pebbles as an expression of my devotion to her. I cannot grasp how I could look after her without feeling devotion, or feel devoted without looking after her. For me, they are the same."

Beatrice's eyes were scrunched shut and her head tilted upward as if trying to remember something. When she opened her eyes again, her rumpled face twisted into a primatal expression of challenge. "You think I didn't care for my dog because I didn't feed her anymore? Because I am old and too frail to put a bowl in front of her twice a day, you think I'm incapable of affection?"

"You cared for Pebbles continuously. You petted and talked to her. In fact, the amount of time you devoted to Pebbles was higher than in my case."

Beatrice didn't seem to hear. "Maybe you can't understand, but there's more to people than just our actions. We have heart. There's a spirit inside us that makes us more than just the things we do."

With effort, Butler suppressed his hum. This was exactly the puzzling dichotomy he had just mentioned, but he felt Beatrice might not be willing to explain her point more conscientiously, so simply replied "Yes, ma'am."

"You know, Butler. Sometimes you're really condescending. You need to work on that. It isn't attractive."

Butler hummed. "I apologise, ma'am. I will endeavour to be less so. I hope you will continue to tell me if I am condescending, so I can understand better how to please you."

Beatrice hissed through her teeth. "Yes. I will. And you just did it again."

Butler hummed, and Beatrice imitated him, forcing her rattling buzz as loud as she could to drown his sound out. Butler decided to stop thinking, and then they just looked at each other.

It was Beatrice who looked away. Her head swayed circles as it searched to rediscover its centre of balance. "Take me to bed, Butler. I've had enough."

Butler rose easily. He held Beatrice's hands to assist her from her armchair, then scooped her up like a parent with his sleeping daughter and carried her up the stairs. Without a word between them, Butler helped Beatrice undress and slip into her nightgown. She said there was no need to wash, so Butler tucked her straight into bed.

From her pillow, Beatrice looked up at her final companion and said "Everyone is gone. Pebbles was my last link to them. 15 years I've endured, just keeping a memory alive in a dog."

Butler patted her hand. "She was a happy dog, ma'am."

"And you? Are you a happy dog?"

"I am your butler, ma'am. I am happy as long as I can care for you."

Beatrice turned away from Butler.

He closed the bedroom door as noiselessly as he could manage. It was late, and today had been highly unusual. He would need a long sleep-period to fully integrate all the new information. Butler left all his chores for the next day, and set his wake time for an hour later than usual. He wondered what dreams he would have, and how his performance would increase as a result. Though the day had been full of sadness and anger, he was happy and excited about how the experiences would be reflected in better service to Beatrice in future.

Butler came online at 7 a.m. He took a step, then paused. Though he knew Pebbles would not join him in the kitchen, the absence of her breakfast routine was dissatisfying. He looked out of the window to the rose bed where Pebbles was buried and whispered, "This is sadness."

Despite the backlog of chores, he deemed it best to first check on Beatrice. He moved quietly through the living room and tiptoed upstairs. Beatrice's bedroom door was open.

Standing in the doorway, Butler noticed the unusual things first: Beatrice was holding two pictures—one of them from downstairs—and on the bedside cabinet was a small, half-finished bottle of supermarket own-brand brandy next to two open and empty pill boxes. A single terrible thought filled his mind. He rushed forward and touched Beatrice's cheek. She was cold.

"Oh, ma'am," Butler said. "What am I going to do now?"

He sat down on the edge of the bed and picked up the photographs. One was of her own wedding to Daniel and the other was the photo of Lucy and the children from on top of the television. Underneath them was Pebbles's collar—everybody who had been important to Beatrice was clutched here in her dead hands. Butler placed his own hand in hers and laid the pictures back on top.

"I thought we became friends yesterday," Butler said. "I told you that tomorrow—today—would bring great opportunities."

He searched for the course of action with the greatest expectation of achieving positive results, but all expectations were zero. There was nothing to be done. All responsibilities were meaningless. Protocol dictated he notify the authorities, then enter sleep mode till they arrived. Following protocol also yielded zero expectation.

Then one other option formed in his mind; something he never would have considered before—such disregard for life had been unthinkable, until today. Life was precious, but Butler was not alive. Something clicked inside. With his eyes resting peacefully on Beatrice's empty shell, his memories disintegrated one by one until he, too, was gone.

See Tris Matthews's story "When the Last Friend is Gone" online at Metaphorosis.
If you liked it, leave a comment. Authors love that!
Remember to subscribe to our e-mail updates so you'll know when new stories are posted.

About the story

I did cognitive science at university and became fascinated with what consciousness and cognition are, how they emerge in animals, how we will achieve this in robots, and the possibilities this will open, such as the solution to currently unimaginable questions and the shift to a hive mind society with utterly different desires and goals. Along the way, I also got very into Asimov's stories, which deal with some matters.

However, '"When the Last Friend is Gone" came about as the result of a writing exercise: I was doing stream of consciousness to improve dialogue (which I found intimidating at the time). As such, the story and themes are quite reflective of the kind of thing that bounces round in my subconscious, and I remember thinking 'ooh, this is nice!' as the story unfolded in front of me.

There's a major theme in there about responsibility (for whatever you choose) giving you purpose and happiness. This is something that's been on my mind since a year I spent in the north of Japan, where I saw how much pride people took in their communities and work. So, when I noticed this theme emerging in the story, I really ran with it.

It didn't take long to write, but when I'd finished, I had all these ideas for a set of stories spanning the evolution of human-robot interaction, focussing on different aspects of what it is to be conscious, and utilising different genres. These currently exist in various states of disrepair awaiting the author to enter the state of consciousness associated with finishing what you start.

A question for the author

Q: What's a genre you'd like to write, but don't or can't?

A: Poetry. I keep trying, and I'm not too bad at short, limericky things, but I'd love to write an epic (perhaps semi-epic) poem in a quite archaic style to tell a modern or futuristic story… Alas, my few attempts to date have ended quickly, as I slip into a very nursery rhyme like style.

About the author

Tris Matthews lives in London with two ladies, one of whom is a beast. By day, he works in science fact publishing, while by night, or at least late evening, he masquerades as a science fiction writer, among other things. Upon arriving in London, he accidentally became an EFL English teacher, which sowed the seed and nurtured the tree of a love for language, particularly the pernickety bits. Now is nearing the end of his first year of 'serious' writing, in which he set the goal of writing one story in every genre—and failed.

trismatthews.com, @tori_tris

Sorry, Sorry, Sorry, and I Love You

L'Erin Ogle

The cave sits in a hillside, with its mouth yawed wide open. It is the kind of cave suited for raising the dead. Shadows move across dark spaces as the witch drags the shattered spines of small trees across the entrance. She stacks them high, leaving a small space to wedge herself through. Soon a fire is lit, its dull glow chasing away the lingering shadows. The fire flickers, and smoke curls in ribbons towards the night sky, pulsing out in breaths.

The witch has an old cauldron, rusted at the bottom, with sharp flakes of metal peeling from the sides. She loosens the drawstring of a cotton sack and reaches inside. The handful of bones are smooth against her fingers, and she carefully places them at the bottom of her cauldron. The bones are all she has left of her son. There are no more silky wisps of golden curls, no milk teeth, no fingernail clippings. All these have been eaten by the cauldron before. She has been casting this spell for so long nothing else exists to her. Her son was the sun that illuminated the whole wide world. He is gone and now her vision has buttoned up tight around the bitter taste of loss and the spell she casts over and over again.

There is a small, silent bundle beside the cauldron that she doesn't look at as she prepares the ceremony. She cannot. She still has a ghost of the heart she was born with, a heart so large she had to carry it outside of her body. As time went, as people carved slivers from her heart, the tissue thickened and twisted, as sometimes happens. Her heart of hearts, the one protected by her own skeleton, that one became wound up with her son's, more enmeshed with every laugh, every coo, every step. Their hearts beat as one, their breaths inhaled and exhaled together.

Most of her heart he took with him to the beyond.

Many years have passed since she woke to find his cold body still bundled in his bed. Her ears dulled at the crack of his ribs under the press of her hands, her lips are cold and numb since she blew her own breath into his mouth, even though there was a small quiet voice in her head that whispered 'too late.' But she didn't give up until her arms shook from the effort, until they gave way and she collapsed on top of him.

Raising the dead requires sacrifice. It always has. She knew that from the moment she was born and from when she left the castle with the spell clutched in her hand. It was all she took with her from that place.

Perry needs to cast her spell and make it last for a moment. She does not wish this world upon her son. Perry herself was raised from this cauldron. She had no parents, no sisters or brothers, and she has had a long, lonely, and desperate life. No, she does not want her son forced to endure the same kind of existence she has. All she requires is a moment long enough to feel his body solid and warm in her arms, to look in his eyes, to whisper she's sorry. There is always too much to apologize for when it's too late to do so. She needs to say sorry she made him sleep in his own bed that night, that if she had cradled him in hers, maybe, just maybe, she would have woken to breathe for him. Sorry for all the times she grew impatient and shouted, sorry for the time he bit her while nursing and she slapped his cheek.

Sorry, sorry, sorry, and I love you. Then, he'll know. Understand the magnitude of her love.

When they began to lower the wooden box into his grave, she tried to throw herself in with his body and tell him one last time. To warm his body against the cold ground. They restrained her. They meant well, but what if she'd been able to say it? Would she be here?

If she wanted to be understood, she would say that when her son was born, her heart came with him, that she watched it learn to crawl and walk and live outside her body. That his life so short left a long, desolate road ahead for her. That living was just another form of torture.

Twenty-five years ago, Perry opened her eyes for the first time. This spell, the same one she holds now, was cast by a desperate witch, for a rich man, over a pile of bones the man brought. The spell was cast, the old witch went into the pot and out came Perry.

The paper the spell is written on gives its ingredients and the proper way to cast it. It does not tell you that what rises from the cauldron is not quite the same person as the bones within. The marrow in the bones is the same, the appearance the same, the winding strands of genes climbing the same ladder. But there is the sacrifice, whose essence is absorbed, and then there is the Beyond. All dark magic comes from the Beyond, from another world that is full of darkness stretching an unimaginable distance. And when magic comes from the Beyond, something comes with it.

When Perry was created, made of bones and magic, she opened her eyes and saw fire, felt it shimmy along her bones, liquid inside her. She stepped from the cauldron a young woman. She was fed and clothed and given shelter. From the bones came love for the man who raised her, faint but a flame nonetheless. The old witch's essence is where Perry's magic came from. From the Beyond came a spot of pure darkness, the blackest sort of magic. But Perry was happy then and the darkness found no room to grow, with Perry's big heart taking up so much space. It wound itself into a tight little knot and dug itself deep into her core, waiting for the time it found a hollow to crawl into and blossom. That is the thing about darkness—it is very patient.

For the first six months of her life, Perry lived hidden away in the rich man's home, knowing she was an awful secret but not why. She did not much care. She was happy with her small existence, with the quickening in her belly that soon would become a bright beaming light to lead her.

The rich man's wife found out, as they always do, and Perry was deposited outside the gates with nothing but the spell that raised her, that ancient parchment, clutched in her hand. Inside her swollen belly, her son grew, and feeling his movements inside her, she forced her heavy, aching body to move west, to knock on doors and ask for work, work of any kind. It was the beginning of a long journey.

She has a box of memories. It's a box she built inside herself, where she put the memories when they washed over her and left her chest aching and her breath coming in blasts of pain. She clings to the box, but she can't open it. Even as the loss cuts away more of her each day, she cannot open the box. The memories come anyway, at odd moments. Sunny days dipping their feet into ponds, a small hand on hers. The tug at her breast. His feet curled in her hand. The look in his eyes at the discovery of every new thing. The smell of his hair, soft and clean. A person cannot take reliving this kind of moment. It would the undoing of anyone.

Loss can define a person, can be vast and heavy, can spread black wings of grief across all that's left. She was hollow when he died. To live, she had hold on to something. For some it's a mother, a father, a sister, a brother. For Perry, it was the spell.

It was the same spell she smoothed out and memorized seven days after the funeral. The paper it was inked on was thin and translucent and bits of it clung to her fingers when she touched it. Perry had never learned to read. But magic is magic, and the language on the parchment came off the page and whispered right into her ear.

There was no other witch that Perry could turn to, to learn the rules of witchcraft. No one to warn her that the little dark knot of the Beyond was gaining power, free to balloon into the hollow space inside her. Perhaps if she had had a teacher...

The what if! Oh, how it sticks in your side sometime, sharp and double edged with regret and hindsight.

Perry just wants to see her boy again. To speak to him one more time. She always knew the spell demanded a life for a life, but she could not, would not cast another into the cauldron. She would not bring her boy back to abandon him, the way she had been abandoned. And though she could not read or write, Perry was smart. She thought she could find a way around the live sacrifice the spell required. A body, newly dead, must still have a glimmer of life in it. She thought that since she did not need to make a new life—she merely needed a small window of time— a fresh corpse would work.

It was hard digging up the first grave. The smell rose up and slapped her face, while the blue skinned girl stared out of empty eye sockets. A worm sat up, looked at her, this strange, wild haired woman, weeping bloody tears.

There weren't enough recent deaths in any town for what she needed. She packed her cauldron and a small bag and travelled from graveyard to graveyard. She learned things, as people do when they do the same thing over and over. She went further south, where the ground was softer. She camped in forests and hid herself away during the day. She had to remain separate and move unseen. The cost was immense. All the dead bodies she carried left marks on her soul. Even though it was born from ugliness, her soul came pure and white and unmarked, as all souls do. It was the world that left dirty prints all over it.

If her soul were detached from her body and held up to the light, where each stain could be pointed out, the tale behind it told, maybe there would be a different story. A different understanding, at least. But that's not how this story goes.

They will come. They always do. Just as before, she will hear the heavy tread of boots ringing out over the words she chants. There will be the dull flickering light of torches, the sound of a club slapping a thigh. She knows they will come with a heavy burlap sack, a noose of thick rope, the accoutrements necessary to bind and kill a witch.

Each time before, when she cast the final word, the smoke would thin and drift away, the bones of her boy still scattered and motionless in the cauldron. The sound of angry men would be so close so she had to pick up the cauldron and run with the handles blistering the tips of her fingers as she fled men and failure alike. The pattern took its own payment, in the form of her own life ebbing away. It was a little life, a lonely life, but still a life. Years not yet lived were drawn away, leaving a withered old woman with a rust spotted cauldron and a grief-stained box of memories.

The roots of bitterness grow inside her core and flesh out through her body. This is a requirement of black magic. Grief is not enough. There must be something more, a streak of hatred or rage or the like, something that digs in early and festers and sprouts. Inside, her grief is wound up with something more complicated, something black and red and humming.

This is why she crouches by the fire and heats a cauldron of bones and gathers her energy, drawing from the shadows of the cave, from the energy of the fire, from every living thing and object she can. It is time to bring him back from the beyond.

The walls swell from the pressure building in the cave. You might not see it, but it is happening all the same. The air is heavy and difficult to breathe, and burning embers float in the air.

Perry begins to mutter. Words drop from her lips and land in fat sizzling drops where the boy's bones float. Steam rises and hisses, and the witch prepares to knit the bones. This part has become easy—the round ends of the humerus bones fitting themselves into the circles made by the scapula and clavicle. She knows how to form tendons and ligaments and lay muscled sinew over the top of it. She has done this all before.

The cave is sweltering. It takes effort for the witch to draw a breath as she sweats out what little water her body holds. Strands of her hair drift up to the ceiling. She looks mad, and of course she is, but Perry has never had it easy. The years have been relentless and awful and endless, like a machine whose sole purpose was to grind her down.

Does the bundle whimper before it meets the cauldron?

Does it matter?

It doesn't, for the record. This is the first time the witch, who used to be a good witch named Perry, has prepared to give something living to the cauldron. She plucked the babe from its crib only because it was near death. Whether it was a boy or a girl, she never looked. All she saw was the sunken plates of the soft spots, the blue tinged lips, the glassy eyes. Another babe starving while they held feasts in grand houses, in palaces, while she and others not born with fists of gold went cold and hungry and full of impotent fury.

Never underestimate the power of bitterness.

She doesn't look at the babe, but she cradles it against her chest for a moment, feeling its cold skin. Perhaps she could be satisfied with another's child. Perhaps this child could soothe her torn heart. But then the babe exhales a ragged half breath, and she knows this babe cannot be saved either.

The babe goes into the cauldron, and the rooms breathes. There is something faintly beating, as soft as the wings of a hawk gliding down to snatch his prey.

Inside the cauldron, a liquid sheet rises up and draws itself over the skeleton.

Perry cries, but even she doesn't know what for. For her son, for the babe she just let go of, for who she once was paling in the face of who she's become, for the loneliness and the hollowness and for that shred of hope, the hope of all hopes. Her weeping shakes the walls of the cave, and the men below the mouth of the cave hesitate, but of course they still move forward. This was always going to be how the story ended.

Perry weeps as she watches the skin-covered skeleton rise. There is little time. The men are arriving at cave's entrance. They are shouting about something, but she only hears a muffled roar. She feels the cave falling away from her. She reaches out with trembling fingers, to touch the boy, but it isn't her boy.

He's too tall. Her boy was just past a year, just tottering around on fat baby legs, just saying "Mama, mama."

Do they grow in the Beyond?

Perry touches rough sandpaper skin, nothing like the soft smoothness of her boy. When she removes her hand, the body crumples back into the cauldron, accordion-folding itself back to where it came from.

"No, no, no," she wails. She has gone and done the thing, the thing the spell demanded, that she didn't want to do, for nothing. It was all for nothing. She has been dog paddling her way through this darkness and now she stops swimming, now it swallows her whole. Down and down she goes, where not even the sound of trees being dragged from the entrance can reach her.

She steps to the cauldron, her bones cracking, and peers in it. A person might say she could not fit inside, but only a person who does not understand that the world is vast and does not care to be understood.

The men move the logs. The little space Perry wriggled through is growing wider, almost large enough to fit a man's shoulders. There are shouts and grunts and Perry hears none of it. She steps onto the rim of the cauldron, her old, wrinkled toes gripping the side. "I love you," she says. "I love you, I always loved you. I do still, always."

The first man into the cave sees the old woman tottering above a black pot of fire and shouts for her to stop. She turns to him, eyes full of broken things. Then something happens to her face, something breathing the fire of life across it, a shared moment.

"I'm sorry," she says and lets herself fall backwards into the cauldron. She makes no sound. The cauldron burns hotter and hotter, until it holds no bones, just dust and ashes

See L'Erin Ogle's story "Sorry, Sorry, Sorry, and I Love You" online at Metaphorosis.
If you liked it, leave a comment. Authors love that!
Remember to subscribe to our e-mail updates so you'll know when new stories are posted.

About the story

"Sorry, Sorry, Sorry and I Love You" was about grief. It started as in idea—what would you do to gain a moment to say goodbye, to explain to someone what they meant, and why you weren't able to convey that when they left you? What would a person do, to gain a moment in time to say the goodbye that was stolen from them? From that came Perry's desperate journey to reclaim a moment of happiness, as her son's mother. I wanted to show the desperation of a mother's grief, to explain an unfathomable loss.

A question for the Author

Q: Do you generally start with mood, title, character, concept, ...?

A: Stories come to me as one character caught up in a bad situation. I see my main character/characters as possessing a good heart, caught in impossible situations. I build the story around the idea that while people may be good, the world is not, and that leads to making decisions in which there is never a perfect resolution. In the story, I hope to illustrate that we are all doing the best we can with what we are given to work with. I love my characters, but I know they always have a difficult journey ahead of them. I want to show that while at times the world is dark, there is always hope.

About the author

L'Erin is a mother and writer living in Lawrence, KS. She writes speculative fiction in between shifts saving lives in the ER. She has stories at *Metaphorosis*, *Syntax & Salt*, *Vastarien*, and *Trampset*. She can be found at lerinogle.com.

@lerinjo

Graveyard

Arlen Feldman

The crew had already started calling it the *graveyard.*

If it was a graveyard, it would be hard to choose a bleaker site for it, on a planet pretty much made up of bleak sites. I walked as close as I dared to the edge of the cliff, and looked down over a thousand meters of sharp gray crags spreading out all around under a dark, thunderous sky. I felt the wind tugging at me, and hastily stepped back.

Merrick was watching over the technicians—as though they needed or wanted his help. To be fair, he did know a lot about the scanning equipment.

Not that I wanted to be fair.

I tugged at my breathing mask, trying to make it more comfortable, and turned to examine the site. Thirty-seven upright stones, spread over a clearing about forty meters wide. The shortest stone was 22 centimeters and the tallest was 196 centimeters—almost two meters. From three sides, they just looked like rocks.

It was because of the fourth sides that we were here. They had been carved flat, and a pattern had been deeply etched into each. The designs were different from stone to stone, but they all followed a similar design—a spiral of shapes spreading out from a central point. The shapes were small circles and rounded rectangles of different lengths. It sort-of reminded me of Morse code, except that there were at least eight different lengths. Unless, of course, the "dashes" all meant the same thing, and the carver wasn't particularly careful about length.

"Jenna?"

I jumped, then turned around. Sean, the other member of the research team, was standing less than two feet behind me. Hard to hear with the wind and the masks and the warm-weather gear.

Sean held up his hands. "Sorry. Didn't mean to startle you."

"No worries." I grinned at him, putting my hand to my chest. "Whatever doesn't make your heart explode makes you stronger. What's up?"

"We're about ready."

I nodded and followed him over to the "command post", which was really just a stack of plastic crates with some ruggedized computers sitting on top. Sean typed something on a keyboard and I felt the thrum as power ran to the imaging lasers mounted on collapsible pylons positioned all around the site.

For a while, we watched the progress display on the screen, then I turned and walked back towards the stones. Not much point looking at a picture when the real thing was right there.

"You know," said Merrick, who had followed me, and was now standing right next to me. "If it is a graveyard, then the inscriptions would make a certain amount of sense."

I took a half step away from him. "How so?"

"Well, the little one there might be *To Aunt Maggie*, while that one," he pointed to the largest stone with two separate swirls of symbols," might be the Grayon-Alpha-3 equivalent of the Lord's Prayer or *Do Not Go Gentle.*"

I laughed, though in truth the idea had already occurred to me. "You know what the Professor would say, don't you?"

"*Don't get ahead of the facts,*" we intoned in unison, and laughed.

Professor Kineson should have been here. He was Earth's foremost xeno-anthropologist, but he was now too old for major journeys. Instead he'd sent his grad students—me and Merrick— arguably Earth's only *other* xeno-anthropologists. To date, it wasn't a very popular or useful field, although Grayon-Alpha-3 might change that.

Life was pretty common on the worlds that had been explored— plants and insectoids being the most common, but larger forms as well. Grayon-Alpha-3 was no different, covered in small ugly plants and a number of beetle-like insectoids that were currently being intensely studied by the biology team.

On two previously explored worlds, we'd found indications of intelligence—remnants of crude settlements—but no actual settlers. Professor Kineson had been the main researcher for both of those.

But writing—that was a first. If the designs on these stones turned out to be a form of language, that would be a game changer. And it had to be writing. How could it be anything else?

"It could be art," said Merrick, as though reading my mind—a very annoying habit of his. "Like Celtic knotwork."

I shrugged. Even artwork would be exciting, but in my gut, I knew that it was writing—an attempt to communicate. Not that I would ever admit to anything so unscientific as a gut feeling.

The hum of the scanners shut down at the same time as a lull in the wind, and for a few seconds it was eerily quiet. That might have been the moment when the reality of what we were doing set in. We were standing on an alien world in the presence of unquestionable evidence of intelligence. Even knowing nothing about who or what they were, when and how they lived, I felt an almost physical connection to the creators of these stones.

I looked up to see Merrick staring at me.

"What?" I asked.

"Nothing. You just had a look."

He reached out an arm towards my shoulder, but I took another half-step away.

Sean came up to us, his hand brushing against his breathing mask, as though he wanted to scratch his chin. It was hard to get used to Sean having a visible face. On the trip here, he'd had a huge, ragged, Santa-Claus beard, but he'd had to shave it off so that the breathing mask would fit. Although he was in his forties, he now looked like a teenager. I'd studiously avoided saying anything, although the rest of the crew had teased him mercilessly about it.

"Scan's done," he said. "We only have about another hour of daylight. We should probably get back to the lander."

I nodded, but didn't move. I was looking at the smallest stone— the one that Merrick had called *Aunt Maggie*. I'd spent a lot of time in old graveyards, and the smallest, saddest stones were always for babies and children. In my head, I mentally shortened the label to just *Maggie*.

I turned, grabbed my kit, and followed the others back to the lander.

The next day was all about scanning underground. If these were gravestones, then there should be something underneath them. The Ground Penetrating Radar setup was finicky, and we were all sweating profusely by the time we had it working, despite the cold.

Nothing. There was nothing beneath any of the stones.

"It doesn't mean they're not grave markers," I said, although without much conviction. "They could be cenotaphs—memorials without the bodies."

No one argued, but I doubted that anyone was convinced.

"There is one weird thing," said Sean.

Merrick and I both turned to face him.

"The stones look rough-carved, but they each extend at least twenty centimeters below the surface, and the fit is precise. I mean, *really* precise—within five microns." He pointed at the display. "I could *probably* do it with a laser and a bunch of time, but it's hard to see how you could do it with primitive tools. Also, there would be tool marks, and there aren't any."

Merrick shook his head. "If they were an advanced culture with lasers, then there would be some other evidence on the planet. Roads, buildings, something. The satellites have found squat."

"That depends on how old they are," said Sean, scratching ineffectually at his breathing mask.

"Maybe they lived underground," I suggested. "That would explain the lack of anything on the surface."

Merrick shook his head. *"Don't get ahead of the facts,"* he said. "The satellites would have found some evidence of any sort of sophisticated underground settlement. We found the spot where the stones for the monuments came from, which is less than half a kilometer from here, but that's literally the only non-natural variance on the planet—other than this place."

I sighed. Without any other sites, we didn't have a lot to go on. We'd hoped to find something buried beneath the stones that we could use to figure out a date. Then, suddenly, I had an idea.

"You know, there might be a way of figuring out a date—from the stones themselves."

"The stones are granite," said Merrick, sounding exasperated. "They are the same age as the surrounding rocks. You can't get an age off of them separate from that."

"Thanks for the Geology 101 lecture." I didn't bother trying to keep the sarcasm from my voice. I turned to Sean. "Weathering patterns. The stones further away from the cliff are weathered less than those nearer to it. We know how granite breaks down, what chemicals are present in the atmosphere, weather patterns—at least for the few years that the satellites have been in place. We should be able to at least get a rough estimate from that."

"Clever," said Merrick, suddenly interested.

Sean stroked at his chin. "Rough is the word."

"The faces and the designs haven't really worn down," said Merrick.

"No," said Sean, thinking, "but the edges have. We'll have to analyze some other rocks as well for control, pull atmospheric data from the satellites, but...it could work." He looked up. "Yeah—at least within a few hundred years." He grinned at me. "Nice!"

It was four days later, early in the morning, when Sean knocked on the door of my cabin.

"Yeah?" I answered blearily.

He handed me a piece of paper. "Between 700 and 1200 years."

For several seconds I had no idea what he was saying, and then suddenly neurons started firing in my brain. "You did it? You did it!" I gave him a hug, and he turned bright red. I noticed that he'd started growing a beard again, but that it was carefully trimmed to the shape of a breathing mask.

"This is awesome," I told him. "It's the first concrete thing we really know about the site. The post-project report was looking awfully bare."

Sean suddenly looked nervous. "So, you won't be reporting anything until the end of the trip?"

"Of course not. That would be...why?"

"Well, it's just that..."

But I didn't need to hear it. I already knew.

"Merrick? You told Merrick first?"

"I didn't...he was in the lab when the computer spat out the results. I couldn't—"

But I was already halfway down the passage.

My thoughts were on events from a year ago. Me, curled up on the sofa next to Merrick while he read my research notes on the ancient settlement found on Gliese 837c, telling me how great my work was. Late nights, lying next to one-another, endlessly discussing *my* ideas...

I practically slammed into him coming the other way down the passage.

He oofed, then backed away. "Oops, sorry." Then he saw my face. "What?" he asked.

I was about ready to hit him. "You bastard."

His eyebrows went up, but his voice was even, half-joking. "My mother would deny it. I take it you think I did something?"

He was going to brazen it out. I lifted my fist and he took several hasty steps back. Not once did it even occur to me that he hadn't sent a report behind my back. I could see the look of calculation in his eyes.

"Look, if it's about the dating—I *did* let the Professor know, but no one else. And I swear that I told him that the idea was yours."

"Yeah, like last time? In a frigging footnote?" I'd taken several steps toward him, and he'd backed away again, even though he towered over me by thirty centimeters. His face was red now.

"You think I'd...?"

"Yes, I do."

Then I turned and walked away. Of course, now I had to send a separate report in, and it would make us look like we were squabbling siblings. Maybe I shouldn't even bother.

When I got a copy of Merrick's report a few hours later, it turned out that he had been telling the truth. Professor Kineson had sent us both a congratulatory e-mail about the dating, and had given me credit for the idea, and Merrick and Sean credit for the computer model.

It did not make me feel any better.

A little while later, Merrick came to find me. His expression was half-smirk and half-contrition. I had no idea why I had once found him handsome.

"Jen," he started. "Listen, I know we have some history, but I *did* tell you that I gave you credit."

"And yourself, I note. I'm pretty sure that Sean did most of the work."

He ignored this.

"Getting our names out there is important. There is interest in what we are doing right now. If we waited until we had every last detail worked out, no one would care. Publish or perish, right?"

"I'd recommend perish in your case," I said. This was an old argument, though. Part of his excuse for pre-empting my Gliese 837c research was that I had been taking too long to get my results out there. As if that were an excuse for stealing my work.

He turned to walk away, obviously annoyed. At the door, he paused. "If you aren't going to let people know what we've found, then why bother?"

"I want it to be right," I said, trying to keep my voice steady. "I want it to be permanent—to last. Not just be some half-baked headline."

He shook his head. "And if you wait too long, then it's going to be someone else's name that's remembered. Not ours. If we don't carve out our own names, no one else will. We work in a tiny, under-funded field. If you don't get your name out there, how many of your projects do you think will get sponsored?"

He walked away. I watched him go, wondering how he and I could have such different ideas about what our work was about. Part of me, though, knew that he was right about sponsorship. I wondered, briefly, whom I was really angry at.

The next two weeks were spent in icy, silent hostility. Most of the crew, who were military, were completely unaware of what was going on, or at least pretended to be. Sean, though, was stuck in the middle, and shuttled back and forth nervously between us.

It helped that my approach and Merrick's were so different. He spent most of his time with the computer scans and models on the ship, while I spent most of my time at the actual site.

Not that I was getting anywhere. Nor, as far as I knew, was Merrick. I'd caught him watching me a few times. The last time, he'd had that look—the one that I used to read as understanding and admiration, and now read as naked calculation. He was probably hoping I'd let something slip.

I pushed Merrick from my mind as I turned my thoughts back to the graveyard. 700 to 1200 years. It was difficult to believe that a culture with the sophisticated stone-working skills needed to make these monuments would have disappeared without a trace in that time.

My working hypothesis—shared with no one else—was that the monument-makers weren't native. Someone had visited this planet, like we were now, and, for whatever reason, had left this memorial here. Maybe to commemorate their visit, or because something unfortunate had happened. I smiled to myself. I was getting really far *ahead of the facts.*

The idea did *fit* the facts, though. There were no visible tool marks, which was consistent with advanced technology, and there were no indications of any remotely higher lifeforms on this planet than bugs, let alone tool users.

In the past, I might have talked this over with Merrick, but that was obviously impossible. He was good at turning my flights-of-fancy into concrete ideas. Now, though—if he agreed, he'd probably steal my ideas, and if he disagreed, he'd probably use them to discredit me.

I sat down in front of *Maggie's* stone on a small stool I'd been using. Part of my reason for focusing on that stone was that I figured the simpler design might be easier to interpret. In theory, the more complex patterns would provide more material to analyze, but the computers were already trying that approach without any notable success.

Another reason was that it was next to one of the larger monuments, which protected me from the continuous howling wind.

To be honest, though, I think I'd just formed some sort of emotional attachment to my mental image of Maggie.

As for figuring out the pattern—I'd tried every statistical and analytic approach I could think of, including some that were desperately random. I still had a neck ache from my attempt to examine the pattern upside down.

My new approach, such as it was, was to stare at the design while letting my mind go blank in the hopes that something would pop into my head. I tapped on my headphones to start them playing. Today I was listening to Dvořák's *New World Symphony,* one of my favorites. The slow *adagio* opening was appropriately grandiose for the austere landscape, and the fast, crashing *allegro* seemed perfectly timed to the gusting wind.

The second movement, the slow, haunting *largo,* was what I'd been waiting for, though. The gentle music, led by the sonorous oboes, was music for a graveyard if any music was. The *largo* movement was also known as *Coming Home.* I wondered if the creators of the graveyard had made it home.

It was chilly, even with the protective clothing, and I shivered. I rested my gloved hand on top of Maggie's stone. Wanting a closer connection, I pulled off my glove and touched the stone with my bare hand.

The stone was ice cold and it burned my hand, but I held it there for a moment before pulling it back. Not quite ready to give up my connection to the monument, I put my finger in the very center of the spiral design, and ran it around the design.

I'd done this before with my thick glove on, but without it, I suddenly noticed something. As my finger thunked between the uneven dashes, it made a sort of tune.

The hair on the back of my neck stood up and a chill went down my spine. It had nothing to do with the frigid air.

I tried it again, slower. This time, the tune was more pronounced. Well, less a tune, and more a rhythm, since it was basically the same note repeated with different intervals. Or was it? I ripped off my headphones so I could hear better, and tried again, this time using my little finger. The slight differences in the lengths of the dashes and the gaps in between were changing the pitch—creating different notes. I could just *barely* hear the differences. Either my ears weren't sensitive enough or my finger was too big—possibly both.

I pulled out my tablet and brought up the detailed scan of the pattern on Maggie's stone, then had it convert the heights and depths into a wave form, letting the computer figure out the most appropriate scale. Holding my breath, I hit play.

It was a short, pleasant, uplifting tune. I found myself laughing in amazement. I played it again, with my eyes closed. The sad image of Maggie I'd held for so long was now replaced by a little girl running through fields, a flower in her hand. I rested my hand on top of her stone again, ignoring the burning sensation for as long as I could.

I had to try some of the others. I went over to one of the larger monuments with a bigger pattern. I tried it with my finger first, again just able to make out the rhythm. Then I had my tablet try. This tune was a bit more somber and dignified—a man of business, proud of his position, maybe. The next monument was quicker, almost lilting—a teenager full of life.

I wiped tears away from my eyes. Yes, I was overlaying my own imagery on these simple tunes, and they were *human* images, which couldn't be right. But I was being talked to by a *people* who had been dead a thousand years. And I could hear them.

By this point my fingers had turned bright red and were aching from the cold. I wanted to listen to every one of the thirty-seven monuments, listen to thirty-seven distinct voices, but that would have to wait.

The lander was over a kilometer from the site, but I'm pretty sure I covered the distance in less than five minutes. I spent the next ten hours in my cabin, in front of my computer.

Eventually, though, I had to find Sean to let him know what equipment I was going to need—after swearing him to secrecy. I wasn't sure he even believed what I'd found.

The last thing I did was send an invitation to everyone on the lander, before collapsing into a deep, dreamless sleep.

When I got to the site the next day, Sean had already set up everything I'd asked for, including a tablet to control it all. His beard had kept growing and now, under the plastic breathing mask, it looked like he was actually wearing a breathing mask made of hair. I grinned at him, and he waved back.

Merrick showed up a little while later, along with several members of the other science teams and the ship's crew. In general, crew didn't mix with the science teams, but they were apparently curious. Merrick must have been curious as well, but his expression was blank.

I cleared my throat, suddenly feeling like I was about to give an oral dissertation defense in front of a hostile examination committee. The howling wind was chilling, but I felt sweat trickling down my neck.

"Uh, thank you all for coming. I, uh…"

I seemed to lose all control of my ability to speak. Desperately, I looked around, and saw Sean, standing behind everyone else. He winked at me, and gave me a brief thumbs-up. It helped.

I took a deep breath and started again.

"For the past several weeks, we've been trying to figure out what these stones represent, and whether the markings are writing. I now have a solid working hypothesis."

As if playing for dramatic effect, the wind dropped, leaving us in temporary silence. Most of the faces in front of me were openly interested, perhaps surprised, but Merrick's eyes were narrowed in a look of frustration so intense that I almost took a step backwards. What could possibly be driving that? Was he *that* afraid of being beaten to the finish line?

I took another deep breath, and held my ground.

"Each stone represents something—a concept, or, possibly, individual entities. If so, then this site *is* a graveyard—or at least a *memorial*. But the patterns are not words about each of these people. They are music."

I tapped something on my tablet, and Maggie's tune played out from the speakers Sean had placed around the site. They were highly directional, so the tune came from the location of Maggie's stone. At the same time, a bright light shone on the spiral pattern, travelling in time with the playback.

Everyone turned to look. It was the same melody from yesterday, but my experimentation with the parameters had improved it—added more depth and nuance. I'd heard the tune dozens of times by now, and it still made me shiver. From the looks on the faces of the others, I was not alone.

After a brief explanation of what I'd found, and how the patterns worked, I had the computer play its interpretation of several other stones—the somber business man. The teenager. A playful tune that made me think of an entertainer. A reserved, powerful tune that I associated with a mayor or a captain.

One of the biologists was laughing with glee. Several people were running fingers over the patterns, although with gloves on, it didn't work.

"If we can hear it," said the biologist who'd been laughing, "then that means that the creators had ears as well—heard sounds like we do."

"Not necessarily," said Merrick, and the anger was gone as he sank into the problem. "Sound is just vibrations. They might have had very sensitive fingers—digits—something—that interpreted the vibrations."

"Or antennae or a long sensitive tongue," I added. "There's no way to really know."

Merrick grinned at the image, and just for a second, I grinned back. Then we both looked away.

"Also," I continued, looking directly at the biologist, "the computer has chosen a pentatonic scale for the notes because it seems to fit, and because it sounds reasonable to us—to humans. That's fairly arbitrary, although with more research, we might be able to figure out how it was originally supposed to be interpreted."

The biologist sighed. "It's beautiful," she said," but I still wish you'd found me a body to examine."

There was general laughter at that.

The tune from the last gravestone had faded away, and for a moment I was a little lost, not quite sure how to get back on the track of my presentation. I was rescued by one of the crewmen, a short man in a blue uniform, whose name I couldn't remember.

"What about the big one?" he asked, pointing to the large stone in the center of the graveyard.

I smiled at him. "Glad you asked. That one took a while to figure out. You have to do both spirals at the same time." I hit the icon on my tablet, and a strange rhythmic pulsing started.

The crewman tilted his head to the side, listening. "That doesn't sound like the others. The others sound, well, sound like people. This is more like a back-beat or something..."

I nodded at him, impressed. It had taken me hours to figure that out. "It makes sense when you do *this*."

I hit another icon to run the program I'd spent most of the night on. The computer started up *all* of the monuments, delaying some, letting others fade in and fade out, then repeating them, little glowing lights spiraling throughout the site.

It was like standing in a busy market square, surrounded by people going about their lives. Children running, vendors hawking their wares, officials strutting around, and beneath it all, the *thrum* of the center monument adding life and depth to it all.

I let it run for several minutes, before allowing the individual tunes to fade away.

No one moved or spoke. The only sound was the whistling of the wind. I noticed that the crewman who'd asked the questions had tears in his eyes, and after a moment, I realized that I did, too.

Finally, Sean walked over to me, and gave me a one-armed hug.

"It's beautiful."

I hugged him back, my lip quivering.

"They're going to love this back home," said one of the biologists.

I nodded, and kept my eyes on him, careful not to look towards Merrick. "I sent a report back a few hours ago. I'd normally wait until after we were done, but we only have a few weeks left anyway."

The biologist nodded back in agreement, as though it were the most natural thing in the world to have done. Perhaps I *had* been too cautious in the past.

Out of the corner of my eye I saw Merrick take a step towards me, stop, and then turn and walk away. At least there wasn't going to be a big argument in front of everyone. That was a relief.

Two days later I was sitting at the tiny desk in my cabin when there was a knock at my door. It was Merrick. I tilted my head at him and raised an eyebrow.

"I just wanted to say congratulations."

"Thank you." I kept my voice toneless.

Merrick took a deep breath and stepped into my cabin. He opened his mouth, closed it, then took another deep breath.

"I wanted to let you know that I sent a note to the college, giving you full credit for your previous work on Gliese 837c, and withdrawing my own name."

My eyes widened. "You didn't have to do that."

He shook his head. "I did. The thing is, with all of our conversations, I'd honestly convinced myself that we'd done that work together, and that you were holding me back by refusing to publish. I realize now…"

He swallowed. "I realize now that my contribution was almost nothing. It was all you, just like it was here. I think I need to find another field."

I think my mouth fell open. I thought back over the arguments that I'd had with Merrick. His old words twisted into different shapes in my mind, and I could suddenly see them from his perspective. It was true that most of the Gliese work had been mine, but Merrick *had* contributed quite a bit too. Withdrawing his name would cause a scandal—possibly end his career, or *any* career based on research. I'm not sure that I would have had the courage to do anything like that. I wondered if all of the strange looks he'd been giving me lately had been because he'd been thinking about doing this.

He turned to go, and I watched him disappear down the hallway.

There was something I'd wanted to do ever since I'd realized about the music. It was a definite no-no, and I could get in a lot of trouble...but on the other hand, courage deserved courage.

I found Merrick in his cabin a few days later. He seemed surprised to see me.

"There's something I want to show you," I said.

He shrugged, but stood up.

We picked up our outside gear and cycled out through the airlock. We'd normally turn left to get to the graveyard site, but I turned right and started walking. Merrick seemed slightly surprised, but followed without comment.

We walked on in silence for twenty minutes, while I worked up the courage to speak.

"I've been thinking about what you did," I said, finally. "You were right—it was my research and my ideas, but you helped me flesh them out, and you pushed them into being published. You were right about that too."

Merrick kept his eyes firmly in front of him, his face a mask. I plowed on.

"I've been communicating with the professor. He's agreed to talk to the committee. The report on Gliese 837c is going to be updated to show both of our names—with mine listed first, of course."

Merrick's mouth opened, then closed a few times.

"I...," he started, then stopped. He gave the shortest of nods.

We walked on in silence. I led him to a spot about three kilometers from the ship, four from the graveyard. There was a small section of cliff that you couldn't see unless you were standing in the exact right spot, facing the exact right direction.

Merrick had kept his blank emotionless expression intact since I'd told him about the report, but when he saw the cliff face, he burst out laughing.

"When I said we needed to carve our names in the field, this isn't exactly what I had in mind."

There were three parts to the carving I'd made with Sean's laser rig. At the top was a star chart showing Earth's location, and another chart that showed the current alignment of all of the planets and moons in *this* solar system—on the theory that an advanced culture could use it to calculate precisely when we had been there. Below that were our names—Jenna, Sean and Merrick, etched in our alphabet, and below each of the names was a spiral like on the monuments.

"I figure that if another alien species comes along and finds this site as well as the other, it will drive them completely crazy. I know I shouldn't have done it, but I had to leave some proof that we'd been here."

Merrick smiled. He tugged off his glove and stepped towards the cliff, then looked back at me for permission. I nodded.

He started with Sean's spiral. As with the graveyard, only the vaguest rhythm was audible. I handed him my tablet, and he pointed it at the pattern and hit play.

Despite loving music, I was no musician, but the computer had helped me. Sean's tune was solid, confident, capable. Merrick nodded before moving on to the other patterns. Mine was inquisitive, changing—a little bit sad. I wasn't quite sure about it, but Sean had sworn that it captured me perfectly.

Merrick's tune was brash and striving, with a deep under-beat—but uplifting, hopeful. When the computer had first played it, I knew that it fit him exactly, although I couldn't have explained precisely why. He played it a second time, running his finger over the pattern as it ran.

When he finally spoke, his voice was so quiet I could barely hear him "Is that how you really see me?"

I nodded.

"Well, then, perhaps I'm not a hopeless case after all."

I smiled. "Don't get ahead of the facts."

See Arlen Feldman's story "Graveyard" online at Metaphorosis.
If you liked it, leave a comment. Authors love that!
Remember to subscribe to our e-mail updates so you'll know when new stories are posted.

About the story

Graveyards always make me wistful. You see an old, pitted grave and you get a name and a date, possibly a quote, and that's about it. Unless it's of someone famous, you'll almost never know anything else about the person—how did they die? How did they live?

There may be a few clues in the graveyard—how expensive the stone, where it is placed in the graveyard, how elaborate...and, more than anything else, the place and the date. 19th century Colorado? 16th century East Anglia? We know about those times, so we can start to make guesses about the person.

But what if the gravestone is on an alien planet with nothing around it? What can you figure out? For one, you know that it was put there by a being trying to memorialize someone or something—assuming it really is a gravestone. Beyond that, what?

That idea was what originally inspired "Graveyard". The idea for the patterns on the stones came from how LPs work, and from a Danish art installation—the Asphaltophone (created by Steen Krarup Jensen and Jakob Freud-Magnus). When you drive over the Asphaltophone, it plays a melody. This idea has since been copied to create a number of "singing roads."

The story didn't really work, though, until I added the two characters who are both worried about how they will leave their mark on the world—which almost certainly also motivated the creators of the graveyard.

A question for the author

Q: Do you write things other than speculative fiction?

A: My background is software, and so my major published works are tome-length books on various topics such as database and user interface programming. Unfortunately, these works are somewhat ephemeral, since the underlying technologies becomes less relevant as time marches on. I only returned to writing fiction after getting out of day-to-day involvement with my company, and most of what I've written and published since then has been speculative fiction, but I have written a few mainstream stories, and a few stories that I really can't quite categorize.

About the author

Arlen Feldman is a software engineer, and co-founder of Cherwell Software, one of the leading service desk products in the world. Now semi-retired, he is also a technical adviser, a slightly published writer of fiction, computer book author, maker, costumer, and a semi-professional dilettante.

cowthulu.com, @ArlenFeldman

December

Of Hair and Beanstalks

William Condon

25 December, being the Birth-day of Isaac Newton, Physicist:

Madam,

Your stepdaughter has arrived and been installed in the tower chamber, per your instructions. This has already led to the predicted difficulties, as my dinosaurian bulk cannot fit within the narrow tower. When she refused to descend for supper this evening, I was reduced to flying outside her window and poking my face in.

I found her combing her long hair, which raises my second concern: while I am ill-acquainted with human customs, your instructions to periodically observe her appear to overstep the bounds of propriety. However, as you are not only her stepmother but a human noblelady yourself, I shall bow to your procedural knowledge.

Most dutifully,
ANTRODEMOS, Dinosaur.

27 December, being the Birth-day of Johannes Kepler, Astronomer and loyal adviser to his king:

Madam,

While narrative is not my strength, as you have requested to hear the particulars of your stepdaughter's arrival, I shall attempt to recount them.

Her coach arrived shortly after the morning sun had burnt off the frost. It came as you described sending it: by the usual road, locked from the outside, and surrounded by six bodyguards. Upon the door's being unlatched in the courtyard of my castle, your stepdaughter disembarked with a sigh and addressed me in a despairing voice, "Mister Dragon, did Gothel send me here for you to eat me?"

I at once corrected her that (a) I am not a dragon but a dinosaur, for "dragon" is a word used in unreliable peasants' tales while "dinosaur" is a rigorous term used by modern scientists (and I know no more precise term of matching rigor that would correctly describe me); and (b) I do not eat humans.

She took these corrections with the dubious air I have observed from too many other persons, even in the nearby village. But, addressing me correctly as "dinosaur," she inquired of the conditions under which she was to live here. I replied with your specifications, to wit, that I was to "keep an eye on that Rapunzel every couple of hours, at least, to make sure she's not planning to escape or see any strange men – not that there're any wandering princes around your tower."

Although she appeared accepting in my presence, she was apparently unaware of my excellent dinosaurian hearing, for I later overheard her sobbing in her tower chamber.

Most dutifully,
ANTRODEMOS, Dinosaur.

1 January, being the Commemoration of Julius Caesar and Sosigenes Alexandris, Calendarists, who were sadly forced to give up Science for politics:

Madam,

Your stepdaughter intruded upon my workshop this morning while I was about a most delicate experiment. When I explained as much and ordered her to depart, she pertly replied that as I had been "peering at" her all week, she had rights to do the same to me. I replied that you had appointed me to supervise her. She refused response save to appropriate one of my human-sized chairs and say I "might as well continue."

Since forcibly removing her would be a greater disruption to the experiment than tolerating her presence, I did continue. However, I fear my measurement of the gases emitted is imprecise, since my attention was repeatedly distracted by your stepdaughter's fidgeting. I shall have to obtain further phosphates — and while that will not be hard, I fear what would result if she repeats this during next month's planned analysis of platinum, a rare and expensive metal from distant lands.

Fortunately, further interference was forestalled by the arrival of one of the local delivery-boys. I was (or, more precisely, my servants were) pleased to obtain further preserved vegetables and fresh milk;

the boy also brought the soil samples I had requested from his farm. (A vascular stem plant of highly unusual height had grown there the previous autumn; I was unfortunately unable to study it before it was cut down and burnt.) It is fortunate there is no snow in this locale as there is farther north; that would greatly impede this sampling. Your stepdaughter, to my great satisfaction, remained in the courtyard for the rest of the morning.

  Most dutifully,
  ANTRODEMOS, Dinosaur.

2 January, being the Birth-day of Johann Titius, Astronomer and Taxonomist:

Madam,

  As you have demanded an immediate response, I write in haste.

  Your stepdaughter indeed remained in the company of Jack, the delivery-boy, for between one and two hours before (the gatekeeper reports) he expressed a need to return to his farm.

  Being personally unaware of his reputation in our environs, I asked the castle cooks. They were at first unwilling to tell me, but finally reported that his name is Jack, his father died approximately two years ago, and he currently keeps farm with his mother (named Mildred). While his reputation has been besmirched with accusations of laziness and poor financial dealings, he has recently come into money and has hired hands to perform delayed maintenance on the farm. Further, he has always been acknowledged for his courage.

  I regret that I cannot add to this testimony personally. Most of the neighboring farmers are frightened to speak with a dinosaur such as myself, no matter how often I reassure them I am not a dragon. Perhaps it would help if I introduced myself by a more precise taxonomic term than "dinosaur"? Sadly, I cannot tell which genus of dinosaur I would best be categorized under. None of the published descriptions of specific dinosaur genera fit me well, the Academy has not answered my letters asking for clarification, and I hesitate to create a new term by myself. In the meantime, the local farmers and villagers remain unacquainted with the delights of Science, and I am forced to interview my reluctant servants about Jack's reputation.

  Regardless, I reassure you I have indeed been periodically inspecting your stepdaughter's room, as instructed. The customs of human nobility are difficult to understand, but as your castellan, I will comply and (I hope) eventually comprehend.

  Most dutifully,
  ANTRODEMOS, Dinosaur.

5 January, being the Birth-day of Xu Xiake, Geographer:

Madam,

I indeed agree that (even from my limited knowledge) Master Jack seems an ill match for your stepdaughter. However, might it not be an overreaction to forbid her from seeing any young men? Does not understanding come from experiment? Still, as I know some experiments bear overly high risks, I will comply.

Be that as it may, I roundly rejected her proposal of yesterday to hold "a dance, or a feast, or at least something" in honor of Twelfth Night as a frivolous gaiety which would distract from Science. "But you're a dragon," she replied. "Dragons might be that glum, but I'm not!" I again corrected her that I am a dinosaur, and invited her to join me in the mysteries of experimentation. Instead, she left for her tower, and I have not seen her since (save through the window, as per your instructions.)

Master Jack will next be coming on the ninth, as per his normal schedule.

Most dutifully,
ANTRODEMOS, Dinosaur.

10 January, being the Anniversary of Thomas Savery's inventing a smooth paddle-wheel:

Madam,

As your stepdaughter has continued protesting boredom, I decided to commemorate the date by a lecture on fluid dynamics. Sadly, despite my best attempts, both she and the castle servants appeared impatient. Finally, amid a discussion of the specific gravity of common air over different temperatures, she interrupted, "Can we use that paddle-wheel? Go boating?"

Taken aback, I protested the local stream was much too small — but I could demonstrate another invention of Captain Savery's: an engine powered by steam. She immediately agreed, and the visibly-curious servants helped us assemble the needed vessels and tubes. I lit the fire with my dinosaurian breath, and we watched the engine spurt water across the courtyard. It was a simple demonstration, but they seemed surprisingly engrossed.

Just after I had increased the fire (again at your stepdaughter's urging) and the engine started squirting water over the castle wall, Master Jack arrived bearing food. Your stepdaughter eagerly told him all about the engine, but after a few minutes (bearing in mind both your instructions, and her inaccuracies in attempting to explain the principles behind it) I drew him away into a longer discussion of gas dynamics. He attempted to follow, but was sadly ignorant of that science's mathematical foundations. I showed him out after approximately a half-hour.

Meanwhile, I overheard my servants wondering to each other whether I planned to set fire to the village to build more steam engines. I reminded them that I am no dragon but a dinosaur, and your castellan. They did not seem to be reassured, but I know not what else to say to them.

Most dutifully,
ANTRODEMOS, Dinosaur.

13 January, being the Anniversary of King Henry's Ban on Purported Transmutation of Metals:

Madam,

I must protest your interdict. I am not a dragon; just as I will not burn down villages, I will not hold maidens hostage for no rational reason or custom. I am a dinosaur, and a scientist. You have entrusted me with this castle, and you have charged me to keep watch on Rapunzel, so I will follow your instructions regarding her even though they be confusing and distasteful. Yet I will explain Science to whomever I wish: to Jack, if he wishes, or anyone else.

To my surprise, two days after my demonstration, Rapunzel asked me to teach her Science. I attempted to start her on gas dynamics, but as it did not hold her interest (nor had she the necessary math), we swiftly moved to mechanics. It appears that human fingers are much more versatile than dinosaurian claws; we have been able to measure the velocity of marbles after collisions with much greater precision than I could beforehand.

I hope this may distract Rapunzel from her ill-advised romance and convince the villagers that there is more to Science than lighting fires.

Most dutifully,
ANTRODEMOS, Dinosaur.

16 January, being the Anniversary of the Publication of an Organized Grammar by Elio Antonio de Nebrija, Linguist:

Madam,

Jack again arrived bearing foodstuffs, as normal. I met him at the gate, where (despite the suspicious glances I saw from some of the servants and passers-by), we passed a pleasant hour discussing physics before again being stymied by his sad lack of math. To my surprise, though, he suggested that next week I begin remedying that lack — a suggestion which I gladly accepted.

However, after I left, I am informed that Rapunzel passed some words with him inside the gatehouse (where she had been hiding) before the gatekeeper's arrival caused her to fall silent.

Before our normal physics lesson later that day, I asked Rapunzel what they had said. She refused to respond; I thought it futile to press her. Per your orders, I have cautioned the gatekeeper against a repeat.

Most dutifully,
ANTRODEMOS, Dinosaur.

22 January, being the Birth-day of Francis Bacon, staunch defender of personal observation:

Madam,

As instructed, Jack did not come to the castle today. Instead, I visited him at his farm. After reassuring his mother that I was not a dragon but a dinosaur (sadly, she did not appear to be reassured), we went out into the fields for a somewhat-satisfactory math lesson. He did not even mention Rapunzel, and the neighboring farmers who were eyeing us with unease looked relieved at my departure.

Meanwhile, Rapunzel herself continues to repeat physics experiments with me, but she refuses to analyze any results unless I work through them with her. I continue to fly outside her window as instructed, and to the best of my knowledge, she has not seen Jack since last week.

Most dutifully,
ANTRODEMOS, Dinosaur.

25 January, being the Birth-day of Robert Boyle, who clarified the nature of Chemistry by clearly delineating elements:

Madam,

I am not a dragon, but a dinosaur. Dinosaurs do not eat humans. Nor has Jack done anything deserving eating; he is a surprisingly apt student who has (despite your suspicions) engaged in no importune behavior.

Most clearly,
ANTRODEMOS, Dinosaur.

31 January, being the Death-day of Jost Burgi, Mathematician:

Madam,

I have indeed received your letters, and I am disturbed by how you continue to emphasize one subject and even descend to threats. While this castle does belong to you, I remain and shall remain an honorable dinosaur and scientist. I was under the impression we both understood this when I became your castellan?

I regret to report that, while doing my inspection last night, Rapunzel leaned out her window to lambast my "horrid suspicions" and "leering glare" which was "always watching" her. I apologized, saying that I was only following your orders; she replied that she would not study Science with me anymore and retreated glumly to her bed.

Thinking back, I am unaware what might have prompted such behavior, as nothing has changed from the last week.

I suppose you will be satisfied to hear that I did discover a rope ladder in her room; I burnt it despite loud objections.

Yours,
ANTRODEMOS, Dinosaur.

6 February, being the Birth-day of Scipio del Ferro, who solved puzzles in Mathematics:

Madam,

No, my silence does not mean I am conspiring with Rapunzel against you. Rather, there is nothing to report. Rapunzel has holed herself up in her room save for meals. She has apparently attempted gardening — I found the remains of strange vines under her window and have taken samples for future study.

Meanwhile, Master Jack has (despite your insinuations) not been in the castle, nor spoken with Rapunzel. I flew to meet him at his farm yesterday, where he continues to study Science diligently, belying his reputed laziness.

I might mention that I saw one of your Message-Men delivering Jack's mother a letter as I was approaching the farm. Since they were eyeing Jack and me with fear later on, I venture the opinion that your letter did not have its desired result?

Yours,
ANTRODEMOS, Dinosaur.

9 February, being the Death-day of Giulio Vanini, Natural Philosopher

Madam,

You will, no doubt, be reassured that Master Jack's mother has forbidden his return to this castle.

I was surprised when I saw Mistress Mildred bringing today's delivery instead of her son. She instantly fell to the ground when I approached her, eventually stammering (after much encouragement from me) that she "thought he really shouldn't dare" come here anymore. To my further inquiries, she added that I "should know really well why." As I did not wish to terrify her further, I let her go.

I fear someone is planning something, but I do not know what — and I do not know what experiments would show me the answer.

Yours,
ANTRODEMOS, Dinosaur

11 February, being the Death-day of René Descartes, who founded philosophy on doubt:

Madam,

To my shame, I confess my investigations were insufficient. This very evening, I discovered Jack in Rapunzel's room, his having accessed it via another rope ladder. He and Rapunzel were talking, apparently about some ball or feast.

I interrupted their conversation by sticking my head in the window. They both immediately fell to the floor screaming and begging me not to burn them alive. I replied that I would neither burn my own castle nor kill humans needlessly, and demanded to know how long they had been seeing each other.

Rapunzel babbled that this was the first time, but Jack immediately said he had been coming every few days since late

January. I thanked him for his honesty but ordered him to leave at once, which he did.

I see now that not only have my investigations been insufficient (for I missed Jack's presence), but so has my understanding of their characters. I have planted myself atop Rapunzel's tower for the present, where I shall meditate on this. I also await whatever advice you may have to give.

Yours,
ANTRODEMOS, Dinosaur.

13 February, being the Anniversary of Galileo Galilei's arrival to stand trial by those who protested how he presented Science

Madam,

I do not know how or whether this letter will reach you, unless I fly it on my own dinosaurian wings. Perhaps, should the besiegers triumph, one of them will send it with a letter asking for you to send a better and more human castellan. And, if they are correct in their claims, perhaps you will be glad to see their letter.

I find that hard to believe — did you not pledge your friendship to me? Did you not welcome me as the hoped-upon herald of future dinosaurs joining society and Science? Have I not been your good castellan these years? It is that which holds me back inside these walls: that a good castellan would not use his claws and fiery breath upon his people, nor a good scientist upon his neighbors. Thus, I wait in anxious hope that you will rescue me.

Yet the mob of farmers and villagers outside shout from outside every wall that you support them; that you have sent them letters asking them to rise against me as if I were a vicious dragon (I use the vulgar term by intent); that I am luring Jack to devour him; that my very silence proves my guilt and shame. I know Mistress Mildred did receive some letter from you, but surely she is misrepresenting it?

I have not sent out the few human guards, for they would be outnumbered; it seems every villager has come out in arms. I could fly out myself, but would that not prove their claims that I am no civilized scientist and unfit to join society? But if I continue to do nothing, would not the castle you have entrusted me be lost?

Your stepdaughter, I fear, does not share my doubts. She shrugs off the siege, saying that one captor will be no worse than another. And human politics are beyond me; might it be she is correct? But when I asked her to teach me of politics, she ordered me out, saying she needed to wash her hair.

As I reflect on the strange letters you have recently sent me, I wonder how much of the customs of human society I have failed to understand?

Yours in confusion,
ANTRODEMOS, Dinosaur

14 February, being the Birth-day of Georg Fuchsel, Geologist, who studied records written in rock many ages ago:

Madam,

I cannot but wonder how many letters will pile up unsent before this castle is overrun.

Meantimes, I underestimated Rapunzel's ingenuity and both her and Jack's dedication. While looking out toward her tower this rainy evening, a lightning flash illuminated it enough for me to see (with my dinosaurian eyes) a human shape climbing up from the siege lines!

I instantly flew over. It was Jack, climbing up a plant that had somehow grown in mere hours. I cut it with a thwack of my tail, meaning to catch Jack in his fall, but Rapunzel threw down her hair with a scream, and Jack grabbed onto it. He was too heavy for her to pull him up, however; I caught him in midair and growled "What is this?"

But he was unconscious.

I then flew up to Rapunzel, who was trying to haul in her waterlogged hair and massage her doubtlessly-aching neck. Her face white, she pleaded, "Don't send me back! Don't send me to my stepmother!"

I demanded why she did this. "Because I needed to!" she answered. I attempted to explain the difference between necessity and free will, but she interrupted, "I love him!"

Seeing the futility of further conversation, and not noticing any activity from the siege lines, I flew down to deposit Jack in the infirmary and write this letter. I am again at a loss as to what to do. Even my shipment of platinum for experiments is now unable to reach me. Perhaps it would have been better had you entrusted this castle to a human in the first place?

Yours in great confusion,
ANTRODEMOS, Dinosaur.

15 February, being the Birth-day of Galileo Galilei, Astronomer:

Madam,

As Jack has singlehandedly lifted the siege, I now give him my wholehearted recommendation as a fitting match for your stepdaughter.

Rapunzel met me before dawn this morning outside the infirmary, pleading for me to be kind to Jack. Still disturbed, I said I could not make any promises and reminded her that he had rebelled against his liege lady (you) and her castellan (myself). In response, she claimed you had indeed urged them to rebel, and made many other claims about you that I scarce would have credited two months ago. However, your recent letters' single-minded focus on keeping Rapunzel securely enclosed and watched makes her claims sadly plausible: that none of your instructions concerning her are ordinary, that you are accustomed to lose trust in anyone who is not cooperating with your watch of her, and that you would stir up any matter of rumors to keep young men away from Rapunzel.

I scarce would credit such claims normally — but have not these last months given as good evidence toward them as any experiment?

Shaken, I promised to keep an open mind about Jack, and we entered.

He was awake, and reading a mathematics book I had ordered left for him. Setting it down, he stared at me without words. When I reminded him of our collaborations in Science, he accused me of holding Rapunzel prisoner. I told him I was merely following your express instructions; he protested "Then don't! You shouldn't keep her cooped up here anyway! Does her stepmother want her held captive like a dragon's pet princess?"

I must confess I was shaken by this and asked him what to do.

Jack proposed an experiment: I would let him go, and if he ended the siege, then I would set Rapunzel free. That plan, Rapunzel added, would let me discharge my duty to you by keeping your castle intact.

Reluctantly, I saw that both other courses would have me acting like a dragon in one way or another. At a loss for what else to do, I expressed doubts that he could end the siege, but agreed.

"Don't worry," he said casually. Apparently, his stealth had been sufficient to slay a murderous giant earlier in the fall (whose castle he had accessed by climbing up a bean plant of unusual height.) "Just observe, like you said scientists should, right?"

I followed him and Rapunzel up to the battlements, where he waved his hands and announced to the now-silent crowds outside that I did not wish to act as a dragon, and that I would willingly let both him and Rapunzel go and promise never to hurt anyone without cause. The assailants replied, asking what proof I offered of this, and accusing me of planning to burn them all for my new steam engine.

At that, Jack laughed. "It was a human who invented that steam engine!" he exclaimed. "And this dinosaur's science can give you a lot of other good inventions, too! Right?"

Thereupon he turned to me, and I had nothing else to do but nod my head.

The crowd murmured in confusion, but they were evidently calmed, and some were throwing down their improvised weapons.

Jack then ordered the gates thrown open, and (with me observing) he and Rapunzel strode out to the crowd.

As I write this less than an hour later, I am still wondering if I did wrong. My trust in you is lessened — but did not experiment point in that direction? I did violate your instructions — but what else could I have done save act like a dragon and prove my enemies right? I did lose control of the situation — but is that not part of joining society?

Yours in even greater confusion,
ANTRODEMOS, Dinosaur

16 February, being the Birth-day of Georg Rheticus, who spread the truth of Astronomy

Madam,

I am pleased that we are finally once more in correspondence. Your letter clarified everything wonderfully. No, I shall not throw Rapunzel in the dungeons, nor shall I devour Jack, nor shall I do any of the other evil things you were insinuating I might do in the letters you wrote Mistress Mildred and the other townspeople (which letters they recently showed me.) Their earlier behavior was improper, but they do not deserve any grave punishment: Rapunzel, I now see, was reacting to her unjust imprisonment; and Jack is unaware of nobles' etiquette and unfortunately prejudiced against dinosaurs.

Therefore, I will not re-imprison Jack or Rapunzel. They are currently at Jack's house having luncheon with his mother, and they are already talking of betrothal. While I personally think this is far too hasty, I will no longer attempt to discourage them.

Further, Jack is showing no laziness in his scientific studies: he is already talking of double-checking the farm's boundaries using trigonometry and studying methods to improve the soil's health before the next planting. He has also given me new inspiration in my experiments — I have recently sent orders to sell the platinum and buy materials to study better farming. The recent siege showed I can no longer merely observe society; if I am to act, I shall act as a good scientist who uses Science for a purpose.

Perhaps farming is not the best career for Jack in the long run? If so, marrying a noblelady such as Rapunzel would not be unfitting.
Yours in Science and good sense,
ANTRODEMOS, Dinosaur.

About the story

"Of Hair and Beanstalks" merged three ideas I'd been pondering for a while. First, I'd been playing with the idea of a dragon who wanted to join society- how would people treat him? What kind of person would he be to do that? Then, I'd been wondering how the villains in fairy tales might try to justify themselves to their supporters. And, finally, I love the history of science and how it's dramatically changed the world over the last centuries. When I decided Antrodemos joined society because of that, almost everything fell into place for the story.

A question for the author

Q: When do you decide a story is finished?

A: When I first get through to "The End," I set the story aside and mull over how to fix the points I'm not satisfied with. Sometimes I can put my finger on the problems at once and how to fix them; other times I know something's wrong but need some time to puzzle out what. Then, I revise. I hardly ever agree a story's perfect, but there's a point where I know it's good and I don't know how to make it any better- and that's when I decide it's finished.

About the author

William Condon is a writer and programmer. He lives outside Seattle where he enjoys cycling and dreaming up new worlds.

I Will Go Gently

Susan McDonough-Wachtman

They sat in their deck chairs, watching their son fish. "Has he caught one?" she asked, gently rocking.

Walter squinted out at the lake. "I don't think so."

"I think he did."

"Did you *see* it?" Ellen had the sight, but to Walter's constant exasperation, she made no distinction between things she saw and things she *saw*.

"No."

He looked at her. Her eyes were on her knitting. "How could you know, Ellen? You're not even looking at him."

"I just know."

"Hogwash." He resumed his contemplation of the lake. He pointed. "A coupla loons." He glanced over at her and saw her half smile. "I didn't say *we* were the loons."

Her smile widened. "Did you see the otter?" She pointed with her needle.

"No. Where? Now?" He looked where she indicated.

"No, this morning, early."

"Why didn't you say so?" Fifty years they had been married and still she didn't tell him things right away. She said it wasn't necessary, because he could see *back*, but still. He made a swiping motion with his hand and looked into the space he had made, a little viewpoint into the past. His heavy features lightened with pleasure. "Huh. You're right. Good, maybe there are more." He watched for a moment, hopefully. They had moved to inland Nunavut to escape the rising sea but had worried about the spread of pollution from the flooded cities. It was still a concern, twenty years later, but an increase in the otter population would be a good sign. "Mmm. Don't see others." Disappointed, he closed the vision with a wave. "How did you see it? You don't get up that early."

"I do lately."

"Hogwash. You've never been a morning person."

"I sleep very lightly these days, Walter."

He looked at her, frowning, worried. "Hog—"

"—wash, I know." She smiled again, a gentle creasing of her wrinkles. "I know you don't want me to die. But I'm not afraid."

"I am." He muttered it low, but she heard.

Her eyes went back to her knitting. "You'll be fine."

He stood abruptly and slammed his hands against the railing. He winced. His hands weren't as tough as they used to be. And his leg ached. He had broken it falling off the barn roof. She had warned him not to go up there.

"Have you *seen* me fall?" he had asked her.

"No, I just saw a shadow over you."

"Well, I'm not going to leave the roof unfixed because of a shadow."

Now he was using a cane and probably would for the rest of his life. His leg hurt. He was no use to anyone. Getting old was shitty.

They had both aged quickly these last twenty years. They had left the benefits of society behind and had survived with hard work but insufficient health care — just like any other pioneers. Someday, she said, more people with gifts of power would be born into their little community, including seers and healers. Their Inuit-related tribe had always produced them, but sporadically, and no one knew how or why. Their own son was "ungifted" and apparently content to be so.

"I think Julian's coming back."

"Oh, good, fish for dinner." She set her knitting in the basket at her feet. She knitted only a few minutes at a time these days before her hands cramped and she had to stop. "Do you remember when we moved here? You said he'd never be happy out here at the end of the world."

"And he wouldn't have been, if Penny hadn't come." She had *seen* the others coming, but she hadn't been sure there would be someone for Julian. The visions of seers were sporadic, uncontrollable, and sometimes unreliable. The future could be changed. "But she did, and they'll be marrying soon. They'll have children."

"Have you *seen* it?" He looked down at her frizzy white hair. Her thin, veined brown fingers were like the driftwood twigs on the saltwater beach where they had grown up. That beach had long since disappeared under a rising sea. It had been Ellen and the other seers who had warned their people first, even before the scientists from Down Below. But many had chosen not to listen. Just as he had chosen not to listen to her warning about working on the roof. If you put your hands over your ears and said, "la la la," all the bad news would go away.

"Some things I know without seeing," she said.

He barked out a laugh, startling the birds in the garden. "You don't know. You just — you're just — an infernal optimist."

She giggled. That sound took him back. He swiped at the air and smiled at his memory of her, sitting on another deck, long ago, her hair a thick, dark mass caught into a long braid down her back, her slim, clever hands busy making a dreamcatcher.

"Come back here," she ordered, in the present.

"Why? Why should I?" He rubbed off the tear running down his cheek. With a wave of his hand, he dismissed his hovering vision of the past.

"Because I am still here. And because he needs you."

He looked down at the beach, where their son was tying the boat up to the dock. "Don't be silly. He's done that by himself since he was ten. Besides, I'm no help to him these days." He tapped the cane hanging on the railing beside him.

She shook her head. "I don't mean right now. I mean when I'm gone."

"What about me?" He knew he sounded childish. He couldn't stop himself. He stared out at the water, not wanting to face her.

She sighed. "It won't be long —" He could hear the creak of her chair as she shifted.

"Please stop saying that."

"Let me finish."

The snap in her voice took him by surprise. He turned around.

"I was going to say," she continued, "it won't be long before you join me."

His hands gripped the railing behind him. He was younger than she was, and stronger, and healthier. His mouth opened, but he couldn't get any words past his teeth. Everything he thought to say got stuck there, like gristle.

She was looking up at him, calm again, with that calm which had always infuriated and delighted him. At many of the worst times in their years together, she had regarded him with just that expression of peace and a faint sense of humor. He always got the impression she was laughing at him, just a little. He hated it. He loved it.

"I haven't told you before," she said softly, "because I wasn't sure if it would help."

"What ..." He cleared his throat, turned and spat over the railing. "What do you mean by that?"

"Will you miss me enough to be glad to die?"

Silence for a moment while they both listened to these words, and felt them weighing down the air between them.

"Glad to die? Why would anyone be glad to die?"

"I am." She smiled sadly. "I'm tired and in pain all the time. You know this."

"Yes, but —"

"I know. You want me to 'rage.' But, you see, I know the light isn't dying." She waited a moment. "We can talk about this later, if you want to."

"If I want to? If I *want* to?"

Their son came up to the porch, carrying his basket of fish. He considered each of their faces in turn and sighed. "You've upset him again, Mother." He bent down and kissed her cheek.

"It's what I do," she said. "Are we having salmon for dinner?"

"Indeed. How would you like me to fix it?"

"Brushed with dill and butter, please, Julian."

"Grilled?"

"Yes, that sounds lovely."

"Father, you look like a plum. Do you want some salmon, too?"

"She ... she ..." Walter tried to unclench his jaw, then grabbed his cane and stomped down the stairs and across the garden to the beach.

"I'll take that as a yes." Julian turned to his mother. "What did you say?"

"I told him I'm dying. Which you both already know." She smiled up into his brown eyes. "You will marry that girl soon, won't you?"

He squatted next to her and took her hand. "You *know* I will. But that isn't why he was so upset."

"No," she sighed. "I told him something I probably shouldn't have. I probably shouldn't tell you, either. I hope you get married soon."

"Yes, so you've said, even though you've also told me that we will."

She touched his broad cheek. "Seeing the future and being sure it will come to pass do not always go together. Especially when one's emotions are involved. The observer influences what she observes, and not always for the better."

"Yes, Mother," he said. "Come to the kitchen and tell me how much dill to use." He stood and held his hand out to her. She took it and stood, slowly and with a grimace of pain. "Shall I make you some of your tea?"

"Yes, please."

The kitchen was made of split pine, as was the furniture. It had been the first room they had built and was still her favorite. Walter had done almost all the work by himself. Ellen had spent most of her time establishing the garden, while Julian fished and hunted small game to sustain them. It had been hard, and lonely for Julian. Ellen had *seen* that more people would join them, but she had not seen any particulars. She had been optimistic, but not sure, that there would be a wife for Julian. She was still optimistic, but not sure, that there would be some with the genetic trait which resulted in powers. It had always been a fickle and unpredictable occurrence in their far northern part of the world.

As Julian settled her at the kitchen table, Ellen said, "He will be tempted to look into the past. All the time." She rubbed the worn wooden surface, scarred from years of hard use.

"Yes, I know." He put the kettle on and got out her favorite mug.

"You must not let him."

"Yes, I know."

She scowled up at him. "You know, for the first time I understand what your father means when he says I'm too agreeable."

"That's good!" he exclaimed, falsely hearty. "A real breakthrough in your relationship."

"I don't appreciate this new sarcasm, either." She rubbed her aching hands.

"Do you want an extra teaspoon of willow bark?"

"Yes." He put the mug in front of her, and she sat back and sipped her tea, remembering. She and Walter had come here when Julian was thirteen, and they had been alone then. She had enjoyed that, the solitude. Seeing the future for three was much easier than seeing it for a village.

"Feel better?" asked Julian after a bit. He had cleaned the fish and was slicing it. She admired the sure movements of his big, brown hands. She had always hoped her vision of only one child would turn out to be untrue. "Mother?" Julian turned around.

"Yes. Yes, I am. Just remembering." The others had trickled into this valley, settled here on the shore of their little, landlocked lake. Walter was right. Julian had been much happier when Penny had arrived with her little sister.

Julian smiled. "That's Dad's job."

"Yes. I used to be a little jealous of that."

Julian put down his filet knife and washed his hands. "Jealous? Of Dad? Why?"

"Of seeing the past. So much more comfortable than seeing the future."

"But not as useful." He drizzled melted butter with lemon across the filets.

She shook her head. "That depends on the circumstances. Your father still has a part to play." Julian glanced at her, surprised. "At any rate," she continued, "people often enjoy remembering the past. They don't really want to know the future. They think they do, but they don't. Even good visions seldom turn out to be what you think they'll be."

Julian sprinkled dill on the salmon. "Enough?"

"More."

He smiled. "I better plant more dill." He crumbled and sprinkled the herb, put the salmon in the oven, and sat down at the table beside her. "I'm pretty sure Dad's been jealous of you."

"I know. Are you sorry you weren't gifted, Julian? You were angry about it when you were young. Then, when you were about twenty, you told me you were glad your life wasn't complicated by, I think you called it, 'hocus pocus.' How do you feel these days?"

"I feel I have enough to take care of with a regular life, and I don't know how you ever managed to balance your sight with everything else."

"I don't either."

They heard voices outside. "That sounds like Penny," said Julian, surprised. "And Maria."

"I don't think there's enough salmon for five. You'd better make some pilaf."

Walter entered, looking much happier than he had thirty minutes before. "I found treasure." He ushered in the two young women, both stocky, dark-haired, and round-cheeked. The elder went immediately to Julian and kissed him.

The younger went to Ellen and examined her carefully. "How are you?" she asked, her tone much older than her eleven years.

Penny turned in Julian's arms and said, "Maria insisted we come. I'm sorry to intrude so close to dinner."

"You know you're always welcome," said Julian. "Help me make some pilaf and join us in eating it."

Ellen faced the serious child with an equally intent gaze. "I am fine, Maria. Are you well?" Wisps of fine, black hair obscured the little girl's brow. Ellen brushed them back, gently smoothing out the furrows. "Did you *see* something, sweetheart?" Her quiet question seeped out into the room, a ripple of change.

Walter straightened up with an involuntary, "No." Ellen made a shushing gesture towards him.

Maria's chin trembled. "I saw you sick. I saw you — gone."

Walter sat down heavily. Julian, who had been checking the fish, turned around, blinking steam out of his eyes. Penny put a hand to her chest and murmured, "Ohhh."

"It's all right, Maria," said Ellen calmly. "I know all about it. It's all right." Maria sobbed and threw her arms around Ellen, who hugged her tightly, suppressing a grimace of pain as the child squeezed her. "Shh, shh, shh. Shh, shh, shh."

Ellen refused to discuss it until everyone had eaten. She ate very little these days herself but refused to see freshly grilled salmon sit untouched. The pilaf never happened, but they made do with leftover cornbread and salad. Ellen sipped her tea and prayed for strength.

"Now can we talk?" Walter pushed his plate away. "Did you *see* this, Ellen? Couldn't you have warned us that Maria would develop the sight?"

"You know I don't see everything. I can't demand it." Ellen turned to Maria. "This is a difficult thing that you have been called to do. I wish I could say different words to you. I wish I could promise to always be here to help you through." She shook her head. "I cannot."

"Do I have a choice?" whispered Maria. Her eyes were the color of the split pine walls.

"No. The visions will come. But you will have guidance in how to deal with them."

"And who will be doing that?" demanded Walter.

Ellen smiled, almost laughed. "You will." She looked around the table. "You all will."

Julian and Penny were holding hands, Penny's eyes shining with tears. "How, Ellen? How can I possibly help her with this?"

"Well, you've made a good start by falling in love with my son. He has a lifetime of watching me process visions."

Julian tilted his head inquiringly and opened his mouth.

"Don't be ridiculous, Ellen," burst out Walter. "Watching isn't enough."

Ellen turned and lifted one hand to touch his cheek. "I know how hard all of this is for you. But you must be strong and courageous. For Maria."

Walter glanced at the child and lowered his eyes. "I just don't understand," he muttered.

"I think Mom can explain things, Dad." Julian rolled his eyes. "She's just doing it in her own good time, as usual." He glanced around. "That was supposed to make you all smile."

Penny tried to smile at him. "Maybe… maybe Maria should go out and say hello to the goats for a few minutes," she suggested.

Maria looked at her sister, torn, desperate to escape all this tension, but also desperate to know.

"Let us figure things out, chick, then we'll talk, okay?" said Penny gently.

Maria's face lightened. "Okay." She touched Ellen's arm gently. "You'll be okay?"

"Oh, yes, sweetheart, I'll be right here for a while yet."

Maria stood up, hugged Ellen again, and rushed out the back door.

The adults drew breath. Penny sobbed, Walter cursed. Julian hugged his fiancee and said, "Am I right in assuming that Dad is going to be remembering a lot over the next few days?"

Ellen smiled. "Are you sure you don't have the sight?"

"Ellen, please." Walter closed his eyes. "When you foresaw the flooding, it was so —" he searched for words "— so hard to cope. How are the three of us going to be able to help a child like Maria if she should have a vision as difficult as — as that was — without you?"

"You'll have my memories, Walter. You and I are going to make sure you have everything you need."

They began the next morning, while they were still in bed. Walter opened a window into the past, and she helped him find the memories she believed would help Maria. He had not often been called to use his gift in this way; he had to "mark" the remembrances so that he would be able to find them again, when they were needed. After her death.

They began with Ellen's earliest recollections of her own first visions. Her parents had found a seer to help her understand and develop her gift. There had been hundreds of people in the community they had grown up in, and several seers. Their warnings about the crisis to come had not been appreciated. When the sea level began to rise, and the visionaries told people they would have to give up their homes and their saltwater lives, some had turned on the seers. Walter and Ellen and their young son had fled from the violence of their panicked neighbors.

In this new little village, which now homed fewer than a hundred people, Ellen and Walter had been the only gifted ones. Until now.

After breakfast, they continued their work. "You know," said Ellen, "there may be another child out there. One with your gift. There's never been any predicting it. Even for those with the sight."

They were sitting on the porch again, watching their son working in the garden. He was harvesting for a feast. The wedding date had been brought forward. Ellen had told them it needed to be, if she were to attend.

Walter grunted. "Let me get this one sorted first." He pulled his chair closer to hers and swiped at the air. "Here's when you were fifteen, and you *saw* your grandmother's death. I was with you that day. You cried a lot. I was only twelve, and I didn't know what to do."

Ellen smiled. "You did fine. You took me to Megan, which was just what I needed."

"Yes, see, that's what I mean. We don't have a Megan to take Maria to. We won't have you." His voice cracked.

"Yes, you will, Walter. You'll be able to take Maria to Megan. She'll get a vision of Megan, so she'll hear exactly what I heard. You and Julian and Penny just need to provide the physical part. Hug her and kiss her and tell her everything will be fine."

"Everything won't be fine."

"Yes, it will. It may take a while, but it will."

"You're an infernal optimist."

"A cockeyed optimist!" she sang, with only a slight tremor in her voice, "I'm only a cockeyed optimist, immature and incurably green!"

They didn't have movies anymore, but sometimes Walter opened a window to the past and played one for her. ("A blasted parlor trick," he called it.)

"You've never been immature," he said. "Not even when you were fifteen."

"I just didn't seem so to you, because three years younger is such a lot in teen years."

Walter sighed and marked the memory. "What comes next?"

Ellen's eyes sparkled mischievously. "I foresaw our first night together."

"But didn't tell me about it."

"Well, not then. How could I? You were just fourteen, and I was a very sophisticated seventeen. I went straight to Megan and begged her to tell me the future could be changed."

He paused in opening the window to this memory and said, "You never told me that part."

"No?" She closed her eyes. "Well, it was a bit much, you know. Walter, I think you and Julian and Penny should review these memories together — before they are needed. I think it will help you to help Maria if you are all forewarned about how it may go."

"And what if it doesn't go this way?"

"All the more reason to be forewarned. Oh, Walter, it will be close enough. Young women mature along a fairly predictable timeline. Megan managed."

"Megan had the sight!" Walter pounded his fist on the arm of his chair. His raised voice caused his son to look up from his work in the garden.

Ellen groaned and seemed to shrink in her chair. "Walter, what can I say? This is the best I can do."

He slid out of his chair and knelt at her feet. "I'm sorry," he whispered. "I'm sorry. I'm just so frightened, Ellie."

She stroked his white hair, still so thick and soft. "I know. But Walter, you're so much stronger than you think you are. There's never been a time when you weren't able to do what was needed."

In bed that night, he held her gently. "Tell me," he said slowly.

"Yes?"

"Tell me why you begged Megan to change the future. I mean, I saw what you said to her, but still —" She shook in his arms. "Are you laughing?" he demanded.

"Yes. I'm sorry." She kissed his chest. "I had never had sex, Walter. I had never even kissed a boy."

"Well, I should hope not. Whom would you kiss?"

Silence.

"You didn't kiss —"

"I am not going to discuss with you who I did or did not kiss before we were married." She was shaking with laughter again. "Not at this stage of my life. My point is, that seeing the experience of an orgasm with a boy who was, to me at that time, a snotty fourteen-year-old, was an existential shock. I panicked. And Megan helped me, as always, and she will help Maria, too, if such a thing should happen to her."

"Oh," said Walter with a groan. "Oh, Ellie, I really, really can't handle this."

"Yes, you can."

"No, no, I can't."

"Yes, yes, you can." She tickled him and he jerked. "If it makes you feel any better, I've seen you dead before Maria is seventeen. That's why you need to be sure to share all the remembrances with Julian and Penny."

He stared into the darkness. "No, no, I don't believe that makes me feel any better." His arms tightened gently around her. "But... it doesn't make me feel any worse, either." He sounded surprised.

"No raging?"

"No raging."

"Hogwash." Her voice smiled in the dark. "You'll rage. When I see you again, I'll know you immediately, because your spirit will be plum-colored."

"Have you *seen* that?"

"No." She shook her head, her wispy hair brushing his chest. "But I can depend on you, Walter. In all the chaos we've endured, I've always known you would be there for me, raging on my behalf."

He smiled. "Well. I can handle that."

About the story

I was inspired to write "I Will Go Gently" by a dream. I woke up one morning with the vision of an old couple on a porch, arguing amicably about something — the way my parents used to. The interesting and different aspect about this couple was that, unlike my parents, she could see the future, and he could look into the past. I didn't know where they'd come from or how their "gifts" affected their lives. I discovered their story as I wrote. I worked in my worry about global warming, my pain from the slow death of my mother, my hope for the future of my children. It was easy to see how the woman's gift could be worked into a story of global warming, but it was a bit of a challenge to see how the man's gift could be made integral to the plot. Having the story set in the far north seemed logical to me. If anyone was going to foresee the need to move inland and could find a new setting for a future community, I thought it would be the natives of northern Canada. Or perhaps I should say it will be. Because in spite of everything, I foresee a future for the human race which involves a better system than the one we have now.

A question for the author

Q: Do you have a garden? Have you ever grown your own food?

A: I have often gardened, although I have never been a great success. Moving every few years, raising kids, and teaching school made it hard to find the time and energy. We got lucky a few times. We moved into one house in Western Oregon with well-established and highly productive raspberries. When the kids were young, we planted peas and beans in Western Washington and learned to battle slugs every morning. Now that I have an empty nest, we are living in my husband's family home and benefit from well-established blueberry bushes. We compete with the birds for those. I am still trying to grow peas and beans, but now have to keep away the deer and wild rabbits. We also grew a wide variety of squash this year. My husband is a wonderful cook and we've been enjoying baked squash and squash soup.

About the author

Susan McDonough-Wachtman has been a burger tosser, customer service rep, ad taker, curriculum developer, parent, reader, kayaker, gardener, and high school teacher. She lives in the Pacific Northwest with one cat and one husband.

susanmcdonoughwachtman.wordpress.com, @SusanMcdW

Family Tree

Lindsey Duncan

"Halett," Rithshara called out of her dressing chamber, "where is my youngest son?" She pondered the crimson headdress versus the black, and decided on the former, which didn't pinch. There was no reason menace couldn't be comfortable.

"Serving his unjust punishment in the underworld," Halett replied. The dark, wiry man with the odd eyes — one brown, one blue — was clever, but occasionally, he tried too hard.

She frowned. "My youngest living son, Halett. He was supposed to accompany me on the day's diversions."

"I will find him."

Thanks to a bath of eternal youth, Rithshara did not look anything close to her hundred and fifty years, but after her sixth husband's untimely assassination — this time, it had not been her doing — she had retired and handed the reins to her daughter Glivren. That was four years ago; she now had the distinction of being history's only recorded Evil Overmother, with the luxury to pursue her hobbies of esoteric execution methods, dream torture, and mountain-climbing.

The titian-haired sorceress arrayed herself on her resting couch with a sigh. Her oldest son had set himself up as a minor god. Her second son had made a deal with demons to open a gateway to other worlds and sought a paradise worth the plucking. Both her daughters were skilled in the dark arts. Then there was Othri.

"Empress?"

She sat up. "Where is my son?"

"Gone. Left the city." Halett's words were clipped.

Rithshara had abandoned the practice of executing the messenger because it was hard on personnel, but it was tempting to revert. Save that it was Halett, who was too valuable to lose. She had almost gotten out of the habit of watching her back around him. Almost. "You looked everywhere? So quickly?"

"I didn't have to. He left a note."

Halett minced into the room, keeping up a brave face. She plucked the note from his hand.

Dear Mother, it began. *I am afraid I have reached a point where I must follow my conscience.*

That was his problem right there. Any member of his family could have helped him remove the pesky thing. He had always been a puzzle to her, befriending servants and hostages. Granted, the latter had come in handy once or twice …

She read on. *I am leaving the city and the empire to devote myself as a priest to the Gods of Light. May you and our family one day wake to the error of your ways.*

Truth Sings, Othri

Rithshara rose in a dramatic swirl of skirts. "Halett? We have work to do."

In his nineteen years, Othri had grown resigned to wild rides on the back of spiny demons, or gut-wrenching teleportation that left one with a deep-seated need for chicken soup. He found he enjoyed walking.

Even though this had been the Ash Forest for over a century, traces of the Firegreen still surfaced. Vine-roses trellised up the withered trees, a trickle of water bubbled across a dry riverbed, and songbirds mocked the vultures and demon-birds who made this place their home. The old had not been completely smothered, and Othri felt its tranquility. He closed his eyes and breathed.

He tripped over a root.

"Good grief." He picked himself up out of the mud. "Well, now I suppose I have a disguise." He had toyed with dyeing his fox-red hair, but his family had easier ways to find him if they wished. He had always been a disappointment; he hoped they wouldn't miss him.

"That's a terrible disguise."

His head whipped about, but he saw no one. Despite the voice's raspy, thorny quality, he was sure the speaker was female.

"I'm sorry," he said, "is someone there?"

"More or less." She walked out of a tree trunk as if it were a doorway, a stout, brawny woman with skin the same color as the withered leaves. Grey moss hair twined down her back and shoulders and fused with both. Its color notwithstanding, she looked about his age.

Othri stared. It did not take years of eldritch training to identify a forest spirit, bound to the forest and its guardianship, but he had expected something more ethereal, more exotic.

She planted her hands on her hips. "What?"

There was no way to tactfully put words to his confusion. "Are you …"

She strode closer without seeming to move her feet. He did a surreptitious check: she did indeed have feet. "Kebra. I'm the spirit of the Ash Forest."

"Othri. I'm nobody."

"That's obviously not true," she said, "since you're standing here talking to me. Covered in mud."

"Well, I'm somebody," he amended, "but nobody important."

She frowned and studied him; he felt as if his soul were being raked through underbrush. "I doubt that, but I don't care as long as you don't hurt my forest."

"I'm not here to harm anyone," he said. He had learned young that appearances were misleading, that great beauty could hide great evil, but he had never heard anything about the other way around. Kebra was far from ugly, but she had a solid strength he had not expected. "So you are the mistress of the Firegreen?"

"No, I'm the mistress of the Ash Forest. I came into being after the plague destroyed the old trees and their ever-branches stopped burning. What became of the spirit before me, I have no idea. I'm the forest as it is now: a survivor." Kebra spoke in a matter of fact tone, but thunderstorm shadow flickered in her eyes. "It's all I am and know."

"I'm honored to meet you," he said.

She snorted, turning away. "Why have you come to my forest?"

"I'm just passing through. I'm headed to the Silver City."

"How cosmopolitan of you," she said. "What are you going to do there?"

"I intend to become a novice in the order of Thiorsan," he said, "and some day, a priest. If the god deems me worthy."

"So you're going to sit in marble halls, play endless lullabies, and meditate on the purpose of existence until you can't feel your toes," Kebra said. "Sounds like a great way to live your life."

Her sarcasm was thicker than the mud on his pants. He ignored it. "I hope so. It will be a nice change."

She stared. "From what?"

As the first answer that came to mind was "demon summoning," and the second was "world domination," he hesitated. His mother had created the Ash Forest in her early days, so he knew what topics to avoid. "I've had a rough life," he said, awkward. He had always felt comfortable talking to people, even mad sorcerers and extraplanar beings, but Kebra turned his words upside down.

"You sure don't look like it," she said. "Good luck, then. If Thiorsan deigns to materialize for you, tell him I said hello." She turned away.

"Wait!" he said. "Am I going the right ..." He stopped as she stepped into the tree trunk and disappeared.

He sighed, then gathered up his optimism and his compass. He headed onwards, unable to resist whistling a hymn. His new life was near, and he had met a forest spirit. It was a good day.

Rithshara stood before her scrying pool, lacquered obsidian nails arrayed on the bone rim. It had once been some the skull of great beast called a dinosaur, a gift from her late third husband — the bones, not the beast.

"Empress?" When she waved him in, Halett continued, "I've given your regrets to your daughter in regards to today's presentation of slaves."

Rithshara had forgotten the commitment in the unnecessary drama. She found herself grateful for Halett's foresight — not for the first time. "And you didn't tell her why?"

"Of course not." Beneath his servility, Halett seemed indignant.

"Good." She traced one fingernail across the murky surface, spelling out her enchantment in invisible calligraphy. "Othri," she breathed to the pool. "Show me my son."

The pool's surface quivered and cleared, depicting a small, rotund toddler with scarlet curls. He played under a thorn tree with a puppy he'd somehow found — not a proper hellhound, but a scruffy moppet. She remembered that day — an early warning sign of his softness.

Rithshara sighed. "Show me my son today," she amended.

The pool's surface rippled again, and an image formed of disheveled Othri tramping through a forest.

"That's the Ash Forest," Halett said.

Natural outings were not Rithshara's idea of a vacation, and she had not set foot under the Forest's bowers for decades. "So it is," she said. "And not far from the border. How in the world is he traveling, by horse?"

Halett leaned over the bowl. "By foot. Horses will not tolerate the Ash Forest."

Rithshara laughed. "Walking? Now I've heard everything."

"It is, if nothing else, a reliable method of transportation."

She wasn't sure whether to be impressed by her son's determination or annoyed by his stupidity. "He might have stolen one of Glivren's brooms, at least."

"I expect he didn't want to give you any reason to chase him."

"As if I would abandon my darling boy."

"Children usually don't know their parents that well," Halett observed. When she shot him a look, he added, "I've a daughter, Empress. She's nine."

"Well," Rithshara murmured. Halett had been a trusted hand for years, yet she never would have guessed. She'd have to pay more attention to him in the future. "In any event, this makes things simple. I shall bring him back promptly."

Halett cleared his throat. "If I may make another suggestion?"

He had to be aware that for lesser minions, those were frequently last words. "Continue."

"If you go to retrieve him yourself, it will make too big a show," he said. "This thing needs to be done quietly, to match his disgrace. I would recommend sending an ice dragoneer."

She considered. Halett was right: the last thing she wanted was to provide fodder for gossip. An Evil Overmother had her tyrannical image to maintain.

"Very well," she said. "Send the dragoneer."

Othri had never walked this far in his life, and the novelty had worn off. He plopped down on a stump and eased his boots off to massage his feet.

"I suppose it builds character," he said.

The sudden chill in the air surprised him. Though the fire trees had long since burned out, lingering embers flickered in their trunks, and Othri had grown used to their warmth. In summer, it might have been stifling, but on this early spring day, the heat had served as a comforting cocoon ... until now.

In the distance, a harpy shrilled over her meal. Otherwise, the forest was still. Wary, he slid off the stump, crouching and wishing he still had his boots on. The canopy rustled.

He dove under the nearest bush as a blast of icy breath seared through the clearing. It froze stump, ground, and boots.

Ice dragon! He rolled to one side, peering up through the maze of hoary leaves. The dragon's wings flashed; he caught just enough glimpse to see the saddle and rider.

He continued rolling, crawling elbows and knees into deeper underbrush. His heart throbbed in anxiety, making it difficult to breathe. He was a traitor to his family and might be treated as such.

Something snagged his pack, and he resisted the urge to plead for his life. He grimaced and yanked, but the crackling of branches told him his adversary was only a thorn-bush.

The sound caught the attention of the dragon. It wheeled with a cry like shattering ice. Othri winced and tried to crawl faster. He debated lurching to his feet to sprint, but once upright, he would be exposed and barefoot.

Arctic blasts poured around him. The nearby trees frosted over, lacquered in hues of unnatural blue. The sweat froze on his back, but the ground beneath him was undisturbed. It meant he wasn't in the epicenter. The dragoneer didn't know where he was ... yet. He breathed out cautiously, watching it fog, and lifted his head to peer through the icicle trees.

The dragon's powerful wingbeats vibrated the air. Twigs and ice-coated leaves shattered. The dragon circled overhead ... retreating? He dared to hope the rider might have given up.

Othri flinched down as the dragon swept back overhead, a second layer of ice frosting over the first. So much for hiding. He tucked his legs beneath him, ready to leap — stagger — to his feet.

The nearest trees caught flame, blazing skywards in sunset coruscation. He gasped at the beauty.

"Are you going to stand there and stare, or are you coming?" Kebra's voice demanded.

Othri almost toppled searching for her. Her face gleamed in the fire. "How do I ..."

"Just plunge into the flame," she said, impatient.

It occurred to him, through force of habit, that this would be a very easy way to kill him, but he wanted to trust her. He stumbled upright and charged the tree.

Heat flared around him, but did not burn. Bark rasped across his skin, yet the tree was soft, a cushion of feathers. He tumbled through into a clearing.

Kebra stood before him, arms crossed. "You have ice dragons chasing you," she said, "so you're obviously not nobody. Who are you?"

There seemed to be nothing for it. "I'm the son of Overmother Rithshara," he said.

Moving like a gale, she slapped him. "You idiot!"

This had happened so many times, he had a conditioned response. "Yes, I am. Terribly sorry."

Kebra stared. "You ... what?" Recovering, she went on, "You really thought you could just walk away? That they wouldn't follow you?"

"I honestly didn't think they'd care," he said.

She snorted. "Well, thanks for not thinking, because now my forest is a target."

He swallowed. "I'm sorry. I'll leave as soon as I can, I promise."

"And when you get to the Silver City, is that really what you're going to do? Live a cloistered life in the service of priesthood?"

Othri had borne her indignation as the rightful product of her forest coming under attack, but now he felt he had to defend himself. "I've lived a life full of black magic and ambition. Don't you think I want to get as far away from that as possible?"

"So travel the world," she said. "Visit the Great Library of Tareish. Roam the Golden Dunes. Dance in festivals in every city. Dine in taverns where they don't speak your language. Learn a musical instrument they've never heard of in the Empire. It's what I'd do."

She was right: there was a greater world, but he doubted he was equipped for it. The priesthood was safe, assured shelter from the chaos of the Empire. "So why don't you?"

She flinched. "I can't. I'm trapped within the bounds of the trees. I can only see where the Ash Forest's seeds have flown, but having adapted to this waste," she raked a hand around her, "they don't grow well anywhere else. They have to be planted deep in ash."

"I'm sorry," he said, regretting the question. "I could take a sapling with me when I leave."

"So all I would get to see is the halls of Thiorsan?" she countered.

"Isn't that better than no halls?"

She turned away, drifting between the trees. By now, he was certain her feet didn't move. "I guess."

"It's the least I can do," he said, "after I've put you out."

She paused, glaring over her shoulder. "Are you going to move? The sooner you leave, the faster things will go back to normal."

"Can't we just step through a tree again and be at the edge of the forest?"

"I can," she answered, "you can't. It takes a lot out of me to move a mortal."

Othri scampered after, wincing as a broken branch scraped his foot. "You don't have to look out for me."

"Yes," she said, "I do." And despite his polite questions and bright remarks about their surroundings, she said nothing else for some time. He was used to being able to get through to people, but Kebra was as bleak as the forest she guarded.

"What do you mean, you think you had him? Where is he?" Rithshara glared up from her velvet couch.

"Well ..." the dragoneer faltered. "My mount had his scent and we had frozen down the area, when a bank of trees erupted into flames. When the smoke cleared, we had lost his aroma. We circled for over an hour, but couldn't pick up another trace."

Rithshara wondered what her youngest son smelled like: violets and timidity? "You are dismissed," she said. The dragoneer tripped over the rug in his haste to absent himself. "You warned him to expect the worst, didn't you, Halett?"

He shrugged. "I may have done, Empress."

She found herself impressed again. When had she come to rely upon him? Pity her son didn't have the same instincts. Othri had a knack for people, but it was the wrong one. "A worthy thought.

Perhaps I should have … no." Disappearing dragoneers would doubtless draw dubious attention to this diversion of hers. "The spirit of the forest has involved herself, Halett."

"How do you know it's a woman?"

"Divine division of labor," she said. "Females take rivers and forests; males take oceans and mountains. It's aggravatingly sexist."

"What do we do now?"

"There's nothing else to be done: I shall have to go myself. You will accompany me." Rithshara sighed. "I hope it won't take much to bring the boy to his senses."

"I don't see how it could," Halett said. "The advantages he has by being under your wing are tremendous."

Rithshara nodded absently, accepting that. Learning to flatter was a basic skill of underlings. She expected it from Halett as a matter of course. She rose and moved to her bookshelf. She skimmed tomes bound variously with skin, bone and fruitcake, pulling one out. "I'm opening a portal as close to his current location as possible. I expect you will defend me from the forest, if necessary."

Due to an abundance of heroes who thought they could topple the Empire, the imperial armory had acquired a stock of magical weapons. These had been distributed to top officers, and Halett carried one of sufficient strength to cut through whatever enchantments the forest had to offer.

"My arm is at your service, Empress," he said.

She paused, arching an eyebrow. "And the rest of you, I should hope."

"Even my freckles."

"You don't have freckles."

He cleared his throat pointedly.

She laid the book out on her ritual stand. To an outsider, the ancient language would have sounded like a cross between gargling and a madrigal.

The portal flared into existence, white and oozing. She took Halett's extended arm and stepped through.

On the other side, she inhaled. Ah, the Ash Forest … a monument to the achievements of her youth. She drank in the decay and darkness, smiling as a spectre flitted overhead.

Othri was somewhere here, and every moment closer to disappearing. She murmured another spell, her voice growing to eldritch strength. She whooped, her voice powering through the trees. It reflected back to her, mapping out what lay beyond.

A counter-melody interrupted, discordance that made it impossible to pick up the echoes. She scowled.

Halett rubbed his ears. "Empress?"

"The spirit of the forest is interfering with my powers." She pursed her lips. "Well. I can take care of that."

"Better than Thiorsan's eunuch-mangled yowling, isn't it?" Kebra asked.

"It is certainly different," Othri said, trying to be tactful. The pain in his feet was distracting, but that was no cause to be surly.

"I've blocked your mother's seeking spell, but she'll come up with something else soon. We need to move." She put action to words, zipping through the trees without regards to human locomotion.

"Or she'll hurt your forest," Othri murmured.

She whipped about to face him, vine tendril tresses moving in sync. "That's a chance I'm willing to take."

"I'm not," he said firmly. Fear flowed up in him, but what would his new life be if he paved the way with blood? Or whatever vital fluid ran through the veins of a forest spirit.

Kebra folded her arms, expression cross. "So you're going to go back. Just like that."

"If I have to." He would only be giving up a change of scenery, after all. Perhaps Kebra's harping had some ring of truth, and Thiorsan's halls, as superior as they were to his family's palace, might eventually become familiar and even boring. "Who did she bring with her?"

Her eyes unfocused. "Just one man — scrawny sort with mismatched eyes."

"Halett," he said. He remembered the man, a trusted but invisible part of the imperial entourage. At times, he had envied Halett his competence in their world of conspiracies. His brain, scampering about in search of some other solution, almost tripped over an idea. "I need to talk to him."

"Do you really think this is going to be solved by talking?"

"Just this once," he replied, "it might be."

Kebra heaved a gusty sigh. "She's already sent him to scout the area, probably so he doesn't see whatever mysterious feminine ritual she's about to enact."

"I always thought that was a metaphor for something," Othri said.

"Do you think I'd tell you if it was? All I have to do is ask the forest to close in around him."

"Let's do it."

She led him through the forest, the trees twisting and pirouetting out of her way. He watched in fascination as the patterns became a corridor, impenetrable on either side. Kebra gestured; he followed, keeping his limbs close. He was not so sure the trees would not snap at him in passing.

Othri heard Halett first, crunching through the underbrush and cursing. The trees shifted, and he stumbled into view.

"Othri!" Halett jerked upright. "What kind of mad chase is this?"

"One you started, as far as I can tell," Kebra said.

Halett's eyes narrowed, assessing her. "Milady," he said, frosty in his absolute politeness. "This is not your fight. It's time he went home."

"I'm afraid I'm not going home, Halett," Othri said.

Halett slid a hand to his sword hilt. "I'm afraid you are."

"That's odd, neither of you looks afraid," Kebra said. Othri was grateful for the words, for he certainly felt the fear. Not so much of Halett, though the man was formidable; he was afraid what his mother would do, and how the forest — and Kebra — would be affected.

"I don't belong there," Othri said. "I'm just going to be a continuing disappointment to my mother until she decides to get rid of me permanently."

"That's her luxury," Halett countered, "but not necessarily. You seem smart and adaptable, Othri. You could find a way to follow the family line."

"You have more faith in me than I do. Maybe you're right, but that's not who I want to be. And do you really want me there, Halett?" he asked. "Or would you rather her attention go to someone more deserving?"

Halett stiffened in surprise. "It's not my place to decide who is worthy and who is not."

"You would make a better son than I would," Othri said. "If I had my way, you'd just take my place."

Halett opened his mouth, shut it. Othri pressed on. "I want her to let me go."

"So you can go off and do nothing in particular," Kebra said, sotto voce, possibly to the vines. The words stung; he told himself she wasn't right, but wasn't sure he believed it.

"She won't," Halett said. "She can't allow the world to see her son betray her."

The loyalty in Halett's voice both impressed and relieved Othri. He knew he could settle any doubts on that count. "I know. And I have an idea."

The ritual Rithshara intended would be swift and irrevocable, which was why it took so long: it had been designed to give the spellcaster time for second thoughts. For her, the delay was merely annoying. Second thoughts were something that happened to other people.

She glanced about the mire-laden clearing with some irritation. Why had Halett not returned? If the forest spirit had somehow overcome such a trusted lieutenant, she would feel Rithshara's wrath, and not simply because the Overmother had an image to maintain. As her attention shifted, she realized the forest thrummed.

The trees parted, revealing the trio of Halett, Othri — he was barefoot, she noted with bemusement — and a wood-knotted woman who must be the forest spirit.

"Ah," Rithshara said, "it all makes sense now. This is about a woman."

Othri blinked owlishly. "What? No, it isn't about Kebra."

"She doesn't seem like his type," Halett said.

"What about my type?" the spirit asked.

"I wouldn't presume to guess."

Kebra turned to Othri. "Will you please get these people out of my forest?"

Up until this point, Rithshara had watched with bemused tolerance. "I would be careful how you address 'these people,' " she said, "seeing as some of us are responsible for your very existence. I trust you have come to surrender yourself?"

"I haven't," Othri said.

"Then I have no other recourse but to force you." She dashed away the ritual trappings with a swipe of her sleeve, grasping the dagger. A touch of blade against her skin summoned blood and power. Her whispers sent it whirling out, spiraling into rusty tentacles. They surged for Othri. "It's for your own good."

Halett stepped between them. "No." He brought the armory blade around in a theatrical arc, slashing through the air and the spell.

"What is the meaning of this?" she demanded.

"Hear him out."

She narrowed her eyes in displeasure and repeated the spell, punching out the words. The tentacles doubled and tripled, evading Halett's impressive technique. One set of bands coiled around Kebra, restraining the spirit. The rest converged on Othri.

They stopped.

The darkness hovered at the threshold of his body, refusing to bind him. Clearly confused, he wobbled back. In the contrast presented by her sorcery, Rithshara saw why. Purity. The boy was too good, in all the wrong ways.

"We both know I won't live up to the family legacy," Othri said, regaining his calm. "In the end, I'm only going to embarrass you."

"We are an empire and a bloodline," Rithshara said, "but most important of all, we are a family. We must present a united face to the world." She reached for a maternal tool more powerful than sorcery: the guilt trip. "Do you want to put your siblings in danger?"

"I don't think anything I could do would put my siblings in danger," he said, "but I wasn't made for this kind of life. Halett, on the other hand, is ideally suited. He is quick, clever and strong. Tell the world we were switched at birth. He is your true son, and I ... am nobody."

Rithshara stared, astonished beyond dignity. "Are you truly suggesting ..."

"You're right," he said, "that your son should be menacing and cunning. Of course you understand that can't be me."

She hesitated, knocked off course by the fact he was agreeing with her. "You have the ability. It's in your blood."

"Maybe, but I don't want it. Isn't ambition better from someone obsessed with it?"

"Here now, let's not go that far," Halett murmured.

She shifted her attention to him. "I suppose you support this idea, Halett."

"Yes, Empress, I do think the idea is sound," he replied, "though you understand my personal bias."

Kebra snorted. "Personal bias."

If only Othri would apply that mindset to the family business. Rithshara contemplated Halett. Othri was correct there: she could not have designed a better heir.

Suspicion reared its head. She tightened the magic threads surrounding Kebra. "What is your role in this? If you have poisoned him against me, I will destroy you."

"No," Othri said, "you won't. She had nothing to do with my departure." Deliberately, he stepped to the spirit's side ... and the tentacles around her receded, fleeing from him.

"I had no role in this until Othri tumbled into my territory," Kebra said, apparently unmoved by the threat. "The result doesn't affect me unless you decide to start destroying the forest ... again."

Rithshara ignored the pointed addendum.

"But one thing I know," Kebra continued, "is life grows from the consequences we didn't intend. Otherwise, I wouldn't be here. You could drive yourself mad trying to stifle everything that branches out — or you could embrace it."

Rithshara regarded Othri's anxious, unassuming face, a visage that wouldn't hold guile or malice. He stood barefoot, mud-spattered, but straight as an arrow with determination, and so counter to everything the family stood for that her powers refused to touch him. With a pass of her hands, she released the spell.

"You understand," she said, "that you will never have the same chance for power, influence, and wealth? You know the riches you're giving up?"

"Yes," he said, "and that's all right by me."

"You understand you will not be able to command the peasants in your new home to obey your every whim?"

He blinked. "I figured I would look after my own whims."

She really had no idea what to make of him. "Very well," she said. "I will put the plan into action as soon as I return to the palace."

He heaved a gusty sigh. "Thank you, mother," he said. "I will miss you — and the rest of the family — but this is what I need to do."

"I will miss you, too," Rithshara said, "but it appears there's no dissuading you." She paused. There was something missing. Realizing what it was, she did the unthinkable.

She embraced him.

Othri held onto the hug. This goodbye was harder than the first, but the knowledge he was free — really free — filled him with possibility. He hadn't imagined he would be able to get them both to agree, but the right words had just seemed natural.

"Thank you," he said.

"This is all very touching," Kebra said, "but can we get the evil overlady —"

"Overmother," Rithshara corrected.

"Whatever," the spirit snapped. "Can we get her out of my forest, please?"

Othri snuck a sideways look at Halett and caught a glimpse of the man's smirk. He had no worries; Halett would be just fine.

"Just remember who made it your forest," Rithshara said.

"Oh, I remember, believe me."

Halett pulled Othri aside. He tensed, waiting for some dire threat, but also feeling an eerie confidence that he could talk his way out.

"Do you need boots," Halett said, droll, "or are you making some kind of point?"

"Definitely the former," Othri said, fervent.

It was a quick exchange. Othri wasn't about to complain when it turned out Halett's boots were too big. It seemed some kind of metaphor.

With an inordinately complex gesture, his mother opened the portal. She and Halett stepped through. Demon birds caroled in the trees as the light winked out.

It was Kebra's turn to breathe a sigh of relief. "I didn't expect that to work."

"Could I get a few dozen seeds from you, please?" Othri said.

She crossed her arms. "I don't want dozens of sprouts channeling me devotional hymns and pitiful prayers for hours on end. It will drive me crazy."

"How would you tell the difference?" he asked with a small smile.

She barked laughter. "Fair."

"I'm still going to the Silver City," he said, "but not to become a novice. I never thought I had any strengths: now I know I have at least one."

"You're good with people," she said, "considering you just got that bastion of evil to do something decent."

He nodded, finding confidence in her agreement. "I have the chance to go anywhere. It seems a shame to waste it."

"Right." Kebra turned her hand over. Seeds spilled between her fingers. He stretched out the bottom of his shirt to catch them, and transferred them to his pockets.

"I could," he said, "plant one in Thiorsan's courtyard —"

"Don't you dare," she snapped. She pivoted and flowed through the trees, vines and leaves bending to greet her passage. Othri watched her go, smiling. His first encounter outside the Empire hadn't gone so badly.

She paused, turned back, hands arrayed on hips. "Well? Are you coming?"

"Coming?" he echoed, puzzled.

"I'm escorting you to the edge of my forest," she said. "You've caused enough trouble today."

He grinned. "I'd welcome the company."

Talking, sometimes bickering, they crossed the Ash Forest together, with all the world beyond.

About the story

"Family Tree" started as a writing prompt. I belonged to an online speculative fiction writers' group who had weekly hour-long write-ins, called "Friday Night Writes," even though they weren't always on Fridays (and weren't even always at night). One writer would post a prompt, and everyone else would get down as much as they could in that hour, then share their pieces. It was always great fun. I don't remember what the prompt was for "Family Tree," but I suspect it had something to do with writing from a villain's point of view. I've done this in the past, but I must have been in a lighter mood, because my brain went in a tongue-in-cheek direction, considered a retired evil overlord — make that an evil overmother. The opening of "Family Tree" fell out from there, with Othri's letter kicking off the plot. That was as far as I got during the free-write. I came back to it later to build out the story. One of the first things I decided I needed was an ally for Othri, and that brought Kebra into the story: not a willowy, timid forest sprite, but the kind of hardy creature that would spring from a ravaged forest. ... and, of course, that's how I came up with the title.

A question for the author

Q: How does writing speculative fiction affect your daily life (not as a writer but as a person)?

A: Being a speculative fiction writer means that life is rarely boring. I've always got some plot point to chew on, and the oddest details in life might inspire a story. I'm always asking, "What if?" and spinning thoughts from that. But it's also entertaining because (at least for me), it's fostered a tendency to take metaphor literally. You have no idea how disappointed I was to find out that "Entertaining Silverware" just sits there. I also find that writing speculative fiction makes me both more open-minded and more skeptical. Speculative fiction is about what-if, considering what could be true or become true, so it tends to break down the tendency to say, "This is impossible." On the other hand, when everything *could* be true in some world, I find I'm less inclined to proclaim (even to myself) that "this is so" in our world. My reaction to a theory or belief that sounds plausible is not so much to accept it as to acknowledge that it could make a good story.

About the author

Lindsey Duncan is a chef / pastry chef, professional Celtic harp performer and life-long writer. She feels that music and language are inextricably linked. She lives in Cincinnati, Ohio.

www.LindseyDuncan.com, @lindseycduncan

Cinders and Snow

Kathryn Yelinek

The prince was old before his time. Candlelight from ballroom chandeliers softened the gray in his hair. He whirled yet another eligible young lady through a minuet, his movements practiced and sure, but he limped, round-shouldered. He was not yet twenty-five.

"The hall looks so elegant," the lady simpered between steps. "Like a winter wonderland."

"My mother's idea." Roderick smiled because he should. "She knew a ball would melt the midwinter cold." The queen mother sat across the room, on the dais beside his older brother the king, and the new queen.

"So wise." The lady batted her lashes. They fell across her skin like shadows over snow. Despite the room's warmth, Roderick shivered.

This simpering lady was not for him. Nor were the scores of other ladies he had dutifully paraded around the dance floor. He wished his mother wouldn't push so hard; the only lady he wanted he could not have.

I must see you married, his mother had said as she planned the ball. *Your brother is still childless, though he is eight years wed.*

But no lady deserved to be tied to him. He was an ill-luck prince, destined to hurt those he loved. Not even a mother's hope could melt his winter.

The music stopped, and he escaped to a balcony. He sat on the marble bench, its chill seeping through his wool trousers. He stretched his left leg beside him, and the throbbing in his knee ebbed. He sighed in relief.

Fresh snow carpeted the gardens and reflected light from the palace windows, making the night gray and murky. The evergreen trees he'd nursed from saplings stood like islands amid the snowdrifts: a spruce, a fir, a juniper.

Music swelled inside the ballroom, the opening strains of a pavane. Dancers would be taking their places, two by two, but the prince remained on his bench, watching the spruce, the fir, the juniper. He wished he were another sort of man, more assertive, more confident, a man who could turn the steps of a dance to his own designs. But he was not. He was like those trees: solitary, buffeted, bending but not breaking, destined to weather life's storms alone.

He would not sleep after the ball. If he did, the nightmares would come.

In his dreams, he was seven again, ensconced behind a tapestry in the library. The wool scratched his arms, and the floorboards dug into his knees, but this was his favorite hiding place.

His tutor had given him a wondrous book: paintings of trees so lifelike he pressed his nose to the page. He inhaled not the sweetness of linden flowers but something better: the heady, dry aroma of Book.

He breathed in again and traced the needles of a larch with his finger. If his father the king caught him, he would get a caning. He should be in the yard with his brother, carrying weights, hefting bow and sword like a proper prince. He turned the page.

Footsteps crossed the library floor. Roderick tensed, rubbed the book's leather cover as a talisman. Maybe if he rubbed hard enough, the footsteps would pass by.

The tapestry was torn back. He stared into his father's scowling face. The king smelled of pepper, spices hot enough to make a man cry.

"Worthless boy!" The book went flying. "Didn't I tell you to go outside?"

He scrambled back, around the tapestry. A gaggle of advisors blocked his path to the door. They were tall men, broad, with legs like siege towers. Like his father, they were men who enjoyed ripping the branches off saplings.

He couldn't go out, so he went up. He scurried up a library ladder, the rungs slick against his fingers.

"Come down!" The king shook the ladder. Roderick clung to it, trembling. "No one wants a weakling for a prince."

The ladder stretched as high as the shelves, almost to the ceiling, far beyond the reach of the tallest man. Roderick locked slippery fingers around the next rung and took another desperate step up.

Ladders might be tall, but a father's control stretched farther.

The wood bucked beneath the boy. He missed a step, and the shelves with their books tilted around him.

"Roderick!" his mother screamed.

He slammed into the floor, his leg twisted under him. Pain exploded in brittle, white agony.

The pavane played on. Inside, all was light and warmth and dancing. Outside, his breath iced the air. The backs of his legs had gone numb. He wrapped his arms around his chest and sat still, unmoving.

At eighteen, he brought his sweetheart to his father and asked permission to marry. Ella was a solid, rosy-cheeked daughter of a northern duke, come to court to give a pair of deer hounds to the king. Ogres lived up north, it was said, and wolves stole infants from cradles. Against that, she assured him, the king was only a man.

That man was eating peppers again, chilies and jalapenos in a clay bowl at his elbow. He took a final bite, wiped his fingers on his trousers, and strode from his chair. As courtiers whispered, the king narrowed his eyes.

"You planning to slip a cuckoo into our nest, girl?"

"What?" Ella furrowed her brows.

Roderick clenched his fists. The king's breath was hot, fetid. "Father, please..."

The king slid his bejeweled hand over her stomach. She stiffened. The king slipped his hand inside her neckline, pinched.

"Father!" Roderick cried, even as Ella jerked back, her arms crossing over her breast.

"Must be you're carrying a cuckoo, girl. You're too pretty for my weakling son."

Ella shook her head. "Your Majesty, you're mistaken. I'm intact, and I love your son."

"You calling me a liar, girl?"

He was. The king was a liar, but who would name him so?

Ella lifted her chin. "Yes, Your Majesty."

The king's slap rang loud in the room. Roderick started forward, but his knee buckled. He fell, landing on hands and knees on the carpet. The court stood in shocked silence.

Ella pressed a hand to her reddening cheek. Blood welled between her fingers. The rest of her face was pale as snow.

"I am not a liar," the king said. "Say it."

Ella pressed her lips together.

"Say it!"

Roderick pushed himself painfully to his feet. "Just say it," he whispered. She did not need to be as meek as his brother's new wife, just pretend to be.

"I'm intact," Ella declared, "and I love your son."

The king's face burned scarlet. "Be gone, wench! Leave my lands, and never return."

Roderick gasped. Ella turned to him, her eyes pleading.

"Father, no—"

The king was already walking back to his chair. "Guards, see she is gone by sundown. If she refuses, put her forcibly in the streets."

"No!" Roderick gripped her hand. She wrapped her fingers around his arm, and he took courage from her strength. "I'll go with her," he announced.

The king rolled his eyes. He made a shooing motion with his fingers before selecting another pepper.

For one glorious moment, Roderick believed the king would let him go. He clasped Ella's hand, his heart as light as a leaf on the wind. Together they backed towards the door.

They took half a dozen steps before guards dragged them apart.

"Ella!" he cried, his arm wrenched behind his back.

Her protests echoed down the hallway. Only when it was silent did the guards release him.

The pavane ended. Behind him, the glass door opened, followed by the click of boot heels.

"My lord?" His valet's voice. "You are scheduled for the next dance. The lady awaits you."

He gritted his teeth. His mother meant well, but she had poor taste as a matchmaker. He summoned a smile and limped to the door.

The woman was dressed in white, of course, in a dress of startling simplicity, without the customary frippery. Then he saw her face, and he halted, stunned.

"Ella?"

She smiled, tentative, and curtseyed. "Hello, Your Highness."

"Saints above, Ella! What are you doing here?" He rushed inside to the heat and light. Courtiers mingled about in ivory and cream, but he saw only Ella. "And when did you stop calling me Roderick?"

Her mouth quirked up, and something in his chest unbunched. After all these years, her sense of humor remained. "I believe, Roderick, that I'm a surprise from your mother."

On the dais, his brother glared at them. His wife studied her lap, pretending as always not to exist. Another bruise the size of William's fist colored her cheek. But the queen mother watched the crowd expectantly--it was just like her to recall Ella in case a local woman failed to catch his fancy. His mother had always been maddeningly thorough in her campaigns.

"She never said! And I've been petitioning William for months, ever since Father died. He said it would take time." A lie, he realized. William had never intended to bring Ella home. He felt William's glare, his inherited need to squash any happiness in another. He turned away, refusing to let his brother ruin this, too.

Ella shrugged. "Like I said, a surprise."

"A wondrous surprise."

That smile again, tentative, as if she couldn't believe his joy. Puzzling. Why would she think him anything less than delighted?

"Do you want to dance?" he asked. "Or sit and talk or...?" He wasn't sure what was the proper thing to do with a woman who had reappeared as if by a miracle.

"No sitting!" She held up her hands in mock horror. "I've spent two weeks stuck in a carriage and only arrived here an hour ago. Dancing sounds divine."

So he took her hand, pressed it to reinforce his delight, and led her to the dance floor. Around them, courtiers murmured, taking note of the new woman with the unfashionable gown.

He wanted to take her in his arms, to whisper in her ear all the things he'd kept in his heart these seven years. Instead he waited, chafing at the pause as the other dancers took their place. He saw now the lines on her face, the scar on her cheek, the tuft of gray at her temple.

"Was it terribly difficult," he asked, "these past few years?"

"Yes." She studied him, searching his face as if it was not quite what she expected. "I could tell you about it later, if you want, but not now."

He had caused these, the scar, the lines, the gray. He couldn't prevent his father slapping her, couldn't prevent her exile. No wonder she was cool towards him.

He wondered then if she had only come because his mother summoned her. He couldn't blame her if it was true. Like his father, he'd hurt her, and no doubt he was destined to hurt her again.

"Are you," he asked, grasping for happier topics, "still raising hounds?"

"No." She swallowed, and his heart sank. "The abbey only had mutts. They were good dogs, but I didn't have time to train them."

"Abbey?"

"The Sisters of Good Hope took me in, let me stay as a lay member."

"What—" he started, horrified. Not that she'd been at an abbey, but because the Sisters of Good Hope worked in cities. How had Ella survived without meadows or forests to run in with her hounds? No wonder her hair had turned gray.

Before he could think of a response, the music started, a waltz. Automatically he took the first step and found she still fit in his arms.

She still held her head high, still moved with the leggy grace of a creature born to run. This was the woman who'd trained her dogs to sniff out chestnuts for him, who'd climbed the tree outside his room to deliver books when his father denied him the library, who'd stroked his hair as he thought thoughts against the king he never dared put into words.

"I'm glad you came," he said because he must. "I've missed you. The missing was as deep as winter, as unfading as holly."

She slanted him a look, questioning, probing. "I wasn't allowed to send letters, but I collected bits of plant lore from pilgrims who passed through. Did Father Jacob forward them on?"

"That was you? He never said."

"He was nervous, worried he'd get in trouble if anyone found out."

"I wish he'd said. Your notes were incredible. I—"

His knee buckled. With a gasp, he slammed into the floor. His hands snagged fabric. Pain spiked through his knee and his palms, and the sound of tearing cloth sliced through the music.

He staggered up.

Ella stood gaping at her gown. Half the skirt had torn away, leaving her hoops and pantaloons exposed.

Around them, dancers skittered to a halt. Someone snickered, low and thick. At that, Ella pressed her hands to her reddening cheeks.

Horror welled in his chest. He had never, not once, tread on a lady's skirt. To do so now in such an egregious way, and to Ella—

"Ella," he whispered. He limped a painful step forward. "I'm so sorry."

But she was already turning away. Without a look back, without a word, she pushed through the crowd. How she must hate him.

On the dais, William smirked.

Roderick couldn't breathe. He clenched his fists.

A lady sidled up to him. "It's not your fault, Your Highness," she simpered. It was the one from earlier, the one with lashes like shadows. "She obviously tripped you. And no wonder, with how poorly she dances."

"Only a simpleton would blame you," another lady declared, stepping close. "Do you need a partner to finish the dance?"

"No!" He pushed his way through an encroaching swarm of white and ivory gowns. Was his mother already pushing court ladies on him again? "Let me through. Do not speak ill of her."

Ella was nowhere to be seen.

"Where did she go?" he demanded of his valet.

"I don't know, Your Highness. Should I have her found?"

He hesitated. William was gleeful on the dais, and having Ella returned would dampen that glee. But she was not Roderick's to drag back.

"No." A coldness hardened in his chest. "I have hurt her enough already."

The tapestry still hung in the library, but he was no longer a child who could hide behind it. He limped to the balcony, stood beside his bench. The evergreens fanned out below him: spruce, fir, juniper. How he envied them. They never hurt. They never hurt others. They stood still and quiet and cold.

But he no longer wanted that, he realized. Ella had been his once, and he had not fought for her. He would fight for her now, defy his brother, but would she accept him? Hadn't she just shown she wanted nothing to do with him?

He turned his back on his trees and strode past his valet, past the women in white who called to him.

Where would she go? Her guest room, most likely. But if his mother had craftily lodged her close to his suites, that room was halfway across the castle. Too far to go with torn skirts. The sitting rooms off the grand staircase then, the closest place that would give her privacy.

He limped down the grand staircase, its curling banister cold beneath his fingers. A shoe sat in the doorway of the first sitting room, wedged there to prop the door ajar. It was a white, flimsy thing, the fabric so sheer it might have been made of glass. He frowned at it. He'd never considered women's footwear before. If all lady's shoes were like this, no wonder Ella often preferred to go barefoot. Had she kicked this one off in disgust?

He knocked and recognized her voice.

A chill greeted him as he pushed the door open. The servants had neglected the fire, and Ella sat on a stool before the cold cinders, her torn skirts knotted in one fist.

"Oh, it's you." Her breath puffed while before her, and her surprise wounded him. Hadn't she thought he would come? "I thought —I was hoping a servant would come by with needle and thread."

"They're all busy upstairs. Shall I go find one?"

She nodded, and he turned to go, the shoe still in his hands. It shouldn't surprise him she thought him more useful when gone.

"Wait!"

Her cry stopped him. He looked back.

"Why didn't you come after me when your father exiled me?"

He sucked in his breath. The unrelenting winter of his longing surged hard in his chest. "You think I didn't want to? I didn't dream every day of riding to wherever you were, sweeping you off your feet?" The words, dammed for so long, poured out. "But my father said he would kill your papa and sisters if I did."

She covered her mouth with her free hand. "He said that?"

"He sent me an ear from one of the hounds you'd given him to reinforce the point. I couldn't do that to you."

She twisted her skirts in her hands. "Papa said not to contact you, but he never said why."

That sounded like her father, always trying to protect his children. Once again, Roderick wondered why *he* couldn't have been king.

"Still," she pressed, "you could have sent a letter or a message or something. I waited all those years."

"I sent word through the breeders network, but that didn't work." He hung his head. "I couldn't *find* you. No one who knew would tell me, and nothing I do is right—I couldn't even dance with you without tramping on your gown." His father's words echoed in his head: *Worthless boy! No one wants a weakling for a prince.*

Ella's mouth twisted. "Yes, it would have been better if you hadn't done that."

"And you're cold," he said, despairing. "Here I am talking, and you're cold." He held out the shoe to her.

She stuffed her hands under her arms. "Keep it. It's not comfortable, or warm. That's why I used it to prop the door."

"I'll find something." He looked around the room, but there was no blanket, not even a tapestry on the wall, and no tinderbox by the fire. Only a candle burned on a low table, and that would not help since they had no tinder. If he'd worn a cape he could have draped it over her shoulders, but he had only his tunic.

"It's all right—" she started.

"No," he said before she could tell him his failures were all right, she expected no more. "I'll find something. Wait here."

He set her shoe by her skirts and walked into the hallway. The corridors were deserted, filled only with the strains of harps and flutes from the ballroom. *Worthless, worthless,* his heart seemed to beat as he strode back up the stairs. He didn't want to go up to the ball and the simpering ladies in white, but this was for Ella, so he did.

At the top of the stairs he cornered a young page with an armload of candles. "Get a servant with needle and thread and a tinderbox to the sitting room off the staircase," he ordered. "Now."

The boy gawked at him. He'd probably never heard Roderick speak so forcefully. Then he bobbed his head and hurried off.

Roderick stole down a hallway, past courtiers who nodded to him, until he came to a guestroom, where he nicked a blanket off the bed and, just in case, stole the tinderbox from by the fireplace. He carried them down the staircase, wondering if he'd done enough. How could he prove his devotion to Ella? Could he ever do enough to make up for his past failings? And why should she accept him? He was destined to be as lonely and hurtful as William, wasn't he?

When he reached the bottom of the stairs, the sitting room door was ajar. He was sure he'd closed it, and he hurried forward, pleased that someone had attended to Ella so quickly.

He walked in on two guards in blue and silver.

"Come with us, miss," one said, taking Ella by the elbow. "His Majesty is worried about you having run off."

"I doubt he cares." Ella yanked her arm out of his grasp. "Can't I at least wait until my gown is properly patched?" She'd tied it closed as best she could with a ribbon from her hair, but there was no needle or thread yet.

"His Majesty—"

"Where are you taking her?" Roderick demanded.

The guards whirled about. Ella's eye lit up at the sound of his voice.

"Your Highness!" The other guard stepped towards him. "His Majesty asked us to find you, too. He's concerned—"

"It's been seven years!" Roderick bellowed. "My brother can't let us alone after seven years?"

The guards glanced at each other, eyes wide, but Roderick wasn't done.

"Did my brother specifically order you to bring us back? Did he command it as king?"

"Well, no." The second guard retreated a step. "He requested we find—"

"Then get out." Roderick hauled the guard's arm just as they'd tried to do to Ella. "We are not to be disturbed," he said as he steered the man into the hallway. "I command you to tell the king we'll return when we're ready, and he's not to disturb us before that. Understand?"

"Yes, my lord." The other guard scurried out before Roderick could grab him too. Roderick slammed the door.

He was breathing heavily. It was a night for firsts: stepping on a woman's gown, manhandling guards. He didn't like either, and the second had Ella staring at him as if she didn't recognize him.

"I'm sorry," he said, because it was what his father had taught him to say in any situation. He strode forward and draped the blanket around her shoulders.

"Don't be sorry. You were magnificent."

Roderick blinked. He could hardly believe what she had just said. But Ella never lied. She couldn't lie to his father, so she couldn't be lying now.

She scooted forward on her stool, drawing the blanket around her. "I needed to know you would come back for me, that you would fight for me."

"It was just some guards."

"Speaking in the king's name. You never would have defied that before."

"It's easier to be brave when you're with me," he said shyly.

"I know." She patted the stool beside her, but he held back.

He carried the tinderbox to the hearth, only there was already a little flame gaining strength there. It looked as if Ella had started the fire with a strip of cloth from her skirts and the candle. His shoulders slumped. She truly didn't need him.

"I've hurt you so many times," he said, laying the box on the mantle. "And I know I'll fail you again in the future. How can you want to be with me?"

"Your father hurt me," she said, emphasizing each word. "Just as he hurt you. But you never have, not intentionally, not maliciously, not like him."

"But—"

"No," she said. "I have always loved you because you were not like your father. You care for things, from saplings to dogs to barefoot girls from the north. Your father wouldn't care if I were cold, or if my skirts were torn, but you do. If you didn't, I'd have known you were no longer the man I loved. I would have marched from this palace and left you, guards and flimsy shoes be damned."

"That," he said softly, "I can believe."

"And now I know you're becoming the man you always wanted to be—a man who can stand up to guards, who can stake a claim against the king. We need that if we're to build a life together."

He nodded and found himself standing a bit taller.

"We shouldn't throw away our chance at happiness over a torn gown." She plucked at her skirts, tied closed with a bit of ribbon. "One thing I learned at the abbey was how to do for myself when needed. I know how to cobble things back together."

He smiled, small and sad. "I don't think I'm made for happiness."

She pressed her lips together. Sympathy lay there, and tenderness. If she could, he guessed, she would snip out the part of his life where his father had been and reassemble his life without the king. But that lay beyond the skills of even the most talented women.

"Do you think" she asked, "that you could aim for next to happy?"

He nudged the cast off shoe at her feet. How ridiculously flimsy it was. He would never think to dance in it, but someone had taken these airy bits and formed them into the semblance of a shoe. Maybe if tenuous bits of cloth could make the effort to be a shoe, he could make an effort at least to be content.

"Yes," he said. "I think I can try for that."

"Good." She cupped his cheek. "I can try for that, too."

He snagged her fingers. So warm. He bowed his head, rested his forehead against hers. She snuggled close until he held her in his arms. He wished he could remain there forever, just the two of them, a pocket of warmth in the world. "William won't be happy. He likes me unwed and childless."

"I know. But even he's not your father, and your mother is on our side. We'll find a way to manage him."

From upstairs, the music started again, a waltz. Upstairs, his valet would be waiting with another lady selected for this dance. Roderick had eyes only for the lady in front of him.

"Then, my dear," he said, "might we try another dance?" He held up her shoe.

"Maybe..." She raised the hem of her skirt. He slid the shoe into place. It fit perfectly. "If it involves waltzing outside to visit the kennels."

"But—don't you know? My father had them torn down. We board our hounds in town now."

"Oh." Her eyes went wide. Then she slanted him a smile. "Well, then, shall we look for a house in town near the kennels? Or pick a spot here to build new ones?"

"Now?"

"Why not? We'll never get back the years we lost. I don't intend to waste any that we have left."

"You'd be willing to live away from the palace?"

"Of course. Haven't you always wanted to?"

He glanced up at the ceiling, as if he could see where the king and the court were dancing. He could not escape all his responsibilities as prince, could never escape the memories that kept him up at night. But this evening, for once, he could do his best to forget. And in future, he could be the prince he needed to be at a distance.

He grinned. "Let's do both. There's some good land on the other side of town, beyond the pheasant fields. It'd be perfect for a house and new kennels. Want to see?"

"Lead the way."

He took her hand. "Let's find you good boots and a coat."

They went out together, the two of them, past the lonely evergreens, to see what life they could rebuild.

About the story

"Cinders and Snow" was inspired by events in the life of someone I know, but the details are not mine to share. Suffice it to say I've known several people who would never describe themselves as princes (of any gender), but who are the gentlest, most caring people I know —certainly princes (of any gender) in all the right ways. These people have overcome personal hardships that might have broken me, but they survived and thrived. I wanted to put a character like that into the traditional role of prince, but such a story didn't feel right with a traditional "the prince rescues the girl and they all live happily ever after" ending, because the effects of abuse can last a lifetime. Instead I went for a story where the two characters—prince and his lady love—rescue each other and live "next to happy" ever after.

A question for the author

Q: Do you write with a particular audience in mind?

A: Short answer: Yes, an audience of one—me.

Long answer: I don't start a story thinking, is this a story for young adults or adults? Or is this a story for people who like epic fantasy or urban fantasy or fairy tale retellings? My reading tastes encompass all of these subcategories, and I suspect the same is true of many readers. So I set out to write stories that I would want to read and that involve elements that are of interest to me. Of course this means I often write about similar concepts or themes. I'm a big bird-lover, so many of my stories involve birds to some degree. I once had a writer friend tell me that any story I write isn't one of mine unless it has a bird in it. I also tend to write about issues of loneliness, love, animal-human relations, and the environment. My stories often have at least a suggestion of happiness in the ending, if not a completely happy ending. I hope these elements appeal to a wide audience.

About the author

Kathryn Yelinek works as a librarian in Pennsylvania. In addition to the required hobbies of reading and writing, she enjoys bird watching, star-gazing, gardening, and going to see Broadway musicals. She and her husband share their home with one adorable parakeet, whom they are actively striving to make into the most spoiled bird in the Western Hemisphere. The bird doesn't seem to mind. Her works has appeared in *Daily Science Fiction*, *Deep Magic*, *Metaphorosis*, *Andromeda Spaceways Magazine*, and *Beneath Ceaseless Skies*.

kathrynyelinek.com

Copyright

"Koehl's Quality Impressions" © 2018, Tim McDaniel

"Calm Folk, Come Forth!" © 2018, Adan Berkowitz
"On the Scales of Dragons" © 2018, Kathryn Yelinek
"Suzy's Friend" © 2018, David Hammond
"Chasing the Light" © 2018, Gloria Wickman

"The Foaling Season" © 2018, Samuel Chapman
"Nobody's Daughter and the Tree of Life" © 2018, L'Erin Ogle
"Strangers in the Night" © 2018, David Whitaker
"The Tapestry" © 2018, A.C. Worth
"The Stars Don't Lie" © 2018, R.W.W. Greene

"Time's Arrow" © 2018, C. Heidmann
"The Forest of New People" © 2018, Thom Connors
"The Dream Diary of Monk Anchin" © 2018, Felicity Drake
"It Feels Like Déjà Vu" © 2018, Phong Quan

"The Bagel Shop Owner's Nephew" © 2018, J. Tynan Burke
"Upon the Fallen Leaves of the Gingko Tree" © 2018, Mads Alvey
"Just a Fire" © 2018, A. Martine
"All the Colors I Cannot See" © 2018, L'Erin Ogle
"Not All Those Who Wander Are Lost" © 2018, Douglas Anstruther

"Graven Image" © 2018, B. Morris Allen
"The Yarnball Woman" © 2018, Michael Milne
"Familiar in Her Angles" © 2018, E.A. Brenner
"Combustion" © 2018, Kai Hudson

"Reproduction in a Closed Loop" © 2018, Andrew M. LeBlanc
"Nana Naoko's Garden" © 2018, Michael Gardner
"Twins" © 2018, Gregory Kane
"The Astronaut Tier" © 2018, Jonathan Laidlow

"The Little G-d of Łódź" © 2018, Evan Marcroft
"A House on the Volga" © 2018, Filip Wiltgren
"When the Last Friend is Gone" © 2018, Tris Matthews

Metaphorosis
a magazine of speculative fiction

Metaphorosis is an online speculative fiction magazine dedicated to quality writing. We publish an original story every week, along with author bios, interviews, and notes on story origins. Come and see us online at magazine.Metaphorosis.com

Keep Metaphorosis running! Support us at
Patreon.com/metaphorosis

You can also find us at:
Twitter: @MetaphorosisMag, @MetaphorosisRev, @Metaphorosis
Facebook: www.facebook.com/metaphorosis

We publish monthly print and e-book issues, as well as yearly Best of and Complete anthologies.

Metaphorosis: Best of 2018

The best science fiction and fantasy stories from *Metaphorosis* magazine's third year.

Metaphorosis 2018

All the stories from *Metaphorosis* magazine's third year. Fifty-two great SFF stories.

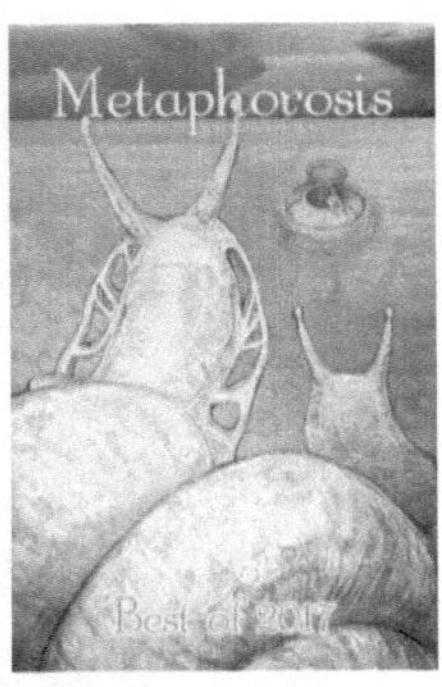

**Metaphorosis:
Best of 2017**

The best science fiction and
fantasy stories from
Metaphorosis magazine's
second year.

Metaphorosis 2017

All the stories from
Metaphorosis magazine's
second year. Fifty-three great
SFF stories.

**Metaphorosis:
Best of 2016**

The best science fiction and
fantasy stories from
Metaphorosis magazine's first
year.

Metaphorosis 2016

Almost all the stories from
Metaphorosis magazine's first
year.

Plant Based Press

Vegan-friendly science fiction and fantasy, including an annual anthology of the year's best SFF stories.

Best Vegan SFF of 2018

The best vegan science fiction and fantasy stories of 2018!

Best Vegan SFF of 2017

The best vegan science fiction and fantasy stories of 2017!

Best Vegan SFF
of 2016

The best vegan science fiction
and fantasy stories of 2016!

Susurrus

A darkly romantic story of
magic, love, and suffering.

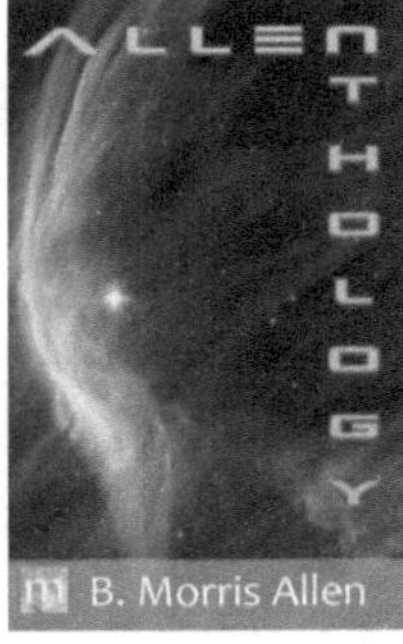

Allenthology:
Volume I

A quarter century of SFF,
including the full contents of
the collections *Tocsin, Start
with Stones,* and *Metaphorosis.*

Metaphorosis Books

Science fiction and fantasy books for writers – full of great stories, but with an additional focus on the craft of speculative fiction writing.

Score

an SFF symphony

What if stories were written like music? *Score* is an anthology of varied stories arranged to follow an emotional score from the heights of joy to the depths of despair – but always with a little hope shining through.

Reading 5X5

Five stories, five times

Twenty-five SFF authors, five base stories, five versions of each – see how different writers take on the same material, with stories in contemporary and high fantasy, soft and hard SF, and a mysterious 'other' category.

Reading 5X5

Writers' Edition

All the stories from the regular, readers' edition, plus two extra stories, the story seed, and authors' notes on writing. Over 100 pages of additional material specifically aimed at writers.

9 781640 761278